THE LIBRARIAN'S COVEN

THE COMPLETE SERIES

KATHRYN MOON

This series belongs to my mother, who offered me patience and confidence in equal measure, and whose pride in me I always strive to live up to.

CONTENTS

WRITTEN

WARRIORS

SCRIVENS

ANCIENTS

WRITTEN

THE LIBRARIAN'S COVEN, BOOK 1

1

―――――

JOANNA

I FELT INVISIBLE, FROZEN IN PLACE. THE CANDERFEY UNIVERSITY campus was *stuffed* with people. They poured out of brick buildings like a sudden flood, trickling over pathways and joining friends to lounge in the grass under the massive trees of the Hand Woods that surrounded us. Most of them passed each other like strangers on the walkways. At home, I couldn't pass a neighbor without making conversation for at least five minutes. And suddenly here I was, people brushing right up against me and never saying a word.

One crossed in front of me, blocking my view of the library, and I rose up on my toes. I knew my jaw was hanging loose, making me look every bit the country bumpkin I was, but I couldn't stop staring. The building was larger than anything I'd ever seen before, and grander, with lamps glittering through the glass panes that stretched as tall as my whole house. Even from the outside, I could see them, lining the walls like invitations—my books. The university's books, really, but they would be something like mine while I trained as a librarian.

My hands squeezed around the handle of my small suitcase. I had brought so little with me. There were people passing me carrying more in their arms than I had in my possession—books and papers

3

and goblets and wands and little potted plants and instruments and artwork still dripping fresh paint.

"Joanna Wick?"

A wind picked up and brushed my hair—now too long to stay out of my eyes and too short to do anything with—across my face and I pushed the dark strands back. My stunned gaping settled on a small woman with bright red hair braided over her shoulder and a pair of round glasses bouncing the glare of the sun into my eyes.

"I can find you a job cleaning the windows if you'd rather," the woman called from the path in front of the building. "Or you might come in."

"Yes," I said, stumbling forward to the enormous wood and glass doors of the library. My voice was practically air. All of it had been stolen out of my lungs at the sight of my new workplace.

"Well," said the woman, eyes flinty behind her lenses. "You look the part at least." Then she pushed the door behind her open and waved her arm for me to enter.

We were dressed similarly, in our long dark skirts and buttoned gray blouses and gleaming black boots. I had never seen anyone dress any different, but this woman and I seemed to stick out for our plainness here.

"It's really all I own," I admitted as a young student passed us in something feathered and flounced.

And then I was struck stupid again as we stepped into the lobby.

A library with a lobby. A giggle burst out of my mouth and I caught my breath, savoring the whispery dry smell of books in the back of my throat. Three chandeliers of candles and crystals hung above a long wooden counter that had fairies, goblins, and ghouls carved into the facade, wolves crouched and snarling along the floor. Behind the counter stood three librarians, stamping books in and out of circulation. Beyond them was one of the most beautiful sets of shelves I had ever seen, full to bursting with every shape and size and color of book.

"Am I supposed to be *here*?" I asked, starting to turn to the woman. Instead, my eyes caught on the roof above me, made of cut and colored glass, casting a scene on the black tile floor of the changing seasons.

"So they tell me, dear," she said.

I glanced at her long enough to catch the curve of a smile. And then was completely distracted by the bookshelves stretching beyond her to the left. The farther up I looked, the more stories of the library there was to see. Another wing soared up to the roof on the right, with wooden balustrades looking over the lobby.

"There are more people in this building than in my entire hometown," I said without meaning to.

The woman snorted and took my elbow leading me behind the circulation desk where the other librarians were smirking down at their tasks. She pulled at the edge of one of the shelves and it swung toward us, revealing a small room of dark armchairs and bright lamps glowing.

"Let's have some tea," she said and the bookshelf swung shut behind us.

❧

HER NAME WAS Gwen Woollard and despite her quirking lips and the dry snap in her tone, she was patient with me.

"You start tomorrow and you'll be shelving for us to start with, so there'll be plenty of time for fondling spines and sniffing pages then," she said as she led me through the stacks, orienting me with the arrangement, pointing out the places students ended up nestled together, and describing the rush hours.

Despite her words, she let me trail behind her, my eyes soaking up the sight of the shelves and their precious cargo. Had I ever even imagined there might be so many books in the world? The trip to Canderfey from Bridgeston, where I'd grown up, had taken the night and the better part of the morning, but still. I would have tried to find my way here sooner if I'd known what I'd been missing.

"These next two floors are for faculty and library staff only," Gwen said.

I had to race up a set of stairs to catch up after staring too long at a painting of a crowd of people in gossamer clothing, twining together under moonlight. The artist's subject was an old fertility festival, and the canvas shimmered with life and magic, and left me blushing as I joined my new boss.

"Even then," Gwen said, pausing at the top of the steps, likely waiting for me to catch up. "Keep your eyes on the professors. They're as bad as the students, most of them. Always trying to sneak books away or cozying up in corners."

"I *know* you aren't talking about me, Gwendolyn," a man's voice purred from behind a bookshelf. I leaned around Gwen and saw him, stretched out in the window seat sunning himself like a cat. He was wearing a vivid green jacket that looked soft even from where I stood. His skin was dark and smooth, and there was silver at the temples of his short black hair. He grinned at me with full lips and a sharp smile, dark eyes flashing.

"Professor King, I absolutely am," Gwen answered, her tone biting. But her smile was easy as she added, "You're nearly late for class and if I haven't been saying that same thing for the last twenty-odd years I don't know what I've been doing."

"*Nearly* late," he agreed, rising up from the bench seat with a grace I envied. He added to me, "Don't let her bully you."

"I'm not easily bullied," I said, and his grin widened as he winked at me and passed us. If Gwen noticed the book he tucked against his side under his arm, she didn't say a word.

"Be careful," she said.

"Of him?" I whispered, glancing back at the man who was retreating down the flights of stairs.

Gwen stared at me, eyes narrowed for a long moment, her lips twitching. "Of the books," she said. "The reason the students aren't allowed up here is because this is our...more sensitive catalogue. It's a devil to keep organized and every last page is ornery and soaked in magic. They'll shift around or go missing entirely."

I wondered if Professor King had anything to do with the latter, but kept the question to myself.

"When you aren't busy elsewhere, this will be where we need you," she continued, walking ahead.

I bit my smile as one of her hands floated up from her side to brush her knuckles across the spines lining a low shelf.

"Do what you can to keep it tidy, but don't be shy or stupid about calling for help if you need it," she said, turning in place on the toes of her black boots.

"Help?" I asked, glancing at a bookshelf. It all seemed to be a smaller version of the organization in the greater library. And while it was on a scale larger than I'd ever had the imagination to fathom, it was the same system we used at home in our own little branch. It would be easy work for me.

"You'll see," Gwen said, smiling at the books. Then she turned and looked over the rims of her glasses at me. "Go on. Say it now."

My forehead knotted, not sure what she meant.

"What's been running through your head since you got off the bus," she said. "Probably since you got the letter of employment."

I took a breath and held it, staring up at the lamps above and then at the deep row of bookshelves surrounding us. There was a shuffle of pages farther off, and a quiet echo from beyond the balcony—steps on tile and whispering voices.

"Are you sure I'm right for the job?" I asked. It was a magical university, and I was…not much of anything as far as I could tell. I'd never shown any aptitude at real magic, not more than the little basic charms everyone knew. I loved books and quiet and walks. I'd applied to Canderfey's library staff on a whim, not a genuine expectation of being hired.

"Yes," Gwen said, without any hesitation. "We know what we're doing here. Soon you will too. Now let's get your suitcase and I'll tell you where to find your rooms."

THE DIRECTIONS GWEN had given me seemed clear enough while we were alone in the quiet little break room behind the circulation desk. But out on the campus grounds with classes changing and people flooding the paths that curled around massive old trees, the words were pouring out of my thoughts as they became flooded with new information. My steps slowed as I stared at the collection of towering buildings of brick and stone. A beautiful variety of people rushed around me, the kinds of people who passed through Bridgeston without stopping. Faces and clothing and lives I would only have seen glimpses of through windows.

I couldn't decide where to look. At the group of young women huddled together on the grass, painting sigils on each others' skin with blue-black ink? Or the boy who was walking up a set of stairs into a building, juggling flames through his hands while no one but me seemed to pay him any attention? I was distracted from them both by the woman coming toward me, book floating in front of her nose as her fingers were busy with small needles knitting a pair of socks.

But the walkways were too crowded for all of my gawking. A group of students, running to class with their bags beating at their hips, knocked into me, and I crashed sideways into a pair of arms full of rolls of paper and weapons.

"I'm so sorry!" I said, and it was echoed back to me just as quickly in a man's tone, low and gentle.

"It's my fault," he said. He was still standing, cast in sunlight as I scrambled on the ground to gather up the mess I'd made. There were maps unrolling and a knife that had dropped, blade down, into the dirt.

"It really isn't," I said, a nervous laugh bubbling up in my throat as he crouched down, plucking weapons up out of the grass with long, pale fingers. "I think you're meant to be walking on that path and I was too busy..." I looked up, arms full of paper and one ragged-edged axe, and my voice caught in my throat. His eyes were very blue. And he was very...lovely was the word that came to mind. Handsome in a gawky, bookish way that made my belly squirm and my cheeks heat. A shy smile grew over his face, framed by a coppery beard.

"Staring," I said. I pulled my gaze from his face, all the long narrow lines of it, and tried not to distract myself with the breadth of his shoulders or the white shirt sleeves that had been rolled up to his elbows.

"You're a new student," he said, hands reaching out to where I was starting to crush the maps in my hold.

"Trainee, in the library," I said, passing over his belongings. I had no idea how he'd managed to hold it all at once. But he was tall and long-limbed and he seemed practiced at the process as he gathered it up into a tidy arrangement. The blades and axes seemed to vanish as he arranged the bundle in his arms.

"Staff," he said, nodding. "You're looking for the housing?"

"Yes!" My breath came out in a relieved huff of laughter.

He came up to my side and shuffled everything into the crook of one arm despite the fact it had been previously overflowing both. His free hand settled at the center of my back, and I held my breath at the touch and the pool of prickling heat it created. He nodded down the path.

"Stay on this as it curves north, head west at the oak, and the housing is a row along the side street at the end. Look for the red doors," he said, and then his hand was gone from my back, plucking up a pair of glasses from his collar and sliding them up his nose. His eyes flicked over my face. "You'll find it," he said.

"I can always knock someone else over if I don't," I said, ducking my chin as I stepped back onto the walkway, letting the traffic carry me forward. I could hear his laugh following behind me—a brighter, livelier sound than I expected.

The directions weren't any more specific than Gwen's, and there were more than a few oak trees at forks in the path. But there was an instinctive tug in my belly at a great mossy old beast of a tree that arched over the path with rounded knots where low hanging branches had been cut away. At the end of the narrow road of shops and a small grocers was the side street of narrow houses pressed together with doors in all shades of red.

I found mine on the left side of the street, in the middle of the block. My heart was doing happy somersaults in my chest as I stared up at the narrow, shabby little building as if it was as grand as the library.

The iron railing leading up the steps was rusting, and whatever plant had tried to make a home in the window box was wilting. The key turned in the lock, and while the space inside was small, it was simple and entirely mine. Just ahead of the front door, a set of stairs led up to the second story, and off to the left was a thin room with a square table and two chairs facing each other. At the end of the room was an empty bookshelf, modest and plain compared to the ones I had just visited. There was a tiny kitchen at the back of the house with a smudged window, streaming foggy light in over the sink.

The bathroom upstairs had barely enough room to turn around without falling into either the tub, sink, or toilet. Still, it was clean and bright, and there was a stack of towels stuffed onto a shelf. I could take a bath and no one would come knocking, waiting for their turn.

My bedroom was as little as of the rest of the house. I could see the street through the window from where I sat down on the bed. I set my suitcase on the floor and scooted back on the mattress, springs squeaking beneath me as I moved. I rested my head against the wall and closed my eyes. For the first time in my life, I was living alone. There were neighbors next door, sharing the same wall with me, and I had no notion of their name or what they did or who their family was. I turned my head to press my cheek against the plaster and tried to imagine them in my head.

Instead, I ended up picturing two people, Professor King from the library and the man from the lawn with the gentle smile and the arms full of weapons.

I opened my eyes and chewed at my lip. Did I *have* to wait an entire day to go back to the library?

2

———————

CALLUM

I was late for dinner. Again.

I tried to kick the front door shut behind me—gently because Isaac listened for that kind of thing—when a knife went sliding out of... somewhere and clattered to the floor.

"Put those away before you slice your damn toe off," Aiden called from the dining room.

I winced and tiptoed to the closet door, lowering myself just enough to keep from dropping the entire mess I had taken into class with me, and doing my best to open it silently. Then I threw the entire lot in at once and snapped the door shut before anything could escape. It would all find its way back to wherever it was meant to go... sooner or later. As long as neither Aiden or Isaac went looking for their coat tonight.

I pushed the hair out of my face before taking the hall down to the dining room.

"I'm late, I'm so sor-" I stopped in the doorway.

Aiden was grinning at me from the table, lounging back in his chair with his feet up in my seat. The *empty* table. How late was I?

"I put off making dinner," Isaac said, appearing from the kitchen,

11

steaming dishes in hand. "Feet," he said, raising a dark eyebrow at Aiden's sprawl in front of the table.

"I was holding your seat," Aiden said, not even bothering to be convincing.

"I've left the wine," Isaac mused, glaring at the table.

"I'll get it," I said. He'd left the bread and the salad as well, but I didn't mention it, just juggled it all up into my arms.

"Did either of you get to the library today?" Aiden asked as I returned. His face was blank aside from the slight wrinkle of his eyes that meant he was fighting a smile.

"I took your book back for you in the morning," Isaac said.

He glanced at me for a moment and we both turned back to stare at Aiden. He'd seemed smug when I'd walked in and he was using the slow, drawling tone he adopted when he wanted to drag a good story out. He blinked at Isaac's words and frowned for a moment.

"Why?" Isaac asked. "Did *you* get to the library today?"

"I…I wasn't *expecting* to," Aiden hedged, eyes widening. "But there was a symphony-"

"Oh, alright," Isaac said, rolling his eyes and stealing the wine from my arms before taking his seat. "Get to the point, Aide."

Aiden glanced at me and I sighed, dropping plates to the table and taking my seat so he could enjoy his dramatic reveal.

"Woollard's gone and found some ingénue from the middle of nowhere and set her up working in the library," Aiden said, grinning at us both. Isaac and I exchanged another look, both of us frowning and Aiden added, "I'm fairly certain she's even given her a set of her very own dour clothes."

"Ah!" I said, remembering the younger woman I had nearly plowed straight through on my way to class. "Tall, with hair," and I waved a hand around my head thinking of the way her hair had floated around her head like dark feathers, unsettling with the breeze.

"An artist's eye," Isaac muttered to his wine glass.

"Face like a startled little woodland fae," Aiden said, nodding.

She had seemed startled at first, those wide dark eyes staring up at me with an ancient axe in her delicate hand. And maybe a little skittish. But there had been a wry slide to her smile as she left, carrying the charm from me on her back that would see her safely home.

"See?" Aiden said, nudging Isaac and pointing at my face. "*He* noticed her too. And he doesn't notice anyone."

"I notice plenty," I said, serving myself. I just wasn't usually *interested*.

Isaac made a little 'hm'ing sound and shrugged at me. "You're picky," he said.

"But you've never been wrong," Aiden added with a toast of his wine glass to me. "Your better judgment is why we are still a lonely three-man coven without our fourth. But at least it isn't the *wrong* fourth."

I huffed softly at my plate. I don't think Aiden had ever bothered being lonely if he didn't really have to. We loved each other, my covenmates and I, but we didn't ask for faithfulness. Not while we weren't complete. And Aiden did his absolute best to search high and low for our fourth, infatuations littering the path behind him as he went.

"Is she very magical then?" Isaac asked us.

"I don't think so," I said at the same moment Aiden said, "She certainly looked so." I laughed despite myself.

She had seemed…*significant*, in a way. Or maybe Aiden was right and I took so little notice of people outside of our coven and the scene of my classroom that striking someone down on the sidewalk was what it took to shake me out of my pattern.

"She wouldn't have to be," Isaac said, more to me than Aiden. "Not with the three of us."

I hummed something that might pass for agreement and took a bite of fish. Isaac was right. Between the three of us, magic was covered. Hell, between Aiden and Isaac even the domesticities of the house were covered. We just needed the right energy to temper us together. Make something cohesive out of all of our pieces. Aiden called it a family. I had a less generous view of the word, but I did know *something* was missing in our home, happy as we were.

"See what you think," I said to Isaac. I tried not to conjure her face in my head but it was right there, staring back at me from the empty place across the table.

3

JOANNA

I WAS BACK IN THE LIBRARY AT DAWN, LOADING STACKS OF RETURNED books into the small elevators that carried them up to their respective floors, unloading them onto wheeled racks, finding their homes on the shelves, and starting over again. I found a student sleeping beneath a shelf of sigil texts and woke him up.

"When does the cafeteria open?" he growled at me.

I shrugged. "I have no idea, but it's morning."

"I *know* that," he said, and then rolled his back to me.

Three students and one professor stopped me in the hopes I had seen books that the circulation desk *swore* were not on site. I found an abandoned pen and notebook on a shelf and started myself a list titled *Books To Find*. Gwen checked on me for the first few hours, nodding at me from the end of a row of shelves, or glancing up at me as I passed the balcony on the third floor.

It was more work than any day in the Bridgeston library but it made the minutes tick faster and I had never had the opportunity to see so many titles, so many subjects, and all of them the kind of magic no one bothered with in the country. Theories and strategies and ancient traditions and symbolism. The section on domestic charms was exquisitely small in comparison to the volumes of weather magic, astronomy, shadow walking, dream travels. Concepts I had never even heard of, and words that I practiced on my lips in silence.

I had just finished re-shelving the east wing and was leaving the art and color magic section, when I stopped in front of a painting stretching floor to ceiling like a window into a scene straight out of the town I'd left behind two days before. I caught my breath, tasting soil and the dry musty scent of wheat, and stared at the stretch of the field reaching across the land to the old line of border oaks. The bristles of the stalks gleamed in the sunlight and all but shifted on the canvas with some breeze of brushstrokes. An ache bloomed in my chest and a longing for the stretch of uninterrupted sky burned at the back of my throat.

But I had only been away from Bridgeston for what felt like hours. I *couldn't* be homesick yet. Or at the very least, I hadn't been up until that moment.

"You look unhappy with that painting," a voice asked from behind me.

"It's making me think of home," I said, frowning.

I turned to see who had joined me and my throat dried at the sight of him. Was it mandatory at Canderfey to be so handsome? At least this time the man at my side was staring up at the painting instead of at me. The angles of his face were strong and broad and there was something watchful and animal in his gaze although I couldn't decide if it was predatory or merely observational. He had black hair curling down to the back of his neck and a shadow of a beard over his jaw.

When he turned to look at me I moved my stare to the painting, avoiding his eyes.

"It looks like Bridgeston," I said. "Where I'm from."

"Really? It's Hammish scenery, but I suppose there isn't much difference," he said.

I looked at him again. He had the dark hair and tanned skin and broad shoulders so common where I grew up in the southern area of Enmairian countryside. I glanced back at the painting and saw how he fit within the frame and realized all at once that it was *his* painting. His homesickness.

"You look Hammish," I said, feeling braver now. Hammish wasn't so far from home, and its people weren't so different from mine. Even if he was wearing the vivid colors and lush fabrics of the university people, he now held something familiar and safe about him too.

"Do I?" he asked, grinning. The smile, and the dimples within it, softened the edges of his face. "You don't look Bridgestony."

"Thank you," I said, and he laughed with open surprise. I blushed and added, "Not that there's anything wrong with...I didn't mean that." Embarrassed, I took hold of my cart and started my escape.

"No, no, I know exactly what you mean. I ended up here, didn't I? Before you go," he said, stepping closer still, smiling with the laugh in his voice. "There's a book I'm looking for."

"Oh, of course," I said. Of course he had spoken up because he'd needed something while I'd been busy looking at art instead of working. I grabbed up my new notebook from where I'd left it in the cart and flipped it open to my list where I'd tucked the pen. He leaned over, peeking at the words on the page, and I could smell the ink and oil from him. There was a spot of vivid blue paint behind his right ear, smudged into the skin there.

"Mmm, you'll never find those," he said, reaching out and pointing to two titles I had scribbled down for a couple of students. "People have been looking for them for ages. Lost decades ago as far as anyone can tell."

I put little stars next to where I had written *Gatekeepers; a Compendium of the Old Guard* and *Resonants*.

"It won't hurt to remember their names," I said, shrugging. "What was the title?"

I looked up and found the studious examination he had given his own painting now focused on my own face. "*Color Magic*," he said, still staring. "By Felix Amesbury. And *Blue in Study*, now that I think about it," he said. He glanced back down at the notebook and I rushed to fill in the words.

"Thank you...what was your name?" he asked.

"Joanna," I said, finishing adding his titles to my list.

"Thank you, Joanna. Isaac," he said, holding out a large hand stained with color. I tucked my pen away and shook his hand, ignoring the heat in my cheeks. "If you find them, would you bring them to my office? Professor Metclaffe in the Burgess Building. Woollard won't mind."

"I...sure," I said.

His lips quirked and he nodded, turning and walking away. There was more blue paint at the back of his neck and for some reason, the sight of it made my stomach flip. I pressed the backs of my palms to my cheeks and grimaced when I found them warm to the touch. A little cough echoed behind me and I jumped, finding a student blocked between two shelves by my cart. I muttered a quick apology and dragged it out of the way, hurrying to move on in my work.

By the time I had finished with my re-shelving I had collected three more missing book titles. Gwen came to find me in the afternoon just as I was heading up to browse and check on the staff only area.

"Take a break. Eat something—before your eyes start crossing," she said, leading me back to the break room.

The shelves behind the circulation desk were already filling up with returns and I wondered when I would ever find the time to work in the restricted section. Gwen was dragging me back through the swinging bookshelf when I saw it, gold block letters glittering down the spine of a thin black spine. *RESONANTS.*

I pulled back and stopped in front the shelf, pulling the notebook from my skirt pocket and flipping it open. Already I could see the two texts Isaac had mentioned waiting on the shelf. I ran down the list, checking off every last title. Gwen glared at the books on the shelf and then down at my notebook.

"What a coincidence," she said dryly, looking hawkishly at me through her lenses.

It was a coincidence or, more likely, Gwen was joking at my expense. Perhaps the library had its own kinds of charms in place, bringing books back when it was ready to or when they were needed. The most it signified to me was that I needed to track down Isaac Metclaffe.

I LOST track of time in the library that evening, finishing my work and ending up nose deep in an old textbook outlining the ancient seasonal rituals. (In the country the rough shapes of the holidays were still practiced, although nothing so elaborate as the festivals and performances of history.) The Burgess Building was closed by the time I remembered where I was supposed to be so I went the next day when Gwen shooed me out of the stacks to eat lunch.

The building was swimming with students when I arrived, classes just letting out, and I felt like a fish battling the stream trying to get myself up the stairs. It cleared out enough by the second story, for the din of chatter and feet on stone to fade and for me to stop by a group of girls leaning against a railing together, paint-stained smocks still hanging over their jewel-tone clothing.

"I'm looking for Professor Metclaffe's office," I asked, trying not to shift as they looked me over head to toe with puzzled expressions.

"Oh!" one said, face softening and cheeks blushing. "It's on the third floor, down by the windows."

"Thank-" I started.

"He won't be there, though," another added. "He was working with us today so he'll still be in the studio for a while. Top floor, on the left."

I hesitated on the third floor. It would be just as easy, easier really, to leave the books in his office with a note. Gwen knew where I was and the errand didn't require me to speak to him. Or to see him. But I turned up the stairs and followed them up two more flights. The top story of the building was surrounded by windows. Even the rooms had windows facing the hall that stretched up the roof and let the light stream through every room in bright sheets.

Isaac Metclaffe sat at a canvas with his back to the doorway, the afternoon sun catching on the palette at his side. There were feathers stretched across the painting and my muscles ached with the urge to run, to flee, to escape, until I fixed my eyes on the back of the painter instead of his creation. I wanted to sit down and ask a million questions. How did he put magic into an image? Did it begin with brush-strokes or sooner, in the mixing of the paint? The stretching of the fabric over its frame?

"It's injured," I said, glancing at the painting again, seeing the way feathers at the bird's stomach were ruffled and stained, feeling a hot tear in my own gut.

Isaac glanced at me once, 'hmm'ing in agreement, and turned back to his work. Then he startled in his seat and spun the stool to face me.

"Joanna!"

I tried not to get carried away, pleased that he'd remembered my name. "Your books turned up," I said, pulling them out of the bag at my side. *Blue in Study* was, from what I could tell, a book made entirely of blue. Every shade and hue shifting from page to page, like moving liquids. *Color Magic* was a crumbling collection of browning pages and curling leather that I was too afraid of damaging to even take a glimpse of. I wrapped it up in a sheet of white paper with *For Professor Metclaffe* written at the front.

He blinked at them for a moment and then at me. "Just like that?" he asked.

"They were waiting on the circulation shelf after you left. You probably just missed them," I said. I held them out to him, wanting both to have a reason to stay and also an escape from the studying look in his eyes.

"Where did Woollard find you?" he said under his breath.

"Bridgeston," I said, smiling a little even though I felt like I didn't understand the scope of the question.

He laughed and shook himself, rising off the stool and walking up to me. "You must be the very best library clerk Canderfey has ever had because *Color Magic* has been missing for hundreds of years. Ever since Amesbury had his falling out with his favorite student."

"Maybe they finally decided to return it?" I joked.

His eyes narrowed even as his smile deepened. "What did you do? Smuggle it out of the library?"

"I told Gwen it was for you," I said, shrugging.

"You call her Gwen?" he asked, taking the books from my hands at last. "That's remarkable in itself." His finger ran over his name on the paper wrapping and a smear of russet paint followed the line.

I winced, wondering if maybe I shouldn't have lent the rare classical text to a painter.

"The others," he said, looking up suddenly. "The other books on your list..."

"They...turned up," I said, feeling the strangeness of the statement as I said it, as I watched his face shift, twitching with interest. "If you know anyone looking for them..."

"I'm sure you'll see them soon. Where did you go to university, Joanna?" he asked.

I shook my head and looked down to fidget with the strap of my bag. "No, I didn't...I'm not a witch. Just training to be a plain old librarian."

"Ohh, don't tell *Gwen* you said that. Her coven is fierce," he said, grinning.

The boyish expression on his face made me want to find a seat nearby to curl up in for the afternoon, as if it were ten years ago and I was sitting on a field fence waiting for Gregory Thatcher to notice me.

"I should get back to work," I said, turning away quickly before I could catch another flash of his smile or answer another question in a way that made him laugh at me again.

"I'm here in the studios a lot at this time," he said to my back. "I'd like it if you came back again. Canderfey has too many city people, stuck out here in the woods."

My hands clenched around the leather strap of my bag. I didn't even know how badly I wanted the invitation until it was ringing in my ears. I nodded at him, looking back over my shoulder. My eyes landed on the canvas and my chest ached as I recognized the bird in flight, copper feathers flashing at me from across the space.

"The hawk..." I bit my lip, not entirely sure what I wanted to ask.

"He'll heal," Isaac said, watching my face.

Somehow, that was the answer I needed and I left the building, hurrying as I realized how long I had dawdled with the man.

4

JOANNA

I wasn't brave enough to visit Isaac again the next day, but I *was* brave enough to gobble down a sandwich at lunch and use the extra time to sneak back up into the staff-only library. I found a text on the pigments used to preserve a life in a portrait—ground bone and dried blood and the ashes of the body included—and the book *Resonants* which was all about the strongest tones in sound for conjuring the instruments that best formed them.

The window seat I had seen Professor King in on my first day was open and I folded myself into the corner, a stack of books I couldn't possibly work through placed in front of my feet. I was mid-explanation of the breed of tree in the northern mountains whose wood was the ideal density for the hollowness required in the bass note that brought the dead back to life, when I was interrupted.

"You're getting quite cozy with my book."

Professor King stood at the far end of the bench seat, an eyebrow raised at the book in my hands. He moved closer and sat down next to my pile of reading material, glancing down at the stack with a tilt of his head.

"That's quite the range of subjects too. Do you have much interest in the influence of ley lines on birthing cycles?"

I was beginning to resent the effect I had on the professors at Canderfey and the way I seemed to draw laughter up in them. I may have been practically magicless and from the rustic country, but Gwen had said I was where I needed to be and I *was* doing my job, even if it was simple compared to theirs.

"I have an interest in everything," I said, keeping my tone even. "And up until this week, I had very little means of finding the information."

His humor settled but the crinkle at the corner of his eyes deepened. "I have students with less ambition than you," he said. "And I'm very jealous that you've gotten a look at that book before I have."

"You must be one of Isaac's friends," I said, closing the book and passing it to him.

"Isaac?" he asked, seeming surprised by the name. But then he added, "I am. Aiden King."

He extended his hand and I took it, watching the way his hold dwarfed mine. His grip was warm and surprisingly gentle, even as he squeezed my hand once and then released me.

"Joanna Wick. Is the information in the book true?" I asked.

Aiden's thumbs were stroking the fabric cover of the book in his hands and he looked down at it, lips twisting in thought. "From what I know, they were at the time. For Wrenshaw, the author, at least. He made all his own instruments, was easily the best luthier in history. But who's to say if the conditions of the materials are still the same now."

"But the part about raising the dead," I said, leaning in to open to where I'd left off. "It seems so...like a story."

"Do you read that fast or do you just know where to look?" he asked, and when I looked up he had leaned in as well and my vision was full of his face, the prickle of stubble on his cheek and the glint in his dark gaze. He leaned away and I realized I had frozen in surprise. "Wrenshaw's wife died very young. He *did* raise her. But it didn't work out, those sort of experiments never do. I expect that portion of the book was why it was stolen from the library in the first place."

A throat cleared beyond us, and I looked up finding Cecil, one of the library clerks, winking at me before leaving a full cart at the sidewall.

I fought down my blush, probably fruitlessly, and stood up from my seat.

"I doubt it was stolen," I said to Aiden, nodding at the book. "A stack of missing books came back at once. Probably a professor had an old collection hoarded away that just got found."

He smiled at me but his brow furrowed as if he were equally puzzled by my answer. "I'll save your seat for you," he said as I grabbed my cart.

I assumed he meant he'd be taking up the spot in the window, but when I passed by fifteen minutes later the spot was empty but for the books I collected. It wasn't until evening hit and my shift was over that I returned. The books were still waiting for me and when I reached my seat I found a charm in place, a sweet little hum of music that faded as I reached it. I thanked Aiden in my head and picked up the next book in the stack, another of the missing titles that Isaac's friends were looking for.

I hadn't answered Aiden when he asked, but the truth was I was both a fast reader and I tended to skip through pages until I found a spot that interested me. *Gatekeepers; a Compendium of the Old Guard*, another withering old book that smelled sharply of dirt and mold, had black ink drawings stamped crookedly into the page and I flipped through the pages until one of the images struck me. It was dark, saturated with ink that wrinkled the paper, faint white lines guiding the picture of a copse of trees that curled up out of the earth and a shadowy figure at the heart of them. The words below the image were blocked out boldly, little faint cracks appearing in the letters.

It Eats.

The lamps in the library dimmed in the evening, although the building was still full of people. It would close deep into the night and only for a handful of hours, open for night owls and early birds alike. The building was warm with magic and the windows on my left were cool from the night air outside. I read the story of the old god-like force of blind destruction, a being that devoured without reason, whose appetite was unquenchable. The chatter of the library fell away into a buzz that lulled me with the rhythm of the words I traced across the page with my finger.

LET ME OUT.

LET ME OUT.

LET ME OUT.

LET IT OUT.

5

CALLUM

AT DINNER, THE NIGHT BEFORE, ISAAC MENTIONED HIS VISIT FROM THE new librarian while I stared down at my plate and Aiden ruffled with excitement. They wanted her, I could tell, and my nerves stirred in anxiety. Would I disappoint them again? Kill another of their romances and our coven's chance for finally being settled, Aiden at last having his family. It left me wondering for the hundredth time if I was really meant to be here, sharing this home and their magic with mine.

Aiden bringing her up at our third dinner in a row was enough. He'd already decided for himself. Joanna Wick had the potential to be our fourth. His stare at me from over the candlelight wasn't subtle. It was time for me to meet her, really speak to her. And if there was no real attraction, no pull—why was there never a pull?—then I owed it to my covenmates to let them know sooner rather than later.

"I left a charm for her and her books," Aiden said, still staring at me. "She has *Gatekeepers*, by the way."

A little carrot to dangle for me. Get the stubborn ass moving in the right direction.

"I've been looking for that text," I said as if I didn't know what they were fishing for. Their shoulders relaxed in their seats.

27

I left for the library as Aiden cleared the table. Their watching eyes were like hands shoving me out the door.

She was asleep when I found her, with one of the most valuable, dangerous, and contentious texts of magic still gripped between her hands. Her temple was against the windowpane at her side, her lips pursed and forehead tangled. Her shoulders were drawn tight up to her ears and my palms itched, body leaning forward and wanting to follow some set of instructions I had no translation for. To wake her or soothe her or both.

I crossed in front of the lamplight and she sat up with a violent shudder and a whimpering gasp that froze my chest. I dropped down to the bench seat, hands reaching out for her even as her back stretched up against the wall behind her. A cornered animal with the whites of her eyes stark in the dim light.

"I'm sorry," I said, pulling away. "I didn't mean to startle you!"

A trembling hand fluttered into the air and then landed over her heart. The terror was bitter in the air, and a sting of bile rose in my throat, bringing back muddy fields from decades ago and the echo of magic and metal crashing.

"I...I fell asleep?" she said. The whisper in her voice of lingering sleep brushed away my memories.

"Are you alright?" There was an argument in every muscle in my body, the urge to leave, and the impulse to move in closer and offer... comfort or at least *contact*.

There was a catch in her breath and I tensed under her stare as it landed firmly on my face after skirting the space of the stacks around us.

"A dream," she said. "It must have been...I don't remember it, but it was just a bad dream." And her shoulders eased as she spoke.

Dreams were significant. A part of me wanted to press with questions, check her symptoms off against the possible causes. Nightmares were one thing, but a disturbance in dreams wasn't limited to the subconscious and if she...

"You're one of Isaac's friends, aren't you?" she asked, glancing at me out of the side of her eyes while trying to smooth her skirt and hair to erase the evidence of her nap.

"Covenmate," I said and then wished I could bite my own tongue as her eyes widened and then shuttered, face going blank.

"Of course," she said, with a wilted smile. "That makes sense. And Professor King."

"Yes." The word sat stale in my mouth with all that I wanted to add to it. That we were only three. That Aiden and Isaac had all but shoved me out the door to meet her. And that for the first time, I could understand *why*. There was a draw, an itch under my skin to be closer to her. That contact I was craving.

"This is yours then," she said, closing the book in her hands and passing it across the bench to me.

The energy around the book pooled darkly like rot and refuse in the air and I hesitated before picking it up.

"Bit of light reading?" I asked, wondering how far she had read.

"I like a spooky story," she said, tone dry and light and coaxing a smile out in spite of my nerves. "But I suppose it explains the anxious sleep."

My fingertips brushed down the spine of the book and a creeping, slithering feeling stirred at the back of my thoughts. But it was chased away as Joanna stood from the bench.

"I should be getting home, my shift ended hours ago," she said, moving to pass me.

I stood too abruptly and forced her to stop in her tracks or run into me again as she had days ago. She stared up at me in surprise, a dark curl falling down one cheek.

"Let me walk you," I said, trying not to cringe at my own clumsiness. "I'm on my way out," I added, holding up *Gatekeepers*.

"We can walk each other down to the circulation desk, how about that?" she said.

I tried to laugh off the refusal, but the sound was closer to a cough. Still, she waited for me to join her at the steps, her hand poised on the stair railing.

"I think this is the kind of building all books should live in," she said after several quiet steps down. I turned to look at her and found her staring up at the wood molding that grew up the staircase walls, rosewood vines crawling up and alien faces peering out from behind glossy wooden leaves. "Where I worked before was nice. Well, it was clean and quiet. But the town I grew up in didn't have much use for books and certainly didn't think to build them such a…shrine." I had seen women looking less seduced by Aiden at his most charming than Joanna did at the walls of the library. And her touch on the staircase was more of a caress than a steadying hold.

"How long have you been a librarian?" I asked. She looked young. Not young enough to be a student, but enough to leave a gap in our ages.

"I'm not really, yet. But I've been a clerk for a decade, about?" she said, shrugging. "Since I finished school. The librarian was working alone and I'd been doing the shelving for her for years anyway. Now she has a couple of council women volunteering. It'll do fine." There was a little wistfulness in her voice.

"Are you homesick?"

"Nooo," she said, sounding disgusted at the idea. "Not yet, at least, but…" she raised her chin and squared her shoulders, "I don't think I will be."

"In my experience you don't have to be," I said, firmly keeping home out of my head.

We reached the first floor and quieted as we passed clusters of students gathered together at long tables, studying in hushed voices. She ducked behind the circulation desk, grabbing one of the open places and reaching across to me, hand outstretched for the book.

"So you can skip the waitlist," she whispered, grinning at me.

I leaned across desk and whispered back, "I'm at the top of the waitlist."

She raised an eyebrow and pulled one of Woollard's massive reference texts up, flipping through till she found the collection of names gathered for holds on *Gatekeepers*.

"Callum Pike," I said as she skimmed past the names that had been crossed away, retired professors and graduated students from years ago.

"Callum…but this is from almost twenty years ago!" she said looking up at me. "You can't have been a student then."

"I was, I attended very young." And for a very brief amount of time. When Joanna raised an eyebrow at me I added, "I was fifteen."

Instead of shock or awe, she rolled her eyes at me. "Well that's not fair," she said. "Wait here, I'll check this out for you and then we can walk out together."

"Let me see you home," I said, and I told myself it was a reflex. I held my breath as she chewed at the inside of her lip.

"I don't want to trouble you," she said.

The tightness in my chest eased. "Staff housing, right? It's on my way." Which was a lie. It was in the opposite direction, but it could have been miles away and not made a bit of difference.

She stared at me for another moment and then nodded, "Alright. I forgot it would be dark and I think I would be jumping at every noise on my own. Did you bring your axe with you?"

I laughed and tried to cover my embarrassment with a hand over my eyes. "I was giving a lecture on alloys in weapons being affected by ley lines. I teach warfare strategy, but I don't generally carry weapons."

"I thought as much," she said, smiling and filing away the check-outs record. "That or juggling. I'll get my coat."

She left the book on the counter for me and walked back into the room behind the circulation desk. It struck me then, seeing the sway of her hips and set of her shoulders and finding that I wanted to follow her in there, and out of the library and anywhere else she might be going. This was what Isaac and Aiden had been waiting for. That gut instinct of attraction and interest that came so easily for them and seemed all but absent in me. Except where they were concerned. And now Joanna.

I was as eager to get back to the house to tell them as I was to see her home.

She returned, a black jacket over her blouse and a canvas bag at her side, nearly overfull with the books inside. I followed her out of the library and into the cool night. I waited for the ease of conversation to return and then realized almost too late that I might have to start it myself.

"Isaac and Aiden mentioned you," I said, which was as close to a hint about the exact direction of our thoughts as I could bring myself to make.

Her face froze as she walked at my side and my stomach sank, wondering if it was a misstep.

"I think I'm a bit of an anomaly here," she said. "I feel that way at least."

"I did as well," I said, rushing to smooth away whatever awkwardness I'd created.

"Well…" she mused, her face relaxing. "You *were* fifteen."

I coughed out a laugh. "I was. But Isaac felt the same too when he got his teaching position. He said you were from similar parts of Enmaire?"

She nodded. "The middle of nowhere parts."

"The only person I know who really feels at ease everywhere he goes is Aiden," I said and she laughed. "Canderfey is full of the unusual."

Her smile dropped. "That's where I'm afraid I differ." Before I could correct her she added, "What dangerous equipment will you be carrying to your next lecture?"

I followed the subject change. Aiden or Isaac would be better at drawing her out than I was. It was enough that she was allowing me to walk with her, to spend a little more time examining this new connection and the way it thrummed with our synchronized steps.

"Oh," I said. "I keep the heavy artillery in my office. Too much of a pain to cart around."

It was enough for me to make her grin.

ISAAC

I ROLLED THE CHARCOAL STICK IN MY HAND, SMUDGING THE BLACK INTO my fingerprints. Every time I set the charcoal to paper the image grew more confused. Aiden's profile, Callum's hands…Joanna Wick's tentative smile, all scattered across parchment in fragments.

Aiden was sitting on the floor in front of me with his back against the couch, stringing and tuning his old guitar. His fingers smoothed down the fret, a whistle following, for the dozenth time that evening. I started to scribble the curve and swell of the guitar in his hands and ended with the familiar silhouette of a woman. I dropped the crayon to the paper and Aiden's head lifted at the sound.

"What if he doesn't like her?" I asked.

"He will," Aiden said.

He had probably known the question niggling at me for the past hour, only waited for the words to come spilling out to give his answer.

"This is Callum," I said, baffled by his certainty. "He doesn't like… anyone but us."

Aiden smiled at that, it was an exaggeration but it was *close*. "Exactly. And he's never been shy about his disinterest." I grimaced and Aiden set the guitar aside, twisting on the floor to face me. "He already met her on the lawn."

"…Yes," I said.

"And he agreed to go see her tonight, which means he's willing to consider her," Aiden said, shrugging.

"Or it means he's feeling guilty, thinking he's the one holding us up in finishing our coven," I said.

"Maybe. That will only go so far," he said, reaching up to squeeze my knee. "I make sure to tell him how grateful I am that he's so determined not to fall in love carelessly," he added grinning. "It saves us so much time. But I think if he's considering her, it's a good sign. It's certainly progress."

"There's a long jump between consideration and love," I said, but Aiden's optimism was infectious and I settled my hand with his, linking our fingers together. "It…it feels different, doesn't it? Not just attraction but…"

"The pull," Aiden finished, nodding. "I remember the early days with you and Callum. Constantly running into each other. Knowing where to find you without knowing why. Making up excuses. Try," he said. "Try and guess where she is now."

The answer felt ready and it wasn't the time of night or any little scrap of information I'd gleaned from the two times of meeting her.

"Home," I said. "Alone, safe."

The front door opened and Aiden and I both stiffened. He pulled away to turn back to the living room entrance, picking the guitar up from the floor and settling it in his lap as if we hadn't been spoiling hours, waiting for Callum to return. It felt like long minutes before the front door shut and his footsteps sounded on the floorboards, drawing closer. He appeared in the doorway, a little windswept and pink-cheeked, with a strange expression on his face. He looked puzzled to find us there, waiting for him. Puzzled to find himself standing in our home at all.

I waited for Aiden to start in, to quiz him about the evening, but no one spoke at all for a very long time. Aiden's shoulders were tight and he was practically holding his breath. Callum seemed to not know which way was up. My stomach was flipping giddily and I was about to launch myself off the couch and…I didn't know what.

"I think it might be her," Callum said, staring down at the carpet as if he'd never seen it before.

Aiden exhaled a shaky breath, and my thoughts went skipping out of my head one by one.

"I don't know what to do," Callum said, frowning at us both. "I don't know what comes next?"

I laughed at that and slapped my hand over my mouth, the taste of charcoal bitter on my tongue.

"They call it wooing," Aiden said, a grin stretching over his face.

Callum crossed the room with heavy steps and collapsed down to the couch next to me, his head dropping onto my shoulder.

"I think she's going to take a lot of convincing," he said, wincing. Aiden scoffed, but I had a sneaking suspicion Callum was right. Joanna wasn't even calling herself a witch, she'd never imagine fitting herself into a coven.

That, at least, I had an inkling of how to solve.

7

JOANNA

THE WEEK FINISHED WITH BUSY DAYS IN THE LIBRARY AS CLASSWORK AND foot traffic picked up in the narrow stacks. I landed in my bed each night with aching feet and settled into heavy, dreamless, sleeping that left me groggy and headachy again by morning. Finally, on Sunday, I woke up to the sky warming with orange light, and instead of dragging myself out, I closed my eyes and rolled over. It was my day off and for the first time all week, I was planning on staying away from the library. I came downstairs hours later to my meager supplies in the kitchen and the still dreadfully bare space of my home. In the whole week, all I'd managed to accumulate was some groceries, a lamp to read by in the evening, and a stack of books.

It was time to get outside.

I gathered up two books—one, a wishy-washy text on everyday symbolism often over-looked due to generally being coincidental, and the other a magical reference of birds and their uses in spellwork—and my broad-brimmed hat to set out for a walk. The campus was quiet in the morning, although I had walked through large groups making rowdy, colorful magics the night before, so I wasn't surprised. I stopped at the campus grocery for provisions and then found a dirt path at the farthest edge of campus to follow into the woods.

I had the book on birds out in my hand as I walked deeper into the wilderness, sunlight mottling down through the tree branches to splash over the pages. At home, we didn't have dense woods like these but we had uneven walking paths, and I'd learned to feel my way over them with a book in front of my nose at a young age. What I wasn't used to was keeping track of which turns I took, since the flat, endless scenery of home made it easy to look out over a field and know where I was. I'd been walking through the chapter on the hawk when I heard my name and looked up, realizing how far I'd traveled and how little idea I had of how I'd gotten there.

"Joanna!" he called again, and I turned to the left, seeing a clearing of trees where the sun was flooding in to land on the drying heads of wildflowers past their season. Isaac stood at the far side, a smaller canvas set up at his side and an arrangement of tools peeking up above the weeds. He waved his arm at me. "Follow the path left and come join me."

I followed his directions like a reflex. I hadn't taken him up on his offer to revisit the studio, but there was no good reason to avoid him now. And I honestly couldn't think of anywhere I'd rather be than sitting in the sun reading, especially not with company like Isaac's.

He was sitting back at his canvas when I reached him, the scene of ringing trees and browning plants building on his painting, the shadows of the woods catching in dark umber browns and blues. There was a brick red coat spread over the ground next to his work spot and he nodded at it, smiling at me with dimples in his cheeks.

"I don't have a seat for visitors but I *can* offer velvet."

"My skirt can handle a little dirt better than that jacket," I said, bending to pick it up.

"Please," he pressed. "I'll feel like a good host. If you'd like to stay, that is."

"I think I better, I was halfway to finding myself very lost," I said. "And you're making those woods look too sinister for me to feel adventurous."

He wrinkled his nose at the painting. "I agree. It wasn't my intention but the woods usually know better when I try to paint them," he said.

"It makes me feel like fall is coming," I said and his smile returned at that, growing as I moved and sat down on his coat, feeling the burn of the sun warming the fabric under my fingers. "You're sure I won't bother you?" I asked.

"I'm certain," he said. "No more than I'll be disturbing your reading, at least."

Which was not at all. Isaac was as studious to his work as I was to my book, and the lack of conversation was filled in with the sounds of birds chattering and the trees creaking around us. It was as easy to sit in the quiet as it was to steal glances of him while he mixed a new color or leaned back and glared at the canvas in front of him. I pulled the sandwich I had bought at the grocery out of my bag and sat half of it down on a clear spot on his side table. He hummed and took it without really seeming to notice the offer.

"Aiden and Callum spoke highly of you," he said eventually.

I had moved through my book into the subject of sparrows, and it took me a few sentences before the words registered and I looked up from the page.

"Your covenmates," I said and he nodded, watching me. "I…you suit each other."

He glanced at his painting for a moment, adding a few brushstrokes, and then looked back at me. "We do." The corner of his mouth quirked up and there was a fierceness in his gaze like he was willing me to keep speaking. Heat was rising up my neck and I couldn't think of a thing to say, couldn't imagine a reason why these men would remark on me at all.

"How did you meet?" I asked, because it seemed the only safe thing to land on.

"Callum and I were new faculty in the same year. Aiden took it upon himself to mentor us." Isaac smirked at his painting and shrugged his shoulders. "At first, I think Cal and I bonded over having zero idea of what to do with Aiden. He fills up the space he occupies and we were attempting to blend into the background." He turned to me and I looked down into my lap, not sure how to speak of the man. Aiden King both intimidated me and had a magnetic pull, leaving me with the urge to soak up the brightness that poured out of him.

"But eventually you learn the gentleness in him," Isaac continued in my silence. "I was happy to find a coven so quickly. I'd pulled up all my roots leaving Hammish and it gave me somewhere to plant myself."

I bit my lip and waited for him to continue, but he was more patient than I. Or he had become reabsorbed by his art just as I had become absorbed in the story.

"And Callum?" I said, finding the curiosity outweighing the shyness.

A line tightened on his forehead between his eyebrows and he fiddled with his paint palette while I waited.

"He has a tendency to fight his own happiness," Isaac said, voice quiet and blending with the rustle of the clearing. He cleared his throat and continued, "But Aiden is determined and I am patient. And we are as settled as we can be until our fourth joins us."

My heart thrummed in my chest and then ached bitterly as my stomach dropped. They would find someone like them, someone powerful and fascinating and beautiful. A witch who would not pale behind their glow. Not a shabby library clerk from the country who could barely keep herself from staring open-mouthed at every new and strange thing she found in the world.

"Would you like to try?" he asked, standing up from his seat.

For a stupid, painful, moment I thought he'd followed where my head had traveled. Then he flicked his paintbrush in invitation, gesturing to the seat.

"I'll ruin it!" I said, glancing to the painting where the woods were growing deeper and the light stark on the canvas.

"You won't and even if you did it wouldn't matter," he said. He jumped forward, walking to where I was sitting and holding out his hand.

"I don't have any magic," I said.

His eyes tightened on my face. "That isn't true. You have charms on your shoes to keep them clean and a charm on your bag to keep it from splitting."

"That's…that's just everyday things. It's not *enough*." And I wasn't sure that I meant that in terms of the painting.

He crouched down to the ground until he was eye level with me. "How do you know? It only takes a little and what's the worst thing that could happen? You apply a bit of paint on the whole canvas that doesn't tell the viewer 'the woods are dark and dangerous today?' Try it."

It was not fair that someone should be so handsome and have a voice that sounded so warm and coaxing. I took his hand and let him pull me up from the ground. His thumb stroked over the back of my wrist and the thrill of the touch twined up my arm like a vine as he led me to the canvas. I sat down on the stool he had waiting, stiff and nervous, and he knelt in the grass next to me.

He passed me the paint palette, full of greens and grays and blues and browns with little flecks of yellow and white and red.

"It won't bite, Joanna," he soothed, holding a brush out by its handle.

"But it doesn't come with a set of instructions, either," I said.

"Pick a color, put it on the brush, apply to canvas," he said, and even without looking I could hear the grin in his voice.

"Is that how you got your teaching position?" I asked, hovering the soft bristles over the paint palette, eyes darting between the painting and the field in front of us.

"I save that speech for my problem students," he said, folding his legs on the ground, sitting down to give me space.

The painting as it was looked complete, sunlight catching at the tips of tall grass with the depth of the woods behind turning darker, like a warning. I hated to alter it in any way. I found a small smear of blue paint sneaking its way over an ashy brown and swirled them together, thinking the least obtrusive addition I could make was adding a bit more shadow near the back. My hand shook as I lifted the paintbrush, but with the first stroke of the bristles against the canvas, the action felt like a circuit connecting me to the painting. The process of painting was less choice and action than it was the follow-through of a background thought into an image on the canvas.

An image that looked less like the tree I had intended, and more like a dark figure lurking in the shadows.

I frowned and Isaac sat up, peering at the painting.

"Sinister," he said, eyebrows raised in surprise but smiling as if he were pleased. "How did it feel?"

"Magical," I said, voice tight. I cleared my throat and asked, "Was that yours or mine?"

"Some was mine," he said and his eyes were on my face as he spoke. "There's magic on the canvas, the brush, in the paints I mix. Whatever power you felt was yours."

My lips pursed and I stared at the figure, passing in dark between the trees and sending a chill up my spine.

"It gives the painting something to say," he said. "Like a story."

"I think you're being kind," I said, rolling my eyes. But when I turned my head back to look down at him he was still staring at me.

"Would you sit for me?" he asked. "I'd like to paint you."

I dropped the paint palette and brush into my lap at the question. "I...what? Today?"

"No," he laughed. "I think I'm done for the day, before the light goes. And Callum and Aiden are useless at making dinner. But I would like to, soon." He watched me for a minute, struggling to find a word to say or even to make eye contact, and then his hand settled gently on my arm. "I promise not to bully you into it like I did the painting. If you'd rather not..."

"Maybe," I said, finding my voice. "Let me think about it."

"Of course," he said.

Some openness had faded in his face, the smile going out of his eyes and I floundered for a moment. I wanted the time with him, but it was a desire accompanied by worry. Of enjoying myself too much, pretending the time meant more than friendly camaraderie.

"Would you walk me back to campus?" I asked. "I don't really know how I got here."

His shoulders eased and he stood, nodding. "I would love to."

I tried to help him with his packing, but Isaac shooed me back to my seat on his jacket. "I have a system," he said.

It looked more like 'tossing everything together in a small collapsible box.' Considering the box was smaller by far than the contents it carried, I figured it must require Isaac's magic more than any organization. By the end, all he had was a light backpack that fit around his stool and over his shoulders, and his painting in hand. He held his free hand out to me and I rose, bringing his coat along with me.

I slid my hand in his, trying not to think too much of the action, to stamp down the lightness that burned through me at the touch. He had a growing coven and it was only a friendly gesture, like two country folk together on a walk. Except then I couldn't think of an example of me holding a man's hand on a walk that *wasn't* romantic enough to start all of Bridgeston gossiping about who was getting grandchildren in the spring or whose heart would be broken before winter.

Even then, it would have been my heart broken. Isaac wasn't the type of man to stay in a place like Hammish or Bridgeston and it was a plain fact. And I...I could barely believe that I hadn't woken up back in my father's house by now, with my brother and his wife and their squalling, darling twins calling for me from downstairs.

"No wonder you got lost," Isaac said, drawing me back. "Your head's always traveling."

"Either in a book or daydreams," I agreed.

He drew me in, wrapping my hand around his elbow and pointing out scenes in the woods I had missed on my walk.

WE WERE BACK on campus in the late afternoon and the bustle of activity had returned. Not only that, but for the first time since I had arrived at Canderfey, I felt something other than invisible. Several groups of students and more than one person I suspected was faculty, paused in their tracks as Isaac walked me back to my little house on the row.

"It's more like a small town than it seems at first," Isaac whispered to me.

I didn't take any comfort in that. "I can find my way from here," I said. We were barely a block away from the street and Isaac probably could have seen me walk up to my door from where we stood now.

He didn't comment and I didn't let go of his arm so the suggestion died in the air.

I spent the rest of the walk considering what I could expect from Isaac. I knew what would be impossible, given who he was and who I was not. But it left so much room, for the possibility of a friendship at least.

"I'd make a very awkward model," I said as he walked up to my door.

His footsteps broke pace for a moment before turning to me. "I beg to differ," he said, eyes widening.

I bit my lip to keep from laughing as his face broke into a full grin. "Well, alright," I said, pulling my hand from his arm and taking the first step to my house. It gave me the inches I needed to be on eye level with him.

"Sometime soon?" he asked.

I nodded and shrugged. I didn't know when I'd really be brave enough, but now that he had offered there was a nervous little excitement in my belly to see what he would paint. To know how he saw me.

"Thank you for the afternoon, Joanna," he said, catching my hand again. And then he leaned in, with the scratch of stubble against my cheek and a soft, chaste kiss at the corner of my mouth.

He pulled away before I'd known what to do with myself and I searched his face for something I also refused to believe would be there. But he was smiling, easy and relaxed.

"See you soon," he said, releasing my hand with a last squeeze and starting off down the sidewalk.

"Yes," I managed, dumbly, after finding my throat too dry to say anything. I darted up the stairs, fumbling in my pockets for my keys as my cheeks heated. A part of me wanted to turn again, watch him walk away, and wait to see if he looked back too. Instead, I focused on turning the key in the lock and making it inside before I made a fool of myself.

An envelope skidded across the floorboards as I opened the door. I let myself droop down to the floor, the corner of my mouth still singing with the warmth of a kiss. I leant against the doorframe and picked up the envelope finding my name scrolled across the front.

Joanna,

The university has finally come through and one of Wrenshaw's last instruments—a horn rumored to gift the listener with the sensation of flight —is being delivered to my office this Tuesday. Come listen?

A. King

My head thunked back against the wood and a dull pounding started in my temples, matching the beat of my racing heart.

8

ISAAC

I was barely drifting off when the stairwell lamps flickered on and the boards began to creak. Then they muted and I sat up, staring at the mouth and waiting. Callum's hair shone fire red in the yellow light, bobbing up the stairs as he tiptoed up to the hall in the dead of night, shoulders hunched.

"Where were you?" I hissed, whispering from my bed.

He froze at the top of the stairs, shoulders drooping further. The stair lights turned off and he shuffled to my door, the moonlight catching at the muddy knees of his pants.

"There was something on the campus," he whispered from the door. "I went…hunting. Came up with nothing. Checked on Joanna's house, the wards are good there. Then-"

"You went to Joanna's?" I asked, the surprise stealing all the quiet out of my voice.

There was a thunk and Callum dropped his bag to the floor, then huff of breath as he walked in, landing in the blue glow of light from the night. He was wrestling with his coat as if he'd forgotten how they worked. I almost snapped at him as the coat landed on the floor too, but he went straight for the buttons of his vest next and his fingers slipped in exhaustion. I sighed and climbed out from under my sheets.

"She's alright," he said as I pushed his hands out of the way and started helping him out of his clothes.

"Was she home?" I asked.

"Think so…" he yawned and his jaw cracked. "Didn't knock."

I screwed my mouth shut and refrained from commenting. It was maybe a misguided gesture, but I couldn't blame him and I was a little too pleased that he thought of her in the first place.

"Are you alright?" I asked, looking up at his face. His cheeks looked hollow. It occurred to me then that he hadn't meant 'hunting' as searching. He'd been using magic.

"Frustrated," he bit out in a growl, then added, "Tired. I've never felt anything like it and then…then it just skittered away. I tracked every inch of campus and then the surrounding woods and town and *nothing*."

"Are you-?"

"I'm *sure*," he said, glaring at me, taking his belt from my hand and pulling it loose. "I don't know what it was or where it went, but I know it *was* there. Can I sleep in here tonight?"

"If you don't you'll have to pick up all your things and take them with you," I said. Aiden might be a laundry chute but I was not.

Callum nodded and bumped against me as he crossed to the bed, practically falling into it.

"Did you eat?" I asked.

"Mmmhmp." He nodded into my pillow. "S'good."

That meant there was a plate of scraps sitting out downstairs because Callum never remembered to put a finished dish in the sink. I rolled my eyes while he couldn't see and kicked his clothes out of the way before following him back into the bed. I settled on my side with my back to him but after one deep sigh of breath, Callum shuffled closer, pulling me down to my back and curling himself up to my side, pressing his face into my neck and hooking his bare leg over mine. I froze in surprise and then shifted to wrap my arm around his shoulder, scratching my nails into his hair and listening to his groan. I couldn't remember the last time Callum had wanted to *cuddle*.

"Are you sure you're alright?" I asked, lifting my free arm to brush at his shoulder resting over my chest.

"Mmfine," he said, voice already scratching with sleep and he settled as I squeezed him tight and set my lips against his forehead.

I WOKE AGAIN in the dark with a mouth sucking at the curve of my neck and Callum's hard length bumping against my back. His arm was stretched over my side, hand gripping at a pillow with a white knuckle grip as his hips rolled into me. He growled into my skin, teeth pinching and making me arch, and then the growl became a word.

"Joanna."

I didn't mean to but it came out all the same, a bright and sudden laugh. Callum froze and then inhaled sharply, breath panting against my neck, before rolling away. I went with him, turning to my other side so I could look at him in the dim light. His face was scrunched up tight in a grimace and he blinked one eye open at me before groaning and swinging his arm up over his face.

I stifled another laugh and bent to kiss at his shoulder, rubbing a hand over his tense stomach and feeling it twitch against my touch. "I'm flattered," I said. "But I imagine her to be much softer than any of us." Then I slid my hand down to squeeze where he was still hard and hot, stretching at the fabric of his underwear.

He snarled behind his arm as his hips lifted up into my hand.

"Don't tell Aiden," he said, words almost muffled by his arm. Then the arm was swung away and he surged up, pulling me into a messy, anxious kiss.

Callum was never what I expected; always greedier for affection, more passionate—his body always wound tight with the craving until it burst out of him. I let him pull me down, trapping my hand against him as his hips bucked and his teeth bit, lips sucking until the sleep at the back of my head was being replaced with hunger.

"Tell him what?" I asked.

Callum pulled back, head landing against the pillow and a knot between his eyes as he looked up at me. "That I...that I-" He stopped himself, kicking his legs between us until they were framing me, my cock fitting against his ass.

"That you're dreaming of her?" I asked, rearing back as he tried to lift up and kiss me again.

"Yes," he snapped, forehead furrowing.

"That you're attracted to her?" My cheeks almost hurt with my grin and Callum's eyes narrowed dangerously at me.

"Yes."

Then his legs knotted around my hips and he surged up, pushing at my chest until we had flipped on the mattress. I landed with an 'oof' that turned into an open-mouthed moan as he lowered his head and wrapped his lips around my ear lobe. He sucked at it with a 'pop' and then moved to the corner of my jaw.

"Do you think about her here?" I asked, low in his ear. "With us?"

He stiffened and then his hips pressed hard against mine, erections nuzzling together through the thin layer of cloth until we were both panting.

"Yes," he hissed into my neck.

"Tell me where you would want her," I said and Callum whimpered, a soft whine as his chest lowered and stuck to mine. "Next to us, watching? Between us? Or like this, like I am now? Squirming beneath you as I fill you up?"

"Fuck, Isaac," Callum breathed. His eyes were huge and dark and fixed to mine as I slid my hands under the band of his underwear and started to push them down his hips. "Yes. That's what I want."

I could taste the words, the way it tore at Callum to admit them. I liked to look at my lovers, watch their faces change with every touch, but I could make an exception for this. To imagine with him, to picture her face on the pillow. I leaned up and kissed Callum, hands busy easing fabric over his stiffness, and he muttered soft begging words against my lips.

I slid out from under him and he kicked his legs free, elbows braced against the mattress and head hanging low as I moved behind him.

"Lay down, love."

Callum settled and I straddled his hips, digging my fingers into his shoulders and working at the tension. He hissed behind his teeth, back tightening, and then sighed as I pushed my thumbs up the back of his neck.

"You'll have me asleep," he mumbled, cheek smashed to a pillow.

"So play with yourself," I said, smirking. It would do half the work for me and keep him distracted. Aiden said that Callum was like a jack in the box, coiling tighter until the strain was too much and he exploded with pent-up kinetic energy. I assumed Aiden just preferred to be the target for that energy. I had tricks for uncoiling him.

Callum's hips twisted and his hand burrowed beneath him. I watched his arm flex and twist as I moved down his back, wrestling with the knots beneath his shoulder-blades until I could see the way he melted into the mattress, eyes drooping and hand growing lazy. I stretched for the bedside table and grabbed the bottle of oil, squeezing some out into my palms and warming it before stroking it down his sides and then up over his ass, barely dipping my fingers between his cheeks.

Callum grunted beneath me. "Is there more oil?"

I added some to my palms and then took his hand to slick it. He sighed as he gripped himself again, moving smoother and a little faster.

"Tell me what you dream about. What you're thinking about right now," I said, bending to kiss the back of his neck. I spread my hands across the back of his thighs and worked up with my fingers dipping again, a little lower.

Callum was quiet for a moment. "Her eyes," he whispered. "Her hips." I hummed and he continued, "The way she looks at me out of the corner of her eye. How she teases. Like Aiden but...sweeter, dryer."

"Your knees," I said, soft so as not to pull him out of his thoughts of her. I coated my hands and fingers in the oil as Callum pushed up to his knees. "How chaste," I said. "You dream of her looking at you and that has you moaning in your sleep?"

Callum sucked in a breath as my hands went to work, one sliding up and down between his ass cheeks, a fingertip barely grazing at the puckered rosebud of sensitive flesh. The other went between us to stroke and pull at myself until I was tapping beneath him, swollen and aching.

"What do you want me to say?" he grumbled.

"Tell me how you would touch her," I said, circling his hole with my fingertip.

"I'm afraid to," he whispered.

"To touch her?" I asked, brow furrowing.

"That I'll mess up."

It wasn't as if I had forgotten that Callum had given up interest in anyone but me or Aiden, only that I forgot that meant he hadn't been with a woman in over a decade. Or anyone new.

"It's not so different," I said. His ass was twitching in my direction, my middle finger just resting at his opening with him nudging back, impatient. I pressed in, just to the first knuckle and Callum released himself to rise up to his elbows, pushing back and fitting my finger deeper.

"Like…right now, I'm thinking about how her legs would look wrapped around your hips as you filled her up," I said, pumping my hand for him and watching his mouth fall open, face grimacing down at the mattress. "Think about how warm she'd be, how wet we could get her."

I pushed my index finger in, adding to the stretch and he buried a cry into the pillow, one of relief. His hips rolled, dipping into the fantasy of a woman, and a whimper echoed from his mouth.

"I need this faster, Isaac," Callum said through gritted teeth.

I tested him, adding a third finger but his face only relaxed and he gave easily. I pulled my hand free and then held him open, his hips holding still while I rested the blunt head of my cock against his entrance.

"I want to taste her," Callum whispered. "Have her soak my tongue." And then a moan broke free as I pushed in an inch.

"I want to know what she sounds like, crying out for you," I said, holding still.

Callum's shoulders tensed, the lines of muscle in his back standing out in shadow. "Want to feel her softness."

"Good," I said, and I entered him another inch, swallowing at the hot grip of him. "And?"

"Damn it, Isaac," he hissed but I held still, rocking away as he tried to push back against me. "I want to suck on her breasts...*oh*." He breathed deeply and continued, "Pull her legs up around our hips and fuck her fast, play with her clit. Bite at her neck."

My hips were settled against him and his head was rolling back and forth. "Would you leave a bruise?" I asked. I wanted to mark her, in secret spots for our eyes only.

"Only if she wanted me to," Callum said and he looked back over his shoulder to smile at me. He'd left hickeys on my neck back when we'd started courting and it'd been free gossip for the campus for weeks. "Please, Isaac."

I slid my hands up and down his sides and then took his hips in a hard grip. "Picture her there."

"Tell me," he said, and our hips rolled down together.

"I want to watch her face as she comes for us," I said, drawing back and surging forward and feeling the first sparking beat of pleasure in my groin. "Watch her take you in her mouth and make you fall apart."

Callum lifted his head from the pillow and one hand braced itself there, leaving room for another face to nuzzle against.

"Her skin," I said, finding a rhythm with the words, with the sound of Callum's breaths and the hiccup of a whine at the back of his throat. "I want to mark it too, to claim her. Fill the bed with the smell of her like... like..."

Like cookies my mother had made on rainy days. The spice of cinnamon and the thick halo of sugar in the air. I groaned as Callum conjured it around us, the cloud of sweetness and spice. I wondered how she would smell with us inside of her.

I pressed my belly to Callum's back as my hips bucked and his rolled forward into nothing. My hand found Callum's already folded around the sheets as if he were holding hers, and we knotted our fingers together and braced ourselves. My other hand stroked down his chest and then wrapped itself around his cock. His pulse was throbbing against my palm and his voice was breaking in the air.

I left wet, licking kisses over his spine, my breaths sobbing out on his skin.

"Fuck, Isaac, I won't last," he growled and jerked in uneven, desperate hitches and thrusts.

There was a spike of white-hot, dizzying sensation running up my own spine. I released his hand on the bed and wrapped my arm around his chest and we fell hard into the bed, gasping and groaning together as we fell apart. Callum burst and spilled himself over his stomach and the sheets and my hand and I buried myself deep and held on tight to him, my teeth grasping at his shoulder.

His arm wrapped over mine and he caught his foot around the underwear, lost somewhere in the sheets, and drew it up to wipe as much away as he could.

"We're going to have to do better than that for her," he mumbled.

I snorted against his skin and left a soft kiss where I had bit. I moved to pull away and one of his hands landed on my hip to hold me still.

"Not yet," he said. So I curled myself around his back and kissed his neck and behind his ear. "Don't tell Aiden, yet." The words were slurring with sleep and I rolled my eyes a little, my own head feeling heavy and drowsy.

"It's all going to work out," I murmured, and Callum sighed and shifted, either to nod or to drop off into sleep.

9

———

JOANNA

AIDEN SAT ON A BENCH IN FRONT OF AN UPRIGHT PIANO WITH A LONG pipe-like instrument, as tall as my waist and narrow in his hands. The wood gleamed red as he polished at the metal fixtures running up the long body that twisted back around itself. Sunset streaked in from the window at the far end of the room, glinting like gold on the pedals and tuning clamps and curving over his broad shoulders like a heavenly silhouette.

"That looks like a weapon," I said, standing in the doorway of his office.

"I would take serious issue with anyone who tried to use it as such," Aiden said. His eyes traveled openly from my boots up to my face, expression easy and eyes slanted with interest. "Thank you for coming."

"I'm flattered you asked," I said, which was true. I was baffled too, and flustered, and nervous. I felt like I hadn't stopped blushing since Isaac had left me standing on my stoop on Sunday, and Aiden's gaze—somehow both casual *and* thorough—was no help.

"Will you come in and sit?" he asked, nodding to an armchair waiting at the desk on the opposite side of the room as his piano.

55

"Why *did* you invite me?" I asked, finding that words came easier if I didn't have to look directly back at him.

"I like an audience," he said. I caught his grin as I sat in the chair. It was too big for me, Aiden was broader and taller by far, but I fit nicely when I curled up in the seat.

"And you've scared off all the other potentials?" I said.

He laughed. "Some of them, yes. Others, I've simply worn out my welcome."

"Settling for a little country librarian," I teased.

He hummed at that, glancing at me out of the side of his eyes, and the sound was almost a growl for how low it was. "At the very least you'll be a university librarian soon, Joanna," he said.

I ignored the flutter in my stomach at the way his voice purred over my name. That was only how he spoke. And I was spending too much time with these men, searching in the conversation for an invitation that wasn't really being issued.

Isaac was bad enough, but at least he had the charm of home on his edges. Aiden was the kind of man I would never have imagined meeting because I could never have imagined a man *like* him. He was style and charm and art in an exquisitely perfect package. Flirting aside, and his interaction with Gwen had made it clear he did plenty of that, I had no chance of keeping his interest past the novelty.

"What's it called?" I asked, nodding at the horn in his hands.

"Ah yes, the Wing Horn," he said, lifting the instrument up off his lap and holding it vertically in the air. Everything from the height and gleam and warm tone of it suited him. "Wrenshaw was a little romantic and he was constantly building new pieces, trying to make it impossible for anyone to really learn his techniques. At least until he published. There are a few Wing Horns of his, each one a different manner of flight, supposedly."

"Have you heard any before?" I asked.

"Once, at a concert my parents took me to when I was young," he said. He was more interested in the Wing Horn now than me, and I settled deeper into the chair, happy to watch him handling the piece while ruminating. "It *did* feel like flying to listen. Dizzying and fast and like the floor fell away right from under where we sat. Then my mother told me to close my eyes and…the music just soared and took us with it."

His face softened as he spoke, shedding the smirk that lingered at the corner of his mouth and the tight focus that left me squirming. The catlike cunning and handsomeness transformed into something open and gentle and the sight left me warm, cocooned in the chair that smelled like spice and the sharp pine of wood polish.

"Would you like to hear?" he asked. The quirk in his grin returned with the glint in his eye, but this time instead of wanting to shy away from it, I answered it with my own.

"Please," I said.

He held my gaze for a moment, eyes darkening, and then slowly lifted the horn up to set the reed to his lips in a kiss. The first note rose, sweet and coiling through the air, and the room spun without moving. I closed my eyes as the sound deepened, reverberating around me and against my skin. There was no seat beneath me, no worn fabric beneath my fingertips, just the glow of the sun falling in through the window and stretching out to stroke at my cheeks.

Aiden spun the single note into several, rising and falling and flurrying around each other. Something like a breeze brushed through my thoughts. I pictured the lane at home that stretched flat and straight through the county and without pulling at the image it began rushing beneath me. The music built and I flew higher, watched the pattern of the fields organize themselves into a quilt of my hometown, all while the wind wrapped itself around my waist and limbs and carried me off like a leaf or a bit of cotton weed.

I was partway between woman and bird and speck of dust on the air, losing the sense of having a form or thoughts and feeling; only *flight*.

Too soon, *far* too soon for my liking, the whirlwind settled. My shoulders were heavy and the roots of my hair ached as I remembered them. There was a soft chair beneath and it felt as hard as landing from a great height. I opened my eyes and the smell of fresh air was replaced with wood polish and dry pages. The sun was shifting lower and casting shadows in the room.

Aiden waited for me to speak, eyes soft on my face.

"Like…floating," I said, then added, "Is there more?"

His laugh was like gravel after the pure notes of the horn. "That's it for now. From me, at least. I'll write you something," he said. "A flight suite."

He could find a better use of that time, I was sure, but I didn't want to argue. I could enjoy the idea of the offer without building expectations.

"I do, however, have a recording I think you would like," he said. He grabbed a case that had been leaning against the piano and started to pack away the horn.

"I should go," I said, but I didn't move to get up out of the chair.

"Stay a little longer," he said, looking at me over from over his shoulder which I had been busy watching shift beneath his jacket. "Or I've dragged you all the way up here for a few bars of music."

"And a few moments of flying," I said, laughing.

His grin turned wicked for a moment and then settled. "My favorite recording and I'll walk you home."

"Everyone is always offering to walk me home," I said. "I must look easily disoriented."

"You *look* like good company," he countered, crossing the room to rifle the contents of a shelf, heavy with records. "And maybe a little bit stubborn."

"The last part's true. But alright, I'll listen."

He had already pulled the envelope off the shelf and turned to the gramophone. I had seen one before in the Bridgeston pub, a rickety old thing that skipped and hissed through the limited collection of stomping tunes the town agreed on. Aiden loaded the record into the player with quick, practiced precision. Even if I had been determined to leave he would have had the music playing before I'd made it to the door.

"I hope you like water," he said, dropping the needle. He came to join me, sitting on the floor in front of the chair and then leaning back, resting his head against my knees.

There was a hiss of static and then we were swimming in music; piano keys bursting into bubbling notes, strings sweeping tidal waves into the room around us, and a low groaning tuba in the background dropping away the world and leaving the ocean beating beneath us.

My fingers reached down and grabbed onto Aiden's shoulder to steady myself and he rested his cheek there. His own hand reached back and wrapped around my ankle as we were swallowed up in sound.

"YOU MUST BE JOANNA."

I was standing on a ladder, arguing under my breath with a group of divination texts that insisted upon organizing themselves by year of publication instead of the last name of the author. And I thought to myself, *must I be Joanna*? Because it seemed as if 'Joanna' had a great deal going on in her life and I wondered if it might be nice to be someone else.

"The new librarian trainee," the voice behind me added.

That, at least, I could not argue. I twisted on the ladder and looked down to find one of the most fashionable women I had ever seen. And beautiful, or at least polished to the point of being inarguably perfect. She was tall, enough so that she barely had to crane her neck to look up at where I stood on the ladder, and statuesque in sapphire blues and charcoal silks that sang against her brown, glowing skin.

"What can I help you with?" I asked.

Her facial features were large and well made-up, and her black hair was piled high, lustrous and smelling strongly of roses. But in spite of all that there was something straightforward about her and she looked less amused by me than most people on campus.

"Gwen sent me for The Arcanary," she said, pointing to a book near my hand. "But I suspect now she sent me up to meet you since we've been gossiping about you."

I turned away to cover my surprise, grabbing The Arcanary as an excuse. She was waiting, her expression even and patient, when I turned back.

"What is there to gossip about?" I asked.

"Oh," she waved her hand in the air and then grabbed the book I held out. "It depends on what you're interested in. For some, it's where you came from. And for others, it's the company you keep," she paused at that, and I suspected she had a little interest there too. She grinned and then shrugged. "Personally, I'm fascinated to know what you can do."

"Most days I'm lucky to manage alphabetization," I said, my voice clipping.

"Who could blame you, with this lot?" she asked looking at the shelves around us.

"Hildy?" Gwen appeared from around the corner. "There you are. And Joanna, of course. Why are you still here?"

Hildy leaned towards Gwen as the other woman approached, and Gwen's arm wrapped around her waist. I noted that no matter how Gwen dressed—a lot like me—*she* never looked drab. Even next to all that silk and embroidery and perfume.

"Just because you work the extra hours doesn't mean you're paid for them, now mark your place and come with me," Gwen said to me. She looked to Hildy and added, "The others are waiting."

"I was going to stay and read," I said. I wasn't the only one who hung around outside of their shift and I hadn't gotten in trouble for it before now.

"And then go home and eat, what? A tomato and cheese sand-wich?" Gwen asked, raising her eyebrows. "Come have dinner with us."

I pulled my notebook from my pocket and came down the ladder steps, writing down the shelf I had stopped at and *needs rearranged to author's last name NOT publication.*

"The other library staff?" I asked, tucking the notebook away.

"Book mice?" Hildy laughed. "Nooo. Dinner with our coven."

"Don't say no," Gwen said as I opened my mouth in surprise. "Or I won't offer again, and you'll miss very good cooking."

"Oh yes, you must come," Hildy echoed.

I swallowed down my excuse and made to follow the two women down to the lobby. "Gwen…how did you know what I was planning to eat?"

"I'm clairvoyant," Gwen said.

"She spied in your lunch box," Hildy said, winking at me over her shoulder.

Downstairs, waiting for us, or at least for Gwen and Hildy, were the others. A man, straight and thin as an arrow who was as elegant as Hildy and as sharply focused as Gwen with moon pale skin and short black hair. At his side was a petite person, beautiful and fae with catlike green eyes and wispy blonde hair brushing high, golden cheekbones. They ignored gender entirely in body and dress, and they looked like a magical creature's best impression of a human. Canderfey seemed the place for that kind of thing and Gwen was probably too matter of fact to care.

"Joanna Wick," Gwen said, gesturing to me. "My covenmates, Hildy Samanta, Tatsuo Ito," she said, and the man stepped forward to shake my hand. She finished with the most curious of the group. "And Bryce Gast."

Bryce smiled at me and it was toothy and edged and left me more certain than ever that they were not strictly human, and neither male nor female. But it was Tatsuo that walked at my side through the campus, while Bryce walked to the front to lead our party.

"How are you settling?" Tatsuo asked, with his hands folded together at his back.

"Alright, I think," I said slowly. The library was enjoyable at least, it was everything else that left me not knowing which way was up.

"Do you enjoy your work?"

"I love my work," I said, happy to have a simple question. "It's the only thing I've ever really wanted to do."

"*That* is a blessing," he said. "I have yet to decide what I enjoy in work."

Hildy looked over her shoulder at that and they smiled softly at one another.

"What have you tried?" I asked.

"Oh, aura healing, astrology, herbalism, phrenology, predictive hallucinations…"

I started to laugh as the list went on, not certain whether or not he was teasing me but enjoying the variety all the same. Tatsuo's smile deepened in response.

"What are you trying now?" I asked, interrupting the list after 'beekeeping.'

"Writing," Tatsuo said, raising his eyebrows at me.

"What kind of writing?" I asked, taking the bait.

"Trance writing, it's a wonderful process for working out the subconscious," he said. "You should try it."

"I'm not sure I'd like what came out," I said and Gwen snorted ahead of us.

"It's only words," Tatsuo said with heavy sweetness and Gwen eyed him over her glasses.

We reached the neighborhood at the north edge of campus where permanent faculty lived. The houses were beautiful, tall and broad and colorful, built for covens and families rather than individuals. There were gardens in the front yards already planted with bright orange blossoms hearty enough for the coming chill of fall.

Gwen and her coven lived in a sprawling cornflower blue house with cream shutters and a porch wrapping from the front steps all the way to the back of the house. The yard was surrounded by a tidy hedge and the view through the windows into the house was obstructed with pale blue lace curtains. It had the look of Hildy about it, but even Bryce, wild and quiet, seemed settled and comfortable as they walked up the steps to the front door.

Tatsuo and I made to turn up the walkway to the house and my eye was caught by another, down at the end of the block. A red brick beast of a house, narrower and taller than the others around it, sat glowing in the sunset. I couldn't see much, just bay windows curving out into a trim yard, and several chimneys stretching up into the sky, one of them spitting a little trickle of smoke. I turned away at the first pang in my chest. There was no reason to feel it, but I was certain that was their house, Isaac and Aiden and Callum's.

Tatsuo had walked ahead without me and the four of them waited on the porch for me. A perfect set, elegant and powerful with a fascinating, delicate, ferocity. Tatsuo and Hildy had their arms around each other's waists and Hildy's knowing smile had been replaced with something fragile and private. Bryce's hand was in Gwen's, possibly an effort on the latter's part to keep them patient while they waited on me.

I hurried up to the steps, begging my mind to quit wishing for something I was not meant for.

10

JOANNA

The next morning I found that someone else had managed to organize the divination shelf I'd been working on, and this time had managed to make it stick. I was a little jealous and a bit disappointed in myself for not handling the work myself. It was as if I was being shown proof that even training as a simple librarian, here in Canderfey I failed to measure up. It put a fire in my belly and I finished my shelving on a tear of speed and set to bullying the books to rights in the restricted section for the rest of the day.

I caught sight of myself in a window near the end of the day—hair in a mess sticking at odd angles around my head, my hands and white shirt smudged with dust and old ink, and my cheeks red with exertion. I remembered that I had agreed to see Isaac, to sit for a sketch, after I was done at the library and I wondered if I couldn't sneak home first. Not that I had much better to wear or any chance of fixing hair that refused to do anything other than what it liked. I tried anyway, combing my fingers through tangled curls as I turned away from the window and found Callum Pike waiting for me at the end of the aisle, eyes wide and startled.

"You look like you've been in an argument," he said.

"Only with books," I answered.

"The rumors are true?" he asked, coming closer with his arms full of books. "They rearrange themselves."

"That or you professors are playing tricks on me," I said, narrowing my eyes at him.

His cheeks pinked and my stomach churned. "I used to sneak up here as a student," he said, looking around. "Woollard always caught me, dragged me out by the earlobes."

"She does that to me sometimes too," I said.

Callum laughed and it was a surprised noise, like I had caught him in a trap of humor he hadn't expected. I thought of the way Isaac spoke of him and wondered if a laugh was a rare sound from Callum.

"Isaac mentioned he'd be seeing you later, for a portrait," Callum said, stepping closer. Closer than librarians and professors really needed to stand, but farther than my skin ached to have him.

"I'm afraid I will be the first person to fail at being the subject of a portrait," I admitted.

"You'll do better than me," he said, grinning like the sun. "He has yet to manage it and we've known each other for over a decade."

From the back of my thoughts came the image of the hawk, wounded and screaming and still soaring, and I realized the color of the copper feathers matched Callum's hair, that the glaring green eyes of the painting were fixed to my face now. I wasn't sure how right he was about that claim, but I couldn't find my voice to correct him.

"I look forward to seeing it, either way," he said and this time I realized I had been the one to step forward, searching his expression for the hawk in the painting.

"I've never been very good at being looked at," I said, which was a thought I hadn't meant to speak aloud, but there it was and it was true.

"You'll have practice," he said.

I was getting practice right now and it made my heartbeat pound in my ears and my skin felt charged and sensitive to the air against it. And I didn't feel shy or embarrassed under Callum's gaze at all. If anything, I felt like I was stretching up to him, trying to catch more of that sunlight feeling. That being looked at should only be the precursor to being touched.

"Joanna," he said, and his eyes flicked down to my mouth where my lips were parted and catching a breath.

The books shifted between us, pushed aside and he had done that trick again; the one where what he was holding seemed to fit itself away. But I was distracted by his now free hand reaching up to cup my jaw and lift my chin. I blinked and my eyelids felt heavy as I watched him bend his head to mine, nose brushing across my cheek before his lips settled over mine, slanted and pulling gently.

It was a kiss, but it felt something like the flying of Aiden playing the Wing Horn and something like the burn of connection while painting with Isaac's brush and canvas. And something like lifting my face up to the sky to feel the scorch of the sun on my skin.

I was on my toes, hands reaching for something to hold onto, when Callum nipped at my bottom lip and heat burst in my belly, and the world—and good sense—returned to my head.

I yanked myself away, steps tripping backward and my hands clapping over my mouth.

"I'm sorry!" I said, and my eyes searched the library around us, seeing no one. The relief was a heavy, queasy feeling in the moment.

"No, Joanna, I-" he started, face torn and twisted with deep lines digging into his forehead.

"You have a *coven,*" I hissed and watched him swallow his words, expression falling. "And I have no right-"

"You have every right," he said. His hand reached out for me and I fell back a step. My stomach twisted as he winced, but his shoulders set straight and he fixed his eyes to mine and said, "We want you. In the coven, with us. I shouldn't have pushed but..."

He trailed off as my head shook, back and forth in the rapid beat of my heart pounding. I closed my eyes, covering them with a shaking hand as bone-deep disbelief battled with the pathetic part of me wishing for the words to be true.

"I'm not a witch," I said, and my voice was dry in my throat.

"You are," he said, but I heard the uncertainty. "Surely there must be something…all the librarians at Canderfey can do something."

I lowered my hand and looked up at him.

I swallowed. "But I'm not a librarian. And I probably won't be. I can barely keep dust off the shelves."

It was something in his expression, the way his eyes darted over the shelves like he was scrambling for an answer as he said, "We'll… think of something."

"Is this a joke?" I asked, flat and low. My stomach sank. Outside the bells for the hour echoed over the campus.

Callum's face went blank with surprise. "A joke?"

It had to be. It made more sense that they were *laughing* at me than that…that I could be of actual interest to them. The knots in my gut hardened to pits.

"The three of you finding the *least* likely person to ever- ever be *worthy* of you," I spat, feeling triumphant in anger, in seeing his face sharpen at my words. "And then you all chase her around the campus. What did you want? To seduce me? You could have done it without the charade of sweetness. Or is me being foolish enough to fall for the fantasy part of the fun?"

"Joanna, stop. None of that is true," he said. But the sweet, earnest bend of his voice was paired with the tight anger in his face.

I *still* wanted to believe. It was in the shake of my hands and the way my heart seemed to thrash inside its cage and the stupid tears gathering at the corners of my eyes. With all the self-disgust I could muster I stared at Callum and said, "I want you to leave me alone. All three of you."

I had to push past him to get to the stairs. It was after five and I was free to leave the library, and I burnt on the inside knowing I would not even want to come back the next day or the day after. He didn't grab for me, but his voice pleaded my name as I edged around him and without the tangle of his expression the tone curled around me, drawing at my weakness. I whimpered as the tears spilled over and I ran to the stairs, steps skidding.

"Please, wait," he whispered, words cracking.

I ignored the stares in the library, grabbing my bag and rushing out onto the lawn as classes let out. It was easier to be invisible, head ducked down, in the crowd of students busy with themselves. I thought I would make it to my house and I knew the walk well enough to follow it with my eyes on the ground, but I forgot where else it would lead me.

"Joanna," Isaac said, a gentle hand on my elbow and a kiss on my wet cheek as I was pulled to a stop. I looked up as he drew back and his wide smile fell. "What's happened?"

"Get away from me," I whispered, but it could barely be heard over the tears in my throat and the crowd around us.

He heard it and the reaction was as sudden as if I had struck him with my fist. But it smoothed away and he huddled in closer, broad shoulders blocking me from the bustle around us.

"Please," he said, head lowering almost to mine. "Please tell me what's wrong."

"Callum kissed me." I hadn't meant to say it, but it was easier than shoving Isaac away in all this crowd. Than making a bigger idiot of myself at this university than I already had managed to.

Isaac's eyes lightened for a moment but they searched my face. He didn't look triumphant or angry or jealous. He just looked…concerned.

I didn't want Isaac to be a liar. More than the others even, I wanted Isaac to be a friend to me. An honest one.

"We can go into my office," he said and I looked over his shoulder. I had walked directly past the Burgess Building on my way home. "I was getting you flowers," he added, lifting up a bouquet of crimson roses. "For the portrait."

They would outshine me by far, I thought, almost spitefully. I had always been a little unsure of myself, even in Bridgeston. I was humble like my neighbors but more interested in the world outside our village than the others. I'd built up a fantasy in my head of finding myself in Canderfey, of growing into someone new, but instead I'd only been seeing how little I measured up. Suddenly I hated this place, and these men, for upsetting the fragile truce I'd maintained with myself, for pulling me out of my books and giving me something real to compare my own life to.

"I only want to help, Joanna, I promise," Isaac said, gray-blue eyes aching like a storm cloud about to burst.

If Isaac was a liar, he was the best of them. I didn't want him to be that. I didn't want to be the person I saw myself as either.

I nodded and whispered, "Alright."

His hand at my elbow slid down to my hand and I followed him up the stairs of the arts building. I kept my eyes fixed to his back as chattering students curved around us until we were up to the third floor. Isaac held the door open for me and left it open by an inch behind us.

He had a corner office with windows on two walls and it looked as though he had converted the small space into another studio for himself. Smaller easels took up more room than the minuscule desk pushed into the corner next to a closet door. The room smelled like him and felt inhabited by him and against my better judgment I could feel the tension easing out of me. He pulled the desk chair out for me and grabbed a low stool for himself after putting the bundle of roses together in a short, black vase. He pulled the stool close until our knees were almost touching, and then he simply waited.

"He said that you want me in your coven," I said, watching him.

"That's true," he said, without any hesitation. He smiled a little and then added, "Although I think we agreed to talk to you about it as a group. After some time."

"Isaac, that's not how it works. You need a witch."

"We do," he said nodding.

I raised my eyebrows, waiting for him to catch up, but his smile only flickered back. "I'm *not* one," I said.

"I think you might be," he said. "I haven't said anything to the others yet. Because you deserve to know first, of course."

I released something between a laugh and a cough. "Do you honestly think I could have missed it somehow? I'm twenty-seven years old."

"Are you?" he asked, smiling. "I guessed about that."

"Isaac," I said, feeling something like panic rising up in my chest. I had been so angry with Callum, at the very idea he suggested. Certain that it *must* be a trick or a lie. It didn't seem fair that it could feel silly and sweet here with Isaac. "I don't understand. If you aren't sure that I am a witch, how can you even think of me being in the coven?"

"I haven't thought of anything else since meeting you," Isaac said and my heartbeat paused for a moment, as if to listen. "Neither have the others, I think. Aiden could care less if you had magic or not, honestly. Callum just assumes you must."

"I don't," I said, trying to press the words to him, into his head. Because it hurt more to think he might really want me when I was so unfit to be in a coven, than it did to think he was making fun of me.

"What did you say to Callum?" he asked.

I looked down into my lap, fidgeting with my bag where it sat. "I thought you were all making fun of me."

"Oh, Joanna." He jumped off the stool he'd been sitting on and came to kneel in front of me, lifting my hands from my lap and fitting them in his own. "It's not that. I swear to you. We may have been clumsy, but I promise we were sincere."

I blinked a new bout of tears away, staring out the window and Isaac waited at my feet, thumbs making patterns over my knuckles.

"If you were a witch," he started, soft and slow. "Would you accept our invitation? At least consider us?"

I chewed at the inside of my mouth for a long minute, and then looked to him. "Yes," I whispered.

He beamed at me, lifting my hands to kiss them, before standing up from the floor and crossing to one of his easels. He brought me a stick of white chalk. "Take this," he said.

I took it, forehead furrowing in confusion at the leap between my confession and this.

"I don't want an art lesson right now," I said.

He grinned and pulled me up from the chair. "It isn't an art lesson, it's a magic lesson," he said. He dragged me a foot over to stand in front of the closet door.

"I'm not sure I want that either," I mumbled.

Isaac's hands were warm around my waist as he stood behind me, and he pressed a kiss to the back of my neck. His breath was in my hair and his hands squeezed once on my sides before releasing me and stepping back.

"Write on the door," he said, and then after I'd stared at him for too long he added, "With the chalk."

I frowned at him and then lifted the chalk up to scribble on the door. *This is sil-*

"No, no, no." Isaac rushed forward to grab my hand and stop the sentence. "Not that."

"But it's true," I said, raising my eyebrows.

He opened his mouth to respond and then shut it again, glancing between me and the door. "Wipe that off and…and write 'door'," he said.

"That's even sillier."

"Joanna," he said, voice dropping. He was at my side, our shoulders brushing and we were close enough in height that I would only need to twist and lift on my toes a bit to be kissing him. His eyes flicked down to my lips and I thought he would do it, but then he looked to the door. "It will only take a minute to humor me. And if I'm wrong it won't change how I feel or Callum feels or Aiden feels about you."

I wasn't sure how to explain that while I returned their feelings, I wan't *prepared* for them.

I sighed and reached up, smudging the chalk away with the heel of my hand. "Door," I said, writing the word out in clear, square letters.

"Now, 'to'," Isaac said.

I wrote *'to.'*

"Now think of a place it might lead to, *other* than the closet," he said, giving me a significant look. "And then write that place."

Like an escape route, I thought. And then I wrote *'my bedroom.'*

He smiled at my work, all four words of it, and then we stared at each other.

"Now what?" I asked.

"Now you open it," he said as if it should be obvious. And his eyes were bright and his grin was twitching, waiting to grow brighter.

I looked at the door blankly. "Isaac, I've read about portals and you don't make them with chalk and a few words in a tidy hand. There's… runes and preparation, and meditation and-"

"Open the door, Joanna," he said, lips pressed to my cheek.

11

AIDEN

"I've bungled it!"

The front door slammed shut and I looked up from the violin I'd been sanding, just in time to watch Callum storm into the living room, fists in his hair as if he were trying to pull the whole lot out at once.

"Bungled what?" I asked.

"Joanna," Callum sighed, collapsing into an armchair. His face was crashing down to the floor with a weight that dripped down his whole body. "I've ruined it. Again. Aide, I'm so sorry. You and Isaac are better off without me. You'd have a prop-"

"Don't be an idiot," I said, cutting him short. "We're all but useless without you. Now tell me what happened."

"She thinks it's a joke," Callum whispered, head dropping to the back of the chair. "Worse, she thinks *she's* the butt of it. I went wrong somewhere and now..."

I set the violin down on the low table in front of me and brushed the sawdust away into nothing before standing. Callum looked as though he were halfway to coming up with a spell to disintegrate himself. It struck me suddenly. Callum looked *awful*. Over a woman.

"You like her," I said, trying and failing not to grin.

75

He groaned and rolled his head to glare at me, but it melted quickly into an agonized twist of his expression. "I want her," he said. "You're right. She's...she feels like she should fit, right here," he said, gesturing to the space between us.

I crossed the room and bent over him, kissing his forehead. "You haven't bungled anything," I said. He was still glaring up at me, but that was fair since I was probably still smiling. But a lovesick Callum? That was new. And worth a little good humor. "Not alone," I added. "We went about this wrong. We'll approach her together. Invite her to dinner. Be the decent gentleman we are rather than cornering her from all sides like a pack of starving wolves."

"I *feel* starved when I look at her," Callum whispered.

I laughed at his grimace. "About damn time, Pike. Now, where did you leave her?"

"She ran out of the library," he said, and his nails were nearly digging grooves into the arms of the chair. "Told me to stay away from her. All of us."

My eyes widened at that. "That's... What did you do to her?"

"Kissed her," Callum said, and I congratulated myself at not laughing at the announcement or the way his bottom lip was threatening to pout.

"I see. Well, we better go get Isaac before we find her," I said.

"Should we?" Callum asked. "Find her, that is. Wouldn't it be better to...give her space?"

"Maybe, but I think Isaac has a better read on her emotions. And they were supposed to meet today so he'll be worrying. Come on. No sulking, yet," I said, grabbing his elbows and pulling him up from the chair.

"Wasn't sulking," he muttered, but his feet dragged as he followed me.

12

JOANNA

My hand was on the door handle when Isaac's office door swung open and Aiden and Callum ran in. It was the first time I had ever been in their company all together and the effect was immediate. I felt settled and excited at the same time, grounded and light. I knew that something inside of me, deeper than my thoughts or the nervous anxiety that twisted me up in knots around them, had made the decision for me. I wanted these men. I wanted the magic that would make me worth being with them.

"Ah," Aiden said, upon seeing me.

Callum behind him froze in his tracks and then stared down at the floor, and I knew I owed him an apology for what I'd said.

"It's good that you're here, but it's important that you don't interrupt," Isaac said to them. And then after turning to me and then back again, he added, "We'd better close the door."

Both men stepped inside and shut the door behind them, but Callum hugged himself to the wall as if he were scared to come closer. The anger I had seen in the library was turned inwards and I wanted to leave the little closet door project behind to speak to him. Isaac caught my eye and shook his head slightly.

"Just to know," he said to me.

I twisted the handle and swung the door out, still staring back at Isaac, prepared for his disappointment. But the sunlight from the street outside my bedroom window hit my cheek and I looked through the doorway, mouth falling open. Inside of the little narrow closet door was my creaky bed with books and nightclothes tossed on the covers, and my small case I had traveled with against the wall, and my tiny dresser. And the window overlooking the street on a part of campus that couldn't even be seen from the Burgess Building.

"That's... What is that?" Callum asked. He was suddenly behind me, next to Isaac staring through the door.

"My bedroom," I said, words dumb on my tongue.

"No, the magic," he said, and all of his reserve from moments ago had been replaced with studious curiosity. "It's not a portal, it's more...refined?"

"It's a door," Isaac said shrugging.

"How much did you help?" Aiden asked.

"I gave her chalk," Isaac said. "Drawing chalk."

"And directions," I added, edging closer to the doorway. Isaac snorted behind me.

"Can I- can I walk through?" I asked.

"Wait," Callum said, stopping me with a hand in my path. "Let me."

He had to bend to fit through the door and he stepped inside with enough caution that I half expected the door frame or my bedroom to collapse in on him. But nothing happened. And standing inside my bedroom, studying every surface, Callum looked more confused than ever. Also, a great deal taller. A half thought at the back of my mind pointed out that he wouldn't even fit in the bed.

"How?" he asked, turning back to us, staring across a few feet of floorboards and more than half a mile of the campus.

"She wrote it," Isaac said, a hand settling at the small of my back. He looked down at me and said, "Just like you wrote 'books to find' and texts that had been missing for hundreds of years suddenly reappeared."

"Or a shelf that stayed organized," I said under my breath. I had always made lists and directions for myself. But they had always been mundane things. A need for a sunny day, a list of ingredients for the market, a return date on a book.

And no one in Bridgeston had missed a due date in all my time at the library.

"And that haunting you added to my painting is yours too," Isaac said. "My students won't even look at it. I thought it would be a good test. Painting and writing have more similarities than most fields of magic."

"I didn't know writing was a field of magic," Aiden said, joining Isaac and me in watching Callum squint and frown at the wall around my bedroom door.

"Runes, sigils," Callum said.

"But just words?" Aiden tossed back.

Callum only covered his frown with his hand, scratching at his beard.

"I imagine giving you a rune would be like giving you a hammer," Callum said to me.

"I never used one, I thought…" my voice tangled in my throat. "I didn't know…"

And then I was nearly crying again for an entirely different reason. Aiden's arm wrapped heavily over my shoulder and I leaned into his side.

"You're a witch, love," he said, and then kissed the top of my head.

Callum stopped his pacing upon seeing my watery gaze and I tried not to laugh as he looked between Isaac and Aiden with a bit of panic on his face.

"Do you mind if we leave the door here a bit longer?" Isaac asked me. "We can go inside and have…"

"Tea," I said nodding, blinking away the tears that had risen. "Or will we be stuck between the office and my bedroom?"

"One way to find out," Callum said. And he looked excited to do so.

I expected to feel something upon crossing the threshold. A push of air or some kind of friction, but it was as if Isaac's closet had always led to my room. And when we were all inside, which only furthered the point that my bedroom was far too small for any one of the men let alone all three, I shut the door behind us. And like nothing, it was *my* door. Wider and taller than the closet's and in a different shade of wood.

"It's a surprisingly elegant construction," Callum said and it took me half a beat to realize he didn't mean anything to do with my house.

I turned the handle again, and this time the door swung in on my room, and waiting outside was the small little alcove at the top of the stairs.

"*That* is magic," Aiden said from behind me and the tone of his voice warmed the back of my neck.

The first floor wasn't much better in terms of fitting the four of us. I only had two chairs at my little table and when Isaac tried to join me in the kitchen to help with the tea we may as well have been dancing for how close we had to stand together. When I put the kettle on the stove Isaac wrapped his arm around my waist and leaned in to whisper.

"Do you need more time? Do you want us to go?"

I reached past him to the counter, leaning into his side to grab the tea tin. He didn't lean away, only brushed the tip of his nose along my jaw until I settled back and started prepping the teapot.

"Yes," I said. "And no. I want to talk."

"Alright."

He moved to go and I reached out, tugging him back by the pocket of his vest. Our lips bumped clumsily together, and I wished for half a moment that I planned instead of acted. But then Isaac hummed a pleased little sound and pressed into the kiss for a soft, sweet moment. I was blushing and he was smiling as he pulled away, squeezing at my waist and then leaving me to the tea.

There was chalk in my pocket, the stick Isaac had given me to write on the door, and I reached in to play with it a moment, thinking of the men waiting for me in the other room. Then I pulled it out and looked down at the dark wooden countertop.

There are four…

I paused for a moment chewing at my lip before continuing.

There are four identical chairs in the dining room.

"Joanna!" Aiden shouted.

"It worked," I said, as the tea kettle started to whistle. I tucked my grin against my shoulder as Isaac peeked his head back into the kitchen, an eyebrow raised.

"Sit," I said.

"Glad to know you're handling that well," Isaac said, smiling back at me.

I had mismatched china to serve the tea in but I at least had four cups and I carried them out to the table. There was an open seat across from Callum and Aiden took two cups out of my hands and passed one to him.

Then he turned back to me and said, "Have dinner with us."

It was somehow both more and less than what I had expected him to say. Although I didn't think I'd have an easier time answering if he'd asked for me to join the coven as plainly.

"I…" I had spent so long trying to avoid familiarity for a reason that no longer existed and now I couldn't think of a word to say. I'd been so angry barely fifteen minute ago, with myself and Canderfey and them, and now it was all just evaporated into a little magic and confusion.

"You're a witch," Aiden said. "So the argument against our request to court you is void, right?"

"Don't push," Callum muttered, looking up from where he'd fixed his eyes to the cup of tea.

Aiden raised his eyebrows at the other man in answer and Callum turned gray and looked back down at the table. Aiden winced and he and Isaac communicated in silence for a tense moment. Here was another thing I was afraid of, not fitting into the space they shared together. Not being enough.

But there was something I could say in this moment. Something important.

"I owe you an apology," I said and Callum looked up frowning, glancing at the others until he met my eyes and realized I was speaking to him. "I was…confused, but I shouldn't have said those things or run off."

"It was my fault," he said, voice tight. "I shouldn't have…"

Kissed me. Although the twist of his face implied something much less innocent and sweet than what occurred.

"It's alright," I said.

I had just kissed Isaac in the kitchen. And it had been clumsy and simple and made the blood in my veins sing. If it had been Callum and his slow, smooth caress just now instead of an hour ago before everything had been turned inside out…before *I* had been turned inside out, we wouldn't be grimacing and apologizing to one another.

Callum swallowed and the subject died.

"Come to dinner, please," Aiden started again, this time more gingerly. "Isaac will cook, so you don't have to worry. It's…dinner, that's all, I promise."

"No," Isaac said. He reached over the table and tangled our fingers together. He looked at Aiden and then Callum before back to me. "We should be clear. Joanna Wick, our coven wants to court you. Please come have dinner with us."

My heart was pounding in my chest and I could feel the heat on my face and the way my feet pinned themselves to the floor, half ready to take flight. The invitation, the weight of it, and pointed intentions behind it had felt so impossible as recently as the morning.

But I had thought about the possibility of them. Had wished for it. Imagined myself in a life where I might have expected such a thing.

"Are you sure?" I asked, barely a whisper.

Aiden was beaming, smiling too hard to speak and Isaac's dimples were growing deeper as he joined him.

"We're sure," Callum said, eyes fixed to mine.

I took a shaky breath and swallowed. "Dinner would be lovely," I said.

13

JOANNA

THE MORNING OF THE DINNER I TRIED TO GO FOR A WALK. JUST A SMALL break away from the campus to clear my head and gather my thoughts about the upcoming evening. But when I got to the path it shimmered a fiery orange-red and my feet stopped in place. Posted to the nearest tree was a small poster reading *Paths Out Of Order; please refrain from exploring the woods at this time.*

I laughed at first. How could a path be out of order? Was it a prank from the students? But it would take a serious effort to close the paths with magic. I could ask the men later.

I thought of going to the library instead, but it was full of people and my coworkers would probably want an explanation for why I was pacing the stacks. Instead, I headed north past Gwen and her coven's neighborhood, into the downtown of Canderfey proper.

The streets were full, the town up earlier than the campus on a Sunday, but my anonymity here was better, and I could stroll and window shop in peace. I found a shop entirely filled with tea, and another solely dedicated to beauty and bath tinctures. At the shop at home there had been two kinds of tea, and one kind of soap. I spent a good hour sniffing jar after jar and coming up with reasons to buy new tea and a small collection of washes that probably wouldn't even fit in my bathroom. I was walking back to the bus stop, debating between walking home for an hour or riding for ten minutes, when I stopped at a shop window full of dresses.

An evening gown stood on a mannequin, the black fabric gleaming red where the sun hit it, with the skirt pooling over the floor like blood. It looked like liquid on the frame of the body, sliding down the shoulders and over the breasts and hips. There was black pearl beading at the shoulders and down the collar, and fine seams down the bodice and it was the most beautiful thing I had ever seen. But I could only imagine myself slouching wrong, tripping over the hem, and wrinkling the skirt with the way I sat.

Hildy passed the window behind the dresses, turned away from me, and talking to a woman who was considering a petal pink dress on a hanger in her hands. She had mentioned her shop while I'd had dinner with them and while I'd imagine something *nice*, this was... Well, it made much more sense when it came to Hildy, I supposed. I doubted there was anything inside for me, but I wanted to say hello.

And I wanted to touch.

Hildy looked away from her customer as the doorbells chimed with my entrance. Her eyes lit up and her smile turned from professional to friendly for a moment. She nodded at me and I returned the greeting before she went back to work. The shop was bright and well lit, the colors of the garments hanging shining against the cream and white stripes of the satiny wallpaper. A table sat in the center with several elegant hats, feathered and topped in silk flowers, as well as a collection of gloves and their glowing pearl buttons running up the arms.

When faced with the dresses in person, each one an individual work of art formed out of decadent fabrics and lace and delicate embellishments, I found myself keeping my hands knotted up in front of me. And when faced with the price tags, handwritten on heavy card stock with the dress's details, I found myself swallowing heavily and averting my eyes. Hildy was finishing with her customer, wrapping up the pink dress in black tissue paper when I finally found a corner better suited to me. Simple dresses and skirts with clean lines out of rich fabrics, and tidy blouses in light silks.

"That's Gwen's corner," Hildy said, as the bells rang and we were alone in the shop. "I started carrying them when I realized I was never going to trick her into lace."

Most of the pieces were in neutrals but my fingers were wrapping around the hanger of a dress the purple-red of cherry juice. It had short sleeves and a full skirt and while it was nicer than anything I'd ever owned or worn, it was still simple by the university standards.

"At least you like color," Hildy said.

I glanced at the tag and decided it would be safe for me to touch. It was a soft, light velvet and it felt downy under my fingers.

"Can I try it on?" I asked.

"I would've wrestled you into it," Hildy said, smile bright.

I knew in the dressing room, as soon as the fabric slid over my shoulders and with the first *snick* of the zipper, that I was going to go home with the dress. The fit was close, just a little loose around the waist and shoulders, and the skirt swished like music around my calves as I twisted in place.

"It's perfect for you," Hildy said. While I knew it would be a sale for her shop, I could tell the words were those of a friend.

I bit my lip and stared at my reflection in the mirror. My hair was a mess and my boots were a little scuffed but I looked good. Pretty, maybe. Less like a book mouse and more like…

"I've just found out I'm a witch," I said, staring at myself in the mirror.

"Just?" Hildy asked, and she was fussing at my waist, fitting the fabric tighter. "We've known since Gwen received your application."

She was grinning to herself and I frowned at her thinking. A slow sinking weight dropped through me.

"My *application*," I hissed, grimacing. My *written* application. Describing why I would be a good fit for the position.

"Ohh, don't fuss," soothed Hildy before taking pins to the fabric at my shoulders. "Gwen saw it right away and it's not as if she couldn't have turned you down with a little de-charming. But with that talent? Who would?"

"You must all think I'm an idiot," I said. My fingers were playing at the folds of skirt at my waist and found their way into a pocket and I twisted in happy surprise, nearly getting myself stuck with a pin.

"There are plenty of strange magical talents," Hildy said with a shrug. "Sometimes they get overlooked, other times they get shoved into a more familiar field of study. You probably would have ended up in the arts if anyone had noticed sooner. *I* almost landed myself in carpentry for goodness sake. Can you imagine?" She made a disgusted face over my shoulder, nose wrinkling in annoyance. "As if carpentry has any of the subtlety of tailoring."

"Think of the wood shavings," I said, teasing and laughing at Hildy's horrified expression.

"You're better off," she said, patting my shoulder. "Who knows if there'd be anyone to really teach you. And now here you are, likely ruining all the romantic hopes of half the students on campus."

I blushed and stared at her as she put away her pins and began to unzip me from the dress. "Gossip travels fast," I said.

Hildy grinned and shrugged. "I have a shop-girl in the arts who had a lot to say about your picnic with her favorite professor this week."

I ducked back into the dressing room, a smile creeping up my cheeks as I remembered Isaac rescuing me from the library for lunch in the grass together. There was a last burst of summer in the weather and the lawn had been full of students and professors. I knew we had been seen, but I hadn't imagined there being anything worth gossiping about. I didn't think anyone else could tell the way we'd made excuses to have our fingers brushing, or the way Isaac wrapped his hand around my ankle as we sat opposite each other, eating in quiet.

"They're very lucky men," Hildy said from the other side of the curtain.

"You don't think it's unlikely? They could do...more than *me*." I almost hated to put my old clothes back on after wearing the dress for only a handful of minutes.

"I'm not sure that they could, darling," Hildy said sweetly. "And it's not as though there haven't been attempts before. But from what I know, which is quite a lot, they've never all been interested in the same person before. Callum Pike is notoriously standoffish. If he wants you in the coven, then that makes you more qualified than anyone. Do you want to be?" she asked as I came back out with the dress, pins still in place.

It hadn't even occurred to me to tell her not to fit the dress. And I couldn't bear to not buy it now.

Hildy was watching my face, waiting on my answer, as I passed her the dress.

"I'm having dinner with them tonight," I said. It was one thing to say it to their faces, that I wanted to be with them, that I wanted to try. It felt like a much riskier thing to share it with others. If the relationship failed, if they changed their mind, did I really want others to know I had thought it possible in the first place?

"Give me ten minutes and I'll have this ready for your dinner tonight," Hildy said. She ducked into an office and a billow of magic, bright and spiky like the tips of tailoring pins, trickled out for a moment.

I thought of what she had said about Callum. He had wanted me, for a moment in the library. I knew that much. What I was less sure of was if he still did after my outburst. He had said the words while we all sat around my little dining table, but they didn't take down the walls he seemed to place between us after the kiss. If I had already ruined things, would he say so? Or was he going along now for the sake of his covenmates?

I wished I could have rewound the week and gone back to the moment in the library. Accepted the kiss or at least not made such a fool of myself refusing it. But it didn't seem like the kind of problem words on paper would fix.

"Here you are," Hildy said, returning from her office with a box wrapped in gleaming cream paper. I joined her at the counter to pay and she pulled a small jar of red lip stain from her pocket. "And this is for you from me. I stash them everywhere so it won't be missed."

And I didn't have any at home, but of course, Hildy could already tell that.

"Thank you," I said, as earnestly as I could. The dress and makeup would feel like a kind of armor to wear at the dinner tonight. A costume of the woman who *could* imagine herself with the three beautiful men.

"Oh," Hildy waved her hand at me dismissively with a small smile on her face. "Just come back. Give me a reason to bring in some colors Gwen wouldn't touch."

We kissed cheeks in parting and I took the bus home. When I closed the entry door behind me and took off my boots I found an idea brewing. I had washed the countertop in the kitchen earlier in the week, erasing the words I'd written. And with them went the two chairs that had materialized. I found my rescued notebook and pen in my bag and open them to write in *my boots are like new again*.

They shone black by the door.

14

JOANNA

Aiden was waiting for me on my steps when it was time to leave.

"I would have found the house on my own," I said, a bottle of wine in hand as his eyes raked over me.

"I wouldn't have had the pleasure of walking with you," he said, grinning. "You're stunning."

I couldn't think fast enough to answer that and his grin grew. Hildy had thought further ahead for me than I had. I had no good coat to wear with such a beautiful dress, but she'd enfolded it in the box in a heavy black and gold wrap for me to wear. After dabbing on the lip stain and draping the wrap over my shoulders I barely recognized myself in the small bathroom mirror upstairs.

"There's a minor security fuss in the woods outside of the campus. Callum was fretting, and I was happy to take the excuse to have a little time alone with you," he explained, sobering.

"Did he want to cancel the dinner?" I asked, hunting for a clue about Callum's changed feelings.

Aiden barked out a laugh. "He wanted all three of us to come get you," he said.

I locked my door and came down the steps and Aiden took the wine from me. He tucked it inside of his jacket and it disappeared.

"I can't do that," I said, frowning at the place where the wine had vanished.

"Callum could teach you," Aiden said.

"Callum?"

"He taught me," Aiden said, taking my hand and leading us down the block. "He said he found it in a dusty old book, but I think he made it up. I've never seen anyone else do it."

"How does it work?"

"Something to do with making a very small space bigger," he said with a shrug. He patted at his ribs and said, "It's still here. I can feel it against me like it's in a pocket I can't see. I lose things this way occasionally because I can't find the pocket again. I just don't tell Callum that or he'll repeat the whole lesson all over again and he's a beast when he's lecturing."

I tried to fight my laugh and failed. In all my interactions with Callum, he had been gentle and direct. Even while we'd been hissing at each other in the library. 'Beast' was not the word I would ever choose for him.

Aiden smirked at me out of the corner of his mouth. "Oh, just wait. You'll see. He's chomping at the bit to learn more about what you can do."

I chewed at my lip and he watched me. I could make doors, chairs, shiny shoes. I could influence a job application.

"Are you nervous about the magic or the dinner?" Aiden murmured, bending his head to mine as we passed students on the common lawns.

"Both," I answered just as quietly.

"We'll follow your pace," he said, squeezing my hand. "Tonight is only dinner. A significant one, for us certainly, but just dinner. Conversation. Isaac will show off his cooking, and I'll probably corner you into listening to more music." I smiled at that and Aiden's brow furrowed as he continued, "And Callum…well he's more scared of you than you are of him."

"That doesn't sound promising," I said, looking up at him. "I think he's upset with me, about the way I spoke in the library."

"He's upset with himself," Aiden said, without any doubt. "He's out of his element. Isaac and I are inclined to find it amusing because it's so rare. But he's sincere."

"You don't think he's just going along? For the sake of keeping the peace?" I asked.

Aiden's grin stretched, wicked and excited. "Not at all. And if you worry, you should talk to him. He'll make himself clear."

It was a slightly cryptic thing to say, but we'd just reached the neighborhood, passing Gwen and Hildy's house, so I let the subject drop.

"How long have you lived here?" I asked as Aiden pointed out the house, the red brick I had seen before.

"Since I got my position," Aiden said. "About eight years before Isaac and Callum started at Canderfey."

"You lived alone that long?"

Aiden's usual smile faded as he nodded, staring up at the house. "I didn't think it would be so long," he said. "I thought I'd start working and meet my coven and we would have a house ready." He looked down at me and said, "That was twenty years ago."

He looked up at the house as it seemed to grow larger the closer we stepped. I tried not to sink under the weight of the declaration. Twenty years of waiting, considering the possibilities. Twelve for Isaac and Callum. I didn't know a lot about covens, not expecting to ever find myself in one, but it was common knowledge that most people found theirs not long after coming of age. Aiden's expectations had been realistic if not a little eager. Twenty years was a long time.

His fingers were stroking the back of my hand and I knew he had said the words with good intentions, but they left me wondering again. Was I here because the wait was too long and I appeared at the right time, strange and unfamiliar?

"You're fretting, Joanna," Aiden said as we turned to the red brick tower house at the end of the street. It was at least four stories tall with something strange and unfamiliar in every window. Every window but the one at the center front.

"I am," I admitted, staring at Callum Pike stretched out in a window bench with a book in his lap. He looked up and jumped from his spot, the book landing with a flutter of pages on the cushion.

"Tonight is only dinner," He repeated, lifting my hand up to kiss at the knuckles. "And there's no majority vote on this. We'll respect any decision you make. But I may try to influence it for my own interests," he added, grin returning.

The front door swung in—an enormous, elaborate door with a stained glass window depicting a rich sunset landing with the stars and moon winking out at the top of the door frame—and Callum stood waiting for us on the step. He was dressed tidily in cool grays and blues, but his reddish hair was sticking out at odd angles like he'd be mussing and pulling at the strands.

"I...Isaac's been waiting," Callum said, and then he winced. Aiden snorted and gestured me ahead of him.

Callum moved out of the way at the last moment, busy blinking at me as I approached, but it was me that held us up at the head of the hallway as I stared down the length of it. Someone, probably Aiden, plucked the wrap off my shoulders and I let it slide away as I soaked in the vibrant jewel blue walls covered almost top to bottom in paintings and photographs.

"You'll have plenty of time to explore," Aiden said behind me.

"Don't lose my wine," I volleyed back, and he laughed. I started at the closest painting, as small as my hand and covered in bright red raspberries that sparkled sweetly on my tongue. I studied another of a small gray house surrounded by pine trees that eased away the tension in my shoulders. I made it as far as a thunderstorm, snapping wind and wet cooling my cheeks, ignoring Callum and Aiden behind me all the while, when Isaac appeared at the end of the hall. His shirt sleeves were rolled up and he had a towel thrown over his shoulder. His long hair was pulled back and trying to escape.

"Hello, love," he said, as I met him halfway. "I like your dress," he murmured in my ear as he leaned in to kiss me, brief and gentle. The heat returned to my cheeks.

"These aren't all yours," I said looking up at a portrait of a sour old man that, incongruously, made me want to laugh.

"No, only a few," he said.

"He likes to give *his* paintings better light to be seen by," Aiden said, passing us in the hall.

"It's part of my collection," Isaac said. "Will you help me in the kitchen?"

"Yes please," I said. I looked behind us, but Callum had already disappeared, probably back to his book in the window.

The kitchen was at the back of the house and it also left me stunned. I had never seen a kitchen this large. Tall, multi-paned windows let in all the evening sun. The stove was at the far side taking up most of the wall aside from a door leading to a greenhouse. There were pots hissing and steaming on the top of it and something glowing in the belly and someone had opened a window nearby to let the cool fall air in as relief against the heat.

"I mostly wanted some company," Isaac admitted as I stopped at a wall where racks of herbs hung to dry.

"Make me useful so I don't fidget," I said. He laughed and dug a spoon out of a pitcher full of utensils, passing it to me.

DINNER WAS EASIER than I expected. Isaac's cooking was too good to ignore with lots of talking and when my words did dry up Aiden had plenty to say. The word 'coven' was never uttered. Callum disappeared after the dishes were cleared from the table and my gut twisted as I realized. He'd been across from me again during the meal and I'd caught him smiling and felt him watching. I'd wanted to believe that the stiffness was fading, but the avoidance was as clear as ever.

I was standing at the kitchen counter, tracing my finger around the rim of a wine glass when Aiden's hand landed on mine, still damp from washing dishes in the sink.

"Go find him," he said.

"He's *supposed* to be drying," Isaac said, glaring down at the plate he was toweling off.

"I don't want to force this," I said.

"Just nudge a little," Aiden said. "He'll be holed up in his office on the third floor, 'researching,'" and he said the last word with a sarcastic wiggle of his eyebrows.

"Tell him to quit being an ass," Isaac added.

Aiden took advantage of the distraction and my laughter to duck down and press a kiss below my ear that brought goosebumps out along my neck. "Go on, you'll both feel better. Second door on the left."

The stairs were at the heart of the house, a round flight that twisted up with dark wood steps and glossy sage green paper and yellowy lamps glowing. I hurried up to the third story to a harvest yellow hallway. There were two closed doors on the right end and three open doors on the left.

The first was a bathroom with bright green and sparkling white tiles that looked cleaner than my own and had a tub big enough for me to go swimming in. The second doorway revealed a bright room with a massive bed, unmade with white sheets printed with charcoal smudges. Isaac's room. The last was an office that looked more like a library. Callum had his back to me, bent over a desk at the far end of the room in front of a window, but I was busy staring at the full walls of bookshelves, bursting with pages. They were stuffed into every available inch, stacked in front of and top of each other like it was a puzzle to see all the different ways they might fit together.

I forgot about knocking completely and walked in without an invitation. "How do you keep track of them all?" I asked, going to a bursting shelf and seeing no rhyme or reason to the arrangement.

There was a clatter at the window and when I looked over Callum was half out of his chair, it tilted dangerously on the back two legs.

"I'm sorry," we said together at the same time. But at least he smiled at me in the pause that followed.

"I don't," he said. "But I usually…I have a charm for getting the book I need to pop out."

"Do you have a charm for making the shelves bigger too?" I asked counting the shelves up to the ceiling and realizing that they didn't make sense in terms of the size of the room.

"Sort of," he admitted, standing and putting the chair back to rights. "Don't tell Aiden, he's fussy about not stretching the house."

"He hasn't noticed?"

Callum shook his head. He took small steps to approach me, as if he was afraid of making me run. Maybe Aiden had been right.

"He has his own office and… You're very observant with magic," he added.

We stared at each other for a quiet moment until I'd managed to steel my nerves.

"Do you want me to leave?" I asked.

He looked around the room, brow furrowing and half shrugged. "I don't mind you being here."

I bit my lip and debated leaving it at that. But I needed to know before I enjoyed the evening any more than I already had, before I found any more beautiful places in the house that made me crave spending time here.

"Do you want me to leave the house, now?" I said. "I can tell Aiden and Isaac that this isn't-"

"What? No!" He rushed forward, eyes wide and nervous.

"If I am here for them and you really aren't…you don't want me…" I tried to dig the words out, but they jammed in my throat.

"Joanna, it isn't that at all," he said, and his own voice was tight. "I sent you running in the library, I don't want to make another mistake like that. Aiden would have my head."

I looked down at the floor at the reminder of what my being here meant to Aiden and what that must mean to Callum.

"It isn't about him either," Callum said, quiet and close.

"The library wasn't your fault," I said, looking up. "I had spent so much time trying not to think of any of you this way, and I had a very strict list of why it was impossible."

"It's not," he said firmly.

But I could see the battle in him, the strain in his muscles. Only this time I knew what he was resisting. And maybe I could fix it by telling him that he wasn't going to scare me off or set me running again, but there was an easier solution than that too.

I rose up on my toes, hands braced behind me on the edge of a bookshelf. I brushed my cheek against his beard, kissing at the bare jaw just past the coarse hair while his head ducked lower. A sigh stroked along the skin of my neck and we held still for a breath together. His hands wrapped around my waist as my mouth searched out his and with the first stroke of the kiss, he pulled me tight against him. I gasped, lips parting and Callum was there filling in the spaces.

I released the bookshelf behind me to hold onto his shoulders as my toes scraped against the floor. He groaned as my fingers tightened and the sound vibrated against me, under my hands and into the kiss. Teeth dragged over lips and tongues followed to soothe, and with every quick clamor for breath we wrapped up tighter in each other's arms. My heart was pounding and the beat was echoing in my blood and down into my stomach and sinking lower still until I was twisting in his hold trying to find friction.

My back hit the bookshelf behind us and Callum's fingers dug into my hips as I stepped wider to make room for him against me. I was surrounded by him, my head tipped back and eyes squeezed shut as his mouth pressed wet kisses down to my jaw, nipping at my throat. I whimpered and his thumbs circled over my hip bones as he shifted closer. I could feel him against me, stirring hard and as restless as every inch of my skin was feeling.

"Glad you two talked."

I jumped at the intrusion and tried to scramble away, but Callum just straightened slowly and soothed his hands up my spine.

Aiden was grinning at us from the doorway, eyes sparkling as he bit his lip. He looked as if he *hadn't* just dined on a beautiful meal, but was now staring at one. Callum was still stroking at my back, settling my surprise and embarrassment. I looked up and found his face relaxed, with a small smile nearly hidden at the corners. But I didn't doubt that Aiden could spot it as well as I could.

"Are we expected downstairs?" Callum asked as I tucked my heated face against his chest.

"Well, you were, but I can make excuses," Aiden hedged, a laugh at the back of his voice.

"Give us a few minutes, Aide," Callum murmured, fingertips drumming softly at my back.

I heard the floorboards creak—and why couldn't I have heard them *before* being caught—and Callum pulled back slightly so he could look down at my face.

"Are you alright?" he asked.

I opened my mouth to joke and then swallowed the words, not wanting to interrupt the tenuous affection of the moment.

"Not used to being caught by anyone other than the town gossip," I said after a beat.

Callum's smile stretched wide for the first time I had seen in a week. "You still haven't," he said.

I laughed, head falling back and he took advantage. Ducking down and kissing at my throat, by my ear, his nose nuzzling until my laughter skidded away. I ended up back against the bookshelf again, but the kisses were slow and sweetly lazy instead of building. Callum's hair was rumpled from my fingers when we eased apart, and I left it that way to make Aiden and Isaac smile.

We turned down the stairs hand in hand and Callum led me midway down the hall to a rosy orange room where Aiden was seated at a massive, glossy, black piano. The music was airy, skipping and trilling, and I watched his hands for a moment wondering how hands so large could play so lightly. Isaac was sitting cross-legged with a sketchbook in his lap, in the middle of a long brown couch. Callum joined him, leaving a gap between them just large enough for me. They were ready as I approached, Callum twisting and reaching out to settle me against his chest and Isaac, dimples sharp in his smile, pulling my legs up to drape over his. Aiden's playing deepened and all the nervous tension in me fled away.

I would let myself enjoy this, this impossible thing, for the evening at least.

15

JOANNA

"We really shouldn't be doing this," I whispered. But I didn't get up from Isaac's lap, tucked away together in a corner of the staff library, and I didn't pull my arms from around his neck.

The coven had found ways of keeping me company for over a week now; bumping into me on campus or appearing in the library in the evening to walk me home. Isaac was especially good at finding excuses. I was especially good at playing along with them.

"I could argue," he said, trailing kisses up the side of my jaw before continuing, "that you shouldn't be loitering in the library so late."

"I've got a better reason than you," I said, grinning and tapping my forehead to his.

"You *had* a better reason. Now you're canoodling. Woollard hates canoodlers." And then he kissed me, fingers digging into the short hair at the back of my neck. I swallowed my groan and wondered how easy it would be to get a massage from Isaac. Probably very.

"I caught Woollard canoodling last week," I whispered against Isaac's lips and he pulled away, eyes wide with surprise. "She and Bryce were having lunch together in the lounge."

"You're on first name terms with Gast too?" he asked, eyebrows raising.

"We didn't speak much, but I had dinner with the coven a couple of weeks ago."

Isaac swallowed, leaning back, his head thunking against the wall.

"What?" I asked, and bent to kiss the corded muscle at the side of his throat.

"They may as well have offered you an invitation into their coven," he said.

I made a rude sound and rolled my eyes. "They already have a finished coven."

"That doesn't mean you couldn't have a place in it if you wanted," Isaac said. His smile quirked at the corner and his arms wrapped tighter around my back as I mulled it over. I suppose I had heard of a coven of more than four, although generally only in stories. "They're a better offer than we are," he said watching my face. But he didn't look nervous as I glared down at him.

"I think Gwen was just being friendly," I said. "They all were. Even Bryce, who terrifies me."

"Bryce terrifies everyone but their own coven," Isaac said. "*Gwen* terrifies everyone but her own coven for that matter. I'll warn Aiden and Callum of our competition."

"Don't you dare," I said, bending and nipping at his chin until he was grinning. "Aiden will take it as an excuse to come around here and start harassing Gwen...and *me*."

Isaac laughed beneath me, stretching up for a smooth, pulling kiss that was sure to lead to another...

And then the library *CRACKED!* all around us, one enormous groan of wood and screech of glass and iron.

The lamps went out with a spitting noise and an electric burn in the air. Isaac jumped up, arms like a vice around me, and twisted us so I was behind him. He seemed to grow, shoulders broadening and back tightening and I stood on my tiptoes to see, but the library was shadowy beyond us. Isaac's hand sought mine behind his back and I gripped it tight, holding my breath in the following silence.

"Do you want to stay-?" he started.

"With you," I said.

The air turned muggy and warm around us as if a thick coating of mist had crawled over shelves and risen up from the floor. It was cloying and dusty in my mouth, like candy left out too long to the air and it scratched down my throat as I swallowed. Below us the library took a collective gasp, every book seeming to shudder on its shelf and a great moaning came from dozens of voices like a chorus.

"Students," I whispered, and my heart was rattling in my chest like a wild animal.

Isaac's hand squeezed mine and I guided him forward through the weave of shelves to the dark stairs. We were running down the flight, just reaching the landing, when a terrorized scream whipped through the air. The sweet fog was sliced and the sound cut at my ears and Isaac stopped in his tracks, pressing me back against the wall. My free hand gripped at my skirt and I felt the chalk stick waiting in my pocket, a thought clamoring forward.

Isaac released my hand, turning, and took my face clumsily in his hold. A kiss landed high on my cheek, over the bridge of my nose, and then hard against my lips.

"Stay here, go back upstairs, climb out the window," he rushed, the words as quiet as he could make them. "I'm going down, but I need you to get out, alright? Get help, but get out safely, Joanna."

A part of me wanted to protest, but the other part was slipping my hand into my pocket, a plan racing to piece itself together.

"Be careful," I whispered.

"Callum will be on his way," Isaac said as if it were a promise of rescue.

And then he let go of me and in four steps he was lost in shadow. I didn't run. I crouched down to the ground, feeling at the floor for the edge of the stair carpeting, for the stretch of clean wooden floorboards. I pulled the chalk from my pocket and it almost glowed in my hand, pure and white. There was another scream from downstairs, another cracking groan of wood and the floor shook against my knees. I set the chalk to the wood grain, squinting to try and see in the dark.

THE LIBRARY I scratched out in blocky, jagged letters, and then the glass roof in the lobby screeched, plates grinding together, and there was a high sprinkling sound. My arms ached and the chalk slipped in my fingers and my breath was short as if writing the words cost me physical effort. *IS* came with my vision spinning in front of me.

"Joanna!" Callum's voice, deeper and harsher, came ringing out from the heart of the library.

"Callum. Here, quickly!" I heard Isaac's voice and let my eyes fall shut with relief. I forced my hand to shape the *A* on the wood, messy and crooked but solid. A headache like an axe split through my skull and I found myself breathing through my teeth, ignoring the shouting from downstairs.

For every letter I managed another symptom rose up, my skin breaking into a thin sweat or my stomach cramping or the walls seemed to bend forward to crush me. *SAFE* looked like a child who was only just learning their letters had written it. I got as far as *PLA-* and then I was on the floor on my side with my hand as hot as flames, fingers twitching and burning where I squeezed the chalk. I twisted out a *C* with tears streaking out of my eyes and the shouts from the lobby banging like the beat of drums in my ears. But with the last four scratches of chalk on the floor everything released like a great pop of pressure.

The front doors banged and the walls and floor rattled in response, shallow and harmless now. The lamps flickered back to life, dim but warm and yellow. I could hear the sobs of students downstairs as my head cleared; still throbbing, but at least not feeling *stabbed* at every second. The floorboards rattled again, now with a clamor of steps running up the stairs, familiar voices echoing with my name in the mix.

I pushed myself up to sitting, my arms wobbling and my breath short, with the white words scribbled on the floor at my side.

THE LIBRARY IS A SAFE PLACE

Isaac and Callum came skidding and tripping around the corner of the staircase and Callum grabbed at the other man by the scruff of his neck before he crashed to the floor, right into my work.

"Don't mar the words," Callum barked, all the edges of his face sharpened into something ferocious and unfamiliar to me. He looked up the steps where Isaac and I had come from, eyes narrowed as he held still for a long moment.

Isaac landed at my other side, arms pulling me in by my shoulders and tucking my face under his chin. He smelled like ash and copper.

"Witch," he murmured into my hair, turning the word into something reverent.

Warm hands wrapped over the tops of my knees and I shifted, Isaac loosening his hold, so I could see Callum kneeling in front of me.

His gaze was sharp on my face, studying me in fast flicks of his eyes. "Are you alright?" he asked.

"It's-" my voice scratched and I swallowed, mouth dry, before trying again. "It's never hurt before to write. Did it...was that happening to you too?"

Isaac's hands were soothing my hair away from my face, his nose pressed to my temple, as Callum stared back at me.

"Some," he said, and the strain in him eased as he rested in front of me. "It would have targeted you when it felt the spell start."

"I asked you to run," Isaac said, tipping my chin up to see the worry digging lines across his forehead and between his eyebrows, jaw ticking with tension.

"This is big magic," Callum said more to himself than to us. "That may have contributed to the strain."

"It's my library, and I had an idea," I said to Isaac, and then looked to Callum to ask, "Is it a ward?"

Callum shook his head, staring at the words. His fingers were tracing circles over my knees, drawing up a sweeter trembling feeling in my skin. "Wards can't kick something out once it's already in. Although it will act as one now as long as it isn't erased. Can you stand?"

As soon as I moved, they were lifting me up. My legs felt shaky and weak, but I was fairly sure that if Isaac took his arm from my waist I would stay standing. Not that he seemed about to.

"I can manage," I said. "What happened downstairs? Was anyone hurt?"

Their faces were grim and Isaac looked away, swallowing and paling almost to green.

"I'm going back down to take care of it," Callum said. "Isaac will take you home."

He lifted his hand from my elbow up to the back of my neck, bending to kiss my cheekbone and then lingering there as I argued. "I'm staying to help, there's going to be…sweeping. Or something. I heard glass breaking and…" I swallowed, thinking of their faces and what they hadn't said. Someone *was* hurt. "I want to help," I added, quietly.

"You've helped," Isaac said. "And you're exhausted."

"I'm *not*."

"You're aching," Callum said, hand sliding down to my back and leading us to the steps. "And still shaking."

"Alright, *listen*—" I started. There was a hiccup in my voice but I was ready to have this fight.

But then Aiden came thundering up the steps, the whites of his eyes wide and his warm dark skin turned gray. He had me scooped up in his arms before the others had time to let go of me. And then he was pulling Callum and Isaac in by their shirts too until I was smashed between the three of them in an embrace. The knot in my throat released and tears spilled out of my eyes. I pressed them into Aiden's shirt.

"They said a librarian had been killed," Aiden croaked from above.

"*What?*" I asked, squirming. I found Isaac's eyes, as wet as mine and still creased with worry. "…Who?"

"Cecil Pincombe," Callum said, voice nearly muted against my hair.

My stomach turned and now I was sure my legs would not work.

"When we get downstairs, don't look," Callum told me. "Keep your eyes down until you get outside."

I opened my mouth to answer, but I couldn't think of a word.

"Woollard arrived. Gast is outside, guarding," Aiden said. "They've gotten the students out and to medical."

"Gwen," I whispered, although I wasn't sure that anyone heard me. I was set back on my toes, but I didn't feel them beneath me and between Aiden and Isaac they had such a tight hold on me, it didn't matter. Callum stopped at the bottom of the steps.

"I'm warding the stairs until Gwen can do something to preserve your words," he said. His hands framed my face and his head bent, filling my liquid gaze as he pressed a long kiss to the center of my forehead. "You saved us," he whispered.

Not Cecil Pincombe, I thought. Callum's words felt like a bad joke.

And then I saw Gwen, over Isaac's shoulder, standing in front of the library doors and looking half lost. There was an explosion of charred books at her feet, mixed with wood and glass shards. Overhead, most of winter and part of spring had been torn out of the stained glass ceiling. I tugged my way out of Isaac and Aiden's hold and rushed across the tile to her.

I saw it out of the corner of my eye. Just a piece, unrecognizable and bloodied, near the circulation desk—now a shattered, torn thing, raw wood exposed and smoking like coals. And in the midst of it, what Callum didn't want me seeing. Smeared like waste at the belly of the room.

I fixed my eyes to Gwen and she turned at my approach, overturned and scorched bookshelves all around us. The other two night-staff were standing behind one, out of sight of the circulation desk, arms around each other as the younger woman cried.

Gwen stared at me as if she didn't recognize me. But then she blinked and said, "I told you there's no good in staying after your shift."

I paused in place at that, hearing footsteps catch up to me, and Gwen covered her face with her hand and shook her head.

"Excuse me," she whispered, and twisted herself toward me, turning away from the giant wound in the library. "I'm glad you're safe."

"What can I do to help?" I asked.

"Joanna, you need to rest," Isaac said, arriving behind me.

"He's right," Gwen said, taking my hand to squeeze it. "I'll need my staff tomorrow morning. Tonight I need him," and she pointed past us all to where Callum was striding across the tile, head up and shoulders straight. He looked ready for battle and I wondered how well he knew his subject. He was too young to have served in the war, but if he'd been in an army…

"I want your best wards, Pike," Gwen growled.

"You have better now," he said. "Joanna wrote on the floorboards. That's why the library is still standing."

Gwen reeled back for a moment before falling forward, small arms snaking around my shoulders. My poor bones ground together in her grip, but I was grateful for the hug all the same.

"Oh, you silly girl," she muttered in my ear. She released me before I could answer, smoothing at her skirts and lifting her chin. "Hildy should be able to fix it to the building. Joanna, go home and rest. I've got plans for you in the morning."

My objections faded with the exhaustion that was building like a brick wall in my body. I wobbled and Isaac was behind me.

"Walk with them to the house and then come back?" Callum asked Aiden.

"Bryce can walk them home and then fetch Hildy," Gwen said. "I need your help now before more faculty arrives."

No one argued with Gwen. Callum's hand brushed at my back, leaving a tingling warmth before he was striding over to where the rest of us refused to look. Aiden pulled me into another bone-crushing hug and I took a deep breath of him, and then Isaac was pulling me outside.

Bryce was pacing the grounds in front of the library like an overgrown wildcat and froze as we approached. Isaac spoke to them as I swayed in place and then we were all walking. Or Bryce and Isaac were walking and I was floating along despite feeling like a lead weight.

"Did Callum charm me?" I mumbled to Isaac, and he pulled me into his side.

His hand spread out over my back and he hummed. "He has a tendency to do that."

"I think it's all that's keeping me upright at this point," I said. Although the cold air kept my eyes open at least.

"I was going to carry you, but I thought you might be mad," Isaac whispered and then, even quieter, added, "Bryce would do it if you asked."

I snorted and it turned into a cracking, panicked laugh. Isaac squeezed me and Bryce glanced over their shoulder at us.

"We're going the wrong way," I said, suddenly realizing we were walking in the opposite direction as the campus staff houses.

"Sorry," Isaac said. "But Callum would have a fit if you weren't with us tonight…we all would, really. We have a guest room you can use. And the four of us won't fit in that little house."

Thinking on it, I didn't really want to be alone in my house either. And their home had felt warm and beautiful and magical and safe. "I want to use that massive bath of yours," I said as we got close to the house.

Isaac's lips brushed my temple. "That can be arranged."

Bryce took a deep sniff of the air as we reached the house, back tight for a long moment, their lips parted slightly. Then they relaxed, turning to us and nodding.

"Thank you, Gast," Isaac said. Bryce passed him with a sideways glance and then stepped up to me and left a dry hot kiss on my cheek. There was a funny smell in the air as they left and Isaac pulled me inside.

"What is Bryce?" I whispered as the door closed behind us.

Isaac grinned, weary but bright, and looked at me. "Would you believe me if I said a dragon?"

"Yes," I said.

He chuckled and shrugged. "It's only a rumor, but I believe it too."

We were smiling at one another and then my chin was wobbling and my eyes were stinging. Isaac's smile sagged and I was folded up in his arms with my hands clutching at his back.

"What was it? In the library?" I whispered against the skin of his neck where I pressed my face and the tears that were spilling.

"We don't know yet," he rasped. "Callum's been tracking it, but this was…it's bigger than he thought. We'll figure it out. Everything will be okay."

Except that someone had already been killed.

16

JOANNA

It occurred to me, watching Isaac fuss with the faucets of the tub—his shirtsleeves rolled up to his elbows—that I'd never seen him look nervous before. He was fidgeting and his knee was jiggling and he hadn't looked me in the eye since we'd walked into the bathroom. I was too tired to be nervous or self-conscious, and still too shaken to be alone. We had stood together in the entrance for a long time before he'd remembered my request for a bath.

When Isaac cleared his throat for the third time, sitting on the edge of the tub, I started to unbutton my blouse.

"Will you join me?" I asked, deciding I could settle the matter.

He looked up from the water filling the tub and blinked at me, and then at the peek of my plain gray slip.

"Are you sure?" he asked, rising.

"Yes," I said, tugging my arms free of my sleeves. I winced at the smell of my clothes, the sour sweat and bitter burn of the events of the library.

He crossed the tile as I left my shirt on their sink counter. His hands folded around my bare shoulders and I sighed at the touch as he bent and kissed the skin next to his thumb. "I don't want you out of

109

my sight," he said, almost a whisper with the roar of water behind him. "But if it's pushing or…"

"I'm asking you, Isaac," I said raising my hands to wrap my fingers around his wrists. "I want you here with me."

He lifted his head and we were kissing, something between comfort and desire. I found the buttons of his shirt with my fingers, which were still shaking, and his hands circled the waistband of my skirt, content to hold me there for a long moment before releasing the zipper. Our lips parted and we watched each other as we finished, him shrugging out of his shirt and letting his pants fall to the floor as I pushed the straps of the slip off my shoulders and tugged it down my waist.

Isaac was built like the men at home, with wide shoulders for tossing hay bales in the wagon and narrow hips to suit their wives' tastes. But he was refined too, as if he had studied the chiseled statues of men in art and become one himself. His eyes were pale as they tracked the path of the slip down to the tile and then traveled up again, slower, to my face. He was wearing a faint smile and nothing else and I mimicked him. Studying the cut lines of his stomach, the dark hair between his legs, and the length of him stirring there. His legs were lean and strong and I imagined fitting him between mine, the way we might twist together.

"Come here, love," he said, words rasping like a touch on my skin.

It was only a step or two and then he was warm against me, our stomachs and chests brushing together and my breasts aching at the contact. Our gazes locked, noses bumping and I twined my arms over his shoulder. His hands spanned my back and traveled down to my waist and then over the swell of my ass, cupping underneath. I could feel him growing against me at the same lazy pace of his smile.

"The tub will overflow," I said. There was a dull ache left lingering at the back of my head, and now a pleasanter one growing in my belly.

Isaac's smile stretched and quirked, and then he lifted me up in his hands and carried me over to the tub. I bent my legs up as he climbed in, and we both hissed at the heat of the water before sinking down, letting it flush our skin. Isaac stretched a leg out in front of us and switched the water off with his toes as I settled at his side. The heat and steam clung sticky but warm enough to burn away some of the fog in my head.

"I can't tell if I've just been seduced or vice versa," Isaac murmured, scattering kisses over my nose and forehead.

"Haven't even gotten that far," I said, and he made a small choking sound in surprise.

I turned in the water, stretching my legs out to bob behind me, and studied the planes of Isaac's stomach and chest with my fingertips and the line of his jaw with my teeth and lips. He gave me a moment's head start before gripping at my hips to guide me over him, then pushed my knees apart with his. His hands skirted the backs of my thighs, traced a line behind my knees that had me squirming closer, my breasts resting just below his chin and the sensitive skin of my sex teased against the narrow trail of hair leading down from his belly.

His head was resting back against the rim of the tub, eyes closed and teeth gleaming in a narrow smile as I scratched the back of his neck and tried to soothe the growing itch in my skin with small shifts of my hips. As if I could find the satisfaction and keep it secret from him. He nuzzled his face down into my wet skin, nosing at the arch of my breasts while his palms squeezed me closer, right below my ass

Just as I thought I might start to beg for more, his lips parted and his mouth latched onto my breast above a nipple. The pull drew deep into my skin and down into my belly, making me throb and cry out while his hand slid forward, fingers teasing where I wanted them most. I tugged at his hair in response and he released me, a red mark blooming on my skin where his mouth had been.

"That's better," I said, looking down at him, as he set his chin on my breast bone to gaze up.

"What would help?" he asked, hand cupped between my legs and fingers pressing in softly against my folds.

"More," I managed, ducking down to swallow his laugh.

There *was* more but at an idling pace as we floated in the tub, hands and lips mapping a terrain of touch, guided by hitched breaths and hums of pleasure. Isaac's hands traveled more than I wanted them to, always returning back to my core to build me up and then move on again before they had finished their work. I repaid him in kind, but he seemed too patient, too happy to be turned weak and moaning at my explorative touches and then denied again.

"You're teasing," I said, panting slightly. Isaac had me arched back over the edge of the tub, tracing his tongue below my breast and across a rib as his thumbs stroked right at the inside edges of my hips. The pressure was beautifully stirring and yet nowhere near enough to satiate me.

"Tell me to stop," he said, and I could hear the grin in his voice. He rose up on his knees, his cock brushing between my legs where I wanted him and our stomachs sticking together.

I braced myself up on my elbows and we stared at one another for a long moment. His lips had just started to twitch, and he was about to pull away when I called the game to an end.

"No more teasing," I said.

His eyes darkened and then he was pulling me up out of the water and out to the bath mat. "Do you want to see your room or mine across the hall?" he asked.

Guest room, I thought, correcting him. But I busied myself by fitting closer against him, nipping up his throat to his ear and feeling him groan against me. A warm towel wrapped around us both, doing a perfunctory job of drying away the water, and then he had me scooped up in his arms.

"Closest," I managed, still tasting his skin.

The hall was cool and we were half laughing as he crossed it in a great rush. A door swung shut behind him and then my back was on a soft mattress and I was pulling him down with me, our bodies pressing heavier together without the buoy of the water around us. His skin was hot on mine and his kiss was deep, tongue seeking and stroking and licking. My legs were hanging off the bed and my hips were arching up, nudging and begging against his.

"Joanna," he groaned, and an arm burrowed beneath my back to hold me tight against him. His pelvis pressed to mine and my head fell back with a sigh, relief and need pooling together at the pressure. "We should slow…" he started, mouth panting wet breath against my neck.

"Not for my sake," I whispered. He chuckled, but his back shook under my hands for a long time after the sound.

The library, I thought, and I placed a hand between us and pushed him back. His face was dry, but the lines were deep on his forehead.

"We're safe," I whispered.

His breath came out unevenly and he pressed back down, lips just barely set to mine. "I want you to remember what you did tonight the next time you're thinking you don't belong with us," he whispered. "We would not have made it out of the library without you."

I didn't think that could be true and I wondered what he had seen. What the destruction I had seen the end of had looked like in action. I was ready to pull him down to my side, to curl up together and let the night be made of up of a different kind of closeness, when his fingers found my center again, one digit dipping in while his thumb swirled over my clit.

"Is this better?" he asked, pushing up on his free hand to look down between us to where he was touching.

My breath caught in my throat as I tried to answer him.

"I need you," he said, and when my head rolled to the side he pressed a kiss at the corner of my jaw by my ear. "If you'll have me."

I laughed at that, turning my face back and pulling him down to me, sucking at his bottom lip and fumbling a hand between us to wrap around his cock. My hips were rolling into his touches, a fluttering heat building in my core and spreading out like waves lapping under my skin. His mouth traveled down my neck, pausing at my pulse and groaning into my throat as I squeezed and slid my hand over him.

I'd had lovers growing up, but they'd been brief relationships with couplings to match—sweet but often bumbling and awkward too. Isaac pressed a second finger inside me, crooking them gently and the stretch and angle was better than anything anyone had tried before.

"I-Isaac, *yes*." My legs stretched wider, feet bracing at the edge of the bed and Isaac's thumb swirled again as his head ducked down and his lips wrapped around my nipple.

With a pull of his mouth and a deep stroke of his fingers, my body was turning loose and tight all at once, my mouth falling open and broken words falling free. The tug at my breast vibrated with Isaac's hum, the rhythm matching the pump and twist of his fingers, the circling pressure of his thumb, all of it a rising pulse building in my bloodstream. I was rocking into his hand, begging without instruction. When Isaac pulled back, his teeth scraping at too sensitive skin, and the pressure broke apart. My fingers clutched at the sheets and my voice cracked and a spiraling flying feeling flooded through me.

Isaac's fingers pulled away before I wanted them to and then he was pushing in, smooth and deep, while I was still flying from the high of bliss. My feet lifted and wrapped around his back to hold him tight and still against me, studying the full feeling as I adjusted to the gentle burn of him inside me. The hair at his groin brushed against my swollen clit and I whimpered as he ducked down, kissing at my closed lips.

"Beautiful," he murmured, and his arms framed my shoulders, fingers digging into my curls.

My skin was still at a simmer, limbs soft and relaxed and I loosened the grip of my legs around his hips. I skimmed my fingernails up his back, scratching lightly and hiccuping a moan as he shifted deeper.

"Your turn," I said, kissing at his chin.

His eyes narrowed and a smirk curled at the corners of his mouth at that but instead of speaking, he sipped at my lips. His hips rocked in shallow, soft thrusts that stirred the remains of my orgasm. My thighs squeezed and I rolled in closer, trying to stir him into action but he only kept his pace and alternated slow teasing kisses with pulling away to nuzzle and watch my face.

"What are you thinking?" I asked, grinning and sliding my hands to clutch at his ass and try and gain control.

He grinned back. "You've had very lazy lovers," he said.

Which was true, I supposed. And with little spikes of heat growing in the stretch and push of where we were joined I could guess his aim.

"What if I wanted to watch you fall apart this time?" I asked. I scratched up his spine again, a little harder, and noted the way his hips kicked in response. But he was watching my face and caught the flash of aching pleasure that snap sent reeling through me.

"Trust me, love," he said, breathless and half-laughing. "You will."

He drew back farther that time, thrusting in deep and quick. My back arched and my eyes slammed shut and there was something like a chuckle or a groan from him. One hand slid down from my hair to the base of my spine and he lifted me there, holding me just so, every push landing his hips against me. I could feel the head of his cock high inside me, tapping at a spot that left stars in my eyes and my brain turning to liquid.

"Isaac," I said without meaning to, voice high and pleading.

"Does it feel good?" he asked, and at least he sounded strained too.

"Please don't stop. Please."

He hummed and then his other hand came down to my hip, fingers fitting between us just so. Not teasing or scraping but only pressing.

"I would do anything you asked, Joanna," he whispered in my ear and I moaned. "Especially that."

I couldn't answer, the feeling inside of me was deeper and tighter than before and it stifled any thinking but the need to hold tight to Isaac. My fingers dug into his shoulder and my legs crossed at his back even as he plunged with longer, deeper thrusts. I was cresting higher, but I could not break, only cling and I didn't have the words to beg for relief. Isaac was pouring sweetness into my ears, praises that were turning into pleads as his strokes broke rhythm. His fingers rubbed, gentle and quick, between my legs and I shattered.

He kept his promise. My eyes opened as I came down, feeling melted and made up of sparks of stirring satisfaction. Isaac was arching above me, a shout on his lips as he buried himself deep, a burst of heat in my belly. His forehead was knotted but his eyes stayed open and fixed to my face, gaze dizzy and sweet, throat bobbing as he swallowed. His forehead dropped to mine as he sagged, the weight and heat of him a comfort for the moment. I kissed his cheek and the corner of his mouth.

"Are you alright?" he asked.

I giggled and pressed a hand over my mouth as he opened one eye to check on me. "Seems like a silly question," I said. I wasn't sure I'd ever felt better. Drowsy and a little sticky with sweat, but practically incandescent.

He rolled us, taking me against his side and pulling us up to the head of the bed. I hummed with the aftershocks. His arms wrapped around me and he peppered kisses over the shoulder resting on his chest.

"You'll stay with me, like this?" he asked.

I blinked my eyes open. His were shut, his face relaxed and tilted to me. I stretched up for a kiss and his lips pursed back.

"I'm not going anywhere," I said, and then added, "I don't think I can walk."

"Sore?" he asked, brow furrowing.

"Turned to jelly."

His smile burst forth and his eyes opened at that. "Aiden and Callum will probably check on us when they make it back."

I hummed and snuggled into his chest.

"They might crawl into the bed," he added.

I thought that over for half a minute, but my clothes were too far away to worry about modesty and I was too tired to really care. Isaac twitched the covers over us and then nothing mattered.

When I stirred in the night there was a dark arm stretched over Isaac's stomach, warm hand resting on my waist, and a lean body pressed up the length of my back. Callum was snoring softly into my shoulder, arm wrapped over my lower belly. He and Aiden smelled clean and they were safe and I had never felt more comfortable sleeping next to someone, let alone plural.

17

JOANNA

I woke up to the door creaking open and sat up with a start. The bed was empty around me and a bleary glance out the window revealed the sky, pink with morning. Isaac stood in the doorway, a tray of food and coffee in his hands.

"Wha' time is it?" I rasped. I stretched under the sheets and smiled at the gentle ache still left from the night before.

He came in, setting the tray on the bed and laughing as I scooped the coffee cup up straight away. "You've got almost an hour before you need to be at the library," he said.

"Where's Callum and Aiden?" I asked, squinting at the dent in the pillow to my right. I was sure they had been there at some point.

"They cleared out a bit ago," Isaac said. "To get ready and…and we weren't sure how you would feel, given…"

"Given I was sex dizzy last night?" I asked, smirking behind the cup as Isaac's eyes flashed for a brief moment, scanning over my bare chest.

"Yes." He scooted forward, bracing his arms on either side of my waist and leaning in, kissing at one shoulder and then the other. "We don't want to rush you."

"I don't want to be rushed. But I didn't mind them joining us to

117

sleep." At Isaac's beaming smile, I added, "And if you hand me that shirt I wouldn't mind a kiss good morning from them."

Isaac grabbed a white dress shirt from the foot of the bed, and I pulled it on over my head, the shoulders hanging loose. I guessed it was probably Callum's if the length of the sleeves was any clue, and I rolled the cuffs up three times. As if Isaac had called for them, Aiden peeked his head in through the cracked door.

"Hello, you," he said. He looked exhausted and his gaze was less playful and more relieved as if he'd needed the reassurance of seeing me again.

I reached a hand out for him and he glanced back into the hall and then came to me. He took my hand and I had to tilt my head far back to catch his kiss on my lips.

"Morning," I said, looking up and searching his face.

He smiled, an attempt at cheer, but there was stress in the lines at the corners of his eyes. "Any chance of convincing you to take the day off with me?" he asked.

"No." My lips twitched in a smile and his followed, even as he rumbled in his chest.

"Worth a shot," he said, sighing and pecking at my lips again.

Aiden stepped back and Callum was hovering in the doorway.

"Thank you for the shirt," I said.

He looked at me, some combination of interest and wariness and hunger until I could feel the heat in my cheeks. "Anytime. I'm heading out early to scout the campus. I'll see you later?"

I nodded, chewing at the inside of my lip. I wanted to jump out of the bed and pull Callum back to join me. But he was already disappearing down the hall.

"Before you go getting any ideas about what he's thinking, he practically arm-wrestled me to crawl in beside you last night," Aiden said, a hand reaching down to squeeze at my shoulder.

"Eat up," Isaac said, nudging at my knee under the blankets. "We'll walk you to the library."

For the first time, I walked into the library that morning and it was truly *silent*. I stopped as the doors swung shut behind me, and stared at the wreckage. It looked worse by the light somehow, the destruction stark and clear. They had done a thorough job of cleaning the night before—the air was sharp with it—and all the dust and shards were swept away. The desk was in pieces with bared teeth, jagged wooden spikes where it had been shattered. I had done my best the night before *not* to see what the scene really looked like, but either I had failed or I had too vivid an imagination. I turned my face up, trying to avoid my gruesome vision, and saw the gaping maw of the broken ceiling. The sky was visible through the tear, and magic shimmered like a temporary pane of glass.

"Oh!" The voice was soft. I looked to my left and Alice Batting, another clerk and a recent graduate was standing between two shelves that had been pushed upright again. She stared at me with wide eyes and then glanced at the desk with me.

All at once, she was flying across the room. My heart thudded in my chest and then I had a set of arms wrapped around mine, pinning them to my sides, and a puff of white-blonde hair in my face. Alice was crying into my shirt—Callum's shirt—and squeezing me tighter with every breath. I searched the balconies for a rescue and found my coworkers peeking out from shelves and…smiling.

The doors swung open behind us and I twisted in Alice's grasp.

"Oh, alright Batting," Gwen said. "Back to work."

Alice released me with a watery smile and then dashed back to the stacks. I stared at Gwen, baffled. She had dark circles under her eyes and her dress was wrinkled and stained, but her hawkish gaze was sharp as she looked back at me. Hildy was at her side although I almost hadn't recognized her without her finery. But she looked ready to work and there was a group of men bringing in a cartload of wood behind her.

"You don't look well-rested," Gwen said to me.

I ignored my blush rising. I may not have gotten a lot of sleep, but it was *good* sleep. I had no complaints.

"I'm fine, do you know why…?" Why Alice had hugged me when we'd barely spoken before? Why the others were still watching me?

"They know what you did last night," Gwen said, and we backed away to give the workers room to move. "You'll have to put up with everyone liking you now."

"Nicely done, darling," Hildy said, greeting me with a kiss to the cheek and a muted smile.

Tatsuo and Bryce were bringing up the rear and Gwen nodded them in our direction. Tatsuo and I hugged while Bryce sniffed at my collar and grinned toothily at me.

"What needs doing?" I asked Gwen.

"Plenty, but I have something specific I'd like to see if you can help with." She led me to the long tables, now stacked with books, some of which were partially burnt or torn in half. "Normally I have a strict policy against our books being marked up. But I'll make an exception if you can fix them," she said.

I picked up a book, *Orientation and Alignment*, that still had its cover and only looked a little dusty.

"Open it," Bryce said, voice light and low like the late echo of a bell.

I flipped it open and found blank pages filling the spine. "Ah," I said.

"Yes," Gwen said. "Those especially concern me. Tatsuo is familiar enough with the catalog to let you know if you're on the right track."

"Do you have a pencil?" I asked, chewing at my lip and drawing up a chair.

Be whole worked to put the torn books back together but it didn't fix charred edges or empty pages. *I am unburnt and fireproof* did the trick for the former but I had yet to find a solution for the latter.

My pages are full brought uninterrupted gibberish that Tatsuo read loudly and with great solemnity. Or in one case, a book stuffed with feathers and dried flowers and leaves. Bryce, who had taken it upon themself to guard me—either from danger or grateful coworkers—

snatched that up and pulled each piece of refuse free, taking experimental whiffs.

I am restored and *My text is returned* brought nothing but my erase marks inside the covers.

I was practicing phrases on a piece of paper like the words were a puzzle. Was *I contain my original text as it was printed* too wordy? I grabbed the book Bryce had picked clean like a carcass and tested the words in pencil and waited.

"Ahh," Tatsuo said, watching small captions appear at the bottom of the open pages. "Yes, that's actually a compendium of natural materials in flight work. It's primarily illustrated."

I sighed and sagged in my chair. "Hence the feathers," I said.

Tatsuo and Bryce nodded. "Hence the feathers," Tatsuo said.

I looked at Bryce. "Maybe we could just paste them back in with the captions?" I suggested weakly.

Bryce snorted. "Ate them," they said.

I blinked at that. Two warm hands cupped at my shoulders and I tilted my head back to see Callum standing over my chair, eyes peering through his glasses to my words in the book.

"It isn't working," I said to him, chewing the inside of my lip to keep from pouting.

"It is," he said. "It just isn't doing what you want it to."

"Same thing," I muttered.

Callum's thumbs kneaded into the back of my neck and I resisted the urge to purr. "Come on," he said. "Take a break, I've brought lunch."

I made to stand, but Bryce growled out, "Ask nicely."

I wasn't sure they were joking, even if Tatsuo was grinning, but Callum only rolled his eyes. Then he turned fully to me, a bright smile on his face.

"Joanna," he said. "Would you please join me for lunch?"

Bryce made a snuffling sound that might have been a laugh and I ducked my head to hide my bright cheeks.

"I'll organize these into text only," Tatsuo said as I stood. "This new spell should suffice for those. We'll plan for the others after your meal."

I thanked them both and then took Callum's waiting hand.

"Do you mind eating as we walk?" he asked as we reached the doors. "There's something I want to show you."

"I need a walk. I'm not used to sitting while I'm working."

People stared at us on the grounds and I kept my eyes on the sandwich Callum passed me from his bag.

"It's because of the library," Callum said glancing between the gawkers and me.

"It could just as easily be because I'm with you," I said, looking up at him. His hair was reddish in the sunlight, his smile nervous, and it gave me a good reason to quit staring at the ground. "It happens with Aiden or Isaac too."

"People like to gossip," he said, shrugging.

"It is a long time," I said, thinking of Aiden's decades of waiting.

Callum was quiet for a stretch, and then he released my hand. I thought for a moment I made a misstep saying anything, but he only wrapped his arm around my waist.

"Worth the wait," he said, so quiet I almost didn't hear.

But it made the nerves in my stomach swoop and spin dizzily, uncertain if I was scared or delighted by the finality in his words.

"Are we...I thought the woods were restricted?" I asked as I realized we were headed to the edge of campus, trees turning dense ahead of us.

"They are and we won't go far in," Callum said. "But Isaac called me out when he saw what was happening."

Before I could ask, Isaac appeared from behind a massive tree trunk in a dark wool coat. His expression, knotted and dark, eased as he spotted us and he jogged over. I accepted the kiss as he reached me, smiling and feeling the night's light sweetness as it lingered. Callum was watching us as Isaac stepped back, looking almost shy. Isaac smirked at me and then pulled Callum in as well, the taller man's eyebrows raising for a moment before his eyes fell shut and his shoulders relaxed. They parted slowly, gazes full of a familiar kind of understanding and I ignored the warm twist in my belly at the sight.

"I didn't think you'd listen to me," Isaac said to him, cheeks dimpling.

"She's safe with us," Callum murmured, eyes soft and sleepy with affection. "And you're right," he said before turning to me, "You've been living outside of serious spellcraft so long, it's better to share as much as we can with you."

"I don't know that I'd call this spellcraft," Isaac said, tone darkening. "Come see."

I followed with Callum, lifting my skirt to avoid catching it on briars as the forest brush turned wilder the farther we walked in. Fall had caught up with the woods, the colors dimming and the smell of growth gone musty and wet. And, somehow stranger, a stillness had fallen. There were no other sounds, no other movement, than ours as we traveled.

"This is far enough," Callum said and there was a touch at my elbow as if he thought of holding me and then reconsidered.

I stopped and stuck close to his side and Isaac backtracked to us, framing me at my right.

"Do you see it?" he asked.

I looked up at Callum, expecting him to answer but his eyes were fixed up, wary and distant, and I realized he was keeping an eye out for any danger. Any sign of what had come to the library. Isaac nudged me and I looked back into the woods. Was it the silence? Was there some kind of familiar scene here that I should recognize? I hadn't walked this part of the woods before, at least not as far as I knew. And it was Isaac that had noticed the change which meant...

"There's no...green," I said. It sounded stupid as it came out of my mouth, but I was staring at an evergreen tree that was a dull slate gray. I thought of home and walking in winter and even on the grayest of days in the deepest of snow, there was still a little life. "And no animals," I added.

Callum stirred next to me, turning to Isaac, "Is it...?"

"Complete," Isaac said. "Not a single spot of green, up until about four yards from the campus. It's like this for miles around. The west end is still good."

"You shouldn't have gone in that deep," Callum said.

"I wasn't alone," Isaac said, and they watched each other for a moment before Isaac smiled. "If you mean I shouldn't have done something dangerous without *you* just say so."

"Mmmph." Callum shrugged and I bit my lip to keep from laughing.

"Is it all dead?" I asked, stepping up to test a little undergrowth sapling. It bent and stretched under my hands, still young but without any of its lively green.

"No, just absent of color," Isaac said. "A significant color. Life, healing, growth, safety."

"And the animals?" I asked.

"That I didn't notice, actually," Isaac admitted with a twist of his mouth, studiously avoiding Callum's gaze.

"I'll come back with Frost, look for tracks to see if they moved to a new territory or…"

Or if they'd gone the way of Cecil Pincombe and the circulation desk.

I swallowed and cleared my throat. "I should get back to the library soon."

They walked with me, Callum sharing more of the sandwiches with Isaac and the pair of them with arms or hands settled around me. It was a solid, safe feeling, and this time I didn't mind the looks from others on campus. I don't think I even noticed them.

"Come back and stay at the house tonight," Isaac said as we reached the library doors.

"I need to get back to mine first," I said. I needed fresh clothing and also to restock on the spelled anti-fertility tinctures, especially if I was going to be a nightly guest with these men. Even if falling into bed with Isaac had been born out of a need for comfort, it was certainly something I planned on repeating.

"Just don't eat dinner before you come in," Isaac said. "If I have to cook for Aiden and Callum you deserve to have some too."

Callum looked as if he was fighting words at the tip of his tongue, but in the end they both kissed me goodbye and I entered the library alone.

Gwen and Hildy were overseeing a repair on the desk. It looked patchy and temporary for the moment, and the loss of the art of the original left my heart aching. Tatsuo was missing from my tables of books, but Bryce was still perched on their stack, picking a bone clean from lunch.

They snapped it as I arrived and sucked on the marrow, teeth gleaming a grin at me as I sat.

I raised an eyebrow. "You'll have to do better than that to scare me," I said and Bryce huffed out a laugh.

I stared at my paper, scribbled with tests of words, and thought of the woods, all the green taken right off the plants. Like words off a page. A bone picked clean…

Words cannot be eaten, I wrote.

"Oh!" Tatsuo shouted, sitting up from behind a table stacked with books. He had one in his hand and twisted it to show me the pages, full of tiny, perfectly lined print. "You've solved it!"

18

JOANNA

I was finishing at home—there were letters from my sister-in-law and the new librarians in Bridgeston to answer—when there was a knock at the door. I opened it and narrowed my eyes at Aiden.

"I *do* know the way to the house," I said.

Aiden only grinned and bent, pressing a kiss to my lips with his soft mouth. I chased the touch without thinking and he chuckled, the low sound ringing in my bones, a thrill low in my belly.

"I wanted to show you a shortcut," he said. "May I come in?"

I stepped back to make room for him and laughed as he crowded in close, arms snaking around me. The door shut behind him with a low, abrupt, hum at the back of his throat. And then I was scooped up, my feet hanging free and Aiden's face pressed into my neck, breathing deeply. I wrapped my arms over his shoulders and tucked my face down into his shoulder.

"How are you?" I asked as the moment stretched.

"Better now," he mumbled into my skin, making goosebumps break out over my arms.

I felt unusually small and light in his hold, and I settled myself more comfortably since he didn't seem interested in setting me down.

"I'm exhausted," he added after another deep breath.

"I almost fell asleep on Bryce Gast today," I said.

Aiden looked up at that, our faces so close I almost went cross-eyed looking back at him.

"Gast let you?" he asked, eyes wide.

"No, they whacked me upside the head with a pamphlet," I said, and the tightness in my chest eased at Aiden's roar of a laugh that shook us both.

"Are you alright?" he asked, kissing my cheek and then my jaw before settling back at my neck and taking a long breath.

"I think so?" I said, and he kissed my throat. "I haven't really given myself a moment to think. And now I just feel…sort of like it was years ago instead of hours." My head was foggy and my body was heavy, and I felt caught between senseless giggles and tears.

"Take a nap with me at the house," Aiden said. I smiled, noting the way Aiden forgot to *ask*. At least he made the orders sound more like suggestions every time.

"Alright, but we should get going or there won't be time. Even with a shortcut," I said.

"Ah yes, that's the other reason I came. Do you feel up to a little magic?" He set me back on my feet, hands rubbing at my back.

"Of course," I said. "I've been writing all day, but I haven't felt anything like I did last night."

"Good, now grab your things and find me a closet," Aiden said.

I knew before he had to tell me what the idea was, and I drew the chalk out of my skirt pocket when we made it to the tiny pantry door.

"Will you even be able to fit through?" I asked, glancing at Aiden's chest. Even if he turned sideways it might be a squeeze.

"Don't be smart, just get us home," he said with a mocking glare.

Door to Aiden's bedroom I wrote on the outside of the door, biting my lip at his use of 'home.'

I opened the door and my jaw fell loose as I stepped inside. The room was scarlet, with an enormous, dark four-poster bed staring at me from the opposite end. The windows were curtained with heavy black material that matched the drapes on the bed, and the only light came from a small golden lamp on a bedside table. There was a glossy blood-red leather armchair holding a guitar and a dark armoire with one door open and revealing Aiden's collection of clothes that would have had Hildy swooning.

"Scoot," he said from behind me and I stumbled deeper into the room, the toes of my shoes catching on a dense, patterned rug.

I was so dazzled by the room, the color and heat and intensity of a beating heart, that I missed watching Aiden squeeze himself through a too-small door.

"I told Callum he could come and look at the portal after we arrived, but since you picked my room and the bed is right here, I think we'll just see if he notices," Aiden said. He passed me, shrugging out of his suit coat and hanging it up in his armoire, along with the tie fixed around his neck. His shoes were toed off next and then he shuffled over to the bed and fell in with a creak of protest and a flutter of sheets.

"Coming, darling?" he asked, face down in the mattress.

I snorted, setting down my small case by the armoire where it would be out of the way and then untangling myself out of my boots. I touched the wallpaper which was stiff and shiny, something like a crest pressed in a matte pattern over every inch. I looked at the art on the walls, certain Isaac had painted the series of constellations that glittered inside of gleaming black frames. I dug my toes into the carpet and felt guilty for even stepping on something that felt like velvet.

"City boy," I murmured, looking around.

Aiden rolled over on the bed, propping himself up on an elbow and staring at me.

"Isaac calls me that," he said.

"But you did, didn't you?" I asked, fingering the crystals hanging from the lamp at his bedside. "Grow up in the city? In the south?"

"Yes," he said, sounding a little wary.

There was more I could say. That the contents of this bedroom probably cost more than my entire house in Bridgeston. Mine and my neighbors. That I had never seen a room like it before. Never met anyone like him before.

"Where can I leave my things?" I asked, not wanting to muss the place. I unbuttoned my borrowed shirt and pulled it free from my skirt.

"Are you undressing?" he asked, eyes brightening.

"I'm not napping in my clothes; they'll get wrinkled," I said.

"Leave them next to my guitar."

I folded them up, standing in my slip, and then went to join Aiden in the bed where he'd moved over to make room for me. The mattress dipped like a cloud under my knee and I froze. Aiden watched me, barely stifling a laugh.

"C'mere," he said, and then he grabbed my hand and pulled me down into silk and feather down.

I held my breath as the bed settled around me like an airy hug and then caught Aiden's grin in the corner of my eye.

"Isaac keeps his bed like a country boy," Aiden said. "I prefer a softer touch."

I wiggled into the mattress and it shifted and curved around me until Aiden's patience ran out and he wrapped his arms around me, pulling my back to his chest.

"Plenty of time to test the give later," he mumbled into my hair.

I covered his hands with mine and he tangled our fingers, his knees drawing up to curve behind mine. Aiden's heartbeat was at my back, the soft puff of his breath in my hair. And the house around us was quiet but active, the creak of floorboards not far off as someone came down the stairs. I was more comfortable than I'd ever been. And *wearier* too. But that wasn't a cure for what happened when I let my eyes fall shut.

The dark of the library and the choking heaviness that had hung in the air. The scene of the circulation desk out of the corner of my eye, blurry and indistinct but no less gruesome. Something small and torn in a puddle of red.

So I kept my eyes open and studied the pattern of the wallpaper until it became abstracted. A red face sneering, and something in flight in the spaces between. Aiden huffed and held me tighter and my eyelids were heavy, but there was nothing good behind them. So I found Isaac's constellations on the wall and matched them with the familiar pieces of the night sky you could see over fields at home.

"You're not sleeping," Aiden rumbled, and I shivered. "Tell me what's wrong?"

"Too much in my head," I answered and he released me a little, pulling at my hip to turn me on my back until he was hovering at my side.

"Would you feel better alone? You have a room here-"

"No," I said quickly, twisting again and draping an arm over his side and propping my head up with the other.

"Then tell me what's in your head," he said, stretching his neck forward to kiss the center of my forehead.

I closed my eyes and this time the backs of my eyelids were simple and dark so I held still. "It's just...nothing has stopped since I got to Canderfey," I said.

"With us?" he asked, and I held him to me before he could try to move away.

"No, well that's only a part of it. I never really left Bridgeston before, not far. Canderfey is new. The kind of place I *knew* existed, but didn't really believe because it was so...outside. And all the people here. And the magic." Aiden's fingers traced up and down my spine and the drowsy peace that followed made it easier to speak. "And yes, there is you and Isaac and Callum, a coven. But there is the fact that I'm a *witch*. A real one. Every time I write something and it works I almost don't believe it. And then...last night—" my voice choked in my throat and Aiden held me tight. I caught my breath and let the handful of tears that had gathered slip out.

"Last night was new for all of us," Aiden said. "Well, for Isaac and I, at least."

I thought of that, thought of Callum prowling through the library like a soldier.

"Was Callum in the Enmaire army?" I asked.

Aiden sighed, a big deep breath that ruffled the top of my head. "Callum was in the war."

I blinked at that. "That can't be right, he's too young." The Red War in the North was nearly twenty years ago and Callum couldn't have been more than a teenager.

"He was too young," Aiden said, voice flat. I thought that if I pressed I could learn more, but it sounded as if it hurt Aiden to speak of it, and I imagined the same would be true for Callum.

"He doesn't like to act the soldier," Aiden said. "Still, it comes out in ways. Over-protective, quick reactions…gut instincts. He's born to it and it suits him, even when he hates the fact."

"That's why I always seem to have an escort now?" I asked, thinking of the way someone seemed to be conveniently placed to walk me to my next destination at any moment.

Aiden hummed in agreement and then added, "And why you'll be talked into staying for dinner and the rest of the night as often as he can manage it. Mind you, I don't disagree with him."

I frowned against Aiden's chest, chewing at my lip. I had a few thoughts about that, but they deserved Callum's ears, not Aiden's so I'd hold onto them for now.

"We just want you safe," Aiden murmured, kissing the top of my head.

I pulled back to look up at him and raised an eyebrow.

"With us," Aiden added, his smile growing. "Happy…satisfied."

He was grinning now and my cheeks ached with resisting the urge to join him. He pulled me up, my slip rucking up my hips as he moved me closer, resting his forehead against mine. He was shifting us in small movements, bodies brushing together until I was on my back, pinned into the decadent mattress by his weight. It was simultaneously tender and carnal, the feel of him pressing me down, surrounding me.

"Do you want to rest?" he asked, and his head bent to mine, lips stroking over mine and then pulling away as I chased them.

"This feels restful," I said, which was a bit of a lie because this felt *stirring* and left me wanting more. But it was certainly better than lying in a bed and staring at a wall.

"Oh good," he said, dipping down again, body stroking mine with the movement and hitching my breath in my chest.

I wriggled underneath him, spreading my legs to fit him between. His body was thicker than Isaac's and the stretch in my thighs traveled up my back and down to my toes as he settled closer. We both took heavy breaths, mouths open against one another.

"Been waiting to kiss you since the day you arrived," he said.

I smiled at that, thinking of him in the window seat. The shock of him to my system, someone so beautiful and teasing. "You have kissed me," I said.

He lifted his head, eyes wrinkled in the corners with his smile. Then he sank back down, taking my lips in a long draw, clasped between his. His tongue flicked out, tasting, and then he dove back in, our hips grinding together as I struggled to find purchase in the kiss. But with every stroke of his mouth and caress of his tongue, I was being swept into a current—a vocabulary of touch well beyond my experience.

His hands framed my face, holding me to him, fingertips stroking along my jaw. Every whimper he drew out of me, he answered with a melodic hum that travelled into the kiss and down into my belly, creating a thrumming warmth. It was magic, a melody made for pleasing. I couldn't answer it with a written word so instead, I wrapped myself around Aiden, clinging and accepting until I had to pull away to breathe. His mouth moved to my neck and I gasped, the music just as strong on my skin as it was on my tongue.

My hips writhed against his and he was stiff and heavy against me. His palms were spread beneath my shoulder blades and he slid down, teeth scraping at my collarbone and releasing a low note that reverberated down between my legs. I cried out and clasped the back of his neck trying to hold him there, to keep the vibration in my bones steady. But he traveled again, soft kisses over my chest as he held a quiet, sweet tone.

"Kisses shouldn't be rushed," he said.

He kissed the gap between my breasts, cheek rubbing against me and stubble snagging at my slip. I caught my breath for the half-beat between one note and the next.

When his lips wrapped around a silk-covered nipple I sang with him, off-key and broken but it did nothing to stop the tremor running through me. Aiden grinned, pulling away and looking up from my chest with a wicked gleam in his eyes.

"That's cheating," I said, voice low.

"I warned you I'd try to influence you in our favor," he said and then he blew softly on the wet spot he left over my slip.

I shivered, tilting my head back to hide my face. Aiden traced the low collar of my slip with his tongue and then sucked on the unattended breast. I held him to me as he started to hum again and I groaned in chorus. He held himself off me then, giving me nothing to seek any badly needed friction from. But every tug of his mouth around my pebbling nipple was an echoing tug inside of me. He reached around a hand to my front, fingers gently pinching in tandem with his mouth. The song burrowing in my skin was turning high and ringing through me, carrying out of my own lips.

"Please, please," I whimpered.

"Patience, darling." Aiden kept up his work, never really touching below my waist, but building up a throbbing beat there all the same. My legs were quaking on the bed as I begged for a release I would have thought was impossible, not with so little stimulation to only my breasts.

He tugged at my slip and it scraped over my skin, exposing me to his hot breath, tongue lashing over one tender nipple while his thumb swirled over the other. My legs stretched up and knotted around his back, tugging him down to land heavily on me. Aiden growled into my skin and the trilling, wavering tension broke in me, music flooding my ears and spiraling out from my aching core.

Aiden kissed his way back up, peppering a warm wet path up my chest and neck and across my jaw. His hands stroked at my thighs, holding me in place. I clutched his jaw in my hold and brought him in for a lazy, licking kiss until he was purring into my mouth.

"S'dinner time," he murmured, pulling away. And there was no apology for the smug smile on his face, although I couldn't really blame him.

"I'm not hungry," I said, reaching up to attend to the buttons of his shirt. My stomach betrayed me with a growl and Aiden laughed.

"You are, and so am I," Aiden said, and he kissed me once more. "Also, I don't want to be interrupted and I suspect if I keep you here too much longer we will be."

"You don't want…" I trailed off biting my lip and righting the collar of my slip, damp fabric sticking on my skin. Aiden raised up and I could see him, stretching at the zipper of his pants.

"Of course I want you to strip me naked and have your way with me," Aiden said, grinning and easing the knot of nerves in my stomach. He settled at my side, hand soothing down my hip while the other brushed the loose curls out of my face. "But I'm patient. The part I was most anxious for was knowing you existed. The rest is icing."

There was a knock at the bedroom door at that moment and then it was opening, Isaac smirking at the pair of us. He glanced down briefly at my chest, eyes darkening, and then looked at Aiden.

"Callum's hunting for you," he said. "And dinner is ready."

I squirmed out of Aiden's hold and pushed my slip back down my hips, rising from the bed.

Isaac stayed leaning in the doorway. "I have a robe," he said to me. "It'll be more comfortable and no one will mind."

I paused at Aiden's armchair. It would be nice not to have to get dressed again. Isaac shrugged as I thought it over.

"Yes, please," I said.

We were leaving Isaac's bedroom with me wrapped in green velvet when Callum came thundering up the stairs and nearly ran into us.

"Where's the portal?" he asked, eyes wide behind his glasses.

I was about to answer when Isaac gestured to me and asked, "Are you completely blind?"

Callum rolled his eyes, stepping forward and sweeping an arm around my waist to plant a swift, fierce kiss to my mouth.

"You're beautiful," he said, words mumbling into my lips. "Where's the portal?"

Isaac made an exhausted sound and started down the stairs as I laughed and kissed Callum again. "Aiden's bedroom door," I told him as he released me.

"You have ten minutes to be downstairs or you forfeit your right to second helpings," Isaac called from a flight down.

I stood at the top of the stairs for a beat, watching Callum race to the door, and debated joining him. But I was starving and Aiden was just emerging from his room, looking as rumpled as I'd left him if not more so. And I wanted those second helpings.

19

JOANNA

Students trickled back into the library as the week went on, suddenly turning up with overdue books as if it might be a consolation to those of us working. Construction continued on the front desk, as well as the glass roof, and for the first time since my arrival, the library was loud with activity. Isaac walked me to work before his classes. Callum brought me lunch and did research in the staff section. Aiden appeared at the end of my shift with some excuse for me to return back to the house with him. He had a new piece of music he wanted me to hear. Isaac was trying a new recipe. Callum wanted to test different writing utensils with my magic. I pretended not to see through the orchestration.

It all felt very regular. Or it did in the moments where I made sure to not look toward the woods that had gone gray. Even the sky hanging over the tops of the trees had lost its color. And now grocers were keeping smaller stocks of food because the fresh would turn to rot overnight.

So I had bought a bag of apples and commandeered the kitchen from Isaac to bake them in dark sugar and whiskey for dessert. We had gorged ourselves on them before they went to waste. And then Callum had disappeared up into his office. Like he did every night.

Just like every night after falling asleep with Isaac and sometimes Aiden, I would wake up and find Callum curved against my back, an arm wrapped possessively around my stomach.

"Do you want to see your room tonight?" Isaac asked. He had dragged an armchair over from the corner of the front room when I'd settled in the window seat with a book. And while I knew he'd pulled out his sketchbook, it was easy to ignore the scratches of a pencil on paper in favor of studying runes and sigils.

"Sick of me stealing your pillow?" I asked in answer, flipping a page but not seeing it.

The room, the guest room as Aiden had first called it, came up often. And always referred to as '*your* room' like there was a permanent place for me here. Everything they said to me offered that, and every time it was offered I felt a swell of panic. That this was a dream that could be snatched away. That they would realize their mistake in bringing me into their fold.

I glanced over at Isaac and he was looking away, a frown on his mouth and a guarded tightness around his eyes. *Just take the stupid room*, I thought to myself. But there wasn't a room in this house I hadn't loved upon finding it, and I knew that would be the case now. But it had only been a few weeks, and things between us so rarely felt real. It was too perfect for me to feel comfortable grabbing onto, and in spite of their insistence that I belonged I didn't see where I fit yet.

"I need to go find Callum," I said, which was true, but it had been just as true days ago. Now was only convenient because I needed the escape.

Isaac nodded but didn't look back. I rose and crossed to the doorway and he caught my hand on the way, linking our fingers and holding me there.

"When you're ready," he said, meeting my eyes with something fierce and tender in his, "We can take my damn pillow with us."

He smiled a little and I dove down for a kiss to thank him for his patience. He held me there for a long, sweet, stretch and I was practically ready to accept the room *and* the coven when he released me.

"Good luck with him," he said, kissing once more at my cheek.

I blinked and then remembered. Callum. I had used him as my excuse to break the tension and now I suppose I had to follow through. It was overdue anyway.

I took the stairs up to the third floor, hearing Aiden practicing from his studio on the second. Callum was squinting down at a text by the dying sunlight from his office window. A pile of books on the floor surrounded his desk chair like a protective wall.

"You need a lamp," I said.

He glanced over his shoulder at me, a furrow on his brow easing with his smile. "Write me one."

I pulled the chalk—now kept in a little cigarette case Aiden had found for me—from my pocket and wrote on the edge of a bookshelf. *Callum has a lamp on his home desk.*

"Ohhh, not *that*," Callum said, and he pushed his chair away from his desk. It was gaudy, a more elaborate version of the crystal one in Aiden's bedroom. "Anyway, there's nowhere for it to plug into."

It is always lit. And so it was. Callum's face went wide with surprise.

"You should have been more specific to your tastes," I said.

"You could fix it with a word," he muttered, prodding at one of the hanging crystals and sending prisms of light dancing over the books around us.

"I'm thinking I'll spend next week at my own house," I said, pretending to study the books on the shelves.

"What? Why?" Callum asked, voice sharp. "What if we...need you?"

"For what?" I asked, laughing. I pulled a small paper bound text on defensive glamouring and disguise from the shelf and flipped aimlessly through.

He was quiet and then I heard him pushing books aside. "Aiden or Isaac will want to stay close—"

"Aiden or Isaac, but not you?" I asked, turning on my heel to face him.

He winced and raked his hand through his hair. "No, of course, I —but—"

I took pity on him and abandoned the teasing offense. "Just say it, Callum."

He froze and swallowed and his fingers swept through his hair again, tangling at the ends. He sighed and dropped his arm. "I'd like it if you stayed with us as long as we're dealing with this threat. Or...or with Gwen and her coven. If you'd prefer. As long as I know you're safe."

The suggestion of staying with Gwen caught me by surprise, I'd give him that. I'd expected more insistence and less...genuine worry.

"I'd rather stay here," I said, smiling.

His shoulders dropped with relief. "You mean that?"

"I do, I was just sick of the play-acting, Callum. You can be honest with me, I promise not to argue for the sake of it," I said.

I had meant to say more, but the words were lost as Callum surrounded me, arms clutching and lips hard against mine. It was an urgent, hungry kiss and in half a breath I was answering it in kind, my fingers clawing at his shoulders. I felt like I was trying to climb him, force our bodies closer, close enough that I could feel his heartbeat against my breast and pounding through my blood. His hands grasped my hips, holding me tight to him and pinned against the shelves.

"I promise to be better," he whispered, pulling away just long enough for me to gasp. I wanted to answer him, to tell him I didn't need *better*, that he could simply be less skittish around me.

But he wasn't skittish now. He was consuming, his tongue stroking against mine, hands traveling, gathering up my skirt so my legs could cling around his waist. I severed the kiss as my nose smashed against his glasses and broke away laughing, pulling them off his nose. Callum barely noticed, intent on sucking kisses along my jaw. His hips jerked between us, fingers digging into the soft underside of my thighs and the glasses went clattering to the floor. There was too much fabric between us and with every aching groan from Callum I needed him more. I wanted to soothe him as much as I wanted to satisfy myself.

"Put me down," I rasped and Callum stepped back so fast I nearly fell to the floor.

"I'm sorr—" he started.

"Don't you dare say it," I said, raising a finger in his face. I dropped my skirt to the floor and pulled my shirt over my head too fast, a button popping and dinging against a book.

Callum stared dumbly at me for a moment and I smiled shakily back, reaching out and plucking his vest buttons loose. There was a sudden hot shimmer and then Callum was bare and I had a second to see him, the long narrow lean of him, muscles corded, and the tangle of scars down his right hip before I was back in his hold. I swallowed his groan; tangling my hands between us to pull my slip over my head. And then he covered my cry as his fingers slid into my panties, fondling at my skin, dipping inside of me and spreading the wetness he found here. I pushed the last scrap of clothing between us off my hips and Callum lifted me from the floor.

I grabbed the shelf above me for balance, laughing and kicking one leg free of my underwear to brace it against a stack of books. Callum hitched my other leg over his hips, fingers guiding himself into place and then he filled me with one swift stroke. I cried out at the stretch and the suddenness. But it brought with it an immediate flutter of relief, like I'd been waiting hours for him instead of minutes. I felt full to bursting, Callum fitting so deeply, pressing into places I'd never found before.

"Oh gods, Jo-Joanna," he muttered, the words were winded. His lips snagged over my earlobe, breath puffing against my skin.

One of my heels was pressed to his ass, holding him still inside me.

"I didn't mean to rush," he said, a whine at the back of his throat and I nuzzled into his cheek.

"I want you to," I said, and I squeezed experimentally around him. His mouth fell open with his moan, and he stirred, hips twitching. "Please, Callum," I said. I kissed his cheek as his hands braced me. My foot stroked down the back of his thigh and I rolled my hips into his, our breaths catching.

His belly quivered against mine, all the tension in his body built up. And then his lips latched onto mine like an anchor and he drank my ragged cry as he gave in, drawing back and surging in again. It was a harsh, heavy rhythm, our bodies slapping noisily together and Callum's hands tight enough on me to leave fingertip bruises. But every push threw stars into my eyes and a hot flutter mounting in my belly.

Books rattled on the shelf behind me and I pulled away from his mouth to giggle and gasp, a moan falling free with every hitch of his hips into mine. Callum's forehead was knotted, mouth open and he looked so desperate and lost. I wrapped an arm around his shoulders, tangling my fingers into the hair at the back of his neck.

"You feel so good," I said, kissing over his brow.

He grunted into my neck, hips snapping. It was a deep, full pleasure, but not the kind that would send me over the edge. Still, I didn't want him to stop. Having Callum turning needy and wild in my arms was a heady enough feeling on its own. As his thrusts became more urgent and the groan held tight behind his teeth turned into an aching, begging sound I only wanted more. I raised my legs higher around his hips and squeezed him with every buck and twist, watching with hungry eyes as his back arched and his cries tore free.

"Joanna," he gasped, gaze fixing to mine. "Joanna—I want—"

"I want to watch you," I said softly, nails scratching into his hair and thighs clasping around his hips. "You're beautiful."

He cursed and the bookshelf dug into my back as his even thrusts turned erratic and sharp. My hand above slipped, bringing two smaller books crashing down to the floor. I was grinning as Callum was grunting, face pressed to my neck as there was a warm, slippery feeling bursting inside of me. His arms twisted up around my back like a fierce hug and for a long moment, I could feel his legs shaking as he leaned into me, with soft little thrusts. Then he straightened, face leaning up to glare at me, and he pulled us away from the bookshelf, a few more texts tumbling down.

"Where are we going?" I asked as we wavered in step for a moment.

"To find my dignity," Callum muttered, taking me over to his desk chair.

"Callum, you don't need—" I said with a small 'oof' as I landed in the seat, the leather cold against my skin.

Callum kneeled at my feet, cheeks still flushed from his orgasm, and a light smile replacing his glare. "I forgot how that felt, if I'm being honest," he said, hands stroking over my thighs, and then sliding between to touch where I was still aching and now dripping as he said, "Being in a woman. But I *did not* forget how to please. And that's all I want, Joanna."

His hands parted my legs, drawing me forward in the chair to make room for his shoulders. He kissed up the top of my right thigh, and then across my belly and back down the left, all while his hands cupped and petted at my swollen folds.

"I'm a mess," I said, squirming under his touch but my knees were falling open for him and his hands were already stirring up sparks in my skin.

"Whose fault is that?" he grumbled, and then his hands slid away and he pressed a tender, open kiss to my clit, tongue flicking out. My fingers dug into the arms of the chair and I held a whimper at the back of my throat. "I want to hear you, Joanna," he said.

He licked a stripe up my center, the hair of his beard prickling at my skin and I let my gasp carry up to the ceiling. His hands scooped under my bottom and pulled me forward, nose nuzzling at the top of my lips as his tongue dipped and swirled. It was a teasing, sweet touch, tickling up the pleasure he had brought to a simmer with his cock. He alternated sucks over my folds with probing licks and gentle nibbles until I was bucking in his hands, now desperate for the pounding pressure. He kissed and soothed and stroked while my whimpers built into sobs.

"Callum, please, please," I chanted, hips rolling towards him even as he backed away, keeping the same delicate touch. "I need *more.*"

He pressed a long, closed-mouth kiss over me, hands stroking at the outsides of my thighs as they crept towards his shoulders. Then his tongue pressed flat, mouth wrapping around me as he sucked and licked. My back bowed as the pressure broke, sweeping slow through me like warm syrup while Callum kept lapping and kissing. I was a trembling puddle in the chair as the aftershocks eased. I hissed, eyes popping open, as he dipped a finger inside of me.

I looked down to my lap, where Callum's cheek was resting against my thigh, lips still shiny. His finger pumped gently, pressing deeper and then easing back again.

"Can you take more?" he asked, thumb brushing over my clit and making me twitch and draw back.

"I...I don't know," I said. My body still felt glowy and soft, but every touch was on the edge of too much sensation.

He smiled, beard scratching at my skin. "I think you can."

A second finger joined the first, twisting and he lifted one of my legs onto his shoulder. He sucked a ring around my over-sensitive lips, stirring up warmth and making my legs shake and my toes curl, all while keeping a shallow rhythm at my opening. I unclenched my hands from the armchair, dipping my fingers into his hair, body relaxing under his ministrations. There was a hum in my ears and it wasn't until Callum looked up from between my legs, eyes smiling, that I realized the sound was coming from me.

"Feels nice," I said, voice slurring with the lazy heat flowing through me. I didn't know if it meant I would come again, but Callum seemed in no rush and it was too nice a feeling to want it to end.

"You taste sweet," he said, tongue flicking gently over me.

I snorted at that and his eyes darkened, fingers delving deeper suddenly and then crooking up.

"Oh!" I shouted at the swelling feeling inside of me.

"I'm not teasing," he said, still stroking inside of me as I squirmed closer, wanting more and less, lips parted on a soundless cry. "I want to keep the flavor of you on my tongue."

And then he was laving at me again, tongue firm and seeking out all the places he had already discovered, but now with intent and purpose. I was riding his hand and mouth, a cracking, pleading noise rising up from my throat. My hands held him tight to me and he groaned against my skin, the sound echoing deeply and making me writhe. I called out his name and his touch grew firmer, tongue pointing and lashing at my clit. The pleasure was spiky and burning and seemed to stretch from toe to head through, one long bright heat content to leave me hanging.

"Come for me, Joanna," Callum said, the words heavy in my ears. "Let me hear you."

And then his lips wrapped tight around my clit pulling and pressing, and his fingers pushed high against me. My legs lifted up around his ears and my belly clenched and I tugged tight on Callum's hair even as I drove my hips against his face, stars bursting behind my eyes. He moaned into me again and all the tension in me splintered as I fell apart and my body trembled into a limp puddle in the chair.

Callum rose slowly, easing my loose fingers out of his hair and settling my legs back from his shoulders. He kissed a slow wet path up my stomach and his arms wrapped around my back as I let out a small, helpless sound that was meant partly in thanks. I felt almost wounded with how thoroughly undone I was, but the tender hold of him around me soothed away the sting and I snuggled into his chest.

He draped my arms over his shoulders lifted me from the chair and I grunted. "No," I said.

He chuckled, holding me to him as he stood up from the floor. "No?" he asked. "I'm taking you to bed."

Oh. I wasn't sure what I had thought, only that I knew I was officially used up for the night. I nodded against him and wondered if it was really possible to *hear* someone's smile. Or if I was just that tired.

He carried us to Isaac's room where Isaac and Aiden were facing each other on their sides in the bed, the sheets low enough that I knew they were naked too.

"I hope you two are satisfied for the evening because Joanna here is done," Callum said, sounding a little too smug. I pinched at the skin under my hand, but he only shrugged and I caught him grinning.

"We heard," Aiden said and my cheeks blushed hotly.

"Come here, love," Isaac said, rolling in my direction and pulling back the covers.

Callum settled me on the mattress and I pulled him down with me, wanting to be surrounded. I got my wish, Isaac pulling me to his chest and Callum sliding in tight behind me. Three hands stroked down my side and I hummed again, eyes drooping.

"What was all the crashing about, though?" Aiden whispered as I sank into slumber.

"Books," Callum said, and then I was asleep.

20

CALLUM

I woke as Joanna twisted next to me, rolling away from a now empty spot and cuddling into my chest. I squinted in the dim light and found Aiden and Isaac rising out of bed.

"Where're you going?" I whispered. My hands were helping Joanna, soothing at the bed warm skin of her back and pulling the sheets back to cover us.

"Groceries, errands," Isaac said, hunting his dresser for clothes.

"It's your turn to come up with an excuse for her to stay here," Aiden said, low voice almost growling in an effort to keep quiet.

"She's staying," I said. "We talked last night."

"For good?" Isaac asked, and both he and Aiden had paused in dressing.

Joanna made a small sound of protest, hands clutching at my skin, and I wrapped my arms around her, marveling in how she settled at the touch.

"Until it's safe," I answered. Aiden's expression fell but he nodded. "But...don't you think? She might...after some time?"

"We hope so," Aiden said softly. "The day she doesn't skirt the subject, I'll feel confident." Isaac and I both frowned and Aiden came around to the bed, bending down and kissing the center of Joanna's back. He smiled at me and leaned in for a real kiss. "She will," he whispered before leaving the room.

Isaac kissed us both before leaving as well. "Let her sleep," he said, but his expression looked as if he didn't expect me to follow the advice.

And a part of me was tempted to wake her—slowly, with lips and hands—if only to have a chance to perfect my efforts from the night before. Mostly to have her in my ear again, her begging words and the pretty broken twist to her voice as I did something right.

But I didn't want to interrupt the sleepy cling of her on my chest so instead, I half-dozed with my fingers in her hair and her toes against my calf. I turned my face to her and took long breaths, the salt and sugar of her filling up my lungs until I was drowsy. She whimpered in her sleep and her back tightened so I stroked my free hand down the length of her spine and pulled the sheet up to her shoulder. Her forehead was knotted so I loosened the tangles in her hair and brushed it out of her face. And when she shivered I rolled us so she was in my warm spot of the bed.

She stirred then, breath hitching and fingers tightening on my sides. There was a half-second of terror in her eyes as they fluttered open and then it faded just as quickly and the frown on her mouth curled up into a smile.

"Morning," she murmured, eyes falling shut again as she relaxed back on the mattress.

"Morning," I said. "Bad dream?"

Her mouth pouted with a sleepy frown and she twisted, leaning into my hand that was stroking down her side to her hip.

"No dreams," she said shaking her head.

"No nightmares?" I asked.

Her nose wrinkled and her hands uncurled from between us, circling to my back. "No. I don't remember dreaming in…weeks. S'like…like I'm not even sleeping. I'm awake and then I'm waking up again. Almost doesn't feel like rest."

All the drowsy lazy pleasure of the morning stilled as she spoke, turning dull and muted as my thoughts started catching up. My brain was cataloging away the warm maple color of her eyes in the morning, and the deep peachy pink of the tips of her breast, in favor of recalling the weight of dreams. And the forces that had the ability to take them away.

"Hmm, I lost you somewhere, didn't I?" she said, smile creeping up on one side of her mouth. A hand appeared between us, one finger reaching up to stroke between my eyebrows. "What did I say?"

"How long have your dreams been missing?" I asked.

There were psychic drains, like parasites, that might take on a host. But that wouldn't explain the woods or even the attack on the library.

"Weeks," she repeated, shrugging. She looked at me for a moment and then thought again. "Since…since that first batch of books turned back up."

"The night I walked you home," I said, stiffening.

"I suppose…probably."

I jumped out of the bed, hearing her laugh my name as I hurried to the door and into the hall. *Gatekeepers* was on my desk by the window of my office, buried under a stack of books. I grabbed my pants out of the pocket of space I'd left them in and tripped my way into them on my way to the window. Soft footsteps padded behind me and Joanna was at my side, wrapped in Isaac's green robe and peering over the arm of the chair.

"You think what was in the library, what's taken over the woods, also has to do with me not dreaming?" she asked. "I've gone without dreams before."

"You said it felt like you weren't even asleep," I said, pushing the other books aside and pulling forward the fragile old beast of a nightmare text I had left stinking up my desk.

"Out like a light," she said softly. "That's significant?"

"Dreams are often a warning system. Something has stolen yours." I flipped through the pages with clumsy fingers. Nails scratched gently into the back of my hair and I paused to shift the book in her direction.

"I skipped ahead," she said, still combing her fingers into my hair. She brought her free hand down, turning in halfway through the pages and flicking ahead to land on a wavery illustration of a figure in the woods. "It eats," she said, pointing down the words beneath the woodblock print.

"Sounds…" I trailed off, the vision of the library coming to mind. A maw of darkness throwing silhouettes in eerie relief. The librarian who sent a cowering student across the room to safety and then splintered in a metallic grind of light.

"Like a boogeyman," Joanna said. She was perched on the arm of the chair and I looked up at her, puzzled. "You know…don't go into the woods, or you'll get eaten up for being a rotten child. What?"

"Nothing. Is…is that what parents say to children in the country?" I asked. "Isaac made it sound rustic but—"

Joanna grinned. "My mother was northern. Every misbehavior was threatened with death or kidnapping by a monster of some sort."

I swallowed and looked back down at the book in my hands. Her mother was northern. Did she know about my part in the war yet? Would Isaac or Aiden share that with her, take the burden out of my hands, or would they leave it alone as my business? I would never share it with another soul if I thought I could. Even Joanna. *Especially* Joanna.

"It does say it consumes everything but dreams seem like a light meal," Joanna mused, tracing her finger over the page of the story.

I shook off my thoughts, leaning into Joanna's side—as if her closeness might burn away old stains from my past, as if I could keep them from her indefinitely.

"Dreams could be powerful," I said. "From the right person. Stronger than a desk or—" I broke off, feeling her tense at my side. "And this story looks a little familiar."

"That illustration looks familiar," she mumbled, leaning in as well.

"You've seen it before," I said, just to tease.

She ignored me, pulling her fingers from my hair and making me regret my joke. She lifted the book out of my lap and held it back from her face.

"That looks like Isaac's painting," she said. "The trees and- and the meadow. The one I…"

"Painted a shadowy figure in the background of?" I asked as she trailed off. Her eyes narrowed and her lips pursed and a low-sinking weighed heavy in my gut.

There were plenty of terrible possibilities behind the current situation. There were *only* terrible possibilities. Someone had been killed already and the color green was vanishing. *Being eaten*, I amended, looking at the illustration in the book. But if what was plaguing the Canderfey campus had a place in *Gatekeepers* then our situation was even worse than I expected. And if Joanna had any special kind of connection...

My chest burnt with how hard my heart began to beat. I needed more information. Answers to questions and a collection of plans to study. I needed a solution to the problem and an action to take. I need Joanna safe and uninvolved.

"Callum," she whispered, and she tilted the book in her hands, brow furrowing. "There's...there's something-"

The front door on the ground floor shut and Joanna jumped up from the chair. I pulled the book out of her hands, leaving it open on my desk.

"That'll be them back with groceries," I said as Joanna watched the doorway. "Go down and fill them in? Let me do a little hunting for more information."

She was chewing at the corner of her mouth with worried eyes. I stood, drawing her into my chest and settling my lips over hers until she answered the kiss, rising up on her toes.

"As soon as I know what we're facing, I'll be able to start coming up with a solution," I said.

"I'll bring you up tea," she said.

Her fingers were fretting at the cuffs of the robe, and I wanted some way of soothing the anxiety out of her. But that was Isaac's skill and she would be better off downstairs in good company. And I would work faster alone.

THERE WERE three drained cups of tea and the remains of a forgotten breakfast on my desk when the sun went out.

I looked up from the pages, squinting at the sudden darkness of the room, Joanna's gifted lamp the only shy source of light. Outside the window, the sky had turned slate gray, but soft clouds lay scattered across the sky as if it should have been a beautiful sunny blue day.

"Callum," Aiden called from downstairs.

I scrambled out of my chair, bringing half a dozen books with me. The stairs were pitch-black and I made it down to the first floor more by memory than by sight. Isaac and Aiden framed Joanna at the front window of the sitting room, the three of them staring up. I pulled up behind Joanna and found the glowing black orb in the sky where the sun should have been. I winced at the burn in my eyes and backed away.

"Don't look at it," I said. The words snapped on my tongue and I clenched my jaw to bury the barking command.

Joanna turned right away, her arms folded tightly over her stomach in a too-large sweater. Aiden's probably.

"Can it eat the sun too?" she asked me as Aiden and Isaac drew away from the window.

"The sunlight," I said. "The books call it things like the Hollow, Consumer, Devourer, Eater, etcetera..."

"Is this happening everywhere?" Isaac asked, glancing over his shoulder to the window.

"No, not yet. Canderfey and the Hand Woods for now. It's...been locked up for centuries, at least that long from what I can find. The library, the woods, Joanna's dreams, this is probably just its way of acclimating back to its appetite."

Joanna was pulling books free from my arms, taking them with her to an armchair in the corner where she curled up in the seat. "If it *was* locked up then it can be again," she said, as much to herself as to the rest of us.

"I told you we'd find a solution," I said, but she didn't smile, just began digging through the pages in front of her.

"There's a food shortage starting," Isaac told me. "I contacted the campus and they agreed to help any locals in whatever way they can."

"What's a true name?" Joanna asked, looking up from the book I had found most useful and swatting away a curl from her face. "This says '*The Hollow was caged by its true name.*'"

I pulled another chair over to Joanna's corner and Aiden and Isaac followed. "It's a name of power, one we're born with. Not the kind our parents give but one that holds the essences of our...our souls," I said. "There are supposedly rituals you can do to learn your own. But knowing someone else's true name gives you power over them."

"Power to trap something for centuries?" she asked. "Something strong enough to eat sunlight?"

"Given what that creature is capable of, the hold of a true name might be the key to keeping it contained," Isaac said. I nodded and Joanna lifted a hand to chew at her thumbnail.

"How do you learn the true name of something so old?" Isaac asked.

"That's the next thing I'll be searching for," I said. "If I can figure out who caged it, I might be able to find research of theirs that would help us."

"If it took the true name to cage the Hollow years ago, would you need the true name to open the cage?" Joanna asked.

I smiled a little, I had thought of the same thing. I wanted to push aside the current disaster and take the day to learn more about Joanna's magical instincts. She found patterns and errors in the world quickly. Once she had a better sense of what she was capable of, what other's magical traces felt like, she would be even faster and sharper.

"I don't know yet, it would depend on the cage," I said. "Whether or not the witch or coven that designed it trusted that it would be left locked."

"If it did take a true name then that means someone opened it intentionally," Isaac said.

"Or experimentally," I argued, thinking of the students. Thinking of the kind of student *I* had been growing up. I would have tested a lock to see if I could break it when I was younger. Consequences were a foggier concept than knowing my own strength at the time.

"We should go to the library," Joanna said, shutting the book in her hands and holding it to her chest. Her gaze was already on the front door and her face was missing any hint of expression.

Isaac and I met each other's eyes at the same time and I could see the worry. Joanna had fallen into the deep end of magic in a very short amount of time. And while it was a revelation that *had* to come sooner or later, a part of me regretted that we had been the ones to lead her there.

"There will be books on true names," she said, looking at us finally. "And Gwen should know. Tatsuo and the others could help us."

I tried to wrestle the grimace off my face before anyone noticed, but Aiden laughed and I was caught out.

"Yes let's put Tatsuo Ito and Callum in the same room together and see who comes out with more research," he said.

"He's a hobbyist," I muttered.

"He's my friend," Joanna said lightly, rising from the chair and giving us her back. "And he's very helpful."

"Get dressed," Aiden said, grinning down at my still bare chest. "We're going to the library."

21

JOANNA

If the tension of the two covens together in the staff library wasn't bad enough—in Callum's defense, Tatsuo *did* seem to be baiting him by voicing aloud every bit of useful information he found—I could feel my bones rattling under my skin. It had started in Callum's office, *Gatekeepers* in my hands and the imprint of the words almost shimmering on the page. An impression of letters scratched into the page like it had been drawn there with an inkless pen. Or a fingernail.

Let it out.

I couldn't focus on any of the books in front of me. I only saw the letters spelled out, a cruder version of my handwriting. Was it still writing without any pencil or chalk? I didn't remember making the words but I remembered the drowsy, drugged feeling while reading. I remembered the icy cold fear of waking, the itchy crawling in my head as I woke. The one I still had some mornings.

Isaac passed me, arms loaded with dark parchment scrolls, and I stirred in the window seat. The library lamps were turned up bright to combat the darkness outside. Aiden and Hildy were a couple aisles away, chatting about the city while they browsed books. I had been trying to read the same page for the past ten minutes. It was only information Tatsuo had already found three times in other texts. A true name might be a word, or a sound, or a symbol, or a color. Usually, they were some combination and the older the name the stronger they became.

Bryce rounded a bookshelf and came to sit at the far end of the window seat. They were empty-handed and watching me steadily. It was as likely Bryce had come to see me of their own volition as it was Callum or Gwen had sent them to check on me. I was snapping my thumbnail against my front teeth and Bryce arched an eyebrow.

"Sorry," I mumbled, stuffing my hand under my skirt.

Bryce leaned forward, taking my bag from where I'd stashed it against the window by my knees. I dove forward to grab it back but I was too late, they were already taking out the book I had smuggled from the house. They flipped straight to the illustration of the Hollow, setting it face-up on the bench between us.

I stared at Bryce's face and they looked up from the page to me, green eyes glinting.

"Your words," Bryce said, pointing to the slanted press of letters on the page. I could barely make out the *it ou* before it faded into shadow.

My breath caught in my chest and I exhaled, slow and shaky. "Is it a spell?" I asked, keeping as quiet as I could.

"Yes," they said.

The start of a sob cracked free, and I fastened my lips shut looking down at my lap while I blinked away tears. Bryce waited quietly for me to settle myself.

"Did you know?" I asked.

"I guessed," Bryce said. "Will you tell them?"

"Should I?" I asked. Bryce shrugged, and for a moment I thought they actually didn't care. But Hildy laughed somewhere in the shelves and Bryce's gaze twitched in her direction.

"Will you help me?" I asked, but Bryce had stiffened in their seat, turning to the stairs and back arching like a cat. There was a low sour note in the back of their throat, and then Callum was appearing between the shelves and the stairs, the same tension in his shoulders.

"It's on the campus," Bryce said, prowling toward the stairs.

"Stay with Joanna," Callum barked at the others.

Everyone shouted at once, Aiden and Tatsuo at Callum, Isaac at me, Hildy and Gwen at each other about which of them would stay with me. Bryce looked at me once over their shoulder, and I skirted around Callum following their footsteps quick down the stairs.

"Joanna!" Callum yelled.

"It's at the staff houses," Bryce said, just loud enough for me to catch the words.

I pressed my hand over my pocket, feeling for the case of chalk, and then lifted my skirt to run faster, hearing the footsteps pounding down the stairs after us. Callum caught my elbow at the bottom of the stairs, Tatsuo passing us both to chase after Bryce.

"Joanna," Callum growled.

"I helped the last time and I will again if I can," I snapped, yanking back on my arm. "But this thing is back on campus, and it's a waste of time and breath to argue about it."

"She's right," Aiden said, pushing us both forward as the rest of the group caught up.

"Everyone in the library," Gwen shouted, hands raised to her mouth. "Find your way to the staff lounge behind the circulation desk as quickly as possible and remain there until the staff calls the all-clear."

I ran to the nearest table of students, ushering them out of their chairs and shepherding them to the center of the building before running back to my...my... My thoughts stuttered at what to call Aiden and Isaac and Callum and I shook them out, focusing on the front doors.

There was a dark outline in the sky past the trees and buildings, over what must be the staff housing. Bryce and Tatsuo were already on the grounds rushing there and the rest of us followed quickly, Gwen leaving last and locking the library behind her, a few startled faces still staring out at us.

"If I tell you to run, you run," Callum said, his hand jamming into the air in front of him and drawing an enormous sword out as he looked back at me. The hilt curved back to his wrist like a pair of wings and half the blade gleamed bright and razor-sharp, the other half dark and heavy.

"I don't need to be your concern in this, Callum," I answered, my words biting out of my mouth.

"Stop," Aiden said to the both of us, jogging to walk between us, hands raised. "We are not having this argument right now. Joanna, you don't have a choice in Callum's concerns. Isaac and I want you safe as much as he does, as much as we want each other safe."

I swallowed and fixed my eyes past them, to the dark horizon, fighting back what I wanted to say. That I would have wanted them far away too. Because this was *my fault*. But they didn't know that yet, and it certainly wasn't the moment I wanted to tell them. If I told them.

Fingers trailed across my back, shoulder to shoulder, and I looked to Isaac at my side. There was a bright, clean glow resting over Aiden's red sweater, something shimmering and white.

"Just a little color magic," he said, eyes fierce on my face. "For protection."

"Thank you," I said, lifting his hand from my shoulder to hold it tight in mine.

A gust of wind carrying a bitter burnt stench swirled around us as we made it to the Burgess building. The ground trembled under our running feet and the shouting started in the distance. Callum and Aiden ran closely in front of us both, and for a moment I couldn't hear anything above the slaps of steps on the pavement. And then I realized that it was matching the cacophony of destruction on the far end of the campus. Dust and smoke were gathering in the air and echoes like thunder carried down the paths we ran.

My ears felt crushed under a heavy pressure that wanted to buckle my knees beneath me. People were streaking by us, others standing on their steps, screaming back at the darkness gathered in front of them, their hands raised to trace magic in the air. There was a storm whipping across the ground as we arrived, a torrent made from a smoke cloud and black shrouded fabric and a dark tear that ripped away the world to leave an empty hole, all swirling on the street in front of my little house.

And on either side of my house was wreckage, buildings turned to rubble and smoldering ash.

Bryce—small, delicate Bryce—was crouched in the middle of the street, shining a faint gold that the shadowy expanse skirted away from. Tatsuo stood at the edge, arms raised with short wooden staffs in either hand. Callum ran to join him, and the storm seemed to coil in on itself, and explosion in reverse. It was gathering into a shape, a figure, and the words fell loose from my lips.

"It came for me."

Isaac stirred at my side, as if he had heard and was about to look at me, when a tangle of darkness slithered across the ground in our direction.

"Look out!" Aiden shouted and both he and Isaac moved in front of me.

I dropped to my knees, chalk already in hand, and scrawled in heavy letters across the pavement.

STOP

The wind was gone from my ears, and the shouting was stilled, and the roar of what must have been the houses crumbling was quiet. Aiden and Isaac were frozen in front of me, Callum and Tatsuo and Bryce in the distance. Between us was the Hollow, something like a body under smoky gauze. A body in the right shape but wrong pieces. All I could imagine, all I could really make out through the shifting film of airy black, was a squirming, twisting split. A mouth waiting to surge forward and swallow.

I held my breath, waiting, hoping I hadn't hurt anyone.

I've waited for you, witchling, it said. The voice was something like Bryce's. Like layers and ringing, but this was more scratch and hiss in my ears than a sound. *You set me free and then you steal the food out of my belly. I wonder if you are friend or foe.*

I had put a stop to the fires in the remains of the houses, and a stop on my friends, but the Hollow was floating through the still-life scene as if it were a piece of refuse picked up by a breeze.

"Foe," I said. I meant to shout it, but it came out as a whisper, my eyes busy tracking its approach.

A brave answer, the Hollow hissed. *But you are not a foe when you are only a small, breakable thing that cannot hurt me. And you cannot hurt me, witchling. You can't even protect your belongings.*

Something like a hand reached out from the shadows, crawling through the air to Isaac.

"No," I whispered, and I tugged at the back of Isaac's jacket. "No, stop!"

Isaac swayed at my pull but stayed upright and held captive as the hand that looked more like a claw or a blade stretched closer. I stared down at the word on the ground, scrubbing my palm over it to try and smear it away and break my spell. But I had ground the chalk into the pavement and *STOP* stayed bright and unbroken, my hand scratched by the rough surface of the road.

I scrambled up to my feet, trying to place myself between Isaac and the Hollow, but I was too late. The smoke scratched over Isaac's right cheek, and into his hair. His eyes winced and a moan escaped his parted lips and his knees buckled. My arms were around him and he fell into me, the Hollow continuing to ooze over the ground on its way past us. It hissed and spat with laughter and the dark clouds over the sky cracked and drummed and rain came spilling loose as I sank down to the ground with Isaac gasping and groaning in my arms, red and gray and white streaking across his cheekbone.

"No, no, no, no," I whispered. "I'm sorry. I'm sorry."

His chest heaved and rain turned his white shirt translucent. I looked down at the ground beside us where I had wasted time, and my word was being spattered and spoiled under the falling drops. I dug my nails and fingers into the chalk, scratching and tearing until the word became nothing more than a white smear, streaks of red mingling where I had ripped at my skin.

"I picked the wrong word," I said, as motion stirred around me.

Aiden landed on the ground, warm hands on my cheeks, and I pulled away. My eyes were blurry with tears and my words came out in hiccuping sobs.

"I picked the wrong word. I'm sorry, I'm sorry."

"Callum!" Aiden shouted, but Callum was already reaching us, with Tatsuo and Bryce.

Bryce grabbed Isaac out of my arms with more strength than someone their size ought to have had and I shouted, reaching for him. Tatsuo stepped between Callum and Bryce and I thought it might come to blows. Isaac moaned in Bryce's hold and we all surged forward.

"Wait," Gwen snapped from behind us. "Wait, Bryce can help."

Bryce held him up, legs limp, and lifted one of their hands to his face, covering the marks made by the Hollow. They shined gold again, and there was a hum that felt like ringing in my ears, but I refused to look away. Aiden's arms squeezed around my waist and Callum strained against Tatsuo. Isaac's breath was ragged and he hissed and squirmed in Bryce's hold for a long moment. And then he went soft, relaxing and turning quiet.

Tatsuo released Callum and Bryce passed Isaac to him. "Take him to medical," Bryce said, green eyes bright and yellowy.

Aiden stood, his hand clasped around mine. I clamped my lips shut and choked down the remains of my sobs.

"Take her back to the house?" Callum asked.

I could see the way Aiden's shoulders drew in, but he started to nod.

"No," I said. I stood on shaky legs. "No, you should both go." Callum's forehead knotted and Aiden looked resigned, prepared to argue for Callum. "I'll stay with the others," I said.

"She's safe with us, you know that," Gwen said.

"Go," I said, flattening down tears that wanted to break free and the anxiety rioting in my gut. "I'll find you later."

I couldn't tell if Callum was angry or worried or hurt or if he simply didn't want to waste the time arguing when Isaac needed care. But he left with quick steps. Aiden pressed a hard kiss to my forehead that left me queasy with guilt and then hurried after him.

"This isn't your fault," Hildy said gently, taking my hands.

"It is actually," I said.

I felt numb with the truth of it. I had been curious and careless and even if it had all been an accident, it was my hands that let the creature out. And if I had not, Cecil Pincombe would have been alive and Isaac would have been safe and the woods wouldn't be dying and the sun probably would have been shining too for that matter.

"Joanna," Hildy murmured.

"Better get to the library," Bryce said, taking my elbow in their hand.

I sagged with a kind of relief. Bryce, at least, would not argue with me.

2 2

JOANNA

IT RAINED FOR DAYS.

The campus kept busy coming up with magical means of keeping the flood at bay. And in the library we watched the rain break against the patched hole in the roof.

Isaac came back to the house sleeping, and I volunteered to keep the night shift of watching over him, shooing Aiden out of the room when he offered to sit up with me. I left early in the morning and came back late at night with excuses about the library. Callum and Aiden watched me passing through the house, but I found corners to hide around when I thought they might be looking for me.

At night I kept vigil in a chair by Isaac's bedroom window and wrote in my notebook. *Put it back. The Hollow is in its cage again and cannot come out. Everyone is safe.* But every morning the sun rose, dark in the sky, and the vise squeezed tighter in my chest.

Isaac slept like the dead the first night, the red mark bright on his cheek with the faintest glow above it, either from the healers or Bryce. The next night was fits and stirring, and I sat on the side of the bed, wiping sweat off his brow and letting him crush my hand in his grip. Finally, on the third night he settled, breath deepening. I leaned my head against the window, glass cool on my skin, and let myself drift off.

I woke choking on air, hands on my arms as I tried to fight them off.

"It's me, it's me, Joanna," Isaac whispered.

I reared back in the chair and caught my breath. Isaac's hands stroked at my sides, his eyes half-lidded with sleep and the scar on his cheek shiny but pale.

"Come to bed, love," he said.

"You should be sleeping," I answered.

"I will. Better with you next to me. Come rest."

I let him pull me up and then ducked under his arm as he swayed in step. "Do you want me to get Aiden or-"

"I want you to come lay down with me, Joanna," he said, words weary as we stumbled back to the bed together. "I just want to hold you." Isaac pulled me into his side under the covers, arm across my back and fingers in my hair. "Quit punishing yourself," he mumbled against my forehead.

I hummed and he squeezed me gently. Everyone had tried telling me similar things. Even Bryce had said, 'It's only a problem that needs solved.' It didn't soothe the heaviness at the back of my head or the clammy feeling under my skin or the guilt that lay bricks in my belly every minute. And Isaac's soft snores brought tears to the corners of my eyes rather than helping me drift into sleep.

Over and over in my head, it ran in a loop.

If I hadn't come here to Canderfey.

If I hadn't sent the charmed application.

If I hadn't met Aiden or Isaac or Callum.

If I hadn't called *Gatekeepers* back from whatever safe hole it had been moldering in.

Everyone would be safe. The Hollow would be in its cage and Cecil Pincombe would be alive and Isaac would never have been hurt.

It was my fault. And if it was a problem that needed to be solved, it was time I set about doing so.

Hɪʟᴅʏ ᴀɴsᴡᴇʀᴇᴅ the door in the morning before the dark sun had finished rising in the sky. I was already soaked through my coat and my boots, just from the short walk to the house.

"Joanna, come in," she said. Her face was clean and tired and she looked surprised to see me, but I thought it was probably beyond Hildy not to be welcoming when it was called for. "What do you need? Gwen is already at the library."

"I was hoping Tatsuo was home, actually," I said, ducking into the dry warmth of the house.

"Of course, we're just having breakfast."

"I'm sorry," I said, covering my hands over the sick clench in my stomach.

"No, don't be silly," Hildy said with a wave of her hand before gesturing me to follow her. "You're welcome at any hour, you know that."

Tatsuo was drinking tea, bare chest pale under his bathrobe, and his eyebrows raised as I entered the kitchen. Bryce sat opposite him and barely glanced over their shoulder at me, unsurprised by my arrival or simply not awake enough to care.

"I..." It seemed silly now, to have come while they were busy having breakfast. "I wanted to ask about...trance writing."

But Tatsuo's eyes lit up at that and Hildy snorted, going to her spot at the table while he rose up from his.

"Absolutely," he said as if it were a natural question for breakfast at dawn. "Come to the reading room and I'll show you some of what I've been working on."

There was a fire going in the reading room, dark daylight coming in through the windows and brightened quickly by Tatsuo turning on lamps. He offered me a seat and then fluttered busily around the room, gathering up stray pieces of paper and heavy books. He brought them back, pulling up another chair and laying it out over the table with a flourish. I glanced down at the scribbles, cryptic scrawling messages in strange directions, and bit my lip.

"I had a few…specific questions," I said.

Tatsuo clapped his hands together. "Yes, please, ask away!"

"The trance, is it hard to…to fall into?" I asked.

He leaned back in his chair, hand lifting to stroke at his chin and I could tell it pleased him to have someone here, asking him questions. It brought me something almost like cheer until I wondered if Callum would hear about this later, that I had come to Tatsuo to form a plan. And then I remembered that he probably wouldn't care after what I had done and I blinked quickly down at my lap.

"I suppose it may be, for a beginner," Tatsuo said. "It requires emptying one's head, making room for the openness needed in a trance. Sometimes though, Bryce will drone for me and then it takes no time at all."

"Drone?"

"Mmhm, it's like singing, but it leads almost directly to hypnotism for most people," he said. He took a breath and I realized he was about to launch deep into the new topic so I hurried to keep him on track.

"Is trance writing a way of discovering a true name?" I asked.

Tatsuo's eyes narrowed at me for a moment at that, the excited collector of knowledge replaced with someone shrewd and intelligent enough to know what I was fishing for.

"It could be. Certainly of the symbolic portion of a true name. But not of anyone or anything. It would have to be your own, or the name belonging to someone you share a connection with. And it is widely acknowledged as being the kind of thing better left unknown. Knowing a true name allows for the opportunity of it being discovered by the wrong hands."

"Of course," I said.

Bryce had not told him then that I already had a kind of connection with the Hollow. It was stealing my dreams and I had let it out of its cage. That may not be enough, but it was more than I wanted, and it was the best—or worst—anyone else could boast of.

I quizzed Tatsuo on the ceremony of the practice, filling in my real questions with aimless, harmless ones that sent him rattling in new directions. I kept him for an hour, saying goodbye to Hildy as she left for work. I hoped that he would forgive me later for pumping him for the information. I hoped that I would be around to receive forgiveness.

"I should get to the library," I said, as Tatsuo finished an explanation on different kinds of plant-based inks. "Thank you for humoring me."

"My pleasure, I love hypotheticals after breakfast," he said, gallant as ever, even in his dressing robe.

"I'll walk you." We both turned to see Bryce lingering in the doorway. "It's not safe out."

"Thank you," I said. I repeated the words to Tatsuo with a hug and then met Bryce in the hall. They walked me to the door, pulling a long black umbrella out of a stand.

"You can't do it alone," Bryce said as they shut the door closed behind us and passed me the umbrella.

I fiddled with it first, opening it out and waiting for Bryce to stand under the cover with me.

"I know," I said, quiet as if someone might be listening.

"I will help," Bryce said. The nerves in my stomach mingled with relief. They looked at me, eyes narrowed. "It is one of my kind, somewhat."

I had wondered as much. It didn't change the fact that I trusted Bryce completely to help. "Do you think it will work?" I asked.

"It will work or we will be eaten," Bryce said shrugging. "Does that suit you?"

I almost laughed, but it was laced with panic and came out like a squawk.

"I suppose," I said.

I LINGERED late at the library, a queasy feeling hanging in my stomach at the thought of heading home. Home to the little staff house for the first time in weeks. And this time no one would come to fetch me back to the coven house.

Callum had explained that he had placed wards strong enough to keep the Hollow out of the small house before they managed to convince me to stay with them. It was why mine was still standing, unmarred, and my neighbors' homes were rubble.

But the neighborhood had made it out at the first sign of the sky turning dark. Isaac was the only one hurt that day.

I didn't want to go back to my house. It was small and empty and I had loved that it was mine and mine alone, but now the thought of it made me lonely. I wanted to put my cheek against lush fabrics and let my eyes soak up the color of bright walls. I wanted to fall asleep next to someone and wake up in a crowded bed.

It was a waste to crave that tall tower house, and the people inside, so badly now when I had given all of it up.

I snuck past Gwen to the main doors as the sun started to set. I didn't want to stay with her and the others either, not while where I really wanted to be was within easy sight.

The rain hadn't stopped once and the sidewalks were drowning, water up to my ankles that splashed and ran into my boots with every sluggish step. There was no busy traffic outside with me now. I wasn't even sure if classes were still in session or if students and faculty were in hiding together. I lifted my chin, shivering in my thin coat, and letting the tears wavering at my eyes roll over, mingling with the rain stinging at my cheeks. If Bryce and I were successful, would I leave campus? Quit the library and wander back to Bridgeston again? It would be too hard to see my...my men. Not that it was right to call them that now.

"Joanna!"

My heart skipped in my chest and my feet skidded in the water. But I clamped my eyes shut. "No," I whispered. Why hadn't I written *Forget me*. Or *We never met*. I didn't want to see them again. Didn't want to offer an explanation or—

"Joanna, stop!"

I didn't mean to listen. I didn't want to hear the crack in Callum's voice. I covered my face with my hands and my feet stilled beneath me. For a perverse moment, I wanted to be going a little crazy and imagining hearing him. Wet splashes pounded behind me, footsteps kicking through the deep puddles as they caught up to me. My street was within sight and I wondered if I could run there faster, hide in my small little house, and refuse to look back.

"Don't do this," he whispered, words blending into the whistle of rain. "Please don't do this to us."

I stifled a moan behind my hands as they slid down to my cheeks. I turned and he was there, getting drenched in rain, hair sticking wetly to his forehead. He pulled his glasses, spattered and wet, off his face and tucked them away, revealing the injured wince on his face. Aiden and Isaac were behind him, a little farther off, but Isaac looked pale and was leaning into Aiden's side.

Why? Why had they come? It had seemed like such a simple thing to do. Write myself out of their lives. It shouldn't have even mattered. Not to them.

"He shouldn't be out," I said looking at Isaac and his slow approach.

Callum looked back over his shoulder. "Tell him that. I tried. Joanna, why?" he asked stepping closer.

I stepped back, keeping the space between us. "Because it's true."

He pulled his hand free from his pocket, the note I had written and left under my pillow folded in his fingers. "Tear it up."

"I can't," I said.

"Of course you can. *I could.* I'm asking you to do it," he said.

I folded my hands under my arms to keep them from reaching out and smoothing away the furrow in his brow and the frown over his mouth.

"Why are you here?" I asked, my heart hammering in my chest. "I… I was never going to belong. This should be—It should be easy. Just go home-"

Callum stormed to me and I didn't have a chance to skirt away. "*Easy?*" he growled. "Joanna, tear it up, *please.*"

"It's my fault," I said, almost shouted, breaths ragged as the tears filled up in my throat. "I let the Hollow out. I wrote it in the book. I should never have come here. I shouldn't have magic in the first place.

I'm just a stupid little nobody from the country whose absolutely in over her head and now everything has gone wrong!"

"It can be fixed, love," Isaac said. He and Aiden joined us at Callum's side.

"Cecil Pincombe can't," I said, voice cracking. "I know- I *know* you wanted someone. You wanted me to be right. But I'm *not* and I can't be."

"If you weren't meant for us then you wouldn't need to write a spell to change it, Joanna," Aiden said, and he sounded angry but I could barely see for all the crying.

"Tear it up," Callum whispered.

"I won't," I said.

"Then you wrote the wrong thing," he said, and he pulled my arms free and stuffed the note into my hand before taking my face up in his hold. His face was blurry and close, but I could make out the blue of his eyes. "If I have to love you without you belonging in our coven then you've cursed me."

The sob tore out of my chest and the pain of it was more relief than wound. I folded forward with the force of it and Callum dragged me against his chest. The note, *I don't belong in your coven* printed inside, crumpled wetly in my fist as I struck it against him. I had told myself it would be enough. To erase whatever fleeting attraction that had fooled them in the first place. To make reality set in and break up all my romantic fantasies. Instead, every word had felt crooked and wrong to write.

"We knew something was broken today," Isaac said, and his voice was faint. "That you'd pulled away."

I wanted to get him somewhere warm and dry as much as I wanted to push them all away. *Thought* I wanted to.

"Callum was getting ready to find you at the library when I found the note," he said. "You can tear it up or leave it, but it won't stop me from *wanting* you with us."

"Tear it up," Callum repeated, a little sullenly. I could feel him nudging at the top of my head and I wiped my cheeks against his damp shirt before looking up. "Did you ever want it to be true?" he asked.

It was such a stupid question! I blurted without thinking, "Of course I did! From the start. But all of this was my mistake and I have to fix it!" Aiden was closing in at my side and I rushed to add, "And I can't stand that one of you might be hurt or worse again if I make another one. I…I thought, maybe, once it was all done…"

"Trying to do this alone is a mistake," Aiden said. He *was* angry. I could hear it now. It didn't seem like a good time to mention my plan.

Callum's eyes narrowed on my face. "You can't stop us from fighting for the campus or for you. We're already involved. Is that enough now?"

"Or did you think we wouldn't fight for you?" Isaac whispered. His hair was down, soaked like inky streaks running down the sides of his face, and his skin was almost as pale and gray as his eyes. But his gaze was sharp on me, pinpricks of heat that burned in my chest.

"Please, Joanna. No more," Callum begged. "If you meant it, if you really want us…tear up the note and come home."

I felt trapped under a weight of emotion I didn't understand and dizzy with confusion. Isaac was right. I didn't think they would come. I thought I could write the words and that would be the end. The only one left hurting would be me. But if what Callum said was true…I wouldn't be able to bring myself to write away those feelings. Not if they were real and I could have them, keep them and wallow in them. I couldn't carve them out of myself either.

The ink had all but washed away on the note, now soggy. But I lifted it between us and ripped through the middle of the words, and then again and again until it was pulp in my fingers. Callum took my wrists in his hands and kissed me, lips and teeth hard against mine, holding me close and still for a long stretch. I cried into the kiss and there were hands at my back until I was sheltered between the three of them.

"Say it," Callum said, drawing back.

"I'm sorry," I said.

"Not that," he said, pecking at my lips. "Say you belong in the coven."

My breath was shaky and nervous in my chest. But his eyes were fixed to mine and Isaac and Aiden were holding their breath on either side. "I belong with you," I said. "In the coven."

"We need to get somewhere dry before we have to swim home," Aiden said as Isaac pulled me from Callum, peppering kisses over both my cheeks.

"My house," I said, sniffling and wiping uselessly at my eyes. "I never got rid of the doorway into your room."

We were a cluster on the sidewalk together, walking as quickly as we could without having to be out of each other's reach. The street was desolate and I wondered how many staff were even still staying in their houses after what had happened on the weekend. There was a second, smaller wave of guilt and then Aiden's warm hand was at my back, leading me up the steps. I dug in my pocket for my key and let us inside.

The house felt abandoned, as if I'd needed further proof at how much more quickly I had settled into living with them than here by myself.

"Do you need anything?" Callum asked, glancing around.

I shook my head. "I left my case at the library and...and I never had much."

Isaac squeezed my hand and Aiden led us all to the pantry door in the kitchen and then back into their home.

23

AIDEN

Joanna's steps squished in her shoes as she walked into my bedroom and she stopped abruptly before reaching the carpet. We were all dripping onto the floorboard and Joanna had a puddle around her from her boots alone.

"Get a bath going?" I asked Callum.

He looked between us, at Joanna fidgeting by herself, and Isaac shivering by the door. "Come in when you're ready," he said.

I knelt at Joanna's feet as they left, her hands landing at my shoulders as I untied her boots and lifted her feet free. They were like icicles and I resisted the urge to lift them to my lips to press some heat back into them. I looked up and she was already peeling herself out of her clothes, that flimsy, awful little slip of hers sticking to her skin and distracting me. I stood, stroking up her side as I went and she leaned into the touch. I took the clothes out of her hands and stepped back.

"Find something warm for yourself," I said, crossing past her to dump her clothes into the hamper and get out of my own.

"Aiden," she said, the sweet mellow syrup of her voice burrowing into my chest.

I wasn't sure if I wanted to be angry—that she had tried to leave, tried to shatter the possibility of being a part of our coven. Or to be grateful she had torn her note, her spell, up into dozens of little pieces. To prove to her once again that I could offer her something worth keeping. That I was worth keeping.

I turned back and she was waiting, holding out my robe and wearing my red sweater, the collar dipping low between her breasts. My lips quirked against my will. I didn't stand a chance. Not against her. She helped me into the sleeves and her arms followed mine around my waist as I tied the belt.

"I'm sorry," she said into my back, words mumbled into the fabric.

I squeezed her hands over my stomach and took a long breath before pulling myself free. She was anxious, wounded looking, eyes red and hair still running wet rivulets down her neck.

"Come sit with me," I said, keeping her hands in mine to lead her to the bed. She climbed up to the coverlet, knees disappearing under the hem of the sweater as she folded them under her. I faced her and kept our hands clasped, resisting the urge to pull her into my lap, to hold her face and kiss her beyond any thought of leaving again. "Tell me your plan," I said. She frowned and I added, "What were you going to do after you had successfully…kept us safe by leaving?"

Her fingers fidgeted in mine and she looked down at her lap, cheeks coloring. "Bryce Gast said they would help me. They… I went to ask Tatsuo about trance writing to find true names," she said.

"Is that possible?" I asked, feeling a panicked kind of temper rising in my chest. "Wouldn't you need-"

"A connection?" she asked, looking up. "I have one. I'm the one that let it out, it's eating my dreams at night from across the woods."

"And Gast was going to help," I spat.

"They offered, yes," she said and her words began to harden, shoulders straightening. "For their own reasons."

I released one of her hands to scrub at my face. "True names *aren't just words*," I said, breathing through my nose.

"I know, but-"

"While you've been hiding from us, Callum and I have been scouring for information. The Hollow's true name is made up of music, color, and…a word. We haven't found them yet, but don't you think that gives us the *right* to help you?"

"Yes."

I pulled my hand off my eyes to stare at her and almost immediately regretted it. She looked so fragile and aching still and it made me want to pull her up in my arms.

"Aiden, I'm sorry," she said, every word heavy with sincerity. She scooted closer and my arms twitched for her. "I *do* think it would have worked. Bryce wouldn't have agreed if they didn't think so too but-*but*," she said, raising her hand to stop my words and continuing quickly, "That doesn't matter. It was the wrong decision and I regret it. I… Aiden, I really didn't think you would all…" her breath hitched, eyes filling up, and my will broke.

I took her face in my hands and held it to mine, foreheads touching. "Haven't we told you? All we've wanted is for you to be a part of us, of this home."

"You have and I heard it and I just…I kept waiting for it to turn out to be a…cosmic trick on me," she whispered, tracing a kiss over my mouth. "I can still barely believe it."

"We need you to," I said, feeling the grip of panic at the back of my throat.

"I know," she said, hands soft on my back as she settled herself in my hold. "I know. I'm not going anywhere, I promise."

The panic shuddered out of me and I took her lips in mine, drawing deeply, holding her tight to my chest. Her hands squeezed at my shoulders before sliding between us to push away slightly, nipping at my lips in quick affectionate nibbles before leaning back.

"That doesn't change the fact that I am responsible for what's happening," she said softly.

"You cannot blame yourself for being manipulated into letting that thing out," I said.

"And you can't deny that I should be the one to put it back in its cage," she said, face steely. "I don't want to be guarded in the tower by three knights when it was my *mistake* that's led to this."

I huffed. For once, I needed Callum here to deal with the problem.

If there was anyone who could talk Joanna out of self-punishment it would be him, and it might do them both good. In the meantime, there was something I could say.

"Joanna, we have waited for you for a *long* time. I know you know that. And I'm not saying that gives us the right to try and shield you. Although it's probably been a motivation for us, you're right," I said. I kissed her mouth before she could argue and then continued, "I'm just saying, we *all* try to shield each other. We've just already had the arguments over it, and you're playing catch-up. If it's any consolation Callum was walking Isaac home every night I escorted you back from the library."

She blinked at that, a faint smile appearing on her lips. "It helps a little."

"We won't let you try to fix this on your own," I said. "That's off the table as of right now. And Bryce Gast isn't enough help either, and if you argue that, I'll tell Woollard and the rest of their coven about the plan, and then the pair of you will both be in trouble. But I promise that we aren't trying to tuck you safely away. We're a coven, and we're doing this together."

"Are you going to tell Callum that?" she asked, smirking.

"I am," I said, raising an eyebrow. "If you're lucky, I won't even mention that you went to Tatsuo for help."

She was turning soft in my arms. I knew we should be finding the others, but there wasn't a cell in my body interested in moving. Not if she wasn't moving.

"I'm sorry, Aiden," she said again, simple and earnest.

"Don't ever do that again," I said.

"Never," she said, easily.

"Are you sure there's nothing you need at your house? You may be in for a long stay here," I said, wanting to ask it. *Stay, stay, stay.*

"I like it better here, anyway," she said.

"Right here?" I asked, grinning and looking down at where she was sprawled over my lap. I stroked my palms down her back to her waist and she rose to her knees, inching closer.

"Maybe…here," she said, pressing our chests together, a small smile growing in the corners of her lips. Her hands were between us, shaking with cold and untying the knot in the waist of my robe.

I teased my fingers down to the hem of my sweater, skimming them over the skin at the tops of her thighs.

"Are you eager for the bath?" she asked, voice tilting and teasing.

"Not especially," I said, trying to keep the growl out of my throat.

"And will Callum and Isaac come looking for us?"

"Would it matter if they did?" I asked.

Her eyes darkened at that and there was a needy clench in my belly. She liked the idea. I smoothed my hands up her skin and found her hips naked, my thumbs stroking over her bare mound. She hummed and closed her eyes, body leaning into the touch.

"My Joanna," I murmured, lifting the sweater to see a glimpse of the pink skin of her pussy before she was squirming down to nuzzle at my cheek.

"My King," she whispered in my ear and my cock jumped, stirring and aching, even as I laughed at her joke.

She kissed a wet trail over my jaw, rocking and twisting herself in my lap, drawing out a groan as I hardened against her. She pushed the loose robe off my shoulders, her hands roaming greedily over my skin as I pulled my arms free. We had both stripped down to nothing and I could feel her growing wet, sliding it over my length and working herself up in the process.

Her breasts were bouncing lightly with her movement, nipples turning to little points. I stroked my thumbs over them, grunting as she ground down against me. But there was something soft building in my chest watching her.

"I can't decide if I want to watch you in my sweater or out of it," I admitted.

She opened her eyes, raising an eyebrow at me. "Is *that* what you're thinking about? I wondered why I was doing all the work."

I barked out a laugh, and pulled the sweater up over her head, ducking to taste the skin I'd found. She rose to her knees again, and I grinned as a breast appeared conveniently before me. I wrapped my lips around a perfect, rosy nipple and then groaned against the skin when a small hand wrapped around me, pumping gently.

"I'm already there, darling," I growled into her breast, my hands gripping at her hips to draw her over me, teasing her opening with the tip of my cock.

"So am I, darling," she said, grinning. I looked up to watch her face as I pulled her down slowly, a fraction at a time.

I knew Callum and Isaac's bodies as well as I knew my own, and I knew that the girth of me would be a stretch for her. A stretch she seemed to appreciate if the way her face went lax and open with every gentle nudge deeper. I rolled her onto me, her hands clutching at the back of my neck.

"Oh, oh gods, Aiden," she said, high and breathy.

She was slick and hot around me and it took all my willpower to keep from surging up into her. I clenched my jaw, bouncing her, stretching and teasing at just her entrance until she was mewling, trying to push herself down farther.

"Darling girl," I said, wrapping an arm around her so I could free a hand. I stroked at her where we were joined and she arched, crying out.

"I want more," she pleaded, still squirming and trying to turn the small careful thrust of me inside her into something deeper.

"You'll have it, I promise," I said.

I sucked at the breast hovering by my lips and fumbled in her slippery folds until I found her clit, rolling and pressing. Her nails dug into my back as she shouted, squeezing in tight flutters around my cock as I finally drew her down. I seated myself fully, swallowing my groan and tensing my thighs to keep from bucking as she quivered around me with small aftershocks. I wrapped my arms around her back, a pleased rumble in my chest as she settled, and kissed my way up to her neck.

"Do you always get your way?" she grumbled against my ear, and then nipped at my lobe, a bolt of pleasure shooting down my spine.

I laughed again, as she pushed me backward into the mattress, and then the laughter died and turned to moans as she took revenge for my teasing. Her hands were braced against my chest as she rose and fell, clasping and dragging over every inch of my cock. She squeezed around the tip of me before sliding down again and grinding our bodies together, broken sounds falling from both our mouths. I braced my feet against the edge of the bed, bucking up to meet her and holding her steady.

"Aiden," she whispered, turning it into a chant as her head drooped.

The pace turned quick, her thighs shaking around me, and every dive and drag of her body pulling straight from my gut. My hands felt hot and an electric current was jolting up my spine in time with Joanna's torrid rhythm. She surged up, back arching and hands moving to my knees, body leaning back and putting me at a new angle inside of her that had her singing. I gentled our movements, pressing in slow, strong strokes until she was trembling with every small brush between us.

"Come again, darling," I begged, needing it as badly as she did in that moment.

She shook, abbreviated little cries and babbling praises, and she was slippery and hot around me, trying to milk pleasure out of me in return. I gathered her to my chest and rolled her onto her back, her legs and arms wrapping around me as heat burrowed at the base of my spine and exploded outward. There was a roar in my ears and a dense blanketing warm rolling out into my muscles. She had me enveloped, sweet heat still clenching around me and hands fluttering and kissing over my back.

Joanna hummed small happy sounds in my ear, kissing the corner of my jaw, and she held me tight to her as I tried to draw back.

"'M too heavy, I'll crush you," I said, squeezing gently at her shoulders while my arms were still trapped beneath us.

"Just one more minute," she said.

She loosened her hold around me as I softened. Her hair was

rumpled and damp around her face and she was flushed red over her chest.

"Hello," she said, smiling and biting her lip. I leaned down to pluck it free with my own.

"Hello," I said. I drew back and she squirmed, a little whimper at the back of her throat as I pulled out. "Alright?"

"Yes," she said, grinning. "But I'll have that bath now, I think."

I scooped her up off the bed and ran us down the hall and into the bathroom. The room was warm and misty and Callum and Isaac were both already submerged in water. There were candles lit on the counter and glasses of wine waiting for us. I set Joanna down and she hurried to the water, Callum moving aside to put her between him and Isaac, drawing her against his chest. Isaac was pink-cheeked, warmed in the water, and leaning back against the lip of the tub with his eyes closed. But he lifted Joanna's feet and set them up on his knees, thumbs digging into her soles and drawing a purr from her lips.

He had looked stricken, almost green when he came down from his room with her note in hand. There had been actual defeat in his expression and I had let it dig into me too, rejection thorny in my chest. It was Callum, of all us, who had refused the words, the spell, the gesture completely. But Isaac seemed content now, if maybe a little reserved. He and Joanna would have their time later, she was watching his face.

Isaac's hand reached back for me and I took it, letting him drawing me in on his other side. The water stung with heat, burning at the lingering chill of the rain and the dark.

"Say it again," Callum whispered and both Isaac and I turned to look at Joanna, reclined in his arms.

She met our gazes. "I belong with you," she said, reaching up to cover Callum's hand on her shoulder. His answering smile was light and simple, a pure kind of pleasure he rarely showed. Joanna was still staring back at Isaac. "Can I see my room after the bath?" she asked.

Isaac exhaled heavily, leaning into me. "Of course you can," he said, words soft.

Joanna smiled, no nerves or shy hesitation on her face. There was a giddiness building up in my chest. A wild delirious feeling that threatened tears at the back of my eyes and made my throat swell shut. She belonged with us and she *would* stay this time. I had my coven, my family.

Now I—*we* just needed to keep each other safe.

24

JOANNA

My bedroom was on the fourth floor of the house. My bedroom *was* the fourth floor of the house with an ensuite bathroom as nice as the one the men shared. The ceiling was high and domed, wood beams dark and exposed and there was a large round window at the far end of the room. An enormous bed sat in front of the window, wide enough to be shared by four, I realized, staring at it.

The men were at my back and I could hear them shifting, waiting for my reaction. And I couldn't come up with one because I was too busy being overwhelmed.

There were cream bookshelves lining the walls and I wondered if they had been added after they had met me, or if they had known they would find an avid reader. Or if they simply had been there when Aiden bought the house. Five small windows hung in the roof, and later, when everything was settled and safe again, I would see the stars out of them at night. There was a set of armchairs over a rug, by a small fireplace, with a low table between them.

"Do you like it?" Callum asked, standing close to my back and resting his hands on my hips.

"It's beautiful," I said, and then realized that wasn't the right kind of answer I added, "I love it. It's so big though. I won't have to stay up here alone will I?"

Aiden laughed and moved over to the fireplace, pulling logs from the rack. We were all fresh from the bath and I was back in his sweater with Aiden and Isaac in their robes and Callum's hips wrapped in a towel. The room was a little chilled, and smelled dry and dusty, unused for too long. But everything was clean and there was a painting of a field of wildflowers on the wall that made me ache with sweetness.

"Not until you get sick of having us in your hair," Aiden said. "This was designed to be the master suite. I just wanted to save it until…"

"Until the coven was full," I said and he looked back at me from the fireplace, eyes bright and crinkled with a smile.

"You mean it," Isaac said. I turned and he was behind Callum, hovering near the door, face shadowed by the stairwell.

"I mean it," I said.

Callum bent his head, fingers tugging at the sweater to pull it down and expose my shoulder to his mouth. Isaac stepped up close, his hands layering over Callum's on my ribs, nose brushing mine.

"I'm sor—" I started, happy to say it as many times as they wanted to hear. Happy to be in the house again, happy to feel stupid for ever trying to leave. But Isaac swallowed the word with a kiss, tongue delving and stroking into my mouth, licking at the back of my teeth and curling over my own tongue.

I moaned into the kiss as Callum's teeth scraped over my shoulder. He traveled up my neck, sucking and licking, hips pressing into my back. Isaac crowded me at my front, lips turning soft and teasing. I wished for more hands, more ways to return their touches as I arched and curved between them.

Callum's fingers stroked over the tops of my thighs, sliding between my legs to brush and pet, dancing away as I tried to chase them. Isaac drew away from my lips and then he and Callum were kissing, one long smooth caress into each other. I was surrounded by them, swallowed up in the embrace and feeling every inch of them against me, cocks stirring against my belly. Their hands gathered up the sweater, dragging it up over my head.

"Take her to the bed," Isaac said. Callum lifted me up, arms around my hips and I squeaked in surprise.

"I can walk!" I said, laughing as Callum layered kisses on my shoulder.

Aiden was grinning from in front of the fireplace, a small flicker of flames already started. He winked at me and offered no help.

Callum kicked the towel away as it fell to the floor in front of the bed. I bounced on his lap as we landed on the mattress and then he dragged us back to the headboard. My back was to his stomach, the start of his erection bumping into me as he spread his knees inside of my thighs, exposing me to the air. He caught my hands before I could cover myself, drawing them back and kissing them both.

"Let us see you," he said against my ear and then kissed at the corner of my jaw.

I shivered and even I didn't know if it was the cool air or the sound of Callum's voice in my ear or the sight of Isaac and Aiden watching us.

Isaac was prowling to the bed, eyes caressing over my skin as he crawled up the mattress. He nuzzled into my belly button, flicking his tongue out briefly and making me gasp at the touch.

"The pair of you are art like this," he said, glancing up.

"You are not allowed to sketch this," I said, but my words were weak and breathy.

Callum's hands were tracing over my ribs, barely brushing across my ribs. His tongue lapped over my neck until the skin was hypersensitive and I wanted to beg him to stop or bite. Instead, I just stretched it, exposing more flesh to the treatment.

"Maybe from memory," Isaac said, grinning.

Isaac's palm cupped over my pussy, rubbing the pads of his fingers across my clit. The tip of Callum's cock was peeking between my legs, just under his hand and Isaac dipped his head down, sucking it into his mouth. Callum arched under me, bucking me up into Isaac's hand while his chest rattled into my back with a groan.

"Tell her," Isaac mumbled, pulling away from Callum and moving his hand away. He nibbled at my lower lips and Callum arched forward to swallow my whimper in a kiss. "Tell her, Callum," Isaac said again and I rolled my hips up to try and draw him back to me.

"We...we talked about you," Callum mumbled into the kiss. "While we were fucking, we talked about how we wanted you."

I moaned and he pulled at my mouth again, Isaac rewarding us both by lapping avidly at me. Callum stretched my hands back around his head, banding an arm over my ribs to hold me for Isaac's efforts. The bed dipped at our side and a large warm hand stroked down from my neck all the way to the hair just above my folds, a finger toying at the top of my slit. Aiden's mouth landed at my breast and suddenly there was too much at once and I couldn't think of what I wanted next, only that I wanted more.

Isaac licked, swirling over my clit, and a finger and then two slid inside of me, testing, before drawing out again. Callum's breath hitched in my mouth and then he was pushing into me, guided by Isaac's hand.

Callum cursed into my neck, knees spreading wider and hips thrusting beneath me. Whatever word I meant to say fell apart into nonsense. He released my hands and they fell into Isaac's hair, tangling and gripping at the strands.

Isaac lay flat on his belly and I watched his back, the planes and knots of muscles working as he mouthed wetly over where Callum and I were joined. He groaned against us as my fingers tightened in his hair and moved up to flick and lap and swirl at the bundle of nerves stirring heat and ecstasy into my blood.

Their names were falling out of my mouth, tangled together in the wrong order. Callum bounced me over his length, mouth panting grunts against my neck as Isaac toyed with us both. Aiden's hands were everywhere while his lips pulled steadily at my breast.

I crested quick and hard, a bright shout echoing out of me as stars lit up behind my eyes, and my thighs clamped around Isaac's ears. I wanted to fix him in place to me and push him away at the same time. Callum fucked through my orgasm, extending and deepening it until I was twitching and boneless and my whole body felt fevered and charged.

Isaac pushed my thighs apart and stole me out of Callum's hold, his hips kicking in chase and a ragged growl breaking out of his throat.

"Not yet," Callum snarled.

Aiden laughed, drawing away from me and pulling Callum to his chest. His hand wrapped around Callum's cock and sliding evenly over it, coated in my juices, and Callum grasped onto Aiden's hold with a grateful moan. Isaac scooted up to my back as I curled up on my side. He pulled my hips into his and raised my right leg up over his, fitting himself inside of me from behind.

I whimpered, twisting my neck to hide my face in a pillow, but Isaac pushed my hair back, hooking his fingers under my chin. He lifted my chin up and kissed at my pulse.

"Watch them," Isaac said in my ear. He was fully seated, hips barely pumping, and free arm stroking over my side and belly. "Watch them with me."

I caught my breath in little puffs and opened my eyes. Isaac settled his chin into my shoulder and we stared at Callum and Aiden in front of us, curled together like a mirror of our own position. Aiden was peppering kisses over Callum's shoulder, one hand stroking softly at the base of Callum's cock and the other working behind. Callum's mouth was opened wide on a soundless cry. I reached out, running my hand down his chest and into the hair trailing down from his navel. His stomach trembled under my touch.

Isaac nudged us closer until Callum and I could reach each other, mouths latching hungrily to one another. Aiden rumbled at Callum's back and the sound echoed out of Callum into the kiss. Aiden pushed forward and then Callum was sliding against me, cock twitching and leaking fluid against my thigh. Aiden's knuckles brushed over my sex as he squeezed and dragged his hand down Callum's length, both of them bucking closer.

Isaac braced himself up on an elbow, one hand holding me open at my knee, hips swirling and thrusting, hitting at my front walls. Wet sounds filled the room and noisy cries. I could feel the echo of them in my throat and mouth, but I couldn't pick the voices apart in my ear. Just like I couldn't keep track of who was touching me and when and where. Only that every part of me was full of hunger and a dreamy kind of satisfaction.

With every rutting push, Callum and I tangled closer, Isaac struck deeper, Aiden's hands were harder against me. I felt frenzied and calm at the same time, riding a torrent that was pounding in my ears and blood. The drumbeat was heaviest between my legs, where Isaac was rutting into me and Callum was bumping and Aiden was nudging.

The first wave of pleasure was slow, had overtaken me before I realized I was under it. I pulled free of Callum's lips to cry out as the crashing warm feeling buried me, catching my breath. The second, as Isaac's rhythm turned erratic and desperate inside me, was sharp and sudden, a stab of pleasure bolted through me leaving me tense, squirming away from the touch. There was a wet splash, hot and sticky against my belly, and then Callum was panting on my throat. Aiden's arms wrapped around us both, tight, as he shouted.

The four of us were limp on the bed, hiccuping breaths punctuating the air. I felt like a sticky, stretched out mess, but a giggling bubbly sensation like champagne was rising up in my chest.

"Someone grab that towel," Callum grumbled, face pressed into my neck.

Isaac's hand slid up my leg, making it twitch, and dipped into the fluid cooling on my stomach. "I'll get it," he murmured, kissing behind my ear.

I hissed as he pulled out of me, and he kissed my hip, stretching to the edge of the bed and digging on the floor for the towel.

"Remind me why we took the bath first," Isaac mumbled after cleaning away our mess and passing the towel to Aiden.

"We were too cold for the necessary blood flow," Callum said. He hadn't moved an inch yet, but he reached up and grabbed at Isaac's shoulder drawing him back down to the mattress, and tight to my back.

"Are you alright?" Isaac asked me.

One of the giggles broke free, and then a second, until they were all loose and I was shaking between him and Callum. Aiden sat up, eyes soft on me and smile only a little concerned.

"I'm fine," I assured them when I caught my breath again. "I'm perfect. Exhausted and possibly bow-legged, but perfect."

There was a collection of kisses laid over my skin where they could reach, Callum pressing several to the bridge of my nose, and then we were all settling. Someone found the edge of the blanket to draw over us. Having them all around me as I fell asleep was like being nested, and it was a feeling I was coming to crave. My skin was still tingling, and I was a pleasant kind of sore, but relaxed and drowsy.

I drifted down to a chorus of breaths in my ear, eyes blinking slowly up at the ceiling of my bedroom.

◦

CALLUM WAS WAITING for me as I got out of the shower the next morning. Out of *my* shower. That felt like warm rainfall and was the size of the entire bathroom in the little campus house.

There was a stack of clothes on the bed next to him.

"Aiden went to the library to get your case," he said. "And they sent me up with these in case you objected."

I scrubbed a small towel through my hair and flipped through the clothes. It looked like they had come from Hildy and my only real question was *when.* How long ago had Aiden started picking out new clothes for me? But they were only nicer versions of what I usually wore, things I had already been saving up for.

"What were you supposed to do?" I asked, passing him my towel and slipping into the underclothes. "Wrestle me into them?

"I will if you need me to," Callum said, watching my skin vanish. "But it's that they think we match for stubbornness."

"Well then we better tell them I was extremely uncooperative," I said. I slid the new slip, heavier and softer, over my skin.

Callum laughed and lifted the dress, a rusty orange with long

189

sleeves and a full skirt, up from the bed and held it up for me to step into.

"I came to talk to you," he said, quieter than before. "About the Hollow. And Cecil and Isaac."

I froze in place and Callum finished dressing me, drawing the zipper up my back, fingers gentle over the nape of my neck.

"I know you want to tell me not to feel guilty or—" I started.

"I only want to tell you the facts, I promise," he said, kissing where his fingers lingered before going back to the bed. He moved to sit against the headboard and patted the spot next to him.

I crawled in slowly as if it were a trap. Callum waited, an arm held out for me to fit against his side. It was an easy trap to fall into when presented that way. His hand wrapped over my shoulder and we sat together in quiet for a moment.

"I know better than anyone how impossible it is to let go of guilt for responsibility," he said and I turned into him to see his face better. His focus was distant and his free hand reached out to fiddle with mine over my lap. "I'll get to that later. I just want you to know I'm not trying to talk you out of your feelings. *But* there are things you should know."

He glanced at me and I nodded for him to continue. "*Gatekeepers* was taken off-campus for a reason. I wasn't aware, no one was. The magic used to write it seems to contain some kind of…preservation of the beings it describes. And in the case of the Hollow, the proximity of the book works like an echo. Or a microphone, even. And if you hadn't been the one influenced, *I* might have been."

"Or the student who requested it," I said, thinking of the younger girl looking for research materials for a paper.

Callum paled a little at that. "Probably the student. Either way, the Hollow would have found a target."

"You *are* trying to talk me out of my responsibility," I said. Because there was a tangled knot loosening in my chest and a part of me—the stubborn part—*did* want to hang onto it.

"You are no more responsible for Cecil Pincombe's death than I or Isaac are," Callum whispered, hands tightening around mine. "We were on the ground floor with him. And he did what he could to protect a student, but nothing and no one was going to be fast enough to protect him. You saved dozens of lives that night."

"Isaac," I said.

"Isaac is fine. He has a little scar and a few gray hairs now. Honestly, he could do with being a little less handsome," Callum said, trying to stifle a grin.

I pushed at him. "He is *not* less handsome. It isn't *funny!*"

Callum sobered with only a small roll of his eyes. "I know. I do."

"I got him hurt," I said. "I don't know what I'm doing and I can do…"

"So much?" he asked, raising an eyebrow. "With just one word."

"And that was the wrong word."

"We don't know what would have happened if you hadn't written it, though," Callum said. "What if Bryce and Tatsuo and I had tried to battle the Hollow then? I didn't know half of what I know now. It might have gone better and it might have gone worse. But Isaac *is* safe. And you should speak to him."

I winced. Trying to abandon three lovers meant owing three lovers a sincere apology when you'd realized your own stupid mistake. And while Isaac seemed to accept that I was here now, that didn't keep my actions from being hurtful. He and I had been closest from the beginning with how much we had in common.

"There's something else I need to tell you," Callum said after a stretch.

His arms and hands and chest were tense all around me. I twisted in my spot to sit close, facing him and keeping our hands tangled together.

"About the war," I said.

He nodded, eyes fixed to where my thumbs were stroking the backs of his hands. "You've heard about the Toy Soldier?" he asked.

"The general on the front lines at the end of the war," I said. Callum looked up, his eyes going flat with anxious lines appearing between his brows. It sank in slowly. "But…Callum you were…you can't have been. You were so young."

"Sixteen," he said.

"How on earth?" I murmured.

"My father, he was- is a general," Callum said, taking a deep breath. "His older sons, my half-brothers, are all in the army. And we're from northern parts so he was home a lot during the war. And at the time I was his last son. He brought me into his office, tried to teach me about war. But I was...I was already learning about it. I'd been listening to him talk about it my entire life, that was all we had to read about and I was..."

"Natural," I said, thinking of what Aiden had mentioned.

"My strategies were crude but effective," Callum said darkly. "He took them with him to the fronts and won battles. So then he took me too. I think it was meant to be a bit of a joke at first. A way to show off to the other officials. They ended up being impressed. And I was an idiot and thought I was a genius. I wasn't seeing the results of my plans, I only heard the news. Battles won, armies defeated. It sounded like a game."

It had sounded like a game in the south too. I was younger and by the time I really knew what was happening, we were winning. There was no chance of the war coming to Bridgeston.

"My mother had died, and the others in the coven...it was different than ours is. And I was making my father proud which was all he or I cared about the time." Callum grimaced and then shrugged. "No. I cared about winning. I was proud of myself."

"You were too young," I said.

"I was. They gave me a brigade and advisors and put me in a tent on battlefields and I...I devised the strategies that would win fastest and by the largest numbers. And they kept bringing me more men because...because I was..." he went quiet and I held my breath, already knowing what would come. "I was having them slaughtered. Just a fraction less than the enemy. I saw it at the end. What I had done to them. And they sent me back home because by then..."

"You'd won the war for them," I said. It was what we had heard at home. The Toy Soldier had won the war. I wondered how many people had known that the Toy Soldier was a boy.

Callum nodded faintly. My hands rose up from our laps, wrapping over his cheeks and his eyes met mine, dull and exhausted and wary. Everything I thought to say I threw out again. I could not say that I was sorry, or that it wasn't his fault, because they were true but they weren't *enough*. And they wouldn't change anything. So I kissed him, pressing my lips gently to his and holding us there as his hands clutched at my back.

"You said your mother was from the north," he said as I leaned back. "She'll know what I did to her people."

I blinked at that. "My mother died a few years ago," I said. "And she was Vermenian." Callum's eyes widened. "My father met her while he was in the army in the north, before your war. And they said that was where she was from, like it would explain the accent. I don't know how she felt about the war, not really. But she talked about it like everyone else in town. Saying nasty things about her own people. Praising our soldiers, *you*. So my brother and I did too. Even though we knew. She spoke Vermenian when she was angry, if we were alone."

Callum's brow furrowed again and I gave him another swift kiss. "You should not have been a general," I said because that was simple and it was true. "And no one is their best self during a war. My mother would have forgiven you."

He studied my face, maybe looking for the Vermenian pieces, and then nodded briefly.

"My mother would have loved you," he said, with the trace of a smile.

His father and I would not be getting along, that much was for sure.

25

JOANNA

"Here...here is something," Hildy said, lips twisted thoughtfully as she leaned away from the book in front of her.

Midterms were put on hold, classes were canceled, and the Library was locked. Hildy and Aiden, apparently trustees of the university, had gotten access to the President's private library. Callum had pulled all the relevant books and brought them back to join us, clustered in the sunroom of Gwen's home.

"It's about the history of the university," she said. *"The Hand Woods, designed and cultivated to contain magical forces,"* she read, *"Became an ideal location to foster growth in students. In addition, the University would act as a line of defense.* It's very vague but-"

"The woods is the cage," Tatsuo said.

Callum and I glanced at each other, our expressions a mirror of puzzlement, and then it struck us both at the same time.

"The Hollow isn't the only thing out there!" I exclaimed as Callum said, "The woods is a prison, Joanna only unlocked one cell."

"Which is why it hasn't left the area," Gwen said, pulling the book to herself from Hildy's lap. "It's still trapped. In here, with us."

"The cage is built of sigils, that's easy enough," Callum said, books open in front of him on the floor of the other coven's sunroom. "But we guessed partly right. There's a coded melody and a swatch of color here. Pieces of the true name. But the word was never written down for safety's sake. And we need the whole name to keep the sigils in place."

"But I have the connection we need to get that word," I said. "Tatsuo said—"

"It's not safe," Callum said without looking up from his texts.

"Neither is trying to solve this with a missing piece and if I can do it, then that's what we have to do." I watched Callum's shoulders draw in as he reached up to adjust the glasses on his nose and acted as if he hadn't heard me at all. "You're being unreasonable," I started again.

"I'm not sure that he is," Gwen said from the loveseat, and Hildy was looking studiously into her own lap. "You've never tried trance writing. You're still so new, Joanna."

My cheeks warmed and I looked at the others. Aiden was studying the page Callum had handed him with the melody and Tatsuo seemed to be avoiding my gaze. Only Bryce and Isaac were looking back at me, and both of them were too inscrutable for me to puzzle out in my embarrassment.

"I can put you in the trance," Bryce said, words slow and cautious.

"No," Callum snapped, looking up.

"If she practiced," Tatsuo tried.

"With whom? Herself? It's something entirely different," Callum said, voice snarling on the words. "Or were you volunteering?"

Everyone stiffened at once, Gwen and Hildy staring at Tatsuo with wide eyes.

"No," Tatsuo said slowly. "And Joanna and I don't share the necessary connection. I was thinking of someone in her own coven."

Callum paled at that, face dropping back down to the floor. Even Aiden's expression became shuttered at the suggestion. Isaac was as quiet and wary as he had been since I'd tried to leave them. He didn't withhold physical affection, but the distance remained clear.

I couldn't blame a single one of them. If it had been my choice to offer up the most vulnerable piece of myself to another person—give them power over my will—I wouldn't volunteer either.

"I'll do it," Isaac said. The whole room stared at him and he stared back at me.

"You don't have to," I said.

"I know," he said, and what had seemed wary now appeared steady and centered. "But I'll do it."

I glanced at Callum and Aiden, expecting them to argue with him. To at least warn him what a terrible idea it was. Callum looked frustrated, but he didn't say a word. Aiden only reached out to squeeze Isaac's hand and then turned to smile gently at me.

Isaac pushed away from the fireplace to come stand in front of my chair. "Come on, let's talk."

I took his hand and followed him back through the house into a small study stuffed with books and smelling faintly of tobacco.

"Are you sure you want to do this?" I asked.

"I am," Isaac said, facing me. "I think you're right and that you have the best chance of finding that missing piece to the name. And I know you writing it will make it the strongest cage possible. But that's not why I'm volunteering."

"I know that it's such a risk and I swear to you I would never abuse the power. I'll never even *use* it, I promise!" I said.

Isaac smiled, faint and flickering, and his hands squeezed at mine. "I need you to know that…I'm still hurt. That you left us," he said and when I opened my mouth to answer, apologize, he darted forward and pecked quick and soft against my lips. "I know you regret it and I…I do forgive you."

"I won't leave again, Isaac," I whispered.

"I believe you," he said, and then he winced a little and added, "I will. Time will prove it. I'm telling you that doesn't change how I feel. I trust you. Even if you had left us and said you didn't want to be a part of the coven, didn't want to belong with us. I would still trust you with this."

"I love you," I said, quick and clumsy because I was afraid he might say it first. And I wanted him to know that I meant it, and it wasn't just an answer.

His eyes brightened and his cheeks dimpled and I jumped forward into his arms, kissing him fiercely. His arms wrapped around my waist, lifting me to my toes, and a weight in my chest lightened.

"I love you, Joanna," he said, pulling away and we both grinned. "I love you and I trust you to know me. Every bit."

It was probably wrong to feel so giddy, walking back into the sunroom hand in hand with Isaac. Especially given how grim Callum still looked, sitting on the floor staring blankly into the books. Aiden was busy transcribing music onto a piece of paper, tracing the notes in the air and grimacing as he worked through them. Tatsuo and Bryce looked up as we entered, and Tatsuo's expression brightened at seeing ours.

"With Bryce leading the trance, it accelerates the process. You'll need to be focusing entirely on Isaac or the results will be aimless," Tatsuo explained, placing a pencil in my hand and notebook in my lap.

"Gast," Callum interrupted, looking up at Bryce. "Is it safe for them?"

"If it doesn't work, I will stop," Bryce said shrugging. "But what happens in the trance is up to Joanna."

"It's just a practice," I said.

"A test," Isaac hedged. "To see if it's even possible."

Callum's jaw worked, but he nodded once. He and Aiden and Gwen and Hildy all cleared out of the room to the kitchen, leaving Isaac and me with Tatsuo and Bryce.

"Now Isaac, you're more of a prop in this situation," Tatsuo said, taking Isaac by the shoulders and leading him away from me to the rug to sit. Bryce guided me over to sit across from him.

"If Joanna were experienced in this, and with a few years under her belt in the coven, she could probably manage this without you. But having you here will help with the focus," Tatsuo explained. Then he came to me and knelt down. "I'm going to leave in a minute. The fewer distractions the better. It's important that you stay as relaxed as possible. You'll want to direct the trance, but it will flow best when you let it carry you. What's important is maintaining your connection to Isaac."

I nodded, trying to fight the grin on my face as I met Isaac's gaze. But he was looking at me with those dimples in his cheek and the shade of his eyes had just gone the blue right before he kissed me. I couldn't imagine *not* feeling connected to him in the moment.

"She'll be fine," Bryce said, smirking at me.

"You may not realize at first when you find his name," Tatsuo said. "It isn't a label, it's portions of our soul. Just be open to what you find."

"I will," I said and Isaac's lips twitched again, mine resisting the urge to answer his. "What happens if I don't find his name?"

Tatsuo glanced at Bryce and they both shrugged at me. "Nothing," he said. "We'll think of something else."

Tatsuo coached me into a slow, regulated breathing to help with Bryce's drone. I watched Isaac's chest rise and fall steadily as he followed along, and that was its own kind of hypnotism. I didn't notice as Tatsuo tip-toed out of the sunroom. And at first, I didn't even notice as Bryce began to hum by the fireplace. It was all white noise, and I had given my attention to Isaac completely.

My heart squeezed in my chest and our eyes linked over the space. The room around me dimmed as if to give Isaac my focus. The hum in my ear became a buzz and then a roar burrowing into my thoughts more than lingering in the air. Isaac was larger and closer in my vision with every second and every echoing wave of sound in my head. Bryce's drone was overwhelming. For a moment, I wanted to tear away and ground myself again, in the sunroom and in myself.

But Isaac's eyes, the familiar dusty blue, were locked to my face. And it was a color I had grown fond of, felt safe surrounded by. The room shifted, blurring into that blue, and I settled. My heart thumped evenly, the beat joining the persistent burn of noise in my ears and head.

In one breath the rug scratched at my ankles and I felt the wood of the pencil between my fingers. In the next breath, I was bodiless. I wasn't in a room *with* Isaac, but I could feel him all around me. The taste of paint was on my tongue and the sharp bite of the woods in my head. The droning was gone and replaced with something that sounded like the ocean, a twin rhythm of waves.

Heartbeats, I realized. Mine and Isaac's.

The gray-blue I was surrounded by fragmented in time with the beats. A flicker of new color appeared here and there until I was in a prism, hues flashing and spinning around me. They tangled and reshaped and overhead, a blinding brilliance shined into a glare.

When it cleared I was in a wheat field, bright golden and shimmering with sunlight. There was no sound and no temperature and no taste or smell in the air, but the colors were strong and abstracted. The sharp yellow-brown of the grain, the near white-blue of the sky, and a trim of green along the horizon.

The sun flared overhead, and a sweep of dark rose up, like a hand shielding my eyes. The field twisted and the brown deepened and the scene shifted into a small kitchen. One like my own in Bridgeston, close and hot from the stove, with a small window and the sunset shining in. There was a faint whiff of cookies and a little melody, one my father had known, but in a sweeter voice. A woman's figure, monstrously tall—no, just large like adults were to a child—and distorted in shadow, passed at my side. She wore a vivid blue apron, and the fabric outshone everything in the room. Its color was saturated and crisp, and it made me feel immediately safe.

She went to the fireplace, back turned, and the blue vanished and the room went dark. The flare of the sun became the red glow of a dying fire. There was a scratch of splintered wood nipping at my palms and knees. A low growling sound rumbled from beneath the floor under me and there was a shattering crack on the stone floor. Bottle green glittered and sparkled by firelight. The color was stark and queasy and made the pain of the wood splinters sharper. A coal hot anger rose up in me as the green gleamed and the room went blue-black with night.

More of Isaac passed through me. A secret stash of paper and pencils kept under his mattress. Heartache for the girl living down the lane *and* the boy who courted her. The blinding, glittering, first moment of stepping onto Canderfey, a blur of colors and so many of them *new*. Gawky, clean-shaven Callum, barely more than a teenager and hiding behind a stack of books. Aiden's hands starkly dark against the white keys of a piano.

White sheets and three bodies in bed, sunlight bouncing off their skin, throwing a pinkish-brown halo into the hair. I ached as the color burned through me, a sweetness so painful it made the outline of my heart in my chest clear again through the trance. It was Callum, Aiden, and I in the bed, legs and arms tangled together. There was a dent on the mattress next to me where Isaac had just risen from. It could have been that morning or sometime in the future but the dawn pink light stretched over us like a fresh canvas until we were lost in the glow.

The pink flushed into the ruddy red skin of a screeching baby, and the noise was high in my ears, ringing like an alarm. The baby was wrinkled and still wet, inky black hair matted down to its head in tufts. It swatted one red fist and there was an emotion I had never known, something beyond love or ferocity or safety. It swallowed me up until my sight blurred.

The tears were hot in my eyes, streaking down my cheeks and my legs were numb underneath me. I blinked and the room cleared around me. Isaac had moved close, sitting knee to knee to me, and he reached up and swiped at the wetness over my cheeks. There was a little frown at the corner of his lips and I leaned forward at once, kissing it away, kissing him just for the sake of it.

"Are you alright?" he asked.

I nodded, swallowing and hunting for my own voice.

Bryce beat me to words. "You didn't write anything down."

I glanced down. The pencil was still in my hand, the page blank.

"We can try again," Isaac said.

I realized that they assumed the trance hadn't worked and shook my head. "I'm fine," I said. "It's fine, it worked. I didn't write anything."

Bryce's eyes narrowed and I thought I probably sounded like I was babbling. "Can you give us a minute?"

They stood and left and Isaac's fingers wiped away the last of my tears.

"Do you feel alright?" he asked again.

I sat up on weak knees and wondered how long we had been sitting together. It was dark outside, but with sunlight missing it was hard to tell evening from midnight. I moved into Isaac's space and he made way for me, pulling me close to his chest.

"I love you," I said and his smile flickered back. "I'm fine. I didn't write anything because there was nothing to write. Just color."

Vivid blue, bottle green, rosy earth, squalling red.

Isaac's eyes lit up at the news. "What—Well, maybe I shouldn't know. Really?"

"Really," I said, grinning.

"And nothing to scare you off?" he asked, a note wavering in the question.

"Nothing," I said, drawing him in for a slow and thorough kiss. "What did it feel like? Did you notice anything?"

"It was like…having you close," he said, smiling. "As if you've known me my entire life."

The others came into the sunroom, and I knew by the relief on Callum's face that Bryce had told them I had failed.

And then Isaac spoke.

"It worked. She found it."

And Callum's face fell.

HE DIDN'T COME to bed when we returned to the house. The trance had taken hours, another point in Callum's argument against it, and there was exhaustion in everyone's expressions. I didn't fight against his refusal and no one else continued the discussion, but it was clear that he knew it was only a matter of time. They would end up needing me in whatever plan we formed against the Hollow, and Callum would be outvoted.

"I don't disagree with him," Aiden mumbled in my bed as we lay down with Isaac to sleep. "I just think we all know he's wrong."

I huffed a laugh at the time and then lay awake until Isaac and Aiden fell asleep. Then I crawled out from the bed with a pillow under my arm and snuck down to Callum's office. The glittering lamp I had written him was lit on the table and he was hunched in his armchair, dark circles shadowed under his eyes.

"If you've come to argue your case," he growled, "I plan on being unreasonable."

"I was thinking," I said, dropping the pillow to the floor. I took a seat in front of the bookshelves and grabbed a discarded book from the pile around his feet. "What do you think would happen if I wrote 'the Hollow is back in its cage and the cage is locked and cannot be unlocked?'"

Callum blinked at me over the rim of his glasses. "I think…we should have tried that already?"

"I did," I said, passing my notebook full of the anxious scribbles of Isaac's sickbed. His expression fell. "Now, since that didn't work, what do we try next?" I asked.

Callum stared at me for a long stretch of silence and I waited. "Did you come down here in the middle of the night to strategize with me?" he asked, the angles in his face softening.

I nodded and waited as he took a long breath and sighed it out. He gathered up a collection of the books in front of him and then slid down from the chair, moving over to sit next to me. He passed me one of the books and flipped it open on my lap, something like sigils staring stark and black up from the page at me. One looked like a crescent moon with a jagged edge of teeth, and the other was twisted like a knot but with no sign of a beginning or end.

"This is an ancient alphabet, supposedly one belonging to gods. Or god-like creatures. I thought maybe they might be…helpful," Callum said, grimacing. "Except I'm not really sure what any of them mean."

"I could try one out on the paper to see what happens," I suggested, hiding my smile.

Callum took his glasses off and rubbed at his eyes. "I'm too tired to tell if you're joking and I'm desperate enough to consider saying yes. Let's talk about what parts of the caging spell we *do* understand."

I left any further writing to him for the night. But we discussed phrases I might try to help stall for time or keep everyone safe. And slowly, and very late at night, we talked about how I might find the missing piece of the Hollow's true name.

26

—

JOANNA

When we opened the cupboards the next morning all the porcelain had been turned to dust. Hildy arrived an hour later to tell us the pack of campus stray cats had been found, injured but whole. Tatsuo was nursing two of the older tom cats who had been injured, and there was a litter of three kittens in need of a home. Aiden made one attempt to object, and I cut him off before he could finish the sentence.

Callum found me and the kittens—an orange and white, a black and white, and a calico—by the fireplace in my bedroom. They scattered under chairs and, in the case of the orange and white boy, my skirt as he sat down with me.

"We shouldn't wait," I said.

He and I had barely made it to bed before dawn and the fresh round of bad news.

"We have a little time left," he said, tapping his fingers on the rug and making the kitten under my skirt peek its head out. "Bryce says the Hollow probably never chose a name for itself which is why we call it by these spook titles. Nothing for your spells to pin down."

Callum held still as the little tuxedo cat rushed bravely out and

205

attacked his pant leg. He reached one finger out, scratched at its tail bone, and the kitten flopped onto its side with a roaring purr.

"What do we try next?" I asked.

He waited to speak until all the kittens reemerged, using him as a playful obstacle to climb and conquer.

"I'm afraid that if you use your connection with the Hollow it will make you more vulnerable," Callum said. "That it may be able to manipulate the connection as well."

"I'm afraid of that too," I said. "But I trust you, the three of you and the others, to keep me safe."

Callum stretched his hand out to mine, linking our fingers loosely, and the calico went tumbling down his leg to paw at our wrists. I smiled in spite of the conversation.

"I think instead of setting sigils, I should be focusing on hexing… distracting the Hollow," Callum said. "Keeping it busy while the rest of you work."

"Gwen and Hildy and Tatsuo can handle the sigils," I agreed. It was what we'd been saying for most of the day before.

Callum nodded loosely and then looked up at me. "If anything does happen, I'll get you out."

"I know," I said, squeezing his hand.

IT TOOK another day of discussion and planning and Callum's wired pacing through the house. But we set into the woods by full daylight, as distorted as it was, armed in every way we could be. Aiden carried his latest handmade violin, stained black for battle. Callum had a knife that looked as deadly sharp as it did heavy with power and runes. Isaac carried the rough slate tile I would write on and the others were all armed with ceremonial wands.

I had a dense stick of chalk waiting in my pocket and it felt as comforting as being left naked in a thunderstorm. I didn't say that to the others.

Storm clouds gathered at our backs the deeper we walked into the woods. The path back to the clearing I had met Isaac in weeks ago was silent, dull and gray and devoid of life.

"What if it doesn't come back?" Isaac whispered as if to avoid shattering the hush of the woods. "Why would it walk back into the cage we let it out of?"

I *let it out of*, I thought. "That's what I'm here for," I said. "To lure it back."

Callum looked over his shoulder at me, eyes flinching at my words, but it was true. It was one of the things we had talked about in the dead of night in his office.

I thought I wouldn't recognize the clearing a second time. That I would rely on Isaac or the others to tell me when we had arrived. But it couldn't be mistaken. The ground had been scalped down to a barren mudscape, already our feet were squelching in the wet earth. In the colorless landscape, the trees ringing around the clearing really did look like bars on a jail cell.

We walked into the cell in silence, my covenmates sticking close to my side. Bryce remained near us and Gwen, Tatsuo, and Hildy continued on to the three farther points, like the ends of a compass. The sky darkened in a ring all around the tops of the trees and I knew we were being watched, tracked. I just wasn't sure if the Hollow saw us as a predator or prey.

"Are- are you sure?" Aiden asked before I could kneel, the neck and bow of his violin in one hand and the other reaching out to me.

Callum's plan, the order of actions, and all the different variables he and I had argued and pored over in our planning rattled through my head. I went to Aiden, pressing myself to his chest and feeling Callum and Isaac at my back. Aiden's arm folded around us and we held each other for several deep breaths.

"I'm sure," I said, starting to pull away. Aiden gave me a hard swift kiss, Callum leaving a softer one at the back of my neck.

Isaac bent as I knelt into the mud; cold, wet earth clasping around my knees. He left the stone in front of me and a long, soft kiss to my temple.

"Be careful," he said, standing again.

It wasn't a careful thing we were doing. I didn't answer him. There was a sound in the distance like a tree trunk splitting open, and it seemed just as likely as a crack of thunder.

I looked over my shoulder and Isaac's hands were held out in front of him, the space between wavering darkly. He had said he didn't need paint or ink or canvas to work color and I hadn't understood what he meant till now. Color was pooling in the air between his palms, the sickly gray-green of the woods around us growing dense and rotten. It was a stagnant, dying shade, the color of the Hollow. It clogged the back of my throat and left a pungent smell in my nose.

Aiden raised the violin to his shoulder and with the first stroke of the bow over the strings the sound was a tear in the air. I turned back to the clearing, closing my eyes and finding the spoiled color behind my eyelids. The melody Aiden had dragged off the page was a slithering, rasping piece running talons through my head.

My stomach rolled and when I blinked my eyes open, the clearing was spinning around me. I slammed them shut again, trying to push past the twist of music in my thoughts and the pounding dark color that hammered through me. I dug for the headache I woke up with in the mornings, right at the base of my skull. It was there, dull and pulsing in time with the Hollow's melody. When I found it, everything tangled together into one blurring, burning cacophony.

And then it was there, lurking inside the headache, coiling around itself like a snake. I opened my eyes, finding the clearing around me, but with the feeling that I was somewhere else. Bryce was watching my face and we nodded at the same time.

As Bryce began to hum, the color squatting at the back of my head spread across my vision, flattening the stone gray of the woods. Hildy in all her rich blues faded away, swallowed up by rotten green. The droning buzz of Bryce's voice joined the music and goosebumps rose up on my skin until I was one tingling, vibrating nerve.

And then I was nothing.

I remained that way for what seemed to be *too* long. There was something at the edges, something crawling in a perimeter circle.

Pacing at a horizon of a color that stopped being a color and a song that had no beginning or end.

I tried to hold onto what Tatsuo had said, to let the trance carry me. But I was afraid now of being left here, rotting in a color gone bad.

Then there were shadows, rising up over my head. My knees were cold and my skin was clammy. The space around me sharpened, the foggy edges of darkness grainy in my sight. I looked up and the shadows became impenetrable. I looked down and saw the faint trace of my own feet, now standing, and a cluttering tangle of dark around them.

That was a very stupid thing to do.

I spun and stumbled back, my feet catching and tripping over uneven ground. The words were in my head, but the language was foreign on my ears, like the thunder of rocks breaking against each other.

The Hollow was behind me. Unshrouded, a naked pale thing that wasn't human or animal, only horror. Its flesh was greasy, body elongated as if it had made an effort to become *something* and then gave up. There was a distended belly, and the suggestion of a face, and pieces that were *like* limbs but were not.

"Where are we?" I asked, and the words echoed, my voice small and useless.

I've been building you a cage, the Hollow said, voice a spider's crawl up my skin. *To keep you in my belly with all the tasty things.*

"This isn't your belly," I said. "You haven't swallowed me down. I've come for your true name. You'll be back in your prison before nightfall."

You think like a human, witchling, the Hollow hissed. *I ate my true name too. And I'll eat your coven and your friends, but I won't keep them. Not for you. I'll spit them out into the dirt after I've chewed them bloody. I'll eat the woods and the brick mountains they built to gate me in and the hills and I'll keep you here to watch it all slide down my gullet.*

The Hollow grinned or snarled and its mouth was a fresh rotting rip in the moon white flesh. And then it was gone as I was catching a sour, humid breath to answer it. I gagged on the taste of the air as it clung to my tongue. My breaths stuttered in my chest and my eyes watered as I waited, hoping for the scene to shift like it had with Isaac. But the space was still and quiet and my heart hammered in my chest.

I fumbled in my pocket and found the stick of chalk still there. I shifted my feet over the floor until the right slid back and forth over something smooth and hard. I bent down and wrote blind.

I have a lamp to light the way.

There was a lamp, a little glass and oil one, yellow flame flickering and spitting at my side. The words were written on a piece of smooth dark wood, half-swallowed in the muck beneath me. I stood, raising the lamp, and shivered. Mountains of refuse rose up around me, bones and brick and glass. There were books, walls, pieces of what looked like an old ship, and more gruesome images I shied away from. I lifted the lamp above my head.

I was in a cavern, dark and massive and held up by spiraling stone gray that resembled something like a belly. My belly heaved and I covered my eyes, breathing into my palm.

It had to be a trick. It *had* to be.

But how long would it be before the others realized I was getting nowhere in my search? Could I leave the vision if the Hollow didn't let me out? Or worse, had I come waltzing into a trap I'd built for myself?

My stare fixed to a scrap of bright yellow fabric snagged on a shard of wood, a carved wolf's face broken into, as panic flooded through my veins. But the wolf was familiar, the yellow fabric too. It was the same yellow as Cecil Pincombe's shocking necktie, and it was flecked with a rusty brown. And the wolf had been one of the animals carved into the desk of the library.

I ate my true name too.

If that was true…and I was in the Hollow's belly…

I released a slow, shaking breath. My grip tightened around the handle of the lamp and the flame brightened. Vision or not there was something I could do while trapped here. I crawled to the top of one of the mounds of churned up wood and glass, picking up the books as

I went, balancing as carefully as I could. I held my breath at the top, afraid of falling in an avalanche of trash, and looked around.

What surrounded me seemed to be from the campus. Several mountains deeper was the ship, and beyond that my lamp glanced off the window panes of a steepled church. The cavern went on and on, and I wondered how far in I would have to go, digging through waste and wreckage to find the word.

I lifted the lamp higher, squinting to see what was dangling from the steeple of the church. Firelight glinted above me and I tore my eyes gratefully away from the shadowy figure hanging. There was a glitter of warmth overhead, tracing over the bone of a rib, and I swung the lamp in an arch, watching more lines glitter.

There were symbols carved into the bone, worn and polished into the twisting arch. One flickered in the glow, a knot that tangled endlessly. I stumbled over trash, wincing as my foot caught in something sticky, but I kept my eyes up, following the pattern of symbols. Most of them were familiar, foggy in my memory, but from Callum's ancient alphabet.

In my head, they made the heavy crashing sounds of the Hollow's language. The sound looped, inverting in on itself. Like the knot letter and the melody. I practiced it silently on my tongue, working out the shape.

"Gvesdrasveg," I tried and everything rattled around me, the hill I stood on grumbling and scratching at my legs.

"*Gvisardrasivg!*" I said, louder and lower, the notes of the word clawing at my throat and grinding on my teeth.

And then the glass and wood and bone dropped out beneath me and swallowed me up.

I was braced, one hand in mud as the clearing reappeared around me. Night had fallen and stars winked overhead and my legs felt frozen in the cold underneath me. My right hand was poised over the stone, my palm sweaty around the chalk in spite of the chill. Books I had rescued lay scattered around me in the mud.

"Joanna!" Callum said, palms on my shoulders.

"*Gvisardrasivg,*" I hissed and a ring of storm clouds snarled in above us, swirling together like a tornado and dropping to touch down in the heart of the clearing.

"You have it?" Callum asked.

"*Gvisardrasivg*," I shouted and Bryce echoed it, the word stronger on their tongue and sounding closer to the right word.

"Sigils, now!" Callum shouted, standing up at my back.

I drew the knot at the top of the stone as the Hollow, Gvisardrasivg, The Belly of Nightmares, poured itself out of smoke and storm cloud, shrouded again and as tall as the trees.

Aiden's bow was screeching over the strings of the violin and Isaac had turned the world the sick gray-green. Bryce shone yellow in the strange light, bellowing the word I had found into the sky. The Hollow bent, lunging at my coven, and there was a flash like orange fire. Callum was behind me like a blaze at my back, the tingling warmth of his protection charm multiplied by hundreds. He was chanting and there was a slice of metal in the air above my head, his knife tracing a ward.

My legs burned and my bones throbbed as I added the next letter, a mass of points like a bursting star. It was like the library all over again, my head pounding and my body screaming in protest. My writing slowed as my hand began to shake while I tried to make the smooth rounded edge of an empty moon. The next shape zigged and zagged and my teeth ground together through a scream. My back bowed and my vision blacked as the sensation of my bones shattering and splintering rocked through me.

"Callum," Isaac shouted. "What are you-?"

"Joanna's failing," I heard him say. "Hold the circle as long as you can."

Arms that burned like fire wrapped around my middle and I writhed against them.

"I have you," Callum said in my ear and there was a cool touch at the back of my neck that smoothed the rough, tearing feeling under my skin.

"The others," I whispered. But my body had calmed enough,

making an X at the bottom of the stone and then crossing at the top and bottom, like an hourglass.

Across the clearing, a tree tore up from its roots, crashing dangerously down to the ground in front of Hildy. But the woman didn't even flinch, tracing a vivid blue sigil in the air that looked like a lopsided clockface.

"Finish the word, Joanna," Callum said, and I could hear the strain in his voice, feel the sweat sticking us together at my back.

My hands felt numb as I worked and out of the corner of my eye, I could see the Hollow thrashing. More trees came crashing, shattering on impact into jagged pieces that scattered in all directions.

The entire world seemed to shake, threatening to break apart, as I finished the second starburst, the last letter. The chalk crumbled against the slate as I joined the last point. Bryce was joining me in the dirt, placing small glowing hands on either side of the name. The letters burned bright with Bryce's touch turning from chalk to fire to scorched carvings on the stone

The Hollow screamed and the sound reverberated at the back of my head like a white-hot poker. My throat burned as I screamed with it, my body seizing and my sight swimming into a blind, bright, burst of empty color. Callum's lips were on my cheek, moving with a word, but I was falling under.

27

JOANNA

EVERYTHING WAS GRAY AND FOGGY AS I OPENED MY EYES. MY HEAD still felt split in half and my vision pulsed like a drumbeat for a moment before clearing. The plaster above me was cracked and stained, a familiar bowing moon white circle above a narrow and lumpy bed.

I took one breath, mildew and charcoal and fresh bread, and I knew. I was back in Bridgeston.

I sat up and my head swam, the room blurring to a cloudy smear and then back again.

The house was quiet and my heart sank, knowing the inherent wrongness of the silence. I teetered out of the bed in bare feet, mud brushed away from my knees so they were still dusted in dirt. I looked out the window by the bed and there was a low morning fog hanging over the yard, hiding the rest of the town.

I stumbled to my bedroom door and out into the hall. The house seemed to have faded since I'd left, like the life and charm had been leached out over time. That or the cheerful pale yellow of the walls was now dull to me in comparison to the saturated colors of my coven's house.

Where were they?

There was a choking panic in my throat. What happened in the woods? Why was I in Bridgeston and not with my coven?

My legs were weak and my feet barely felt the grain of the floor underneath me. But when I made it down the hall to the stairs I saw gleaming black shoes under the rickety kitchen table and for the first time since waking I took a full breath.

"I was afraid- afraid you weren't here," I said, coming down the stairs and finally seeing Aiden, Callum, and Isaac crowded together in my family's kitchen.

Their faces turned to me in unison, but instead of relief or smiles, their expressions were smooth—a placid smile on Aiden's mouth, a sneer over Callum's. Isaac only blinked at me.

"Why are we here?" I asked, at the bottom of the stairs. "What happened with the Hollow? How are the others?"

"The Hollow is caged," Isaac said, and there was nothing in the words, no joy or feeling.

"Come sit, darling," Aiden said. "You must be tired."

I wanted to go to them, fold myself between the three of them. But there was no room with the way they linked together, Callum sitting in the chair with the others framing him, hands on shoulders like the twist of a knot. And Aiden was pointing to the seat across from them. I walked to the table, trying to catch my feet on the ground to settle myself, but instead left wading in a murky dread.

I made it to the free chair and then stopped, hands grasping onto the back of it. I didn't want to sit, I wanted to resist the weight sinking into my gut.

"Why are we here?" I repeated.

Their faces turned to face each other, something so synchronized in the movement. They had been together so long, it was as if they were a single unit. And I was still an outsider.

They looked back at me and it was Callum who spoke, head tilting and eyes squinting at me through his glasses.

"You were right. About everything."

I stared back, my breath locked in my lungs as I waited, feeling that dread shaping underneath me. A familiar fear that I had tried to give up as if it were an addiction.

"It's so much clearer, seeing you here," Isaac continued. "You're such a simple creature. So small."

"Canderfey was swallowing you up," Aiden said. "And here you look so at home."

"I'm at home with you," I whispered, because it was a promise they had given me.

"Do you think so? Or did you just want to be more than you really are?" Callum asked, voice gentle and poisoned.

I swung around, facing the small stove where dented pots were hanging overhead and a ragged, stained towel was dropped carelessly on the counter. I squeezed my eyes against the tears and pressed my hand to my chest where my heart was trying to crack open.

"Joanna."

I spun again, fixing my eyes to Callum, hearing the urgent plead in his voice, but he only looked bored. My head panged and the room darkened, the three of them blending together into one dark and menacing shape, and then the pain faded.

"You're an awful lot of trouble, darling," Aiden said, his grin cruel.

"Writing is an… unusual gift, but it doesn't mean you suit us," Isaac said.

"You don't belong in our coven," Callum said, firm and final.

My lips parted and I didn't know what would come out, a scream or a sob or protest…or an agreement. I stared at them, vision watery and body feeling trembly and useless. Plain and small and pathetic.

"There you are girl," my father said, coming in from the back garden, hands dirty and face distracted. "This kitchen is a mess. What have you been doing all day?"

"I—" My brow furrowed. I had only just woken up.

My sister-in-law, Rose, came rushing down the stairs, two squalling children in her arms. "Could you take Aggie for just a minute? She's got a tooth coming in and she's impossible and Donny needs changed."

"Quit gaping and daydreaming, mouse," my brother said, appearing through the front door.

My niece was screaming and wiggling, arms reaching out to be held and bounced and my father was frowning at me and my brother was rolling his eyes. And through it all my coven sat, watching me with narrow eyes and patient smiles as if to say 'See? This is what you are.'

"No!"

The activity in the room paused, my family's eyes wide as I dug my nails into the chair in front of me and braced myself.

"No. This is not what we agreed," I said. "We fight for each other. We do belong together. It's as much my coven now as it is yours."

"You can't be in a coven, honey, you're not a-"

"Not *now*, Rose," I hissed, without tearing my eyes from Aiden's face. "And it isn't up to any of you whether or not I go back to Canderfey. I have a job there."

My coven looked at each other again and there was something strange in the movement, the pace slow and smooth and regular. Callum turned back to me, a twist of annoyance in the purse of his lips.

"We really don't know you well enough to be sure you're worth it," he said.

But he had said so, from the start. They had all said so, even when I refused to listen.

"You do," I said, but the protest was weak.

"You would have to prove it to us, darling," Aiden said.

My stomach was twisting around itself and my knees were shaking. These were not the men I had found too easy to fall in love with. I didn't understand what had changed, but I felt needy and desperate to change it back.

"How?" I whispered.

My family was hanging back by the stairs, the children gone quiet in their mother's arms, and all eyes fixed to me.

"Your true name would tell us," Isaac said, the usual sweet rasp of his voice now honeyed.

"My... I don't know it," I said. My gut stopped rolling and turned to stone.

"You could find it," Callum said. "If you wanted us, you could find it around here somewhere."

"Around...around here?" I stepped back from the chair and Callum rose up, Aiden and Isaac's hands still on his shoulders.

"Just look, darling," Aiden purred.

I blinked at them and then let my eyes wander slowly around the room, thoughts scrambling.

These were not my men...these were not...

"I can't find it," I murmured.

"*Look*," Callum snapped.

I bit my lip and avoided their gazes. The fog was still hanging outside the window, dense and dark.

"Gvisard-" I started.

"Stop!" The room shouted as one, my coven in front of me and my family behind.

I should have felt afraid or threatened, but instead there was only relief. I looked directly at the men, not into any of their faces, but at the twisted, hulking shape of them together.

"You were too impatient," I said.

"I can find it myself now that I'm here," it said from a half dozen voices.

I backed up another step and the table and chairs vanished between us, the image of my covenmates starting to congeal together at the shoulders. I had seconds.

"Gvisardra-"

Callum lunged and pulled the bodies of Aiden and Isaac with him. I scrambled back, spine hitting the edge of the stove as six hands— dark and tan and pale—wrapped around my throat, choking off the sound.

Joanna, breathe.

Callum. They were with me. Not here in the vision the Hollow conjured to torture me, but out there in the woods, waiting.

"Gvisardravig," I said, or tried to say, air squeaking out of my lungs. Aiden's face was smashed to Callum's, eyes bulging together as Isaac's jaw fell loose, and looser, long and gaping and grotesque with too many teeth.

The room was going black and my voice was strangled but I kept my lips moving even as nails clawed at my face and neck.

"Get into your cage and *rot* there."

Fingers punched into my throat like blades and I choked on on blood or air or nothing.

I thrashed as voices shouted in my head, too many voices. My hands swiped through the hair and were caught up in a firm grip.

"Joanna! Joanna, it's us. It's us. It's alright."

I tried to lunge back but arms were banded around my waist. A cool hand brushed over my forehead and the black cloud in my vision washed away. Callum and Aiden and Isaac were surrounding me and I screamed, the shout burning in my abused throat.

Callum reached up to my neck and I flinched away. But his hand was gentle where it landed.

"You're safe," he whispered. "You're safe. It's over."

I was gulping for air, finding that I could breathe again, and the sudden introduction of oxygen made white stars burst behind my eyes. I sagged in Isaac's hold and Aiden's worried face leaning forward to leave a warm kiss on my cheek was the last thing I saw.

I WOKE up in Isaac's bed, an emptiness in my head. And in my stomach. There was a kitten sleeping on my shoulder, the orange and white one, and the calico was snuggled against my side. Callum was asleep in the chair I had taken vigil in while Isaac was ill. I froze at the sight of him, panic and relief warring in me, afraid to find myself under a new trick.

There was a little mewling chirrup from the end of the bed, the tuxedo kitten, and then Callum stirred. His head lolled in my direction and for a moment he only blinked at me. Then he was out of the chair, tripping in his bare feet on the way to the bed.

"Is it you?" I asked, and the words came out sticky and slurred. I pushed myself up on the pillow and the orange kitten growled and rolled away.

"Here," Callum said, pulling over a little mug of cold tea and lifting it to my lips as he climbed onto the bed with me.

The tea was sweet and icy on my aching throat, carrying away some of the burn and parched dryness.

"You kept kicking and pushing at us while you slept," Callum said, with a goofy smile on his face. "The healers said to leave you to it."

I 'hmm'd and then reached out a hand, brushing my fingers over the rise of his cheek. It felt right, the warmth and softness instead of the hot and sticky fever of the Hollow. I tugged him closer by the front of his shirt. He laughed and scrambled up to the pillows, tucking me into his side. I felt a little stiff and a little weak, but none of the lingering pain that had struck me unconscious.

"How long's it been?" I mumbled into his shirt, smiling as I heard the house groaning with running footsteps up the stairs.

"Just a day," Callum said.

I blinked at that and then realized that the sun was shining and there was blue outside the window. "It really worked?" I asked. "It's...is it gone?"

The door to the bedroom opened and Aiden was charging in, straight for the bed. I stretched and arm out for him and he slid underneath it, heavy over my stomach and face pressed to my neck.

"It worked," Callum said. "The Hollow is locked up tight."

"Hello, love," Isaac said from the doorway, carrying a tray in his arms. "How are you feeling?"

"Okay, I think," I said. I waved a hand towards the back of my head. "A little like I'm...missing a headache I've grown used to?"

Callum's fingers combed through my hair and I let my eyes drift shut at the touch. "That'll be the connection gone now."

The connection that had let the Hollow into my head, my fears.

"'S a relief," I murmured. Aiden shifted up to my side, an arm joining Callum's over my shoulders. I folded my legs, up making room for Isaac and reaching out for the tray of food. I was starving. "How are the others?" I asked.

They hesitated for a moment and I froze, a muffin halfway to my lips, stomach sinking. Aiden sighed and spoke first.

"They're alright, really," he said, trying too hard to be reassuring. "Tatsuo was hit by a piece of tree falling. Got a nasty shot through his left leg. But he's healing, quickly if Hildy and Gwen have anything to say about it. And Bryce was a little wavery at the end yesterday, but I expect they're rested up by now."

"Altogether, nothing serious," Isaac said, hand stroking at my leg over the blanket.

I eased and Callum kissed at my temple as I took another bite of food. "So…what's next?" I asked, looking at each of them.

"You take time off, a week according to Woollard," Aiden said, fingers tracing a pattern on my belly.

"What?" I snapped, sitting up and jostling him. "No, I'm fine—"

"A week," Isaac said, tone firm.

I sulked back against the headboard. "I'll play it by ear." I hurried on before they could correct me, "And what I meant was I've agreed to be in the coven so now…there's supposed to a series of trials right?"

Callum grinned at me. "Those are old traditions."

I fidgeted. "I only read about them. And I wasn't *expecting* to practice them. But I remember that there was an Invitation and…"

"A Union and a Trial?" Isaac asked, head leaning to one side. "I think we covered those, love."

"Isaac issued a formal invitation," Aiden rolled onto his back to look up at me. With a sly grin, he said, "We've had unions. And if locking the Hollow back up wasn't a trial, I don't know what was."

"I assumed we covered that when you tried to leave," Callum said shrugging.

"So…that's it?" I asked.

"There are formal commitment ceremonies, coven marriages," Callum said, watching my face. He glanced at the others and back to me. "When you're ready, we can talk about that."

"For now," Isaac said, squeezing at my leg. "I would like to simply enjoy the company of my coven, complete and safe as it is now."

And strangely enough, there was something thrilling in the suggestion. Without the threat of danger, and with my promise to stay and be open with these men, a relationship seemed suddenly exciting. And I had agreed to move into the house.

I pushed the tray aside and Isaac immediately leaned in closer, stretching forward to kiss me. "I may get bored at home for a week," I mumbled against his lips.

He leaned back, eyes rolling, and Aiden laughed.

"I'm sure we'll find ways to entertain you," Callum said, voice dry and eyes hot on my skin.

EPILOGUE

CALLUM

I stood in the doorway of Joanna's bathroom with a forgotten book in my hand, watching as she and Aiden kissed under the falling water. I'd come upstairs to show her notes I'd found on Scribes, a rare breed of witches whose magic centered around their writing, but the new information wasn't half as interesting as the sight of the pair of them. Aiden's dark arms twisted around Joanna's narrow waist, her soft hips rolling forward, seeking friction. His hands skimmed down her back, over her ass, and his mouth trailed down her chest to her belly as he dropped to his knees.

Joanna's small cry echoed against the stone of the shower walls.

I was ready to drop the book and join them when a hand settled on my shoulder.

"This came in the mail for you," Isaac said.

It took a minute for the hungry fog to clear out of my head before I could tear my eyes away from Joanna arching back as Aiden held her against his mouth. Isaac was holding out a letter in his hand.

My stomach sank and the desire fled my blood. The writing was my father's.

"Did you tell him about Joanna?" he asked, voice lowered.

"I don't tell him anything if I can help it," I said. But he might have heard by now. It'd been almost a week since we'd put the Hollow away. Joanna's part in it—and her place in our house—was no secret on campus.

"Probably news of war," Isaac said. Because it was almost always news of war with my father.

"Or a summons," I said.

Isaac and I looked at each other for a long moment. "If it is, Aiden and I will come too."

A little bit of tension leaked out of my shoulders. I knew what it cost Isaac to offer, but I would need him if I had to go North. *Joanna* would need us all if she had to meet my father.

Joanna was calling from the shower, not for us but for release, and Isaac's attention shifted, a dark smile replacing his frown.

I flicked my hand and the letter vanished. If I was lucky, I would forget it ever arrived.

Isaac pulled his shirt over his head. "Come on, Aiden looks like he could use a hand."

I snorted. Aiden seemed to be fine. It was Joanna that was begging. I started to strip.

I didn't want to think about war or monsters, and my father crossed both categories. I just wanted to lose myself in the touch of my coven for another day. The book I'd been carrying dropped to the floor with my pants. I would tell Joanna about the Scribes after.

Isaac was walking into the shower, steam billowing out from the glass door, and I followed quickly. Joanna reached for me, face tangled with pleasure and frustration, and I banished my worries with her kiss.

WARRIORS

THE LIBRARIAN'S COVEN, BOOK 2

1

CALLUM

"Do you know, I think Aiden could play music to your pacing."

My feet stuttered and I spun, finding Isaac in the doorway to our front parlor.

"Are you rehearsing the part of the metronome for this evening?" he asked, mouth quirking up.

I wanted to ask him not to tease me, but that would be revealing a softer underbelly than I cared to share at the moment. "I'm impatient," I said and then grimaced.

Isaac's lips twitched again but I caught his eyes glancing out the hall to the front door. "You don't say." He watched me for another minute. I crossed the room as if I might find something on the other side of it to distract myself. He sighed and came to me, reaching his hands up to dig tension out of my shoulders. "She'll be fine. There's not an exam Gwen could throw at her she wouldn't ace at this point. It's only the first semester."

"It's not that," I said, waving my hands through the air between us before stuffing them back into my pockets. I leaned forward and he wrapped his arms around me, a small surprised sound in the back of his throat.

"Your father will…" he trailed off, thinking about our upcoming trip.

I stifled a snarl into his shoulder. "Not that either," I mumbled.

I didn't want to think about *what* my father would have to say about Joanna. *To* Joanna. And I would happily put off thinking of it until the minute we stepped off the train in Dannsedge next week. Maybe not even until we reached the manor, depending on whether or not my father sent a car for us or met us at the station.

"You've got me stumped, Pike," Isaac said, softening the flat tone with a kiss on the side of my throat.

I rolled my forehead over his shoulder for a moment, trying to shake off the anxious feeling, before pulling away.

"It's our…our first showing, as a coven," I said, shrugging. "Tonight, at Aiden's concert."

Isaac raised an eyebrow up at me. "Oh really?" he asked. "What was dinner at The Cup and Dagger last month? Or all those picnics on campus."

"You know what I mean," I said out, huffing a breath.

Isaac's whole face stiffened for a moment before relaxing and I knew the tell too well. He was resisting the urge to roll his eyes at me.

"It's an event," I said, my voice rising in volume as if that might make me sound more reasonable. I knew it didn't. "An event with school governors and our colleagues and-"

"The local elite, yes," Isaac said, and this time he did let his eyes roll. "Why should that bother you?"

"They all know what Joanna has done, how…how rare she is." Because when it was clear that there was no one in Canderfey who could *write* magic, we'd sent feelers out through Enmaire. And while friends of friends had heard the term Scribe, no one knew one. One other than Joanna.

"Do we really measure up?" I asked.

Isaac groaned, long and loud, his arms releasing me completely as he reached a hand up to rake fingers through his hair. "Don't you dare start that," he said pointing a finger at me, eyes wide. "You've been spending too much time with Joanna. Is it contagious? This- this whispering little voice asking about being *worthy?*"

My face felt hot and Isaac sighed, glaring at me out of the corner of his eyes. The hand in his hair came down over his face, dark strands following as he scrubbed the frown away, gathering a deep breath.

"If you think you're any less rare," Isaac started before interrupting the thought. "Or Aiden for that matter. Have you ever met another Aiden? Oh gods, now it's started in my head. Poor me, a measly painter with a coven of precious jewels."

A snort escaped me. I backed up to the couch and collapsed into the cushions. "Oh, fuck you," I said, the words entirely half-hearted.

Isaac grinned at that, prowling forward like a cat. He pushed my shoulders back and I grunted as he landed roughly in my lap, knees around my sides. He kissed me hard on the mouth and I let him hear my groan of relief in exchange for the distraction.

"Everyone at the concert will know how lucky we are to have found Joanna," Isaac purred against my lips. "Just as, while we listen to him play, they will know how lucky we are that Aiden waited for us. Just as you and I both know how lucky we are to have each other."

"Mmm, that's very sweet," I said, a smile growing wider at the smug fullness in his cheeks.

"Yes, well, if I hear you mention a single hint of insecurity in front of Joanna tonight I will be considerably *less* sweet," Isaac said, before taking another hard kiss, his teeth snagging over my bottom lip. "Honestly, the pair of you."

"She *should* be back by now," I said, glancing out the window.

"Has she written?" he asked.

I hummed, shifting to reach my back pocket and Isaac slid off my lap to my side. I pulled a small notebook out, the leather cover impressed with the four-pointed knot sigil for Coven. They had been her idea, a set of four notebooks, one for each of us. She'd written on the insides, *For every word written, Every word appears inside,* rotating the words across each of the four notebooks so the inside cover of mine said 'every word' in her spiky script. And it worked. We had a little way of communicating with each other, like students passing notes throughout the class time. I flipped past pages of our handwriting, questions about meals mixed in with tantalizingly intimate promises.

Been captured.

I coughed on air and Isaac leaned over to read the page, laughing.

By Hildy. No ransom yet. Please send help. But not before six-thirty this evening. And then a little lopsided heart.

"If Hildy has her then we'd better spruce up," Isaac said, patting my chest and rising up from the couch. He held his hand out. "Come and shower with me, take the edge off."

I stood up at that, the suggestion was enough to chase away any lingering nerves. But I preferred Isaac's more hands-on methods if he was offering them.

⸭

Isaac and I were dressed fine enough to impress even Aiden—mostly in clothes he'd purchased for us as gifts—as we crossed the street and made our way to Woollard's coven home. Our breath filled the air in white puffs and the last falling leaves before winter crunched under our feet.

I'd always found it interesting that with covenmates like Bryce Gast and Hildy Samanta, the group had taken Gwendolyn Woollard's name. The university knew what a prize they had in their head librarian but in most circles the name was unknown, missing the social weight of the other witches in the family. Even Ito, loath as I was to admit it, was a fairly familiar… character. Respected, believe it or not.

I understood it a little better now. When I'd found Aiden and Isaac, I'd looked forward to throwing over Pike for King, Aiden's name being the obvious choice. Now I wondered what he might think of our coven taking Joanna's last name. Not that she had offered it, not that she was ready to think about marriages and coven names. Not that she was likely to agree, given her habit of shying away from any recognition. But I liked the idea of being known by her name.

Isaac knocked on the door and Bryce opened it as if they'd been waiting for us.

"You're in trouble," they said ominously, one pale eyebrow arched and sharp like a razor.

"How do they look?" Hildy called from deeper in the house.

"Tasty," Bryce said, stepping aside to allow us entry.

"You look very elegant," Isaac answered. He'd taken Bryce's word as a compliment. I thought it might have been a threat.

"Yes," Bryce said, smoothing a hand down the intricately embroidered overcoat that framed their thin limbs. The black fabric was covered in green and russet feathers and talons, birds swarming and devouring themselves down to where the hem skimmed the floor. It was a tight fit, buttoned down to Bryce's narrow waist and flaring out to reveal pants that clung and glimmered like scales.

"Like a predator," I added, and Bryce grinned widely at that.

"Don't flirt," they warned and I held in my nervous laugh.

"Come now, Hildy. Quit torturing the girl," Gwen called up to the stairs, her arm linked with Tatsuo's as they came down together, matching in a velvet blue so dark it may as well have been black.

"Torture?" Hildy squawked. Her head appearing around the corner, long black curls hanging over a jewel-studded shoulder. "I'm doing her a favor, as her friend."

She disappeared as Tatsuo answered, brow furrowed. "You told her she was doing *you* a favor." He glanced back at us to add, "Hildy has designed a new collection for the shop and Joanna is playing model for the evening."

Hildy 'hmph'ed from the top of the stairs, stunning and regal in emerald, gold vines crawling up the bodice of the dress, blossoming into glittering flowers at the neckline. "Yes, well, favors are much nicer when they're tidy and rounded out, I think."

I lost track of the conversation after that. Isaac too, if the sharp intake of breath was any indication. Joanna appeared at the top of the stairs behind Hildy, her hair pulled into a dark crown of braids around her head, leaving her neck long and shoulders bare. Her expression was terrified and stricken and for a moment all I could do was hunt through the house, sending out tendrils of magic to search for whatever threat had her frozen like an animal caught in a predator's gaze. And then I grinned. It was the dress. She was terrified of the dress.

The bodice stretched in a straight line across her chest and around her arms, sleeves fitted snugly down to her small wrists. Sky blue and gold flowers fluttered down the pale yellow fabric like they'd been caught up in a breeze. Joanna was gathering the skirt up in her hands like she was afraid at any moment the fabric might disintegrate at her touch. In her defense, it did look especially diaphanous. Isaac nudged me as she took a few careful steps down, bright blue shoes peeking out from under layers of skirt.

She grabbed our outstretched hands gratefully when she could reach them, cheeks bright. I wondered if Hildy had wrestled Joanna into the dress or if the older woman had a trick for coaxing our covenmate into following her lead. Would she teach me?

"You are a work of art," Isaac said, his thumb brushing over the back of Joanna's hand.

My tongue went gummy instead of gallant and all I managed was, "Stunning."

"I'm afraid to breathe," Joanna said with an anxious laugh. And she sounded winded as she added, "Or move."

"It's charmed against little accidents," Hildy assured her from behind us. "Of course, if someone were to *intentionally* rip it, I would expect them to be prepared to purchase."

I smiled up at Joanna after the warning and her cheeks turned another shade darker of pink. I didn't want to *damage* the dress, but I could almost guarantee that when Aiden saw her in it, he'd be determined to keep it for her. Hildy was probably expecting as much.

"Behave," Joanna growled at me as she reached the floor. Isaac and I bumped into one another in our efforts to keep her close.

"Why warn *me*?" I asked.

"Because," Isaac answered under his breath. "Every time you two are left alone in a room together, suddenly something starts crashing."

Joanna and I grinned at each other, unrepentant, and I bent my head to nip at the curve of her neck.

"Don't you dare leave a mark," Hildy snapped and I sighed, my breath raising tempting little goosebumps on Joanna's skin.

Tatsuo brought over a brilliant blue velvet coat and passed it to Isaac to do the honors of sliding the fabric up Joanna's arms and over her shoulders.

"Come on, darling," Gwen coaxed, as Bryce herded Hildy to the door. "We don't want to be late and miss the good seats." Over her shoulder, to Joanna, she added, "I want to see King's face when he spots you in the audience."

Joanna's nose scrunched in an uncomfortable little grimace, lips firming. I wanted to kiss her, to smear a little of that lip stain, darker and richer than she usually wore, onto my mouth. But I was fairly sure Hildy would let Bryce take a chunk out of me if I did.

"How was the exam?" Isaac asked, settling our arms crossed over her back so she was snug between us.

"Gwen went too easy on me," Joanna said, shrugging and then startling at the way fabric whispered against her skin.

"Never in my life," Gwen snapped from ahead of us.

I stepped ahead of my covenmates so we fit through the front doors to leave the house, Joanna's finger's linking with mine. Two open carriages waited on the street in front of the house, with smartly dressed drivers and horses whose black coats gleamed.

"Are those for us?" Joanna whispered to Isaac.

"It seemed silly to hire cars for such a short distance, but we're not walking through campus dressed like this," Hildy called over her shoulder.

"She doesn't trust me not snag my hem," Joanna said under her breath. After a pause, she added, "Neither do I."

As Woollard's coven filled one carriage I turned and lifted Joanna into ours. Isaac and I hesitated, looking at the bench seat, and then Joanna smiled at us, placing herself in the center and patting either side. It was a squeeze to fit the three of us but it was worth the closeness.

Three months together and the impulse to keep near, stay in the spotlight of her affection, had yet to fade. At least I wasn't alone. Isaac and Aiden orbited around Joanna as much as I did, the three of us drifting through the house together to find where she had landed. And we hadn't worn out our welcome yet. She leaned into my side, pressed her knees to Isaac's and twined her feet with his under the skirt of her dress.

"Gwen wants to keep me up in the staff library," Joanna said and I craned my neck to catch the hint of a curve at the corner of her mouth.

"That's a very good position," Isaac said, his hands over her legs as she played with the buttons on the cuffs of his coat sleeves.

"Mmm," she hummed, nodding.

"Have you thought more about focusing on study?" I asked.

Isaac and I held our breath to give her time to answer. We both had opinions. I thought she should be enrolled at Canderfey, learning as much about magic, *her* magic, as possible. Isaac agreed but was afraid she would either end up adapting her skill to one of the more familiar magical focuses or leaving the University in search of someone who could really teach her. Part of me thought she should, but I knew how easy it would be for me to follow her. I wasn't sure how Isaac felt and I had a guess about Aiden. He wanted to be settled, building our home up and starting a family.

"I have," Joanna said, the words very slow. I reminded my shoulders to stay relaxed as I waited. "Gwen thinks that there are texts she can hunt down through the University connections that might help me. I don't know that I want to make it an official thing but I would like to study independently. Make my own coursework to follow and pursue."

"There are advantages to the University's introductory structure," I said, on reflex. Isaac raised an eyebrow at me in warning and I swallowed the rest of the words down. I'd sworn to myself that I wouldn't push or try to influence her, but the nudges slipped out when I wasn't careful.

"I know," she said, and she reached an arm back to stroke at my jaw. "Luckily I have three wonderfully talented and intelligent professors in my coven." She still said the word 'coven' like it was a word she never expected her tongue to learn. "They should be able to help me round out my education."

Isaac looked pleased, lifting her hand up from his sleeve to kiss at her palm. I felt a little nervous. Joanna had asked me to teach her how to tuck things away into invisible little pockets of space, an old charm I'd found when I was a student. For more than a month we'd lost one penny after another and hundreds of notes of paper in the effort. The lessons usually ended with her huffing away, frustrated with herself, or at least one of us naked in the effort to distract the other. She had small victories with the task now, keeping writing utensils handy, but resisted my efforts to practice with more challenging items.

"If not us, there would certainly be colleagues willing to help," I said, thinking I would rather be her lover than her teacher.

"For nothing?" she asked.

"The whole campus is curious about you, what you can do." I regretted saying it as soon as I saw her grimace. Worse, we were pulling up to Edelsburg Hall, a crowd of faculty, donors, and the local elite milling outside the massive double doors.

And sure enough, at the sight of two horse carriages, all eyes turned to greet us. Isaac glared at me briefly before stepping out of the carriage and reaching back to help Joanna out. She fussed with her skirts, head down as the chatter started around us. I slid my arm across her back and Isaac linked her arm around his elbow.

"Just be Hildy's model for the evening," Isaac murmured against her ear.

Joanna straightened at that, chin lifting. Bryce crossed in front of us, grinning too white teeth at the onlookers and making stares skitter away. The dragon's preference for Joanna was occasionally nerve-wracking. Joanna seemed as unafraid of Bryce as their own coven was and she was probably the only other person who could claim as much. But as an ally, Gast was undeniably effective.

Joanna's smile brightened at the way the crowd parted for Bryce and then us and for that alone I was grateful.

I checked our coats and we made our way into the theater. Joanna's neck stretched as she gazed up at the marble columns surrounding the circular room, vast domed roof glowing with theatrical candlelight above us.

"Aiden will you tell you all about the acoustics later," Isaac told her as she twisted in step, studying the celestial paintings covering the ceiling, the ivy carvings that climbed the columns, the intricate tile swirling over the floor.

"Does he play here often?" she asked as we led her up to the rows of reserved seating for family at the front of the auditorium.

"A couple of times in the school year," I said. "Lots in the summer when most of the students are away."

She hummed, eyes searching the stage where half-rings of seats were set out, a massive piano waiting for Aiden under a warm spotlight. "The campus will be so quiet then," she said.

Generally, I preferred the school year, the full classes and busy schedule. But I found myself looking forward to the summer holiday now. We could take Joanna away, to the sea or up into the mountains. She had an endless list of places she had never been and her coven had the urge to spoil her. Aiden had done as much in the early years with us. Taking Isaac to all the museums in Rhodantis, the capital city, and filling him up on the finest foods. Dragging me out to the middle of nowhere, a cottage on a small lake, and teaching me how to rest and lose myself in the music of crickets at night.

I ached, wishing we were going anywhere other than Dannsedge for the winter solstice. The North was undeniably beautiful in the winter, but my father's home was harsh and cold regardless of grandeur.

Joanna pulled me into the seat next to her, brushing away bitter thoughts. I kissed her bare shoulder again as Hildy and the others took their seats in the row behind us. I would have to tell Hildy later how much I liked the cut of this dress, leaving so much exposed to touch, although I doubted she'd bothered designing with me in mind. Joanna turned her head, the tip of her nose against my cheek.

"I missed you today," she said, just barely audible as the room began to echo with the bodies arriving to fill the seats.

I beamed at her and reveled in the way her eyes lit up at my smile. I'd forgotten this newness, the neediness of falling in love. She brought my hand into her lap and twined it together with Isaac's and hers.

"Now you have a month to get sick of us," I said, feeling strangely giddy at the prospect.

"Speak for yourself," Isaac muttered from her other side.

She hushed us as the firelight ringing the room from above dimmed and the lights from the stage glowed brighter. The Canderfey Orchestra filed out of the wings, instruments in hand as they found their seats with quiet rustling and the dull plucking of strings. When they had settled under light applause, Aiden appeared.

Joanna's breath caught in her throat and she squeezed our hands. I couldn't blame her. Aiden was a powerful figure, drawing the stage lights into his dark skin until he shone with them. His black suit fit perfectly, hugging at massive shoulders, nipping in tight at his hips. Only the three of us knew that he'd gone back to the tailor three times to get it exactly to his liking, and I smirked at the thought. He was vain but I didn't blame him. He was stunning; graceful and animal all at once.

He stopped at the center of the stage in front of the piano and his eyes found us immediately, heat sharpening their richness until it felt like an actual touch on my skin. And it wasn't just Joanna his gaze fell into. It was the three of us, his coven. Finally together and here for him.

2

———

JOANNA

I FELT LIKE I WAS DANCING, WEAVING THROUGH THE CROWD OF PEOPLE in the lobby, hunting out one of my covenmates. Preferably all three if I could catch them together. Eyes watched me as I slipped between two groups of conversation, voices hushing as I passed and I lifted my chin a little higher. I was Hildy's model tonight, not the witch who hadn't known she was a witch, and who'd released an ancient being to terrorize the city.

I'd also had, very thankfully, several glasses of fizzy, tart alcohol and was feeling rather lovely. And a little dizzy.

I floated past another group, not really paying attention to who was around me, only knowing vaguely that I was looking for one of my men. An arm circled around my waist and pulled me back, and I lifted one foot to slide, careful not to spill a drop of my glass onto the gauzy skirt of my dress. Hildy's dress. Our dress.

"Joanna," a voice purred in my ear and I shivered, twisting in his hold.

"Aiden!" In the back of my head, I thought, *Oh, you sound ridiculous,* but Aiden looked so pleased it didn't matter. I rose up on my toes, leaning into his chest, and stole a quick kiss, smiling at the rosy hint it left on his mouth. "Hello," I crooned up to him.

"Hello, darling," he answered, squeezing me closer. I snuggled into his side and felt him shake with a little laughter. "Joanna, you know Margery and Ethan Dagwood. And this is Pablo Banaker, the concertmaster."

I grinned at the Dagwoods, musicians I'd met through Aiden, and then the other man. He'd been the first chair violin and played a soaring duet with Aiden whose fingers flew across the piano keys during the concert.

"It's wonderful to meet you," I said.

"I've heard so much about you, Miss Wick," Pablo said, reaching out a fine-boned, strong hand. I shook it and he held on. "Aiden's coven is very lucky to have found you. What an extraordinary talent."

Aiden stiffened slightly in my hold and the Dagwoods, familiar with me and my reticence to discuss my own magic, glanced at each other. But I had lost my filter for shyness a glass ago.

"Oh, thank you," I said, voice too bright. "I'll have you remind them of that when I'm being 'charmingly impossible.'" I smiled up at Aiden, delighted to find him blushing, dark skin coloring richer. Those had been his words for me. "Have you seen the others? I want to gather you all together."

"We could find them," he said. "Why?"

"Because it would make me happy," I said.

Aiden's blush faded under the warmth of his stare and he bent, pulling me up to my toes to catch my lips again. "Then that's what we'll do. Excuse us," he said to his friends before I took his hand and dragged him blindly into the crowd.

"I don't know whether or not to take that glass from you or fill it higher," he said, catching up to me.

"Neither," I said, rising up to my tiptoes to see over heads. "I like where I'm at just now."

"And do you know where you're going?" he asked, a laugh in the back of his throat.

"Instinct."

Aiden made a skeptical sound as I wove erratically through the hall, heading closer to the front doors by way of long zig-zags across the room.

"Ah, there!" he said, pulling up me short and turning me, pointing over the crowd.

I saw the bright gleam of Callum's hair, like burnished gold and copper under the lights of the chandelier. When the crowd parted for us Isaac appeared at his side and I ran ahead of Aiden into Isaac's arms.

"Oh, hello you," Isaac said, grinning back at me.

"Oh, hello," I parroted.

"How many times did Bryce refill your glass?" Isaac asked. "You're looking rosy."

And now that he mentioned it, my cheeks did feel warm. I'd blame the packed room over the mead Bryce had been sharing with me. "When are we going home?" I asked, ignoring his question. "I can't stay in this dress much longer without disaster."

Isaac's hand skimmed down the buttons laying over my spine. "Then we'd better get you home."

"I'll go hunt down the others," Callum said and kissed my shoulder for the hundredth time that night. "Find out where those carriages went."

"No," I said, spinning in Isaac's hold to catch at Callum's sleeve. "Hildy swore she wouldn't be ready to leave for hours. Isaac's office is just down the row. We can use our shortcut."

I had written a portal from Isaac's office closet door to my bedroom door at the very beginning of our relationship, my first conscious spell. When I had finished really moving from my little University-provided housing and into the coven house, the portal had moved too. The magic didn't care where it had started, it only looked for the room I considered mine. And right now I was looking forward to being back in that room. With my coven.

It still gave me a nervous, happy thrill to think the word. Coven. I'd grown up in the quiet countryside *knowing* I was dull and nearly magic-less, never expecting to come to a place like Canderfey. Absolutely never imagining to find a coven.

I'd been *wrong*, and it was wonderful.

"Shortcut it is," Callum said, lifting up the brilliantly blue coat Hildy had loaned me for the evening.

"I'm already warm," I said.

"But it's snowing out," he argued.

"Oh!" I looked through the doors and saw the snow floating down through the black night, landing on the walkway and melting away in a moment.

I turned and let him help me into the coat but caught his hands before he could draw away. I wrapped his arms around me, soaking up the glow of heat that always seemed to hover at his edges, and leaned back, arching my neck so I could kiss underneath his jaw. He swallowed, neck flexing against my cheek, and looked to Aiden and Isaac for help.

"There are people in this room who have never seen Callum blush before," Isaac said, grinning at us, leaning into Aiden's side.

"Turnabout is fair play," I murmured into Callum's skin. "He loves to make me blush."

Aiden snorted at that and started leading the way through the doors. Isaac stole my glass from my hand, downing the remaining contents in one swallow as I squawked a protest. Callum all but lifted me from the floor as he swept us both after Aiden.

"Am I being embarrassing?" I asked as we hurried down the steps.

I let the words go quiet under our feet but Callum squeezed me closer. "You're being too adorable to share. And now that you've mentioned undressing we're all a little impatient, as nice as you look."

"Why have we never given her apple mead before?" Isaac asked cheerfully.

"Because it'll leave her with a wicked headache," Aiden answered. He took my hand as Callum and I reached the sidewalk and Isaac brought up the rear.

"I drank all five Terrence boys under the table when I turned twenty," I said, as clipped as I could, which was not very at this point, words muddling on my tongue.

"I hope you left them there," Callum muttered under his breath.

"All but one," I said, beaming up at his surly glare. Out of the corner of my eye, I saw Isaac wink at me from behind.

When the coven had first approached me about how they felt—like I was their missing piece—I'd thought Callum hadn't really wanted me. Now I knew better. His affection was rare but it was also ferocious. He'd been worried about scaring me off just as much as I'd been worried about disrupting his harmony with the others.

Now that affection appeared easily and often, tempering into something sweeter as we found our footing as a group. But sometimes it was fun to tease him and find that anxiously possessive interior.

When we made it to the Burgess Building, Callum scooped me up off my feet.

"There's ice on the stairs," he said.

I considered pointing out that him carrying me didn't make either of us *safer* in that case. But since the snow was still melting as it hit the ground and our coats, I let his excuse remain an excuse. Also, my feet hurt from the shoes Hildy had put me in.

Isaac ran up to his office ahead of us with Aiden, unlocking the door. By the time Callum made it there with me, I could see the red glow of the fireplace from my bedroom pooling out of Isaac's tiny little closet door. Callum set me on my feet and I locked the office behind us before we squeezed through the closet and into my enormous room on the top story of our tower house on the other side of campus.

I shut the door and from inside my room, it looked just as large and welcoming as usual. That was my favorite part of the spell, that a doorway could be a sliver on one side of my portal, and wide enough to let Isaac and Aiden through together on the other side.

There was scratching from the bottom of the door, a small black and white spotted paw appearing from under the gap, and I opened it again.

"Oh don't let the dust balls in," Aiden groaned as our three cats tangled their way into the room together, the orange tabby crawling over the other two to reach me first.

"You love them," I said, crouching down to scratch between Molly's ears. "Oh, you little pests! No claws."

Callum shooed them away from my skirt and then picked me up again, carrying me over to the bed where Isaac was kicking off his shoes, already out of his jacket and vest.

"Look at all these buttons Hildy's left us with," Callum said to him.

"Don't tear it," I said. "I can't afford it."

"I can," Aiden said joining us at the edge of the bed. His fingers went for the buttons, pulling them free of the delicate loops with deft care. "But I'd rather see you wear it again than tear it off."

The others left the bed and my eyes drifted shut, leaning back into Aiden's touch. "You were wonderful tonight," I murmured.

"I was, wasn't I?" he said. His breath was warm on the back of my neck and I grinned up at the beams on the ceiling. He wasn't even joking. He simply knew how talented he was and wasn't interested in balking or feigning modesty. "I was happy to see you in the audience."

"I'll always come to see you play," I said.

"Mmm, I know," he hummed, and I shivered as his lips landed softly at the top of my back, slightly damp as if he'd just licked them. "But it reminded me that you're here now. We've found you."

The last button, low on my waist, fell loose, and Aiden's hands swept the fabric forward, sleeves sliding down over my wrists. His palms caressed up my ribs and then around to cup over my breasts, drawing me back to his chest with a gentle squeeze of his fingers.

"They've gone to get us water and feed your little beasts," he murmured, kissing my jaw and ear and cheek as he spoke. "Do you want to wait for them?"

The warmth of mead that had landed in my head and cheeks now sank like a weight to where he held me in his hands, into my belly and down into my hips, making me clench on nothing. I both loved and hated that feeling, enjoying the needy urgency but missing the feeling of having one of my lovers inside of me more.

I pulled his hands loose and stood, wobbling on the soft mattress, Hildy's silken, airy confection of a dress falling free of my hips into a puddle on the mattress. I turned, stepping out of the fabric, and Aiden stared up at me like I was a queen.

"They can catch up," I said, fighting the giggle in my throat.

Aiden grinned, smile bright against the depth of his skin, and he lifted the delicate dress up from the bed, and moved it into my closet for safekeeping, out of the reach of tiny claws or urgent lovers. He shrugged out of his suit coat as he crossed back to the bed and as soon as he was within reach, I caught him by the collar.

"I said I didn't want to wait." And then I pulled him sharply down onto the bed with me.

Aiden let out an 'oof' as he landed on the mattress, but he was ready for me as I crawled up over his chest, my thighs around his hips.

"This is a lovely little contraption Hildy's fitted you into," he said, snapping at one of the ties of the garter belt.

"It would be if I knew how to get out of it," I admitted. But I thought he would like it, they all would, and I purchased it directly.

"I happen to have some practice with these," Aiden said, looking meek for being two hundred pounds of muscle and man trapped beneath me.

"Then put it to use," I said.

I bent forward, drawing his full lip between my teeth to worry and nip. My fingers rushed clumsily over the buttons of his white shirt, pulling the dress collar free and tossing it away from the bed. Aiden hummed under me, breaths hitching as my mouth trailed after my hands, mapping my favorite planes of his skin.

By the time I was scooting farther down his thighs, to open the front of his trousers, he'd only managed to loosen the ties holding up my stockings. It would do. I watched his expression still as I left my work half done, the dark coarse hair of his groin peeking out from his waistband, his erection pushing the buttons and plackets aside with its stretch. I shifted to one knee, pushing the silk and lace underwear down and nearly toppling to the side. Aiden caught my waist in his hands, holding me steady with his eyes fixed to the skin I revealed. I shimmied one leg free and then Aiden moved me, balancing me to shake the other loose.

"Lift your hips," I told him.

It was clear on his face, eyes wide and mouth parted on heavy breaths. I had such power over him like this, catching him by surprise and pushing my pursuit before he could get his bearings. His hips rose up off the mattress, nearly carrying me up with them, and I pulled his pants down, gathering them down to his knees.

"Joanna," he groaned.

I pressed the bare skin of my sex, opening already wet and leaking, to the length of his cock. I wrapped my hand around the base of him, stroking myself against his heat and hardness, prepping him to fill me up. His head fell back to the center of the bed, feet dangling down to the floor and I watched his stomach tremble and clench beneath me, muscles flexing, resisting the urge to steal the control.

"Be good," I warned him. He huffed, eyes peeking open to narrow playfully at me.

But when I lined him up at my entrance and sank down in slow, steady bounces, we both sighed gratefully. This stretch. I was addicted. As much as I was addicted to the sudden strike of passion that hit with Callum and the depths he could reach inside of me. Or Isaac's patience and care that undid me.

I heard the bedroom door open again when I'd seated Aiden fully inside of me. He gave me a soft smile, with just an edge of smug boasting, and I wiped it off his lips, rising and falling swift and hard. He groaned, back arching and hips bucking beneath me. I heard Isaac's laugh from the other end of the room but I was busy chasing pleasure. My skin felt too hot, stretched too tight, and I braced my palms against Aiden's chest, giving my body the leverage to lift and plunge, every stroke of him inside making the motion smoother, slicker with my arousal.

Callum landed naked on the mattress next to Aiden, quickly swallowing up his moan with lips and tongue, one of his hands reaching out to cover mine over Aiden's heart. I watched them kiss, timing my rhythm with Callum's thrusting tongue until Aiden was squirming in the sheets. Callum paused when I pulled my hand free and then I listened to the moans chorus together as I wrapped my fingers around Callum's cock and squeezed myself around Aiden's.

"I'll charm her headaches away," Callum rasped, panting into Aiden's neck as his hips kicked into my hand. "Apple mead suits her."

Having them close suited me. Having them whimpering at my touch felt like the strongest magic, an orgasm careening closer with every second.

When Isaac's warmth was at my back I slowed, putting that moment off, and grinning at the way Aiden's forehead knotted in frustration. Callum's hand wrapped over mine, trying to force my grip tighter, faster, but I wiggled my hand loose.

"I want all of you," I said, turning my head so Isaac's nose nuzzled to my cheek. I hissed as I felt his hand sliding between the cheeks of my ass, one chilly and slippery finger nudging at the tight ring of muscle hidden there.

"I was hoping as much," he said. A hand reached up to my throat, bowing me backward to his mouth. He licked at my lips and Aiden nudged himself softly into me, distracting me from the other intrusion, a gentle finger coaxing its way in from the opposite side, the touch slick with oil.

I'd begged for this early on, but with the first careful effort I'd realized *wanting* wasn't going to be enough. My body needed preparation and I needed to chase away any lingering nerves.

But there were no nerves now. And Isaac had been working me up for months. When I tensed with the excitement, his fingers brushed over my pulse, reminding me to relax. I grunted as a second finger joined the first. Aiden was thick inside me, barely moving, but this was a new kind of fullness. The heat on my skin erupted into beads of sweat and I breathed into Isaac's mouth.

"Bend forward," he said, swiping a wet lick over my lips once more.

Aiden's arms lifted up to embrace me, and I moaned the whole way down to his chest, every inch of movement a new sensation inside of me. There was a burn, but it was a heat outside of pain and more centered around awareness. Everything from my scalp to the soles of my feet felt sensitive. Callum shifted, starting to move away, and I caught my hand around the back of his thigh as he knelt up.

I needed something to distract myself, something to focus on before I floated off in feeling. He shuffled closer and I lifted my head. My ears sharpened around the sound of his stuttered cry as I took him in my hand again and brought him to my mouth, lips tucking around my teeth and tongue stroking the underside of the tip of his cock.

"Gods, Joanna, that's-" The words died fast on his tongue as Isaac began to pump his fingers inside of me and I muffled my cry around Callum's tender skin. His hands reached out, fingers shaking as they reached out to help support my head, careful not to demand.

I was happy to be loud around him, happy to have somewhere to send the fiery energy of Isaac at my back and Aiden pumping softly inside me. I thought I might explode when Isaac added another finger, just the hint of raw pain sneaking in. I sucked at Callum and he twitched under my touch, trying to hold off, trying not to force. But then Isaac's fingers drew away and the tip of his cock replaced them.

I pulled my mouth off, my head falling heavily to Aiden's neck, and Callum's fingers followed, combing through my hair and soothing.

"Oh god, yes," I whispered, and Isaac took it as his cue to slide deeper in. He was smoother than his fingers had been, no knuckles to stretch and snag, and I found myself moving into the touch, rolling my body between his and Aiden's.

"Fuck," Aiden hissed around clenched teeth. He bucked hard into me and for a moment everyone went still and quiet. Then Isaac groaned and sank in completely. "Fuck, this is better than- better than I ever thought," Aiden groaned, his whole body hard and tense beneath me.

They had never done this with anyone else. I smiled into his skin, and then pushed down onto him, Isaac drawing back an inch or so. When I drew off Aiden, my spine arching up into Isaac, Aiden chased me.

"I can't- I can't," he stuttered.

I lifted my head to find his eyes wide, nostrils flaring, looking almost scared.

"Finish," I told him, already imagining what it might feel like. For me, for Isaac. What Callum would feel like replacing him. I felt starved for this. The bright heat under my skin had turned into a wonderful, boiling feeling, traveling fast through my blood and singing all the while.

His hands clasped my hips as Isaac's arm wound around my shoulders. Isaac drew out of me a little, giving Aiden room. And then my beautiful, elegant, polished man turned frantic and desperate underneath me, hips slamming noisily up inside of me as he grunted, chasing release. Isaac's thrusts were shallow and slow in response, his face tucked against my neck, breaths uneven. Every time they nudged together inside of me, barely separated by the barrier of my body, they both lost their breath.

Aiden pulled my hips in, and then he was striking against the front of me and I was shouting and thrashing between them, his hot spill filling me as I came.

Isaac's teeth were tight on my shoulder as I settled, his body tense and still over my back, like he was holding off, afraid to follow us. I kissed over Aiden's collarbone as his chest heaved beneath me. Callum was watching the three of us, his hands fisted in the sheets, and thighs ready to spring. Isaac or Aiden would have to move to give Callum room to join us, and I wasn't sure either man was capable.

When Isaac's bite loosened I tapped at Aiden's chest, pushing up on my hands. He grunted and opened one eye, looking dazed and shattered.

"Callum's being patient," I said, kissing his chin.

Callum was *barely* being patient. He looked ready to rip me out from between them.

Aiden sighed. He and Isaac lifted me, Isaac hissing as we went, still rigid inside of me and making little aftershocks bloom brightly in my blood. Aiden wiggled out from under us and Isaac trembled around me with every movement. Callum was fitting himself under my shaking legs as soon as there was an inch to spare for him.

"That was torture," he murmured, leaning forward to catch my lips. His hands smoothed over my hips and then behind, over Isaac's ass, and I had a stifled grunt of warning before Isaac was tight against my back and we were both hovering over Callum's lap.

"I won't last long," Isaac warned him.

Callum hummed, looking down between us to where Aiden's release was dripping out of me. He pulled me down in one long, smooth drop.

Isaac and I both cursed. With all three of us sitting up, Callum and Isaac were nestled closer together, the friction zinging through me with every breath one of us took. The hairs of Callum's groin scratched against my swollen clit. I drew up again, just a few inches, and Isaac followed me with a whimper, barely moving.

"I'm close enough as it is," Callum said, leaning back on his palms. He thrust up into me and stars flashed behind my eyes.

Isaac held me upright, arms so tight I thought he might have been hanging on for his own sake as much as mine, as Callum surged up from between our legs. With every little nudge of Isaac inside of me, Callum was pushed against my front walls, dragging himself over the most sensitive spots. And with every lift, Callum made sure to grind his pelvis against my clit.

I was making obscene sounds, the wet slap of bodies against me, but also wordless begging noises, more wild creature than woman. Every snap of Isaac's hips was more urgent, and also farther apart like he was trying to stave off a finish that was chasing him just as eagerly. I gripped his arms over my chest and let my body take from the both of them, unable to find its own part to play in the pass and take of my hips between theirs.

Isaac came first with a shuddering moan in my ear, and he pressed us both in against Callum's chest before releasing me and falling to the side on the bed. Callum pulled me tight against him, movements turning fast and hard now that there was no compromise to be made. I twisted against him, keeping my clit striking hard with every drive of his hips.

One hand clasped tight around the back of my neck as I came

again, drawing my shout into his mouth. And then Callum had me flat on the bed, our chests sticking together with sweat, arms clinging to my back. He buried himself once, twice, and then a final time hard and high inside me, coming with a yell and his neck arching for me to take with a biting kiss.

At first, I thought the slow drum was my heartbeat, ringing in my ears. Then I peeled my eyes open, my body crushed under Callum's, and tilted my head back to see Aiden. Clapping. And grinning, stretched back against the headboard.

"That performance might just have exceeded my own at the concert," he said.

Callum made a rude gesture, rolling off me to the side and then cuddling me close, apparently disinterested in moving us higher up on the bed.

"Well done everyone," Aiden said, and Isaac snorted, still catching his breath.

3

———

CALLUM

I woke up to the rattle of the train on the tracks and Isaac's elbow nudging at my gut; the pressure warning me it was time to go find a restroom. I sat up and I found myself pressed between Isaac and Aiden, who had rolled to fill the space Joanna abandoned. I scrubbed my face and looked out the window, finding that yesterday's stretching fields and meadows and forests had transformed into craggy hills, frost blue trees battling for ground with monstrous, twisting roots that jutted up out of the snowdrifts.

I climbed off the end of the fold-out bed, Aiden grumbling as I went and both he and Isaac rolling in again. We'd piled together like this every night when the three of us first got together. Over time those nights had grown rarer. There were times when we all needed our space, when the tension of not finding our fourth grew too tight.

I slept better like this, even with thin train mattresses that could barely hold us.

I dressed enough to be halfway presentable, it was barely dawn and the rest of the passengers would have to excuse me. After the restroom, I went in search of Joanna.

She was alone in the observation car, body leaning into the

255

window as her eyes bounced over the country, soaking in the gray light and the fog lining the valleys like blankets.

"Too squished in our car?" I asked her.

She reached her hand back for me without tearing her eyes away from the view. I took it in mine and let her pull me down the bench, wrapping my arm around her waist and nestling close against her back. A red fox raised its head to watch us pass, and then scurried down into the roots of a tree.

"Too much I've never seen before," she answered. She lifted our hands, knotted together, to her mouth and kissed my knuckles.

I softened against her, resting my cheek on her shoulder. These familiar shapes and horizons left my stomach tangled, reminding me of my mother...and my father. We'd be pulling into the station soon and there'd been a warning bell ringing at the back of my head ever since we stepped onto the train.

"We could get off at the next stop," I said, only half-joking. "Travel around this part of the country. It's cold but-"

"If that were an option, we never would have agreed to go to your father in the first place," she said, tearing her eyes away from the window to twist and face me. "We have to get this out of the way, don't we?"

I opened my mouth to disagree, staring into her bright brown eyes, and then shut it and swallowed. "Eventually," I admitted, the word weak in my ears.

Her smile was thin, but she leaned up and I met her halfway for a gentle kiss. "Then we'll do it now. I want to see where you grew up."

I thought of Joanna in the manor house and winced. It was too cold for her, I was afraid all the stone and dark would sap up her warmth.

"Is there a library?" she asked, tapping over my chin with her fingers.

My smile grew slowly at the question. My little bookworm. "One on warfare," I said.

Her eyebrow rose. "Magical warfare?"

I scratched my fingers through my hair and nodded. "I took a lot with me, but there are still plenty left. Probably in my room where I left them."

My father was a powerful witch but he preferred the crash of weapons and thunder of cannons to any spell. "There's a stable, too," I said, distracting myself. Searching for the pieces of the manor I wanted to share with her.

"Oh, are you going to take her *riding?*"

We craned our necks to find Isaac and Aiden joining us, Aiden's hands wrapped around a mug of steaming tea, eyes still half-lidded.

Isaac's eyebrows were arched at me and I blushed. "If you do," he continued. "I'd like to join you."

"You left me out last time," Aiden grumbled, the words stringing together. "Bastards."

"What kind of riding are we talking about?" Joanna asked. I wondered if I'd ever mentioned the way that dry snap of her voice got my cock stirring when she was teasing me.

"There was bucking but I never sat on a horse," Isaac said, taking the window seat opposite Joanna.

"Poor lads were getting desperate," Aiden said, landing heavily next to Isaac in a slouch, stretching his legs across the space and propping his feet up on either side of Joanna's lap.

"Desperate?" she asked.

"My father..." I stalled and Isaac filled in for me.

"Doesn't approve of me and Aiden."

"Why not?" she asked and all three of us smiled at the way she sat up straight, words sharp enough to cut.

"We're men," Aiden answered smoothly, lips quirking up to one side.

Isaac turned his grimace to the window and Joanna stared at all of us, color high in her cheeks. I started to feel bad for my father or worried for her, not sure who might win in a battle of wills.

"There was a bit of a Pike tradition of...wives. Wives and sons," I said. "Obviously, I broke that tradition."

"It's a coven," she said, almost a whisper. "It's not as if you...choose."

I chewed at the inside of my mouth, staring down at where our hands were still twined together.

"Duncan, Callum's father, chose a new wife after Callum's mother died," Aiden said. "Not for the coven but-"

"For himself," I finished. "One of my brothers, Ivan. He chose too, I think. There were soldiers in his regiment...they felt like a coven when I met them. But he's married with wives now."

"That's terrible," Joanna said. "That's so..."

"Asinine," Isaac snarled, making the word sound much ruder than usual.

"Well yes, but I was going to say sad," she said, snuggling deeper into my side. I wrapped an arm over her shoulder gratefully, tucking my face into the top of her hair, still messy and curling from sleep. "Covens belong together."

Our eyes met over her head, each of our expressions filled with warmth at her words. She'd tried to run from the coven, more than once, and every reminder that she was here with us, *staying*, was another balm over the initial wound. I checked on Aiden, knowing his parents and their coven had split households, but his eyes were soft on her face.

"Will he be relieved we have Joanna?" Isaac asked. "Or more frustrated now that we're complete and you're stuck with us?"

I felt Joanna's head tilting back to look at me and I turned my face to the window. I'd been asking myself the same questions since receiving his first summons in the mail, and I still wasn't sure.

"I don't care," I said, wishing it were true.

EVERYONE WAS silent in the car that picked us up from the station. The driver stood out front, cranking the engine into life again. The cold was proving too much for the machine and I wish my father had sent a carriage instead. But he liked the show of wealth, sending a car when no one else in Dannsedge could. The car roared and rattled back to life and the driver rushed into the front seat.

"Just a little ways more, Sir," he said.

Joanna was still drinking in the scenery, but her fingers played impatiently in the fabric of her skirt and I could see her jaw working in her cheek as if she were already preparing the words she would need to tear at my father. Aiden had taken Isaac's hands in his, both of them looking out opposite windows.

Every familiar curve of the road, every hanging tree branch I remembered climbing, made my heart pick up a beat. We were close to the Vermenian border and the forests were turning dense again with evergreens, winning the fight against the rocky terrain. I started to create a list in my head, trails to show Joanna, landscapes to explore that would keep us out of the manor and away from my family. And I *did* want to take her riding, not just hide away in a stall of the stables no matter how tempting it might be to lay her down in the hay up in the barn eaves.

Which was a distracting enough thought to keep my mind off how close we were to the manor. Joanna gasped at my side and we all turned toward her as the low hedge appeared from around a bend. An enormous, dark, stone fortress squatted in the snow and fog at the end of a dragging lane lined with hawthorns, their sharp talon branches rising high into the sky, thorns glittering with frost.

"That's a castle," Joanna said. "You called it a manor."

I smiled in spite of the dread pooling in my stomach. "We'll take you to see a castle someday."

"It's a beast of a house," Isaac said, nudging her knees with his. "Suiting its owner."

The driver coughed in the front seat, hiding a laugh.

Joanna's fidgets grew more urgent as we turned up the lane, the driver on the other side of the little partition apparently unaware of our general anxiety as the car rumbled over the stone. But Joanna's nerves gave me something to focus on, and Isaac and Aiden chose the same, drawing ourselves up in our seats. I knew the visit wouldn't be a pleasant one, but we would do what we could for her. Shield her or distract her from my father's derision of our coven, my family's sour curiosity and judgment.

"I changed my mind," she whispered as the car pulled to a stop in front of a set of stone steps better suited to a giant's stride than her small tread. "Let's go traveling."

My smile flickered until the front doors swung in, my father—grayer and more weathered than I remembered—bracing them open as if to invite in the cold.

"We'll take one hundred vacations before we come back here," Aiden promised her, and then he opened our own feeble little car door and stepped out, shoulders back in a challenge.

He's shrinking, I thought, as we traveled up the steps. I could never separate the bellowing, fearsome giant of my childhood with the reality of my father now that I was a man. He was a few inches shorter than me, making up for it in width, but now the weight of strength had turned into the weight of rich food and drink. The fire was going out of his hair and turning to ash, a bright streak still running down his chin like blood. The stony gray spark of metal crashing still flashed in his eyes, though, and I forced myself not to flinch as I met his gaze.

We'd almost reached the top step when the downturned snarl of his mouth twisted strangely. For a moment I thought he was baring his teeth.

That's a smile, you idiot, I realized.

"Joanna!" My father let the doors swing wide and behind him, his wives shivered and drew their wraps tighter.

Joanna stiffened as he grabbed her up from the last step and embraced her like a daughter. Aiden made a strange choking sound from ahead of me and I wasn't sure if it was laughter or shock or both.

"You've no idea how long I've waited to meet you," my father said, grasping Joanna's arms in red hands and holding her back. He made that grimacing smile again as if it might charm her. Joanna's shoulders were high, hands fisted, and I couldn't see her face. Whatever the expression was, it had his smile faltering and his hands dropping away again.

"How do you do, General Pike," Joanna said. I hadn't heard a cold clip like that in her voice since the day she rejected me after our first kiss, rejected the whole coven. I nearly flinched. And then something proud and warm bloomed in my chest and I stepped up to Joanna's back, my palm wrapping around the curve of her waist. Aiden appeared on her right and Isaac just behind my left shoulder.

"Father," I said, and the word fell out of my mouth without any meaning. "It's good to see you."

"Callum," he answered, still staring at Joanna like she was meant to be some spoil of war I'd brought home to boast of. Something to make him proud. "Come in, come in. The women are waiting, likely whimpering in their little dresses."

I might have heard Joanna's teeth grind.

My father's wives stood at three points of the entrance hall. Margaret, Ivan and Thomas's mother, was to the left, arms folded over her chest with an expression of endless impatience. The same she'd always had around any of the children who weren't her own. Beryl, James's mother, stood at the right, with a flicker of a smile for me and my coven, waiting on the tips of her toes for the whole charade to end. Ahead of us, on the grand staircase up into the wings of the house, was Robin, the young woman my father had swept home with him after my mother had died. She stood with her hands on the shoulders of two young girls with honey blonde hair, their bodies shying away into their mother's skirt.

Joanna's expression softened for them as my father made the introductions, their names Leona and Emily, and they studied her like she was an exotic bird. What had he been saying about her, why the warmth in his greeting? He caught her again by the elbow, ignoring Isaac and Aiden entirely, and pulled her across the room to the portrait of his father hanging over Beryl's head.

"There are two rooms waiting for you up in the east wing," Margaret snapped to me. "Your brothers are down the hall." And then she swept away.

"Two instead of three," Aiden mused, his eyes tracking Joanna with my father.

"Can't decide if it's an improvement," Isaac added.

"It's an insult," I said, stuffing my fists into my pocket.

Joanna's face was uncharacteristically blank as my father tried to entertain or to charm her, I wasn't sure what his aim was. Only that his effort made me uneasy. When I looked at Aiden and Isaac I knew I wasn't the only one.

"Welcome home, Callum," Robin stuttered from the steps.

"Good to see you, Robin," I said, trying not to let my face show how little I meant it. I didn't dislike Robin, only the way her marriage to my father had made my mother's death feel like an afterthought. But she was so young and had just started working at the house. She was still barely older than Joanna.

When I caught her daughters peeking out from behind her hips I tried to smile, "Hello, girls."

"Hello Uncle Callum," they said together.

"Brother," Robin hissed, cheeks flaming.

I cleared my throat, the awkward thought making me queasy, and swung away from them, crossing to Joanna.

"Are you tired?" I asked, cutting into my father's tale of my grandfather's firm hand, as if the older generation's cruelty might make his own bad parenting seem generous by comparison. But I could hear the pride in his voice and Joanna looked somewhere between bored to tears and ready to scream.

"Exhausted," she said, leaning into me—away from my father.

"Of course you are," my father said, clapping his hands together, and then he grinned to add to me, "She's a delicate thing, isn't she?"

"Like steel," I said, snapping my mouth shut before any more sarcasm might sneak out, afraid of punishments I'd grown out of decades ago.

My father's eyes narrowed and I could hear the crack of discipline echoing in my own head. "I've given you and Joanna your old room," he said. He glanced over at Isaac and Aiden but said nothing.

Joanna was rescuing herself, crossing the hall in quick steps to our covenmates but I stood, swallowing bile and anger and rough words, even as my father was following Beryl down the hall to his study.

"Coming up?" Isaac asked. He looked calm as if he either didn't notice or didn't care about every possible slight my father could come up with in a span of five minutes.

"In a minute," I said because even if he didn't mean for me to, I could see the lines at the corner of his lips where he tried not to frown, and the higher than usual tilt of Aiden's chin. Joanna's eyes were wide, calling for me to join them. "You know the way?"

Aiden nodded, gathering up our cases from the front door and stopping by my side to kiss my cheek before trudging up the stairs.

"Don't bother," Isaac whispered.

I wanted to tell him, tell all of them, that I knew it wouldn't work. Nothing would change my father, he was an immovable mountain and his prejudices were piled as high. But that didn't mean I wanted to accept his dismissal of the men I loved, or his covetousness of Joanna. Instead, all I managed was an awkward shrug and heavy steps down the dark hall after my father.

Beryl was leaving his office as I arrived and she hurried to shut the heavy oak door behind her, stopping with her hands behind her back, still wrapped around the handle.

"Hello, cub," she said, smiling and staring up at me. I wanted to erase her wrinkles, smudge away the gray in her black hair. Remember her always as the towering guard of the classroom, the only wife my father trusted with his sons' education.

"Hello, bear," I said, my lips curving up. I bent to kiss at one of her cheeks, rounder than when I was a boy.

"Whatever it is, you won't win," she said, nodding her head back and raising an eyebrow.

"I know," I said, nodding. "But what am I to them if I don't try?"

Her cheeks grew rounder with her smile and I knew I was making the right decision. "For what it's worth," she whispered, "I like her. Maybe not as much as Aiden, but we'll see."

I stifled a laugh. "I'll let him know to watch out for his spot of honor," I said.

Beryl released the door and patted my arm as she left me in the hall, heading deeper into the house toward the kitchen.

I raised my fist to knock and then flexed my fingers out, taking the handle and turning it without announcing myself.

The room was just as I remembered it, dark stained wood and weathered green leather furniture, too worn at the edges now but what he was accustomed to, so it would not change. The windows facing out to the drive were nearly shuttered behind deep red curtains and the only light was a dying fire in the hearth and two lamps lit at either end of my father's desk.

He looked up from the map spread wide over the flat surface, a stack of correspondence close at hand, and cocked his head at me.

"Shouldn't you be seeing to your pretty little Scribe?" he asked, humor lining the tone.

I stopped just inside the door, the word sinking in. "Scribe. Is *that* what this is about?"

His face froze for a heartbeat and then he leaned back into his armchair, exhausted boredom taking over, drawing down that strange smile he'd been wearing back into his usual frown.

"Is what about?"

"This whole *show*, for Joanna. I can't remember ever seeing you hug anyone before, certainly not one of our covenmates," I said crossing my arms.

He sighed, bracing his hands at the edge of the desk. "They're very rare, you know. And powerful from what I've heard. You did well in finding her."

My insides turned to stone, a harsh flame rising up my spine. Magic, I realized, heading in the wrong direction. I tamped it down and said the first thing I could think of that might discourage him, or at least set him straight.

"We didn't know about her magic when we realized she was our fourth. In fact, we thought she wasn't really a witch at all."

His expression soured a little more. "What is the point of this, Callum? Are you disappointed that I am pleased with you?"

I gaped at him, even as I scrambled mentally. In a way he was right. His greeting was far and away better than anything I had expected from him. So much so, it left me nervous, angry even.

"I'm not asking you to be pleased, not about Joanna's magic," I said after a slow breath, trying to find a way through the riot of emotions in my head. "I am...not unhappy that you were so welcoming to her but, Father, there are two more in my coven. Can't you extend them *any* courtesy?"

"They are guests in my home, they eat at my table, they drink my wine," he rattled off, rising up from the chair. "Whatever your romantic notion of a coven is, whatever *choice* you've made with those men, with Joanna, it is your business. I owe them nothing."

"We sleep together," I said back, lips snarling over my teeth. "At home, we share *one* bed. If you want me to believe that you gave *Isaac* and *Aiden* a separate room out of the goodness of your heart you must think me very stupid."

"Oh pile together then, what do I care?" he shouted at me. "Sleep with your men and leave Joanna in peace. Where you put your cock is nothing to me. There's a war coming and you're too busy fussing over bedding to look at the damn map in front of you and see what's coming."

I clenched my jaw tight and glanced at the desk, Vermenian orange blocks piled over the map at the edge of their border with Enmaire. The imaginings of invasion played out with colored wood chips, like a child's toy.

"I don't think there's war coming," I said, voice going quiet as his knuckles turned white around the desk ledge. "I think you wish there was, you'll always wish for one. But even if the armies are gathering, I'm not going to stand at your side and make you look good to your superiors this time. I had enough of that last time."

His expression was as hard as stone for a moment and rather than feeling as if I'd won, as if I had struck him, I waited for the inevitable blowback to knock me down again. When he cracked it was with a great roar of laughter, falling back into his seat again. It didn't matter that I towered over him, I felt as small as the little boy who had offered compromise as a solution to his battle puzzles decades ago and been mocked for the suggestion.

"Oh to be a young man again," my father said, with that grimacing grin. "As if it were you and not me who lead campaigns, gained ground for the country, fifty years ago. As if you had put the ribbons on my uniform before you were even a thought in my head. You had one war, Callum. I've slept in the military's bed for half a century."

"Your best marriage," I said, without thinking.

As a boy, that kind of comment would've gotten me a belt across my ass but now my father only shrugged, a slight nod of acceptance. "I do love war, it is my trade," he said, eyeing me shrewdly. "But I am not a fool. I know the patterns. I know Vermenia's armies as well as my own. They are *moving*."

I swallowed and drew up my covenmates' faces in my mind, forcing away the memories of war.

"You shepherded eight sons through your armies and five are still alive," I said, thinking of the way Joanna's fingers clutched at my shoulder while she slept. "There are three who would still follow you again. You don't need me."

"You know as well as I do they are good men in combat, but they offer very little to strategy. I don't care if you never step foot on a battlefield again, but Blackthorn and Merchant are staying here for the holidays-"

"You're hosting *generals* for the holiday?" I said, not entirely sure why I was surprised.

"As well as Sabine York and her coven. And tomorrow evening, Ambassador Carras arrives," he continued as I covered my face with my hands as if it might erase the lunacy of this visit. Not just generals but war heroes and the Vermenian Ambassador too.

Strategy. He called me here under the guise of family unity for the Winter Solstice. It gave him a chance to curry favor with Joanna and set me into position at a dinner table with all of his military cronies. I had spent too much time worrying about him mistreating my coven and not enough time planning my counter moves. *Defend*, I thought.

"Just listen tonight," he said, making an awkward effort to coax. "Drinks after dinner and a bit of chat. After the women move on to their pianos and cards."

I swallowed down my next comment. Aiden and Isaac would be

expected to leave with the wives, with Joanna. At least in this, I envied them. Sabine York and her coven of soldiers would no doubt stay at the table.

But it would keep Joanna out from under father's nose for an hour or so and it might be a bargaining chip.

"Treat my coven with respect," I said. My father grunted, looking down at his desk. "Use their names, introduce them when it comes to it, don't pass over them like you did earlier."

"Very well," he said, waving an irritated hand through the air.

Too easy. He may have slighted them in the first place, expecting me to ask this. I'd been teaching strategy and battle for too long and forgetting how to use it.

"I'll listen," I conceded, turning to leave.

"She *is* valuable, Callum."

I froze, dread trickling down my back like ice. "I'm very aware of this, father. But I think you misunderstand what makes her so precious."

My guts were churning and my heart was hammering too hard, heat rising up my neck into my face as I crossed the room to open the door and swung it shut with a snap behind me. I'd accomplished what I'd set out to, in seeing him, but I couldn't help feeling like somehow I had still lost my position in the process. I needed to play chess again, but he had always been my best opponent.

I took an old shortcut to the upstairs, rushing through the kitchens with my chin ducked low, and sneaking up the service stairs to my bedroom floor. I tread softly past Ivan's room, not wanting another reunion, especially not from a brother who still lapped at our father's heels like his word was law.

I heard Aiden's laugh echoing from inside my bedroom and I released a sigh that had been strangling in my throat. When I opened the door, I stopped short in my steps. Off to my left, where previously had been a double bed, barely wide enough for Joanna and I to share together, was now a monstrous sleigh bed, so wide it left my corner lamp tilted against the wall, and trapped my childhood dresser shut.

Joanna giggled, propped against piles of pillows at the headboard with a book covering her smile. Aiden lay sprawled across the center of the mattress, Joanna's feet propped on his stomach as his fingers dug into her arches. Isaac's head popped up over the frame at the end of the bed, his hair rumpled and his smile full. In white chalk above Joanna's head read the words *This bed is big enough for Callum's coven.*

"You wonderful genius," I said, the strain of nerves bleeding out from between my shoulders. "But that's even larger than ours at home."

"I didn't have a ruler handy," she said, with a shrug. "But I think we should leave it as is. Let them sort it out after we leave."

"Our solstice gift to your father," Isaac said, falling back into the mattress as I hoisted myself over the frame to land in their pile, collecting a bit of touch from each of them as I relaxed.

4

JOANNA

It was the most obscenely long dinner table I had ever seen and yet every available inch was filled; with candles and wreaths of evergreen and food still steaming from the kitchens. Every possible seat was in use too, as if Duncan Pike had planned his holiday dinner not to fill his house with family, but to fill his table with an audience. A king staring down at his collected subjects, lined on either side of his table.

Beryl sat on his right, with Callum at her side. Margaret sat to the left of the head of table, sticking me between her and the eldest son Ivan, and the pair of them took as little interest in me as they possibly could. Far down at the end of the table was Robin, and I wasn't sure if I was jealous that she had Aiden and Isaac at either side of her, or relieved for all three of them to be so far out of range of Duncan's demands. My covenmates coaxed shy and surprised smiles out of the quiet woman and every so often Isaac looked back up, through the maze of platters and winter floral arrangements, to catch my eye and share that peace.

Between us all, were the sons, the wives, and the militia. Just as I looked at one man, whose auburn hair was streaked with gray, and thought it must be Jordan the second eldest, I'd see another and think

I must have confused them. Who was Thomas and who was James and which of the women in fine but modest clothing was married to either of them? It was dizzying.

The only person I could name with any certainty sat to Callum's right. Sabine York, Enmaire's infamous warrior who'd taken Vermenian General's heads as trophies during the Red War. Even knowing that she was a woman, I'd imagined her as someone ferocious and masculine, muscular and gruff.

She was exceptionally beautiful, and I felt like such a silly idiot for my surprise.

Her hair was chestnut ropes, knotted together at the top of her head, darker than the fawn brown tone of her skin, like earth baked under the sun. Her eyes were heavy-lidded, the color a surprisingly light hazel and freckles smattered over her wide nose. For all her beauty, there was no disguising the power of the body under the glossy drape of black silk. Her arms were wired with muscle, shoulders broad, and body lithe but structured.

She met my distracted gaze over the top of the table, lifting a goblet of wine to her lips as she watched me scramble to look away. Her coven, scattered in the seats down the line of the table, were equally imposing and equally handsome, but they faded to a backdrop behind her in the hall before we gathered for dinner. She was their commander and for that alone, I think I liked her best of all the strangers I'd met in this house so far.

"York," Duncan said, mid-chew around his still bleeding steak. "Have you had much trouble with the boys in the barracks? Getting them to follow your lead?"

Sabine's stare traveled up the table as she lowered her drink and she swallowed slowly, her fingers clenching around her dinner knife.

"No," she said, and then she turned back to her plate, spearing a roasted carrot with her fork.

Duncan waited a beat and then nodded, blinking at his own food, Margaret and Ivan both humming with senseless agreement on either side of me.

Callum's leg stretched beneath the breadth of the table to rest his foot lightly against mine, his toe twitching against my ankle. We hid our flickering smiles behind our glasses.

No, Sabine was my favorite because she seemed to not only openly dislike Duncan, but to actually make him uncomfortable. I glanced at her again, wondering why she'd come to be part of his collection in the first place.

I had a sneaking suspicion what my part to play was. I hadn't decided if I was relieved that it seemed to have nothing to do with me being the only woman in our coven.

"What is the part of the teaching you enjoy most?" I asked. Was it possible to draw the woman out at all?

Margaret and Ivan, who'd held pieces of a conversation over the top of my head for the better part of dinner, stopped their words to stare at me. Beryl looked up from her lap where I had a sneaking suspicion she'd hid a book to read. Callum's foot nudged affectionately at mine and he leaned back in his chair.

Sabine stared at me for a long moment and against my other cheek, I could feel the force of Duncan's stare.

"I like flipping them onto their asses in front of all their friends when they think they can best me at training," she said, a faint notch of a smile appearing on her thin lips.

I grinned at that and a throat cleared down the table. One of her coven, a scarred, red-headed, giant of a man named Samuel, leaned forward from my side of the table, his eyes fixed to her face.

"Her favorite moment is when they've trained hardest and can win against her," he said. I hadn't heard him speak before and his voice was soft, a whisper that carried even over the last bubble of conversation in the room. "She knows she's done her work for them then."

Neither Sabine nor Samuel smiled at each other, but there was an intensity in their eyes as they watched each other that was more intimate than if they had stretched across the table to kiss.

"High advertisement indeed," Duncan said with an imperious nod, barreling through the warmth of the moment. "York's one of the best in combat you'll ever be lucky enough to see."

"She *is* the best," said another from her coven, Geoff, who kept his blonde hair shielding his face as he hunched over his plate.

If the words ever reached Duncan's ears he made no expression to show it.

With every dish that arrived, Callum grew a little more agitated. He'd tried to convince us that joining his father and the others was an easy decision. 'It'll keep him peaceable and there's really nothing I'll have to contribute,' he said with a shrug as we'd all curled together on the oversized mattress I'd spelled.

But he shifted in his seat at the table, glancing up at the clock that hung over the fireplace behind Duncan, shifting the bites of a dense chocolate cake around on his plate. I tapped back at his shoe and he offered a crooked smile that faded too fast. By the time the meal was finished, I could feel the vibration of the wood underneath Callum's bouncing leg.

His father stood first, pulling out Margaret's chair and Callum was quick to follow with Beryl. I nearly jumped out of my own chair when Ivan started to pull it out for me.

"You'll take our wom—our guests to the drawing-room for drinks," Duncan said to Margaret, glancing down the table at my other coven-mates, the men who would not be invited to sit in on military talk.

Margaret answered as Callum left a swift kiss on Beryl's cheek before rounding the table to me. I pressed my hands to his chest as he cupped my elbows.

"Would you like us to assemble a rescue campaign?" I whispered once Ivan was out of earshot.

His smile flickered again and he tilted his head down for one brief, brushing kiss. "Not necessary…yet. Keep Isaac and Margaret apart," he added in his own whisper.

I nodded, taking my orders and hurrying down the length of the table to take Aiden's arm where he was waiting for me. Isaac was just ahead of us, leading Robin into the hall.

The manor was cool at night, our feet scratching over old carpeting and still the chill rose up from the floor. I leaned into Aiden's side and he bent his head to me.

"How's he doing?" he murmured.

I glanced behind us to find a trail of the brother's wives, too many to keep straight. "Dreading it," I said back, just as quiet. "Do you really think his father's trying to get him back in the army?"

"Definitely," Aiden answered, as we entered a parlor dense with brocade and velvet furniture and thick carpets, with a roaring fire going in a hearth that took up the majority of the left wall.

"Will Callum listen to him?" I asked, glancing up into Aiden's face before being distracted by the painting of a brawny god who held fainting women over his thick arms. I wrinkled my nose at the painting. It reminded me too much of its owner, as if it were painted to suit Duncan's ego.

"He would say no but...I'm not sure," Aiden said, frowning. "There's more influence there than he'd like to admit."

I pulled him with me to the armchairs and loveseat taking up a corner by a set of grand bookshelves. Isaac had already seated Robin in the chair closest to the fire and I was quick to pull him and Aiden down on either side of me, pressed close together on the love seat.

"Miss us?" Isaac asked, stretching his arm out over the back of the couch, running his fingers over the back of my neck.

"I did," I said, even though he had meant it as a joke. The gentle smile that appeared in answer was my reward.

"I'm always glad to be placed at the end of the table," Robin said. She added in a lower tone, "Duncan puts the fun people down there because he doesn't have a sense of humor and he hates for anyone to see that he doesn't get the joke."

A little shock of laughter burst out of me before I could catch it but my covenmates just grinned as if they had learned as much about Duncan in the past.

"It suits me fine to be left out of the important talk," Robin continued. "I never understand it anyway. And oh, Sabine York gives me the shivers. She'd put me off my cake for sure."

"Really?" I asked. "I think I might like her. And her coven."

"They're so surly," Aiden said, brow furrowing.

"But they don't pretend not to be," I said. "Not even for our host."

"You know," Robin said, leaning forward. "They aren't really *her* coven. Her coven died in the Red War."

I gasped, quiet and sudden, the suggestion of such a loss enough to make me snatch up Aiden's hand where it rested between us. "That's awful."

"Mm, it's very sad," Robin agreed, but her shrug was careless and she leaned a little farther forward. "What's worse is she replaced them, with men from other people's covens. Stole them right out of their homes."

My brow furrowed. I thought of the way Sabine's eyes had locked with Samuel's, the way Geoff had growled with pride and defense.

"Covens break sometimes," Isaac said to me, glancing over my head at Aiden. "Not often but it's not unheard of."

"But it isn't the coven that breaks," Robin insisted, with an irritated twist of her lips.

"She collects warriors."

All four of us looked up to find one of the wives—and I really hoped someone would clue me into *which* wife it was before I embarrassed myself—falling into the other available armchair near us. Behind her, the rest of the family had gathered around a table together to play cards.

I chewed at the inside of my lip, trying to guess who she might be.

"Aiden, Isaac, good to see you back again," she said.

"Valerie," Aiden said with a nod and a squeeze to my hand as if he knew what I'd been waiting for.

Valerie Pike, wife of James who was the son of…Beryl, or at least that's what I was guessing for now. She was fairly glamorous—a pile of fire-red hair curling atop her head, and wearing a shimmering rust-colored dinner gown I would have saved for the party tomorrow night. No doubt she had something even better planned.

She smiled faintly at me, but it didn't strike me as sincere while her eyes were busy picking me apart from head to toe. "Are you concerned about her pulling Duncan out from under you?" she asked Robin, while still studying me. The words had a nasty twist to them and I didn't think for a minute they weren't intentional.

Robin only snorted though, "Not in the least. Think James might catch her eye?"

Valerie's gaze released me and I realized after that my hand was wrapped too tight around Aiden's fingers, and Isaac had pressed his knee to mine to offer support.

She rolled her eyes and said, "James is hardly a warrior, though I suppose he's alright with a hunting rifle. The bank suits him much better. No the only one who really needs to worry is Joanna, I think." She smiled at me as if it was a compliment. "Callum *is* a prize."

Isaac laughed. "Luckily we all know firsthand just how bad Callum is at talking to women," he said, his shrug brushing his shoulder against mine.

"I'm sure good looks and his reputation will hold more enticement for Sabine York than any conversation," Valerie said, with false sweetness strong enough to make my teeth hurt.

"I'm sure the prospect of Duncan as a father in law may hold an equal but opposite influence," I said, instantly regretting the words as silence struck our little corner.

Robin broke first into a fit of giggles, covering her grin with her hand. Aiden's shoulders relaxed at my side as Valerie's facade of a smile cracked into something a little more genuine.

"She does really seem to hate him," Valerie agreed, and I liked her much more when she wasn't feigning friendliness. "And he pretends not to notice because she's so powerful and it makes him look more impressive to know her. I wonder when she'll lose interest in insulting him at his dinner table."

"Hopefully not before the holiday is up," Aiden said and Valerie laughed brightly, giving him a blinding smile.

"Val, come and be our judge," another wife called from the card table.

Valerie huffed from her seat, but there was a hint of smug pride in her smile as she rose and left us.

"She loves to make people anxious," Robin whispered to me. "When I first had Leona she came to stay for weeks constantly 'reassuring' me that Duncan wouldn't mind a daughter. Unfortunately for her, she was right. He takes his pride from his sons but he dotes on the girls when no one is watching. They'll be good for him if he ever decides to retire."

"I suppose being the newest, I expected to be a part of the holiday entertainment," I said, trying to relax back into my seat.

Isaac's eyes were crinkled at the corner, just the hint of a smile on his lips, and I knew what he was trying to tell me, wordless and private. And I knew he was right. We had nothing to fear from Sabine York. Certainly not where Callum was concerned, who had only ever loved the three of us and in such a determined, fierce way as if loving each other came with knowing each other.

Also, he really was terrible at talking to women. I still read the majority of his feelings through the things he *avoided* discussing.

"Oh the real entertainment will start tomorrow when the Vermenians arrive," Robin said, worrying at her lip with her teeth. "Just wait till you see how civil we can all be," she said, making civility sound like warfare.

CALLUM'S CHEST rose under my palm with a deep breath and I blinked into the dark, the outline of his shoulder blurry in front of my nose. I turned my hand over and he was quick to lift his, linking our fingers together, his slow sigh brushing warm air over us.

I shifted carefully on the mattress, Aiden's arm over my waist falling away with my movement.

"Tell me," I whispered into Callum's ear.

He held his breath for a moment, and then looked to either side of us, his hair tickling at my nose. I saw the foggy gesture of his head nodding forward and we both sat up, slowly and gingerly to not wake the others. He climbed over the end of the sleigh bed and then lifted me to land soundlessly on the cold floorboards. I hissed and followed him on freezing toes over to the door I had taken for a closet, on the opposite side of the room.

It was even darker inside and I groped at Callum's back as he shut the door behind us and the blackness was complete.

Light flared over us and I winced, tucking my face between his shoulders as I adjusted to the glare.

"Sorry," he said, turning in my hold to wrap his hands around my waist. "Should've warned you."

I blinked slowly and found us in a long, narrow room lined with shelves loaded with books, naked spots where Callum had taken texts to Canderfey with him. A bare light bulb swinging above us cast eerie looming shadows up the walls.

"You turned your closet into a library," I said, studying the corners and feeling the seams where Callum had expanded the space.

He went and settled into an enormous armchair that looked in danger of one arm falling loose if not for the fact it was wedged between the shelves. I followed, folding into his lap and tapping lightly at the hint of a smile it granted me.

"I didn't want to wake the others," he said, keeping his voice low and wrapping his arms around my back.

He was wearing a pair of sleep pants I'd never seen him bother with before, but his chest was bare and I gave in to the urge to lean into it, curling against him. There was a dusty blanket over the back of the armchair and I pulled it loose, shaking it out over the floor before draping it around our shoulders.

"So what's going on up here?" I asked, kissing his temple.

He'd told us before bed that the meeting had been nothing, dull. Aiden, Isaac, and I had shared brief glances together but let the subject drop. If Callum wasn't expounding on a subject, then he was probably hiding something, but he'd come to the truth sooner or later. Except that he'd been lying sleepless even as the others fell into soft snores around us. And if Callum wasn't sleeping, then I was worrying.

"The meeting was...not nothing," he said slowly. His fingers gripped a little tighter to me so I shifted until I was draped close and soft around him.

"We sort of assumed as much," I said.

"I think…I think my father might be right," Callum whispered, head tilted back against the back of the chair to stare up at the ceiling. "I think Vermenia actually *is* making moves against Enmaire. Or preparing to."

Something inside of my chest froze at the words and I held still against him, a hollow white noise in my ears.

"There *are* troops gathering around the border and they aren't even disguising the fact. They've doubled the guard at all entrances and they've put it on the record as precautions against illegal international traffic," he said.

"What does…what does this mean?" I asked.

"If the people here are as influential as I think they are…war, probably," he said. "It isn't as if it's something they aren't looking forward to, and there's enough evidence to support taking action. At least preparation for action."

I chewed at my lip and Callum lifted his hand up over my shoulder to pull it loose and soothe it with his thumb, not even needing to look to know what I was up to.

"What does this mean for *us*?" I asked, stretching to meet his eyes.

He blinked at that and lifted his head, as if he hadn't started thinking of this yet. "I don't know," he said, and my heart sank. "I'm not going back to war," he added after a beat, and the words were firm enough to ease some of the terror that had struck at me. "It cost too many lives the last time."

Oh, I felt horrible and queasy. I knew what I needed to say but I was so afraid it might make him change his mind. I wanted to keep him away from any battles, safe with me, with our coven. But more than that, I hated the way the guilt from his youth still controlled his decisions.

I swallowed, reaching up to cup his face in my hands and hold his gaze. "You were very young and you'd been encouraged to win at *all* costs. But that doesn't make you any less a brilliant leader or strategist. I don't want you to go to war…but if your goal was resolution with as little loss as possible, I have no doubt you would succeed."

His gaze was brilliant on my skin and the uneasiness churning in me faded as I saw that a ragged edge had smoothed out of his expression.

"I hate that his opinion holds any sway over me," he said.

I combed curls off his forehead and he leaned into the touch. "Maybe someday it won't," I said. "For now...I trust your instincts to do what's best for you."

He smiled a little, "It's not me I want to do right by. The three of you mean more to me than anything. Joanna..."

He trailed off so I leaned down, pressing my lips to his until I realized he wasn't answering the kiss. I pulled back and found his eyes worried all over again.

"The way they spoke about Vermenia," he whispered, flinching. "It was vicious and crude and I couldn't stop thinking about..."

"My mother," I finished for him, nodding. "I knew they might."

"I said things like that while I was in the war," he said, still bracing for my anger.

"So did I, Callum," I said. "So did we all. I love you, I know what kind of man you are."

He exhaled a shaky breath, eyes lighting up with the words the way they always did, reminding me that I wanted to say it more often and to each of them. He drew me back down for a deep kiss, lips pulling but instead of our usual urgency there was something softer and searching. I sank into him, offering up every bit of affection I could, stroking my thumb over his jaw and running my free hand into his hair.

The door creaked open and Aiden growled up at the lightbulb.

"The two of you," he rasped as Callum pulled away with a last peck at my chin. "Always getting frisky with the books. Come back to bed and do that, it takes at least four bodies to keep the mattress warm."

Callum scooped me up with him, rising from the chair.

"Do you think we should tell your father I'm part Vermenian?" I asked as Aiden pulled the light's chain, dunking us into darkness again.

Callum nearly fell over, stubbing his toe on air.

"Only if you want him to decide he likes Aiden and me best," Isaac said from the bed with a throaty laugh.

"I do," I said, completely sincere. And then I shrieked as Callum tossed me onto the mattress, he and Aiden following shortly after until we were all a pile of laughter turning to sighs.

5

JOANNA

AFTER LUNCHEON, ISAAC BROUGHT ME UP TO A LITTLE ALCOVE IN THE attic, built up by trunks stacked around the large round window that faced down onto the front-drive. We watched as Callum and Aiden rode out with Callum's brothers for a short hunt and then settled into our respective work. I'd carried up a stack of reading I couldn't possibly get through but also hadn't decided in what order to attack. He sat in a small wooden chair with his sketchbook and pencils, across from where I was curled up in the belly of the window, legs crossed at my ankles and feet propped in the curve in front of me.

"You really are stunning, you know that?" Isaac asked, after an hour or more of quiet.

It took me another minute to pull myself out of the book and realize I had been his sketching subject during the quiet.

"I appreciate your bias," I said, looking back at him.

"It's not bias," Isaac said, narrowing his eyes at me, pencil pausing in his work.

"Oh, look," I said, watching a dark car pull up the drive to the manor.

"Don't play coy and change the subject," he continued, flicking a dark curl off his face.

"No! Really." I laughed, pointing out the window. "I think it's the Vermenians."

He joined me at the window for that, pulling my legs into his lap as we both pressed our noses to the glass. The car stopped, longer than ours had been, and loaded with an awful lot of trunks for just one dinner party. (At least to my mind, though Aiden would probably have disagreed.) At the very bottom of the window, I could see a warped view of Duncan, gray hair and red-streaked beard twisting in glass, waiting on the steps with his coven close at hand.

Ambassador Carras and a small party slid out of the wide door of the black car. He was a tall, fine-boned man who looked about Aiden's age, maybe a little older, with honey-colored hair that shone too brightly not to be charmed.

"Do you think that's his staff or his coven?" I asked, studying the small handful of people that trailed behind the ambassador, all crisply dressed in black coats and trousers.

"You know, I don't even know enough of Vermenia to say for sure that they form covens," Isaac murmured, craning his neck to look down at the procession.

"Neither do I," I said. And I wondered about all the things my mother might have told me about her home country. Had she kept them secret to protect us from Enmaire's animosity, or had it been easier to let go of the past when she could not go home again?

Ambassador Carras looked up from the steps below. It was difficult to tell through the thick glass if he was seeing us but I thought he might have been.

"It's strange that we don't know more about them," I said. "Or is it because we're southern folk?"

Isaac snorted, that was what Aiden and Callum teased us with. Two little country farm kid transplants in Canderfey. I was fairly sure they included Isaac in the teasing for my sake. He'd had plenty of time to adjust.

"It's because we've been fighting for borders for so long," Isaac said. "Although I imagine Callum knows more than we do. Maybe Aiden too, his fathers are both in politics."

"The hunting party is coming back," I said, pointing out the window to the left where a flurry of horses and riders were coming in, hats dusted with snow.

"We better start to get ready," Isaac said, with just a hint of mourning the end of our peaceful afternoon. "Before we get caught up here like naughty schoolchildren."

I'D TALKED Aiden out of buying Hildy's confection of a dress for me with a compromise of a few more practical dresses—some I would be less self-conscious about spilling or tearing or simply wearing. I picked out the most formal of the bunch for the evening; a sleeveless, dove-gray gown with a skirt that hung heavy from my waist and swished decadently around my legs as I moved.

I took advantage of the swish, moving through the crowded room with an intentional twist in my steps. I met Aiden's eyes across the room for a moment as the path to him cleared and he gave me a lazy smile, watching my hips as I tried to reach him. I carried a deep glass of wine carefully in my hand, although Isaac had promised he could get a stain out of anything—he'd had plenty of practice with his paints.

"Joanna, there you are!" Duncan caught my elbow and nearly put Isaac's skills to test, snagging me to his side and wrapping his arm over my shoulder. His face was red with good spirits, or the alcoholic kind, and his arm squeezed too tight, calloused fingers scraping unpleasantly over my skin.

Ambassador Carras stood in front of us, his hair even more obnoxiously bright up close and contrasting with the grooved wrinkles lining his face, nearly filled with powder. Sabine's third coven member Darin stood with the group, suntanned skin and dark hair like Isaac's, but quite a bit taller and broader. He took up the space around him with a kind of electric energy that seemed to vibrate out of him, something wilder than friendliness or humor. He nearly dwarfed one of Carras's staff, a smaller and younger imitation of the ambassador.

"What do you think of this, Carras?" Duncan said, yanking me closer again. "I've a Scribe in the family now."

"Scribe?" Carras said, staring at me out of round, black-rimmed glasses. His assistant, whose name I had learned before dinner and then promptly forgotten, glanced urgently between us but Carras appeared as if he had never heard the word before. Darin, one of Sabine's coven, just grinned. The expression was a tad too sharp, and I wasn't sure I'd seen him stop smiling since being introduced the night before. Perhaps he was more jackal than man.

"Very powerful magic," Duncan said and I ripped myself out of his grasp before he could jerk me again in emphasis. "She writes the words and they have to happen."

Carras blinked, his assistant looked terrified, and even Darin's head cocked the slightest bit to me.

"It's not really that straightforward," I said, grimacing. "Makes more of a mess than is helpful."

"Very good girl, too," Duncan went on over me. "Modesty's quite becoming in women."

I nearly said something very immodest in response when there was a light touch at the center of my back.

"Come with me," Sabine said, appearing between me and Darin in a dress that looked as if it were made of armored scales. She made the words sound simultaneously friendly and imperative. Or maybe I was just that desperate to be rid of Duncan's company.

I followed her away from the men, not bothering with a polite excuse or goodbye. She led me over to the leaded windows looking over the vast wilderness behind the house, the silky black reflection of a pond farther off glittering through the panes. It was drafty in this corner of the room but I was grateful for the chill burning off the hot irritation in my cheeks.

"As much as I would have liked to see what barbs you might have conjured against Duncan I thought I'd better rescue him instead," Sabine said.

My laugh was more of a small cough and I covered my face with my free hand. "I never would have imagined having someone pleased with me would be so infuriating," I said, shaking my head.

"This family is a nest of snakes," Sabine said, gazing over the room, and her tone was factual instead of hard. "And their wives aren't much better. They're all half hoping I find a way to steal their husbands out from under them. You're a pleasant exception."

She turned to stare at me but my guts had turned to stone at her words and I couldn't think of an answer. Somehow, even though I had thought the very same thing about the Pikes, it upset me to have Callum's family spoken of in that way. Perhaps because Sabine was a stranger and I felt no more comfortable around her than I did Margaret or Victoria, however much I appreciated the rescue from Duncan.

"I think Callum's mother must have been a saint," I said eventually. "He's nothing like any of the others from what I've seen. They don't do him much credit."

Sabine's eyes narrowed, studying my face with an almost tangible focus and there was a long silence before she spoke again. "You forget, I was in the war. I know a very different side of that man. My coven and I served under him."

The room carried on around us, but I was fixed to her stare, feeling as if we'd closed a door on the rest of the world. "Your...first coven?"

"Yes," she said, and there was no guard up against the ache in her voice or the pain at the back of her eyes.

The coven that had died in the war, serving under my covenmate who carried the guilt of the men whose lives he'd unknowingly bargained and lost in battles.

"Callum doesn't know," I said, not sure who I was telling.

She scoffed a little. "No, I doubt very much he does," she said. "He didn't bother much with us at that time."

I swallowed several times as my brain searched and failed for the right thing to say. It seemed a waste that I should have a magic so closely tied to using the *right* words when I never seemed to know what they were.

"I'm very sorry for your loss," I whispered. I bit my lip wondering if I could add to it. Callum was sorry for *every* loss. But that didn't excuse the past and it seemed wrong to present her with his pain when she was confessing to her own.

"So now I break up homes and covens," she said, turning back to the room, with false brightness in her voice.

"They seem very devoted to you," I said, because I couldn't tell how much she meant the claim. And whatever the gossip was, those men had chosen her as much as she had chosen them. They were as guilty as she was of any fracture in their previous relationships.

An edge softened on her face and she looked back at me. "I like good men at my back," she said.

I thought of my own coven and almost smiled. "I can understand that."

She was studying me and I tried not to squirm under the stare. My eyes found Callum, sitting in a chair tucked behind a line of his brothers. He was blocked off from the room, a book in his hands and a furrow on his brow. Whatever Sabine York thought, I knew what I had in Callum and it brought a fuller smile to my lips.

"I'm not sure they deserve you, truth be told," Sabine said, and I barely caught sight of her expression, predatory and curious before she pushed off the window and crossed in front of me on a path to Callum. Candles and firelight caught on the scales of her dress, making her look like a shower of sparks, and Callum looked up at her approach.

But his eyes slid past her to me and his eyebrows rose in pleasant surprise. He stood from the chair and even as Sabine eyed him, almost as if he were dinner, he dodged out of her way without a glance and joined me at the window. I wanted to laugh, to feel triumphant, but Sabine looked back at me over her shoulder and there was a smug satisfaction in her smile that held some kind of ominous promise.

"You're alone," Callum said, covering me from the room as he reached me. He ducked down for a firm, breath-snatching kiss. "How did you manage it? I've had to use cloaking spells the entire night."

I laughed and nestled close against his chest, looking over his shoulder and seeing a number of people spotting us in our embrace. We wouldn't be left alone for long. Sabine had found her coven and she was whispering in Geoff's ear, the lot of them gazing our way. I wasn't convinced she really wanted to catch Callum for her collection, not with the way she'd spoken about him, but she seemed to enjoy dangling the threat in front of me. Unfortunately for her, Callum was more than a good man. He was an obtuse one and notoriously unmoved by those outside of our coven. I didn't think she was up for the challenge.

I rose on my toes to kiss him again, even if the whole room was watching. Even if it did make damn Duncan Pike pleased with himself.

"What did I do?" Callum asked, voice a little dreamy as I pulled away. "I'll do it again."

"I love you very much," I said, because I had promised myself to do so more often. "But you're probably going to want to run, someone is coming to talk to us."

Callum skirted away with my lipstick smeared over his mouth, vanishing into a shadowy corner of the room where there were more books to hide behind. Ambassador Carras appeared just in time to see him disappear.

"Ms. Wick," he said, with a deep nod that I answered with one of my own. "I hope you don't mind my curiosity but...Scribes aren't very common here in Enmaire, are they?"

I raised my eyebrows at that, he'd acted as if he didn't know what Duncan was talking about earlier.

"We haven't found any," I said. "There's mention of them, but no one I've been able to speak to yet."

He nodded as if he'd expected that answer. "You see," he said, and his accent was a little clunky and careful over the 'ss', reminding me of my mother who lisped when she was agitated. "Vermenia has almost no magic to speak of and what there is we regulate quite strictly.

Scribes however, written magic, was once quite common in our country."

He looked pleased with my surprise and nodded as if I had said something. "Yes," he continued. "It's not like the magic of Enmaire which manipulates the world around the magician. Written magic is... creative, which is to say it creates, seemingly from nothing. You sound as if you might be one of those rare witches who conjure directly from their words. It was a very revered kind of magic, but the trait died out years ago."

"Died out?" I asked, feeling something freeze in my chest.

"Decades ago, maybe over a century," Carras said, his gaze fixed to my expression. I tried to stay blank, offer him nothing, but I needed to know more. "The Scribes were Vermenia's best defense. There was no battle we could not win if they wrote it. Of course, then they were captured and killed. Our leaders were too confident in them, and not careful enough. They began to vanish after that. The good bloodlines were lost in those wars. We coveted those who remained until they too were lost. I haven't mentioned any of this to General Pike, yet."

"Oh, please don't," I rushed to say, feeling dizzy in the wake of all the new information. "I'm not- I'm really more of a...a Scribbler. My writing hardly ever works the way I mean it to."

He stared at me for a beat and then he grinned, revealing a set of perfectly even and perfectly white teeth. (I wondered what kind of magic he had to aid so well in his vanity.) He laughed a little.

"That is not a word we use for the magic in Vermenia but I like it very much," he said, with a little shrug. "And it suits your modesty, as General Pike would say."

There was a burn in my cheeks, both of embarrassment and anger. Damn Duncan Pike. Although Isaac might almost approve of him if my new hatred of 'feminine modesty' tricked me into speaking with more self-assurance.

"I thought from how he bragged of you that you were one of his," Ambassador Carras said, pretending not to see the way I bristled in response. "But now I see you are his son's."

"His son is *mine*," I said, too sharp. A wavering hand rose to my eyes to cover them as my embarrassment deepened. "No— I only mean… his father has nothing to do with it," I said, finishing lamely.

"I see," Carras said, looking terribly smug.

I scanned the room looking for an escape route. Aiden and Beryl were together by the wine giggling and I mapped myself a path through the room that would keep me away from Sabine York and Duncan Pike and about half of Callum's brothers and sisters-in-law.

"It's very surprising, I think, for an Enmairian to have a Scribe's magic," Carras continued.

A corner of my mouth rose up as a potentially terrible idea came to mind. "Well my mother was Vermenian," I said, not bothering to speak quietly. One of Callum's brothers, Thomas, glanced over with wide eyes at my words. Carras looked dumbfounded at the announcement.

I smiled at him, wondering how long it would take for this to reach Duncan's ears, and stepped quickly, cutting my way through the room to my covenmate.

I ought to warn Callum, I thought. But before I could find him in the crowd he appeared at my side, popping out of whatever shadow he'd been hiding in.

"Now you've done it," he said, but his grin was lopsided and giddy as he wrapped an arm around my waist and hauled me close.

6

CALLUM

JOANNA WAS SKIPPING AHEAD OF US ON BERYL'S MARE WE'D PICKED OUT from the stables, her cheeks lifted to catch the snowfall. We'd snuck out of the house after an awkward breakfast where half the residents were nursing hangovers and my father was staring at Joanna as if she'd sprouted horns overnight and he hoped he might be imagining them. Someone, probably Thomas, had made sure to inform him of Joanna's parentage after the party and I could see the struggle in his expression every time he looked at her.

The boast of rare magic in his family versus the wariness of having one of 'the enemy' in his son's bed.

He'd peeked his head out of his study before we left, got one look at her dressed in my mother's thick wool coat and hat and gloves, opened his mouth to object, and then vanished again with an irritated grumble.

If I'd known the effect Joanna's parentage would have on my father —turning him uneasy and nervous—I would have sent it to him in a letter months ago. Then maybe we never would have needed to make the trip north.

Isaac nudged his horse into a trot, catching up to her easily, the pair of them natural on their rides. We'd left with the excuse of seeing the property, but I'd packed us a lunch and we'd long since crossed the boundaries of the estate into public land. No one suggested turning back to the Manor no matter how red our noses were now.

"How far is the border?" Joanna called over the shoulder.

I looked around for Aiden, the least comfortable of us on a horse, and found him rocking side to side in his seat as if it might convince stodgy old Stinger to pick up his pace.

"Hours at our rate," I answered her. "But there isn't much to see, really. They have a fort not far off from there but it's more of a 'they can see us' than us seeing them."

"I suppose it's silly to think it'll look…different just because it's a different country," she mused.

"If we turn north a bit we might see their mountains with another hour's ride," I offered. "Depending on the snow."

Aiden huffed, although I wasn't sure if it was at the suggestion of a longer ride or the fact that Stinger had stopped in place to root his nose into the snow as if searching for grass. I clicked my tongue to the roof of my mouth and the horse perked his head up again, hurrying over and nearly unseating his rider.

"Do you mind?" she asked, turning in her seat to strike Aiden with wide, hopeful eyes.

"Course not," he said, quick and easy and I could see Isaac's grin flicker.

Would we ever be immune to the impulse to please her, the way we had grown into each other? Or would she always have the upper hand? I didn't mind, not when her touch was still so gentle.

"I'll do unspeakably delicious things to you if you keep this old goat moving," Aiden muttered to me as Stinger caught up.

I snorted. "You love doing unspeakably delicious things. But I'll keep your loyal steed on track or Joanna's toes will freeze in her boots before we get back."

"Good enough for me," Aiden said.

Joanna raised a hand as she passed under a tree branch, snow crashing down in clumps after her.

"I always wanted the Solstice to look like this," she said. "It never does back home."

"It just rains in Hammish," Isaac said. "I used to try and draw it, our house and the lane covered in snow, wishing it might change the weather. Drove Dad mad. We never had enough money for firewood in winter."

"If I'd known I could Write snow we'd have had white solstices every year," she said, smiling. "And if they didn't come to Hammish you could have come to us."

Isaac's hand stretched across the open space and Joanna's met it, Beryl's mare Rose pacing agreeably alongside Isaac's ride, one of my brother's stallions that probably wouldn't be missed.

"We *are* lucky," Aiden said, nearly a whisper. And I think he meant all of us.

I thought of my father and brothers, my mother, the uneven and often one-sided affections my family seemed to cultivate. It seemed impossible that I should have ended up in the coven I did, but when Isaac and Aiden approached me I'd been greedy for the affection and attention. Greedy enough to ignore how disappointed it would make my father.

"We are," I said. I would disappoint my father a thousand times for this coven, happily.

With gentle clicks and pats to Stinger and the occasional bribe of an apple, we kept up for another hour. I led us through the evergreens until they thinned, meeting the Dannse River that came out from the mountains. Our steps were quiet, the horses' footing careful, breaths puffing white in the cold. But the snowfall broke and the gray sheet of the sky cracked as we rode, revealing a bright blue seam in the clouds.

"That flash of white above the river," I said, pointing straight ahead of us. "That's a peak. There are higher views further off but with the weather, I doubt we'd see much more."

"They mine rixon in the mountains, a heavy metal that dampens magic," Aiden said, stopping near me.

Isaac continued ahead, slowly weaving back into the trees at the edge of the river.

Joanna settled her ride with Aiden and me, eyebrows raised. "All kinds of magic?" She'd told us in bed the night before about Carras' revelation regarding Written magic being common in Vermenia.

"I was wondering the same thing," I said. "My magic leaves a trace, almost like a heat signature."

"I remember," Joanna said while smiling, thinking of the warm tingles of the protection charms I'd placed on her during the fall while we'd guarded ourselves against The Hollow.

"But when you turn a pantry into a portal there's no sign of a change," I said. In a small way, I understood my father's inclination to pride regarding Joanna. Her power was magnificently vast and beautifully tidy... when it worked the way she wanted. "If rixon weren't illegal in Enmaire I'd say we should experiment."

"Callum." I swiveled at the whisper. Isaac was waiting in the trees, face pale from cold or shock. "There are...there's something you should see."

"What-"

"Quietly," he said, and my spine prickled. "Come."

I slid off the back of my horse and I could hear the whoosh of fabric and the crunch of feet landing, Joanna and Aiden following close behind. Isaac glanced at them once, a nervous twinge in his expression before he dismounted too, leashing his horse to a tree trunk and ducking away.

I stopped Joanna before she could pass me, crouching down and tracing sigils for heat and silence on the toes of her boots, and then my own and Aiden's. We followed Isaac back into the trees, steps soundless. My stomach turned anxiously but the hairs on the back of my neck stood and I recognized the spark of sharp focus bursting in my veins.

I glanced back at Joanna and Aiden, Joanna's hands wrapped around his coat sleeve as they tiptoed behind me. I winced and Aiden raised an eyebrow at me in answer. I gestured to his coat, a deep crimson that shone like blood against the white and green and brown scenery around us. He let out a quiet gasp of understanding. Isaac was waiting for us behind a wide cluster of evergreens and when we reached him, he set his hand on Aiden's back, the coat shifting from red to a deep gray that matched the sky above us.

"There's a clear shot through there," Isaac whispered in my ear. "Can barely see from here but I don't think all four of us should get any closer."

"I'll go," I said.

Joanna 'oof'ed' behind me as Isaac caught her round the waist and stopped her from following when I cut through the tree line. Our brave witch.

I ducked out of sight as quick as I had appeared. It was a long way off but even then I could see the strange hulking shape, a shadow of bodies moving father off. I pulled a glove off and raised my fingertips up to the corner of my eyes, a little sting of heat spreading around my lids until the world sharpened and grew larger around me. The figures in the distance cleared even as I felt my way forward. Men in dark clothing, digging into the earth, guards standing around them with guns strapped to their backs.

A rock hardened in my stomach.

Branches stretched across my vision, warped and wide from the spell on my sight, but I kept my gaze on those guns. My heartbeat pounded in my ears. These weren't soldiers. Not in uniform, at least.

I tugged at my earlobes, strengthening my hearing in case they had scouts watching who might sneak up on me. It was just enough of a boost for me to catch the words floating in the air, the syllables hard and foreign.

Vermenian. Not soldiers, unless they'd kept them in plain clothes for a reason. But Vermenian men to be certain.

I stopped, as much out of sight as I could be while still being able to watch them working. There were men digging, cracking spikes into the frozen earth, and others carrying cargo closer—closed wooden crates. I knelt down into the snow, ignoring the cold soaking into my knees, trying to count the men in the woods.

Twenty at least.

There was a persistent impulse burning through me, to charge forward and attack, like a dog nipping at my ankles. I stood, washing the sight charm off with a handful of snow, and turning back to follow my footsteps to the others. I hushed Joanna when I reached them, her lips parted and eyes bright with questions. My hands rubbed my ears to get rid of the hearing charm and raised my finger to my lips before anyone could speak.

When Joanna's gaze turned stubborn, mouth opening I bent my head, kissing her lips closed again, and then ushered them back to the horses.

"We follow the river back," I whispered. It would take us a bit in the wrong direction but at least not any closer to where the men were working. We would stop in Dannsedge, get a drink before going back to the Manor and it would give me time to think.

⊙

THE DANCING BEAR was a dreary old tavern in Dannsedge. The dust on the tables was thick enough to pillow your head when it landed there after too many cups of their dangerously sweet mead, and the grime on the windows made for excellent privacy. Joanna—perfect, strange creature that she was—beamed at Terrible Troy, the barkeep who'd helped my brother James drink me into a sick stupor after the war ended.

"Back corner table," I said to my coven, nodding my head in the direction, a table too dark to see from the front door with the white snow still bright behind our eyes.

Aiden cursed as he ran into a chair.

"Soldier," Troy greeted.

"Professor now," I said, although I'd said as much the last time I came in, and the time before that and it never made any difference. He only snorted, the whiskers of his mustache wiggling with the expression, and went back to wiping out a mug with a dingy rag. "Four meads, please."

I set the coin for our drinks down first and Troy brought the clean mugs out from under the counter. My eyes adjusted enough to the dark by the time he'd finished pouring that I could see we weren't alone in the tavern. There were a few familiar local faces at the tables by the windows—Troy wouldn't bring the candles out until the sun had gone down—and they nodded to me as I spotted them. But the table in the corner was private enough and the people drinking here were men and women my family had employed for decades. They wouldn't listen in, and if they did they wouldn't repeat a word.

I put a privacy charm up all the same after setting the mugs down at the table.

Joanna squeaked and then coughed with the first sip of the drink, but she took a hearty gulp immediately after and shivered with the warmth that followed.

"Why didn't we have this to drink last night?" she asked. "I think it would have improved everyone's mood quite a bit."

"Who was it?" Isaac asked as Aiden said, "Well, what did you see?"

"A Vermenian troop, I think," I whispered. "Mercenaries, maybe."

Joanna coughed again at that. "But… we weren't at the border?"

"No, they were well over onto Enmaire soil and they knew it," I said. "They were burying something. I'm not sure what."

Aiden sucked in a breath, tugging Joanna close to his side. She fiddled with the edge of her mug, chewing at her lip.

"It can't be good, can it?" she asked.

"No," I said. "No, this can't be good."

"You'll tell your father," Isaac said, almost a question but more resigned to the fact. I was involved now. All my father's hopes for intrigue and conflict and I would be the one to hand over the proof of it.

"Yes," I said, equally resigned. "But not until Carras and his staff leave. I don't think… I don't think there'd be any chance of peace if he and the Vermenian Ambassador were in the same house when he heard this news."

Joanna was watching my face, a worried crease folding on her brow. "How long will you stay?"

I huffed out a sigh. She'd found the words before I could, before I was really even certain of the truth of them.

"I don't know. Term doesn't start again for three weeks."

"I'll get word to campus, rearrange a few meetings," Aiden mused.

Isaac flinched at the thought of staying for longer than the next two days.

"No," I said. "The three of you should go back. Gwen's expecting you back at the library while the student aides are home. And the pair of you left all your curriculum planning in Canderfey. I'll be home in a week or two. Before term starts for certain."

"I could stay," Joanna said, leaning forward. "The library will be so quiet and Gwen would understand."

For anyone else Gwen Woollard probably would have found a way of wordlessly expressing extreme disappointment and irritation. But for Joanna, yes, she would understand. Maybe even for my sake.

"No," I repeated. "I know now why my father is so excited about thinking you're a Scribe. The Vermenians used them for wars, designing battle plans. I'm sure he's thought of a dozen ways of using you the same way. I'll stay, investigate the crates, and that should distract him from trying to turn you into a chess piece."

"Be careful," Isaac said, voice harsh with the order. But it was confirmation that he agreed with me, and I knew he could help convince Joanna to leave with them on the train after the Solstice.

"I'll be fine. Besides, Sabine York is here and I'm sure she'll be just as curious as to what those troops were burying," I said.

Joanna opened her mouth and then shut it again with an audible click. She lifted her mug to her lips, wincing as she drank, and her eyes skittered over the surface of the table.

"Be careful," she said, setting the mug down. "Around Sabine."

My eyebrows shot up and I almost burst out laughing. "Joanna! You haven't been listening to the gossip, have you?"

She fidgeted in place, her eyes rolling and I wasn't sure if she was irritated with me or with herself. "No one wants to talk of anything else," she said, waving a hand through the air. "But it isn't that. She-she really doesn't like… your family."

I smiled. "I'm aware and I respect her more for it." I reached across Aiden to grab her hand in mine. "But she is a very loyal soldier to this country. And while I am now quite rusty in battle, she and her coven are not. I'll be safer having them nearby with me."

She just chewed at her lip until Isaac and Aiden settled their own hands over ours, tension draining out of her shoulders at the touch.

"I don't like it," she said, but the words were weak and she sounded resigned.

7

———

JOANNA

I kept to the edge of the party, Callum's family and their guests gathered around the enormous fire. In Bridgeston we burnt a wheel at Midwinter, but it was usually some old rickety wheel someone had taken off their wagon and saved for the event. Just a small, quick-burning fire, often in rainy weather. Here in the north, they built a wheel especially for the holiday, beautifully carved with stags and hares and wolves, wide enough to host Callum's family and their guests and many of the Dannsedge locals who were associated with the family all standing in a ring around the blaze of heat.

Snow fell from the stars and steamed in the air long before reaching the ground, a heavy mist blanketing the ground. It was magical and animal and wild but instead of filling me with strength to face the dark winter days, I was left with dread in my belly. There were too many unfamiliar and untrustworthy faces, and I wished we had decided to spend the holiday at home in our house with the cats and the fireplace. We could have made the little bread wheels my mother liked to bake on the fires and then drench in butter and honey and chocolate syrup.

I swallowed a sigh, hovering in the shadows behind Isaac and Callum who stood together, Callum's arm across his shoulder. My

301

fingers rolled back and forth over the stick of chalk I now kept constantly near. My pinky finger wiggled against the folds of my skirt, nail catching on that single, invisible thread Callum had taught me to find, a pocket of space. I slid the chalk inside, running my fingers over the surface of my skirt and finding no interruption in the fabric, and then found the opening again to pull the chalk out. It was about all I could manage at this point and it had come with many hours of frustration and many kisses meant to distract me from my own failures.

Now it was turning into a nervous habit, my fingers hunting out the chalk while I worried, thoughts racing over how I could use words to protect the men I loved. Could I write that Callum traveled back to Canderfey with us? That nothing could harm him and he never returned to war?

I tucked the chalk back into the secret pocket as Aiden broke away from farther down the ring of people and came to join me. He curled around my back, and I grabbed at his arms, crossing them over my front and warming my hands in his.

"That's a very beautiful fire if you can keep yourself from fretting long enough to enjoy it," he whispered in my ear.

"I know that," I said, and then added, "Theoretically."

He huffed against my cheek and the breath drew shivers down my spine. "We're all worrying. And we'll all feel very silly for it when he arrives home to us in a few weeks."

I nodded but my throat had sealed shut and my sight was blurring, figures being swallowed up by the orange glare of the bonfire. Aiden kissed my temple but squeezed me tighter against his chest while I blinked away tears. When my vision cleared I found that Isaac and Callum had turned to us.

"Let's go inside," Callum said, watching me carefully. "My room's view of the fire will be just as good and much warmer."

He led us in through a service entrance and grabbed us a bottle of wine out of the corner of the kitchen before we snuck upstairs together. Despite the lovely view of the burning wheel and the reflection of the fire on the frozen pond, we huddled together on the bed, greedy for touch.

When the others had fallen asleep it was my turn to lay awake sighing, although I tried to keep my breaths shallow. Callum was hooked around me, his head pillowed on my breast. When a sigh turned watery—frustration from my spinning thoughts keeping me from sleep when I was *so* tired—he nuzzled against me.

"Tell me," he whispered, shifting up against me until our noses brushed together.

My breath hitched and I swallowed. Callum kissed a sleepy trail across my cheek.

"I don't want you to stay," I answered.

He only nodded, lips catching over mine, swallowing a little cry with a kiss. I pulled him to lay over me and we tried to be quiet, not wake the others, but Isaac's hand brushed sleepily down my side and Aiden took my hand to kiss my palm as I clutched Callum against me. He filled me up, barely moving, and I kept him held close until neither of us could resist the building need.

BREAKFAST the next morning was a sour meal. The majority of the household was sleep-deprived and hungover again and my coven still had crust in their eyes from a sleepless night spent soaking up each other.

Duncan didn't say a word when we seated ourselves together, at the far end of the room but he glared down the length of the table like we were plotting against him. I was, but only in my head.

The Ambassador and his party had left in the night for an inn and Sabine York and her coven of knights did not come down for breakfast. It was only the family together. And my coven, which I was deciding to consider outside of that dynamic.

"Tell me about your family, Joanna," Duncan called down the table, abrupt and rough, the words echoing up the high walls of the hall.

I looked up from my place, all the faces of the table swiveled to watch me, eyes hooded with exhaustion.

"Just farm people," I said, barely raising my voice. My father and brother were masons but I didn't believe for a second he really cared.

Duncan leaned into the words eyes narrowing. "Your father's people?"

"Yes."

"And what of your mother's?" he asked.

I opened my mouth to snap 'Vermenian' and then thought better of it. I meant to say I didn't know, because my mother spoke very little about her family. But I didn't want Duncan to know that, to know the way my mother had abandoned her family and her heritage after her marriage. So I scrambled through foggy memories to find something true to use.

"Blacksmiths," I said, remembering a spare mention of her brother's apprenticeship with an uncle.

Duncan grunted, turning down to his plate. "There's good profit in war for a blacksmith."

I wasn't sure if it was meant as praise or condemnation so I only took my tea, hoping the subject would drop.

"And your father was a soldier?" he asked.

"Conscripted," I said, eyeing his frown. "But he met my mother in Vermenia and here we are."

He grunted again. "I suppose the Red War was not very popular in your house then."

I lifted my chin and set the cup down into its saucer, staring down the length of the table, the frozen faces on either side lost in my focus on Duncan.

"War was never a popular topic in our house," I said, and this time I let my voice carry. Callum stiffened on the other side of Aiden and even Isaac looked at me warily at this announcement.

Strangely enough, Duncan only grinned at me. I thought perhaps I had finally decided for him the matter of whether or not he would like me—because of my magic and in spite of my mother. He was now free to disapprove of me as I disapproved of him.

Good riddance.

CALLUM HIRED the car to take us back to the train station in the evening and I hated that we were one suitcase short with our luggage. The drive away from the Manor—where Duncan Pike had neglected to wish us goodbye—was as quiet as the one we'd taken in.

We surrounded Callum on the platform as the train loaded, our arms layered around him.

"Just a couple weeks," he said and I heard Aiden kiss him and murmur a 'see you soon' over my head. Isaac pulled him down for a kiss and their foreheads bumped gently together before stepping apart. I tried to meet Callum's eyes but I was too embarrassed by the sudden urge to cry again.

He bent, taking my face in his hands and kissing me three times, brief and soft and quick. "You won't get rid of me once I'm home again."

"I'll manage," I said, throat tight and forcing a smile.

We pulled apart quickly, Callum holding himself still as the three of us hurried onto the train car before it pulled out of the station without us. I caught sight of him a few times as we passed compartment windows but by the time we'd found our own place he was gone from the platform. Isaac made space on the bench for me against his side, tucked under his arm, and I folded my legs up under my skirt. Aiden took the opposite window seat, but turned away from the glass, propping his feet up next to mine on our bench.

I had a book I could not bring myself to read and Isaac was sketching aimlessly—evergreens and wine goblets and crates piled in the snow. Aiden's eyes were closed but there were worry lines on his forehead so I knew he wasn't sleeping. When the sun sank under hills and a manager announced there was only a half-hour left before the dining car closed, not one of us moved.

Aiden sighed, eyes opening at once, obviously never having dozed. He sat up and rubbed at the stubble over his chin. "I'll get us something simple to eat."

Isaac tossed his sketchbook aside after Aiden left and bundled me into his arms and I went gladly, turning my back to the window to ignore the dark silhouettes of the scenery. Aiden returned with sandwiches, drawing my legs up over his lap so we could all sit together. He tapped out a rhythm on my knee with his fingertips.

"I think your mood might be contagious," Aiden said, turning his head to me.

"*My* mood?" I asked, as if I wasn't very well aware that I was sulking not to have Callum returning home with us.

"Don't tease her," Isaac said, with a hint of a smile at the corner of his eyes.

"I'm not," Aiden said, barely disguising a laugh. "Well, I'm partly serious. I don't remember ever feeling so... *bereft* when one of us left for a conference or research or any of those kinds of things."

"This isn't a conference," Isaac said, and that sobered us all a bit. It cost Callum to have to work with his father like this and therefore it cost us to leave him to the job.

"I think it's cause he's her favorite," Aiden said, lips tight with the force of hiding his grin.

"Are you- you silly oaf!" I spluttered, kicking my legs over his lap.

"Don't be absurd," Isaac said. "I'm her favorite."

I snorted and relaxed back against him.

"You're both absurd," I said, but I was smiling and grateful for it.

"Well if it's not Callum or Isaac it must be me," Aiden said, looking at me with that fixed gaze and the hint of a smile right before...

He pounced, snatching me off Isaac's lap and drawing me to his chest, my legs falling to either side of him, skirt tangling between us. Isaac stood from the bench and drew the compartment's shades down before we accidentally scandalized someone's grandmother. But Aiden only kissed me, soft and chaste, arms wrapped around my waist and holding me close.

"I didn't realize it would be so tangible, to have one of us away. Like a missing limb," I said. "I feel as if I should be able to turn and have him across the seat."

"Yes," Aiden said. "I remember the feeling. Except for so long, I did not know what shape that missing limb would take when it arrived."

He meant me, and the twelve years it had been just the three of them together, wanting and not finding their fourth coven member.

"I knew you would be beautiful," Isaac whispered in my ear, kissing my cheek and falling back onto the bench seat beside us.

Had I felt their absence the way they had felt mine? I thought of growing up a little too quiet for my peers and a little too studious for the boys that surrounded me and a little too strange for my family. Yes, I had missed them before I even knew to dream of the idea of a coven of my own. Certainly long before I dared to imagine falling in love with men like the ones I had found.

"I'll do my best to make sure you don't miss him too much," I said, kissing the bridge of Aiden's nose as he scoffed at the suggestion.

He and Callum enjoyed a friendly antagonism at home that usually leant itself to bickering over petty topics for days on end. But I'd once caught them after a more explosive end to an argument and the culmination was not hard feelings, but Callum pinning Aiden to his rarely-used mattress, Aiden groaning into his knuckles as Callum set a punishing pace inside him.

I couldn't replicate that exactly, although a secret part of me wished it were possible, but I could take Aiden's teasing and respond to it in kind. I knew already he liked when I made demands of his hands and mouth and cock rather than waiting for his seduction.

I landed another kiss against his mouth, drawing his full bottom lip between my teeth to worry it gently. His chest rumbled under my palms, a pleased, low, purring sound. Isaac moved up from the bench and I pulled away, leaving Aiden's mouth trailing hungrily down my neck.

"Where are you going?" I asked Isaac.

"To pull out a bed before all three of us are naked and messy and tired and can't be bothered," Isaac said, bending to kiss me as Aiden found the spot over my pulse that had me squirming over his lap.

The train was rumbling pleasingly underneath us. I'd thought of it, almost embarrassed to wonder how it might feel during sex, on the trip to Dannsedge. That compartment hadn't felt private enough with a baby crying through one wall and an elderly man coughing through the other. Now, at least, I hadn't seen our neighbors in the corridor and there'd been no sound from either direction. I wanted connection with Aiden and Isaac to fill the gap of Callum missing. I could be quiet and pretend we were really alone.

Aiden's hands caressed up my calves, ducking under my skirt and brushing over the tops of my thighs until they reached the edge of my underwear, tugging until it slid down my hips. I sat up on my knees and he pulled them down as far as they would go without me moving, and then released my neck with a nip. He was grinning and I was fairly sure he'd given himself permission to leave a mark on my throat.

He lifted me up from the bench and then knelt down between my legs, hands tugging my underwear down the rest of the way. I balanced myself with my hands on his shoulders and stepped free of the fabric.

"What are you up to?" I asked with a giddy expectation brewing in my stomach.

He took my hands from his shoulders and stretched them behind him to settle on the bench, bending me forward.

"Improvising within the space," Aiden said, finding the zipper at the waist of my skirt.

"I think I'll join you in this," Isaac murmured, sinking down to his knees behind me and helping Aiden tug my skirt down.

I felt silly and exposed, bent over and undressed from the waist down, wishing for the apple mead that had made me so brave with their touches. Their hands petted and stroked up and down the lengths of my legs, lingering when they brushed together, and soon the silliness was being replaced with longing.

Isaac kissed up the back of one thigh and then the other while Aiden nuzzled his face against my stomach, stray kisses landing over my mound, the stubble of his beard just barely teasing at my folds. I shivered, feeling the scratch echoing down my legs to where my feet were trembling with the vibration of the train. Isaac's hand smoothed over the curve of my ass, and his fingers spread over the base of my spine, pressing down.

"What- what do I-?" I started, arching my back under his instruction. And then Isaac licked a stripe over my slit and my breath caught with an "Oh!"

My head dropped and I could watch them, upside down, as Aiden shifted forward some, spreading my legs apart more so his could stretch out over Isaac's lap. My hips ached and Isaac's hand at my waist held me in place for a few moments until I was rocking back to the slow kisses of his mouth against me. He slid his hand back down my hip and then between their laps, Aiden grunting a moment later.

"Together?" Isaac murmured to him, the word tingling over my sensitive skin.

Aiden hummed and shifted forward an inch, and then arched his neck. His tongue swiped at me, higher, brushing over my clit and then trailing down to swirl and press. I whimpered, trying to catch the sound behind closed lips. When Isaac pressed forward, copying Aiden's push and swish until they were kissing me at my opening and kissing each other all at the same moment, the whimper became a startled, delighted cry. My fingers dug into the back of the bench and I swayed over them, not sure how to remain upright under the assault.

Aiden's hands braced my waist above his head as Isaac pushed two fingers into my clasping channel, pumping and slicking the digits as his and Aiden's tongue caught every drop of me. He pulled his hand free, and Aiden hissed against my clit as Isaac used his slick hand on him. Aiden's fingers replaced the gaping need inside of me, pumping and pressing down. I couldn't see what Isaac was doing to Aiden but I could guess. Aiden's mouth was harsh over my clit, his fingers urgent. My toes were curling in my boots and the reminder that was I still wearing shoes left me giggling and wiggling between their hands, gasping for breath.

"Please," I breathed, begged, trying to find the words and only able to repeat myself. "Please, please."

Isaac's licks followed Aiden's fingers, stroking over the stretched opening that was sparking with heat. Aiden lashed at my clit, his face nuzzling hard against me, a long and ragged groan burrowing into my skin. I came, laughing and sobbing all at once and Aiden growled victoriously, pulling his fingers free before I had finished, and jumping up from the floor, cock bobbing free from his open pants. We all three fumbled together, me trying to kick off my shoes and tear away my blouse as they tried to undress themselves and each other.

Despite Isaac giving Aiden a head start on his pants, he was free first, his simpler clothing making an easier job of it. He pulled me backward onto the bench turned cot, and slid into me from behind, the both of us laying on our sides, my leg braced backward over his hip. I craned my neck to take his kisses, finding the taste of myself and Aiden's kisses on his lips. Aiden landed heavily in front of us, wrapping his arms around us both, his cock sliding between my legs to nudge against Isaac's as if he could find a place for himself there.

I was melting onto the cushions under Isaac's slow press and retreat, my hands cupping Aiden's cheeks to kiss him, messy and sweet.

"How long can you stand to wait?" Isaac asked and I let my head droop, watching them above me, braced on their arms, hips working in opposite directions to strike softly at me in tandem.

Aiden's face smoothed, like he was pushing away the urgency from a moment ago with just a flick of will. He glanced down at me and grinned.

"Until she begs us to quit," Aiden said. His head bent and he kissed my cheek, nose bumping softly against it. "And we all know how much you can take, darling," he said to me.

I preened a little at that, trying to find more friction at the same time. I could take as much as they could give.

Isaac pulled free and I frowned, turning to glance at him, but then Aiden shifted, filling me up with a few short thrusts, and my mouth fell open on a moan.

They worked in short stretches, one building me up with smooth, slow strokes inside while the other petted and played with us both. And just before I reached a peak, hands clawing at Aiden's back, and throat stretched for Isaac's kisses, they would switch again. I was sweating and shaking between them, Isaac's breaths harsh in my ear, and his thrusts becoming more urgent, for the third time.

"Poor darling," Aiden cooed against my lips, sounding not at all sorry as I sobbed with complaint, Isaac gathering control and drawing free of me.

"No," I whimpered, nearly swallowing the word. I didn't want to be the one to give in. But I hadn't thought they would tease me with release and then carefully deny it. Aiden and Isaac both held still as I caught my breath. Aiden's forehead was beaded with sweat and his hands shook on my hips, but I could see the hard glint in his eye. If I didn't beg he'd find a way to continue the game even if it took the whole rest of the ride home. Which was both a wonderful and terrifying thought.

"No more," I whispered, hoping he would be hungry and swift with me now that I'd given up.

He huffed, relieved, and smiled, darting down to sweep his tongue into my mouth, pushing and plunging the way I wished he would inside my aching cunt. He pulled me forward and then rolled me down onto my belly. I almost cursed him until he covered my back with his chest, hands parting me just so, and then he lined himself up and thrust deep and hard. I wanted to arch, away from the sudden onslaught or into it, but I couldn't move an inch, pinned to the thin mattress that was rattling with the train running the tracks. My thighs parted just a bit more and then *there*, my clit was pressed to the fabric, friction buzzing through me. Aiden had barely started when I was coming, hands fluttering open and shut. Isaac pulled my face to his, swallowing my cry with a kiss.

Every rutting snap of Aiden's hips dragged me against the scratch and buzz of the cushion, licking at me like flames. His breath puffed hot on the back of my neck until he was grunting with each dive inside of me, his mouth brushing over my skin. His rhythm turned harsh and uneven in the next beat and he clamped his teeth around my shoulder, bellowing into my skin as he finished.

He drooped to the side, barely falling free of me and Isaac shifted me closer, his fingers knotting with mine on the seat above my head. He groaned as he slid inside, the path slippery and smooth with Aiden's release mixed with my arousal.

"I love this," Isaac said, mouth against my hair. "Love you soaked like this."

I'd thought at first that Isaac was the patient one of the group, and that was why he waited for the others to finish in me first, took his time when we were together. Now I grinned into the cushion, knowing he liked the mess and the sounds. Even more, he liked to see if he could draw more out of me even after I thought I had nothing left. He was usually right.

He seated himself fully inside of me and then moved in a shallow rocking, kissing over my shoulders, paying special attention to the sensitive marks Aiden had left on me. I sighed, turning my head so he could stretch up to kiss my cheek and my temple. He widened his stance between my legs and my folds spread a little too, leaving my clit more exposed to the friction of the rocking and the train.

"Oh *yes*," I whispered and I caught Isaac's smile out of the corner of my eye.

My eyes fell shut and I gave into the slow build. If he could be patient so could I and this was a softer, sweeter ache than I was used to. Aiden's hand lifted, combing my hair back from my face as he sat up, kissing and stroking down Isaac's back with his other hand.

"You won't make me hurry," Isaac said, teasing. "I know you can't go again and I've nothing to rush for."

"You aren't the only aesthetic animal," Aiden said, and his voice was so low that when he was quiet it was more of a vibration than a sound. "I like to watch too."

Isaac hummed at that and then shifted a bit, giving Aiden access to my back. It moved him inside of me too, bumping at my front walls and leaving white stars blooming behind my eyes.

"Oh gods, right there," I gasped, stiffening. "Right there and don't stop."

Isaac grunted as I started to clench around him, but he continued, soft and steady, a drumbeat inside of me that carried up into my ears with my heart pounding. I wanted more, exactly that way, but my body was fighting at the same time, trying to pull away. Aiden's hands braced my shoulders and Isaac's hands freed mine to clutch my hips and hold me steady.

I buried my face in the cushion to muffle the broken, begging sounds that scrambled up from my throat. I could hear Isaac, breaths puffing as I started to flutter. There was the urgency now, his cock striking the same perfect place, his fingers digging into my skin. I came with a buried scream, heat rushing through me and my body turning limp. There was a wet rush inside of me and Isaac shuddered and groaned at the feeling and then echoed it as he finished, fitting himself deep and tight, body covering me head to toe.

The train was still vibrating underneath me and I was pressed hard into the bench and it was too much, but it was grounding too, having something almost painful follow something too unearthly.

Isaac slid away soon enough, drawing me into his chest, and Aiden curled up at my back. I felt a little raw, and a little weepy somehow despite the pleasure, but their hands were soothing down my side and soon that ragged edge was brushed down into something drowsy and relaxed.

"Sleep, darling," Aiden said in my ear, kissing the spot behind my lobe. "Soon we'll be home. And then not long after so will he."

Ah, yes. That was why I still felt off-kilter. But Aiden was right, not much longer. I lifted his hand to kiss his knuckles and then Isaac's, and I think I fell asleep before taking another breath.

8

CALLUM

I was trying very hard not to watch the clock over the mantle in my father's study. General Blackthorn was droning over military roles while Councilman Cosgrove, equally dull, answered with the strain of tax levies in the northern regions. There wasn't much else to do but watch the hours drag through the evening, not with so many 'important men' determined to give their insight.

I had been spared this during my war, odd as it was to think of my father sparing me from anything. This careful negotiation reminded me of setting up toy soldiers in tidy lines on the carpet, arguing over who took which little carved piece, only to sweep them all down with raucous shouts and a great deal of stomping. Great petty debates that all ended with nothing accomplished.

There was a twitch by the window and I looked over, Sabine York and her warrior coven were sitting in the drafty frame. The movement came from Darin, massive frame stretching and jaw yawning, openly bored but easily ignored by the older members of the party. Samuel was sleeping, fire-red hair turned blue in the shadow of the window frame, lips barely parted. I hoped perversely he might start snoring. Geoff sat glowering with his hair curtaining his face, hands braced lightly on his thighs. I had passed him in the hall and felt the metallic snag of at least eight weapons hidden on his person. Even here, he looked ready to spring into action at any moment, as if he expected my father's study to be attacked, or for the lot of us to suddenly turn on one another. I supposed the latter was possible.

Sabine York was watching me, watchful but expressionless. I had seen her rescuing Joanna from my father during the dinner party, which was enough to earn my respect. I nodded to her in acknowledgment and Geoff caught the gesture, turning to her. She didn't acknowledge either of us.

"Callum," my father barked. I glanced at him but his back was to the room, the map from his desk spread up over a wall, clustered with pins and notes of where Enmaire and Vermenian troops were positioned. "Tell us again what you saw."

I was starting to think I'd been left here in a dull, repetitive nightmare. I started the story again, the one I'd told every day of the week since my coven had left. There were no new details and I'd found no further insight since being trapped in this study for days on end. But they liked to hear it all the same so I answered, thinking all the while that I could be at home in Canderfey instead.

We broke up late after too many glasses of whiskey and nothing decided. I didn't hurry out of the room. Joanna had left the bed massive in my room and I simultaneously loved the change because she created it, and hated it for leaving me alone in such a wide empty space.

Beryl dragged my father off to bed and I stayed in the study as it cleared, hoping to get a chance to read over the correspondences he'd been coveting. If I could find any clue, anything scrap of information he'd overlooked, maybe I could accelerate the glacial pace of their so-called investigation.

"Old men like to plan their maneuvers more than act on them, I think."

I looked up from rounding my father's desk and found Sabine and Darin still in the room with me, the others having all cleared off. I thought they might have used a little cloaking magic because I'd barely noticed them until Sabine spoke.

"They've forgotten *how* to move," Darin said, more in answer to Sabine than to me.

"It does seem that way," I said, shrugging.

"Do you remember where to find the crates?" Sabine asked.

I thought about it, fingers flicking at the edges of the papers on my father's desk. "I think so," I said. We'd taken a winding path, my coven aimless together, but I knew how to follow the river and roughly where to stop, what direction to turn. With the number of men that had been in the woods, there ought to have been tracks to follow after that, even after a snowy week had passed.

"Then we should go and find out what cargo they've brought over," Sabine said.

She was wholly warrior, like I had been during the war, impulsive and lethal. She lacked any technique of persuasion—something Aiden had coaxed into me over the years—or she lacked the interest in the effort. But I knew why she hadn't suggested as much to the whole meeting. They would dither or they would gather up a mess of horses and troop clumsily into what might easily be a trap. Old men were also not as good at stealth.

I scratched my hand over my beard. Finding the contents of the crates might lengthen my stay to the full three weeks, but at least they would give a purpose to me being stuck here instead of free to go home.

"They should sleep to luncheon," I said, counting the empty glasses around the room. "The whiskey ought to take care of that."

Darin grinned at that and I thought Sabine might even have spared a twitch of a smile.

"The five of us can go out at dawn," I said. "On foot might be better, but if we need to rush away it could be good to have horses."

"Our horses are stabled here," Sabine said, with a shrug. "We'll leave it to your judgment. Toy Soldier," she said, with a deep nod.

I wasn't sure if I liked the gesture of the nickname; it was meant to be respectful, but I had a sinking feeling that Sabine didn't respect anyone outside of her coven. I didn't answer and she and Darin, who had grinned again—a toothier, meaner expression than before—left the room before me.

I thought of heading up to my room, it was after midnight and dawn was only a handful of hours away. But it would be better to be prepared, and if there was anything worth finding in my father's notes then I wanted to be armed with it before the morning.

GEOFF HAD a curious ability to follow my lead while keeping his horse in front of mine. I assumed I was being watched out of the curtain of that pale hair of his, but just to be sure I took a few circuitous routes on the way, making sure *I* wasn't the one being herded. He followed from ahead, glancing at me with icy irritation after we went out of our way a couple of times, like he could see the nonsense but didn't understand why it was employed.

I knew Sabine, Samuel, and Darin by their reputations in the war —their medals and acclaims. As far as I had found there was nothing to know about Geoff York other than that he was the first warrior Sabine York had collected for herself; the pair of them walking off the Enmaire battlefield together at the end of the Red War. Maybe her tastes changed after, looking for higher lauded coven members, but I couldn't shake the sense that there was *something* worth knowing about the man. Perhaps because he was so obviously hiding something.

We followed a bend in the river and a faintly familiar tree appeared, evergreen branches scalped away from the trunk, up as high as the head of my horse.

"Here," I said, swinging down from the saddle. "East through the trees but I'd rather we go in quietly."

"Darin will stay with the horses," Sabine said, jumping down and passing her reins to him.

I glanced at the man. He was a giant and I thought I would have rather he was *with* us than waiting for us if anything were going to go wrong. He had a vicious reputation in battle and a bright grin that seemed friendly until suddenly it wasn't. But that friendliness was taking up the horses now, patting their necks as they snuffled in search of treats around his pockets.

I had a vicious reputation too, I thought, but I didn't relish it now. Sabine knew what she was about with her own coven. I passed him my own horse's reins and led the way into the trees, this time Geoff was content to follow, now at the very end of the line of us.

There was no sign from here of men or crates, not even a mound of cold earth or a snowdrift where they might have buried the cargo. They had covered their tracks which made the discovery more imperative. This wasn't something that could be excused away with a wave of politics or trade. I traced a cloaking spell over me and felt echoes of them behind me, Sabine's magic a sharp slash through the air, Samuel's feathery. Geoff vanished without magic, his steps going unnaturally silent as he slipped away. So that was his skill. Most likely used well for spying during the war.

Samuel joined me at my left, the warning snag of the sword hanging over his shoulder nicking at my arm. When I'd met them in the stable while the sun was rising it was like being pricked by dozens of knife tips. They were armed to the teeth. I had a single knife in my boot.

"Keep your eyes on the ground for any sign of disturbed earth," I said. "We should be getting close."

Geoff found it first, appearing ahead of us, snow dusted over his shoulder. There was a drift after all, that he brushed away with a tree branch before we reached him, and a shallow mound of overturned earth below.

"Is anyone nearby?" Sabine asked, and Geoff shook his head.

"Not for miles," he said, voice rough and stilted from disuse.

"If you hand me that branch I can raise the earth," I said, holding out my hand. "Save us the trouble of digging."

Even then he turned his gaze to Sabine, waiting until she nodded with permission. I imagined Joanna waiting for permission to do anything and nearly snorted. No, more likely she was our commander than I hers. Geoff passed me the branch and I broke away the smaller twigs, pine needles shedding onto the pile and sap sticking to my fingers. I found the very edges of their digging, tracing a ragged oval in the earth where their shovels had struck with the tip of the branch. I scribbled sigils over the lines I'd made, testing the work by gripping the middle of the branch-turned-staff when I was done and wiggling it in front of me. The ground shuddered, pine needles trembling down the mound.

I turned to Sabine and raised my eyebrow to wait for her command as a joke. She didn't look startled or pleased, or even confused. She only stared back and nodded once.

It was a deep hole and the effort of lifting burned straight up my arm to my shoulder. I grabbed onto the branch at either end and hoped that I'd guessed the depth well enough or I'd have to ask one of the others to lift me so we could take the whole pile out at once. Sweat frosted on my forehead, the weight of the earth dragging on my magic. The ground was frozen cold and holding tight to the edges.

Geoff was staring over my shoulder at Sabine. He may have been thinking I was pathetically weak, or maybe he was impressed with the feat. The whole damn coven was impossible to read. Darin with his grinning, Geoff with his silence, Samuel stoically glued to Sabine's side.

My arms were shaking by the time I'd raised them over my head, and a thin gap appeared between the enormous load of dirt I'd dragged out of the hole. Samuel stepped back as I turned to the right and my cargo traveled through the air, little pebbles of earth falling loose as it shifted.

Lowering the branch was a relief and when the pile touched down I released it with a clatter at my feet. The dirt slid around the edges, trickles of it falling back into the hole, but the work was done. Sunlight landed on dull wooden crates, stacked in a pyramid, and we all stepped closer. I released a tendril of hunting magic, but there was no answering warning, there was no answer at all.

"I think I know what this is," I said, glancing at Sabine.

Her arms were folded over her chest and she seemed relaxed as she shrugged at me in answer.

I bent and lowered myself into the hole, as deep as my chest, and Geoff dropped down in with me at the other end. The crates were nailed shut and I pulled the knife from my boot to wedge open the solitary box at the top.

Chains lay bundled together inside, the strange oil slick black of rixon metal shifting colors under my shadow. Even without them touching I reached for a scrap of my power and found only a faint whisper in answer. The others were quiet around me.

"Imagine how many of these they might have buried around the border," I said, taking a link of the chain between my fingers and lifting it reluctantly, like rotten trash.

"This will certainly spur action," Samuel mused. "We're lucky your coven ran into this."

I dropped the chain back into the crate, my heart drumming in my chest. The search this would take would be extensive. And surely the Vermenians had some way of scouting, of checking on these crates. They might already have spotted us. How could we clear the border of any rixon? If it was used by the Vermenian troops, it would ruin the magical defenses on our armies and any major maneuvers made by Generals like my father.

And how would I keep my father from charging into battle *before* the rixon was cleared? Because this would be taken as a declaration of war. Illegal border crossing by Vermenians, mercenaries or troops. Burying an unlawful substance on our land.

There was a restlessness running up my spine, the urge to *act*, and I tried to bury it quickly. My responsibility was to finish here and return to Canderfey, not war. Not again.

"Does this make things easier or harder?" Geoff asked.

I looked up at him, brow furrowing, puzzled. He was staring over my shoulder at Sabine.

"Easier, I should think," she said.

I turned to face her and saw it coming out of the corner of my eye, too late. The blunt handle of her sword, swinging straight into the side of my head, a burst of pain like a firework going off behind my eyes. The world went black but my brain kept running for a moment, feeling my body turn limp, the crash of elbows and knees landing too hard against wooden planks.

"For my coven, Toy Soldier," Sabine said, voice fading into a whisper.

9

JOANNA

Alice Batting passed me in the stacks while I was supposed to be shelving returns. She stopped to watch me lift an old book to my nose and breathe in the dust and ink and dry leather. She didn't laugh, but smiled and nodded instead, moving on with her own cart.

It had only been a week in the north with Callum's family but I had badly missed my library and my quiet. And a fragrant book was not to be ignored.

"Joanna?"

I turned around and found Gwen leaning around a shelf, a stack gathering in her arms. "I promise I'm working, not just fondling," I said quickly.

She snorted. "It's not that. I'm looking for any texts on husbandry or breeding for magical amplification," she said. She waited while I let the words sort through my head. "If you see anything, will you grab it for me?"

I was still wrapping my head around the concept—breeding live-stock for specific magical traits—but I nodded and started scanning the titles around me as I returned books back to their homes. I collected as I replaced, dropping off a pile with Gwen who'd taken up the favored window seat. I had a sneaking suspicion that this was as much a test of my ability to find relevant texts on a narrow subject, as it was a way for me to help her, and I was treating it like something I might be graded on.

I was stretching up to reach for a collection of magical almanacs to take to her when a lightning bolt of pain, zipped from my temple to shoulder. I cried out in surprise and crumpled forward, dropping the books in my arms and falling into the shelf, grabbing on to brace myself. My knees shook and panic rushed through me along with a heavy, sleepy weight behind my eyes.

"What's happened?" Gwen asked, hurrying over and trying to catch me.

I only fell harder onto the floor, pulling Gwen along with me as the pain rushed up in a wave through my head.

"I…" I wet my lips and blinked my eyes in a slow, determined way, trying to shake off the urge to sleep or faint. "I don't know. I…pulled a muscle?" I waved my trembling hand up to where an ache was pounding like a drumbeat from my temple down to my shoulder.

"Check in with your coven," Gwen said, arranging me on the floor to rest against the bookshelf.

It took longer than usual but I found them eventually. Aiden and Isaac, near and nervous with a pale echo of what I was feeling that made my vision swim. Callum was distant, faint and quiet, probably still sleeping at this hour without the rest of us to rouse him.

"Something happened…maybe?" I said, words slurring. It was hard to tell if I was reacting to them or their echoes were in response to me. Harder when I felt so drowsy and any focus made the pain in my head bloom bigger and brighter. Something cracked, like a lightbulb going off right between my eyes, and I was out.

There was a long pause where everything was dark, and then I was alone on the floor against the shelf, my eyelids drooping. After another dark moment that stretched and stretched, my eyes opened again and I was being led down the staircase, my arms hanging over someone's shoulders and my toes slapping against the steps limply.

"…can't get in touch with…" Gwen was saying.

The edges were clearer when I came to again and Aiden was

sitting over me in the small dark staff lounge, his face relaxing as my eyes opened.

"Headache," I said, although the word was more of a whine.

He bent forward and pressed a warm kiss to my forehead. "I know darling, I can feel it." His fingers ran over the shoulder that had hurt so badly and I groaned at the touch, both painful and relieving.

"What'd you do to yourself?" he asked. "Felt like someone struck me in the head with a rock."

"I don't know but I feel terrible," I said. I tried to swallow the tears rising up in my throat but they came too quickly.

"Oh, I'm sorry," Aiden said, bundling me closer with tender care. "I know. I shouldn't have teased. Come on, let's get you home. You terrified poor Gwendolyn."

I heard a sniff and looked over Aiden's shoulder. Gwen was waiting by the door out to the main library, looking not at all terrified. Maybe a little pale.

"I think you should check in with Pike," she said and my eyes widened.

"I will, don't make her nervous," Aiden answered in a lower tone.

"Callum?" I asked, my hands going to my skirt pockets to root for the notebook filled with our messages to each other. It was there, safely sitting alongside a stub of pencil and I flipped to an open page. *Are you alright?* I stared at the words, willing Callum to answer.

"He's probably still asleep. We'll call up to Dannsedge," Aiden said, hands running down my shoulders. "Let's get you home first. Isaac's there resting, you nearly knocked him out too."

I frowned and I felt every fraction of the movement, like my skin was taut and swollen down the right side of my head. Every shift of my hair a stinging pinprick on my scalp. There was a half-formed thought at the back of my head that refused to shape.

Aiden moved to brush away the hair falling into my face and I flinched, only seeing a shadow reaching out. "Sorry," he murmured, "Are you ready?"

He helped me up, moving to my left, and I leaned into his side as his arm wrapped around my waist. My hand went to my skirt, and for a moment I was sure I would not be able to reach my chalk, but the pocket appeared and the chalk stick was safe inside.

I pulled it out and looked to Gwen. "Do you mind?" I asked, not relishing the idea of a long walk back to our house.

"Not at all," Gwen said, stepping aside. "I'll wash it off after you leave. And don't rush back tomorrow if you aren't well. The books can have their fun on the shelves for a day."

I tried for a smile and hoped it didn't end up too wobbling and pathetic.

Aiden all but carried to me the door. "Do you think it will work if you're…"

"Barely managing?" I suggested. "I don't know, I hope so."

There was no heat to my magic, like Callum's, and no trilling note of music or glow of color. But I thought I was learning the feel of a gentle landing with each letter added, as airy as a snowflake striking the back of my hand.

The words were spiky and uneven but I managed them. *Door to home.*

And then the lounge door, which usually swung into the room from this side, opened in the opposite direction. Our narrow hall, full of Isaac's collected paintings, waited for us inside.

"Take care," Gwen said. "I'll check in."

I kissed her cheek and Aiden scooped me up into his arms and carried me inside.

"Where's Isaac?" I asked as Gwen shut the door behind us.

"Upstairs," Aiden murmured.

"Kitchen," Isaac called from the end of the hall. I heard the strain in his voice, the way he kept it lowered to keep from ringing too loud in his own ears. "Tea?"

I tried to jump down from Aiden's arms but he held me tighter and carried me down the hall. Isaac was slouched over the little table with three cups steaming in front of him. He looked almost as rough as I still felt and he snatched up my hand in his when Aiden finally set me down in a chair.

"You're alright," he said, almost a question.

I nodded, stretching my neck to one side and the other, testing the hollow ache. "Are we…are we sure it was me?" I asked.

Aiden stood between us, drinking from one of the cups of tea. He and Isaac looked at each other, both frowning.

"Callum feels… alright, I think?" Isaac said. "Sleeping?"

I looked out the window. It was later now, I wasn't sure how long I'd been asleep in the staff lounge but the sun seemed higher. Would he still be sleeping?

"I'll go into town, make some calls," Aiden said, and he sounded weary too.

"I can go," Isaac offered, half-hearted and Aiden snorted.

"It didn't hit me as hard," he said. "I'll go. The pair of you get some sleep."

"You didn't…didn't find another book, did you?" Isaac asked me and Aiden froze at the thought.

"If I'm being haunted it's by the spirit of farm livestock," I said, and this time the smile came easier. They both sighed and I rolled my eyes at my own cup of tea.

Set a menacing god-like being free from its magical cage one time and no one lets you forget it, apparently.

The tea washed away the worst of the pain and my shoulder relaxed from where it'd pulled tight to my ear. Aiden finished his cup and kissed us both before leaving again. Isaac and I made it as far as the front room before giving up on the idea of stairs and settling for curling up together on the couch for a nap.

SUNSET WAS TURNING the house orangey when the front door opened and I woke. My head felt gummy but the pain had turned dull and faint. Instead, there was a trickle of dread running up my spine. I scrambled again for the notebook but there was no answer yet from Callum.

"He may be far enough off he didn't feel anything, he might not check for a message," Isaac said, the pair of us sitting up, eyes fixed to the page. His voice sounded weak, stretching for reassuring and falling short.

Aiden appeared in the doorway, face drawn tight with tension.

"It was Callum, wasn't it?" I whispered, and Isaac's breath hitched behind me.

"The town is in the woods north of the manor," Aiden said. "A search party, but the woman who answered didn't know who for."

Isaac sat up at once, arm circling my waist and hand clutching into the fabric.

I covered my face with my hands, my breath coming short, and scrambled within to find Callum. There was nothing. And then after the echo of nothing, there was dread but I didn't know if the creeping terror was his or mine or Isaac's or Aiden's.

"What do we do?" I asked, lowering my hands.

"Bryce is waiting to hear back from Dannsedge for us," Aiden said, coming closer.

"We should go," I said, rising up from the couch with a weak step. "We should go back."

Aiden met me in the middle of the room, cupping my shoulders to stop me. He had an apology in his eyes but he looked set, determined. "We don't know yet who is missing. We're going to wait to hear back or we might miss a call from Callum himself," he reasoned.

"I can't really feel him," Isaac said, staring up at us from the couch. "Not like...not like he's gone. There's just..."

"Please," I whispered up at Aiden.

He grimaced, wet tears flooding his own eyes, and I knew what his answer would be. "Not yet, darling. The second we have any confirmation, we'll take the fastest route I can find us."

I wanted to pull away, be angry, but he bundled me up, pressing his lips to the top of my head, and the comfort was more persuasive than the anger.

"We'll know before morning," he said. "Bryce will come as soon as they hear."

BRYCE CAME in the middle of the night, opening the front door I was sure I had locked, and appearing in the dining room like a specter. I jumped in surprise, but I'd never felt more grateful to be shocked out of my wits.

"Is he missing?" I asked, leaping up from the table we'd been holding an excruciating vigil around.

Bryce licked their lips, eyes skirting around the room before landing back on me. "Taken," they said. "By Vermenians."

The silence landed like an anvil in the room.

"Vermenians?" Isaac whispered after a long stretch, his hands braced against the tabletop as if to balance himself.

"They crossed the border with him," Bryce said. "General Pike and his sons have left for the capital to bid for troops."

Aiden's voice was in my ears but I couldn't make out the words. Puzzle pieces were scattering through my thoughts. The members of the holiday party in Dannsedge, the crates we discovered in the woods near the border, Duncan Pike's readiness for battle.

"They're going to start a war over him," I said, without meaning to speak. My whole body felt numb with shock. Callum was *taken*. I wanted to run right out of the house onto the street to find him, as if I could catch up to him on foot, motivated solely by panic.

Aiden trailed off and Bryce stared back at me, a wary agreement in their silence.

"I'll go to the capitol," Aiden said. "My fathers will have access to the discussions, maybe even a voice in the decision. They would share any news with us."

"We'll all go," Isaac said.

Aiden opened his mouth as if he might object, and then shook the thought away. "Of course," he said, nodding slowly. None of us could look at each other.

"I'll tell Gwen," Bryce said. "Our coven will help in every way we can."

Aiden asked Bryce to get us train tickets into Rhodantis for the morning and I was halfway to the stairs to start packing.

With every step up, my heart beat a little harder, sensation returning. With it came a painful fear. Callum had been kidnapped. *Callum.* Of all of us, he seemed the least likely to be threatened. Hiccuping breaths, sobs that I tried to bury, came up like gasps as I ran up the flights to my bedroom. Callum wasn't safe and if Duncan Pike had his way, Enmaire wouldn't be either. We would go to war.

I wanted my covenmate back and I wanted him safe, and I wasn't even sure if that was possible. He was already in Vermenia, a country he'd battled and beaten violently as a near boy. What would they do to him as a man?

I sat on the bed, taking uneven breaths until my eyes focused in my lap, my fingers still tight around our notebook. My hand gripped so tightly around the pencil I thought I might break it as I scrawled helplessly.

Callum, be safe. Please, be safe. Callum, come ho-

But the word 'home' would not come no matter how hard I tried to force my own hand.

Isaac found me not long after, sobbing and heaving into the page, tears nearly blurring the words I had managed.

"Hold on, love," he said, soothing hushes between words. "See? He's safe. Hold on. We'll get him back."

10

—————

CALLUM

I WOKE IN A HEAP, TANGLED AND SHACKLED IN RIXON CHAINS. MY HEAD was throbbing, my eye was swollen shut, and my body felt heavy and dull without its connection to my magic. Worse, I couldn't trace my bond back to my coven.

Canvas stretched overhead around a squared frame and even that was made of rixon. The crates from the pit I had unearthed with Sabine surrounded me, and one jumped and rattled as the cart hit a pothole, threatening to slide off its stack and land on top of me. A hand reached out from the end of the cart, pushing the crate back in place and I stretched and shuffled, my chains clanging, into the corner to see. There was a uniformed man riding at the far end of the belly of the car, hair dull in the shadow and eyes fixed to me, watchful. The cart went over another bump in the road and the canvas flap opened, flashing his face.

"Werrfur?" I said, voice thick and rough around the Vermenian word. Why? Why had they taken me with the rixon?

The soldier ignored me, only watching in response. He looked young and the whites of his eyes were bright even in the dark. Had they told him the rixon would be enough to keep me contained? To keep him safe? Evidently, he didn't believe them.

I wished he was right to be afraid of me. I didn't want to hurt him but if I thought I could get myself free of these chains I might have been feeling more optimistic. As it was… *my* chances as a prisoner in Vermenia weren't good. They had taken away my coat and I was certain Sabine hadn't returned my knife to me after knocking me unconscious.

Sabine York.

She had *hit* me. The thought of Sabine and her coven of Enmaire's finest, being in any way involved with Vermenia was laughable. Was she covering up the presence of rixon in Enmaire or was selling me out to the enemy her goal from the start?

For my coven… Her words after the strike sank in slowly, nausea rising up my throat. Not her current coven but the one before. I understood now, or I guessed the truth. Soldiers in my troops had been spent carelessly under my lead. My father and the other generals had made sure I didn't meet the men and women serving under me, never more than a passing glance before the battle began. They didn't want me sympathizing, seeing my chess pieces as living and breathing.

I had sent Sabine and her coven to the slaughter. More than a decade later I'd sat next to her at a dinner table, wholly unaware of our history.

My father knew. I thought of Joanna too, her wary nervous gaze at Sabine York, her warning to be careful, trying to protect me from the consequences of my past. I should have listened.

Does this make things easier or harder?… Easier, I should think.

They hadn't been expecting the rixon. It had been a surprise, but a convenient one. Strike me and chain me up, that way even if I came to I couldn't act against them. Would it matter to them, what the dig site could potentially mean? Or was their only concern Sabine's revenge?

"Werhar?" I asked, trying to sit up but too laden to manage. I waited but the soldier only ignored me, still watching from his seat, safely out of reach. I eased back onto the floor, wincing as the cart thumped and pain rang like a bell in my head. Where? Where were we? Or where were we going? I didn't care. My best chances would be if the cart was caught at a border, or overturned from another one of those damn potholes.

"Wermenya," he answered.

Vermenia. I swallowed back a retort he wouldn't understand. They wouldn't tell me where I was going. They likely wouldn't even tell me where I was when they locked me up.

I closed my eyes and tried to draw out wisps of magic, imagining them escaping through the links of the chain. But there was nothing. I shifted restlessly and felt friction at my back, a muffled whisper of pages. I froze on the floor, pressing my back down. The outline of the small notebook from Joanna pressed into my skin, and I released a silent exhale of relief. I had something. Something of my coven. Even if I had no way of answering, at least I had the pages.

Either from the strike on the head, or boredom, or exhaustion—from wasting magic against a metal that absorbed and deteriorated it—I slept. Fitfully, waking with a groan every time the cart thumped over the ground, but dozing. My body was tense and shivering when I woke in the dark, the metal of the chains doing nothing to fight against the increasing cold. Every breath stung at my nose and throat. We were getting closer to the mountains, the air drying out and starting to thin.

"Werhar?" I asked again, knowing I wouldn't receive an answer but hating lying still and only waiting.

Silence answered the question and I shifted and jerked myself up into a sitting position. There was no shadow at the end of the cart. I squirmed my way through the narrow gap between the crates, chains clanging and scraping and clattering noisily with every small move-ment. It was not a stealthy process, and the canvas at the end of the cart parted by the tip of a blade.

This was a different soldier, older and looking not at all afraid to see me sitting in chains while he stood with a rifle and bayonet in hand. I froze and we studied each other for a long minute as he considered a violent alternative to whatever orders he might have had to guard me.

But he turned away at the murmur of a voice. "Awake," he said, in

Enmaric, accent thick. He stepped away from the cart and the canvas fluttered shut for a moment before being drawn back by a short, round arm in deep brown wool. There were lamps lit in a dark space outside and the sudden brightness left me wincing, exploding brightly in my right eye especially.

"General Pike," a clear, weighty voice said at the opening. I could just make out a rounded, portly frame, backlit from the blue-white glow of the lamps.

"Professor," I corrected, more out of an irritated habit. I would always be a general, but it gave me some sense of control to insist on my academic title.

"Of course," the man said. "I'd forgotten."

He stepped to the side and light fell over his face and suit, and for a moment I was too busy wondering at the fact that he was Enmairian, not Vermenian. And then, finally, I recognized him.

"Ambassador Pearce," I said, with a huff of relief.

Were we stopped at the border? Had they sent for him that quickly?

"I don't want to get your hopes up, Pike," Ramond Pearce said, rolling back on his heels for a moment, his belly stretching far out ahead of him. "You see, I'm a part of this arrangement." Then he turned to the soldiers and said something in Vermenian and disappeared, two soldiers taking his place and dragging me bodily out of the cart.

11

JOANNA

AIDEN HAD NEARLY HIRED US A CAR TO DRIVE THE WHOLE WAY TO THE capital, but none would take us until the morning. The first train into Rhodantis beat that time by nearly an hour anyway.

I was so tired, so stretched thin from worrying the night away, that as the train rounded the edge of the city I barely noticed the glittering, cascading buildings running down the hill to the sea. It wasn't until we were out of the station and Aiden was pulling me and Isaac onto a trolley after him, that the vision of Rhodantis struck me.

The city was all but falling into the ocean, glimmering roof tiles sparkling under the morning sun, passing us as the trolley descended the hill that led to the docks and then the ocean. All the buildings were brightly tinted plaster; clean white, or buttery yellow, or sky blue, or a faint and friendly shade of peach.

"It's impossible," I breathed, staring at the gold-trimmed doorways and windows, at the rush of people. Dawn had barely broken, the sky still dark and rosy behind us, and already the city seemed busy.

I thought I might have been imagining the way we sank over the hill, the buildings turning grander with stone but making up for color in their stained glass windows and bright shutters and banners. But I was tired and heart sore and after the night we had my imagination wasn't up to creating a place so beautiful.

Aiden squeezed me to his side. "We'll come again, all together, and really enjoy the city. I wish this weren't your first time here."

Which was a reminder that we were going to his family, who I had not met and knew very little about aside from the fact they were in some way important. And wealthy, judging by Aiden and his own tastes. And the farther down the hill we went the more I knew it must be true because the houses grew wider, instead of taller, still offering a view of the ocean for the smaller tighter buildings above them. There were electric lamps lit down the sidewalks and fewer people out on the streets. The docks were far enough off to our left and all down below in front of us was a long boardwalk with brilliant white stone buildings and cobalt blue and copper tiled roofs.

Isaac shifted his bag from one hand to the other, and then wrapped his arm around my waist, linking the three of us together. There were already dark circles under his eyes, and he'd been reticent on the train, only hanging on to me and Aiden. His sketchbook sat open in his lap during the ride, his fingers tracing over a sketch of Callum's profile.

Aiden tugged at a wire at the top of the trolley and a bell rung out as we slowed to a stop, just two blocks above the boardwalk row. My legs had turned wooden with exhaustion as we rode and I concentrated on lifting my feet as Isaac and I followed Aiden down to the sidewalk. We walked halfway down a block and he paused in front of a wide brick house, built low and deep and painted white with emerald green shutters.

"My father lives here with Lissa, my covenmother," he said. "He's the Regional Head for the capitol in Congress. He'll do what he can to stall Duncan for us."

I stared up at the tall green door but Aiden was continuing to the next house. Covenmother, not birth mother. Their coven had split, although amicably enough that they remained living next door to each other. But when Aiden spoke about his home growing up he only ever talked about one house, and one family, the only child of four doting parents.

A light went on in one of the windows and I hurried after Aiden and Isaac, not wanting to be caught outside of a stranger's home in the early morning. Even if it did belong to my covenmate's family.

Aiden's mother's house was smaller and I could see a lush green yard through the narrow alley between the houses. The building was brightly tiled, glimmering glass and porcelain shards pressed into mortar, whorls and waves of color blending into one another. The swooping colors stretched up halfway to the roof before receding, revealing the same brightly painted white bricks and vibrant blue shutters over the second-story windows. She was the director of the Rhodantis Museum of Art and all my men spoke of her in warm, affectionate tones. Callum had been gratefully adopted by her after his mother had died and Isaac spoke little enough of his own parents that I suspected he felt the same.

A bright yellow door, more modest than their neighbor's, opened and I knew at once this was Aiden's mother. She looked tiny standing in front of Aiden, still an inch or so shorter even though he was a step below, but she beamed at him, that same wide and bright white smile inside full, dark lips. Her hair was salt and pepper, twisted into fine braids that hung in one long fat braid over her shoulder. She was standing in a white shift with an oversized plaid robe barely wrapped around her, just out of bed, and she spread her arms wide with a laugh as Aiden lifted her up in a hug.

"Ohh," she said, voice breaking. "It's wrong to say how happy I am to see you at a time like this," she said into his shoulder and I saw Aiden's eyes squeeze shut. "But I am and that's the sorry truth of it. Go inside so I can hug my babies."

My heart clenched unexpectedly at the words and I knew this woman was going to have just as much an effect on me as she did my covenmates.

Isaac didn't wait for me, rushing up the steps into her arms, not lifting her as Aiden had but falling into her hold. She cupped the back of his head like a newborn's as he kissed her cheek and then held him back to look him over with a mother's careful eye.

"Hello Claudia," he said.

"Hello, honey," she said, seeming satisfied with what she saw in him. They both smiled weakly at each other, a sympathy for the missing of Callum. Then she patted his cheek and he went inside.

I was suddenly anxious, standing at the bottom of the steps and looking up at the woman my men all loved so dearly. I was meeting Aiden's mother for the first time and without any warning. But she didn't stare at me or study me, sizing me up to see if I was worthy. She smiled, eyes and lips wrinkling at the corners, and came down the steps in her nightgown and robe.

"Oh it is *good* to finally meet you, honey," she said, with a warmth that tightened my throat and brought pricking tears to my eyes.

"It's good to meet you, too," I said, having trouble catching my breath. Then she was wrapping me up in a tight hug, with arms so strong they seemed to squeeze away the tension from the past day and lend me strength.

She was pulling me up the stairs, our arms linked together before I had any more time to worry about impressions.

"Aiden, you forgot to tell me how beautiful Joanna is," she said, in a sharp voice, even as she winked at me out of the corner of her eye.

Aiden spluttered, standing shocked in the doorway where he'd been keeping an eye on our introduction. "I absolutely- I *did* tell you-"

"Well you didn't say *enough*, baby," Claudia said, shooing him back inside.

The house was colorful inside, an open entrance hall filled with trinkets and art and portraits—several clearly from Isaac's familiar hand—and it reminded me of our tower house on campus. My shoulders eased as Claudia closed the door behind us while Aiden continued to protest that he *had* talked about how beautiful I was, the whole conversation turning my cheeks red with embarrassment.

"Well, never mind," Claudia said with a feigned sigh and a little hint of Aiden's own smirk on her lips. His eyes narrowed as he caught onto her jest but she barreled ahead. "Marcus left before you got here, he's getting all the information you'll need. The only thing I want you to worry about right now is getting some food in your bellies and a bed under those tired feet of yours."

We all glanced at each other, feeling that gut-churning need to *go*, to *find Callum*. But Claudia was right. He wasn't in Rhodantis. And I suspected if Aiden or Isaac had known where to find Duncan Pike then that's where we would have gone first no matter how tired our feet or how empty our bellies were.

"No arguments," she added, and this time the strict edge wasn't a tease.

We followed her back into the house, and I collected every little detail my tired eyes could manage to hold onto. A glass cabinet filled with ancient wooden figures, dragons and wild faced masks and lush female figures. A garland of dried roses strung in a net that hung from the ceiling of the hall. Glittering strands of mirrors and beads hanging in every window. A cozy room piled with pillows and books and an elaborate glass and brass hookah, sitting dormant.

"Your home is wonderful," I said, seeing the wild garden out the window, full of small grass trails that wound around herb and flower and vegetable beds.

"Oh, it's a never-ending project," Claudia said as we reached the kitchen, but she said the words fondly as if it was a project she would prefer *not* to see the end of.

There was a young woman in a simple blue dress and white apron, putting food from the stove onto four plates for us.

"Grace, thank you," Claudia said with a deep sigh. "You're a good girl. And tell Darrell and Lissa we said thank you too."

"Of course, Mrs. Cole," she said, curtsying deeply.

My brain sorted the names into my head. Darrell King was Aiden's father. Marcus Cole was Claudia's husband and covenmate, and another member of Congress although not one of the Heads. I wouldn't give my coven up for anything but a relationship did sound simpler with just *two* people and fewer names to keep track of, especially when you were tired and emotionally worn out.

Isaac took my shoulders and put me down into a chair around a small table, a plate of steaming food waiting in front of me. The three of us ate with automatic movements at first until the spice and salt of the food caught up with our taste buds. Then we ate like we hadn't seen a meal in days. I was almost embarrassed, but Claudia only hummed with sympathy and stroked her hand over the back of Aiden's neck, eating more slowly and keeping a watchful eye on us.

By the time I finished, my eyes were drooping, the room feeling hazy and distant around me. Aiden's mother left her food to cool, helping us up from the table and taking us to a set of narrow stairs. My eyes glazed over the small miniatures that ran up the stairs, family portraits and little scenes of what looked like Rhodantis. There was more to see in the hall but I missed it as Isaac helped carry me along while my feet dragged. Aiden's room in the house was much like his own at home. Decadent, dark furniture, plenty big enough for the lot of us, and heavy black curtains hanging shut over the windows.

I fell gratefully into the bed, hearing Claudia call me a 'poor dear.'

"She was hit the hardest when… whatever happened to him," Isaac whispered, the words creaking with his own exhaustion. His hands were at my ankles, taking off my boots as Aiden wrestled me gently into the blankets.

"We'll have news soon," Claudia assured him. "And that boy won't let anything get in the way of getting back to you three. He's too strong for that."

I sank into sleep after Aiden and Isaac stretched down into the mattress on either side of me, our arms going around each other. I reached down the bond for Callum with my last thought, but found nothing.

<hr>

"WAKE UP, DARLING."

I sat straight up, glaring at Aiden. I had gotten minutes of sleep if any at all. He frowned back at me, wiping a sweaty lock of hair off my forehead.

"I'm sorry," he said. "I know. But Marcus just got back."

"How long?" I rasped. How long had I been asleep?

"Four hours," Aiden said. "Not long enough."

I rubbed the sleep out of my eyes, trying to also rub away the irrational anger at being woken up. Marcus was back which meant…

News of Callum!

I shot out of the bed, nearly tripping over Isaac who was still blinking blearily up at Aiden's velvety canopy, like it was absurd that he should wake up under such a thing. He sat up with a grunt, lifting me out of the tangle of sheets and we went downstairs together, barefoot and clumsy.

Marcus surprised me when I finally saw him, slurping coffee out of a deep mug. He looked almost like an older version of Callum, not so much in the shape of his features but in his height, the faint traces of red left in his gray hair, and the thin-framed spectacles on his nose. But he grabbed Aiden, who was almost twice the width of the narrow man, and squeezed him tight, clapping at his back the way my father did with my brother.

Isaac shook his hand, not with the same affection he had with Claudia, but a warm and familiar greeting.

"And this is Joanna," Aiden said, guiding me forward as I tried to finger comb the sleep tangles out of my hair and brush the wrinkles out of my clothes.

"Joanna, *yes*," Marcus said, nodding and bobbing on the balls of his feet as if he had just remembered I existed. He glanced over my face and I felt almost certain that he was trying to decide if he had met me *already* or just now.

"It's very nice to meet you," I said, clearing my throat. "I've heard a lot about you."

He smiled, cheeks flushing a little, and shrugged, humming. "And I you," he said. I suspected he *had* heard a great deal about me but had forgotten almost all of it, and I liked him for it as much as I liked Claudia for her unconditional affection.

"Tell them what they came for," Claudia prompted Marcus when he looked about at all of us as if he was waiting for someone to pick up the thread of conversation.

"Ah yes!" he said, snatching up his coffee and taking another long gulp from its contents. "Duncan Pike has arranged a hearing with Congress tomorrow. I expect, given what he is proposing—being war, again, and unexpectedly-"

"Yes, Marcus," Claudia whispered, a gentle nudge back to the path he'd wandered off.

"Yes, well, decisions won't be made quickly no matter what his aim," Marcus said, nodding along with himself.

I glanced at Isaac and we shared the same conflict. I didn't want Duncan to succeed, just as much as I wanted to march into Vermenia myself this very instance and demand they give up Callum. I would use whatever force was needed, too. If I'd thought Duncan only wanted his son back, I might have supported him. For now, I was relieved he'd be delayed.

"There will be at least a week, of Pike and his cronies bringing forth their claims and evidence, I'd guess," Marcus said. "That's if everyone agrees quickly at the end. But Pike's arranging his plans. There's a Congressman holding a dinner party this evening and he'll attend, grease palms and plead his case on a more personal level. I'm sure that's where he'll speak most urgently about Callum's being captured."

I sucked in a breath and Claudia's hand swatted into Marcus's stomach. But I shook my head and waved away his apology. It was the truth and it was why we'd come to Rhodantis after all.

"Can we get an invitation?" Aiden asked, voice tight.

"Of course," Marcus said. "I've already arranged for you to come with me. And if we talk to your father he may give up his own place for Joanna and Isaac."

"That's alright," Aiden said. "Let them rest here."

It took me just long enough for the suggestion to sink in that I caught Claudia's eyebrow raise skeptically at her son.

"I'll do no such thing," I said, head swinging to stare at Aiden.

"Joanna," he said, hands stretched out to soothe me.

"You won't get anywhere with Duncan on your own," I said.

He huffed and Isaac glanced back and forth between us. "You're not his favorite daughter-to-be now that he knows your mother is from Vermenia," Aiden reminded me with false patience.

"That doesn't mean he doesn't still see me as a useful tool," I answered. "I can press the issue of my magic if I have to. Gladly, if it helps us track down Callum. Or learn what happened to him."

Aiden chewed over that, eyes narrowed down at me. I knew what he was thinking. I was not the most diplomatically minded member of our coven. I might be clumsy or the weight of the past day might catch up to me and leave me emotional in a pit of unsympathetic men and women, seeking to further their own cause. But I knew what I would do for Callum, for any one of my coven, new as they were to me. I would hound Duncan Pike if I had to, but I could just as easily speak sweetly to him. He was only a man, and from what I had seen of him in his own home, it took very little effort to please him if you appealed to his ego.

"You haven't brought anything to wear," he said, a feeble effort.

I huffed and threw up my hands. "Oh, buy me a dress then, you know you love to."

Claudia appeared at my side, smiling with motherly pride. But this time it was for me. She wrapped her arm around my shoulders and squeezed me to her side, hardening my resolve against her son.

Aiden's eyes narrowed at me but a smile flickered in the corners of his lips. "Very well then, darling."

12

CALLUM

THEY WALKED ME THROUGH THE MINE, BLINDFOLDED, AND PUT ME IN A room without windows. I didn't need to dig for my magic to know that every inch of the walls surrounding me was made from rixon. I could taste it on my tongue, bitter and sour, feel it weighing in my bones. My body ached for my coven, unable to find rest or peace when the connection between us was severed. But when I rolled over onto my back the notebook was still there, tucked carefully into a little pocket on the inside of my trousers against my spine. Safe.

The soldiers took the chains off me, holding me at gunpoint the whole time, watching every twitch of my body. Even if I wanted to brave a bullet I wasn't quick enough, or strong enough at the moment, to have a chance at gaining the upper hand against five of them.

They left me in the dark and I felt my way through the shadows until I found a bed, surprisingly soft. I bent over it, palms braced on the mattress, waiting for the trap to spring.

It already has, idiot, I thought. I'd walked into it that night in my father's study as Sabine suggested riding out together. *Joanna told you to be careful around her,* I reminded myself for the hundredth time since I'd woke up in that cart.

I was in the trap. I might as well make myself comfortable. For as long as they were planning to keep me alive.

And despite my misgivings and good sense about falling asleep when surrounded by enemies, I slept soundly on that bed. No one woke me, not even when they opened the door and slid a tray of food across the floor. When I finally did open my eyes again, there was a lamp lit, sitting on a small table by the door to my cell. If it could be called a cell. I didn't recall seeing any Vermenian soldiers in a room this nice in our jails after the war.

I felt groggy but only in the way that meant I'd slept for a long time, without interruption. My stomach was rumbling and I eyed the tray of food with wary hunger. An apple, a small loaf of bread, and a chicken leg, the latter two still faintly warm to the touch. There was a cup full of water waiting on the table too, made of rixon of course, so I could not manipulate it with any magic. Not that I had any magic to be found in this cell.

A rixon cup would keep a potion from working, so at least I knew I wasn't about to be spelled. Enmaire had used those kinds of magics on prisoners to draw out information during the war. I didn't think I had any information worth knowing anyway, so the cup wasn't reassuring. Not being spelled didn't mean I couldn't be poisoned. There were always simpler concoctions to put in the food, killers made of herbs or toxins.

I took a longer look around the room. There was an armchair near the lamp and table, and on the opposite side of the room was a sink and toilet behind a short partition wall. Basic but courteous, more than I had expected when I'd entered in the pitch dark. I went to the sink, and when the water poured free of the faucet I lifted handfuls up to my mouth, taking great gulps as I realized how long it'd been since I'd had any water.

The door opened and I froze, twisting the handle on the sink and spinning to face the door. Ambassador Pearce walked in, without escort and unarmed. I wiped the dripping water off my face with my shirtsleeve. I may not have stood a chance against five armed soldiers but I could certainly overpower this man.

And then what?

I was in a rixon mine and not anywhere near in shape enough to take on a small army of mercenaries, even if the man paying them was dead.

"Callum," Pearce said, nodding respectfully at me.

"Ambassador," I said, the word slow on my tongue as if it were fighting the dozen other names I would have liked to call him.

"Are you comfortable?" he asked. He glanced down at my tray of untouched food, and nodded again, confirming something to himself. "I told them you would not eat. Here." And then he sat down in the armchair as I watched him. He handed me the loaf. "You choose the piece, I'll eat it. I know it's no perfect guarantee but... what can we do?"

I hesitated, staring at the loaf in his outstretched hand, and then stepped closer, grabbing it up. I broke the bread into quarters and then lifted them up to my nose. They all smelled the same, clean and yeasty, making my mouth water. I grabbed a chunk blindly and passed it back to him. He ate it without really looking at it, humming and chewing. I put the rest back on the tray and picked up the cup. He let me lift it to his lips and pour some into his mouth, eyes patient on my face. I set that down too and repeated the process with the rest of the food, picking apart the chicken into smaller pieces off the bone before handing one to him at random, pointing to the spot of apple he should bite into. But I left all the food and the water back on the tray.

"Still won't eat?" he asked, staring at the mess I had made. "After all that work."

"I will in a while," I said, moving back to the bed.

I waited, watching him, but he didn't rush to the door, to leave me with the food while he went in search of the antidote. Even if the poison were slow-acting, he would know it was there in his body; the anxiety would show on his face. No man would trust an antidote with his life on the line, the nerves would show.

But Pearce seemed relaxed.

"I thought you'd put up more of a fight," he said, a perverse sort of disappointment on his face. "I left the dispensable guards at your door, just in case."

That's why they'd all looked so nervous. They knew they were not enough against me, against my reputation at least. The Toy Soldier. But instead of regretting my willingness to fall into the bed, to sleep, when I could have fought, I was relieved. Maybe I would have made it out of the room last night, but not out of the mine. All I would have accomplished was entertainment for a man like Pearce.

"I suppose I am curious what you mean to do with me," I said. "Since I'm not dead yet."

Pearce raised an eyebrow and looked around the room. "You are… my guest." I smirked at that and he added, "With restrictions."

"And have I been brought here for a reason?" I asked, relaxing back against the rixon wall behind me even though it made my skin crawl and my legs feel weak to be so near.

"To be useful," Pearce said without hesitation.

Frustration was rising in my chest, with claws and sharp words and I took in a long breath to settle myself. Whatever he expected of me, I wanted to be the opposite. If he was expecting a young warrior, wrestling his way out of the cell, then I would be meek and cooperative.

"And what do I need to do to be useful?" I asked, trying to relax my face, make my voice light.

"Oh." Pearce laughed and waved his hand through the air. "You're already doing that just fine, my boy. Don't worry about that a bit."

So the capture *was* the purpose. My going missing would stir up my father and the other generals into action and would make a persuasive argument to Congress on pursuing action against Vermenia. Not Enmaire's Toy Soldier! Not the hero!

He moved to stand and I gambled. "You and Carras have been discussing this for a while, I take it?" I said and watched his face. He flinched, bending to hide his face as he heaved himself out of the chair with a grunt.

He looked at me for a long time after he stood, eyes narrowed. I guessed he was trying to decide if I had unexpected insight, or if Carras was loose-lipped.

"I always thought your common interest was peace between our countries," I said.

He snorted at that, shaking his head. "Look at a history book, Pike. There's never been peace on that border. Peace is a common interest for fools. Now, I take my leave of you. Is there anything you need, anything I can bring to entertain you? You're in for a long stay."

He didn't mean to relieve me, but he did. They weren't putting me in front of a firing squad anytime soon. Maybe he would keep me in the mines through the whole war, the one he was putting together with Carras while men like my father unknowingly cheered him on. Maybe I would see my coven again.

But war could carry on forever and I wanted to be with them *now*. I needed to maneuver myself into position. Because what if he only needed me to precipitate the war, to add urgency to my father's argument to invade.

So I pulled up what little I knew about Ambassador Pearce, from my father's admiring comments made on the man, and asked, "Could I have a chessboard?"

Pearce's eyes narrowed at me. It wasn't a popular game in Vermenia but it was at home, and Ramond Pearce was well known for being a champion at the game. My father had hissed and spit and cursed the man the one time he'd played him. And Pearce had thanked him for the game, a little smile on his lips, and said that he could convince no Vermenian to play properly.

"And who will you play, *Professor*?" he asked, with a sly slide in his voice as if he had caught out my trap.

"Myself," I said. "To keep from growing bored."

He looked irritated but he bowed a little and nodded. "Well it's a rare game here, but I'll see what I can do." He left with a backward glance at me, a suspicious squint in his eyes and it was small comfort to think he might not know who won the game of our first conversation.

I stared at the food where I'd left it, wanting badly to grab it up and fill my hollow stomach as quickly as possible. Instead, I took up the cup of water first. If it were poisoned it would have acted faster than any of the food. And after the conversation with Pearce, who'd never shown a sign of even thinking of the food again after he ate it, I didn't think I was going to be poisoned.

The water wasn't enough but I made sure to drink slowly and not spill a drop, resisting the urge to lick the cup dry. I took the apple next, carrying it back to the bed with me. I watched the door as I took a bite, reaching behind me and pulling the little notebook free from its pocket.

I read the words covetously, taking careful nibbles of the apple with every flick of a page, hoping the crunch would cover any sound.

Dinner at seven and if you are late Joanna promises there'll be no dessert for you.

Whose trousers were in the hall? And why?

I ran my fingers over one of Isaac's sketches of Joanna's lips, partly because of my love of the subject and partly because it was done by his hand.

I hurried through the notebook as I neared the end of the apple and at the end of all our love notes and written bickering I found new words, my heart breaking at the sight.

Callum, be safe. Please, be safe. Callum come ho-

We'll find you. Going to Rhodantis.

Can't sleep without you.

My throat closed up as I held the last bite of apple in my mouth. Their words were here. Words after rixon chains and maybe even after being put in the cell. Written magic didn't work the same as my magic though, there was never a trace or tingle left behind. Whatever energies Isaac and Aiden and I used, Joanna didn't need. And maybe it was those energies that rixon blocked.

Maybe...

I stared at the empty gap of the page underneath their words. I took the corner of my thumbnail and pressed it into the paper. Would this work? The space grew cramped as I worked, letters made crooked and silly with my fingernail. But I squeezed it in, pressing all the love, all the horrible ache of not having them near, and not feeling them close, into the word.

Safe.

13

———

JOANNA

Darrell, Aiden's father, squeezed my hand gently, and I relaxed my grip, an apologetic smile flickering over my mouth. We were walking up the tall stone steps into the Congressman's home, Congressman... Whitworth, I reminded myself.

Aiden and Marcus were just behind us, which had something to do with Marcus's position vs. Darrell's and I felt a thread of panic rush through me at how little I understood of the layers of our own government. I needed to spend more time in the history section of the library when I got home, and less in the magical research. The men and women inside this house would be the ones making decisions about Duncan Pike's war tomorrow, about Callum's supposed rescue, and I would have liked to know more about them. I wished it was Isaac's arm I was holding, he was better at keeping me calm than anyone else. But when it became clear that we needed Darrell King to gain entrance to the dinner and there was only room for one of us, Isaac had quickly begged off.

"There's nothing to warm Duncan to me," Isaac said to Aiden. "You have your father's influence, which will count for something to a man like him. And Joanna has her magic. I'll be in the way and, honestly, I'll feel better here."

351

"We'll take care of things here together," Claudia said in his support.

And for all that Darrell looked like an older, and maybe heavier, version of Aiden, I saw now that Aiden's warmth and charm came from his mother. Darrell King was imposing and while he'd gone along readily enough with our plan for Aiden's sake, or Callum's, he was not a soothing escort.

I drew my shoulders back and glanced down again at the dress Aiden had procured for me. I'd expected something from the city, hastily gotten, but instead Aiden had called Hildy and she'd expressed a package straight to the house by car. I remembered the dress as soon as I saw it again, a black-red like blood, embellished with silver threads and beads, flowing liquidly down my skin.

I lifted my chin high and imagined myself as the kind of woman who would own a dress like this. Someone like Hildy and Sabine, and a little of Bryce too. Feminine and seductive and dangerous. Aloof. *I am poisoned cherry wine*, I thought to myself, and then grimaced a little at the idea of it.

The doors opened at that moment, and the mingling attendees of the dinner party looked out onto the steps and saw me. Me, with my nose wrinkled and thinking to myself that, really, I was more like pressed apple juice than anything so exotic as poisoned wine.

I tried to erase the expression but already the women were looking me up and down and the men passed over me with quizzical expressions, probably only wondering why I was here and Lissa King, who I'd only gotten one elegant daunting glimpse of, was not. Well done, Joanna.

I glanced over my shoulder at Aiden, whose eyes were fixed to the open back of my dress, frozen and goose-pimpled from the short walk out of the carriage, and wished we were walking in together. A footman announced my name, that I was Darrell's guest, and I heard a familiar growling throat clear.

I scanned the room, the milling figures of aristocracy and diplomats, and found Duncan Pike in a tight black suit with a dark tie too tight around his red neck. His eyes fixed to mine, glaring and wondering all at once. And now I did not care whether I was wine or juice, or seductive or silly. I smiled at Duncan and had no doubt in my mind that tonight, where he was concerned, I was the predator in the room.

"You'd do well to make him sweat," Darrell said under his breath to me. "He'll guess you're here to work against him, but for now the rest of the room thinks you'll have come as his ally. Avoid him. Speak to the others. The women will listen to you."

"Thank you," I whispered back and he nodded without glancing at me, leading us to the grand woman standing on the steps.

Congressman Whitworth's wife, Juliet. She was younger than the man she stood with, a jaunty old fellow with a hooked nose and a thin comb of white hair over his pale head. Her hair was honey gold and the streaks of silver there were carefully arranged to shine under the lamplight. She was draped in silks and lace, a silvery blue trimmed with delicate pink threads, entirely feminine and gentle. She kept an affectionate hand on her husband's shoulder, smiling at his guests with a warmth that was either sincere or close enough to be believed.

"It's good to see you, Darrell," she said, and her voice was smooth and full that I thought at once there must be magic in it. She could be a singer, and the songs would be a spell of their own. Aiden would know.

"You look lovely as ever, Juliet," Darrell said, stepping up as she lowered her cheek to be kissed. He stepped back and gestured me forward and I panicked for a moment, wondering if I should curtsy or bow. "This is Aiden's covenmate, Joanna Wick."

Juliet saved me from my panic, reaching out an elegant hand to shake. I answered it with my own, suddenly spotting ink under my fingernails. "Thank you very much for allowing me to join you this evening," I said, knowing that she had nothing to do with it, really.

"Of course, I am very happy to have you," she said, the sweetness in her voice matching her smile and almost lulling me into believing the welcome. But her gray eyes were sharp on my face and it cleared some of the magic of her words. "And you are a covenmate of Duncan Pike's son too, I believe," she said, her eyes glancing over my shoulder to where I guessed Duncan might be circling me around the edge of the crowd.

"Callum," I said because I wanted the room to remember his own name more than his father's. "Yes."

"Here to help his case," she said, watching me with those knife-bright eyes. The words might have meant Callum as much as Duncan and I didn't want there to be a mistake of my purpose for the evening.

"I'm here to learn as much as I can about what happened to my covenmate," I said and I felt the blade of her focus recede a little. "And do what I can to ensure he returns home safe and soon."

I glanced at Darrell who nodded in support, and saw Aiden watching me over his shoulder, pride in his gaze. Words needed to be used carefully in this room but this was something I had been practicing, not in speaking but at least in writing. I hoped it would be enough.

"Come," Juliet said, stepping down to me. "I'll introduce you to some of the others. It will be better if people know you before the real talk begins."

Juliet may not have been my ally exactly, I couldn't tell for sure if she cared one way or the other about Callum's disappearance, but she maneuvered me carefully through the guests. We avoided Duncan with a deft step between one politician and the next, and I tried to collect the names in my head. She introduced me mostly as Aiden King's covenmate, and occasionally as Callum's as if she knew who would understand the connection.

I made it back to Aiden as we moved to the dining room for the meal and I leaned into the arm he offered me, feeling weak already from the scrutiny of the party.

"Duncan cornered me already," he whispered against my cheek, looking like a lover rather than a conspirator. I soaked up the affection regardless. "He wants to know what we're doing here."

"He knows exactly what we're doing here," I said with a roll of my eyes. "Did you learn anything about Callum?"

"He went out to investigate the crates we found," Aiden said.

"Didn't come back. When they went to find him the pit was empty and Callum was missing."

My forehead furrowed and I ignored the dining room—the murals on the walls of boats at sea and mermaids on rocks and glorious faces peering down at it all through the gleam of stars above—in favor of searching for Duncan. He was at the other end of the room, pouring words into Charles Whitworth's ear who looked somewhere between attentiveness and a nap.

"I don't believe him," I whispered. "Callum wouldn't have gone alone. He knows more."

Aiden grinned down at me, squeezing at my waist before we had to part again to take our seats. "Then you'll pry the rest out of him. After dinner. I'll do what I can with the men to keep him in check."

"I love you," I said, brushing a quick kiss over his lips.

"I love you," he answered. "And you look fearsome tonight. We'll win. We'll get him back."

We parted with my chin held high, remembering that for the evening at least I was a warrior too. For Callum, I would fight.

DUNCAN HUNTED me down when the men returned to the group after drinks. Aiden was close at his heels but he stopped when I shook my head, only slightly, and turned back, joining his father and Marcus where they were speaking with Charles Whitworth. Hopefully, as a group they would be able to undo whatever rallying cry Duncan had built up with Congress members, using Callum as an excuse to march on Vermenia.

"Do you *want* my son to die?" Duncan hissed at me.

I'd moved away from the card table of women, who'd hummed and fretted sweetly over my concern for Callum, when I saw Duncan enter the room. He caught up to me by the bookshelf, a thankfully empty area of the room, and did his best to loom over me and pin me into the corner. I braced the heels of my shoes hard into the floor and held as still as stone. He'd nearly knocked our faces together before he realized I would not move, and retreated quickly with a huffing breath.

"I was going to ask the same thing," I said, watching him carefully. "Tell me what happened."

His eyes flinched and he almost turned away from me. My hand flexed at my side and I nearly reached out to grab him but he spun back to me.

"He went out to look at the dig site you found and-" Duncan started, the words automatic.

"Who was he with?" I asked.

His head snapped to stare at me. "What?"

"Who was with Callum at the dig site?" I asked, watching every twitch of his eyes, every flickering twist of his mouth behind that beard. "He wouldn't have gone alone, he's not a fool. So who went with him and don't tell me you don't know."

"You *would* go looking for someone to blame other than your people, wouldn't you?" Duncan snarled at me, all but spitting the words.

"I will blame *every* person responsible including the Vermenians who crossed onto *our* soil illegally," I answered, lowering my voice. "But what matters to me, what *should* matter to you, is who allowed Callum to be captured?"

"No one allowed-"

"Who was he with?" I said, and I let my voice raise this time because I didn't really care if I made a scene. I was Callum's emotional covenmate, his grieving lover. Duncan was the one trying to play politics with his son's life.

He jumped, glancing over his shoulder to see that we had caught the eyes of a few of the other party attendees. He gave me a warning glare but I only opened my eyes wide, tears welling up so easily— they'd been waiting there all day and night really and I would use them as my weapon if I had to—and parted my lips to speak again.

"No one, you silly girl," he hissed, eyes darting over my face.

I stared at him, waiting for him to change his mind, and when he didn't I pulled out a stick of chalk.

"What are you-?" he started, but he was too late.

Duncan Pike cannot lie, I wrote on the side of the bookshelf, white chalk dusting onto my beautifully dark skirt. His hand snatched for my wrist gripping it tightly.

"Who was Callum with?" I asked.

Duncan's teeth ground in his jaw and his fingers squeezed so hard on my skin I could almost see the bruise beginning to form.

"I want you to take your hand off her," Aiden growled from Duncan's back. "No one has seen you yet but me, but I'd gladly step aside so the room can watch you."

"Who was Callum with?" I repeated, ignoring the ache in my hand.

"Sabine York and her coven," Duncan whispered, his face red with the effort of staying silent. He threw my wrist back at me, releasing it, fingerprints bright on my skin. "They went with him and were attacked. Callum was grabbed. They could do nothing."

It was a flimsy story and it sounded even less convincing on Duncan's tongue. No wonder he wasn't sharing that version. Oh, I believed that Sabine York had been there with Callum. But I didn't for a second believe that she or her coven had been attacked. She *did* want to take Callum from me, but not for herself. Not to keep.

"You don't believe that," I said.

"No, I don't but it doesn't matter," Duncan growled. "If they are traitors, we know now. We can prepare. What is important is that we move quickly against Vermenia before they are able to finish any more plans they have in place." I blinked at him in shock and he rolled his eyes at me, face red and tight with anger, a vein popped on his forehead. "You don't understand."

"I do," I said, quiet and weak. "What is important to you is that Enmaire goes to war with Vermenia, the sooner the better. And I imagine that is what was important to the people responsible for Callum's kidnapping, too. You have more in common with your enemy than you realize." His face grimaced and his teeth bared at me in anger, but I continued. "What is important to me is that your son is safe. And that he makes it home. The sooner the better."

"You haven't seen him," Duncan said, words whispering and a

manic gleam in his eye. "You don't know the best of him. You're worrying and weeping for a man, a boy, that destroyed *armies*. This is nothing. This will do nothing. Callum will *always* survive."

I was tired from head to toe, weary of Duncan and of worrying and missing Callum. But I drew myself up and realized I was not smaller than the man in front of me, no matter how he wanted to see me. I stepped into his space and he fell back a step, nearly bumping into a still glowering Aiden.

"You should want more for your son than survival," I said.

His expression hardened. "There's nothing you can do, now. This war is your best hope of his return."

"Tell me where to find York and her coven," I said.

He opened his mouth to deny me and in the breath, he realized that the room beyond us was growing too quiet. Soon there'd be no privacy in our conversation and I already knew more than he wanted made public.

"In the north, west of Dannsedge. Near the barracks. I haven't kept their address on me," he said, sneering.

I stepped around him without answering, wiping my palm over the words I'd written on the bookshelf until they were only a faint smear. Hopefully, Juliet would forgive me.

"There's nothing you can do," he repeated, firmer and it sounded like reassurance for him more than me.

Maybe he was right, but I looked up to Aiden's gaze and he looked hopeful, a strength of belief in me without even knowing the outcome of the conversation. Because he knew I wouldn't give up. So maybe there was nothing I could do. But I thought there was plenty we could try.

☾

ISAAC WAS WAITING for us by a small fireplace in the nest-like living room of Claudia's home. His head shot up from the small notebook in his lap and he jumped up from the chair as we rushed to him.

"Joanna pried it out of him," Aiden announced, grin tight with tension and full with pride.

"You'll want to see-" Isaac started.

"We need to leave as soon as we can," I said. My thoughts had been running with a building momentum ever since we'd left the Whitworth's and there was a rattling urgency inside of me now.

"Just look," Isaac said again, holding the notebook out to us.

"It was York and her coven," Aiden said over him. "We're going back north. We'll figure out a way into Vermenia."

"We have to go to Bridgeston first," I rushed to say.

Aiden twisted to me, a baffled openness on his face. "Why on earth would we go to Bridgeston?"

"*Look*," Isaac shouted and we both snapped back to attention.

It was the notebook we passed messages in, opened to the most recent pleas to Callum to be safe, to be home again. But the page was blank beneath our messages.

"There's nothing," I said, burying the ache in my chest. I opened my mouth to answer Aiden when Isaac's hand shook, and I saw the glimmer on the page, the impression of words. I snatched the notebook up out of his hand and turned my back to the fire, twisting the page in my hand so that the firelight played over the indentation, a fingernail scribble.

Safe.

Something broke in my chest, a cage that I had built up against all my fears and anxieties, a way to survive an evening amongst strangers who didn't really care one way or another if Callum made it home to me. I sobbed and Aiden caught the notebook up in his hand as Isaac's arms circled my waist and hauled me into his chest. The cage crumbled in small doses, hiccups of relief and a sudden ability to breathe deeply again as I hadn't since fainting in the library.

"Is it him?" Aiden whispered, thumb stroking over the page. "I can't...I still can't feel him."

"It felt like his markings," Isaac answered, fingers digging into the back of my head, undoing the elegant twist of hair Claudia had put up for me. "It might have been wishful thinking."

I sighed into the skin of his neck and took another deep breath.

With Isaac's magic, the art of color and shape, he could feel the impressions of a person in a bit of handwriting. If he believed Callum's hand had made the word, I believed it too. I *needed* to believe it.

"I could use a little wishful thinking," Aiden said, stepping closer to us. I heard him kiss Isaac over my head, an anxious huff of breath released with a trembling rhythm.

"If it weren't him they would have used a pen," I said. "He's safe but he doesn't have anything to write with. Oh!" I dug around at the silk skirt of my dress, over my hip. My hands were shaking and my fingers were a little numb from the cold or from the shock of the news, but I found the gap of magic I was looking for, drawing a small nub of a pencil out. "Give me the notebook."

Aiden passed it to me and I stayed tucked between them, lifting the notebook up to Isaac's chest and flipping up the page. *Where are you?* I wrote. *We love you. We'll find you.*

Aiden bent to rest his chin on my shoulder, nudging my cheek with his and kissing at my jaw. "It will take time for him to answer," he said.

"I know." But still, I stared at the page as if I could will him into seeing our message and answering right away.

"Joanna bullied Duncan into giving up the information we needed," Aiden said. They both had hands on me that squeezed gratefully, Isaac almost laughing as Aiden described the scene of Duncan cornering me at the dinner party. But when Aiden told him about Sabine York, Isaac stiffened in our embrace.

"We can't go up against them," Isaac said. "Even if Callum were with us, it would be dangerous. They're not infamous warriors for nothing."

"I think Sabine's made her point," I said. "This was some kind of retaliation for her coven but-"

"And if she decides a better retaliation would be a coven for a coven?" Isaac asked, forehead knotting.

I sucked a breath at the thought. I'd thought there had been respect between Sabine and myself, but clearly, there hadn't been enough to keep Callum safe and I would be an idiot not to be careful. Isaac was right. All her poisonous words may have been against Callum and his family, but she'd held that grudge for more than fifteen years. What if it wasn't satisfied by one act?

"We don't even have an idea of how to get into Vermenia yet," Aiden said, running his hands down my sides.

I lifted my head at that, looking up at both of them. "Actually, I do, a bit," I said. "We need to go to Bridgeston. My mother's papers are still at the house. I think I could work just enough magic to be able to use them myself."

Isaac and Aiden stared at each other, their faces barely shifting, exchanging words without having to speak. And they were leaving me outside of the conversation. A spark of frustration flared in my chest. I had just found the information we needed about Callum's disappearance. I deserved to be included.

"Don't," I snapped and they both looked at me, eyes wide. "Don't make a decision together without even having to say the words aloud. I know that I am new, still-"

"Darling, it wasn't-" Aiden said.

"*But* we will need papers to get into Vermenia and I have access to some," I continued.

"We weren't-" Aiden protested again, raising his hands to his side, with an edge sharpening in his voice.

"You wanted to come here without us," I said, rounding on Aiden. "Were you planning on going into Vermenia alone too?"

"I was planning on coming up with a *good* idea, one with more than a few minutes thought," Aiden said, raising haughty eyebrows. "One that doesn't send *you* into Vermenia alone, which is what it sounds like you were planning."

I opened my mouth to shout, although I had no idea what words might fall out when I did when Isaac stepped between us.

"You're both half-cocked," Isaac said. "And we're all exhausted." Aiden and I stared at each other watchfully over Isaac's shoulder as he turned to face Aiden. "For what it's worth I think we should take every option we have and go to Bridgeston. It's an opening, even if it isn't the one we end up using. And maybe we'll need to speak with York too. We'll decide that as we go. *Together.*"

I held my breath and this time as Aiden and Isaac stared at each other, I let them have their silent conversation. After a beat, Aiden's shoulders sagged and he looked exhausted, older. My stomach felt a guilty kind of twist as he seemed to wilt.

"We could call Gast," he said, with a glance at me. "Bring them with us to York's coven if Joanna thinks they'll have more information about Callum for us."

"I do," I said.

Isaac was quiet for a moment before saying, "Even if York did have plans for us, I think Bryce would be a shock, and certainly a safety net for us. That's a good idea."

Bryce never said one way or another if they *were* a dragon but they enjoyed the game of me trying to ask the right questions to get a straight answer. Callum had said once that dragons were covetous of their magic, that they used it rarely and sparingly. But Bryce had used it earlier in the fall against the Hollow that came to campus and I had no doubt that if they agreed to come north with us, they would be able to keep us safe from any potential threat, even a coven of warriors.

"You're trembling," Isaac murmured and I looked up. His gray eyes were pale with that studious focus of his that could have meant he was sketching me out in his head or trying to decide on the best way of approaching my feelings.

"We're all exhausted," Aiden answered for me. "And now that we have this, I feel as if I might actually sleep tonight. I'll go next door and make the calls we need. Bryce should be able to meet us on our way to Bridgeston. The two of you should go and get some rest."

Isaac loosened his hold on me so I could turn to stare up at Aiden. His eyes were getting bloodshot now and there was a pinch around his lips I had never seen before, and my heart clenched. He had taken on the heaviest burden of planning amongst us so far, without any hesitation. I realized I wouldn't have known what to do when Bryce told us the news from Dannsedge, wouldn't have had any idea of where to go or whose door to knock on for answers.

I stepped into Aiden's chest, pressing my nose into the hollow of his neck, and his hands clutched at my back.

"You'll be up soon?" I asked and felt him nod against the top of my head. It wasn't an apology on my part for snapping at him, but it wasn't one from him for trying to control the decisions either. A truce, maybe.

"I'll set us up to leave in the morning and come right back," he said, kissing my hair. He lifted a hand and loosened my mess of hair a little more, plucking out a few pins. "Don't wait up, I'll hop into the bed as soon as I'm done."

I didn't remember the way back up to Aiden's bedroom, having been half asleep both on the way up and down the stairs. Isaac's fingers tangled with mine after Aiden left out the backdoor of the house to cross the yard to his father's house.

"I knew you would do it," Isaac whispered to me as we tread quietly through the upstairs hall. "Duncan didn't stand a chance against you."

14

ISAAC

IT SEEMED LIKE THE WORLD WAS BEING SAPPED OF COLOR AGAIN, AS IT had in the woods around Canderfey when the Hollow stole shades of green. This time it was only my own mood, my head too heavy with worry and wondering about Callum to enjoy the sight of Rhodantis, of Claudia's beautiful home.

Joanna's feet were stumbling as we made it into Aiden's room, her eyes heavy-lidded, and in the dark even she was turning colorless, skin going moon white and hair losing its bright sheen.

"Come here, love," I said, leading her over to the bed and sitting down in front of her. "I promise you only have to stay upright long enough for me to get you into something to sleep in."

She hummed and swayed a bit in front of me before stilling. The room was a gray-blue, moonlight slipping in from a window facing the garden. Her dress was black and inky over her skin in the darkness, and I tried to imagine dipping a paintbrush into the color and spreading it over a canvas, a color of secrets and aching.

"I'm trying to remind myself that I don't hate everyone but our own coven," she said, her back to me as I undid delicate black pearl buttons at the base of her spine.

I swallowed a laugh at the declaration. "You didn't have a nice time

365

at the party?" I asked, dripping sarcasm. I'd been a little relieved not to go, although the evening alone had seemed to run at half speed while I waited for them to return.

Her shoulders shook and for a moment I thought she was laughing too and then I realized that she was shaking with dry, silent sobs. I abandoned the buttons in favor of pushing the dress off her, and she twisted out of it, climbing into my lap even as the fabric slid down her leg to land on the floor. Her arms tangled over my shoulder and I pressed my nose to her shoulder, breathing her in and smelling the perfume of the party on her skin.

"He's safe," I said to her, and it felt like a prayer more than a promise.

She nodded, pulling in a deep breath and pressing up close to my chest, her hands reaching up to frame my face.

"We'll get him back," she said, the words every bit as wishful as mine had been. Her eyes scanned my cheeks, my mouth, and then rose back to my own, tears shining on her cheeks. "Tell me how to make this easier for you and Aiden."

"Don't," I whispered, chest burning. "We don't think this is any different for you than it is for us just because we've known him longer. We're *all* a coven."

Her expression crumpled for half a beat before smoothing again. I leaned in, resting my forehead to hers. "I need something else to focus on," she said, words small. "Just in times like this, when we can't move faster than we already are. When we can't get to him yet."

He's safe. He's safe. The words repeated on a loop as I drew Joanna to my chest, laying the pair of us back against the mattress. I wrestled with the worries—of *where* Callum was, and *what* was happening, and *how* we were going to rescue him—and buried them at the back of my thoughts. Joanna's fingers fussed at the buttons of my shirt, pulling the top free and sliding her palm inside the collar to rest against my chest. Her touch was warm and my heart skipped in its rhythm, a little flash of feeling stirring.

"If he were here," I said, closing my eyes and drawing Callum up in my imagination, trying to put the copper color of his hair back into the world. "He'd be sitting up against the headboard with the lamp lit and his glasses on his nose and a book in his hand, staring at the pair of us. Waiting to see if we'd invite him closer." Silly man was always *waiting* for permission. Never taking what any one of us was all too happy to give him. Until we told him to, and then gods help anyone who tried to stop him.

"I'd make him watch," Joanna said, and her cheek swelled against my shoulder, a real smile swelling up.

We were quiet and when I opened my eyes again it only reminded me that the room was dark and Callum was not here. I sighed and Joanna chorused it, breath trailing over my skin. I didn't like speaking of him this way, as if he was gone from us and couldn't return.

Joanna pushed herself up, palms pressed over my chest, her hair an amusing, dark halo of curls around her head. "I'll Write him back to us, or us to him. Whatever it takes."

The moonlight was over her cheek like silvery highlights and I could see the set of her lips, firm and straight. I reached up and rubbed at the light on her skin with my thumb.

"I know you will," I said, because even if it took every last stroke of my magic and every last drop of paint, if I could have pulled Callum free through a canvas, I would have done it too. "Focus here, on me tonight. I need you, too." And it wasn't until the words were out I knew how much I meant them.

"Thank you," Joanna sighed out. She rolled over me, her legs sliding around my hips, all bare except for the delicate underwear she wore. I pulled her down to me, hands in her hair, rooting for pins, and slanting my lips across hers.

It was a guilty kind of relief, the comfort of her against me. I chased the small, pleased sound she made and drew more out with my tongue against hers, pulling back to suck at her lips. Callum was in our thoughts as we touched but there was no apology needed. It was an even exchange, trading pleasure and distraction. There was a watery choke in every little moan she made and my forehead was knotted, focusing on her sounds and taste, the salt and the bitter, tart stain of wine on her mouth.

She was pushing my shirt open and before I could pull my arms free, she bent her head to nip a line down my chest. Her fingernails scratched teasingly on their way to the zipper of my pants, drawing out goosebumps and shivers on my skin, one of her palms rubbing over the top of the fabric against my cock as the other undid the fastenings.

There was hunger building in my blood and I drew her face back to mine, kissing her out of gratitude and a *need* that I had missed in its absence.

I sat up, lifting her with me, moving just enough for her to push the pants off my hips with my underwear, down my thighs to my knees. Her hand wrapped around my length, and the touch was like a rush of life and awareness back into my system. I groaned at the feeling of her fingers around me, warm and soft, tugging sweetly. I braced myself on the bed, kicking my legs free of my clothing as Joanna coaxed my cock into a stiff, aching state of arousal.

I wanted to touch her, to finally take advantage of all the skin she'd left open for me to touch, to kiss and lick. But before I got the chance, she pressed our chests together, pushed her underwear to the side, and sank down on me, stretching herself open on the way.

It wasn't a smooth, slick descent. She hadn't been patient enough and I could see the anxious little line between her eyebrows, the bite of her teeth into her bottom lip. I lifted one hand from the mattress and pressed it to her clit, swirling quickly, trying to make up for her impatience. The drag of my cock inside of her was a shocking kind of friction, and I hissed at the feeling. I wrapped my free arm around her waist, holding her to me, watching her face as the tension turned slack, her mouth falling open in an 'o' of understanding.

"That's it, love," I whispered as she started to squirm in my hold. "There's no rush. You have me."

"Isaac," she whimpered.

I kissed at her lips, her chin, her neck, until I could nudge her back over my arm, leaving her breasts pointed up to me. I kissed them too, flicking at her nipples with my tongue. She had a smoother flavor here, a little salt of sweat but something sweet too, and infinite softness. I traded one breast for the other and back again until her chest was rising and falling in a quick rhythm, fingers tight in on the back of my neck.

I braced my feet on the floor in front of the bed and rolled my hips up into hers. She sighed, and I could feel her body relaxing around me. I released my tight hold on her waist and softened my touch on her clit, teasing with my fingers and chasing the shallow bounce of her hips over mine. She sat up again and her mouth landed on mine, with wet lazy kisses, fingers tangling in my hair, gripping and pulling every time I thrust up a little harder.

"Oh stars, Isaac, I've missed you," she murmured.

I'd missed her too. We rarely got time alone and I could never resist watching her with one of the others if they were near, but I was suddenly grateful to be selfish with her now.

Her muscles fluttered around my cock and I ached to roll her over on the bed, to snap my hips into hers until there would be crescent bruises on the backs of her thighs from my hip bones. She was squeaking, the sound held tight behind her lips. I groaned as she pulled hard on my hair, rutting up into her, the movement easy now that she was dripping and so close to falling apart for me. I pressed hard on the little bead of nerves between her legs and she came, burying the sound into my neck, her thighs squeezing tight around my waist.

I wrapped my arms around her back and rolled us, unable to stop myself from thrusting, from falling into the way her body milked mine. All my noble plans to draw her pleasure out again faded as she clutched to me with legs and arms and cunt.

"Yes," she whispered in my ear. "Yes, I love to feel you."

She was flattened beneath me and I buried my cry into the mattress, shocked by the sudden spiral of ecstasy that burst out of me. Her hands soothed down my back as I shuddered, hips jerking in a finish until I was too sensitive to move at all.

Joanna's legs loosened from around me, lowering to the mattress as I grunted in protest. Her eyes blinked up at me, lids low and barely moving.

"Alright?" I asked, pulling out and scooping her up in my arms to pull us back to the head of the bed, my knees shaking.

She only peppered clumsy kisses over my shoulder, soft and limp, already falling asleep. I huffed a laugh but managed to slide her under the sheets with me. My heartbeat slowed as I curled around her back. I called down the bond to Callum and the empty echo answered, but it felt less hollow now that we'd heard from him. And I believed in Joanna and Aiden to find our way back to him as much as I believed in Callum to keep himself safe until we could get to him.

Joanna's breath was puffing against my back as Aiden finally returned to the room. He whistled a sweet note of magic under his breath and the silk of the dress on the floor slid up into the air and then across the room to drape over an armchair.

"Everything okay?" I whispered.

He froze in place for a moment, before reaching his hands up to cover his face. I almost got up out of the bed but I heard the huff of his sigh release and then he was shrugging out of his coat, his hands rough on his clothes as if he were trying to escape them. No, he wasn't okay. No more than Joanna and I were, and possibly worse. He'd slept less than either of us, constantly pushing to get us closer to Callum.

"There was a train in two hours or one at ten..." he said, keeping his voice lowered."I...I got us tickets on the later one. Did I choose wrong?"

I didn't think Joanna would stir, not with the way she'd fallen to sleep so easily after we'd finished. Still, I scooted out of the bed with careful movements. Aiden eyed me with a weary kind of interest as he threw the last of his clothes on a tidy pile.

"You chose right," I answered, wrapping my arms around his chest and holding steady as he leaned into me. I pressed my face against his neck just under his chin and drew in a long breath. He still smelled like the cigar smoke of a parlor room, and the cedarwood oil he usually wore beneath that. "I know we want to rush every bit as much as Joanna does, but a few hours won't hurt. We need to be thinking straight when we go to see York. Never mind crossing into Vermenia."

"Earlier, when she said..." but he trailed off, leaning back and looking up at the ceiling. I waited for him and after a long silence, he continued. "I'm not trying to shut her out. I don't think we love him any more than she does. And it isn't that I love him more than her, I just..."

"Want to be the one to fix this," I said. "And it chafes when she has a solution before you do."

He looked back at me, frowning, on the verge of disagreeing. Then he swallowed hard and nodded. "Tell me that's stupid," he said.

"That's stupid," I said, trying not to smile.

"She can do things we can't. Not just dealing with Duncan but the Written magic, it's different too. It can reach him when we can't," he said, frustration lacing the words.

"I know," I said, reaching up to squeeze his shoulders.

"So I'm being petty," Aiden growled quietly. "Resenting that she has the tools to save him and I don't."

I shrugged. "Probably," I said.

Aiden's eyes narrowed at me. "You're just going to stand there and agree as I work through this?"

I grinned and he grimaced at me. "Well I'm very tired," I said. "And you were doing so well on your own."

He tried for another moment to stay annoyed but the laugh came out, stifled just enough not to disturb Joanna.

"She has tools we don't, but Callum needs us every bit as much as he does her. I don't doubt that she would have hunted Duncan down to that dinner party, but I know having your fathers' assistance helped. You have connections and influence we don't have." I turned and looked at the bed, Joanna was curling into a ball without either of us there to press against. "She doesn't feel any more in control than you do," I said, pulling Aiden down to kiss him, a firm press of the lips. "If you can give her a purpose, words to Write, or another stubborn old man to railroad, you'll be taking care of all of us."

Aiden's face softened as I pulled away. "And you'll be holding us all together," he said, drawing me close for another kiss, slower and lingering. It wasn't leading, although even if I was exhausted and spent from my time with Joanna, I'd have offered any piece of myself to soothe him. Instead, he only held me to him, kissing and breathing together for a long stretch, until he wobbled a little as if he'd almost fallen asleep in the embrace.

"Bed," he said, without any of his usual seduction to the suggestion.

"Bed," I agreed, smiling and following him back to the mattress.

Joanna hummed in her sleep as Aiden scooped her up in his hold, dragging her up onto his chest like a child with a beloved stuffed animal. She stayed soft and relaxed on top of him and I laid down at his side, drawing the blankets up over the three of us.

15

CALLUM

I HEARD THE MINERS WORKING FROM INSIDE MY CELL AND JUDGED THE hours passing by their dull clanging. I woke to the sound of gated elevators humming down to their destination and knew it must be morning. A meal of bland oatmeal in a bowl with a side of lukewarm sausage arrived. Then the thin vibration of pick-axes striking began, a quick steady tempo.

There was a metallic kind of cold burrowing into my chest and a strange prickle of discomfort that lingered on my skin. Was it the absence of my magic or was rixon toxic to my physical health too? Or was it just the anxiety of being trapped?

As the day stretched, I was left alone and the *crack, tremble* of activity underneath my feet gradually slowed, the arms of the miners growing weary. Before they were done, before the rhythm turned so slow it wasn't worth the pennies they must have been paying the men, Ambassador Pearce arrived, a tray of food carefully balanced on top of a glossy wooden case.

He took my bait.

A whistling siren went off in the background and all at once the rumble of work stopped.

"Is this rixon for the war? The one you're hoping my being here will start?" I asked. "Or is the war for the rixon?"

Pearce paused in the doorway. He looked a little less smug than the day before, almost distracted. Instead of an immaculate suit like the one he had greeted me in, he wore gray trousers that were wrinkled and faded, and a white shirt dusted with the dark rixon finish, faintly purple and glittering. I couldn't imagine him with a pick-axe but he looked as if he'd been working with the men; maybe not mining, but overseeing.

He stepped out of the way, nodding out the door and ignoring me, as a soldier entered with a second chair, wider and more comfortable looking, and set it down next to the small table in my cell. I caught a glimpse of maps on walls and a low bookshelf. It wasn't a hall outside, but another room. Pearce's office?

"Temké," he said in thanks. The soldier glanced at me with a frown before backing out of the room. Pearce turned back to me, nodding down at the tray and I stood from my seat on the bed to take it from him.

The spread was better, thin slivers of still hot meat and roasted potatoes dressed with gravy. I considered setting it aside again, but I was painfully hungry and I believed that Pearce really had no intention of killing me. Not yet, at least. Maybe if he succeeded and the war began, I'd see the end of my usefulness.

"I forget that your specialty is strategy," Pearce said. He took a seat and opened the case to reveal a beautiful chess set, cream and red-stained wooden squares with golden trim around the edges. Half of the pieces were a marble white, streaked with gray. The others were the shining iridescence of rixon. I had no doubt which he would make me use in the game.

"My father raised me in the subject," I said. I cut the meat on the tray with the side of a spoon, the only utensil they had offered me. As if the lack of an edge would be a deterrent against brute force. Pearce's safety was ensured by my own disinterest in stabbing him, not my lack of fork or knife to do it with.

"Yes," Pearce agreed. "But your father's excellence relies on force rather than observation or finesse."

It wasn't a feeling I was very familiar with, but I couldn't help thinking that Pearce was giving my father too little credit.

"You don't mind playing black do you?" he asked, setting up the board with the rixon pieces facing the open seat.

"Not at all," I said. Because even if I could have used magic to lodge a chess piece into Pearce's throat, I still wouldn't have. Although maybe it was a sign of concern that I was even thinking up these scenarios. I'd sated any bloodthirst I might have years ago as a teenager when I'd walked out of the strategy tent and saw the aftermath on the battlefield.

"Take your time," Pearce said, as he finished arranging the pieces, but his leg was jiggling impatiently and his eyes were scanning the game board as if he was already planning his attack.

I had no magic in the cell and very little personal power, but I could take my time eating my meal, enjoying every bite and chewing more thoroughly than ever. No, I was certainly not being poisoned. Pearce was far too impatient to finally have someone to play chess against to be thinking of *killing* me. I only made it through half my plate before he seemed to have had enough of planning the game, and nudged a pawn forward two places. He glanced at me out of the corner of his eyes and I kept my own on my plate, pretending not to notice. His heel tapped on the floor, faster than any miner's rhythm, until I finished my meal and joined him at the table.

Pearce was an excellent chess player, but he'd been playing against himself for over a decade. I hoped that meant he forgot how to think outside of his own habits.

I played wildly to start with, watching his reactions. He hid them poorly, openly scoffing when I skipped opportunities, grimacing in disappointment when I allowed him to take two pawns instead of working to advance them.

"You must miss your coven," he muttered as if it would excuse my terrible playing. "I hear it is very difficult to be separated, that the rixon interferes with the bond."

It was a lonelier feeling than any I'd ever known, and I had the deepest sympathies for whoever had originally tested the theory.

"I prefer to be here without them than have them here with me," I said, watching as he took a pawn, too distracted by my disappointing strategy to realize he'd opened room around my bishop.

I took my first white piece at the opening, an advancing pawn, and he went still. A smile grew over his face, plumping his cheeks and he looked genuinely giddy.

"Ah, I see, I see, yes. Learning, are we?" he asked, but he didn't glance at me and I didn't feel obliged to answer. "The war is for rixon," he said, eyes fixed to the board. "The answer to your question, earlier."

It was probably a bid to distract me from the game but it was also the goal of my conversation so I held my tongue and waited. As a boy when I would get into bruising trouble with my father for arguing, my mother always told me that men liked to be listened to. I thought it was just a way of warning me not to talk back to my father during his lessons, even if he *was* wrong, but as I grew I realized she was offering her own methods of strategy. I didn't have to ask every question I wanted answers to, just the correct *first* question.

I started a contrary maneuver with one of my knights, leaving the bishop vulnerable. I wouldn't be able to feign ignorance of the game again, but Pearce was following his own game in his head and every move I made that broke his structure made him plan from scratch again.

"There's more rixon in Vermenia than anyone realizes," he continued. "We've been mining small pockets of it as if it were a very rare material, when in fact its veins spread through almost every inch of our terrain, even into parts of Enmaire. It's why there's no magic here."

I studied the way his hands hovered over a knight, refusing to flinch at the news. It wasn't the presence of rixon in Enmaire that worried me, it was that *Vermenians* knew about it, that they'd been studying our ground materials without our knowledge. Or had Pearce been doing it for himself?

"As common as tin?" I asked as he skipped his knight closer to my rook, a less predictable and risky venture. It was my turn to study all the possible outcomes of the position, but I kept my attention focused on the conversation.

"Perhaps even more so," he said. "Of course that would greatly devalue the material. Just another metal. We'd have to *make* people want it. Not just for bowls or forks or chess pieces." He nodded at the pawn in my fingers at that. "But for safety, for security and peace of mind."

"Protection from the wicked magicians in Enmaire," I said, following the train of thought. "A high-commodity indeed. Especially if we're invading."

He shrugged, smiling down at the game between us. He wasn't disappointed by my not sounding cowed or concerned. He didn't need to worry, it was a very ingenious plan on his part. Costly, both in financial terms and in *lives*, but I had no doubt it would make him and any partners a great deal of money if they succeeded.

"Carras has investments in the mining?" I asked.

"We own separate properties," Pearce confirmed. He grinned at me conspiratorially and added, "A bit of friendly competition."

And neither would give up the scheme without losing their investment. Looking at Pearce, dusted in rixon and looking exhausted, as if he had put his own weight's worth of work into the mine that day, I had no doubt he had invested all he could. Certainly more than he could afford to lose.

When I took one of his bishops, and then a knight, with my next two turns, Pearce went quiet, turning his attention entirely to the game. That was fine, I had learned plenty for the day. If I could be patient, I would learn more. I wasn't sure how much time I had before a war began in earnest, but it had only been a couple of days.

Pearce was a talented chess player, and I *was* rusty. He took more than I had planned on awarding him. But I was learning from his attack quickly and while he was playing to win, I was only hoping to disappoint him. When I took his queen he seemed genuinely excited, as if he looked forward to the inevitable defeat. When his king sat still at the end of the game, with no move to make and not yet in check his expression soured. I didn't say a word, waiting for him to call the game.

"Stalemate," he said, with a note of disgust. He looked up with his eyes narrowed and his head tilted, suspicious of me for what I thought might be the first time.

There had been other routes I could have taken for a victory, he knew that as well as I did. But he wouldn't have been upset at a loss and I wanted a *real* victory, not a gleefully given win.

"Thank you," I said, leaning back in my chair. "I needed that distraction."

He 'hmm'd, staring down at the board again as if he might find a new route in the pieces, but there was none. "Tomorrow?" he asked. "A rematch?"

"Please," I said, nodding.

He cleared away the pieces, and I watched his fingers tapping at them, counting to make sure I hadn't pocketed anything, as if I could make much use of a pawn or a rook piece in this barren room. My dinner tray was balanced back on top of the case and Pearce rapped on the doorframe. A soldier opened it and stared at me until I got up from the table and backed away, palms raised and an innocent smile on my face. Pearce left the room without another look at me and the soldier picked up the extra chair and retreated quickly, the lock snapping shut behind him.

I tucked my hands back into my pant pocket, fingers wrapping around the spoon Pearce had forgotten about. I would leave it out on the table tomorrow morning but for tonight I had a message to write.

Where are you? We love you. We'll find you.

I touched the words, Joanna's handwriting again but the entire coven's thoughts. I wasn't even sure if they were a response to my first message or a type of comfort for themselves. But I wanted to believe they had read my answer, that there was a thread of communication between us even if our bond was painfully absent. Beneath Joanna's message was a note from Aiden.

Watched Joanna go up against Duncan at a politician's dinner party tonight. Magnificent. Be safe.

I flipped the spoon in my fingers, trying to think of the right message, the right amount of caution and assurance to keep them safe. If our positions were reversed, if it were Isaac or Aiden in here, there would be no comforting phrase that would stop me from hunting down whoever was responsible. If it had been Joanna the three of us probably would have *led* my father into the war he was hoping for.

Rixon mine, blocking magic, I wrote, using the dull handle of the spoon. *Captive but well. Too many mercenaries for rescue. BE SAFE.*

With the scratches fat and clumsy from the spoon, the words took up all of a blank page and left deep indentations on several behind them. I left the spoon on the small table by the door and tucked the notebook back between my mattress and the wall, wedged into the bed frame.

16

———

JOANNA

There'd been no way to get in touch with my family and let them know we were coming, not in all the rush. Aiden had wanted to hire a car to take us from the station a town over into Bridgeston since the train didn't run to my hometown. But I couldn't imagine pulling up to my little house, riding down the dirt road in a *car*, so I'd talked him out of the idea. There would be a farmer picking up a load of meal at the station, there always was, who would take us into the village.

Neither Isaac nor I found it worth mentioning to Aiden that this meant we would be riding in the back of an open farm cart.

Bryce, who hopped onto the train as it stopped outside of Canderfey—just long enough for us to take long hugs from the rest of their coven—seemed delighted with our transportation. They sniffed at the bags of grain and trilled a strange lowing sound out at a herd of cows we passed. The sun was setting early into patches of snow and muddy fields dormant in the winter chill.

Aiden had his arms wrapped around his knees as if he was trying very hard to avoid coming into any kind of contact with the hay that lay in the bed of the cart. Isaac and I both made cushions for ourselves

381

out of the stuff and I discovered that I had missed the smell of it in all my time away.

"Have the pair of you played a joke on me?" Aiden asked, nose scrunching up as a dusty feed bag thumped over into his shoulder, leaving a print of dry dirt against his deep blue wool coat.

"If we drive through Bridgeston in a car, my father's house will fill up with guests before I finish introducing the lot of you," I said. "We'll be asked to a half dozen meals and someone will throw together a village dance by the end of the evening."

"I excel at dancing," Bryce said, wiggling their pale eyebrows.

"And before you ask, a carriage wouldn't have been any better," I said seeing Aiden's gaze sharpen. "We don't have the time for every one of my neighbors and all the councilwomen to quiz you each on how you met me and what kind of magic you use and whose mother's ring I'll be wearing."

Aiden grinned at that. "Don't be silly, we'll get you a new one," he said.

"Scandalous," I said. "Even more scandalous if you let it slip I've already moved in with you. Then you'll have a *great* deal of questions to answer."

"Your family knows though, right?" Isaac asked, an eyebrow raising in sudden nervousness. "About our coven?"

I had written it in a letter not long after we defeated the Hollow and I moved into the house for real, and then I mentioned it again in a letter telling them where I would be for the holiday. I'd received answers to both the letters, although there was never any mention of my being a witch or having a coven, and I wasn't sure what type of reception we would find at the house. The idea of my having a coven probably seemed so removed from possibility that no one knew *what* to think, and my father had always been a matter of fact person.

"They know," I said. "Not that we're coming, though."

"And there are babies?" Bryce asked, chin propped in their hand as they watched the countryside pass, nose turning pink from the cold and a more than usual amount of steam produced with their breaths.

"Yes, twins," I said. I added, in a tease, "But you can't keep them or eat them."

Aiden's eyes went wide but Bryce only snickered back at me. "Spoilsport," they said as the farmer's head twitched on his shoulders and he flicked his horses to move faster.

I put the hood of my coat up as we reached town, but Bryce and Aiden and even Isaac gathered enough stares on their own.

"I feel as if we've accidentally driven into Hammish," Isaac murmured at my side.

"They look a little different," I said, glancing shyly out at the familiar view of the small town I'd left behind. The dusty plaster and wood buildings, every gas lamp and pothole coming back to me now that I was here again. It hadn't been *so* long away.

"They do," he said, smiling and nodding once at a group of young boys who had given up spying into the tavern window, instead staring at our passing. "But I haven't been back to Hammish in… a very long time. And I could almost mistake them. There are details of these little towns I'd forgotten."

He squeezed my hand, and our rattling pace slowed as we reached the first small road that led to a small line of houses at the edge of town. Aiden passed the farmer a small fortune of coins as we stopped, more than the man would ever even have thought to ask for, and we hobbled our way out of the back of the rickety cart. I pretended not to notice Bryce pocketing some of the grain; Aiden's payment had more than made up for the small theft.

"Safe travels," the man said, marveling down at the coins in his hands. Now he was probably suspicious of our motives if we were willing to pay so much.

Isaac and Aiden carried our cases as I led the way down the lane. I slowed as we came closer. It was the first time I'd be home again since moving to Canderfey and I had a sudden strange reluctance to return, as if I might not be allowed to leave again. The Hollow had manipulated that fear before finally releasing me, and I refused to be cowed by an old memory, and an imaginary one at that.

I opened the front gate and the four of us trailed in on the uneven stone steps leading to the front door. The house looked warm, light glinting through the diamond pattern of the window panes and woodsmoke trailing out of the chimney. The yard was blue in the dusk light but I could hear my family inside, the babies chattering loudly over lower conversation. I knocked on the door, and the conversation paused. I flicked my hood back as I heard the knob turning.

Rose opened the door, Donny on her hip, and stared at the set of us for a long moment before blinking and shaking her head.

"Oh, la, Joanna, don't you look fine," she said, eyes widening and stepping back to make room for me. "Well come on inside, then."

"Hello, baby," Bryce greeted Donny, reaching out hands for him. And Rose, without so much as blinking, passed him right into Bryce's willing arms. Donny and Bryce grinned at one another, ignoring my warning glare.

"Joanna." I looked up as I stepped inside and froze at the sight of my father, pushing himself up from his seat at the table. He looked exactly as I remembered him, dark hair turning light with gray speckled through, wide shoulders and round belly, forearms and neck dark from the sun.

"Hello, Pa," I said, feeling strangely shy as if he might not recognize me, even though he already had. Isaac's hand touched my back in support for a moment but then my father and I were both moving forward.

He scooped me up off my feet with a grunt, even though he was hardly an inch taller than me, and a giggle broke free from my lips. His arms were tight, squeezing my ribs the way he did when I was just a little girl complaining of a bad mood. *I'll squeeze it out of you yet, little lady*' he would say.

"Well look at you," he said, setting me back on my feet but not letting me go long enough to look. "A proper lady now."

I blushed and tugged myself back, smiling back at him. My father's smile was all in the eyes, the wrinkles in the corners and the rise of his cheeks, his lips barely curling at the corners. Those eyes slid over my shoulder and hardened.

"And this must be your coven," he said, staring at Aiden, and Isaac —and Bryce, who had sat down on the floor in front of the table and currently had Donny and Aggie climbing all over them.

I bit my lip as I turned and found my two beautiful men looking uncharacteristically nervous. Isaac was actually *pale* with anxiety, wide eyes staring back at my father. Aiden—careless, graceful Aiden, who was *always* charming—stood stiffly, almost grimacing at the sight of my father.

"Aiden King," I said, gesturing to him with a lift of my eyebrows and an encouraging smile. "And Isaac Metclaffe. And that's our friend, Bryce Gast, playing with the twins."

Bryce snapped playfully—I hoped it was playful—at little Aggie when she pulled at the dragon's fluffy blonde locks. Rose didn't look the least bit concerned and Aggie squealed with delight.

"Our other coven member is…" I blinked at my men, not sure how to explain our situation just yet. "Away," I finished lamely.

"Haven't got enough food to feed the lot of you," Daniel, my brother announced, glancing at each of us.

My father scowled at Daniel who was busy scowling at Aiden's jacket. "Then go to the inn and rustle some up for us," Pa said to my brother.

Daniel's frown deepened until Isaac spoke up. "Can I come along? Haven't seen a decent inn since I was home in Hammish."

Both Pa and Daniel brightened at that. "Hammish?" Daniel said, giving Isaac another, longer examination. "I can see it now, farm boy." When Aiden laughed at the name Daniel lightened even further. "Sure, you can buy me a pint too."

"Daniel," my father warned, but it was half-hearted.

Isaac interrupted him with a grin at my brother. "Gladly," he said and Daniel clapped him on the back and went to grab his coat. Rose crossed to the stove, turning off the pot of boiling water that had probably only been waiting for potatoes or vegetables. I hoped Isaac would pay for the dinner from the Inn too. My father wouldn't have heard of it, but Daniel would be glad to accept.

I nodded at Aiden and he crossed the room to meet my father's outstretched hand with a firm shake.

"It's very good to meet you…" Aiden started before trailing off, eyes narrowing as he struggled with what to call my father. He started a word that sounded suspiciously like 'Sir,' which seemed strange even to me considering that Aiden couldn't have been a great deal younger than my father.

"Frank," my father said, staring up at Aiden with a similarly disgruntled expression. He broke the handshake and turned to me, face sharpening into a stern set I was familiar with as a child. "Now where's this fourth *away* to? If he's…jilted you or-"

Aiden coughed on air and I shook my head quickly. "No, no, no," I rushed. "It's, it's nothing like that. He's been…" It was my turn to struggle with what to say and I turned to gape up at Aiden.

"Taken prisoner," Aiden said, staring back at me with a helpless shrug. "By Vermenia, as far as we can tell."

My father rolled back on his heels, hands in his pockets as his eyes grew huge as he stared at both of us.

"It's…he was the Toy Soldier, in the war, you know," I said, my hands waving about in front of me like a pair of birds caught in a net. The whole story sounded a little ridiculous as I tried to explain it and I only hoped my father would continue to take everything in stride. "And now his father is trying to make it an excuse to start a war. We just want him home safe."

My father's hands settled on my shoulders, and I lowered to the floor, not even having realized I was rising up to my toes. He took my hands in his next and they fell still with a simple squeeze of his fingers around mine.

"Well I know you think the world of your Pa," my father said, face tight as he forced his mouth to quirk into a smile for my benefit. "But I take it you're not here for my help?" He looked between us to Bryce on the floor, still playing with the babies, and I saw the realization that the person he'd invited into his home was more than what they appeared.

"I was hoping I could take Mother's papers," I whispered.

Rose was sitting by the fire watching her children, but practically dozing with the relief of someone else minding them for a change. I wasn't sure how much she really knew about my mother but I didn't want to share any surprises if my brother hadn't said anything.

Pa's face turned grave and he looked up at Aiden for a long moment, before turning back to me. "What are you planning, lady?" he asked, in a low tone that was just as firm as it was quiet.

"She won't go alone," Aiden murmured to my father. "I promise that."

"There's no other way in," I said. "And if we don't get Callum *out* there'll be another war. *Daniel*, Pa. He'll get called out."

My father took a deep breath, exhaling slow and even. "Give me a tick to think about this," he said. "You'll stay the night, we'll make the room. I've a solstice gift to give you, anyway."

"I brought some for you all, as well," I said. Aiden had Bryce pick them up from the house for us and someone, I suspected Hildy, had carefully wrapped each one in glossy patterned paper.

Donny began to scream and we all turned, Rose sitting upright with a start. He was stumbling across the floor as Bryce crawled behind him, growling fairly authentically.

"Oh, Donny!" Rose gasped. "Oh, la, he's finally walking!"

Aggie pulled herself upright by tugging on Bryce's coat, and proceeded to climb onto the dragon's velvet-clad back.

"Your niece is a dragon rider," Aiden whispered and I snorted as my father's eyebrows shot up into his hairline.

*

ISAAC AND DANIEL came back to the house with more food than we could all possibly eat together. There would be plenty of leftovers for my family after we left the house, and while my father looked suspiciously between the two men, he didn't make any complaint.

The twins squalled when Rose tried to take them up to bed and only stopped when Bryce asked to sleep on their floor. Rose and Daniel were too relieved to argue but my father looked to me for assurance that this was safe. I nodded, partly because I trusted Bryce with the safety of my family and partly because if they wanted to eat my niece and nephew, putting them downstairs on a cot wasn't going to stop them. Mostly because I trusted them.

When the fire was dampened in the stove and my brother and Rose had retreated for some much needed peace and quiet, I led my coven up the stairs to my old bedroom. I wasn't sure how we were all going to fit in my childhood bed but there was nowhere else to put us.

"Joanna," my father called from the other end of the hall before we turned into my room for the night. He nodded his head to his bedroom and I left Aiden and Isaac in mine. My father had given Rose and Daniel his old room after my mother had died and it never ceased to feel strange walking into Daniel's old room to find him. He stepped inside and I followed him over to his dresser, a small, familiar jewelry box sitting out.

It was my mother's, the silver finish tarnished with age and the lapis-blue rose embedded on the lid was thick with dust. There had been just a few trinkets kept in the box when I was a child—a pair of pearl drop earrings, a silver chain, a perfume tin with a smaller blue rose on the lid. My father wore the chain against his neck and the earrings were in my own jewelry box in Canderfey. Now when my father lifted the lid I saw a stack of parchments. He shut it again and lifted it up, passing it into my hands.

"Her papers are there," he said. "And a few letters from her family. They were just over the border, the address is on an envelope."

My head shot up from where I'd be staring at the box, my thumbs stroking over the tarnish of the metal. "Her family?"

"Jessa and I left them on good terms," my father said, nodding. "I don't know if they're still there but… if you need anything, I think you could go to them."

"Thank you, Pa," I said, tucking the jewelry box under my arm and leaning in to kiss his cheek.

"I hope this lad is worth it," he grumbled.

My smile felt shaky but I made sure to meet his eyes as I nodded. "Callum is. He's… he's worth everything to me. They all are. And once we're all home again you'll meet him. You *could* come to Canderfey," I said, and the smile turned into a grin at his grimace.

"I suppose I'd better," he said, scratching at his chin. "This house barely holds the lot of you as it is."

Our coven house would be a shock to my Pa, but he would like the woods around the campus and I knew he already liked Isaac and Aiden well enough for the three of us to set both him and Callum at ease during a visit.

"I can bring the twins too and your-" he stuttered over what to call Bryce before deciding on "Friend, can watch them. Give Rosie and Dan a bit of a break at least."

I nearly swallowed my tongue thinking how Bryce's coven might respond to a pair of toddlers, how their beautiful home would stand up to the twins. At least Gwen could always escape to the Library with me.

"Be careful, little lady," he said, turning grave again. He wrapped his hands around my forearms to hold me still. "I don't know how you'll get your covenmates into Vermenia, but even if you manage it remember that this is… political. That kind of thing spreads wide and deep, you can't just ask nicely for him."

But maybe I could *Write* nicely. That was my hope. Vermenia may not have had magic, but they'd had Scribes once, and with Callum's message reaching us I had hopes that my words would have some effect in saving him.

"I'll be careful, Pa," I promised. He kissed my cheek again before releasing me, nodding even as he looked at me with a frown that sank into every groove of his face.

The house was quiet as I left him for the hall but I could hear Isaac and Aiden, soft laughter and murmurs, as I reached my room. They were squeezed together on my little bed, broad shoulders almost overlapping and Isaac's foot was braced into the edge of the mattress as if to keep himself from falling off.

"Your best bet is to jump in on top of us and we'll strap you in," Aiden said, grinning and raising an arm up.

"We have a bedtime story and everything," Isaac said, waving our coven notebook in the hand that was laying over Aiden's stomach.

Word from Callum! I stripped as quick as I could, snatching up Isaac's discarded linen shirt, and wormed my way between them on the bed. They didn't make the most comfortable mattress at first when all I had to cushion me were shoulders and hipbones. We shifted together, Aiden and I holding on tight to Isaac so he wouldn't roll off onto the floor, the three of us muffling our laughter so we didn't wake the twins. We ended up on our sides, their arms cradling me between them.

I raised the notebook up over our heads and flipped until I found the new page, the pressed words wavering in the candlelight.

"Rixon," Aiden said on a sigh. "That's why we can't feel him."

"It's not blocking Joanna's charm," Isaac said, reaching up to the page before dropping his arm again when the shadow blocked out Callum's words.

"Mercenaries," I said, staring at the word. "Mercenaries, not soldiers. Does that mean it isn't the Vermenian government?"

"If it is, they're making some attempt to hide it," Aiden said. "I'll call my father at the station tomorrow. This won't make it easier to get to Callum but it might mean less of a conflict *if* we are able to get him out."

"We have to," I whispered, stroking my finger over the words, blocking out the part where he'd told us not to come.

"Do we really need to go to York's coven?" Isaac asked.

I couldn't see his face, especially not when he bent and kissed the back of my neck. But I saw Aiden looking over my head at him, tense and waiting and face fixed into a neutral expression. He wouldn't try to influence me either way.

"I want to speak to her," I said. I didn't know how to explain the hard knot in the pit of my stomach when I thought about the woman, about what she had done. I understood her need for some revenge for her lost covenmates. I really did. I felt it too, now.

"I want to face her," I said, and my covenmates' arms tightened around me.

17

JOANNA

It had never occurred to me to be nervous about my family and my coven getting along. I loved my family, had an irreversible connection to them. My father and brother knew all the little instances, all the skinned knees, and weeping heartaches, and perfect lazy days with a stack of books under the shade of a tree that made me who I was. But my coven was an extension of myself now. I loved my men more than anything and they were drawing me out into a person beyond my own expectations. Showing me strengths and weaknesses I'd never discovered on my own.

Watching my father hug Isaac and Aiden goodbye, though—clapping them on the back the way he did with Daniel, seeing Isaac's open relief at the approval and affection—a warmth ran through my chest so deep into my bones I felt lazy with it. All I missed was Callum here. Pa would like him too, and Callum would be an utter wreck, happy and nervous, with the acceptance.

"When you have babies I will watch them while you work," Bryce said in my ear after the twins delivered their wailing goodbye and could be pried off the dragon's legs.

My eyes grew so wide it almost hurt. "Watch your mouth," I said, quick and sharp without thinking. Bryce only snorted and I hissed at them under my breath. "Aiden will have us halfway home if he hears you talking like that."

Aiden had brought up children only a week or so after we'd defeated the Hollow and I'd properly moved in. He'd promised not to press the issue, only checked to make sure I *wanted* children. But he'd gone soft-eyed at breakfast when Aggie had climbed into my lap and I didn't need Bryce encouraging him when we were in the middle of a crisis.

Bryce chuckled, a rattling inhuman sound that made the hair on the back of my neck stand up in warning. I laughed too after a moment, releasing some of the tension of traveling and worrying and the ache over leaving Bridgeston—dusty little Bridgeston of all places. Bryce grabbed up our bags from the ground and we took our leave with my covenmates behind us.

I CHEWED at the dull end of the pen in my hand, staring down at the words. The country was racing past us out the window of another train. My covenmates sat on either side of me and Bryce across from us.

Jessa Kershaw... Ramshden, Vermenya... 13.8.1571

"You shouldn't change much," Isaac warned. "If they have any way of checking, you'll need it to be something that almost vanishes."

I nodded absently, hovering the tip of the pen over my mother's birthdate. I curved the seven on the year into a nine and exhaled a slow breath. She'd been in her mid-twenties when she had me so this put me a few years older than I actually was but it was the simplest change I could think of. I altered another date, the one of her leaving Vermenia, with a minor correction that put it three years before.

"Will that be enough?" Aiden asked.

"I don't think so," I said. I turned the page over and flipped the pen in my fingers, thinking of Callum's pressed messages. In the fall of the year, I had released the Hollow not by actually writing out the words, but by tracing them over the page during a trance until it had left an impression.

A believable disguise, I wrote onto the back of my mother's papers with the blunt end of the pen. Hopefully, no one would see the words, only feel their effect. I looked up and Isaac had his mouth covered with his hand while Aiden was staring hard down at the words.

"It will work," I said, pressing a certainty into the words that I was still working on feeling. Callum said that the intention should make a difference in my Writing. So I intended with every bit of my concentration that this simple sheet of paper would get me safely into Vermenia so I could find him.

"And will I be enough against York?" Bryce asked me, raising an eyebrow.

"I have an idea for that too," I said. I reached across Isaac's lap to the small art case he'd brought for traveling, opening it and pulling out the heavy oil pastel crayons.

IT WAS the guards at the barracks outside of Dannsedge that told us where to find York's home.

Bryce was bouncing on their toes as we stood at the end of the home's footpath, but I felt frozen in step. It was strange to stand out in the cold and not feel it biting my skin, hear the wind but not have it ruffle anything. To wear clothes that never landed on my skin. To take a step without my feet touching the ground.

There had been consequences to the spell of *Untouchable* I'd drawn onto our skin with black crayon and it worked almost too well. It was like existing inside of a stifling bubble. Every time I thought to reach for one of my covenmates hands I was reminded that I would not be able to really take hold. But without the chill of winter reaching me, I was starting to grow warm. I wondered if the word would smear or sweat would mar it soon. We couldn't stand outside York's house all day and find out.

The building reminded me of home although I couldn't say why, only the feeling that it was lived in, shared by a *family*. And I didn't want to think of Sabine and her coven in that way. I was holding onto my anger like a blade I could use to fight against them.

The house was brick with tall peaked roofs and a wide paneled window facing the front yard. It was far enough from the town and the barracks that it felt secluded. The snow was melting in patches on the ground but the day was bright and I could see the small border of a slumbering garden that ran around the house. Just like Sabine York herself, it did not look as I expected it to. It was somehow sweeter, more like a home and less like a military base than I expected.

"If we are surprising them, we should move faster," Bryce said and Isaac choked on an anxious laugh behind us. Bryce had tried my spell on for a few minutes before wrinkling their nose and *licking* the word off. 'Too sticky,' they had said. 'I'll take yours off when you're ready.'

The front door opened and we all went silent as Darin stepped out from the shade of the eaves.

"She said you'd turn up," Darin said, grinning and looking pleased with us. Or maybe with Sabine for predicting our arrival. "Well, come in then."

Bryce strolled ahead, hands tucked behind their back, glowing faintly golden, magic bright like the sunlight bouncing off their hair. That glimmer of strength was enough reassurance for me to follow, feeling my covenmates close at my back.

When we reached the doorway Darin stood back to let us in, watching Bryce with almost as much suspicion and caution as they deserved.

"Our friend, Bryce Gast," I said, watching the smile sharpen on the enormous man's face as Bryce stared back at him with a silver-green gaze and a dangerously placid smile.

Bryce took a deep breath as we stepped into the house, shoulders stiff in their jacket, and I paid more attention to the way they studied our surroundings than I did the house itself. The wood was silent beneath our feet since we never reached it, but Bryce stepped deep into the entrance hall with a creak. They moved to Darin's far side before turning out and staring into the next room, a wall at their back.

I followed Bryce's gaze through an archway at my right into a long open room, brightly lit and filled with comfortable furniture. The rest of York's coven sat lazing together in the sunlight shining through their wide windows. They must have been staring at us the whole time we stood outside.

"Joanna Wick," Sabine said, rising up from a huge leather armchair. I supposed when you had covenmates the size of Darin you *needed* exceptionally large furniture.

"Sabine," I said, finding my throat dry as I tried to speak.

"You got Duncan to talk then," Sabine said, smiling faintly. "I knew you would."

She looked pleased, too. I didn't know if Isaac was right and I had walked us all into some kind of trap or if, to Sabine, throwing Callum to the Vermenians was light but necessary retribution. She certainly wasn't *worried* to see me. But the anxious, queasy feeling I'd walked into the house with was fading back behind my anger. Anger for what she'd done to Callum, and anger because she wasn't even *worried* about what I might do to her.

"I want to know exactly what happened," I said, and my voice was lower than I expected, my hands fisted so tightly at my side I could feel the pressure in my palms without the sting of my nails being able to burrow into my skin.

"Of course," she said, smile fading. There was something strange in her expression, something almost like sympathy. Not an apology, but an understanding. My hand hurt with how badly I wanted to strike her for it. "Come sit down."

I tried not to see their home around me as I walked, frustrated and disgusted and confused by the fact that it seemed *warm* and comfortable. There was art on the walls, the furniture was stylish, the space was clean and bright and welcoming. If I hadn't known who lived here, I would have been very happy to be visiting. As it was, I didn't want anything to interrupt my focus, certainly not appreciation for decor.

Samuel and Geoff rose as I approached, moving to stand at Sabine's sides. We weren't surrounded as we moved to stand across from them, Darin stepping up to his coven's back, but I could see by Samuel's thin smile that he felt confident they could take us if it came to it.

I glanced back at the chair behind me, it would swallow me up and make me look like a little doll. I ignored the instruction to sit, instead take a step closer to the warrior coven.

"He could have been killed," I said to Sabine.

"To be honest," she said, face slack with honesty and green eyes open, "I thought he would be."

That was enough for me. The coil of anger I'd been holding onto so dearly sprung loose inside of me, everything white-hot in my vision.

"Joanna!" Aiden snapped, but I was already across the divide of floor between our two covens, my closed fist flying.

I wasn't sure what my spell would do. I wasn't even *thinking* of it; I would have hit her without a protection spell. Geoff snarled and reached for me but he never caught me, fingers slipping through air, bouncing off my charm.

I never touched her. Not skin to skin. But something had to answer for the force behind my punch, even if it couldn't land directly.

Sabine's head snapped to the side, that open honesty turned to shock. She fell into Samuel's side and Darin leaped over the couch, the four of them crowding me as Sabine straightened. There was a knife at my throat, Geoff's, and my heart thumped wildly as I caught the shine of it out of the corner of my eye, but it never scratched.

Sabine flexed her jaw, staring watchfully at me from the side.

"It's alright," she murmured. She pushed back at Samuel's stomach but he didn't so much as shift. "I said it's alright," she said, voice rising. "I deserved that. Put the knife down Geoff, it was just a punch. A good punch," she added turning to me.

My brother had taught me the art and then served to regret it when his teasing grew too persistent.

"May I?" Sabine asked, raising an open palm up and reaching it toward my shoulder. She didn't wait for my answer and I could feel a tickling prickle at my shoulder, like when the kittens kneaded at skin with barely present claws. "That's a good shield. Could it be used for soldiers?"

"Maybe," I answered, a little caught off guard. I still had adrenaline and anger pumping through me, and she was asking about bits of magic while a red bruise began to swell over her cheek. "I only made it up this morning."

She hummed, and the prickling grew stronger for a moment before disappearing altogether. "Can you call off your dragon?" she asked.

I turned and found Bryce glowing bright behind me, the leafy silver-green of their eyes gone molten and electric. Aiden and Isaac stood stiff behind us, edgy and cautious but trusting me and Bryce to handle the conflict. "Call off your coven," I countered.

Darin stepped back at once, falling into the cushions of the couch behind him and Samuel followed after a beat. Geoff lowered the knife away from my throat slowly so I added, "I'm not taking my shield off any of us while we're here, so you can quit waiting for your chance to stab me."

He huffed, nearly growling, and stepped back, the knife vanishing with a flick of his wrist.

"I was going to say, before you punched me," Sabine said slowly, "That I am relieved to know he's not dead."

"He was barely more than a *child* when he lead those battles," I said, wishing I had said these words when we had been standing together in Duncan Pike's parlor. "They never let him know what it cost the soldiers, not till the war was over."

Sabine's expression was stony but I caught a flicker of pain, barely there at the corner of her eyes. "If you want an apology, you've come to the wrong place. But if you... need help, I can offer that much. And... if it'd been Duncan Pike they'd asked for, I would have gladly turned him in instead."

"Who are *they*?" Aiden pressed, stepping up to my back. I wanted so badly to lean into him but when I tried, the spell stopped us from reaching each other.

Sabine sighed, taking Geoff's arm and dragging him back to the couch with her covenmates as if they could force us to relax by offering an example.

"Ambassador Carras," Sabine said, curling up between Geoff and Darin, her legs folding up beneath her, making her appear suddenly small between the gigantic men.

I let Aiden usher me back into a chair that I couldn't really relax in, feeling as if I were balancing on thin air. Part of me wanted to ask Bryce to take the spell off my skin, but Geoff was still staring at me as if *I* had been holding the knife to his covenmate.

"What would Carras want with Callum trapped in Vermenia?" Isaac asked.

"I don't know," Sabine admitted, some of the certainty washing off her face. "I didn't ask enough questions, if I'm being honest. I was too hungry for an old grudge."

"We all were," Samuel said, from the end of the couch. "We all lost people we cared about in that war, under the Toy Soldier's games. The Pikes didn't lose anyone."

"Callum lost *every man* that died," I snarled, trying to rise, but Aiden and Isaac were quick enough to stop me with hands above my shoulders, our spells bristling against each other. I settled instead for holding tight to Samuel's dark gaze. "He *carries* that. They were strangers to him, but don't think he doesn't count those losses every day. He *didn't know* what he was asking you to pay."

Samuel stared back at me, unreadable until I thought I'd have to really fight my covenmates off so I could go strangle the man. Then he shrugged and turned to Sabine.

"I see why you like her," he said.

Aiden and Isaac's shoulders appeared in front of me, not standing, but shifting us all together until I was less visible. Sabine's smile flickered up at their posturing and she and I seemed to share an exhausted thought. *Men.*

"We were only asked to deliver Callum near the border," Sabine said. "When he brought up the dig site the four of you found, it was an easy location to give Carras and a simple way of getting him alone."

She glanced at the others around her and I bit down hard on the inside of my mouth to resist sharing my very noisy opinions on her plots to shuck off Callum to the Vermenians.

"The crates at the site were full of rixon," Sabine said after a silent conference with her men. "It wasn't meant for him, I know that much. But when he stepped into the pit where they'd buried it, there was enough there to dampen his magic."

"Made the whole thing a little too easy," Samuel grunted and I narrowed my eyes at him.

"Carras was annoyed we'd found it," Sabine continued. "When they came to collect Callum they packed the lot up with him. But my coven and I have gone scouting. There's at least four more sites like the one you found, all with rixon underground."

Aiden and Isaac both glanced at me. "They're keeping him in a rixon mine," I said.

Sabine sat forward at the news, elbows landing on her thighs and eyes turning feline and dangerous. "How do you know this?" I straightened in my seat, unwilling to share anything more with her than I already had. She only laughed, leaning away again and raising her hands in surrender. "You can cast a better shield charm than anything they bother teaching in the academy and you're getting news from inside Vermenia. From inside a rixon *mine* in Vermenia. I can't help but be curious."

I resisted the urge to lay my hand over my pocket where the notebook was hidden with a pencil and the black pastel crayon wrapped in a handkerchief.

"You said you would help," I said. "I have papers to get me into Vermenia but-"

"Into Vermenia?" Darin asked, sounding near laughter. "You want to go into Vermenia. *You?* And what? Go digging around in the mines?"

"I want to get Callum out, back home, so we can stop Duncan before he starts a war no one wants to be in," I said.

"You and what army?" Darin asked. "Because I'll tell you right now, I'm not going in Vermenia. Not for the Toy Soldier."

My jaw clenched. "I can cast a shield charm you and your coven can't break and I can speak to my covenmate inside of a rixon mine. I'll manage."

Isaac's hand tried to find mine until we both realized we couldn't touch. He looked down at our hands, feeling the clash of magic between our palms, and his face was full of doubt and desperation and a firm kind of pride. Aiden was staring at me with heat and humor in his eyes. I hadn't gotten as far as the how of getting Callum out of the mine. Or even the where of which mine he was captive in. But I hated Darin laughing at me, and I hated having to ask these people, the ones responsible for Callum's capture, for help.

"There is Vermenian rixon being buried on Enmairian soil," Sabine said, her voice falling low and stilling the smile on Darin's face. "If they crossed before our armies were prepared, they could use those chains and those traps and landmines to render our protections useless."

"Going in without papers is a death wish," Samuel said. "We'd have to declare war, rush the border with troops, and even then she'd have to find her way through the ensuing battles to get to a mine. A mine probably *guarded* by the army, if they're involved in the project."

"Callum said they were mercenaries," Aiden said.

Darin rolled his eyes and slouched back into the cushions, "Mercenaries aren't any better news."

"They are if it means the Vermenian army *isn't* preparing for war yet," Sabine said.

I didn't want to worry about the why and who of the situation. I only wanted a clear path to Callum and damn the rest of it. Every day he was away, the gap in my bond with my coven felt wider, the whole tangle of us looser without him. Now that I knew where to find that emptiness, it was like my thoughts couldn't help but dwell on it, picking at a scab to reopen it time and time again. And at this moment, unable to actually touch Isaac or Aiden, that gap felt even more obvious.

"I have Vermenian papers," I said, and the conversation across the room about numbers of troops and distance between dig sites and advancements artillery went silent. "I have my mother's papers," I said. "They'll get me into the country."

"I can take her," Geoff said from the end of the couch and all together his coven turned to look at him. But he was staring at me. "I am Vermenian," he said and from his mouth, the word sounded the way my mother had pronounced it, the V softening and the end of the word almost trilling. "I have papers. And I can make inquiries, see if anyone knows which mine belongs to the Ambassador."

Aiden and Isaac both looked stricken and I thought they would refuse the offer. Instead, it was Bryce.

"I will take her," Bryce said, stepping forward from where they had patiently been listening to us argue. Between one step and the next, fair and delicate Bryce transformed into the wide and rigid form of Geoff, hair turning long and darkening to a honey yellow. Geoff jumped up from the couch and the two of them faced off, identical as far as I could tell.

"Do you speak Vermenian?" Geoff asked, eyes narrowing even as Bryce mimicked every twist of posture and flinch of gaze. "They won't just let you through smiling and nodding. One of you is going to have to answer questions."

I had never heard him speak so much before and I realized now it must have been his own attempt at hiding the accent. He was Vermenian, he *looked* Vermenian. How had he even met Sabine and the others?

The war, I realized. They probably met on the battlefield.

Bryce's transformation faded slowly and they turned to me, a rare knot of worry folding on their brow.

"It's alright," I said to them. Aiden glared at me so I amended, "We'll think about it."

"I will look into the mine," Geoff said, still watching Bryce carefully. "Give me a day."

"You can stay here while you wait," Sabine said, sounding almost hopeful.

Isaac only scoffed and then went silent as he realized she was sincere. She smiled at him the same way she had smiled at me in Duncan Pike's parlor, playing at seductive threat.

"We'll take a room at the Blue Waters Inn," Aiden said, leaving no room for an argument. Not that I had planned on giving one.

As determined as I was to take any help we could get, including Geoff's, I could see that the suggestion had pushed my covenmates a little too far.

They rose and I hurried to follow them to the front door, Bryce taking a defensive position at our backs.

"I am sorry," Sabine said. The words were given quietly and I wasn't sure that Isaac or Aiden took any note of them as they passed. She was only looking at me.

"For Callum's sake or mine?" I asked, not knowing why but feeling already certain of her answer. I stopped in place to wait for her answer and Bryce waited with me.

"Yours," she said, almost smiling. She glanced over at the others and then back to me. "Just yours."

I could feel the beginning of a blush starting to creep up my neck so I hurried to follow my coven. I couldn't wait until Bryce could take the spell off our skin again. I badly needed to throw myself into Aiden's arms for reassurance, have Isaac circle my back. I only hoped Bryce didn't have to *lick* the words off each of us.

18

AIDEN

"Wʜᴀᴛ ᴏɴ ᴇᴀʀᴛʜ ᴀʀᴇ ʏᴏᴜ ᴛʜɪɴᴋɪɴɢ?" I ʀᴏᴜɴᴅᴇᴅ ᴏɴ Jᴏᴀɴɴᴀ, ᴍʏ blood pounding under my skin.

Bryce left us in our room at the inn, closing the door after running a glowing hand over the words Joanna had written on us. I tucked away the fact that Bryce had the power to undo Joanna's magic for later. Joanna too looked relieved by the revelation, as if she hadn't been certain how to undo the spell after casting.

Now she looked at me, eyes tired as if I were a child throwing a tantrum. *Me.* When she was the one who'd all but agreed to travel alone with one of the coven that had attacked Callum when he'd been alone with them. Never mind that Geoff seemed especially suspect, even for York's lot of men.

"You absolutely are not going into Vermenia with Geoff...damn it, what even is his last name?" I continued, my breath coming in short as if I'd gone for a run.

Joanna was silent, watching me with that weary patience like if she waited long enough all the fight would burn out of me. There were dark circles under her eyes and she seemed paler, although it could have been the dingy light of the inn. I tried not to think about how healthy she'd looked at Sabine's home, cheeks bright with anger and sun striking her deep brown hair with shimmers of red.

"York," Isaac answered me, going to land heavily on the creaky bed we'd rented for ourselves. He set his elbows on his knees and ground the heels of his palms into his forehead. "They all took her name."

Joanna's eyes scanned me, my arms crossed over my chest and a tight purse to my mouth. My back was to the door and all but *daring* her to try and run out of the Inn and back to York's house. Then she turned and joined Isaac on the bed, curling into his side with a grateful sigh.

"It's a terrible idea," she said, looking back at me.

Some of the temper wilted out of me with her words. Was she agreeing with me? I bristled at the idea, feeling like I was being tricked out of my anger.

Isaac's arm wrapped around her shoulder and he pulled her tighter against him, his nose pressing into her hair. "Couldn't even smell you with the charm on," he said, words muffled against Joanna. "Didn't even realize how awful it was. Did you know you smell like beeswax?"

It was in the solid perfume I'd gotten her that she rubbed into her skin each morning. She turned back to Isaac and took his face in her hands, meeting him halfway for a soft kiss.

"Oh, that's not fair," I muttered and then the floorboards creaked beneath me and I dropped down on her other side, my arms circling them both in a tight hug.

Isaac's kisses trailed over Joanna's right cheek and then his face appeared, eyes gentle. I leaned in over Joanna's shoulder and kissed him hard before we all went still, surrounded by each other.

"We could try just...sneaking across the border," Joanna said, words muted from inside our huddle. "I could write 'very difficult to catch' on our skin."

I huffed, my breath ruffling her hair at the back of her neck. I kissed there too and nuzzled the goosebumps that appeared in the wake of my touch.

"Extremely difficult to see," Isaac suggested.

"Oh good, yes," I said, rolling my eyes. "Let's all lose each other in the woods on the way to Vermenia."

I sighed, and with a slight nudge, the tangle of us toppled over onto our sides on the mattress. "I don't know which of that coven I trust with you *least*. Sabine at least seems to like you," I added.

"Too much," Isaac said, and I tilted my head back. He raised an eyebrow, waiting for me to contradict him but Joanna nodded between us. Oh. I supposed I'd taken it for granted that if Sabine was going to set her eyes on anyone in our coven it would be Callum, the warrior. But Joanna was just as much of a fighter. I warred between pride and worry.

"I think Darin would rather let Callum rot than do anything to help him," she said. "I'm glad he doesn't want anything to do with the idea."

We lay together, listening to the rhythm of the inn around us, the thump of feet on stairs, and the occasional shout from the bar below. There was a small wood stove in the corner, to heat the room, and the hickory smell distracted me with thoughts of food.

"You can't go into Vermenia untouchable," Isaac said, the announcement stopping my heart in my chest.

"I know," Joanna said as I hissed, "Isaac!"

I sat up, untangling my arms from around them, and stared down at them on the mattress. Joanna's head was cradled on Isaac's shoulders, and he adjusted his hold on her, twining her closer. They both gazed steadily up at me. Ruthless manipulators the both of them, looking at me like that.

"She's not going without us," I said, a panicking drumbeat going wild in my chest.

"How are we going to get across the border?" Isaac asked, and I wanted to shake the calm right out of him. I knew him too well to believe that he was taking the idea of Joanna going into Vermenia without us in stride. That calm exterior of his had always been for the rest of us, an anchor to keep us from flying loose when things went wrong. "We don't have any way of faking more papers, and unless you want to try crossing on foot, without any idea of where we're going…

This is the best option we have right now. And we don't know how much time Callum has."

I scrubbed my face with my hands, staring up at the beamed ceiling. "And if she travels with Geoff, that's so much better?" I asked. "He could turn her in at the border. He could lead her-"

"I'm right here," Joanna said with a huff.

I glared at her and continued, "He could lead you into a trap. He could throw you into the mine *with* Callum and make sure you didn't get back out again."

"Any of that could happen if you were there too," Joanna said.

"Yes! But we would be *together!!*" I shouted, voice breaking. I had leapt to my feet and I felt as if all the oxygen had been removed from the room.

Joanna and Isaac exchanged a look and a rush of snapping, biting heat flooded under my skin. I opened my mouth, wanting to appear calm and knowing I was ready to shout again, and then Joanna stood. She stepped into me, arms circling my back, and pressed her face to my collar.

"We will be together," she said. "All of us. If something happens in Vermenia I will get word to you. No one knows about the notebooks but us. And the only way I'll make it out again if Geoff does betray me, is if you and Isaac are safe and can plan for help. I know it's not a *good* idea, but it's the best we have."

It was a stupid idea and I hated it. I scooped Joanna up until her toes were barely touching the floor and held her to me, searching her eyes. They'd gone faintly hazel green in the dim light of the room and I wanted to resent the sympathy that I saw there.

"I only want to keep you all safe," I said, almost whispering.

"I'll use every protection on myself you can think of," she said, her hands rising up to frame my face.

I looked at Isaac just in time to catch him smooth away the rough tangle of worry on his face. "I'm not saying I trust Geoff or York or any of the others. But I trust Joanna to do this. I don't think Callum has a better chance than her."

My knees felt weak as I sighed, and I carried Joanna back to the bed, settling her between Isaac and myself again. "Alright, let's brainstorm the words you'll need."

I WAS WAITING in the bar for meals to take up to Bryce and my covenmates when Samuel entered. The scar streaking across his right cheek shone as red as his hair in the candlelight. He scanned the room with the same wary suspicion he'd worn while staring at Joanna standing in his home. His gaze froze when it landed on me and he let the bar door swing shut behind him, nodding once in my direction. I turned my back to him. Maybe it was a bad idea to turn my back on someone like him, but he could have me on the floor with a knife at my throat just as easily if I were staring at him, so I would take my chances.

"Geoff just stopped by the house before going on another errand for your coven," Samuel said with open resentment, appearing at my side at the bar. A bartender left a customer waiting, mid-order, to start over to the warrior but Samuel waved him away with a quick hand. "I came to bring you the map he's made up."

"Map?"

"Of the mines, the likely routes. Carras' mine is deep into the country, nearly a week away," Samuel said. "That's if you're traveling quickly, and I don't see how anyone travels quickly with a cart of rixon and a kidnapped Enmairian."

I frowned, "It didn't take that long for Callum to get in touch. How could they have made it there in time?"

"Geoff thinks it's a different mine," Samuel said, glancing quickly over one shoulder and then the other. "Is there somewhere else we can talk?"

"Waiting on food," I said, mulling over the idea of taking Samuel up to the rooms. Not ours maybe, although I was sure he could find it if he wanted. But the York coven seemed wary enough of Bryce so I would take him up to the dragon's lair... so to speak.

Samuel grunted, turning his back to the bar to watch the room.

"He put together a route for you too," he said, lowering his voice. "If you decide to try and get in on your own. But you'll get yourself killed before you ever so much as make it anywhere near a mine. Border folk aren't a friendly lot and the towns are riddled with soldiers. Retired and otherwise. Besides, you don't look like you're up to... roughing it," he added with a grimacing glare over the length of me.

I snorted and rolled my eyes down at the surface of the bar.

"I don't feel guilty over conspiring against the Toy Soldier," Samuel said.

"His name is *Callum*," I growled, looking up from the counter to glare at the man. He wasn't really taller than me, and not much broader, either. I didn't think I would *win* in a fight against him, but I thought I might at least be able to get a good punch in. Certainly a *rougher* one than he might expect from me.

"But if the result of our actions is another war put together to entertain a man like Duncan Pike then we made a mistake," Samuel continued as if he hadn't heard me, frown deepening.

"If we get Callum back we might be able to do something to stop that from happening," I said, watching his face.

He looked as if he was studying the room, counting the crowd at their tables, but his jaw clenched, a vein popping in and out. He was thinking.

"I have connections in Congress and Callum has influence. He hates to use it, hates how he got it in the first place. But he, more than anyone, would want to avoid another war." I wondered if I would be better off beating the words into the man than hoping the reasoning would stick.

He turned his head to me. "You can trust Geoff. He'll get her there and back again safely, and nothing further will happen to your coven. Any member of it. You have my word."

"And he won't try to sneak Joanna back to Sabine for you?" I asked, half-joking and half... well, a little intimidated at the thought of it.

Samuel grinned, just a flicker, the scar snagging at the right side of his mouth. "Not if she doesn't want to," he said.

I tried not to grimace at the answer. "Joanna isn't that easily caught," I said, thinking of all the trouble she'd given us before accepting our bond, her own feelings.

"I know what they say," Samuel said, softening. "Sabine didn't *steal* me from my coven. Not any of us. I went home after the war and the pieces didn't fit the same. Something had broken inside of me and it fractured in the bond too. My coven had a hard time accepting that. I did too. But I found Sabine long after that."

"People love to talk," I said, shrugging.

His eyes tensed and that crooked, twisted smirk returned. "Oh, but she'd take Joanna in if she could. You're right about that much. Luckily for you, Geoff isn't much for seduction so he won't make any progress for Sabine's suit."

The food arrived, thankfully interrupting the snarl I was working up. Joanna held grudges, and I suspected the one she was nursing against York would last a nice long time. Certainly long enough to get the whole pack of us out of the woman's attention. We were happily bonded, Callum's separation was our only strain. And Joanna would fix that. I believed in her even if I felt nauseated at the thought of letting her go without us.

When we're all together again maybe we could start discussing the idea of marriage. Just as a nice finishing touch to our bond. It was too soon now, but…eventually. The summer even?

Samuel followed me up the stairs but when I led us down the hall I found the door to Bryce's room the door was open. Joanna, Isaac, and Bryce stood huddled together and jumped when I cleared my throat.

"Samuel brought us a map," I said. I was blocking his view of the room from the hall and Joanna's eyes widened as I nodded back over my shoulder. She tucked the notebook in her hand into an invisible fold in her skirt and their huddle broke apart as we stepped into the room.

"We know what mine Callum is being kept in. It's not Carras'," she said.

"We guessed as much when Geoff brought the map. Carras is too far off," Samuel said. He pulled a folded paper out of his coat pocket and spread it across the small table in Bryce's room.

"Which one of those is Ambassador Pearce's mine?" Joanna asked, hands at her hips and lips in a hard line.

"Pearce?" I asked. "Ramond Pearce? He shouldn't even be owning an industry property like that."

"Maybe his name isn't on the paper, but he'll be the one in charge," Joanna said, her tone solid with certainty.

Samuel looked between us before back down at the map. "His embassy is here," he said, pointing to a southern city, Argathe, on the map. There was a mine circled on either side of the embassy. "Chances are it's one of those two. I'll talk to Geoff and it should be easy enough to find out from that. Even if it's a secret, it'll be poorly kept for a man like him."

"Ask him to see what kind of traffic has been there recently, how many men might be on-site, when it will be quieter, that kind of thing," Joanna instructed.

Samuel's arms crossed his chest and he stared down at her for a long stretch. She looked up from the map at him, wide-eyed and waiting but when she saw his expression she only folded her own arms and narrowed her eyes. His mouth quirked and he nodded.

"Yes, Commander," he said.

She huffed and turned away again but I saw the way her shoulders straightened. I found Isaac's gaze and we shared a terrified moment of wondering what trouble Joanna could get up to with a pack of weathered soldiers under her command.

"If you decide to leave with Geoff, be at the house tomorrow morning. You'll want to get an early start," Samuel said. Joanna nodded absently at the map underneath her hands as the man saw himself out.

"Callum wrote?" I whispered.

Joanna nodded. "It's Pearce and Carras, not the Vermenian army," she said. "But they're hoping that it's only a matter of time before Enmaire or Vermenia makes a move." She pulled the notebook free of her skirt and passed it to me.

I flipped through pages of scratched notes. He had no access to sunlight where he was being kept but he thought it might be near an office. My throat felt clogged and my stomach churned in anger and grief. At the end of the message was a clumsy press of words.

He's coming for chess. It's rixon for profit.

"What's this mean? Rixon for profit?" I asked.

"That Carras and Pearce don't care who wins the war or if the borders are moved again. They just want to sell as much rixon as they can in the process."

"Then why already bury the rixon?" I asked, sitting down on Bryce's bed and studying the pages in my hands. "If the army doesn't know about the dig sites, what was the point of them?"

"They can sell the locations," Bryce said, moving to lean against the wall by the small gas lamp lighting the room. They had picked up one of the plates of food I'd brought in and was dining while the rest of us fret. "Tell the army that there's rixon to be found and used, but make them pay per site for instructions on where to find it."

"I hate politics," Joanna snarled. Isaac wrapped an arm around her shoulder and pulled her to his side.

"Sit, eat," I said. "If you're leaving in the morning then we only have tonight to finish planning your words."

Isaac picked up the remaining plates and passed them out, Joanna taking a seat on the bed next to me and turning the table around so the map faced her again.

"That's about where my mother's family lives," she said, pointing to a small dot on the map near the border, almost directly north of where our inn was. "But I don't think I'll be stopping for a visit."

She didn't sound sad exactly, wistful maybe.

"Someday," I said, taking her hand for a moment to squeeze it. I wished it was something I could promise her but a trip across the border wasn't something so easily managed. If it were, I wouldn't be feeling like all my muscles had been tied in knots and my stomach was sitting up inside my throat.

19

CALLUM

HAVE YOUR BAGS PACKED. ON MY WAY SOON.

My heart thrashed in my chest and I landed heavily on the lumpy mattress in my cell. Joanna. *Joanna.*

On my way soon.

My way.

I was going to strangle the lot of them. Joanna for daring to try to get here, it was too damn dangerous. Aiden and Isaac for letting her. If she managed it.

But if she didn't?

The room spun around me and I leaned against the wall, my back curving uncomfortably. There were wild spots in front of my eyes. I'd spent too many days locked in a room barely big enough to move around in. Playing chess and listening to the hours pass with the crack of rock and metal meeting. The sense of being caged had sunk into my thoughts and I resisted the urge to throw myself against the walls. There was no wisp of magic in my chest to find and no thread of the bond to follow and now even my physical strength seemed to be vanishing.

All at once I snorted out a laugh and slapped my hand over my mouth. Have your damn bags packed. That brat. I was going to…

413

Gods, I was going to snatch her up into my arms and never put her back down again when I saw her.

Reasonably, I knew that hoping for Joanna's arrival was possibly fatalistic. I should want her as far away from the mine, from Pearce, as possible. But in the moment all I could think about was the feel of her wrapped up against me again, the taste of her—tea bitter and sugar sweet. I was filled with a vibrating dread and a cloying need at the thought of her traveling here.

My breath was coming short, already thin in my chest after being stuck underground. I needed to get a handle on myself before any guards came to check on me.

I shoved the notebook back into its hiding place and took as deep a breath as I could manage before holding it for several beats and releasing it slowly. *Get it together, idiot,* I thought. Sitting here panicking wouldn't do Joanna any good. If she made it into the mine, made it to me, I wanted to be ready to make sure we made it back out again.

There was a rustle from outside the door and I sat up with a snap in my back, nearly wincing. The lock...locks. I listened more carefully this time, turned, and a bar slid across the front of the door before it opened.

Pearce stood in the doorway, holding his chess case and a small plate with a sandwich. What time was it? It hadn't felt long enough since my last meal, or the last game, for it to be time to see him. I was sick to death of chess already and it had only been a handful of days. I was running out of ways to draw the game or to simply throw it and lose intentionally. Pearce was running out of ways of trying to force me to win.

"You look pale," Pearce said, not sounding especially concerned.

"I do miss the sun," I said, shrugging, and pushing up from the bed.

"And your magic," he said.

Yes, I very much missed my magic. And my coven. I thought that if there were a breeze in this stifling room I would be able to feel it travel through the hollow spaces forming in me.

"Do you have any magic?" I asked, sitting down across from him and picking up my meal.

Pearce's forehead furrowed as he opened the chess case and began to set the board as usual. "I… yes."

"How do you stand it?" I asked.

"I walk out of the mine," Pearce said, and then he looked up at me, smiling.

He walked out and I could not. Very well. Apparently, he wasn't feeling friendly today either.

"And living here in Vermenia… has it taken a toll?" I asked.

His face twisted as if I'd just waved rot under his nose. "I suppose it has," he said through a tight jaw.

I wondered when was the last time he'd even tried a spell. Did living in Vermenia, working in the mine, deteriorate a person's magic to a point of losing it altogether? For my own sake, I hoped it didn't act too quickly.

"I hope you won't take too long to lose this one," Pearce said, sullen. "I have a great deal of work today."

On my way. Yes. I didn't have much time either. The thought of leaving surged through me, drawing my spine up straight, and brought with it a thin current of the strength and assurance that'd been leaving me over the days.

I set the sandwich to the side and faced the board. I was beginning to feel an odd kind of fondness for these rixon chess pieces I played with. They were the only thing in this mine I had any control over.

"Is Congress taking longer than you expected?" I asked.

Pearce flicked a pawn forward and I balanced it, moving quickly as he'd asked.

"We knew they wouldn't come to an immediate decision," Pearce said, frustration turning his tone to gravel. "No matter how your father pressed."

He played now with the expectation of me finding a way to lose and I didn't want him to realize my own plans before it was too late. I leaned back in my chair and tried not to watch the board, picturing it instead in my thoughts, playing out maneuvers so that I could answer each move of his within a few moments.

"Why not manipulate Vermenia to invade Enmaire instead?" I asked as Pearce arranged his knights and bishops into a hard advance forward.

"We've been sowing suspicion but the pieces were easier to manipulate from the other side," Pearce said. He took two of my pawns and gave up three of his own without seeming to notice. "It's easier to keep our own interests out of the spotlight this way."

Because Vermenia might want a cut of the profits if they went to war just for rixon.

I had enough now, I hoped. Enough to take to Congress if Joanna and I made it out of Vermenia safely. If they hadn't already made a decision to go to war.

"And how long am I valuable to you?" I asked.

Pearce grinned, still not paying close enough attention to the board between us to care when his advanced attack was outmaneuvered.

"Until Vermenia is invaded," Pearce said. "After that, I can't afford you returning to the troops. It works out so much better for me if Vermenia wins the war."

"And if no one else knows why it was started in the first place," I said. Pearce agreed with a 'hmm' and spent another piece.

My priority would be getting Joanna out safely, over myself. I couldn't afford the both of us getting stuck in here together. Especially since she wouldn't hold the same value to Pearce as I did.

I distracted Pearce with my rook and then took his queen before he finally really looked at the board and saw that he was losing. His eyebrows furrowed as he stared at the arrangement, his king isolated and my bishops advancing with my queen.

"I see," he said, mostly to himself. He'd finally gotten the game he wanted and he hadn't been paying attention. I'd taken away all the satisfaction of any win from him and now I'd taken away the challenge of losing too. "I see," he said again.

We played the game to the conclusion, only a handful of steps left before I declared checkmate. We didn't shake hands and Pearce didn't thank me for the game, simply cleared away all the pieces and folded the case. He stared at the lid for a stretch of silence and I waited for his response. But it wasn't what I expected.

"Carras told me about your covenmate, the young woman. A Scribe, I think he called it?" Pearce said, looking up at the ceiling in an imitation of innocence that made my blood curdle in my veins. "A supposedly extinct kind of magic, from Vermenia itself."

He looked up at me, eyes flat, and now he was waiting for me. I didn't speak. I wasn't sure I could speak. I only tried to keep the anxiety off my face.

"It seems strange that a magic which has vanished should suddenly appear again," Pearce said. "So we've been looking into the matter. It appears it was not as extinct as we were lead to believe. Are you interested in the form?"

I swallowed and there was a knot in my throat. "I've always been interested in forms of magic," I said, worried I was giving him too much even in that little scrap.

"I thought you might be," he said. "So I've been looking for another Scribe. They're very secretive here. But money talks, and I've had a little success. Wait here." He left out the cell door without another glance at me.

My pulse was pounding in my ears, my fingers clenched tight around the top of the table, eyes darting between the chess case in front of me and the closed door. Minutes passed with the cracking sounds of the miners at work in the background. I stood from the chair and paced the small room, feeling my heart hammering in my chest again. They'd discussed Joanna. Did they know she was coming? Did I have time to write a message? For every second I considered scribbling out a warning, I spent another certain the door would open again any second.

Time passed and while it felt like it could have been an hour or more, my ears lost track of the miners' beat. It might only have been a handful of anxious minutes.

When Pearce returned, he wasn't alone. Four guards followed him in with grim faces, dressed in their gray uniforms, and behind them was a younger man in plain, rough clothes.

"I'd considered this for later, after the war started," Pearce said, returning to his seat as I edged towards the wall, guards tracking my movement with their eyes. "To ensure you couldn't escape back to Enmaire and share what you'd learned before I'd taken full advantage of your visit," he explained. He looked at one of the guards and nodded once.

I was cornered against the wall on the far end of the bed and for the first time since I'd arrived in the cell, I felt myself in genuine physical danger. I glanced at every man in the room. These guards weren't afraid of me, that much was clear in their gaze, in their smirks.

The one Pearce had signaled stepped forward and the others followed. I jutted out an elbow, catching the closest one in the stomach, but he took it with a grunt, and then his fingers wrapped around my upper arm, holding me tight. I tried to jostle him off but another had me by the other elbow.

There was an exchange between them, in Vermenian words I didn't know, and then they were tugging my shirt over my head.

"Tell me what's happening," I growled, teeth gritting as I thrashed and tried to escape their hold. I was weaker than I thought, weaker than I had been when I'd been thrown in this rixon trap. Was it the metal infecting me? Or just inactivity?

"Josef here is an artist, although we'll be using him for cruder methods," Pearce said.

I caught a glimpse of 'Josef'. The young man was watching the guards wrestle me down to my knees with wide eyes, his hands gripped with white knuckles around a leather case. The guards shoved me, bare-chested, to bend over the mattress and I bit my own tongue trying to escape them, the hot copper flavor of blood vivid in my mouth.

"He also happens to be a Scribe. He'll be using those talents together to ensure we don't lose you."

I felt bile rise up in my throat as Josef took a nervous step forward, setting his case down on the ground.

"Have you ever gotten a tattoo, Callum?" Pearce asked.

My stomach dropped and for a moment all the fight in me slipped away, the strength of the guards smashing me to the mattress and pressing the air out of my lungs. Joanna's power but in a stranger's words, trapping me in the mine, ink burrowing in my skin. I roared but the sound was swallowed by the thin cushion and I had given the men holding me down too much grip now; I was fixed beneath them. The only thing I could see was a bit of the wall ahead of me, a scrap of the sheet on my bed.

One man's breathing was echoing in my right ear, and from the left, I heard the snaps of the leather case opening, the click and tap of metal. A hesitant murmur of Vermenian words. I gasped for a breath, eyes turning watery with anger and frustration and fear. I squirmed, tried to twist out of the hold of the hands. They held me fast.

"Try not to move," Pearce said, "Though I've heard it burns terribly. But it will take Josef more time if you don't hold still."

The motor of the needle was the loudest thing in the room, and the second it touched the skin of my back it echoed up my spine and into my brain. I clenched my jaw until my whole face ached, trying to hold in my shout of pain, of rage. It did burn, like hot nails scraping over my skin, vibrating into my bones.

Permanent. Whatever this was. Whatever words were chosen, they would be permanent.

A howling noise escaped my throat, rang against my latched teeth. The needle traveled in lines down my back, a phrase written, each word stacked on top of the other. Under the blur of pain was a steady tapping feeling, like the click of a typewriter key landing against a page. The Scribe's magic hitting my skin.

How would I tell Joanna? She had to stay away and yet I was selfishly yearning for her, for my coven, with a need so strong I almost thought I could feel them reaching back for me in the bond.

The torture stopped abruptly and I realized that my face was wet, a wounded sound choking off in my throat, collapsing in the quiet of the room.

What did it say? I wanted to ask and I was afraid to know.

The guards released me but I remained where I was, fingers tearing holes in the sheets of the mattress, body bent forward. They'd dropped my shirt onto my pillow. My father's voice in my head told me to stand up, to face them. My mother's—Joanna's, Aiden's, Isaac's—soothed in quiet whispers, to stay still, to breathe.

"That should do it," Pearce said, a little taunt.

I sat up, straightening my spine and feeling the tight ache where the tattoo was now printed as if the sun had burnt my skin and left it swollen and raw.

"You can play yourself at chess tomorrow," Pearce said as the cell door creaked open, Josef and the guards retreating. "I'll have work to do."

I clenched my jaw, stared at the mattress beneath me, refusing to meet his gaze. Would I be here tomorrow? Would I be *trapped* here with the force of these words? Would Joanna be trapped here tomorrow, because of me?

The door clicked shut and I stood up from the floor, my knees aching, feeling a wet trickle run down my back. Blood, probably. I went to the sink to wash and thought of what to write to my coven. Hopelessness felt like a dull, lead, weight in my chest.

2 0

———

JOANNA

The sky was barely turning pink when Geoff halted the small cart he and I sat in on our way to the border, and the procession of horses and covenmates behind us.

"Head back before the border sees you, we'll attract less attention without a crowd," Geoff said to the others. Darin had left the house to train in the barracks, but Sabine and Samuel followed us with Isaac, Aiden, and Bryce.

I jumped down from the wagon seat just as Isaac slid off the back of the glossy russet horse Sabine found for him. He caught me quick in his arms as I ran to him. His hold was tight around me and for a moment I pretended that he wouldn't release me. I knew he would, I knew he trusted me to do this for us, and there was no way I was changing my mind. But it didn't mean there wasn't a small part of me —maybe not so small—that was terrified, running through all the possible flaws in this plan of mine.

"Be...be safe," Isaac said in my ear, and then dropped his voice. "Don't let him see any of your magic. Not even the notebook."

I nodded, even though it would mean I was cut off from them, from Callum, while I traveled with Geoff.

"I love you," he hissed, his voice sounding tight.

421

"I love you," I said, not surprised to find my own throat choked with tears.

He took my face in tense hands and kissed me, lips firm, holding hard to mine as we exchanged a shaky breath. He left me with a softer kiss and then one brushed across each cheek.

Bryce was waiting behind him when he stepped away.

"Keep them safe," I said, blinking away the tears that rose up with Isaac's kiss. I smiled, or made a poor excuse for one with my sorry face.

"Don't be stupid," Bryce said. I couldn't tell if they meant that it was stupid of me to think they couldn't keep my covenmates safe, or if they just meant it as general advice for my travels.

"I'll try my best," I said, and at least this time my smile was honest.

Aiden was just managing to get down from his—Darin's, really— horse without it trying to move away when Bryce left me standing alone. He stopped a few feet away from me and I had to fold my lips in and bite down on them to keep my chin from quivering. He wasn't faring much better, jaw clenched tight and hands fisted at his side.

I took mercy on us both, walking up to him and rising on my toes. Just as my kiss landed on his lips he released a shuddering sigh, arms scooping me up to hold me to his chest.

"This is a terrible idea," he grumbled into my cheek.

"I'm going to bring him back and then we're all going back to Rhodantis to stop a war," I said like it would be that simple.

"If it comes down to you making it back safely or you getting stuck in Vermenia with Callum, I want you to come back," Aiden said. I tilted my head back to argue and he continued, "I'm not saying that we won't immediately try getting him out again. I just... don't want you both lost."

I thought it was pretty unlikely that I would find myself making a decision like that. More likely a decision would be made for me and I'd end up caught despite my best efforts. But I nodded, meeting Aiden's eyes, and covered the tears that were sneaking out of the corners of his eyes with my thumbs when I stretched up for another kiss. His hands were tight around my waist even as the kiss was gentle, tender and lingering.

"Time to go," Geoff said, waiting back at the cart behind us.

Aiden ignored him for a long moment before setting me back on my feet.

"I love you, be good, and don't do anything we wouldn't let you get away with," he said, smile hitching at the corner.

"I love you, and I won't make that promise," I said, grinning weakly and jumping out of reach when he made to catch me up again.

Sabine and Samuel were standing near the cart and I regretted for a moment that I had probably missed their own goodbyes with Geoff. I wondered what they looked like. I had a hard time imagining tender words exchanged, but I generally had the wrong instincts when it came to Sabine York.

"Good luck, word witch," Sabine said, smiling at me with a warmth I didn't share. "Geoff will keep you safe."

Geoff sat stonily on the bench of the wagon and did not look at either of us. I felt less confident of this fact.

"Put in a good word with your soldier for us," Samuel said and I raised an eyebrow at him. "You know, so he doesn't try to retaliate as soon as you all make it back."

I looked back at my covenmates and none of us said a word. I didn't think Callum *would* retaliate, I doubt he'd even thought of it, but they didn't need to know that. Isaac stepped forward and gave me a hand as I hauled myself back onto the wagon seat. His fingers clutched hard at mine as Geoff lifted up the reins, and I thought for a moment he might not let go. Maybe he'd changed his mind even after helping talk Aiden down. But as the horses kicked forward he winced and released me, gray eyes following me as we pulled away.

"How far to the border?" I asked, twisting in my seat to stare back at the grim faces of my lovers and friend.

"Couple miles," Geoff answered.

I turned around again to glance at him, expecting more information but he was silent, staring ahead on the road even though it was only miles of snow and hills and skeletal trees waiting for spring. I dug into the bag at my feet, pulling out the map he'd sent to us with Samuel. His head twitched in my direction, profile hidden by a curtain of blond hair.

"Don't have that out at the border," he said. "We should look like we know where we're going."

I didn't have a real reason for looking at it, I only wanted something to do with myself if my companion was going to sit in silence.

"What will I need to say at the border?" I asked.

"Don't speak," Geoff said, and it sounded like a general kind of instruction. "Be shy."

I chewed at my lip and studied the map as if there were some clue I could discover in the lines.

"We'll stop at nightfall, outside of towns to see a contact who has details about the mine," Geoff said. "Now put that away."

I wanted to argue with him, more to annoy him than to defend myself from his prickly nature. But I could see a structure in the distance, probably the border post, so I folded up the map and tucked it back into my bag. I pulled out my mother's papers instead, checking with Geoff—who nodded at the sight of them—before drawing them up into my lap, holding them against myself underneath my coat.

One hundred worries raced through my head in the quiet of our ride and I wished that it was any of the other York coven members sitting next to me. Even Darin grinning meanly and laughing, as long as he would fill the silence and distract me from the thoughts that clamored for attention.

The border gate was only a series of outpost buildings stacked together on either side of a bridge at the Danns river. I could see the rust orange waistcoat uniforms from here, a handful of men milling around the road.

"Not much traffic since the war," Geoff said. "Soldiers get bored sometimes. If they give us trouble we'll turn around."

"And come back later?" I asked.

"Later. Not too soon."

Long enough for them to change shifts or to forget us altogether? Either way, I didn't want to wait.

"Won't the ones on the Vermenian side recognize you, the Enmaire soldiers? Don't they know you?"

"Don't worry about that," Geoff said. "You'll see."

I bit my tongue. We were getting too close to the border for me to be yammering questions. I reached back to pull my hood up but Geoff shook his head at me.

"They'll push it down again," he said.

So I left it and wrapped my scarf tighter around my neck, wishing that I had Written *invisible* on my skin. But I was a little afraid of what those consequences might have been—would I ever find the words again to wash them away if I couldn't see them?

The Vermenian soldiers marched into position as we approached, two on either side of the road. I wanted to look at their faces, see if they seemed bored or looked like they'd give us trouble, but Geoff had said to act shy. I folded my hands over my lap and kept my chin ducked down as we rode closer. My heart was pounding in my ears in time with the *clomp clomp* of horse hooves beneath us.

"Hatte, hatte," the soldiers called and Geoff pulled on the reins, slowing the horses just a few yards before the bridge planks.

I could see the river out of the corner of my eye, frozen an inky blue with sweeps of snow across the surface and thick white cracks like jagged veins. And then black boots appeared on the ground at my side and I looked back down into my lap.

"Karthers," the soldier muttered, another echoing it from Geoff's side. I pulled my mother's papers out of my lap and kept my arm tucked close to my side to keep my hand from shaking as I passed the page over.

Geoff was answering questions at my side, low voice rumbling in chorus with the soldiers. Every second ticked by with excruciating slowness and I glanced over at the man holding my papers. He was young, looking barely older than the students at Canderfey, with red acne still bright on his cheeks beneath his black fur-trimmed hat. He frowned at my mother's papers and I felt bile rise up in my throat.

What if they didn't just refuse to let me pass but arrested me for false papers? Would I be held here at the border where Aiden and Isaac would be able to reach me, or deep into Vermenia?

Then the soldier grunted, and passed back my papers, stepping away. I folded the page with numb fingers, feeling my blood rush warmly under my skin. It had worked. I was safe.

"Shurruck eten," Geoff's soldier said, gesturing to the two still waiting by the bridge.

Geoff's hand pressed over mine in a staying motion and then he lowered himself out of his seat. All four Vermenian soldiers surrounded Geoff, asking rapid questions. I sat frozen, alone in the cart, watching avidly and forgetting that I should be pretending to be demure. Geoff looked nervous, face pale and eyes wide and I wished I knew whether it was an act for the soldiers or if something was going wrong.

But I had been approved. If they kept him detained would they still let me cross? Geoff looked up between their heads at me and I thought I saw a flicker of caution in his stare. Would I leave him to it, take off into Vermenia on my own? There'd be hell to pay if I made it back, I'd answer to Aiden and Isaac if not Geoff himself. I *would* do it though. I would leave without him.

Two soldiers broke off from their circle, looking aimlessly into our bags in the back of the cart. If Geoff had packed weapons he hid them well enough not to be discovered. I only had a few simple garments in my bag, enough to look like a traveler and more than I really needed with me. Geoff had packed grain and food and boxes wrapped in simple paper—gifts for our pretend family. Maybe that was where he had tucked his weapons because the boxes rattled as one of the soldiers shook them.

Another soldier, older, closer to my age, looked up and caught me watching. I flicked my gaze back to my lap, red rising in my cheeks. He murmured something to me, and while I didn't understand the words I heard the teasing invitation in them.

I looked up again and he was grinning at me with a lopsided smirk. Geoff was watching us both while he answered more questions and this time I was *certain* he was nervous. What would happen if I drew my notebook out of my pocket and Wrote us safely across the bridge? Probably I wouldn't even get the chance to finish the sentence with the way they were watching us. Instead, I looked back at the flirting soldier and gathered up my best impression of my mother.

"Net," I said, sliding the n and e together. A snapping word I'd heard plenty in childhood when my mother's temper rose. I was firm even while blushing harder, and the young soldier who had checked my papers snorted, elbowing the other lightly in the ribs before pulling him away.

Instead of cornering Geoff again, they returned to their post at the bridge border, and within another minute Geoff was crossing back to the wagon. He gave me an uncharacteristic smile, but I suspected it was for the benefit of the watching soldiers, so I answered it with more sweetness than he really deserved. He said something to me as he hopped back into his seat and I nodded, hoping that was an appropriate response.

Then he clicked his tongue, flicked the reins, and we were moving forward. I had to hold my breath tight in my chest to keep myself from looking too relieved. The soldiers on the road didn't move, and we passed them with inches to spare. For the sake of our disguise, or for my own personal relief, I sagged into Geoff's side and he patted my arm as we started to cross the bridge.

"Good," he whispered.

"And this side?" I asked, keeping my voice quieter than the rattle of our progress over the wooden bridge planks. The bright ivory uniforms trimmed with blue stood ahead of us, the Enmaire soldiers gathered together around a small smoking fire.

"Watch," he said.

The Enmaire soldiers looked up as we reached them, their gazes settling on me first with a blank kind of acknowledgment, but when they slid across me to Geoff their eyes widened. They nodded at him, a simple gesture that could be taken for polite if seen from the other side of the bridge. But there was wary respect on their faces and they skirted quickly back to their fire without a word.

"They know better than to ask questions," Geoff said to me, raising an eyebrow at me as if to say 'You could learn something from this.'

WE RODE for hours and at one point I decided to walk alongside the cart instead of sitting in it and numbing my bottom for another hour. Geoff was terrible company. I'd tried at first to make conversation, if not for my own benefit than only to irritate him. But he was steadfastly reticent and by the time it was afternoon and the sun was beginning to set for the evening I found myself opening my lips to speak before thinking better of it.

Save it, I thought. It was cold enough now to freeze the inside of my nose and make my teeth hurt when I opened my mouth to speak. I walked until my feet felt like ice cubes and then sat in the wagon until the rest of me did.

"Almost there," Geoff said, as dark took over.

I almost asked where 'there' was, but in my head I heard him answer me. 'You'll see.'

'There' was a sheep farm, dark and quiet and secluded. I could hear the animals bleating sleepily from inside a barn and there was a small farmhouse, dark but for three candles winking through a window. Geoff guided the wagon straight into the yard and around to behind the barn.

"I'm putting the horses in for the night," Geoff said, jumping down from the bench. "Go to the house, they'll let you in and there will be hot food."

I wasn't sure how I felt about the idea of approaching a stranger's home in the dark of night and asking to be let in for food. I imagined all the little details Geoff might have neglected to mention.

These are old friends of mine who know everything about the local mines. One is a very good cook. They often take in strangers traveling in the night. Absolutely none of us are planning on turning you into the local authorities and betraying your coven a second time.

With that imaginary reassurance, I stepped carefully through the snowdrifts up to a narrow back door. There was another thin candle burning in the window by the door and I caught a glimpse of a warped, orangey face passing in front, ghastly in the shadow and firelight. My heart stuttered and I stopped, steps away from the house, frozen fingers going to my skirts, ready to root out the only tools I had for defense.

The door opened and a small, elderly woman stood in the door frame, wrapped in a thick shawl, her gray hair hanging over her shoulder in a braid.

"Camma, camma," she said, waving her hand at me, gesturing inside. She looked a little impatient but smiled all the same, deep wrinkles growing around her mouth and eyes.

I hurried inside and she shut the door behind her with a huff of effort before taking my elbow and dragging me into the house through the dark. She led me into a small room without windows in what must have been the heart of the house. A fireplace sat to my left, burning brightly, and there was another tiny old woman, putting two steaming bowls of stew down onto a nicely dressed table in front of the fire. The two women chatted briefly to one another before the one holding my elbow peeled me out of my coat.

The other took my shoulders, pushing me down into a chair and within moments I was gently bullied out of my shoes and scarf and gloves and socks. A tight laugh worked its way out of me and the pair of them smiled at me.

"Esse," said the second woman, taking my hand and wrapping it around the spoon, warm from sitting in the bowl of stew.

"Gladly," I said, lifting up a heaping bite of carrots and meat and gravy. It was just on the safe side of scorching, warmer in my mouth for how cold I was.

I grinned at the women, cheeks full of food and they both grinned back, leaving me to my meal and sitting down in a pair of rocking chairs at the other side of the room. I watched them as I ate, one pulling open a notebook of scribbles that I suspected was accounting and the other picking up her knitting.

Geoff entered the room in another few minutes and the women

abandoned the work, rushing him and pulling him down by the shoulders to kiss his cheeks. There was a rush of Vermenian, mostly from the women, and even if Geoff didn't look *happy* exactly, he looked much less stony around them. They squeezed his arms and wagged their fingers in his face and I took a big bite of stew to keep myself from laughing. He too was pushed into a seat across from me, handed his spoon, and watched quietly as he started to eat.

The talk picked up then, and while I couldn't follow the words I realized they were sharing information with him. The one with the braid scoffed at the other and then spoke quickly over her. Geoff asked a few questions which they answered with arguments that ended with them both nodding together.

"Pearce's mine is to the west," Geoff said to me. "About eighty men stationed at night. Only fifteen of whom work at the mine. The rest are new, the mercenaries your soldier mentioned."

"And in the daytime?" I asked, feeling worry burrow in my chest. My spoon scraped the bowl for the last of the gravy which was wonderfully rich and salty. Eighty men was too many.

"Hundreds," Geoff said and my stomach dropped to the floor. "But not many more of the mercenaries. They run in shifts all day and night."

"Guarding Callum?" I asked and Geoff grunted and shrugged.

"Him and the rixon, the production," Geoff said. "If the war is counting on it Pearce will want it safe."

"So we go at night," I said.

Geoff looked up at me from his stew. The women stood at our sides watching us eat and I set my spoon down in my bowl. "Thank you," I said to them, smiling. For the food and the information, however much it terrified me.

"We go at night," Geoff said, with a barely-there sigh. I wondered if he regretted agreeing to bring me already. If he thought eighty men was too many also. Probably, but I didn't want to hear it spoken out loud.

"These women are-" I started.

"Gossips," Geoff said, with a tiny curl of a smile that flickered on and then vanished just as quickly.

"I was going to say 'your family,'" I said, as Geoff nodded at them both with a few words of Vermenian. They went back to their seats and Geoff watched them for a moment before turning to me.

"My aunts," he said, going back to his stew.

It took a measure of trust, I realized, for him to bring me here to his family. Family he still clearly cared for, all stoniness aside. Also, I found it fairly charming that his insider information came from a pair of doting aunts.

"They have a three-county gambling circuit and they'll drive a man off the property quicker than all the mercenaries in the country," Geoff said under his breath. "Don't be fooled."

I glanced back at the accounts book with a new understanding and then quickly down at my lap again.

"Your family," Geoff said, clearing his throat to add, "Your mother's family. They're close?"

"On the border," I said. "Across from Dannsedge."

"You think they'd keep you safe if it came to it?" Geoff asked.

I thought of what my father had said and nodded. "Would it be safe for them?"

"Probably, if things go right," Geoff said. "I may send you there. Let me think on it."

He spoke to the aunts briefly and the one abandoned her knitting again for us, coming and pulling me up from the chair.

"Go sleep," Geoff said to me. "Your bag is by the stairs. We've got traveling tomorrow and a long night to face."

His aunt took me upstairs to a small bedroom, letting me stop at a cramped bathroom on the way. There was a small stove in the corner of the bedroom and she put together a little fire and then stacked the mattress with heavy blankets. I thanked her again and she patted my cheek goodnight.

Either I was too tired to lay awake worrying or—more likely—the aunts had slipped something into my stew because the second my head hit the pillow I was asleep.

21

⎯⎯

JOANNA

I slept late into the morning and when I woke the aunts stuffed us both full with another hot meal. I don't think I'd ever seen so many sausages out on the table and I know for certain I'd never eaten as many in one sitting. Even Geoff looked impressed.

Our wagon was full of warm blankets as we left and I gratefully wrapped myself up in one, waving to the miniature pair of women standing in the yard.

Geoff kept us on the roads that edged around towns rather than traveled straight through and every quiet hour that passed where the sun sank a little further into the sky behind us made me sit tenser in my seat.

"I can't take eighty men alone," Geoff said at one point. We had just started to reach the base of the mountains, the horses pulling us slower up the incline.

"I know," I said. I'd been thinking the same thing for the whole of the day. Isaac told me not to take out the notebook, to Write in front of Geoff for any reason, but I couldn't imagine us making it in and out of the mine without more magic.

"And you don't look up to covering the difference for me," Geoff said, slower.

I snorted and shook my head. We were both silent for a stretch, bitter snow falling around us. We were rounding a curve and the sun was being tucked away behind the side of the mountain.

"I have an idea of how to help," I said.

Geoff clucked encouragingly at the horses for a moment before turning to me. "Care to elaborate?"

I laughed loud before clapping my hand over my mouth. It would serve him right if I didn't. His brow furrowed in confusion and I resisted the urge to tease him.

"I can put the men to sleep," I said. "I think I can. It doesn't mean they won't wake up while we're there, I thought of trying that but I'm afraid the spell wouldn't come off again. I don't want to hurt anyone if I can help it."

Geoff nodded. "Sleep is enough. It will make the difference."

I sucked in a shaky breath at his confidence. I hadn't had it before that moment, hadn't believed we might succeed.

"How do we find Callum in the mine?" I asked.

Geoff fished inside of his jacket and pulled out a folded piece of paper, passing it to me. "From the aunts," he explained. "It's based off what workers have said so it won't be an accurate map, but their best guesses for where he might be. I have an idea of how to get more information but for now, this is what we have. Study it as much as you can and keep a cool head when we get inside. It won't feel as clear once we're underground."

I didn't think the map was clear enough to start with, meaningless wobbling lines with three small, circled 'x's. Down which corridor should I wiggle roughly to the right to find my covenmate? But I did study the lines while we rode. It was the only guide I had. The only *hope*.

"The aunts… did they know this is all for…?" I trailed off.

"The General who helped defeat Vermenia in the red war?" Geoff finished for me. "They do. We don't call him the Toy Soldier here though. No one talks much about it. Better not to remember."

"They didn't lose anyone?"

"We all lost someone," Geoff said, and with that, the topic died.

WE STOPPED in a small mountainside town at nightfall. Geoff stabled the horses, propping me against a barn wall and warning me in muttered tones not to speak to anyone. When we were alone in the stable he unpacked the small gift boxes. I had been right, one by one he tucked knives away, so fast I couldn't even say for sure where they were now hiding. Out of one, he pulled out wrapped sticks, almost like candles with longer wicks.

"What are those?" I asked.

"Diversion tactics," Geoff said.

We went to the local tavern and after directing me to an empty corner with a gesture, he ordered us some dinner. It was quiet and empty for this time of evening and most of the people sitting inside seemed to be waiting for time to pass.

"We sit and we- I listen," Geoff whispered to me, bringing over plates of steaming potatoes and a bony looking chicken leg.

I was too wired to eat. The night felt up in the air as if anything might happen, or nothing at all. What if I got lost in the mine and *never* found Callum? What if I was caught and we were separated and our covenmates had twice the rescuing to do for my efforts?

Geoff had cleaned up half his plate and I'd barely taken a bite when all at once the tavern seemed to come to life. Groups of men walked in by the handful, rushing up to the bar and being greeted by the patrons. Shift end, I realized. Within minutes the room was crowded, men covered in an almost glittering purple-black dust, milling together and shouting over one another.

I looked to Geoff and he appeared to be wholly focussed on his plate but I remembered what he said. He was listening into the end of day conversation of the workers. His eyes flicked up to me and he frowned, nodding down at my plate so I returned to my food, forcing down cold bites.

Geoff's arm stretched across the back of my chair and he leaned in close, nearly pressing the words to my ear. "Clear your plate and we'll leave. We have what we need."

I gobbled down what was left in front of me and together we stood, our seats quickly being taken up again by a group of men. Geoff and I squeezed ourselves through the crowd and I kept my eyes down on the floor, stepping cautiously around feet and trying not to bump into anyone for fear of being noticed. I bit down on my tongue to keep from issuing apologies in the wrong language.

Stepping outside again hit me with a wave of relief, even in the bitterly cold air that dried my throat as I took a breath. The world outside of the tavern was still and silent, snow crunching under our boots as we walked up the street without a word. A few straggler groups of men passed us on our way up the mountain road but their eyes were bleary, faces streaked with rixon dust so that they almost shimmered in the dark. They didn't do more than nod at us as we crossed each other.

When the road ahead and behind us was clear Geoff spoke. "The men mentioned a room built for their 'visitor' and I heard that term mentioned more than a few times," he said. "It sounded like it was close to the overseer and foreman's offices. It'll be deeper into the mine but at least it's not some unidentified supply closet." I hummed in agreement because it felt as if my heart was stuffed up into my throat. Geoff added, "It's a clear shot to that area. You just march straight and you'll find it."

I nodded, my head jerking unevenly on my neck. *Get to Callum, get to Callum,* my thoughts chanted.

"He won't be able to use magic and it'll be weak until you get farther off the mountain," Geoff said, and somewhere in the back of my head, I wanted to tease him for turning chatty on me. "So it'll be up to you to get the pair of you down undetected."

"Me?" I asked, voice sharp. "Where will you be?"

"Making sure you have time to get to the cart," Geoff said. When I stared at him he shrugged. "Don't worry about me. I'm better on my own than saddled with watching the pair of you."

I narrowed my eyes, a small scoff at the back of my throat and his lips twitched, but at least I felt like I could breathe again.

"How will we get back across the border?" I asked.

"Not the way we came," Geoff said. "Can you use the map to get to your mother's family?"

I nodded and told him the address, a blacksmith's house outside of a town called Ewenson.

"Alright, I'll meet you there," Geoff said, stopping us on the road. "The mine is close. Do your spell before they can see us."

I hesitated. Despite making it across the bridge, and despite the aunts' hospitality and the fact that I had made it this far without Geoff handing me over to Vermenian authorities or worse, I still felt nervous and vulnerable about drawing my pen and notebook out of my pocket. The gap of magical space was harder to find and I realized it was because I was standing on a rixon mountain and relying on the kind of magic the metal dampened, but my nail snagged and with that, I had found it again.

Geoff watched me carefully as I flipped to a blank page. Callum's handwriting shimmered on the page. *Don't come, it won't work.* My heart banged for him, for his worry. It would work. I would make sure we made it out.

Everyone inside of the Getchrechek Mine except Callum Pike is sleeping, I wrote.

"That's it?" Geoff asked, frowning.

"That's it," I said, shrugging and then added after a beat, "I hope."

He gave me a long studying look, a frown line deepening on his forehead. "Then we'd better hurry," he said finally.

I had to jog to keep up with him and where I was taking clumsy crunching steps and deep puffing breaths, Geoff moved with perfect silence. As we moved a jagged, craggy shape appeared around the edge of the mountain. Wooden beams stretched out of the face of the rock, lit from beneath by two yellow lanterns. We both slowed as the entrance to the mine faced us clearly from the road. There was no one outside and no sound coming from the black mouth opening.

"I'll go in first," Geoff whispered. "Count to eighty and then run back down the mountain if you don't see me."

He waited until I nodded and then ran ahead of me into the dark maw of the mine. I stuttered through numbers in my head, barely putting them in the right order, my heart beating too wildly to keep the count. Before I reached forty, Geoff reappeared in the dark, waving an arm to me and lifting a finger to his lips.

I had returned the notebook and pen to my real pocket and I pulled them out again, flipping back to the spell.

We love you. Be careful. Isaac's handwriting. My chest ached, a burst of warmth cutting through the freezing cold of the night. They were watching for my words. I wanted to answer them but there wasn't time.

My steps are silent, I wrote. At least if that couldn't be undone later there wouldn't be serious consequences. None that I could think of.

When I reached Geoff at the entrance, the darkness inside was less solid. There were more lamps deeper inside and from here I could make out shadowy pathways and halls. Geoff stopped me with a hand on my shoulder and then pointed to either side of the entrance. I nearly jumped out of my own skin. Slack bodies were crumpled on the floor. I held my breath until one sighed, sleepy and low, and then exhaled shakily.

My spell. It was working.

Geoff took me by the shoulders, pointing down the corridor directly ahead of us. "Straight ahead," he whispered, so quiet I was watching his lips move more than hearing the words themselves. "Left before the elevators down. Good luck, word witch. I'll see you in Ewenson."

"Thank you," I said, reaching up to squeeze his arms. He nodded at me, smile almost invisible in the dark, and we released each other.

I marched in quiet down the hall feeling my pulse pound in my head, in the tips of my fingers, all the way down to my toes. I could hear it rushing in my ears. I reached into my skirt pocket and pulled out my chalk stick in case of any emergency and my hand trembled in front of me.

Get to Callum, get to Callum.

There were more men sleeping in the hall, some toppled down to the floor as if they had dropped all at once, others were slumped against the wall, heads back and snores echoing. I tiptoed over legs and around heads and torsos, expecting at every moment for one of them to wake up and catch me by the ankle.

A light bulb flickered through a grate at the end of the hall and an elevator sat waiting, three bodies sleeping on the floor inside, a shadowy pile of men visible through the cage door. A hall broke off on my left, a man stretched across the berth of the opening. I lifted my skirts to step over him, my breath still in my lungs.

A few yards away a door stood, hanging open and flooding light into the hall. I blinked against the glare and crept up. Inside, four guards dressed in gray uniforms lay on the floor and against a wall with a large rixon door bolted shut. To the right of them was a glossy wooden desk, a large man collapsed forward onto its surface, papers sticking out from beneath his rosy face. There was a wool coat draped over the back of the chair he sat in and his clothes were finer than anyone else's in the mine, or in the little town below. This was the Enmairian ambassador who was selling out his country for a profit.

Which meant that rixon door, built like a bank safe, was probably the door to Callum. I rolled the chalk in my fingers again, hand now dusted in white, and stepped carefully around the guards directly in front of the door. I lifted my hand to the metal and even though it was cool to the touch, still and silent, I wanted to believe that the fluttering in my chest was our bond stretching through the small space to reach for Callum.

Unlocked, I scratched over the door's surface, the white standing out stark against the dark shimmering metal. A tumbler thudded inside of the door and there was the faintest rustle of movement from the other side. I glanced over my shoulder as I reached out to the bolt, a guard was grimacing on the floor but his eyes were shut. I was certain that Callum and I wouldn't make it out of this room without waking the inhabitants. If I left now I might make it out of the mine, I might follow Aiden's instructions of coming back with or without Callum.

"Who is it?" I heard from inside.

My free hand clapped over my mouth to trap the sudden sob that tried to burst out of my chest and I slammed back the bolt with too much force. It was him. The bolt sliding back was like a crack in the silence of the room but I was already shouldering open the door. The light from the ambassador's office spilled into the small, stale cell, stretching across Callum's pale face and I was speechless.

His eyes were wide, the blue-green shockingly bright in the light. His hair was dark with grease and his clothes were stained and none of it mattered. He rushed forward and I was surrounded by him, burying my face into the skin of his neck, his hands so tight on my waist, my back, my shoulders that I thought it might leave little bruises. He tore me away for half a breath and then his mouth was slanted across mine, the heat of the kiss blistering and a terrible, weak sound rising up from my throat.

I was streaking chalk through his hair and over the back of his shirt, my arms trying to cling around him as he pushed me away, my back bumping against the edge of the door. He jumped in front of me just as a guard staggered up to his feet, kicking another of the guards awake as he lurched toward us.

I was gasping, thoughts racing for a solution, the right words to combine, when Callum struck. He lunged for the guard, a fist swinging and landing with a gruesome crunch against the other man's nose. His hand pulled back, blood on his knuckles. On the floor around us, the guards groaned to life again as one stumbled up and the man Callum had punched fell backward with an echoing thump to the floor.

I glanced over to the desk where Ambassador Pearce's head was rolling back and forth, drowsily lifting from the surface. As Callum grabbed a guard rushing toward me, bodily throwing him into another, I ran to the desk crouching down.

"Guards!" Pearce said, but the words were raspy and broken with sleep and I hoped they wouldn't reach any of the unconscious men in the halls. He fumbled in his desk, shooting a baffled frowning glare in my direction. "What are you doing?" he asked.

Ambassador Ramond Pearce, I started, writing on the side of the desk so quickly that I had to pray the words would be legible enough to hold the magic.

He pulled a handgun out from a drawer and I rushed even quicker, hearing an agonized grunt behind me and hoping it meant Callum was still winning.

...cannot move. His arm was lifted, fingers wrapped around the gun handle, barrel pointed over my head at Callum. And now he was frozen, eyes wide and unblinking.

"Joanna, quick," Callum hissed as I rose up from the floor, keeping a watchful eye on Pearce. I glanced over my shoulder and the guards were on the floor around Callum, lips and noses bleeding, and one with his arm twisted in a painfully *wrong* position.

I reached out to Pearce and lightly twisted the gun out of his grip, his fingers still too loose around the handle to keep hold. Callum's hand was stretched out to mine and when I took it I felt the fullness in my chest of our coven bond connected again. His lip was swelling and there was a scratch across his nose and over his eyebrow but he was whole and in front of me and I couldn't shake off the lightness in my chest.

"Joanna, I don't know if I can leave," he whispered, taking my hands and helping me jump over the prone, groaning body on the floor to step closer to him.

I opened my mouth to speak but before I got the chance the mine seemed to rock and tremble at once, an enormous noise building under our feet and crashing through the halls.

An alarm began to blare overhead and my chest froze at the sound, a quieter collection of grunts and voices sounding from outside the room. Callum dragged me quickly across the room into a dark corner and I could hear under the screaming, wheeling notes of the alarm, feet stumbling and running away from us.

"An explosion," Callum whispered, glancing back at the stirring figures he'd left on the floor, at immobile Pearce. "They're heading down into the mine."

"Geoff," I answered, quickly scrawling on the wall behind me *The guards in this room are sleeping.* I heard a thump of a body going slack behind me. "It's Geoff," I said. "He said he'd draw them away."

Callum only resisted a little as I pulled him back to the door, glancing out and finding the hallway cleared of sleepers.

"Geoff? Geoff *York?*" Callum hissed.

"Yes, but we can trust him, I promise," I said, equally quiet. "I know they're the reason you ended up here, but I promise that he's the reason you're getting out. There's no one in the hall, we have to go."

"They wrote on me," Callum said, holding me still. I blinked up at him in confusion and he added, "Pearce found a Scribe. They had me tattooed. I can't read it."

I stood dumbfounded. They had *tattooed* him. With Written magic. It made my stomach queasy to think of it. Callum turned, lifting up the hem of his shirt just enough to show me a glimpse of black in spelled out in careful, foreign letters, their outline still red and irritated.

"I'll- I'll-" I stuttered, trying to think of what I could do to fix this.

"You should go," Callum said, turning back to me, taking my hands again, sorrow stretched across his face. "Go without me."

That drew out words. "I'm sorry but I'd sooner cut that ink right out of you," I said and Callum looked startled. "I won't. We don't even know what it says, for goodness sake! I'll do *something*, but we are leaving here together."

Callum's hand squeezed tight around mine and I looked up at him, a whole new wave of relief and aching happiness sweeping over me again at just *seeing* him. His eyes traced my face, weighing my determination against his. But he nodded after a moment and we ran out of the office together. I swung the door shut behind us and wrote with the chalk *Locked*. I hoped no key would open it. Let them tear the door down before they got to Pearce and sorted out how to wash away my words.

I really didn't care.

22

CALLUM

We needed to be fast and quiet and unnoticed. I needed to focus more on getting Joanna out of the damned mine than I did on the fact that she was *here* and in front of me and beautiful. But when I wrapped my arms around her, stopping her from running into the next hall before we listened for activity, I couldn't help but revel in having her close, smelling the salt on her skin and the whiff of rose in her hair, the softness of having her against my chest again. I didn't know if the tattoo on my back would allow me to run or not, but there was no way I'd get Joanna near the exit if I didn't try and escape with her.

Outside of the rixon room, I felt a whisper-thin thread of magic curling in my chest, coming back to life, but it wasn't enough to draw down to my fingers and cast with. Joanna tugged at my hands and I had to release her from my embrace so we could run again.

"We have to get down to the next town," she said, huffing a breath as we rounded a corner. "The horses are stabled there."

There was smoke wafting up from deeper in the mine, shouts echoing from where the men attended Geoff's explosion.

"Where are the others?" I asked, checking behind us to make sure we weren't spotted. I felt a whip of cold strike my cheek and looked ahead again, realizing the darkness in front of us was the clouded night sky.

"In Enmaire, just over the border, waiting for us," Joanna said.

Up ahead of us there was a shout, a figure appearing at the opening of the mine and I pulled Joanna back behind me as the guard rushed for us. He was a blurry sight without my glasses but I thought he was holding the blunt end of his gun raised to strike instead of shoot. They probably had instructions *against* killing me if they could help it.

I barreled forward into his stomach, knocking him onto his back and wrestling for a grip on the weapon. Our legs grappled and the man rolled us until my back hit the floor, a grunt escaping my gritted teeth. He was stronger than me and I needed an advantage but my magic was still too thin while we were inside the mountain.

Over his shoulder, I saw a swish of Joanna's skirt and I wanted to shout out to her to keep running. I would follow or get locked up again, but at least she wouldn't be trapped with me. And then she was behind him, striking him in the back of the head with the wooden handle of a miner's pick-axe. The guard slumped forward and I heaved him off my chest and onto the floor.

"I should have grabbed one of these when we came in," Joanna said, a little breathless. She reached her hand down to me and helped pull me up off the floor, the pair of us grinning. I now had no doubt in my mind that she was sincere when she'd threatened to cut the tattoo on my back. And if it came to it, I thought I might let her.

"You're a fearsome creature and I love you," I said, picking up the guard's gun.

"You'd better," she said. "Grab his coat and boots too, it's cold out and you're underdressed."

"Did you have a secret past as a highway robber?" I asked, rolling the unconscious man and peeling off his coat as Joanna wrestled him out of his boots. She was right though, they'd taken my coat and boots to I don't know where when they'd put me in the cell, probably knowing I'd never make it down the mountain in winter without them.

"I'm just a very practical person," she said, grunting as she tugged first one foot and then the other free.

She stood with the pick-axe raised, ready to strike, as I tugged on the scavenged coat and shoes. I wished I had the time to kiss her silly. Instead, I swung the gun over my shoulder and took her hand as she dropped the axe. The open gate was ahead of us and every step closer was another painful shard of hope burrowing into my chest.

"Don't think about the words," Joanna said. "Just keep walking with me.

I turned my face to hers, taking in her smile, feeling it warm me, letting it distract me.

The cold snapped as we stepped outside together and even as a gust of wind wrapped around us and back down the road, I felt a strange burst of energy. I was outside with the sky above me instead of rock and rixon.

"I hope the town can't hear the alarm," Joanna murmured, her fingers wrapping tighter around mine.

I flexed my magic, feeling a small spark of heat flare in my blood. Even better, I felt the threads connecting me across the miles to Aiden and Isaac. The relief nearly made my legs shake as we walked with quick, careful steps, and it echoed back at me from their end of the connection. The rixon mine hadn't stolen this from me, not my power, and not my coven.

I traced my free hand over Joanna's shoulder, giving her a little bit of shadowing magic, and then did the same to myself. The guard's coat would help some if anyone glanced over me, but the sight of Joanna with me might give a witness pause if they looked too long.

"How did you get across the border?" I asked.

"My mother's papers, I spelled them," she said. Then she went back to the beginning to share the whole journey. Joanna's story skimmed over speaking to my father with a kind of airy avoidance. I was going to have lots of questions to ask our other covenmates.

"I think we can trust Geoff," she said, finishing. "I hope so. We need him to get back across the border."

I was fairly certain I could sneak us across the border if it came down to it, but if Geoff York really had helped free me, and kept Joanna safe in the process, I would try to trust him.

"Here's the town," Joanna whispered, silhouettes of stucco buildings outlined by the glow of yellow lamps appearing in front of us through a blurry sheet of snow.

I could hear a noisy roar of people inside one of the central buildings but Joanna pulled us into a dark barn that stank of hay and horses.

"Fit them up while I get the cart," she whispered.

"Wait," I said, catching at her waist. "Wait."

She stopped in front of me, horses chuffing in their stalls, and the tension in her face bled away as we stared at one another. I pulled her close and she rose up on her toes and I bent my head to kiss her. It was a soft, brushing meeting of lips. A reunion. Aiden and Isaac were somewhere along the bond, distant but present, showering us with a warmth that filled the kiss. We pulled away after another minute and she kissed my jaw.

"It's good to see your face," she said, smiling, almost shy.

I dressed the two brown horses after she left, and led them out to the alley where Joanna was pulling a canvas sheet away to reveal a small wooden cart. We hooked the horses up and Joanna lifted herself into the driver's seat.

"Maybe you should hide in the back under the blankets?" Joanna said, chewing at her lip.

I joined her on the bench, pulling one of the blankets over our lap. "I'd rather be next to you." I thought I saw the hint of a blush in the dark and I wished I had my glasses again so I could enjoy the details of her face. "Besides, I might need you to fight someone off of me again."

She snorted and shook her head, pulling her notebook out of her pocket and flipping it open.

Callum and I will travel safely and secretly until Geoff finds us.

A safe ease wrapped over my shoulders. I trusted Joanna's Writing, her magic, to overpower anyone else's. The tattoo stung on my back, under the weight of the heavy coat, but whatever the words said, I tried to believe we'd make it home safe. Joanna lifted the reins, flicking them and nudging the horses forward down the mountain road.

A MILE away from the mountain and I started to layer our skin, the horses, and the cart with spells. Partly it was to keep us safe, unseen, warm. Partly it was because having my magic at hand again was such an enormous relief and I didn't want to stop, afraid it might drop away again.

Joanna drove until dawn, softening into my side and eyelids drooping. I took the map out of her hands and followed the route she'd traced, the roads curving around towns until we reached a small, wooded valley. Joanna all but fell out of the cart, hurrying to build a fire, melting snow for water while I fed the horses.

"You're tired," I said, my own voice scratching in my throat. "Lay down and rest."

"I will," she mumbled back at me, kneeling down by the fire until her skirt was nearly soaked with snow and mud.

My heart swelled large and hot in my chest at the sight of her, almost toppling over as she poured out steaming cups of water for us and then brought over the rest of the pan to the horses, pouring it over the snow to make puddles for them to drink from. I joined her, tracing a spell on the ground and the puddles remained full and warm.

"Rest," I said, wrapping my hands around her waist before she escaped again, pressing a kiss to her neck.

"You rest," she snapped, but without any real heat.

"That's a very good idea," I said.

I lifted her up off the ground and carried her to the back of the cart, pushing aside her pack of food and clothes and tossing her in on the two blankets we hadn't bundled up in during our ride. I jumped in after her, crawling over her and snatching the blankets from the front of the cart, dropping them on top of us.

"Oh! Callum!" Joanna said, trying to sound sharp and failing as she broke into laughter.

"I've run a ward around our camp and hid the smoke from our fire, the horses have grain and water, and if I let you loose you'll end up tripping into the fire half-asleep," I said, shifting the blankets until they tented over us, bracing myself over her body on my forearms. Little pinpricks of sunlight snuck in through the weave of the blankets, just enough light to make out Joanna's smile.

"I missed you," she said, a crack in her voice. "You've no idea."

"I do," I said, letting my head droop to rest my cheek against hers. "Very much. I will lecture you, Aiden, Isaac, and *myself* later on what a terrible idea it was to have you come into Vermenia to find me. For now, I'm just grateful."

Joanna turned her head, nudging her nose over my cheek until our mouths brushed. Her arms linked around my shoulders, careful of my back, and pulled me down to lay full against her. I cupped her face in my hands, kissing her in long, deep caresses, licking the taste of her off her lips. She nudged me away and I only traveled far enough to find her neck, pushing the scarf out of my way to suck at her pulse, feeling it thrum against my tongue.

"My skirt," she said, catching her breath. "It's all wet. I should take it off."

That had me cooperating at least, rolling to my side. I traced heat sigils on the blankets above and below us as Joanna squirmed out of her shoes and coat and skirt, then her blouse. I followed her example with help from her hands. My borrowed boots were muddy, the knees of my pants wet, and all of it was a perfect excuse to strip, to have more of my skin touching hers.

"Callum," Joanna whimpered and I brushed my hand over her cheek, find wet tracks. "Please," she said, tugging me close.

"I'm here," I said. "We're safe." It was an affirmation as much for me as it was for her. We twisted close, legs and arms tangling. I could feel her heart beating under my chest and I closed my eyes for a moment, savoring the sound of her in my ear. And then I needed more.

She kissed me, hard and needy, pulling me against her as she wrapped her legs around my hips. "I want you closer," she said against my mouth. I answered with another kiss, sliding my tongue in to stroke against hers as together we pushed her underwear back down her hips, kicking it away into the blankets.

I hooked my arms under her knees, pulling her close and pushing her legs back to leave her open to me. It never failed to amaze me the way she fit to me, the way I could hold her mouth with mine while I fucked her. I kissed her, teasing her tongue with mine while I nestled my cock against her folds, sliding myself against the outside to stroke her clit. Wetness gathered between us, making my rhythm slippery. Joanna shivered beneath me, pulling away to gasp and throwing her arms around my shoulders.

"Now, please, now," she begged, legs trembling over my elbows. I released one so I could line myself up, fitting myself inside of her as we both moaned at the connection.

"Find Isaac and Aiden," I said in her ear. "Let them feel us."

She smiled until her face collapsed as I bottomed out inside of her, lips forming a wide 'o' of pleasure. There was a happy irritation at the back of my head—Aiden, both jealous and delighted at our teasing call down the bond. Next to that was Isaac's ferocious tenderness, a simmering desire. Joanna's leg hooked over my hip, drawing me present again and spurring me into action. I drew back and then pressed forward again, joyous at the sound of her hiccuped sigh, at the satisfaction from our covenmates, at the heat and warmth of her clasping around me.

I couldn't make up my mind of whether or not I wanted to kiss her through the pleasure or hear it ringing in my ear. I sucked and nibbled at her lips as I swirled my hips into hers until I felt heat pooling at the base of my spine. I arched over her, aiming every thrust to nudge higher until Joanna's eyes opened wide, showing the familiar surprise she wore when an orgasm began to rush towards her. Her eyes fluttered and I snapped my hips into hers so they popped open again.

"Look at me," I said. "I want to see your eyes."

Her nose scrunched and I grinned, balancing on one arm so I

could use the other to pluck at her nipples, tugging at them lightly while a blush spread over her chest.

"You're too far away," she said, but her bottom lip was trembling and she was starting to flutter around my cock, so close to coming for me.

She was right though, I wanted to feel her closer. I drew out, almost completely, arching my back down so I could kiss one breast and then the other, before sliding in again. Joanna huffed and moaned as our stomachs pressed together and I ground myself into her clit as I pumped inside of her. I held her face in my hands and as our eyes locked, and she began to squeeze around me in earnest, Aiden and Isaac echoed in the background, their own pleasure mingling with ours.

"Oh, gods! Callum!" Her eyes fell shut at the last moment and I kissed her through her orgasm until the tight clasp of her dragged my own finish forth. We lay wrapped around one another, barely nudging each other for the last little dregs of pleasure until our breath came back in shaky gasps.

I hummed, kissing salt off Joanna's neck as we settled on our sides.

"Not a bad rescue mission when you think about it," Joanna said, words beginning to slur with sleep.

I snorted. "No, you did a very fine job," I said to her. "But let's not tell my father how tidy you made it or he'll enlist you in the army."

Joanna huffed but I couldn't tell if it was irritation or sleep and my own exhaustion was catching up with me too quickly.

23

CALLUM

I WANTED TO BE MAD AT MYSELF FOR DOZING OFF IN THE BACK OF A horse cart while we were on the run, but it had done us too much good. The heaviness of the mine was gone, the hollow gap in my chest filled up. I was breathing deeper and even without my glasses, the world appeared clear again. Joanna's nervous energy of the night before was softened and we sat together in the cart as she steered us through the Vermenian countryside, the world turning honey-colored in the late afternoon sun.

She gathered up the reins in one hand and reached the other over to set it on my bouncing knee, stilling me for a moment. Maybe I had taken her nervous energy from her. I'd been casting charms for safe travel and secrecy all through the ride. Each one felt a little stronger than the last, the muscle of magic flexing under my skin the farther we rode away from the mountain. The burn of the ink in my skin had softened, almost muted enough to let me forget that I had been marked.

"You're going to turn the cart over with your nerves," Joanna said, glancing at me with an indulgent smile.

"How close are we?" I asked, not for the first time.

The sun was starting to set behind a mountain, even though it was

451

barely evening. I wondered if we could stop early for the day, before reaching Joanna's family. Maybe Geoff would find us on the way and we would never have to ask for hospitality from the strangers. And I wouldn't have to face a family of Vermenian's I had no doubt done some kind of harm to during the Red War. What if they turned us out if they realized who I was? Or worse, turned us in to the authorities, to Ambassador Pearce himself?

"Not far," Joanna said. "What has you so jittery?"

"Doesn't it seem… risky? Just to ask strangers to take us in like this?" I asked.

"My father said he thought they would help us," Joanna said with a shrug. "I would help them."

She would. If some distant relative showed up on our doorstep, Joanna would invite them in and serve them tea. And then I would corner them for extensive questioning until I was certain my coven was safe from them.

"We don't have to tell them anything," Joanna said, taking my hand. My leg started bouncing again almost immediately. She nudged me and I forced myself to hold still.

"They deserve to know who they're inviting in," I said. "What if we've been followed?"

"First we need to find out if they're even still living in the same place," Joanna said, squaring her shoulders. "We'll worry about one thing at a time."

I huffed a laugh. I worried about everything at once. About whether or not she was too cold, if Geoff would find us, if we could trust him when he did, if a wheel on the cart would break. If I'd had any real say in Joanna's coming to Vermenia it never would have happened in the first place. And I'd still be locked in a rixon cage.

I leaned into her side, wrapping my arm around her shoulder. "You saved me," I said against her ear.

"I know," she said, grinning with a teasing pride. "You're very welcome."

I pushed her scarf out of my way so I could kiss her neck and she hummed happily in answer. I trusted her as much as Aiden and Isaac, certainly more than myself. Even if her mother's family wouldn't give us shelter for the night, together Joanna and I would make sure we were safe until Geoff came to take us over the border.

"I see lights," she said, and I looked up, eyes squinting into the gray-blue of dusk.

All I saw was a darker shadow against the sky, everything too milky and opaque at a distance. Pinpricks of orange firelight appeared as we rode closer until the night blue shadow began to separate into a house and a series of barns. There was smoke lingering in the air and a metallic tang, maybe the smithy Joanna had mentioned. We drove up to the yard and I heard the creak of a door from a brick outpost building. Red oven fire outlined a hulking figure standing in the doorway.

"Allo?" the man called to us. He walked forward, boots crunching in mud and grass, slapping in icy puddles, and then stopped in front of our cart. "Jessa?" he asked, voice winded as if the breath had been knocked out of him.

He was almost as tall as me, leaning a little to the left, with broad shoulders, a barrel chest, and a rounded belly. His hair was a little fairer than Joanna's and speckled through with gray. The lines on his face made him look severe and my magic was nearly sparking at my fingertips, ready to protect us.

"Joanna," she said, staying seated by me as she spoke down to the man. "Jessa dottar."

"Jessa dottar," he said, rolling the idea over his tongue. All the severity of his expression transformed to delight as he grinned at us. Then he released a great belly laugh, arms spreading wide. I stiffened, half expecting him to scoop Joanna off the bench, but he stood waiting for her and Joanna jumped down from the seat herself, stepping into his hug. He squeezed her, still laughing, and lifted her off her toes for a moment before setting her down again. "Uncle Myles," he said introduction, tongue clumsy over the word 'uncle'. He pointed up at me and asked, "Husband?"

"Covenmate," Joanna said and the man 'oohed' with another easy laugh.

"Camma," he said, waving to the house. "Come. Dinner time." He deftly unhooked the horses from the cart and led them into the yard and over to a barn, limping on his left foot as he went.

"Myles?" a creaking voice called from the house. "Wur es?"

"Jessa dottar et mannar," 'Uncle Myles' answered, swinging the barn door open and clucking to the horses, leading them into stalls with empty troughs but a nice amount of hay.

"Jessa dottar!"

I hesitated for a moment, and then stepped forward, spelling the troughs full of water. Myles clapped me on the back.

"Good, good," he said.

"Oh!"

We both turned to look and there was a tall and rounded woman, hunched forward with a cane, short-cropped gray hair curling at the ends. She had Joanna's long, narrow nose, although a little bigger. The two women stared at one another for several breaths and then the old woman hobbled forward, sliding the cane down to her elbow so she could raise her hands, taking Joanna's face in them. Her thumbs stroked over Joanna's cheeks.

"Little girl, like mottar," the woman said, words stilted before sliding back into Vermenian.

Joanna sucked in a shaky breath and then bent, the pair of them enveloping each other gently. I swallowed hard around the knot in my throat. Maybe Joanna was right and we shouldn't tell them anything about who I was. It would be a waste to spoil a reunion so sweet.

"Camma," Joanna's grandmother said, pulling back and patting Joanna's shoulders.

"Dinner time," Myles repeated. As if we were expected guests rather than a strange surprise come in the evening.

Joanna smiled at me, eyes watery, before taking her grandmother's arm to help lead the woman back to the house. I kept pace with Myles as he lumbered, not much faster than his mother with his limp.

From the outside, the house looked like a modest farmhouse, stucco white walls around aged wooden beams. But once we stepped inside there was a richness of time to the place, a loved and cared for home. A wide room opened in front of us with a warm burning stove and beautiful furniture. Nothing was 'in style' so much as it was well-made, a care of craftsmanship that I wished Isaac were here to see and appreciate.

Myles and his mother took us through a doorway straight ahead into a warm, fragrant kitchen where herbs hung from the ceiling and pots steamed at the attentive hands of a middle-aged woman. Myles crossed the room to her as Joanna's grandmother bullied us both into seats at a round table. I heard him explain to the woman who we were and she looked over her shoulder to smile and nod at both of us before going back to her work. I assumed she was his wife and she seemed as little bothered or surprised by our sudden arrival as her husband and mother-in-law.

"Good family table," Joanna's grandmother said, patting her hands on the surface and grinning at Joanna. It was a sturdy table, the polish worn with time and use, and much larger than needed for just three people. Maybe the older woman had meant it was good that we were here joining them. Either way, Joanna was beaming back at her, their hands joined fiercely together.

I found her free hand and she squeezed at the touch, leaning her shoulder into mine. No one asked us why we were here, it was as if we had come on invitation. Why *shouldn't* Joanna arrive unexpectedly at their home? She was family after all. Myles brought out five crystal glasses and a dusty bottle of wine and before I could think of how to say that it wasn't necessary, he had it opened, filling glasses for each of us. He made the official introductions, his mother Adele, his wife Irene, and together we toasted.

It wasn't until we'd been served—seasoned potatoes, lamb in gravy, peas and rich butter, and bread rolls still steaming when we broke them open, so much food I thought I might burst but I didn't want to stop enjoying—and were savoring our meal that anyone spoke up.

"Why in Vermenia?" the grandmother, Adele, asked. Joanna and I both looked at one another and reached for our wine glasses to stall.

I wasn't even sure where to begin, or how much they would understand, but Joanna started, picking words as carefully as if she were writing them down. The rixon we found in Enmaire, my getting kidnapped and taken to the mine, her using her mother's papers to come find me. Her family watched us with wide eyes, only occasionally stopping her to clarify a word or ask a question.

"General Pike?" Myles asked. "From old war?"

I set my silverware down and forced myself to meet his eyes, he didn't look angry but I didn't know if that would change from my answer.

"Yes," I said.

"Ahh," Myles said nodding. He wagged a finger at me. "You were very smart. Beat us well and good."

I choked on air as Myles pulled his chair back and raised his pant leg to show me the wooden leg he'd been limping on.

"Took my leg, too," he said grinning.

All the blood rushed out of my face and Joanna coughed noisily at my side. "I'm so sorry," I said, trying to catch a breath.

Adele scoffed and waved her hand at her son until he laughed and clapped my shoulder.

"I made out of one war with all my pieces," Myles said. "Then I enlisted again." At that, he shrugged as if two wars and half a missing leg were about as well as you could hope for. Maybe that was true.

"Stupid boy," Adele said, carrying on with her dinner.

Joanna reached over, squeezing my knee hard enough to bring me out of my shock. Everyone else had returned to their food as if there was nothing very remarkable about a family of Vermenians dining with me.

"Always going to be wars," Myles said to me, gentler, as he shrugged again.

"You're safe here," Adele said to Joanna. "Good to see your face."

JOANNA MADE A SMALL, broken noise at the back of her throat and I tried to twist to face her. Adele's hands on my shoulders stopped me, fingers looking frail but with a surprising amount of strength left in them. They'd put me on a stool in front of a warm fire in the kitchen,

Myle's wife heading upstairs to prepare a room for us. The family looked at my bare back together.

"Just words," Adele said, patting my shoulder. "I have something for healing."

Myles hummed agreement, the whole family staring at the tattoo running down my back. I'd gotten a glimpse in a mirror, clumsy handwriting in foreign words, nothing I could read. Myles rounded my back and came to face me.

"What does it say?" Joanna asked.

"'Where I run, they will find me'" Myles said, scratching his chin.

My stomach sank, they would be on their way to us already, I had doomed Joanna *and* her family by trying to leave the mine. Joanna only hummed behind me.

"That's very vague," she said. "The 'I' could be Callum or the one who wrote. And the 'they' could be anyone. And there's no time frame. If he'd wanted to he could have written 'I cannot leave this mine.'"

"It's very wrong to do, but he could have done worse for you," Myles said, agreed, and the dread in my chest lessened. "Probably he did not want to write at all. You know anything about him?"

I could remember his face exactly, the crooked nose and hollow cheeks, the dirty spikes of dark hair. He'd looked hardly older than me when I'd joined the Red War.

"Josef," I said, not wanting to share too much. I felt guilty for him, my anger was saved for Pearce. "He was very young."

Myles nodded and shrugged, moving back to a chair of his own. "We can help him if he needs helping," Myles said.

"We?" Joanna asked, stepping up to my side and running gentle fingers over the top of my back.

"Scrivens," Myles said.

"Scrivens..." Joanna's eyes widened. "*Scribes?*"

"Written magic?" I asked.

Myles looked between us and then his eyes settled on Joanna, a grin blooming and filling his cheeks. "You have it too, leina? A family gift for us."

"Someone told me there weren't any Scribes- Scrivens, left," Joanna said, voice thin with shock.

"Ah," Myles said, nodding and winking. "We keep that secret too. Scrivens hide here."

Joanna and I both stared at each other. Her uncle had Written magic. It ran in her family. There was something like pleading growing on her face and I knew she was suddenly less eager to be on our way home, away from her family.

"My mother? Did she have the Scrivens magic too?" Joanna asked, looking to Myles.

His face softened and he shook his head. "You and I, leina."

"Leina?" she asked.

"Little one," Adele said, returning to the kitchen with a jar full of a greasy salve that cleared my sinuses with just one whiff. She scooped a large portion out and smeared it liberally over my back. I sucked in a breath and leaned into Joanna's side as the burn from the tattoo vanished, turning almost chilled, a wonderful contrast to the dull ache I'd been feeling.

"We have until Geoff finds us," Joanna said to me. "That's what I wrote. If the tattoo works they'll find us, but only after Geoff does. I think Myles is right and those words were the best Josef could do for you."

"You should rest until your friend comes," Myles said, pushing up from his chair. "The trouble will be quick after that."

There was a small guest room in the upstairs that looked like it had once been used as a nursery. The bed was narrow but that was just a good excuse to hold Joanna close. We hugged Uncle Myles and Adele fast to us before sliding inside together and making our way into the bed.

"I told you it would be alright," she said to me, her hand tucked under the hem of my shirt, fingers stroking over my side.

I smiled into the top of her hair. She was draped over my chest and I had propped up my copy of our notebook on her back, filling Aiden and Isaac in on our progress. I tapped the end of the pencil against Joanna's spine before adding, *Joanna is always right.*

In another moment the words, *of course she is,* appeared and I snorted. I suspected it had been a joking kind of sarcasm on Aiden's part.

Uncle Myles thinks he can get us across the border if Geoff doesn't arrive soon, I wrote.

Just be safe, Isaac wrote.

Come home, Aiden added.

We trust him. See you soon.

I flipped the notebook shut and Joanna hummed against my chest, voice drowsy and fingers turning lazy and ticklish against my skin.

"Do they miss us?" she asked.

"Just you," I said and then jumped as she pinched me.

"Don't be an ass," she said, snuggling tighter to me. "We'll be home soon."

And when my head tried to conjure up all the ways things could still go wrong, all the worries we had yet to face when we did cross the border, I took another long breath of Joanna and closed my eyes for sleep instead.

24

JOANNA

"JOANNA, WAKE *LEINA*."

My head was heavy with sleep and when I tried to open my eyes the world was dark and grainy. I started to drift off again until bony fingers reached out and shook my shoulder. Callum grunted beneath me and sat up with a start, dropping me to the mattress.

"Adele," he rasped.

"Wake, friend is here," she whispered. "Camma, camma."

I dug the sleep crust out of my eyes as Callum jumped up from the mattress. "Stay here," he whispered. "Get our things together. I'll come back if it's safe."

That had me up in a flash, Callum already halfway to the bedroom door. I scrambled out of the bed, my skirt twisted around my legs, and grabbed my bag from the floor. Adele stood in front of me, hands twisting.

"You will be safe, leina?" she asked, creases deeper on her face.

I scooped her up in a tight hug, hearing Callum's feet stumbling down the steps and wanting to chase after him.

"I'll be safe," I said. "And I will write."

"Good girl," my grandmother said, squeezing me back just as hard.

Then she pulled away, brushed her thumb over my cheek, and nodded. "Hurry."

Callum was halfway back up the steps when I made it into the hall. "It's Geoff," he said.

My feet were still silent since I hadn't erased the spell I'd used in the mine, and I rushed soundlessly over the floorboards and down the stairs after Callum. Myles was standing in the kitchen with Geoff. I hadn't really imagined ever feeling *relieved* to see the man again but when he glanced up it struck me all at once. I wasn't fond of him exactly and I didn't think we had the temperaments to be friends. But I was grateful for him, and for his help. He was a good man.

"It didn't go as… smoothly, as I hoped," Geoff said, wincing slightly. "They're not far after me."

"I never expected this to be easy," I said, shrugging. Callum passed me my coat and scarf and I dressed quickly.

"I have better route," Myles announced, and I saw the map spread out over the table between him and Geoff.

"If the tree is still there," Geoff growled. "If it isn't rotten. If it is as well hidden as you say."

Myles frowned at the other man and it reminded me of how formidable he had looked coming out of the smithy barn. "Is secret by magic," he said, voice just as dark by Geoff's. "I share the secret with you so now you find it. You're welcome."

Myles winked at me and my own smile was full of regret, I didn't want to be leaving these people so soon.

"If this is going to work we need to go," Geoff said, and either he sounded slightly sympathetic or I imagined it for my own benefit.

I swallowed down the urge to cry, grabbed Myles for one last hug and then hurried across the room to where Callum and Geoff were waiting for me.

"We're leaving the cart and horses here," Geoff said. "I'd never get them across a river in this cold anyway." The fact that now there would be horses in the stable for my family was unspoken but I was pleased.

I followed them through the house to the front door, before

looking back over my shoulder. Adele and Myles stood together, barely lit by candlelight, the both of them smiling softly. I would have gladly stayed with them for another a week, feeling like I'd barely had time to ask about them, about my mother.

Callum tugged gently on my hand and I blinked away the tears in my eyes before walking out the door and shutting it behind me.

"If your uncle has a secret border crossing, we can always use it for family visits," Callum suggested with a lifted eyebrow.

I laughed and then caught sight of Geoff frowning and watching the horizon, a black smear beneath a deep purple sky.

"How far are we?" I asked.

"Not far, ten or twenty minutes on foot," he said.

"And how far are the mercenaries following you?" I asked.

"On horseback? Maybe the same." Maybe less. It was unspoken.

Callum and I glanced at each other. They would find us, of course. But the words on his back didn't promise that they would capture us. Callum started casting charms over all three of us as we walked, feet cold in the muddy road. I felt the heat of his magic blanketing over my shoulders and then soaking into my bones, a charm for warmth on top of whatever protections he laid over us.

"We need to cut into that wooded area up ahead. We'll meet the river through it. Your uncle says there's a fallen tree crossing the water that will act as a bridge," Geoff said, glancing behind us again as if he might see our tail before they caught up to us.

"And it's just been left there?" Callum asked.

"They use it for smuggling goods," Geoff said with a slight grin. "And information. I wondered how they were getting across."

"You won't report it?" I asked.

"I rely on the information that travels across," Geoff said. "So, no."

"Do you spy for Enmaire or Vermenia?" Callum asked, carefully crossing a step in front of me. I wondered it if was a subconscious gesture, that habit of protecting, or if he was still worried about Geoff's motives.

"Both," Geoff said without hesitating. And then, more reluctantly, he added, "I want what you want. To avoid war."

We reached the curve in the road where the trees turned thick and dense, brambles guarding the way off the road. Geoff charged ahead of us but Callum stopped me and then with a slash of his hand the brambles were cut and crumbling away. I beamed at him and Geoff gave us both a surly look.

"You could have waited," Callum said, trying to hide his smirk.

Behind us, the sound of horse hooves sounded at a distance. We stared at each other in the dark for half a beat.

"Cut us a clear path or guard our backs," Geoff said to Callum.

Callum looked into the woods and then back the way we'd come before pushing me towards Geoff. "Keep ahead of me."

"If you don't keep up I'll come back and drag you after me," I snapped to him before following as Geoff barreled ahead into the woods.

Twigs and briars pulled at my skirt and scratched at my coat sleeves as I chased ahead until the sound of ice cracking and water trickling was just as loud as the wet slap of horse hooves and boots on the road behind us.

"Fire!" A man shouted from the road.

"Illusion," Callum hissed to us. "Keep running."

My foot snagged on a tree root but before I could finish falling forward, Geoff was jerking me back up by my elbow as Callum snagged me around the waist and lifted me again. Mud squelched beneath our feet, dead leaves sliding as we tried to move faster, ducking around trees and carrying broken branches with us.

There was an echoing *crack!* from behind us and a flare of light and Callum grabbed me in his arms, covering my back completely and hunching us down.

"Are you alright?" I tried to say but the words were too airy to be heard.

"Stay low," he said in my ear, pushing me forward again.

"It's clearer by the bank," Geoff called through the trees. "I see it!"

I reached back for Callum's hand but he shook me off. "Go," he said. "I'm going to put up a shield."

I turned, finding him in the dark preparing to face the men

coming for us. I clutched at the back of his shirt and tugged him close again.

"Joanna," he growled.

"Callum," I said, just as fiercely. "You're coming with me, or I'm staying with you."

He glared over his shoulder and I wasn't sure if I was imagining shadows moving farther off or if they were that close to us now.

"They'll catch up to us," he said. "You know that."

"You have a Scribe fighting for you. I can help, step back," I said, reaching into my pocket for chalk.

Callum stood at my back, hands on my waist as if he might have to carry me away if I weren't fast enough. The chalk was sticky on damp wood as I wrote on the tree trunk to my right. *Do not cross this point.* I turned to my left and repeated the words on the next tree trunk and then ran to another and wrote it again. I repeated the phrase on seven trees in a line before Callum took my wrist and pulled me away after Geoff.

It was another minute of running before we broke through the tree line and nearly skidded from slick mud onto thin, crackling ice at the shore. Geoff was west of us, waiting at the uprooted end of an enormous tree that crossed the width of the Dannse river.

"They'll find a way through your trap," Callum said running firey patterns over my back as we tried to catch up with Geoff. He was right. Pearce's men would only run after us until they were past my charmed trees. I just hoped it'd bought us enough seconds to make it over into Enmaire.

Geoff was practically twitching with impatience by the time we made it to him.

"Go," he said, rough and edgy. "I'm not making this trip a pointless endeavor by not letting you make it home."

Callum opened his mouth and I yanked him after me, climbing over the roots to the smooth, scalped surface of the tree. Whoever had been using it for so long made sure that it was easy to travel at least, carving away a flat pathway that looked polished with use. Down the center of it were Vermenian words, carved into the surface. My uncle's words.

"Thank you, Myles," I whispered, taking careful steps forward until I could feel Callum behind me, toes barely nudging my heels as we walked together. I tried to check on Geoff but Callum's chest was blocking my view.

"We'll need to be quicker if we're going to give him a chance," Callum whispered.

I nodded and tried to be fast, but my foot slipped on a thin layer of ice almost immediately. Callum and I were both ready, steadying me again, but it made gaining speed difficult. After a few more steps that nearly took us off the tree and into the water Callum crouched behind me, murmuring words and writing sigils on the wood until steam was rising up around us and ice was hissing and running off the surface of the tree.

I walked quickly after that, my boots soundless, Callum's steps quiet snaps behind me.

"They've broken through," Geoff shouted.

"He's on the bridge, keep going," Callum said, hands gentle and urging at my back.

The men on the shore shouted in barking voices and I nearly jumped right off the tree when I heard more gunfire.

"They're firing in the wrong direction," Callum said, keeping me steady, pushing me ahead. "Up the shoreline instead of at us."

"They can't see us," I whispered at the same time as Geoff. "They can't see us because of Uncle Myles's spell. It's a secret."

"They'll see us when we get to the other side," Geoff said. "Stay low and wait for them to move on or give up."

I got down on my hands and knees at the Enmaire end of the bridge, sliding off onto the wet ground and backing away to make room for Callum and Geoff. I kept low behind the height of the fallen tree and watched over the top as the men across the river continued west down the shore, voice echoing and guns hanging limply at their sides.

"Look at that, word witch," Geoff said, sinking down to me,

balancing in on the balls of his feet. "Your terrible idea of a rescue actually worked."

Callum coughed, trying to disguise his laugh, as I finally gave in to the urge to punch Geoff in the shoulder.

I'D THOUGHT we'd be walking all night after making it across the river into Enmaire. Dannsedge and Geoff's coven were miles away from the border, and the adrenaline of running in the dead of night wore away quickly. But Geoff was leading the way and I should have known he would have neglected to offer useful information.

We walked for an hour, Callum taking me under his arm as I stumbled through snow, before making it to a road. A road where Samuel, Sabine, and Darin were waiting with two horses for us to ride. I could have cried in relief until I felt Callum stiffen at my side.

That's right, I thought. *This whole mess was their fault.* But it was their help that had saved Callum too.

"No hard feelings, Pike," Darin said, tossing over a set of reins.

Callum caught them at the last moment, a creamy white horse clomping over to us and nudging my shoulder before huffing a warm breath in my face.

Sabine sat stiffly in her seat, watching Callum's face as she kept her own carefully blank.

"No hard feelings," Callum repeated after a moment, looking down at the reins in his hand and then over to me. Then, with a very intentional and slow movement, he turned his back on Sabine and her coven, taking my waist and lifting me into the long saddle of the horse. He followed, wrapping an arm around me, all the while leaving himself vulnerable to any strike Sabine might have wanted to take. Again.

I squeezed his hand and knotted our fingers together and Geoff's lips twitched as he pulled himself up onto his own dark horse.

"We'll take you to the Inn," Geoff said, nudging his horse ahead. "Nice surprise for your coven."

25

JOANNA

Bryce was in the bar of the Blue Waters Inn when we stepped inside. They looked up from their quiet card game with two rough-looking men and grinned at us in greeting before turning back to their hand.

"We'll say our thanks later," I whispered. "Let's get upstairs."

We were as fast and as quiet on the steps as we could be, but our feet were tired and there was an excited urgency rushing through us at the thought of reuniting the coven.

Callum waved his hand over the lock of the rented room and it clicked loose, the crooked door immediately swinging in a few inches. Callum waited, staring at me, before I rolled my eyes and pushed him in.

"Whosit?" Isaac whispered, sitting up as the sheet fell from his chest, a little light from the hall spilling through the open door behind us to reveal Aiden's dark back still prone, snoring into the mattress.

Callum sucked in a sharp gasp and then he was rushing across the room to the bed. I shut the door behind us, hearing Isaac's grunt of surprise and then the small, shattered sound of the pair of them kissing, mouths remembering each other. I found the lamp on the small table in the corner and turned it on in time to catch Aiden rolling over in the bed, face twisted in sleepy irritation until he saw Callum. His arm reached out and faster than anything, Callum was on his back between the both of them, kisses landing everywhere and hands roving.

Half of me wanted to join them and the other half was just as happy to watch them, see the clasping hand over the hip that drew out the whimpered moan, the fist clutched in dark hair. I started undoing the laces on my boots—caked with mud—and when one hit the floor Aiden sat up from the tangle on the bed as Isaac started to peel Callum out of his clothes.

"What're you doing over there?" Aiden asked, words gravelly and deep enough to give me goosebumps.

"Watching," I said, smiling. "Trying to get out of these mucky clothes."

"Well get over here so I can touch you," Aiden said, frowning and reaching out.

I laughed and Isaac lifted his head long enough for Callum to tear his shirt off.

"We'll put on a show for you later," Isaac said, voice rasping. "Right now I want the both-"

Isaac's words dropped off as Callum turned and the light of the lamp landed on his back. The room went quiet as Aiden and Isaac both stared at the marks. Unfamiliar words stacked in a line down Callum's spine, a little sheen left from my grandmother's salve still on his skin.

"What does it say?" Aiden growled, a hand running along the outside of the letters, raising goosebumps on Callum's back.

"It doesn't matter," Callum whispered, looking over his shoulder at them. "I'm here. Joanna's own words fixed that."

"I'll fix those marks too," I said, standing. "But not tonight. Tonight I just want to enjoy us all together again."

Isaac bent his head, kissing a line over Callum's shoulder, drawing him into his chest with careful touches. I shrugged out of my coat and got as far as letting my skirt drop to the floor before Aiden was crawling down to the foot of the bed and dragging me against him.

"I ought to spank you for how worried I've been," Aiden said, but his face wasn't angry, it was reverent.

My eyes widened and a squeak escaped my lips before he was covering them with his own, teeth and tongue and mouth greedily taking from mine. I was melting into the mattress as he arched over me, my head still skipping over the threat of Aiden's hand turning my bottom red. It was as if the idea had turned my blood hot. He nipped at my lips, drawing my attention back to him, and I thought I would save the offer for later when we had time alone.

A hand appeared under my neck cradling my head and then Aiden was nudged away.

"Spank Callum," Isaac said and Callum barked a laugh. "He's the one who went and got himself captured. I want to kiss our little hero."

"*Little* hero?" I said, frowning as Isaac's face hovered over mine, upside down and smiling as his hair fell out from behind his ears. I hummed as he ducked down, peppering kisses over my chin and lips and neck as his hair tickled my cheeks.

"Missed you, love," Isaac murmured against my lips.

"Missed you," I said, squirming as one of Aiden's hands slid up under my blouse, rubbing at the aching muscles along my sides and up my spine. Another covered my mound between my legs, heel rubbing into my clit. I groaned and Isaac grinned, lowering to me to suck kisses again.

"I'll save punishment for later," Aiden agreed, sliding off the bed to the floor, taking the sheet with him. His breath was dragging across the tops of my legs above my stockings and he left wet, nipping caresses on the skin there with lips and teeth before, rolling the stockings down to my soggy feet and tossing them aside. "She can have her reward first," he said, rubbing at my feet, his hands burning hot in contrast to my cold toes.

I heard the bed shift behind Isaac and I reached a hand out. Callum caught it with his, squeezing. Isaac's mouth was traveling down my cheek, beneath my ear, and across my neck as Aiden sucked marks on the inside of my thighs. The hollow sensation, the broken limb behind my heart that had been there since we left Dannsedge without

Callum, was gone, replaced with the warm glow of being with my entire coven.

"Did you miss me too?" Callum asked as Isaac's breath hitched on my skin.

"Very much," Isaac hissed. "Although I think I'm still angry. You'll have to make it up to me."

Callum laughed at that and then Isaac's lips were shut tight, his cheek pressed to mine and an eager sound trapped behind his teeth. Aiden leaned out from between my legs, quick fingers pulling my underwear down over my knees and off my feet. Then he pushed me open again, wider than before until the stretch began to burn in my hips.

I lifted my arms above my head, reaching for Isaac's sides, and found his ear to bite the lobe gently, listening and smiling as he groaned in answer. Before I could tease him more Aiden licked a stripe up my center, nose nuzzling me against my clit, warmth bursting under my skin. Behind Isaac Callum released a shaky sigh and I twisted so I could see him, arched over Isaac's back, his fingers tight on the other man's hips, cock nestling into Isaac's ass.

My heart clenched and I blinked away tears. We were together. We were safe. Caution to anyone who tried to change that now.

Aiden's hands wrapped around my legs, lifting them up over his shoulders, thumbs running a line down the tired muscles at the backs of my thighs. My toes curled against his bare back, trying to pull him against me, make him tease me with kisses and licks again. He laughed against my skin and it ran right up inside me, making me clench and my breath gasp.

"Touch me," I said, demanded, and then whined as Aiden covered my aching opening and sensitive flesh with his palm again, rubbing flat circles.

Isaac grunted above me, jerking forward as Callum thrust inside of him, and then his lips were wrapping around my pebbled nipple, sucking and biting gently. I arched my neck to kiss his chest and then fell back again as Aiden gave up teasing, pushing two fingers inside of me, stretching me quickly, and lips landing to kiss my clit. Either Isaac and Aiden could read each other's minds or they had planned this, their mouths perfectly in tandem, pulling a cord of pleasure taut straight through me.

I clung to Isaac with one hand and dropped the other to the back of Aiden's head, holding him close to me, as I spiraled out to the edge. Isaac's moans vibrated into my chest and down to where Aiden's own hums of smug satisfaction were ringing inside me, in time with the pump and twist of his fingers. I was going to fall apart embarrassingly quick but I had an idea or two of what to do next. Isaac's breath was puffing into my skin, his mouth on my breasts urgent and rough.

"Come, sweet girl," Aiden said, lifting his head for a beat, fingers crooking inside of me and making me shout. "I'm so hard I can barely stand it."

He bent his head again, lashing my clit with his tongue and that, combined with the thought of him filling me up, had me squirming and shaking, coming with a muffled cry against Isaac's chest. Aiden licked me through the last of the tremors and then I shrugged out from under Isaac, twisting myself onto my stomach before Aiden could take me.

"Sit back," I said to Callum, pushing up on Isaac's chest.

"What are you up to?" Aiden asked as Callum drew Isaac back, practically onto his lap. Callum's hand was fisted around the base of Isaac's cock—now red and swollen, weeping arousal from its head.

"Making sure everyone is taken care of," I answered, scooting forward on my belly and bending my head to wrap my lips around the tip of him, swirling my tongue over the fluid and against the delicate seam on the underside of his tip.

"Isn't she sweet?" Aiden asked, laughing as Isaac shouted wordlessly. I could feel Aiden's own swollen length nudging between my legs, just dipping inside of me an inch at a time as I bobbed, sinking Isaac deeper between my lips.

"Isaac's a wreck," Callum said, voice choked. "I can barely move."

As Aiden's hips settled against the backs of my thighs I reached underneath Isaac's legs, teasing at every little sensitive spot I could find. He shivered and sagged in Callum's arms, his hips churning between us.

"That's it," Callum hissed, hips picking up again, bouncing Isaac on my tongue.

Aiden's chest pressed over my back for a moment. He kissed my neck and said in my ear, "Will you wave your hand if it's too much?"

I pulled back from Isaac, pumping him with my hand, and nodded for Aiden. He didn't wait or ask again, only immediately started to thrust in earnest. He pressed my legs closed and a startled sound escaped my mouth at how full I felt now. The bed was rattling underneath us from the force of Callum's and Aiden's fucking. Isaac's fingers were carding into my hair, drawing my lips back to his cock and for a moment the whole thing felt chaotic and overwhelming.

And then Aiden found Callum's rhythm until the rattle of the bed turned into a rocking that I could feel echoing in my oversensitive clit. There was magic swirling from Aiden to me to Isaac to Callum and when I searched for the bond, I was swept up in a current of our magic and our pounding pleasure as it built higher. A moment ago I'd been nowhere near cresting again and now I was teetering at the edge, right there with Isaac and Callum, dragging Aiden along behind us.

"There's nothing like it," Aiden breathed, barely audible as I began to flutter and clasp around him. "All of us together." He was rutting into me, fast and sharp and hard, racing to catch up to the others even as I felt Isaac's body tensing, trying to hold out.

I didn't have his control or his patience. I whined as I started to come and the feel of my voice vibrating against his aching cock undid Isaac. He shouted out, fingers tightening just a little on the locks of my hair, and salt flooded my tongue as I rushed to swallow. Callum came next, shaking with his arms wrapped around Isaac's chest and teeth buried in his shoulder. Aiden followed us all, hands squeezing my hips and pulling down onto him until I thought I might burst with the feel of him swelling and filling me.

Isaac was quick to pull out of my mouth, sliding down to the mattress to kiss and wipe at my cheeks. Callum flopped down across him, a hand reaching to stroke Aiden's back as it rose and fell with quick breaths. Aiden huffed and clutched at his hand. He picked me up, the others scooting out of the way, and made room for us both on the bed, all of us piled in strange shapes so we could touch a little of each person.

"I was barely managing without all of you," Callum said, and maybe it was the sex but even now I thought he had more color in his cheeks again.

Isaac's hands stroked across Callum's head. I rested my head against his stomach and Aiden kissed at his hip.

"We weren't much better without you," Aiden confessed.

We were quiet for a few minutes, enough that the travel of the past week was catching up to me, turning my eyelids into heavy weights.

"My father?" Callum whispered.

"They'll make a final decision in two days, unless he can push for tomorrow," Aiden said, draping an arm over Callum's hip to trace patterns on my shoulder. "We'll call in the morning with news of your rescue and take the first train south."

"What a mess," Callum said.

"We'll fix it," Isaac said.

I tried to hum my agreement but it was several seconds late and I was asleep before anyone said another word.

CALLUM

"ARE YOU READY?" AIDEN ASKED ME, HIS HAND ON MY SHOULDER AS WE reached the top of the steps. The massive oak doors sat in front of us, the rumble of Congress arguing muffled behind the wood.

We hadn't given ourselves time to hesitate since rising in Dannsedge the day before and taking the fastest train south to the coast. At least the travel had been peaceful.

"Of course," I said, as Isaac and Joanna caught up to us.

Aiden nodded at a clerk waiting in a chair by the doors who stood and pushed them open for us. For a moment I couldn't move as the wave of sound rushed over me. Men and women in black robes stood, shouting in every direction, carrying arguments over each other's heads. The words crisscrossed until I was uncertain how *anyone* could understand each other. They probably weren't bothering to, only shouting louder to be heard.

Those in the ring of desks closest to us quieted first, staring at me and my coven framed together in the doorway. The quiet seemed to roll forward one row at a time as if Congress was so surprised by a pause in the shouting that it interrupted their trains of thought. As the politicians fell back into their seats the silence carried up to the front of the room. The last man left standing, still berating the room at large, was my father.

"It's good to be home," I muttered under my breath and Aiden huffed a laugh at my side as Joanna squeezed my hand.

My father's back was to the door as he faced the four Regional Heads seated in a raised dais, with the Head Speaker Russell Harley seated at the center. Harley had been the Head Speaker of Enmaire since an election after the Red War. I thought the fact that we'd avoided landing ourselves in another war since his election was a good sign but in truth, I knew very little about the man. He was tall, square bodied, with tidy gray hair and beard, and dark eyes that were now darting between my father and myself. His lips were shut tight and almost invisible beneath his peppery gray mustache.

"If Ambassador Carras cannot speak for his countrymen then what are we to think?" Duncan bellowed.

"We are to think he has betrayed them, as our own Ambassador Ramond Pearce has done to Enmaire," I called out, hushing the last murmurs of conversation in the room and freezing my father's spine in shock.

"Your much anticipated reunion, General Pike," Darrell King said from his seat on the dais, tucking a smirk behind a large hand, and nodding to me.

I'd liked Aiden's father from the beginning, especially once I'd learned his policies often opposed my own father's plans. When he'd run for Head of House in the Capital region, I'd exerted what little influence I could to help his election. I was especially grateful for his position in Congress now, certain he had done what he could to stall any decision on war.

"Callum," my father said, turning on his heel and staring at me with a stony suspicion as if I might have been *turned* by my time in enemy company. "I would have come for you sooner if I hadn't need to waste time arguing the point with *politicians*."

"I think I rather prefer my coven's method," I said, shrugging my shoulders and walking up to join him at the dais. "And it is for the best, given Vermenia isn't guilty of any breach in our treaty."

"Ramond Pearce is as loyal to Enmaire as I am," my father snarled at me. "Whatever you think you heard."

"Be careful what you say because what I heard came from his own mouth," I said, staring down my nose at my father.

He was dressed in full uniform, with all the medals glittering on his chest, so many I wondered how he managed to keep his chest puffed out with all their weight.

"They were keeping Callum in Pearce's office at his own rixon mine," Joanna snapped, stomping up to my side. "What other proof of conspiracy do you really need?"

"I do think Ambassador Carras's absence since the time of Callum's rescue has a great deal to lend to their statement," Darrell King said to Head Harley, who'd remained quiet and watchful.

"They have yet to give a formal statement," Harley said after a moment, his voice heavy and deep.

I had not seen him give speeches during his election, too busy wallowing after the war, but I could understand how a voice like that, steady and solid, would appeal to the nation after such a violent period.

"I think it's time we heard what your son had to say before we hear your opinions on it again, General Pike. You may take a seat at the side or you may wait outside if you feel yourself unable to resist making another interruption," Harley said, speaking slow and even.

Well, that decided that. I did like him.

My father went to the open seats at the side of the room, my coven heading to the opposite end of the room without being asked.

"We'll hear you next, Miss Wick," Harley said, looking down at papers in front of him.

Joanna paused in step, catching my eye, her own widening for a second. "Yes, sir," she said as I nodded to her. She took her seat and Harley looked back up from his papers at me.

"In your words, from the beginning," Harley said, staring at me as the room held its breath behind my back.

"What do you think you're doing?"

My father wrapped his fist around my elbow, tugging me out of the hall at the end of the day and dragging me away from the listening ears of Congress. My coven was quick at our heels and out of the corner of my eye, I saw Isaac haul Joanna back to his chest, keeping her from going after Duncan.

Without thought or planning, I conjured up a clumsy shield around myself with a flash of heat. My father hissed and shook out his hand, a red burn bright on his palm as he staggered back a few steps.

"I came to tell congress what happened to me and who was responsible," I said. I tried to convince my magic to recede, for the shield to fade, but my heart in my chest was beating a heavy anxious rhythm and the shield would not budge.

"You shouldn't have interfered," he hissed, but he was trying to move around me, toward Joanna and the shield only flared again, blocking him from her.

I was protecting her, protecting myself, from my own father. Maybe only from his vitriol and combativeness but that was enough. We'd had enough conflict for the year, although it'd only just begun. I didn't want to argue with my father, I didn't want him to sneer at Aiden and Isaac, I didn't want him to covet Joanna's magic or disdain her family. The family that had saved us.

I didn't want my father in my life.

"She did what she needed to do," I said, stepping in front of my father's view. "What I needed her to do. Her choices, my choices, aren't up to you."

He scoffed at me, rolling his eyes and watching Congress trickle out of the conference hall, trying and failing to act as if they weren't listening in on their way downstairs.

"Maybe I did introduce you to battle too young," my father said, eyes narrowing at me. "You've never really understood what a victory could *mean* to a country."

"To you," I said. "What it meant to you."

"You've wasted every bit of potential I ever planted in you," he said, voice lowered to a quiet rumble, the condemnation meant for my ears alone.

"The only useful things you ever taught me were the rules of chess," I said.

The shield was gone but my father took another step away, expression fallen with disgust and disappointment. But there was no regret curdling in my stomach, no fear of the repercussion of my words or what move he might make next. I had given him power with every little bit of influence I allowed him over my life. He disappointed me too now, as a father and as a man whose position was meant to help protect his countrymen.

"I let your mother coddle you," he said, but some of the fight had withered in him. He'd loved my mother, in a way I didn't quite understand, and it cost him to speak of her.

"Present the facts you've collected," I said, shrugging. "Joanna and I will give our testimonies. The rest is up to Congress. Now if you'll excuse me."

I turned away without waiting, trying and failing not to blush as I caught the looks on my coven's faces. Pride and support and love. Joanna still looked just shy of spitting at my father but she slipped her arm through mine as I continued to the stairs.

"Claudia is expecting us," Isaac said as he and Aiden joined us, but the look in his eyes said 'I know how this feels.'

It felt like I'd cut away rot and now I had somewhere new to fill with the love I had for my coven.

I STOPPED outside of the building, Isaac bumping into my back. The front door of the shop opened and out stepped a demurely dressed young woman with kohl black around her eyes. The buzz that followed her out, trailing into the sea salt air this close to the dock, sent chills down my spine.

"Joanna?" I asked, feeling my heartbeat turn unsteady as I looked inside the window, watching an older woman with hair piled on top of her head apply a tattoo needle to a young man's arm, a rose growing out of the tip, beading red on his skin.

"We don't have to go in," Joanna said, taking my hand in hers as Aiden looked in through the glass on the front door. "But I had an idea of how to fix those words on your back. If you'd rather not, that's fine."

"I-" I hesitated. I could see the way Joanna held her own eagerness in, trying not to push me one way or another and I wanted to agree, for her sake if not mine. "I don't think I want any more strangers wielding needles at me," I said finally.

"I thought of that," Joanna said, still trying to keep her excitement bound up. "So I'd be the one doing the work."

All three of us, Aiden, Isaac, and I, raised our eyebrows in interest at that.

"I've been practicing," Joanna said, with just a hint of defensiveness. "I wanted to make sure I could do it right before I offered."

"I'd have your words on me?" I asked, and now the uneven drum of my heart was something other than anxiety.

Joanna pressed her lips together and nodded. Her nerves weren't about upsetting me, or not just that at least. She was worried I wouldn't want her magic on my skin.

I clutched her hand tighter. "Lead the way," I said.

Her face brightened, a smile bursting forth before she wrestled it back. "Are you sure?"

"Positive," I said.

I met Isaac's gaze over Joanna's head and I could see the happy envy on his face as he smiled at me. Any one of us would *gladly* take Joanna's words permanently.

Aiden didn't wait for any more discussion, only swung the door in, bells ringing as he went. The tattoo artist looked up from her work, squinting at us over her glasses, her hair a vibrant shade of red. When Joanna stepped inside behind us, the woman smiled.

"I've saved the back room for you," she said to Joanna. "Let me know when you're done and I'll tidy up."

Joanna thanked her before leading us back behind a dense, green curtain to a smaller room. A leather chair with a narrow back waited, easy for me to sit backward in while Joanna worked. There were lamps in every corner, warm and bright, and lush prints of flowers and mermaids covering the walls.

"Are you nervous?" Joanna asked as I stared at the chair.

I smiled at her, my stomach flipping. "A little," I said. "Are you?"

She blushed. "A little," she said. "But I've thought of a few things that might help."

She moved to sit on a stool and there was a rolling table at her side, fitted out with shining tools. She pulled a piece of chalk out of her pocket and lifted the heavy looking tattoo needle up from the table, scratching words onto the surface. Aiden and Isaac took up a spot by the wall where a bench waited and I moved to Joanna's side to see the words she'd written.

Gentle touch.

I laughed out loud, some of the nerves escaping with the sound. "Will it work that way?" I asked.

Joanna looked up at me, nodding. "Eve tried it out a day ago. I came while Duncan was testifying."

I'd assumed Joanna had avoided Duncan's testimonies at Congress because of how much she disliked—'abhorred' was her word—my father and I was a little jealous that I'd missed her frequenting a tattoo parlor by the seaside.

She set the needle back down on the table and took my hands. "This is up to you. It doesn't have to today, or even at all."

I bent, kissed her forehead, nose, and lips, and then stepped away, shrugging out of my coat and starting on the buttons of my shirt.

"I'd much rather have your words than another's," I said.

"If he's not sitting in the chair, I am," Isaac said to Aiden who grunted in agreement. They grinned at me as I narrowed my eyes in answer, pulling off my shirt and settling myself down backward in the chair.

Joanna spoke to me as she set up, a hand frequently coming out to brush over the skin of my back as metal clinked together. The sound had me tensing at first but soon the even steady tone of her voice left me relaxed in the chair. She warned me before she started the rotary motor and I held my breath as the buzz sounded loud in the room.

"I'm just going to turn these words into flourishes so they won't hold magic," Joanna said, stroking a soft finger over the lines of text on my spine. "And then, if you want, I'll replace them."

"I'm ready," I assured her.

She counted to three before the needle landed, and no matter how much I tried to stay relax, my body was hard as stone, tense with a fear I couldn't shake. But it wasn't the scratching burn of memory, trapped in that cell. Joanna's chalk on the handle had worked and the tattoo needle on my back was something harsher than a tickle, the rumble of its work in my bones more like a cat's purr than an engine's vibration.

I sighed and went limp in relief, Joanna's free hand running up and down my side.

"This is…nice, actually," I murmured, feeling suddenly exhausted as all the anxiety burned out of me.

The needle in Joanna's hand seemed to swirl, leaving a cool softness behind with a quieter, duller ache than the first time I'd been marked. Isaac stood and came to stand behind me.

"She's joining the lines so there are no words," Isaac told me. "Hmm, looks a little esoteric. I quite like it."

"Don't go getting yourself into trouble just to get your own," Joanna warned, moving quickly down my back, leaving a quiet little sting behind with each new mark.

I didn't know if Josef's Writing had left more than a visible mark, but I felt something lift off me as she finished. A sense of being watched, of having someone at my back and chasing my heels, vanishing at last.

"That part's done," Joanna said.

"Finish," I said, twisting my neck to see her, the line of concentration between her eyes as she looked at her work. "I want your words."

The frown cleared and she smiled. She kissed my shoulder, careful not to brush against the new tattoo, and then started again from the top. I was turning drowsy and Aiden joined Isaac to watch Joanna's progress so I let my eyes drift shut, feeling the rattle traveling down my spine. Joanna's hand was quicker than Josef's and even if I couldn't see the words forming I felt the spike and curl of her letters, almost able to trace her handwriting behind my eyelids. A little bit of the scratch of the tip of a pen against paper, a little bit of the softness of Joanna's own touch on my skin.

The process stopped with a flourish and my eyes popped open. I wanted to see my back immediately, in a way that I'd been avoiding for the week since my rescue. I moved to sit up and Joanna held me still.

"Let me wash it up a bit. It's still red and swollen."

"I don't mind," I said.

She ignored me and finished, spraying water lightly on my skin and wiping the excess ink gently away. Isaac and Aiden helped me up from the chair. I was a little light-headed, almost giddy as they led me over to a mirror on the wall. Joanna carried a smaller mirror for me to hold and use to see my back. My hands shook as I lifted it and her fingers covered mine, steadying me.

Where I travel, my...

There was a knot there, four points twisting together infinitely. "It's a sigil," Joanna said. "For 'coven'. There are other ones but I wanted it to be ours, so there's no confusion."

I saw it all together then. *Where I travel, my coven is with me.*

I looked down at her, my smile so fierce it made my face ache. The words were careful, open enough not to have us tripping over each other's heels, but they were a promise of us together, in our bond if not in body. And the bond was shining bright in my chest, more brilliant than ever.

"Come here, clever girl," I said, pushing the mirror away from us. I wrapped Joanna up around her waist, resting my forehead against hers as Aiden and Isaac circled us both in their arms.

"It's perfect," I said. It was more of a whisper, I was having trouble finding my voice. "Thank you."

"There you are."

I looked up from the book in my hands to find Gwen Woolard staring down at me with a little twist of a smile on her lips.

"You made it back," she said.

"From Vermenia or the congressional hearing?" I asked.

"Both," she said, eyes glinting behind her glasses.

"I'm still not sure which was more of a trial," I admitted.

"Glad to see you in one piece then," Gwen said, patting my shoulder. "And don't just walk out of the building with that book. I want it checked out and accounted for."

"Yes ma'am," I said. Joanna would make sure of it anyway.

"Callum? There you are." Isaac appeared, half-breathless, at the top of the stairs in the faculty wing of the library. "Where's Joanna?" he asked. There was an envelope tight in his fist and the sight of it had me sitting up straighter in the window seat.

"I'll go fetch her," Gwen said, with a glance at the envelope.

"I thought it would take longer for them to come to a decision," I said.

Joanna and I had given testimony for the better part of four days and then remained, stuck listening to the ensuing arguments pick up again before Harley had finally excused us from the trial and let us return to Canderfey together. Talk of war had been put off 'indefinitely' during the trial. I suspected Harley would refuse my father the troops to invade he'd asked for, but there was still the matter of finding the rixon buried, and of dealing with the Ambassadors.

Isaac landed on the window seat next to me, offering up the envelope but I shook my head, wanting to wait for Joanna and not trusting myself to keep from ripping the thing open.

"Well?" Aiden said, still stomping up the stairs as he called out to us. "What's it say?"

"Haven't opened it yet," I said. "Joanna's coming."

"Oh for goodness sake," Aiden said, rolling his eyes and hurrying up to us. He snatched the envelope out of Isaac's fingers and ripped off an edge.

"Don't tear the damn letter," Isaac said.

"Wait for Joanna," I said.

"I'm here!" Joanna's boots skidded across the floorboards as she ran to join us, and I reached out to grab her around the waist before she slipped and fell to the floor. "What's it say?"

"The treaty stands," Aiden said, eyes fixed to the page. "Vermenia's even offering up some concessions they refused previously. We're re-signing."

"That's good," Joanna said, sitting down on my lap and glancing at me to confirm her guess.

"Very good," I said, nodding.

"And Carras? Pearce?" Isaac pressed, his palms braced on his knees.

"Criminals," Aiden said, still reading. "Missing criminals. Maybe if they hadn't taken such a damned long time coming to the decision-"

"They would have run the second Joanna and I made it out of the country," I said, waving my hand. "What about York and her coven?"

Aiden's mouth twisted into a frown and I felt a strange conflicted twist in my chest before he said, "Pardoned. Your testimonies worked. Not sure that's such a good thing."

I sighed, flicking away the faint twinge of resentment. It was for the best. I was guilty of crimes too and they had saved me in the end.

"Darin really is an ass who hates you," Isaac said.

I shrugged and said, "He didn't do more than watch the horses while I was captured. That's only conspiracy."

"I'm glad for Geoff at least," Joanna said, words small as if she were worried they might offend us. I kissed her cheek and she relaxed against me.

"So it's settled then," I said. It wasn't, not really. Pearce and Carras were unaccounted for. But I didn't think they could hurt me or my coven while in hiding.

"There'll be new Ambassadors," Aiden said, sitting down next to Isaac and stretching his hand out to cover mine. Isaac set his down over ours and Joanna's landed above them all.

"I'm staying out of politics for a while," I said.

"Has there been any word from...from your father?" Joanna asked.

Her face was close, dark eyes full and fixed to mine, our noses nearly touching.

"There was a letter," I said. "I threw it out." There was a heavy silence around me with the announcement so I worked to draw up a smile and found it easier than I expected. "Don't worry," I said, kissing Joanna's cheek again, then her jaw. "We'll just have to spend the winter solstice somewhere else next year."

"Somewhere warmer," Aiden suggested, with a grin.

"We've never done it at home," Isaac said. "Joanna's family can come."

I glanced at Joanna, wondering if she was thinking of Adele and Myles, missing a part of her family she'd barely had time to get to know.

"Speaking of family coming," Joanna said slowly, raising her eyebrows. "My father is planning on coming next month. To...to meet Callum."

I nearly choked on air and Isaac tried and failed to stop himself from laughing. "Me?" I sputtered.

"Don't be nervous," Joanna said quickly.

"He's very intimidating," Aiden said.

"Handshake tight enough to break your fingers," Isaac added, grinning.

"Oh shut up," Joanna said, rolling her eyes. "He's sweet and you'll like him."

And with that tone, there was really no room for argument.

EPILOGUE

AIDEN

"I think it's going well," Joanna whispered in my ear. I pulled her closer to me on the couch and together we watched her father, Frank, nodding along to an enthusiastic lecture from Callum about what weather charms worked best with each season.

I thought Frank looked a little dazed by Callum's rattle but he was patient and encouraging and Callum at least was relaxing after his earlier panic about meeting Joanna's family.

The twins rounded the corner of the hall into the parlor, Tatsuo and Bryce quick behind them, growling and pulling faces. Donny ran directly for his mother, giggling all the while, but Aggie came tearing over to Joanna, her aunt scooping her up off the floor. Aggie's eyes were wide and her breaths quick, a little true panic lacing behind all the play and Joanna turned in her seat so that Aggie was safely tucked between us.

Warmth flooded my chest and I tried not to look too hopeful when I smiled back at Joanna.

"Ohhh, slow down, you," Joanna said to me, narrowing her eyes.

I laughed. "I haven't said a word."

"I get a year or two, at least," Joanna continued, even as she rubbed Aggie's back to soothe the little girl, the very picture of maternal care.

"And a lovely coven marriage ceremony," I added into the bargain, wondering if I should tell her what it would mean to me, and knowing it wasn't the time. A marriage ceremony wasn't a guarantee of any relationship staying whole, I knew that. But it was a promise my own parents hadn't made to each other and if she was willing, if they all were, it would be a promise that meant a great deal to me.

Joanna curled back into my side, leaning her head onto my shoulder as Aggie seemed to go limp and relax over our laps, not sleeping but that easy, childlike relaxation of knowing nothing could be wrong. And then all at once she squirmed and wiggled away, running after Bryce's heels out into the hall again.

"There's a letter for you," Hildy said, sweeping smoothly around the racing children, walking in from the hall with the paper pinched between her fingers.

"Oh, no letters," growled Joanna. "They bring bad news."

I reached out for it and frowned at the name in the top left corner.

"You're getting letters from Geoff York now," I said, giving her a teasing, accusing glare.

"Joanna collects covens," Bryce said from the hall.

Joanna's father looked a little lost in the conversation, as if the notion of being an attractive figure to a coven was a concept well beyond him. I thought Bryce was right though. Joanna was coven bait.

"Leave it for tomorrow," Isaac said, but he leaned into Callum's side at the other side of the room, and there was a worried crease between his eyes, his sterling gray going pale. "We're all here together so at least we know it's not one of us captured again."

Callum rolled his eyes, shifting in agitation in his seat.

Joanna tucked her hands under her skirt, refusing to open the envelope so it was up to me.

"It's tomorrow's problem," I decided, kissing Joanna's head and standing up from the couch to take the dreaded letter out of the room.

I heard the conversations pick back up when I was out in the hall and I'd waited till I'd made it safely far enough away before tearing open an edge of the envelope. Inside was a single folded note, words sparse on the page.

Vermenia knows there are still Scribes. No action taken yet. Keeping in touch with Uncle Myles. -G

Joanna was right. Bad news. But Geoff hadn't made it sound urgent at least. It would have to wait a few days. Joanna and the others, *we all*, deserved this time of rest together. I slid the letter in a cabinet drawer full of receipts and forgotten notes for the evening and returned to the living room, determined that my coven would have a wonderful evening together.

A wonderful life if I could manage it.

SCRIVENS

THE LIBRARIAN'S COVEN, BOOK 3

1

AIDEN

"You are being impossible." The words came out from gritted teeth, and I didn't know if I was trying to stop myself from shouting or too irritated to speak freely.

"*You* sound like everyone we've been fighting against!" Joanna cried out. The red was high in her cheeks, brown eyes shimmering. I wasn't fooled. Those weren't tears begging for pity, but a viper's spitting anger gathering and I was in the firing zone.

"This is never going to work if you won't *compromise*!"

"They've left Vermenia to avoid being tagged, and you're telling me that's exactly what we'll do to them when they arrive here!"

"Morning," Isaac said, voice sleepy and mild as he passed us in the dining room on his way to the kitchen. Neither Joanna nor I broke eye contact at the interruption, and Isaac didn't bother looking concerned that we were shouting before breakfast.

Weeks ago, when the news arrived that the Vermenian Scribes were looking for safe passage into Enmaire, and the arguments began, Isaac and Callum leapt between us to keep the peace. Now I could hear Callum murmuring a hello to Isaac and pouring the coffee, the pair of them too used to our bickering.

"I am not the one making this decision," I said, feeling winded by the pause.

Joanna's jaw flexed, her eyes watching me as she turned away. Frustration warred with a crumpling defeat in my chest. We'd had a good day yesterday. She'd taken lunch in my office, the pair of us curled up in an armchair listening to an old Yewmen recording. But today I was meeting with President Anders about the incoming refugees and Joanna couldn't help herself from pushing.

Or had it been me who'd brought the subject up first this time?

"I don't want to fight."

"I don't know why we *are* fighting," Joanna said, her skirt twitching around her legs as if she was thinking of swinging around again. Her back still faced me.

"We have to make a concession. I know you don't want to believe this, but inviting the Scribes is a risk for the campus, for Enmaire."

Joanna's head shook and a curl fell loose from her braid. "I think you do want to argue. I'm leaving for work."

Irritation streaked through me like electricity. Stubborn little brat. Why was she so determined? So naive?

"Breakfast!" Callum shouted from the kitchen, but Joanna's steps took off in the wrong direction, a fast snap against the floorboards.

"I'll grab something from the canteen." And then the front door swung shut behind her.

Callum's shadow appeared in the doorway and I glared at him, daring him to pick up where she had left off. "Don't."

Callum sighed, head knocking against the wall. "You're both running yourselves ragged on this. You should be on the same team."

My words burst out, too loud for the early morning, "We *are* on the same team!" Callum only blinked at me and a strangled growl caught in my throat. I swallowed it down and tried again, forcing or faking calm. "You know as well as I do, she's being unreasonable."

"She's being Joanna," Callum said, lips curling fondly. "Forceful optimist. Determined to make the best of this for everyone."

"Anders, Mayor Sewell—they'll never let them in if something happens and—"

"And they need someone to blame," Callum finished, one obnoxious eyebrow raised.

"You really think this will go smoothly, with *no* hiccups, like Joanna does?" I asked. I couldn't imagine a scenario that easy, there were too many variables and possibilities. Callum, of all people, should have felt the same. Joanna and her magic had come to Canderfey, releasing the Hollow, and she'd been entirely innocent in her actions. What would happen when a magical population, so used to hiding, realized they were free to use their powers here?

"I believe that the Scrivens are just as at risk with us, as we are with them," Callum said, pushing off the wall and crossing the room to me. "It takes away one of their only defenses by putting them on a register."

"What am I supposed to do, Callum?" My shoulders sagged. I was *tired* and the closer he stepped, the more I had to resist the urge to cringe away. My body ached with sudden and unwarranted exhaustion.

But Callum hadn't woken up bristling with fight like Joanna and I had. His hands plucked at the front of my shirt, barely enough to wrinkle me, just an invitation. My feet stumbled forward like he'd tugged at my spine, my forehead landing against his.

"She's their strongest advocate, and she's *Joanna,* so she won't give up on them. Anders and Sewell are... advocating for the university, the town, and Enmaire too I suppose, in their way," Callum mused, mint and coffee on his breath.

"Where does that leave me?" I asked in a quiet growl. Trapped between two opposing forces, one of whom I had to make peace with every day to live happily in my own home...our home.

"Applying your brilliant mind to a compromise," Callum whispered, and I glared at him as he kissed me, a brief, soft peck. "This isn't warfare, it's politics. You're the best of us for the job."

And then he left the room, grabbing his bag from the hall and heading out the front door. I trailed into the kitchen and Isaac was there, passing me a coffee and wearing that patient expression he had when he was watching us all in an uproar, knowing exactly how the pieces would land by the evening.

"Aren't you going to say something maddening too?" I asked, watching him over the rim of the coffee cup.

He only watched me and smiled. "They've poked the bear and abandoned me." I resisted the urge to growl and prove his point, and his smile softened. "You know me, I agree with everyone all the time."

"And Callum agrees with Joanna all the time. I'm left outnumbered," I said.

His head cocked and his eyes narrowed. "Does it bother you? How close they've been after Vermenia?"

It had been a few months since Joanna had rescued Callum from the Vermenian mines and the pair had been inseparable since. Callum had lowered his guard so far, I sometimes barely recognized him, and Joanna, who still occasionally showed a nervous footing in our coven, was as natural in his company as I had ever seen her.

"Of course not, it's good." I wondered if I had taken too long to say the words, although they came out quick and nervous on my tongue. I took a swig of coffee to cover the grind of my jaw.

"I think they play favorites sometimes," Isaac said with a shrug, looking at me with wide eyes as he took a sip of coffee.

I shook my head at him. "Don't try to draw me out, Isaac."

"Okay, you're right." He finished his mug with a last gulp and left it on the counter, wrapping an arm around my back and kissing my jaw. "The Scribes will be here soon and one way or another, things will have to start to settle. Joanna is trying to fight the unknown right now."

My back bristled. "And I'm fighting Joanna?"

Isaac narrowed his eyes at me. "This morning you're fighting everyone," he said, tone low. "I'm not accusing you, Aiden. I'm asking you to find your patience."

Shit. *Time to rein it in, King,* I thought.

My coven deserved better and if I went into the meeting with Anders like this, there would be trouble, probably for the refugees more than me. As naive as I thought Joanna was being about how the influx of Scrivens would go in Canderfey, I wanted it to work every bit as much as she did. Her family—her uncle, aunt, and grandmother —were coming, a connection to her mother she'd lost until months ago. I saw what that meant to her, and wanted it almost as badly for her as she did herself. Not only that, Enmaire prided itself on magic's freedom within the country. The Scrivens deserved that same freedom.

I released a long breath I'd trapped in my chest and Isaac's tension eased with mine.

"Sorry," I muttered.

He patted my chest, appeased. "I love you. Now go polish yourself up or whatever it is you do in the morning and have your meeting."

"Not all of us wake up looking so pretty," I said, flashing him a grin. Isaac rolled his eyes and took my quick kiss before I hurried upstairs to finish dressing.

My father taught me the power of a good suit—and the value of a tailor—and for most of my life, I'd used the knowledge for attracting romances. He'd been as pleased with my use of clothing as he was with my use of the piano lessons. His son, meant to follow in powerful politics, grown into a romantic musician. At least it pleased him now to hear from me on matters like these, negotiating the arrival of the Scrivens refugees in Canderfey. It suited his policies and gave him something worth boasting over in his clubs.

I left our house, umbrella in hand. Canderfey was damp this time of year, but at least winter had thawed, and spring was arriving with warm rains. I whistled at my shoes and the puddles skirted away from my feet as I walked. The closer I came to the library, the more I forced my eyes away from the windows, even as they ached to search the panes. Joanna was working and anyway, she wasn't the type to sigh wistfully after an argument. She would be in the stacks, hunting down reference material, making dozens of lists in her head, and lecturing me under her breath.

My lips quirked at the thought. I would find her at lunch. Sooner if the meeting went well.

President Anders' office sat at the top of the West Building, a palatial Redstone packed with little offices for administrators all the way down into the basement. I took the small cage elevator up to the tenth floor, where a long hall of secretaries and assistants faced a wide staircase leading up to the top story and Anders' office. It was a pretentious display to walk up to, the banisters designed to mimic the ones in the library, a still forest carved out of dead trees.

Elizabeth Bonde, the university's rather odd choice for a Vice President, came ducking out of her office, arms loaded with paperwork and hair twisted into some kind of frantic nest atop her head.

"Morning Bonde. Seeing you in this meeting?" I asked.

She blinked, and for a moment I wondered if she knew what I was talking about, or even who I was.

"No? No, not this one. Good luck, he's rather made up his mind, I'm afraid," she said, and then she was sliding into the elevator I'd just left, descending before I could ask what she meant.

It didn't leave me with a strong outlook for how things were going to go, neither in the meeting nor later with Joanna. I walked up the grandiose staircase to the rather preposterously large doors of Anders' office and knocked, waiting outside until I heard him call out.

Anders wasn't responsible for the design of his office or where it sat in the building, but it was a good representation of the man. Boastful, staring down at the campus from large floor-to-ceiling windows, the space pristine and rich, devoid of personality. He'd fought against Vermenia two wars previously, and become a bit of a show pony with a reputation for raw power. He'd returned, the only remaining son of his parents, and gone into academia and then... shown no real aptitude for anything but strength. He seemed to be a point-and-shoot kind of man. He could follow a set of directions well enough, but I was beginning to think critical thinking was beyond him.

Perhaps that was too harsh. He hadn't been my favorite person recently.

"Professor King, there you are," he said, turning from his windows, hands clasped behind his back.

Stuart Anders was about Isaac's height, average and unremarkable looking aside from his blatant glamouring to disguise the gray hairs or wrinkles in his skin. It created a faded look about him like he was draped in a hazy filter, aside from the rich colors of his clothing. A silk cravat, the color of mustard, was wrapped around his collar, the elaborate knot like a blossom against his throat. I tried not to stare.

"Good morning, President Anders." I glanced at the clock on the wall, I was five minutes early. He'd hardly been waiting for me.

"I've asked Mayor Sewell to join us this morning too," Anders said, gesturing over to a low set of chairs by a fire. There was a shimmer of magic in front of the fireplace, one of Anders' wards keeping the room mild and comfortable, the fire burning only for show with heat glimmering behind the shield.

"Of course," I said, following him to my seat.

I knew why Sewell was coming. To reinforce the demand for the Scrivens to put their names and residence on a registry. Maybe even so the pair of them could again express their 'concerns' about the project as a whole. Part of me wished Joanna was here, witnessing these meetings with me, seeing the personalities of the men who opposed her goals.

When my coven came forward to advocate for the refugees, with my fathers backing the cause in Rhodantis, Joanna was at the lead of the argument here. Somewhere along the way, I became the go-between, representing half-measures Joanna would never have settled for until we had the promise of an offer of safety for the Scrivens and their families. Canderfey was remote enough for the Enmairan government, had enough magical staff, students, and residents on hand to serve as a kind of defense, and donors like Hildy and I backing the project for housing. But the negotiations were one step backward for every two steps forward, and it was coming down to who could hold out the longest.

Mayor Sewell arrived with a young man carrying a coffee tray, pleasantries passed around in a tense ceremony. The Mayor of Canderfey was a quiet, grave man, with olive skin and silver-streaked black hair. He was generally satisfied to let Anders deal with me, watching from the sidelines. I expected if he came to this meeting he was about to break that silence, and I didn't imagine it would be in my favor. My stomach twisted at the thought of telling Joanna bad news.

As the last drop was poured, my opponents shared a glance, and I sat up straighter in my chair. I *was* on Joanna's side. Not only for the peace of my house but because she was such a morally pure creature I needed to succeed for her. The registry might win, but I was determined to steal something back for her in return.

"There's no budging on the registry, King," Sewell said, words even and almost without intonation.

My gut felt like a brick inside of me, the cheap, office coffee bitter on my tongue, but in response, my chest burned and my brain raced toward a solution, Callum's words in my head. Time for politics.

"I understand," I said, finding my father's smile on my mouth, a placating gesture to fool them. "Joanna will have the numbers this evening. Hildy and I will look at the housing we've gathered and arrange a system for their arrival. A check-in process. Joanna will send word about the registry so they will be appropriately informed."

Anders' expression flinched. *There,* I thought. They never intended the Scribes to know. It could give any Scribes too wary of our hospitality the opportunity to vanish on the way.

"I'm not sure that's wise," Sewell said, eyes narrowing.

"I don't believe the alternative would be," I challenged, meeting his gaze and leaning forward with my elbows at my knees, hands spread in feigned supplication. "If we are doing this for the right reasons, for their safety, then transparency is our ally."

"And if that transparency costs Enmaire?" Anders jerked his chin at me, voice too loud for the intimate arrangement of the room. He'd run for mayor before long, I suspected. He was already practicing his grandstanding to an audience of two, but I doubted his campaign would come to anything. A good university President would have the support of the campus during an election, but Anders was an ambivalent one at best.

I slouched in my seat, turning my smile crooked and feigning relaxation as if I were amongst friends. "Gentleman, I'm not arguing the need for the registry." Now I could be glad Joanna wasn't in the room. "I'm simply reminding you that we are promising to be *better* than Vermenia."

Anders sneered but it wasn't him I was concerned with. Bonde had made me nervous with her words earlier, she'd only been hearing from Anders, however. The Mayor seemed more willing to be swayed. Sewell watched me, practiced neutrality in his expression, but the flick of his eyes gave away his study. He was either weighing my suggestion or, if he was smart, calculating how much further I would push.

There were sympathetic ears in Canderfey, it wasn't just my coven and our friends—the students alone would be a powerful force in the argument of equality for the refugees. And my covenfather Marcus would exert influence for us, my father too if my mother got into his ear.

Sewell nodded once, and I turned immediately to Anders. "This has the potential to benefit the college too, President," I continued, sitting up in my chair as the man frowned at me. "An unknown magic, unpublished on, being nurtured here at Canderfey."

"You've certainly been thinking of everyone," Sewell said under his breath, but I thought I saw a flicker of a smile.

"They need a representative," I said, raising my eyebrows.

"A *what?*" Anders asked.

"Other than yourself?" Sewell asked, sarcasm stuck behind his feigned surprise.

"I'm not a Scribe," I said.

"Not your little librarian again," Anders bit out.

It took every bit of my control to wrestle down the urge to turn on him and drop attempts at charm in favor of intimidation. This was not the place or the time to let Anders know exactly what I thought of him, and he would certainly afford me another opportunity.

"No, not Joanna." I brushed the thought away with my hand. "She's a Scribe, but she's Enmairan. They need one of their own."

Anders scoffed, a noisy sound that went on longer than needed, his body shifting in his chair.

"Would it have to be a Scribe?" Sewell asked over the other man's blustering.

"It's their interests they would be protecting," I reasoned. "Yes, it would need to be one of the Scribes." Because if I left room for it to be an unmagical member of the community, Sewell and Anders would latch on and not let go. And while a family member might be trusted to look out for their own relations, I wasn't certain they would protect the others in the same way.

Also, I could guess based on our correspondence with Geoff who the Scrivens would pick. Creating a position for Joanna's uncle Myles to lead his people in Canderfey was a much better apology for our argument this morning than coming home empty-handed.

"Representatives from Canderfey will weigh in on the candidate," Sewell said, and finally Anders seemed to accept that the argument was not *his* to lose.

"Given that I am a major donor to the project—" I started.

"Yes, yes. You and Samanta will be part of the decision," Sewell said, eyes rolling slightly. "Well, King, I hope you're satisfied."

"I genuinely believe this will be a benefit to our community," I said slowly.

Sewell nodded, a hand reaching up to rub over his jaw, his eyes traveling the room. There might be a counter move in the near future, but for now, at least I had won something for us, for Joanna.

"That will be all, Professor King," Anders said, his voice curdled.

I stood and was surprised to find Sewell joining me. Anders' eyes widened.

"You're not staying?" he asked the other man.

"No, I'll walk out with Professor King. I should have been at the office by now." Sewell gestured for me to walk ahead of him.

Anders more or less ignored me in his goodbyes, and I debated on whether or not to wait for Sewell as I made my way to the door. The Mayor caught up with me on the steps down to the elevator.

"I hope you feel successful with that outcome," Sewell said as we waited for the elevator.

I considered my answer carefully, uncertain what response might be welcome or not, but he'd sounded sincere enough. "I do." My body strained to hold still, keep from shuffling nervously, and Sewell played an equally convincing statue next to me. "I hope the refugees will feel they've made the right choice in coming to us."

The Mayor grunted at my side, head bobbing in what might pass for a nod. "I won't be wholly altruistic in this, King. I hope you realize that."

"I do, sir." He'd already proven as much.

"And it would be best if you made good on that promise to Anders, regarding the benefits to the university."

I didn't see how it was possible for an entire group of Scribes to arrive in Canderfey and *not* have it capitalized on by the university. I suppose that was where I would come in, with Callum and the others. We needed to find ways to convince the Scribes to work with the campus. I would turn the problem over to Joanna and Callum first, so they could dream up their ideal scenario for everything to work. Hopefully, it wouldn't come to bickering again when those ideals had to be bargained down to succeed.

"Shouldn't be an issue," I said, conjuring my best smile as the elevator arrived.

Sewell heaved a heavy sigh as we stepped inside, shoulders rattling the cage wall behind him. "I wish I could say I'll be glad when this is all over," he said. "But of course, it hasn't really begun yet."

* * *

I CAUGHT Joanna at the front doors of the library at her lunch hour. She looked pale in the rain, and more tired than she had hours ago in the morning.

"I'm sorry for putting that on you," she said as I approached. The fist in my chest unclenched a fraction and then she added, "But I sent word to Myles about the registry."

I could see the lines around her mouth, her lips pressed tight as she waited for my reaction.

"Good," I said, raising my umbrella over both our heads and

dipping down to her face, kissing across her hairline, and then against her temple. "I told them we would."

She sagged into me and I wrapped my arm around her shoulders, holding her close and feeling the tired tremble in her bones.

"I was hoping you would pass something else along," I murmured in her ear. "They will have a representative in any decisions made after their arrival."

"Oh, Aiden!" Joanna leaned back in my arms, surprise bringing a little color back to her face.

"Will it be enough, do you think?" I asked. I was thoroughly wrapped around her finger if that bright-eyed look of hers was all it took to leave me feeling proud and contented.

"Myles already said they were prepared," Joanna said, eyes sliding over my shoulder as she chewed the inside of her lip in thought. "But this will be a relief, I think." She relaxed again and tucked her head beneath my chin.

"I don't know why I fought you this morning," she said, shaking with a weak laugh.

"Neither do I, darling." I nuzzled into her hair and grinned as her fist thumped lightly against my back. "You're fighting for something you care about. Just know that I never want to stand in the way of that. Do you think I can keep you to myself this evening?"

"If you promise to get me out of the house," she said. "Otherwise Callum and Isaac will just laugh right in our faces."

2

———

JOANNA

"Settle, love," Isaac soothed in my ear, his hand clutching mine as my feet started toward the road again.

My smile wobbled as I glanced at him, moving back into the line of onlookers peppered along the outside gate of campus. "I wish we'd gone to meet them in Gretcham," I said, biting down on the corner of my mouth.

Callum stepped in front of me, blocking my view of the road, and his hands landed on my shoulders, stopping me from rising up to my toes to see past him. The racing excitement in my chest settled at the touch, the pale blue of his eyes washing over me, calming me. I never knew if it was his magic or our connection.

"You'll take care of your family today, and we will handle the rest," he said and his face wrestled with amusement at my expense. I could forgive him for it, I knew how silly my anxiety was, I'd nearly left the house half-dressed that morning.

"I should help with—"

"I will be on campus with Gwen and Gast to see families into the housing, Aiden and the others will be in town," Callum said, spelling out the very plan I had been a part of creating just days ago. "You and Isaac only need to see the Kershaws into their home and *relax*."

I wrinkled my nose and looked away from his face, staring up at the edges of Hand Woods that hung over the road. It was a perfect day, the warmest of spring yet, and the trees were bursting with the first flashes of green we'd seen since the Hollow had stolen it away in the fall. I held my breath while branches rustled overhead, and tried to catch the sounds of horses and carts plodding closer to Canderfey.

Geoff York had called from the road, he and his coven would arrive with the Scrivens and their families today. Over a dozen new witches and at least as many unmagical Vermenians with them. There was a bit of truth in Callum's teasing, I *was* impatient to see Myles, Irene, and my grandmother Adele again. But it was just as important to me that the transition into Canderfey go well for all the others whose names I'd yet to learn.

"Do you trust us?" Callum asked, tilting his head into my view again.

I sighed and leaned into his touch as he brushed his fingers down my cheek, trying to send some of the tension running through my back out with the breath. "Of course I do. I'm settling, see?"

He smiled, unconvinced, and moved back to my side, wrapping his arm around my waist until I was pressed to his side, grounding myself in his calm. Aiden was at my back and his hand came to rest on my shoulder, thumb against the base of my neck. Isaac still held my hand and altogether it did the trick, the three of them touching me, their magic resting at my edges in invitation. I relaxed and breathed deeply.

Under my sigh came the sound of horses.

"They're coming," Aiden said, as the group around us, a small collection of faculty, students, and townspeople, carried the same exclamation down the line. My head whipped to look down the length of the crowd, where President Anders and Mayor Sewell were stepping away from the gates of Canderfey University and out onto the road.

"They look ready to lock the campus," I hissed.

"They won't," Aiden assured me, but when I glanced back at him, he was watching the two men with narrowed eyes as well.

"They can't," Callum whispered and winked down at me. "Took care of that last night."

I laughed, unsure if it was born from relief or frustration. My coven was the best support I could ask for, but I wished the *entire* community was behind us.

Nothing is ever unanimous, Callum's voice from weeks ago echoed in my head.

"Joanna, look," Isaac said, his hand squeezing mine, my head whipping back in the other direction.

Sabine York was leading the convoy up the road to us, with Samuel and Darin on horseback just behind her. My eyes glanced over theirs, it wasn't the warrior coven that made my heartbeat stutter in my chest. There, behind their horses, was a covered wagon—my uncle Myles sitting at the front, reins in his hand and a huge, familiar smile spread over his mouth.

He was sunburnt, and even with the grin I thought I saw dark circles under his eyes, but he caught sight of me right away, lifting off his seat a little and waving his arm over his head.

"Aloo! Aloo!"

My covenmates released me, hands lifting away in unison and my feet took off down the road, boots slapping through puddles and over pebbles. Samuel skirted his horse around me and Myles was there at the end of his bench, catching my hand and helping me lift myself onto the carriage seat. My arms wrapped around his shoulders as he laughed. Embarrassment struck me—I had only met the man once before—until his arm circled my back, tugging me close and releasing me after a tight squeeze.

"Aloo, leina," Myles said, eyes crinkling with sincere happiness. His face was tanned to red from the days on the road, and I could almost feel the exhaustion hanging around him like heavy outline, but we smiled at each other until our cheeks hurt.

"Joanna?"

I heard Adele, my grandmother, from inside the wagon and Myles leaned back, letting me part the curtain. It was dark inside and it took my eyes a moment to adjust, my cheeks grasped in cool and knobby hands and then tugged further in, to receive a kiss on either side of my face.

"Hello, Adele." My eyes adjusted, taking in the light that bled through the canvas and I waved at Irene, my uncle's wife, at the far end of the wagon, propped between an overturned couch and a stack of trunks.

"Aloo, sweet," Adele said, patting my face with her fingertips once more.

My eyes skimmed over the belongings surrounding them, and I thought of their home over the border with a pang of loss. It had been full to the rafters with beautiful belongings soaked with family history. The wagon was packed with light, simple furniture, as much as could be spared now left behind in Vermenia.

"Almost there," I said to Adele and she nodded, a smile cracking across her face, eyes even more worn and red than Myles'. She couldn't have been sleeping well along the road like this.

I ducked out of the wagon as Adele sagged a little, nodding at my answer. Myles caught my eye as I emerged and he shrugged at my frown.

"She needs her mattress," he said, winking at me.

"You'll move in on the campus," I told him. "In my old house."

I hadn't lived in the little staff house long, barely a couple of months, before I was in the tower house with my coven, but it remained empty for the following months and Aiden had pulled the right strings for me. We'd wanted my family in the house with us, but Adele and Myles couldn't take the stairs and Callum negotiated for permission to spell the staff house to accommodate more room for her.

"I'd move into a stable, leina," Myles said. "If there was a door. And hot food."

"Isaac will cook for us tonight," I said, pointing him out to Myles in the crowd.

"Irene will be glad to hear it." Myles bumped his shoulder against mine. His eyes flicked to the dusty, tired looking man, with a backpack on his back, shoes caked with mud, who walked alongside the wagon. "The others will…"

"We've put a basket in every home." I watched a line vanish from between his brows as he listened. "Supplies to help them through this first week at least."

"Thank you, Joanna," he said.

"Have you talked about who will be a representative for you?" I asked, lowering my voice as we reached the edge of the crowd.

"Ehnnn, me, I suppose." He shrugged and scrunched his nose, but I caught the pleased twitch at the corner of his mouth. "If they agree."

He was watching ahead of us to where the Mayor and university President stood waiting.

"They will," I said. "I'll bully them into it, if I have to."

Myles laughed at that, patting my knee. My coven was right, this was where I needed to be tonight. Not just because it would help me reacquaint myself with my family. Myles was my connection to the other Scrivens, and all my wild, stray thoughts that had kept me up at night for weeks could now be bounced off him for advice.

"Hop down, leina," he said, using the Vermenian endearment and nodding down to the side of the road where Callum and the others were waiting for me. Sabine and her covenmates stopped ahead of us on their horses, swinging down to greet Mayor Sewell. "Time for us to be…"

"Cooperative," I finished for him, the word leaving a sour flavor on my tongue.

"Yes," Myles said, a wry smile pressing his lips white. "Go find Geoff. He's hanging back somewhere. I'll see you inside."

I pressed a kiss to Myles' cheek and turned away. Isaac was there as I jumped down from the seat, hands wrapping around my waist and placing me gently onto my feet.

"Where are the others?" I asked as he tugged me off the road. My eyes skipped over the crowd from campus, and then back to the travelers rolling slowly forward over the road, their faces and clothes dusty, some of them dragging on ragged shoes.

"Making sure everything goes smoothly up front," Isaac said.

"And you're here to distract me from harassing Anders and the Mayor?" I asked, raising an eyebrow.

Isaac smiled, leaning in and kissing my lips softly. "Maybe."

"I have to find Geoff," I said. "You can help with that."

Finding the spy under the shadow of the woods and the mix of people was easier said than done, and when we did reach the end of the caravan the expression on Geoff's face was smug. Like he'd chosen the exact moment for us to find him.

"Did you miss me?" His smile was sly, with his hands in pockets and feet treading silently over the road to meet us.

"I have questions for you," I said, watching Geoff's feet pause and his face grimace.

"Of course you do."

GEOFF SPOKE to my grandmother in Vermenian, voice low and coaxing in his own tongue, herding her back to the armchair we'd pulled from the wagon first.

"This is the last of it," I told Myles as he met me in the doorway, my arms burning under the weight of the boxes.

I was sweaty and tired and covered in dust, and my knees were wobbling where I stood. But Myles' limp had grown steadily worse with every trip in and out of the house, and Irene was pale white with bright spots of red on her cheeks. I'd been working double-fast with Isaac to try and keep them off their feet, and finally, we were done with hauling.

Isaac slid between us. "Let me, love." He lifted the boxes out of my arms with perfect timing, my hands sweating and slipping, wood splinters scratching my palms. Adele snuck up out of her chair when Geoff wasn't looking and waved Isaac into the little closet nook that had been transformed into a modest bedroom for her.

"Easier work than leaving," Myles said, with a hint of a smile before closing the door behind us.

A grimace tore through the expression as he rocked slowly over to the couch pressed to the far wall, where Irene was sitting and fanning her neck with a hat. He lowered himself down with a hiss and I winced in sympathy.

"Can the pain be written away?" I asked, thinking out loud more than anything.

Myles and Adele stiffened, studying me, and my throat squeezed until my uncle finally blinked and looked at Irene, translating my question to her.

"Maybe," Myles said to me after, looking down at his leg. "Scrivens try not to write after they know what they are."

Irene glared at her husband and spoke. It was too fast for my limited study of the language to follow, but I understood the tone and my body relaxed as Myles grinned at her.

"She thinks if he can't feel the pain, he won't know when to stop," Geoff translated for me.

"Don't know when to stop *with* the pain," Myles said, grinning and then grumbling as Irene lifted his wooden leg up to her lap.

Geoff caught my eye and nodded in the direction of the kitchen, and I followed him out of the room, giving Irene privacy to berate her husband and tend to his aches. Callum had used a little magic in here too, I noticed, the space now feeling useable rather than cramped. The house still felt *mine* somehow, though I'd spent so little time here—far more in the library and in the coven house, even before moving out.

"Do you think the Scrivens will get used to writing again?" I asked Geoff, moving to the counter.

Isaac had put together the food for my family, planning on cooking their meal to let them rest from the road. I didn't know exactly what he planned to cook, even with the elements sitting in front of me, but I could at least wash the vegetables for him.

"Yes," Geoff answered, propping himself up against the wall as I started to unpack the basket. "Some of them are itching to do it."

I smiled at the thought and Geoff kicked my heel lightly.

"You should be more cautious."

I wrinkled my nose and glared at him briefly. "You sound like the Mayor."

Geoff didn't sigh at me or scoff. "Ask your uncle. He knows who to trust," he said, folding his arms over his chest.

I cracked the window over the sink, letting the cool air from the alley trickle in and cover my embarrassed flush. "Did anything happen on the road?" I asked. I was going to have to eat all my indignant arguments with Aiden if there was already trouble, but it would be better to be prepared. And he might take pity on me. A little.

Geoff shrugged. "Not like you're asking. A wheel broke in the mud once. Sam left to get help before Myles talked to the Scrivens. I never saw the words, but the wheel was fixed after that."

"That just seems…cautious," I said, frowning down at a bundle of arugula. I looked over at Geoff, his face stony but flexing in the smallest details. "What aren't you saying?" When he shuffled, edging closer to the doorway, I pushed, "Oh, come on. I know you're thinking and I'm not your coven so I can't read you."

Geoff let out a brief surprised laugh. "You think my coven can?" Geoff's eyes wrinkled with humor. "I missed you a little Wick."

"A very little, I know," I said, dropping the vegetables in the sink and rounding on him. "Tell me."

Geoff grunted and kept his eyes forward. "Talk to Myles. He knows them better. And you are one of them, in your way."

In my way…I had thought of myself as a Scribe, a Scrivens, since the moment I'd known there was a word for my power. Geoff made it sound as if the Vermenians may not feel the same. I chewed at the inside of my lip, half tempted to leap at him and bully the truth out of him like I might have with my brother when we were kids. Geoff stared back at me, something almost like nervousness in his eyes, when Isaac joined us in the kitchen, stopping short in the doorway.

"Am I—" he started, an eyebrow raised.

"You can cook, I'll leave," Geoff said, taking the opportunity for escape and dashing out of the room.

I glared at Isaac as he came to the sink, but he ignored me, pressing a kiss to the corner of my mouth. "Interrogating the spy, Joanna?"

"I'm inviting him and his coven to stay at the house tonight," I said, and then raised a hand to stop Isaac. "Not to interrogate him. Really. They've done a lot to help."

He mulled over that, frowning at the scattered vegetables in the sink. "Alright," he said, "but I want to see their faces when you offer. And Aiden's."

I decided it was better to warn Aiden of the invitation, but both he *and* Isaac enjoyed watching Darin choke on his salad when I asked them to stay with us.

"Do you think this will work?" I asked as Callum's arm circled my waist and Aiden's draped over my shoulders, his fingertips brushing the back of Callum's neck. "The Scrivens staying here in Canderfey?"

"I think it's time for you to put the project out of your mind and get some rest," Aiden said, and together they lifted me up the stairs to our bedroom. Downstairs, Isaac showed Sabine and her coven to Aiden's bedroom, the tidiest of our rooms to offer them.

I'd asked the same question one hundred times at least in the last few months since hearing the Scrivens were in danger, but I'd never felt less certain of the success of the project than I did at that moment, weary from the day and with Geoff's cryptic warnings floating in my thoughts. Aiden's words weren't an answer at all, but a dismissal of my question, and I hadn't found another opportunity to speak to Geoff or my uncle about the trip to Canderfey.

Although I couldn't regret the cozy evening with my coven and family, Isaac's delicious meal taken from an odd assortment of dishes, many of us standing against the wall as we ate. It was an odd collection of people. I could almost say that I liked Geoff, but I was less certain about the rest of his coven. I, at least, respected them and was grateful for their help. But it was interesting to watch them orbit guiltily out of Callum's way in such a small house.

I slid my shoulders away from Aiden's touch, darting up a handful of stairs and turning to face him. It seemed as if Aiden was *always* telling me to give my concerns about the Scrivens a rest. And now of all times, when they were finally here, ignoring the myriad of details surrounding the project was the last thing I wanted to do! All I wanted to hear was that they had faith this would work and Aiden refused to ever say the words. Callum sighed and caught my hand before I escaped.

"We know better than anyone what you're capable of, Joanna," Callum said, that tired rumble in his voice softening my spine. "It will work. But Aide is right. There's nothing to worry about before tomorrow morning. Time for rest."

I caught half a glance of Aiden's frown before Callum was sweeping me up the last of the stairs.

"Shower together?" Callum asked, his hands on my waist.

I hated to admit defeat but my steps were leaden when we reached the bedroom. "Maybe in the morning," I said, wrestling with my own yawn.

The cats sprang off the bed as we arrived, circling our ankles and crying in soft mewls.

"I'll take care of them," Aiden murmured behind me, before chasing the cats back down to the kitchen.

I rounded on Callum who was rubbing at his eyes beneath his glasses. "You'll smudge them." I pulled the frames down from his nose and rubbing my thumb over the little mark left on the bridge. "He doesn't think this is going to work."

Callum tilted my chin up to meet his eyes. "He doesn't want to promise you something none of us can control." He stroked his fingertips over my bottom lip, feeling where it had stiffened, and he grinned. "Even though we know you'll give it your best effort. Did you get anything from Geoff?"

"Not really. He's very opinionated for someone who refuses to actually say anything," I groused, frowning and pulling away. I stretched my arms and something in my back cracked.

"I'll see what I can get out of him before they leave tomorrow," Callum said, plucking at the buttons that ran down the back of my dress.

I reached back and caught his hand, squeezing it in mine. "Thank you."

Callum's arms circled my waist and I fell back into his hold, my body turning loose with exhaustion. "Just one step at a time for a few days," he said in my ear, lips on my skin leaving the whisper of warmth and shivery pleasure. "And just sleep tonight. No sneaking out of bed to raid my library."

"Hypocrite," I said, but my jaw cracked with another yawn, undermining all the bite.

3

JOANNA

"Your uncle is downstairs."

I jumped down from the ladder where I was pulling texts for a professor, almost knocking noses with Gwen. She held her hand up to stop me in place.

"He's only reading, Joanna, with a few of the others. I just thought you'd like to know they found the section you put together and seem to be making themselves comfortable." Gwen's faint firm smile teased at the corner of her lips. "Would you like me to let you off your shift an hour early?"

Part of me wanted to say yes—run down to check on Myles and the others. But it had been a quiet week since the Scrivens arrived in Canderfey and they didn't need me hovering just because a few had come to the library.

I shook my head. "No, of course not. Here are the books for Professor Timson." I passed the stack into Gwen's arms and plucked the next list out of her fingers.

"Those and anything else you can find on transformative gifts, the more inherent the better," Gwen said, patting my arm in parting.

I slid into the stacks of the faculty library, trying to remember where Bryce had shown me the texts that touched on their own shapeshifting abilities. Nothing was more transformative than a dragon. I turned the corner on a shelf and nearly knocked into Isaac.

"There you are." He caught my mouth in a kiss before I'd recovered from my surprise.

"What are you doing up here? I'm not off for an hour." My mouth followed his for a moment, wanting another scratch of his facial hair against my skin.

"I know, I came to sketch," he said, and the next kiss landed on my neck.

I blushed, still not entirely used to Isaac's attention when he wanted to sketch me. I nodded down to the end of the row where a chair sat in front of a window. "Sit over there, I'll hunt for books very slowly."

He grinned and I tried not to let the third kiss, a slow press and a flick of his tongue over my pulse, go to my head, but my blood was pumping faster and the glint in his eyes meant he knew the cause.

"You're dangerous," I said, narrowing my eyes at him, warmth pooling inside of me. A stray thought about the well-disguised nook around the corner ran through my head. No. I only had an *hour* left. I could behave.

"Nonsense," he said, but the magnetic tug I felt as he drew away proved that wrong. "Let me take you out to dinner tonight."

I opened my mouth to say that I planned on walking over to see my family, but the slightest twitch of his eyebrows stopped me, his silver gaze flashing against the sunlight from the nearby window. I'd taken dinner with Myles, Irene, and Adele every night since their arrival. Most nights my coven was with me. Maybe it *was* time for a night off, for Adele if no one else. We all did our best to give her as little work with our visits as possible, but she was a determined hostess.

And it had been much longer than this past week since I'd had more than a cursory dinner alone with my coven.

"Alright," I said, nodding. "Are we inviting the others?"

Isaac shrugged. "If you like. I just want a little time with my girl. Candlelight is a bonus."

How could Isaac, who I knew as well as myself, still make me feel like a giddy school girl? "It's a date," I said, laughing and hiding my blush as I spun away.

With the evening in mind came stirrings of excitement. I would be sure to let Isaac know how grateful I was for the reminder to be romantic. And as nice as it might be to soak up his company alone, I was equally guilty of neglecting Callum and Aiden recently too. Dinner out of the house, away from the thoughts of Scrivens and university presidents, would be good for us.

I caught glimpses of Isaac while I worked, studious and smiling between his notes and glances at me. It had taken me months of finding myself the subject of his focus before I grew used to the feeling of being studied so intimately. Now it gave me a thrill, remembering the way his attention to my shape and expression was just as devotional on a page as it was when we were in bed together. There was a flush starting at my collar, every one of my movements made with my skin hyperaware that he watched me.

The quarter-hour chimed from the clock tower on campus and I had just sent down a collection of texts for Gwen. I was debating sneaking into Isaac's arms for the remaining time of my shift—there was hardly ever faculty in the stacks this time of the evening and it would take a very brave student to try and sneak into this part of the library—but the thought was interrupted as I turned to find a young woman hovering at the shelves near Isaac's seat.

"Can I help you?" I asked, walking down the row of shelves to them.

Isaac was turned in my direction, his back to the girl, but she stood close enough to his chair to have her skirt nearly brushing his shoulder. She was tall and well-dressed, with a doll's porcelain complexion and long, honey-blonde curls to match. She reminded me of the illustration of a princess in books, all pale and pristine and romantic. Her eyes slid from Isaac's face, which she'd been studying with rapt focus, to mine, in a slow, cool sweep. She smiled, just a curve of her lips, without any real warmth, and shook her head, shifting back to the shelf with a swish of her hips that seemed directed to catch Isaac's eye.

He leaned out of her way, tucking his pencil behind his ear and marking his place in his sketchpad with his finger. I met his gaze, the smile in his eyes and the slight wrinkle of tension in the very corners. Isaac had a particular effect on people, his beauty and internal calm working as a lure to the eye. Flocks of art students, girls and boys alike, had very strong opinions of me for arriving earlier that year and finally taking the coven of handsome professors off the market. He knew how others saw him and accepted the admiration with a kind of grace that still managed not to encourage more.

Whoever this girl was, even if she was a very young professor, I suspected her aim in being up here in the faculty section had little to do with the books.

"Are you a student?" I asked, walking up the aisle to where she stood, trailing an elegant finger over the spines of books as to make a pretty picture were Isaac to look her way.

She flicked her eyes to me again, not bothering with the smile, and shook her head, hair flipping over her shoulder as she dismissed me. Isaac choked on a laugh, rising out of his chair and coming to my side as I narrowed my eyes at the younger woman. She watched him with a hunger that was more akin to a dragon than a princess.

"If we walk very slowly down the stairs, Woolard will never know you stopped book fondling five minutes early," Isaac said, an arm circling my waist. I ignored the girl in favor of leaning into the touch, letting him brush two kisses against my lips, his eyes laughing. Maybe I was a bit of a dragon too because I preened at this extra affection he displayed while she watched.

I would laugh later when the coven teased him for luring girls up into the restricted faculty area of the library.

"I can't leave her up here," I whispered to him. "She's not staff. Why don't you just go downstairs and let her follow you?"

"I was hoping you'd make some grand possessive gesture," Isaac said with a shrug and a teasing sigh.

"Maybe after my shift ends." I patted his chest while my heart flipped at his grin.

I walked up to where the young woman was now standing,

reaching up to the top of the shelf with a stretch better suited to a dancer.

"Are you new to the University?" I asked. I doubted she was faculty, a bit because she looked too young and she was dressed more like one of the students, parading a new fashion.

"No, I'm fine," she said, words clipped and cornflower blue eyes rolling at me. She had a Vermenian accent.

I resisted the urge to roll mine back at her, my jaw clenched in annoyance. "I'm sorry but this part of the library is restricted to University faculty and staff. I'll have to escort you back into the open stacks." I stepped to the side and gestured out toward the stairs, not sure how much of my little speech she would understand. Her Enmairian was at least good enough to try and put me in my place.

She lifted her chin, staring down a fine and pert nose at me. "I am guest of Canderfey," she declared, eyes searching the end of the aisle, but Isaac had thankfully ducked out of sight.

I forced a smile on my face. "Yes, you are. But you are not faculty or staff."

The bells chimed the hour outside and I wondered which of the other clerks might come to relieve me. I could leave this girl in their hands and hope they might have more success.

"Corina," a familiar voice barked from the stairs.

For a moment, the girl's face transformed into something so hostile that her beauty was lost, but the expression smoothed away, and she passed me in a breeze of airy fabric and mild perfume. I followed close on her heels, to make sure she left in the right direction, instead of slipping back into the shelves.

When we reached the stairs I saw my uncle halfway up, face twisted in a grimace. Isaac was there, letting the older man lean on him. Myles barked a few words up at the girl, Corina, who shrugged, somehow making the gesture both petulant and regal. She fluttered down the steps, passing Myles and Isaac without a glance.

"Are you alright?" I asked my uncle as I reached him. There were fine beads of sweat around his temples and Isaac took his weight as we moved carefully back down to the main floor.

"Fine, fine," Myles said. "Wearing myself out chasing that—" He used unfamiliar words in his own language, but I got the gist and agreed, privately. "I'm sorry, leina. She knew not to go up there."

Yes, that had been fairly clear even as she ignored me. "It's alright," I said, grasping onto his arm to help him down the stairs. "She wasn't really reading anything," I added, with a glance at Isaac out of the corner of my eye.

"She does as she likes," Myles growled. "You see her on her own, write for me or Nora."

I now had a second notebook, used for exchanging messages with Myles and one of the other Scrivens, a woman he trusted who was also fluent in Enmairian. He hadn't told me which of the refugees to watch out for in the past week, promising that if anything came up he would let me know. It felt like a dismissal, a reminder that I was not one of them and couldn't be trusted to keep them safe.

"I'm sorry, leina," Myles repeated on a sigh. "I wanted them to be good."

I softened, leaning my cheek onto my uncle's shoulder as we reached the main floor. Maybe it hadn't been mistrust at all but optimism. The same optimism I clung to, hoping every facet of the transition would go smoothly.

"No harm done," I said, seeing Corina at a table, her chin propped in her hand as she stared up at the stained glass ceiling of the library in affected boredom. Other refugees sat around the table, a collection of the Vermenian texts we gathered sitting in front of them.

University students at nearby tables watched the Vermenians over the tops of their books, or some even gave up studying altogether for staring. At least their expressions were less suspicious and more open curiosity, although the attention seemed to be unnerving one of the older men.

"Are they all Scrivens?" I asked, nodding to the table as we approached. Myles was walking on his own again, panting a little and looking like the trip up the stairs had cost him. An idea occurred to me, one to run by Gwen first chance I got.

"Just Corina and Daniel," Myles said, nodding at the nervous man sitting at the far end of the table from Corina.

The two Scrivens were opposites, Corina was young and beautiful, and Daniel… well he wasn't old or young but he certainly had none of Corina's elegance. He was a scruffy looking man, his hair a mix of hay blond and copper red, streaks of gray running down to his untidy beard. I had met him twice before and had yet to make eye contact with him, the icy silver gaze darting constant and quick around him and never landing. He was alternately absorbed with the book in front of him, and glaring at the students watching him—but if he was a book lover, then I could not help but like him. Certainly more than Corina.

It's not as if she was the first woman to fall for Isaac at first glance, I reminded myself. I was guilty of it too, I'd just been lucky. I reached to him through the bond, felt his pleasure and surprise, an answering affection traveling back to me. As Myles settled into his seat with a muffled groan, Isaac and I exchanged a warm glance.

"Aloo," I said, turning back to the table. There was no response from Corina or Daniel, but the others answered in soft voices. I recognized a few of them as Myles' neighbors from the staff row housing. That was good, convenient for my request to Gwen. I turned to Isaac and whispered, "Will you wait here for me? I need to speak to Gwen before I leave."

He nodded, a hand brushing over my back as I turned, fingertips flicking to catch my hand once before releasing. I smiled, Isaac was always a little more affectionate in public than me, but I suspected this was a demonstration of a different nature. Either for Corina's sake or mine.

"Enjoy your evening," Gwen said with a glance, as I reached the circulation desk.

"Thank you, but actually, can we speak a moment as I grab my coat?"

She raised an eyebrow and followed me into the empty staff lounge. "What's your scheme?" she asked me as the door shut behind us.

I stopped short. "Why do you assume I'm scheming?" When she only stared back at me, I shook my head and continued. "Well, alright. I just wondered if you'd mind if Myles wrote his way back home from in here. He can take the others with him, I think most of them live on campus. His leg is bothering him and I don't know how he'd take the walk back."

Gwen glanced at the door out to the library. I had used it once before as a route home when Callum was captured and the shock of pain knocked me out.

"I suppose," Gwen said, with more reserve than I expected.

"If- if you're not comfortable—" I started.

"I am," Gwen cut in, voice firm again as she turned back to me. "I know… these are things you find… simple acts of magic, Joanna. But I wonder if any of the Scrivens have ever felt safe enough to do such a thing. It may be more significant to them."

I opened my mouth to object. I had only known I *could* make such a thing for a handful of months. It was hardly insignificant to me now.

"Offer," Gwen said, nodding. "I'll let them in and clean up if Myles agrees."

I returned to the table of Vermenians, finding Corina attempting a stilted conversation with Isaac who looked like he was warring neutrality with his naturally charming nature. I gave him a sly smile and then crouched down by Myles.

"I'm leaving for the evening, but Gwen Woolard said that you could write yourself a door home in the staff lounge when you're done here," I said. Myles froze in his chair, eyes fixed to mine, and I added, "She'll wash the words off after you've made it home."

I felt another set of eyes on my face and looked up. It wasn't Corina, she was batting her remarkably long, pale eyelashes at an oblivious Isaac. I turned and found Daniel's gaze on me, startled and wary like an animal in the line of the hunt. He turned to stare at Myles.

"Thank you, leina," Myles said softly, but his expression was an intricate, complicated thing—brow furrowed, but eyes bright, and lips pressed together until they were barely visible.

"Come on, love," Isaac said, taking my hand and keeping me from quizzing my uncle on his worry.

I kissed Myles goodbye on the cheek, gave a shaky Vermenian parting phrase to the others, and left with a tug on my hand from my covenmate.

"Did you and Corina arrange a time for you to sketch her?" I asked when we were out of earshot.

Isaac glared at me as he opened the door out of the library, the weather damp and chilly again. "I don't do vanity portraits, Joanna, you know that," he hissed in my ear, before leaving a kiss beneath my lobe. "Don't tell me you're worried."

The question was sincere and I leaned into his side, holding his gaze. "No," I said, lips twitching. "A little offended, but not worried."

"Good. My artist's eye is more than satisfied with its recent subjects," he said, his arm squeezing tight around my shoulders. "My heart is full too, for the record."

I grinned and rewarded him with another kiss, our feet stumbling a little on the path.

"Aiden and Callum are meeting us in town," he said, nose brushing against mine. "I will do *anything* you ask if you promise not to bring this up over dinner."

I laughed and bit my lip, weighing the choice in my head.

4

———————

AIDEN

"Surely you see the bias of your covenmate's uncle being elected to this position?" Anders said to me, his voice amplified to reach the audience below.

The representative decision was originally planned to take place in Anders' office until Mayor Sewell announced that there was serious interest on the issue amongst the townspeople. Now the City Hall chamber was full to the rafters with people, eyes focused up to the small stage where Myles sat under a spotlight like an interrogation subject. I'd wondered at first if Sewell and Anders had drawn a crowd intentionally to cause some kind of commotion on the topic, but the audience was quiet and observant so far. Anders, less so.

"It was neither I nor my covenmate, who recommended Mr. Kershaw for the position, but his peers," I said through a tight jaw, staring down the table of decision officials to Anders at his podium

My eyes landed briefly on Joanna, seated at the front of the hall, her knuckles white around Callum's grip. Her cheeks were red with anger but the flashing gaze was directed at Anders, and I felt a little smug and a great deal relieved that her ire was turned elsewhere at last.

Myles sat to the left of us in a chair, on his own, polished up by his

529

wife and mother until he almost gleamed with trustworthy responsibility. Anders had decided to grind his heels into this decision and resist any common sense on the subject, and I could see that even the crowd of townspeople were weary with the discussion by now.

"He's also one of the few who speaks Enmairian," I added, trying to slow my breathing and keep my voice cordial. Anders seemed to be performing for the crowd more than anything, and I suspected that Myles and I were not cooperating with his expectation of the script by remaining calm and logical.

Myles leaned forward in his chair catching the eye of the councilmen and women lined along the table. "If there is general concern about the appointment, would a pro- probationary period be considered as a compromise?"

I had to clamp down the muscles in my face to keep from reacting. He had clearly practiced the phrase, but it hadn't been under my direction. I wasn't sure it was a wise decision to give the council any room to avoid Myles' appointment. Especially not when he was the best possible choice for everyone involved.

"Is that necessary?" Councilwoman Jones asked. She was a friend of Hildy's and clearly not a great fan of Anders. I didn't know her well, she wasn't one of the more vocal members of the council, but if she ever ran for further office, she would have my vote.

"It is a welcome compromise," Mayor Sewell announced, speaking up for the first time that evening.

A look passed between Myles and the Mayor, a bare nod of understanding. Somewhere along the line, Sewell must have paid Myles a visit, arranging the deal. I found Joanna in the audience, frozen in her seat, and her eyes flicked to mine. I shook my head, the smallest fraction of movement I could spare, willing her my thoughts.

I didn't know.

Her focus went back to the other men and I did the same, wondering if I needed to start preparing my defense for our next argument.

"Three months without incident and—" Anders began rattling off terms.

"This is Canderfey, President Anders, there will always be incidents," I said, rushing over him and drawing a chuckle from the crowd.

Hildy cleared her throat at my side, chin lifting and voice ringing out in a smooth, calming tone. "Mr. Kershaw's position should not be solely devoted to prevention, but to addressing any issues and working to help the community integrate. This project was designed to build a relationship and provide safety."

Anders leaned in my direction, a stubborn refusal ready on his lips when Sewell picked up the train of thought.

"I agree with Professor King and Ms. Samanta. This is a co-operative effort, not a policing system." It was Sewell's announcement, and not all of the arguing, which stirred the crowd into agitated whispers.

I thought I could feel Joanna's sigh echoing in my chest. I relaxed slightly in my seat, listening with a close ear on the rest of the proceedings, but not wanting to butt in at every opportunity. I was Myles' advocate, not his puppeteer. And he did his own work at charming the townspeople well enough, with his boisterous voice and crooked grin, a deferential nod to the Mayor and the council as the meeting adjourned.

"You are responsible for explaining that to your niece," I said in Myles' ear as we moved to the stage stairs. "I want my name cleared."

His smile was rueful as I helped him down to the ground floor where a bustle of Vermenians met us. Joanna was on the edge of the group, rising up to her toes to see over their heads, and I pointed her in the direction of a door out to the back hall.

She caught me by the sleeve as I followed her in, a door swinging shut behind us and the roar of the hall muting with the latch.

"When would that have happened?" she asked, running her fingers through her curls and then tugging on the strands. That was Callum's gesture. Were they so close now they were becoming the same person?

"I have no idea, I thought Myles and I were on the same page," I said.

Joanna drew us back to the side of the hall, but it was quiet and empty, and I heard her head thunk against the wall. Her hand yanked free of her tangles and then fisted in the front of my jacket and drew me closer until I was shielding her, my arms framed around her shoulders.

"If Sewell planned this ahead of time, we may never have reached a decision without that compromise," I considered, as Joanna's exhausted stare landed on the faint stubble on my chin.

"We might have, but he wouldn't have spoken up for it," Joanna agreed, one shoulder shrugging and bumping against my wrist. "I am more concerned… I don't think Myles really trusts me."

She tugged me a little closer, bringing my body in to press hers to the wall. *She likes this*, I thought. She wasn't even thinking about sex, I could see that much from the worry lines on her forehead, she just found comfort in having me so close. It settled a ragged nerve in my chest and I bent my head to rest it atop hers.

"If Myles' goal is to be the best possible representative for his people, it may be that *they* are who he is listening to first and foremost," I said, moving my hands closer to her head, spinning a curl around my finger without her noticing.

Joanna hummed at that, eyelashes against her cheeks. "That's a very wise and neutral thing to say." I started to pull away, not sure whether or not that was a compliment from her, but her arms twined around my back and held me there with surprising strength. "I mean, I think you're right. And Myles is right. Sorry."

Her head tilted back, face lifting up and stroking against mine until she found my lips, drawing them into a slow, delicate kiss.

"I have to earn my way into that community," she said, sliding down to her feet again. "I'm adjusting my thinking."

As she rose up to her toes again I hid my smile in another kiss, not wanting her to think I was being smug. I had been fighting Joanna's expectations for over a month now and it was a relief to hear that she was caving under the pressure of them too.

"You have their interests at heart. That will do the work for you, it just takes time," I said.

She was curving into me, an unconscious relaxed motion, but I slipped my hands down across her back and to her waist to keep her close. The hall was empty and I was greedy for her attention.

"All of this is going to get in the way of your plans to take us away for the summer," she said, rubbing her cheek against mine, not seeming to mind the scratch of my stubble.

"There will be other summers," I assured her, pressing my lips to her jawline and smiling at the sound of her sigh in my ear. "Lots of them."

"We should go find the others," she said, but I was familiar with the little tremble at the back of her voice and she wasn't moving out of my arms.

"Let me have a selfish moment first, now that my civic duty is done for the day."

Joanna was pressing her mouth to mine before I'd finished the words, a soft whimper vibrating on her tongue as she swiped it across my bottom lip. I hummed at the back of my throat to set a charm around us to alert me before our privacy was broken. When she took my lip between her teeth I hummed in earnest.

The kiss was made out of contrasts, needy nibbles and lazy draws on each other's mouths. Joanna's hands found their way under my jacket, nails digging into the fabric grain of my vest, tugging at the tie as she arched in my hold. I bent over her, felt her grin against my mouth, and sucked her searching tongue until her breath caught in her throat.

"Aiden," she whispered, panting for breath.

That was all it took, my heart fisted in my chest as if her hand was wrapped around its rapid beating. Whatever she said next would be taken as solemn orders, binding me to follow the words.

"Don't stop," she breathed.

Her toes left the floor as I lifted her and her giggle was swallowed in the kiss, tongues teasing and stroking each other as her arms wiggled free and wrapped around my neck. It was bad enough that we were acting like horny students, hiding in a hall and all but waiting to be caught. Worse, I wasn't sure if I would even feel embarrassed if Anders walked in and found us like this. Joanna would though, so I pulled away, pressing my mouth over her pulse and humming a second note, warning bells before the door opened.

Joanna released a soft trembling cry, hands cupping the back of my head as I sucked at the spot, marking my place for later. The wall scraped my knuckles as I pinned Joanna against it, her knees rising to bracket my hips. She was wearing one of Hildy's voluminous skirts she liked so much, and there was only the faintest feeling of her body cradling me, my cock twitching, craving more of her.

"I'd find a dark corner and have you right here," I said against her skin, feeling her blood pounding against my lips.

Her hips pressed forward, hard against me, and she moaned. "Tenured professor, caught with his pants around his ankles?" she teased.

"Promising library clerk, debauched before dinner," I answered.

She wiggled in my arms and then leaned away, laughing as I followed her. "Callum is coming," she said.

I blinked, drawing back from her throat, and finding her cheeks flushed and her eyes dark and happy, studying my face.

"How can you tell?" I asked. My wards hadn't noticed anything yet.

She hummed, focus going distant, and then shrugged and smiled at me. "I think it's my words on his back. It's a bit like… catching sight of yourself in a mirror you pass? Just the double-take of knowing something familiar."

There was a strange flavor on my tongue and then, sure enough, the bells of my ward rang and Callum's head appeared in a crack in the door. He smiled at the sight of us, and then slid into the hall, Isaac close on his heels.

"There you are," Callum said. "Everyone has more or less left out the front. Irene and some of the others have already taken Myles, Joanna. I think he's concerned he upset you both with the…"

"Compromise?" I suggested, eyebrows raised.

"I'll leave him a message in the notebook," Joanna said, and there was a twinge to the words. Myles *had* upset her by not sharing the plan with us. But that would be between them. I had done my part and was willing to be satisfied with the result.

"Did you want us to leave you to it?" Isaac asked, raising an eyebrow at me.

I still had Joanna crowded against the wall. My coat was askew and Joanna's lips and neck were marked red from the shadow of my beard. I looked down between us and realized the hem of her skirt was tangled up around my belt too, and I flicked it back to her knees before she noticed.

Joanna raised her chin, not realizing it gave them a perfect view of the mark I'd left on her neck.

"Maybe I was looking forward to sex in a hallway," she said and I choked on air. "It's been ages since someone ravished me in a horse cart or a train compartment."

"She's right," Isaac said, grinning and pulling Joanna out from between the wall and me, to take her arm, head ducking to drop a kiss on the growing bruise. "We've become boring old men. How are we expected to keep our young lover entertained?"

Callum's eyebrows raised. "Did the three of you have sex on a train without me? Oh... of course you did. That doesn't seem fair."

"We can always take another trip," I offered, draping my arm over Callum's shoulder, the pair of us admiring Joanna's mussed hair as she walked ahead with Isaac to the exit.

I ignored the bitter squeeze in my chest. It hadn't been that long since I'd had an evening alone with Joanna. This was what I'd always wanted, my completed coven, whole and happy.

"I say we don't take her to the bed tonight until she begs for rest," Callum said, and then he leaned into my side and kissed my jaw, sniffing at my skin until Isaac opened the door and the cool night air came shivering to us down the hall.

I shoved away the itching, creeping worries at the back of my mind about whether or not our love for each other was balanced—it was, wasn't it?—and vowed to enjoy the evening wherever it ended. Hopefully the bed.

5

———

JOANNA

"Erm…" I bit my lip and glanced across the borrowed classroom to where Tatsuo and Hildy were chatting with one of the Scribes, and then back down to the little girl in front of me. Bekka. Adorable with the world's largest blue eyes that were currently staring at me as if I were an idiot. The top of her head barely reached my waist and she was also chewing her own lip, staring over at her mother and then back at me. My uncle was settling Daniel into a seat, although the other man looked a little wild-eyed and uneasy surrounded by the rest of the Scrivens. Callum sat at his desk and shrugged when I glanced at him for help.

I wondered if I could write myself fluent at Vermenian. Except Tatsuo Ito had made the language his new hobby and was excelling at it without the help of magic.

Bekka whispered her question to me again, as incomprehensible in her child's lisp as the first time. Or maybe it wasn't a question at all, but something along the lines of "Why did you drag us all to this drafty room today, you fool?"

Why *had* I brought them all here? Before they'd arrived in Cander-fey, I'd been fantasizing up a scenario where we all learned our magic together, feeding off each others' experiences, learning the bounds of

537

our abilities together. That seemed naive now. Even my uncle wanted to keep secrets from me. How could I communicate to them that I was trustworthy, that they and their magic were safe here with me, when I couldn't even speak their language?

An idea struck me, a solution to the language barrier and a demonstration of… not power exactly, but of how we might use it together. I glanced at the chalkboard mounted on the wall to my left. Perfect, we could erase what we wrote there with no harm done.

I walked over and Bekka jogged by my side to follow me. I picked up the chalk from the ledge of the board and the room fell quiet as I began to write.

Words written by Scrivens are… I squinted at the board, trying to ignore the echoing quiet behind me as I searched for the right word… *understood by Scrivens regardless of language.*

I turned back to the room and then looked down at Bekka. Oh dear, was she old enough to write? I held the chalk out to her and she stared at it with enormous eyes. Farther back in the room, her mother said something.

Bekka took the chalk from my fingers and then stepped up to the board and wrote out her question in Vermenian, the words shifting in my head.

Where is the toilet?

The room laughed and I blushed, covering my eyes for a moment with the back of my hand. When I peeked, Bekka was grinning at me.

"Come on, camma, Bekka," Hildy said, hurrying over to the girl. "I'll show you."

Callum pushed out of his desk chair and walked over to the chalkboard, Daniel, Myles, and Nora coming to join him to stare at my words.

"Very tidy, leina," Myles said.

Daniel ran his finger through Bekka's question and then wiped it away entirely. I didn't think a simple question like that could carry much magic, but I suppose caution wouldn't hurt. It got them this far.

"Why not spoken?" Nora asked me. She was somewhere between Myles and my grandmother's age, with thick hair the color of steel twisted at the back of her head. She was sharing a row house on campus with Daniel and an elderly couple—Ella and Kristin, both Scrivens. I suspected she was in charge of keeping the three other Scrivens in line, or at least fed and taken care of in their new environments. Ella and Kristin were knitting quietly in the corner by a window, not seeming like they could be much trouble to anyone.

"I thought it might...feel heavy?" I hesitated, thinking over the words. "It would be more physically manipulative."

"Joanna and I have experimented some since leaving Vermenia," Callum said, his fingertips landing gently on my back, touching the same spot that I had tattooed on his. "It taxes her to control others, and there's a pressure for them."

"You control others?"

It was Corina. She'd been sitting at the front of the classroom, ignoring the rest of her peers, and Callum and I too for good measure. But now she was propped up on the front of her desk, staring at me with a keen and hungry focus.

"Not without their permission."

It was a lie. I had controlled the mercenaries in the Vermenian mines, had used my magic like a weapon when I needed to, but Corina didn't need to know that. I wasn't sure she should know. Not of that look on her face was an indication of her likelihood of manipulating others.

"I've been recording Joanna's magic," Callum said, to Nora and Myles. "Mostly for academic reasons. We know so little about how it works, the limitations, boundaries of time or space."

"What did you do to them?" Corina asked me, her voice somehow prettier for its careful approach around the words. When I spoke Vermenian I only sounded plodding and simple.

Nora glared at the other girl and Myles swatted the air in her direction to hush her. Callum glanced at me, a little furrow in his brow, and his fingers stroked softly along my spine.

"I asked her to change my hair color, and then to restore it without erasing the words," Callum said to her.

Corina ignored him and I was both relieved not to have her

mooning after another of my coven, and a little offended on Callum's behalf. He was just as lovely as Isaac, although he stubbornly resisted all of Aiden's attempts to groom him.

"What did they feel?" Corina asked me, and I suspected she was not referring to Callum or our experiments at all.

Callum sent a tendril of calm and love through our bond and it snagged inside of me, catching on tangles of anger, nerves, and a prickly dislike. My chest was tight and with a second nudge from Callum, I remembered to breathe, turning my back to Corina.

"I felt a bit of an itch," Callum replied, answering Corina for me again.

The hair change hadn't been so bad and I'd successfully written his own color back after a few miss-tries. The other experiments—ones to limit Callum's ability to move, to see, to taste, or speak—took tolls on both of us. Without the adrenaline of a fight coursing through me, I carried the weight of what I'd stolen from him like physical aches in my bones.

"Most of us know less than you do," Nora said to Callum. It was difficult to read the woman. She reminded me a little of Gwen, but even my boss and friend shared hints of expression, amusement and annoyance and worry. Nora was as well guarded in her manner as a fortress. "Hiding doesn't make room for experiments," she added.

"Of course, but if we could all share," Callum said, gesturing to the room. "The result of a childhood accident is as valuable as an intentional test in learning your capabilities."

"Maybe in time," Myles cut both Callum and Nora off before they could continue. "We don't want to cause problems."

"It wouldn't be a problem, Myles. You're safe here and you should be allowed to understand your own magic, finally," I said. It wasn't our first time discussing this same argument. It wouldn't be our last, I was sure.

Nora gave nothing away but my uncle beamed at me, that joyful crooked grin, and loped across the tile to press a kiss to the top of my head.

"Thank you, leina."

There was a scratch, and as a group we all turned to find Daniel at the board, chalk in hand. Nora made to stop him and Callum caught her by the arm just long enough to pause her.

"Let him, please," Callum urged. "The room is warded and there's enough of us to solve any problem, I'm sure."

I watched Daniel, the whole room watched him, even Corina. He seemed to stare at the blackboard, chalk poised in his hand as if waiting for the words to appear on their own, one white line marking the beginning.

Myles murmured something to the other man, quiet and gentle, and then Daniel scribbled in a rush. The magic took before my own spell had corrected the language in my head.

The board I write on is green. And it was—a slightly obnoxious, grassy green. Daniel frowned and stepped back, dropping the chalk back on the ledge.

"I haven't sorted out yet why it works this way. Why one shade of green over another, if there's anything to do with subconscious intent on the part of the writer," Callum said, immediately thrilled at the opportunity to discuss the mechanics of the magic, while the rest of the room seemed to be holding its breath, waiting for a consequence.

Daniel wiped his hand across the words and the board faded back to the original dusty black. He grimaced and slapped his palms together, chalk dust puffing into the air. I joined Daniel at the board, retrieving the chalk.

"Specifics help," I told him, as his eyes watched my fingers holding the chalk as if it were a dangerous blade instead of something I could easily crumble in my fist.

Hildy and Bekka returned to the classroom, hand in hand with Isaac in tow, Bekka's little hand wrapped around his fingers, his eyes wide and nervous.

He spotted me, crossing the floor to kiss my cheek in greeting. "Hello love," he said, silvery eyes bright on my face with his wobbling smile. I took inspiration and wrote on the board.

This chalkboard is the color of Isaac Metclaffe's eyes. The effect was immediate and fascinating, catching the room's attention as the board became transformed to spears of grays, pale blues, and the faintest brassy neutrals, like all the threads and textures of color, spread out in large scale.

Isaac blinked at the magic, his smile growing wide and delighted. "Well… do you think I could borrow you for a class demonstration?"

"I can, Professor Metclaffe," Corina said.

My teeth clenched as she appeared at our backs. Isaac's eyes crinkled, a private smile for me, and he glanced back at the younger girl.

"That's alright, I have a Scrivens at home with me," he said, in his gentle way. Callum caught my eye, lips twitching, and I unwound a little. We would tease Isaac together this time. At home, well out of Corina's reach.

She acted as if she hadn't heard him, walking with swaying steps up to the chalkboard, her skirt swishing around her ankles. She picked up a piece of chalk from the ledge and behind me, Nora and Myles barked in Vermenian. I didn't know the words but I understood the meaning. Corina was not allowed to write.

"It's almost five, love," Isaac whispered, his back to the girl and his eyebrows raising. Time for me to be back at the library.

"Go on," Callum said to me. "I'll stay here with them. See if we can practice a few phrases. I'll erase everything before we leave."

"I'll walk with you," Nora said, passing us and snatching the chalk from Corina's fingers. The girl spun and pressed her back to the board behind her, chin raised and turned away in a coquette's sulk.

I made my goodbyes to the group and left hand in hand with Isaac, feeling Corina's stare against my spine like a mean pinch from a temperamental child.

"What can you tell me about Corina?" I asked Nora when we were out of earshot of the classroom. Isaac's arm wrapped around my waist as we walked, wide hand spreading over my side.

"She's the daughter of—" Nora chewed over the right word and settled on, "a man in charge."

"Politician?" I asked and she nodded. "Her family didn't come with her."

Nora snorted. "No. Shipped her off. Now she's our problem."

Isaac and I frowned at that as we reached the door to the outside.

"Don't worry, Miss Wick," Nora said, shoulders squaring. "She'll behave. It's Daniel I wanted to speak with you about."

"Oh! Of course," I said, although my thoughts were still skidding around Corina. Had her father sent her to Vermenia for her sake or his own? I supposed it was just as easily a combination of the two.

"He wrote in the Red War," Nora said.

My steps stumbled down the front stairs. "He *wrote?*"

Nora nodded. "For Vermenia. He volunteered."

"But then—" How had he escaped working for them later? And… why hadn't Vermenia won the war with Scrivens working for the cause?

"Our words *do* have limits," Nora said, her voice lowering even though there was no one close enough to listen. "And there is magic that can guard against it. Your Toy Soldier proved that during the war."

Callum. Callum and his faultless wards and defense magic. Isaac and I shared a wide-eyed glance. Callum had no idea, and who could guess how he might feel at hearing the news. We would have to tread carefully in sharing.

"Daniel wrote many terrible things that came true, and many more that did not. In the end, he was let go for too many failures. They suspected he was lying about being Scrivens to get out of serving on the field," Nora said.

"How did they explain when his magic worked?" Isaac asked.

Nora shrugged. "Chance. However they wanted to explain it." She stopped on the sidewalk in front of the library and overhead the bells started to chime the hour. "Vermenia doesn't know much about Scrivens magic either. And what we know, we keep secret for one another."

"I only want to help," I told her.

"I know," she answered, assessing me from head to toe. "And you might. I'll get back to the others."

I sighed as she left. "I know it's going to take time," I started.

"They *will* learn to love you," Isaac said, turning me by my waist to face him. I was going to risk being late with Gwen if I stayed much longer, but I craved Isaac's comfort. His hands reached up and cupped my face, bending down to feather kisses on my lips. "Just like we do."

"I can take or leave Corina," I muttered against his mouth and opened my eyes as he grinned.

"Don't forget to eat on your break," Isaac said, reaching into the air and retrieving a small bag he'd packed for me. "Don't just read. I'll be back to walk you home."

"Oh, am I getting a chaperone again?" I asked, my voice tart. "I thought we were past that."

"Maybe I just like walking with you in the evening," Isaac said, words as soft and seductive as his stare on my face.

I blushed and took the bag, and he squeezed my hand in parting as I ran to the library.

THE CLOCK HAD long since signaled midnight—my ears deaf to the sounds while my nose was in a book—when Bryce found me in the stacks, standing on a ladder and propped up against a shelf, lost in reading a book I'd meant to shelve an hour before.

"Time to go home," they said, gold-green eyes bright like lamplight in the shadowy rows of bookshelves.

"Isaac's on his way," I said, not really paying attention to them. "He'll take me back when my shift ends."

"Your shift has ended." Bryce pulled a little round watch out of a pocket, a glimmering silver trinket inlaid with pearls and rubies. They did love their glitter.

I blinked at the time as Bryce pushed the watch up to my nose, not reading the hands properly in my stupor. "Oh. Oh, alright." I shelved the text and winced as my hips twinged after standing awkwardly for too long.

"I'll walk you," Bryce said, a small hand reaching up to help me.

My legs felt stiff as I descended the ladder. "Did Isaac send you?" It wasn't like Isaac to not appear without a word. Callum maybe, if he was lost in his own book. I pulled my notebook I shared with my coven out of my pocket but didn't see any new messages inside.

"I was here reading," Bryce said, with a faint roll of their eyes. And then they added, "Smelled you."

"What a lovely thought," I answered, glaring, and they grinned.

There were only students and the night clerks left in the library. It was nearing finals week, so there were more students than usual and twice as much quiet tension. We passed a table and there was a zinging electric shock in the air near them.

"Energy spell," Bryce whispered to me.

"Is it safe?" I asked them.

"Not for the books," they said.

I stepped over to the table and one of the students, a young boy with a round face and red hair that stuck straight out of his head, wiped the charm out of the air at my approach.

"That's all well and good in the dorms, with the textbooks you've purchased outright," I scolded, "but keep it out of the library."

The students slunk down in their seats, books covering their faces and one of them whispered, "yes, ma'am" from behind the pages. Maybe my impression of Gwen was improving.

"My magic feels different than most, right?" I asked Bryce as I caught up with them by the doors.

"Tastes like the air before a storm." Bryce held the door open for me. "Change."

I smiled at that comparison. "And the other Scrivens. Does it feel the same or are we each different?"

Bryce shrugged as we started our walk home. "Haven't tasted them yet."

"I'd like you to be there next time, no one understands magic quite like you," I said.

Bryce's eyes slid sideways at me. "You can't flatter me into obedience. I hate to be useful."

"In exchange for your help," I continued as if they hadn't spoken, "I will allow you to terrorize one of them."

Bryce's laughter was a skittering scratchy sound, but it made me smile all the same. "Did you have one in mind?" Bryce asked.

I thought of Corina's pert nose lifting into the air as her wide eyes ate up the view of Isaac. "Maybe," I said.

Bryce giggled again, hands knotting behind their back and steps bouncing along the sidewalk. "I'll consider it," they said.

It must have been near one in the morning, and the street was dark and shadowy, whispers of activity appearing from bushes and the woods not far away. But with Bryce Gast at my side, it was impossible to feel any nervousness. There was nothing that hid in the dark that Bryce would not gladly take a bite out of, if I had to guess. So we walked in companionable quiet, and even if it wasn't a lazy stroll with Isaac's warmth, it was pleasant.

"Would you know how to block my magic, if you needed to?" I asked as we turned onto our street.

"Block it, borrow it, steal it," Bryce rattled off as if they'd already thought of all the possibilities. "Quit daydreaming up work for me."

"I'm only curious. No practicing," I said firmly.

Up ahead, the light at the entrance of our house turned on and the door swung open, revealing Callum stepping out onto the steps before stopping at the sight of us.

"Thank you for saving him the trip," I said to Bryce as Callum waited for me on the steps.

Bryce skipped off the sidewalk and across the narrow street to their house, with a wave and a glowing glance. Callum met me at the bottom of the steps as I hurried the rest of the way home.

"I thought Isaac was coming to get you," Callum said, street lamps reflecting orange off his glasses as I ran up the path to him. His arm snaked around my shoulders as soon as I was close enough, guiding me to his chest.

"I thought so too, is he alright?" I asked, kissing the hollow of his throat.

Callum frowned and looked up at the house. "I think he was drawing after dinner in his studio. He must have lost track of time.

Get inside, it's late and Aiden's snoring on the couch, pretending he can stay awake long enough to see you get home."

Aiden must have woken up when we shut the door behind us, because he was rubbing a pillow mark off his cheek as I walked into the living room, his legs stretching out in front of him.

"There you are, darling," he said with sleep still clinging in his throat. "Did you eat or just read?"

My chest went soft and warm at the sight of him trying to blink away the grogginess from his nap, and the feeling traveled through my blood as I closed the distance between us. I bent to where he was sitting on the couch and rested my forehead against his cheek before pulling away just far enough to kiss him.

"I remembered to eat," I answered, kissing the corner of his mouth. His fingers slipped through my hair where it hung over my shoulder and I took his hand, tugging lightly. "Come on. Let's get some sleep."

Callum was already on the stairs when we made it out of the living room. "Someone should check on Isaac," he said.

"I'll do it, see if I can lure him out of his work," I offered.

Isaac tended to be an early riser, and he usually preferred to work in daylight, so it was unusual for him to be holed up in his studio late at night. But he had charms to mimic sunlight if he needed them, and I suppose if inspiration was striking hard, he would follow. Aiden and Callum continued up to the top floor as I trailed down the hall of the second to Isaac's room at the back of the house with the southern exposure windows.

He was working by candlelight, creating a romantic picture with his dark hair falling loose from its tie, his focus pinned to an enormous sketchbook propped up on his desk. I peered through the crack in the door, admiring and wondering if I should leave him to it, when he huffed, digging fingers through his hair and leaning away from the sketch.

The sweet tip of the nose was familiar, as was the delicate chin rising high above the swan-like neck. Cascading over the page was pale hair painted in watercolors, shades of gold and blonde and moonlight.

That burning pinch was back, this time in my heart, and I tried to laugh myself out of the feeling. Corina *was* beautiful and Isaac had an artist's eye. We had laughed over her behavior just hours ago and he didn't need me feeling jealous when his love for me was so openly displayed at every moment. But there was a reverence in the sketch and a turn in her cheek that had transformed that bratty expression into something almost queenly.

I turned away and retreated down the hall without a word. Inspiring his work didn't have to mean serious admiration. And Isaac must have had hundreds of equally appreciative sketches of me by now—*more* appreciative. Surely he was due a new subject.

"Is he coming along?" Aiden mumbled, already tucked under the sheets, a spot saved for me between him and Callum, who was reading a book by an illumination charm on his glasses.

"I decided not to interrupt him," I said, and wished I hadn't spoken. There was a hollow sound in my voice, something near to breaking.

Callum slid his glasses down his nose and peered across the room at me, so I turned my back to them and undressed in the dark.

"Don't leave that on the floor," Aiden mumbled into his pillow as I stepped out of my skirt.

I smiled at the reminder, the expression wobbling a little. No, I refused to be stressed over one silly little drawing. Not that I would call it that to Isaac's face. I tidied my clothes away and crawled into the bed, Callum drawing the sheets over me as Aiden pulled me against his stomach, arms wrapping me up in his hold. Two of the cats came bounding from nowhere onto the bed to curl up over our feet.

"He'll come up as soon as he hears the house is quiet," Callum said to me, eyes back on his book.

I hummed in feigned agreement and closed my eyes, letting Aiden's warmth consume me. I lay awake as Callum shut the book and clicked his glasses closed, setting them on the bedside table and then sliding closer to me in the dark. And when the house was entirely silent and entirely dark, I remained awake and waiting, with no sign of Isaac coming to our bed.

6

AIDEN

Joanna was balled up on the mattress when I woke, frowning behind her fists as she slept. There was no sign of Isaac. I slid out from under the covers and Joanna squirmed into the warm space I left behind, Callum rolling after her until he had her unfolded and held against his chest, some of the trouble washing off her face.

That same strange jealousy and affection warred in me and I put it to the back of my mind, pulling a sweater over my head and going on a hunt for our fourth. The cats we had adopted, against my better judgment, followed on my heels and over my toes, tumbling down the stairs ahead of me in a furry mess of gangly limbs and tails and hungry chatter. Isaac was in the kitchen, dark circles under his eyes and wrinkled clothes, drinking coffee.

"You had Joanna a bit worried last night," I said, joining him at the counter. He hadn't brought the other cups down yet so I reached past him to the cupboard. "You alright?"

"Just tired," Isaac rasped, eyes on the counter as I clanked mugs together, grabbing one for Joanna and Callum each. He was usually in charge of making sure we all woke up to coffee, but if his head was elsewhere, I could make it my job for the day.

549

"I'm glad you've got a new project," I said. "Inspiration hit hard, I see."

"It's not a project," he said, the words harsh out of his throat, and he pushed his cup away with trembling fingers. "Just sketches."

I snorted. As if simple sketches kept *Isaac* from his bed all night. Art was his sanctuary, not the beast riding his back to exhaustion. "Alright," I said. "Keep your secrets."

Isaac finally looked up, lines of anguish written over his face for a half-beat, and then his fist wrapped around my collar, pulling me across the counter. His teeth grasped at my bottom lip, tugging with rough force before his tongue was claiming me, a rare strain and hunger in the kiss. My eyes were open on his face, struck with surprise, and his were slammed closed. I reached out, soothing my palms up his shoulders to caress his neck, trying to soften some of his stress out of the touch, but he tore away with a growl.

"I love you," he said, words fierce and almost angry.

"I know that, you fool," I teased, catching my breath and raising my eyebrows.

"All of you," he added, forehead creasing in worry, eyes glancing up at the ceiling

"Isaac, what on earth—"

"I have to get to the classroom," he ground out, face turning down to the floor as he all but ran out of the kitchen.

"Whatever's going on—" I started, watching his shoulders rise high and his back tense as he grabbed his coat out of the front closet, the door shutting with a slam and the sound of Callum's stash of oddities unbalancing from inside.

"Isaac?" Joanna called from the stairs.

"I'll be back at dinner," he said, and then he left the house.

Joanna's feet slapped down the steps until she was swaying in the hall, her nightdress floating after her. At the sight of her slumped shoulders, I had the urge to run out after Isaac and drag him back into the house, force him to make up for his coldness, or at least offer an explanation.

"Come here, darling," I called.

I thought at first she might ignore me, her face turning between the door and the stairs, but then she spun and ran down the hall, meeting me at the counter.

"Oof!"

She knocked the air from my chest as she pressed against me, face burrowing into my sweater as I wrapped my arms around her shoulders. I hushed into her hair, but she wasn't weeping or whimpering, simply clinging as tightly to me as I suspected she wanted to cling to Isaac.

"We'll sort it out with him this evening," I said to her, and when she stayed stiff in my arms I added, "This is Isaac, remember? He probably won't make it through the day without breaking down and letting us in on whatever's bothering him."

"Does Isaac fall in love easily?" Joanna whispered into my chest.

I froze at the question. Fall in love? What on earth did the girl think Isaac was up to?

"Infatuations, I suppose, when we were younger," I admitted, choosing my words carefully. Isaac had been more open-hearted than Callum or even I, while we were waiting to find Joanna. Maybe he had fallen in love with the women, but he'd fallen out just as easily and I wasn't sure that counted for much. "Nothing that stuck after it was clear they weren't the one for all of us."

I stroked up Joanna's back, lifting her curls off her neck and bundling them into my fingers until her chin finally tilted up to meet my gaze. She hadn't slept and her lip was quivering, eyes blinking too fast. I was going to give Isaac hell for this if he didn't deal with it straight away.

"If he fell in love it was not *deeply*, as he is with us," I promised her.

She still looked drawn and tired, but she offered me a smile and rose up on her toes to meet my lips.

"Tell me what's wrong," I said before she could catch me.

"No, you're right," she said, pressing her mouth sweetly against mine in a series of light kisses. "We'll talk to him this evening."

I swept a thumb over her cheekbone, just below the dark shadow beneath her eyes. "I don't like your late nights at the library. Especially not when you have to be back first thing the next day."

"I know," she said, with a flicker of a grin. "But you'll have me back this afternoon and all day tomorrow."

I hummed in agreement. Callum had convinced her *not* to schedule another meeting with the Scrivens for the weekend. Our coven would have a Saturday alone together for the first time in weeks. Callum and I had been working on classwork late last night just to avoid it for the next few days. That furthered my resolve to settle whatever was plaguing Isaac this evening so it didn't carry over into our day off.

"Speaking of, I need to dress," Joanna said, peeking over my shoulder at the coffee mugs, sitting empty on the counter.

"Go on, I'll have it ready for you," I said.

She pecked my mouth again before darting back to the hall. "Thank you, Aide. Love you!"

I smiled and then whistled at the kettle. Flames kicked on the stove, and soon the kettle was whistling back, the morning looking brighter with the first drop of coffee against ceramic.

"Is it just me or are the students more rabid than usual this year?" I asked, after snapping the door to the faculty lounge shut.

Pablo Banaker looked up from his sheet music at my arrival. "There's a rumor going around that we're going to audition sophomores for the orchestra based on their exam performances," he explained.

I frowned. "That rumor goes around every year."

"And every year a new batch of sophs fall for it," Pablo said with a shrug. "Anders is on the prowl today. Do you know what that's about?"

"In classes?" I asked, crossing to the table by the window where Pablo was tweaking notes on the page.

"On campus," he said, nodding to the window.

I dropped my bag to the floor and leaned backward in the chair, scanning the campus grounds outside the window until I spotted him. Prowling was right. Anders was out, glamour failing and face flushed from the sunlight and exercise, pacing up and down the walkways. He studied every person that passed him on the path, eyes glaring and watching like he was searching for misbehavior.

"Was there an incident?" Pablo asked, glancing out the window.

"Not that I know of," I said. "How long has he been doing this?"

"At least an hour, but he's been making his way over to the Burgess building so I suspect the art students are next for inspection."

I grunted in acknowledgment. After the Burgess building, he would be near the little community of staff row houses where the Vermenians were housed. I exhaled a long sigh, sinking back into the chair, and then twisting it so I could watch him out of the corner of my eye.

"He doesn't come out of his high tower very often," I muttered, digging student work out of my bag to finish grading.

Pablo huffed a laugh. "Look at the students. I don't think they even recognize him," he said.

It was true, those on the sidewalk skirted around Anders as if he were some mad professor on the hunt for a tardy student. He had never put much time into interacting outside of the faculty and donor circles.

"Tell me what this looks like." Pablo slid the sheet music across the table to me.

I glanced down at the notes in measure and frowned. "Fowler's fifth movement, opus nine."

"Damnit," Pablo hissed, fingers wadding up the paper.

"Oh slow down! Not every bit of it!"

"No, it was a waste of an hour," Pablo growled. "I hate Fowler."

JOANNA'S FINGERNAIL was scraping up the corner of the book, drumming the pages in an interesting, fretful rhythm. As the front door clicked shut her nail stopped and her back straightened on the couch, but her eyes remained fixed out the window. There was a brief glimpse of Isaac marching down the hall to the stairs and I called out.

"Stop!"

His steps stalled on the floorboards and then creaked back to the front room where our coven had sat for hours, pretending to occupy ourselves while we waited for him.

"I'm sorry about dinner," he said, arriving in the doorway, looking twice as unkempt as he had leaving the house this morning. His clothes were wrinkled, stained with paint and charcoal, and his collar was crooked like he'd been tugging it off his throat all day. It was a nervous tick of his and one I hadn't seen in years.

"You know we can manage a meal for ourselves anytime you need a break," I said, trying to sound light while feeling my heart pound in my chest, thinking of Joanna's question this morning. Had Isaac fallen in love again? Too easily and with someone who wouldn't suit us?

Isaac nodded, reaching up to his hair with charcoal black fingers. "I'm going upstairs to work."

"Not yet," I said.

Callum, who was stretched out over the couch with his head in Joanna's lap, dropped his book face down onto his chest, twisting to see Isaac.

"Are you alright?" he asked, voice tinged with confusion.

Joanna must not have mentioned anything to him after all. There was a warm burn of pride that her distress from the morning had been shared with me alone for once. And then that feeling turned painful. I was just as guilty of jeopardizing our harmony with a thought like that.

"I'm fine," Isaac said, his eyes skittering above our heads.

I turned to look at Joanna and found her frozen, eyes watching out the window as if she was waiting for *our* Isaac to come home, rather than the edgy version we'd had all day. I heard the wood creak again and caught Isaac trying to sneak his way out of the conversation.

"No, come in here, Isaac," I said, firm enough to see his spine snap straight. I softened my tone and added, "Whatever this is, work, or old worries or new, just share with us. Now, here, while we're all together. We won't try and force a resolution, but you're not yourself and we deserve some kind of explanation. Something."

Isaac was in profile, jaw ticking, throat flexing, and hair knotted and I thought that if I were him, I would want to paint the moment, however horribly it made my chest squeeze, the weight of his silence like a boulder on top of me.

"I'm in love," he said to the far wall. Then he turned, every muscle in his expression falling as he spoke to us, finally meeting my eyes. "I'm in love."

The room was quiet as I stared back at him. It was as if the words, something so sweet, had been dropped into the room from a completely foreign source for how impossible they sounded. But Isaac's eyes were clear and gray, the same open terror as I had seen there when he said the same to me for the first time before I had wiped the worry away in a kiss.

"You're *what?*" Callum hissed, sitting up next to Joanna, body turning broad and protective as he leaned forward.

If he attacked, would I try to intervene?

"I love you," Isaac moaned, the silver in his gaze glittering tears. "Of course, I love you."

I glanced at the others, and Callum's brow was furrowing almost comically as he tried to sort the confession out. Joanna was as still as a doll in her seat, eyes distant, face blank, and there was a horrible rolling in my stomach. I hadn't seen her so far removed from us since the beginning when she refused to believe she was a part of our coven. It was worse now to see that expression returned, after thinking that we had banished it for good in the fall.

"But I've...fallen in love," Isaac whispered, some fragile joy breaking through the words.

I rose out of my chair. "Where have you been?" I growled, studying the rumple of his clothes for some clue I didn't want to see.

"No," he gasped out, stumbling forward toward us.

Callum rose too, blocking Isaac from Joanna's view, but she didn't so much as flinch.

"No," Isaac pressed the word to us, body bowing forward, black fingertips reaching. "I would never- You know I would never. I've just… I don't know what to do. I would never break your trust."

Callum was trembling with tension, and my fists ached for how tight I clenched them, my stomach churning as I fought for breaths.

"You don't understand," Isaac said, tears welling up in his eyes. "It isn't sordid. She- she- You would love her too, I think, if you just considered—"

I was going to punch him, my arm twitched with the need.

"Who?"

My breath caught as Joanna spoke and I twisted to look at her. Isaac rushed forward and Callum's palm landed heavily on his chest, stopping him from reaching her.

"I…she's…I," Isaac choked on air, his head shaking wildly before he swallowed hard. "I can't say."

Joanna's blank openness sharpened, her face lifting slowly to study him with slitted eyes, a cold examination in her expression I had only seen once before, while she sliced words at Callum's father Duncan like a dagger.

"Is it Corina?" she asked, her teeth and tongue as careful as a knife around the words. Isaac's face went white and Joanna surged up from the cushion, steps hard and precise against the floor. "Can you say her name?" she asked with quiet care that made me think of a predator.

Isaac swallowed again, jaw working, and all he released was a whispered, "Joanna."

She rushed past the three of us, marching away from the scene.

"Jo, where are you going?" Callum called, grabbing Isaac's shoulder to stop him from chasing after her.

"She's written this," Joanna called with scathing precision, shuffling in the hall, the sound of her boots knocking against the floor.

"No!" Isaac shouted, tearing out of Callum's hand. "You don't understand. It isn't like that. I know you would love her. You must because I—"

Callum muttered quickly, fingers glowing in the air and then Isaac heaved, as if he were about to be sick, and fell silent.

"What did you do?" I asked Callum.

"Spelled him silent, the idiot," he growled, "before he said something he'd regret. Joanna wait, I'm coming with you."

"You're all coming with me!" she snapped from the hall, appearing in the doorway with high color in her cheeks, her hair curling out of her braid as if it was possessed by her anger.

"Where are we going?" I was feeling a bit old and slow suddenly. Isaac had fallen so deeply in love... all from words. *Scrivens magic*. My head ached with the weight of understanding.

"We're going to find the words and I'm going to burn them out of existence," Joanna said. She blinked, lips pressing together until they were white, and then she spat out, "I haven't decided what to do about *her* yet."

Isaac thrashed, pushing at Callum's chest, but the other man only pushed back, face tangled in anger and annoyance. Their bodies wrestled and Callum's expression turned fierce and cold. It wasn't just Isaac who was capable of going too far tonight, if we weren't careful, we all would.

"Enough!" I barked at them. "You think she's wrong?"

With Callum's charm silencing him, Isaac's face was a rioting mix of emotions, angry lines, and then pleading collapse, turning to weary despair.

"We'll go to her, together," I said, and Isaac's chin lifted. "If Joanna is wrong then we'll... have to deal with... your feelings."

I was trying to project calm, perhaps only for myself, but instead my thoughts spun. I'd imagined fractures in our coven for weeks, seeing the way Joanna and Callum had become an indivisible unit, how they orbited each other without Isaac or I. I'd never imagined Isaac being the one to shatter our structure first. Where would it leave me?

The words. Let Joanna be right and it only be a scrap of paper somewhere with a girl's daydream scribbled. Let us destroy them, and then somehow find our way back to peace with one another.

7

JOANNA

Anger felt something like terror. Or maybe I really was trembling and shivering with fear, and not just vibrating with determined rage. Fear of losing Isaac, of having our love interrupted by magic. Of what that would do to the entire coven.

Callum caught up to me down the walk on my way toward town, his fingers glowing brassy and green as they traced around my shoulders. The color landed with a bright tickle on my skin, and under any other circumstance it might have been nice, but I was *raw*. My skin was already crawling.

"What are you doing?" I asked, my voice snapping out from behind my lips like a whip.

"Warding you," Callum said, continuing in his work.

I stopped dead on the path. "From what?"

Callum's heels skidded as he stopped before crashing into my back. He finished his warding, a familiar flickering rushing over my skin, warring with the sensation of bugs skittering in my heart.

"From harm," Callum answered, turning me to face him.

It was the very beginning of night, the sky behind him was still streaked with a dark coal red from the sunset, the temperature beautiful and crisp. It would have been a nice night for a walk out with my

559

lovers, if only this were so simple. Over Callum's shoulder, Aiden escorted Isaac after us, a hand around his arm and a strange stilted space between them as they walked. Isaac looked near tears again, shoulders sinking to the ground, but just seeing him and knowing that sorrow was for *her* made my eyes sting.

"I'm going to… to bind her up so tight she can't even *think* of words," I whispered.

Callum's hands cupped the back of my neck, thumbs tipping my face up to his. "I know you must be right, Joanna. You have to be. This isn't Isaac. This isn't our coven."

I shuddered and fell forward into Callum's chest. My thoughts were everywhere at once. The shredding, broken feeling of Isaac's announcement. The boiling rage at Corina's meddling, her manipulation of one of the men I loved. The private, petty worry that news of this would reach those in Canderfey who already feared what the Scrivens were capable of. And underneath everything, the dread that I wouldn't find the words. Wouldn't fix this. Would lose Isaac and then the others in the wake.

"How could she do this?" I groaned into Callum's shirt. "How could anyone do this to another person?"

"Unfortunately love spells are fairly common on campus," he said, his hands sliding to my shoulders, and pushing me back so he could meet my eyes again. "It's not even the first time someone's tried to spell Isaac."

There was a terrible tremor in my bottom lip and I bit it away, before straightening my back and turning away.

"It will all be well soon," Callum whispered. "And then we'll just have to care for Isaac. He won't like this."

"What if I can't find the words?" I asked. "What if she's hiding them somewhere?"

"We'll make her tell us where," Callum said, and nothing comforted me more in the moment than the dark tone his voice took on with the words. His hand clasped mine and I held on as tightly as I would have if he were keeping me from falling into a pit of my own worries.

"Take the charm off Isaac," I told him, listening to the steps that followed ours, Aiden's clapping shoes on the pavement and Isaac's shuffling drag. Callum glanced at me and I added, "He shouldn't have so much magic controlling him all at once. And not from us."

"He may end up saying something he regrets more. Or we regret hearing," Callum cautioned but I only stared back at him. "Alright."

He turned in step, his arm waving, a faded glitter washing off Isaac's mouth as he gasped, a garbled sound falling loose. Isaac tugged himself free of Aiden's grip and ran to me, my heart slamming wildly in my chest. I couldn't explain the urge I had to flinch away from him, to duck as if he might hit me. Isaac was the gentlest, sweetest, most loving person I knew. But I skidded out of his reach as he neared.

"Joanna," he said, my name a sound of exhaustion from his mouth. "Please. Don't do this. Don't be so…jealous."

"Careful," Callum growled, fingers stroking over my knuckles.

"Why can't you all trust my *feelings*?" Isaac shouted.

My eyes flickered around the street, but for the moment at least we seemed to be alone.

"Your feelings that started when? Last night? After you dropped me off at the library?" I asked, words rushing out as my steps quickened, my heart raced, my eyes stung and filled, blurring the street in front of me.

"It-it must have been… slower," Isaac whispered, and I could almost imagine the way she had written the magic, tangling love into a fictional past that he *felt* but couldn't actually remember.

I want to kill her.

I wanted to leave scratch marks over both her perfect doll pink cheeks, push her into a pit of mud she would never wash off, and tear every one of her pretty dresses to pieces. I wanted to break her little snub nose and her fingers too for good measure.

For putting Isaac through this fantasy of hers.

For putting *me* through it.

Bile was in my throat and when we reached the corner of the main part of town, I didn't know where I was or which way to turn, everything had flipped backward in my head.

"Which way?" Callum barked at Isaac.

"I don't know! I keep telling you, nothing happened."

I regretted asking Callum to take the charm off, the tear in his voice was too much for me, and I turned my back on Isaac as I swatted away the angry tears spilling over.

"She's with the Grivet family in an apartment, this way," Aiden murmured, a warmth at my back, and he brushed his hand against my side as if he knew more comfort than that would leave me crumpling to the ground. At this moment it was my anger holding me together.

Town was busier, with families out in restaurants and familiar faces from campus. I thought at any moment someone—one of Aiden's or Callum's colleagues—would stop us to chat. My hair was half undone and I'd run out of the house without a coat. I wondered again if it was a mistake to have taken the charm off Isaac. What if he told someone what we were doing, what had happened to him? Not that he believed me.

I had to put this right, but if we accidentally cost the Scrivens their safety, it would be just another mistake.

"Joanna," Isaac whispered, feet rushing to catch up with me as I stormed after Aiden.

"I can't. I can't right now." I pulled my arm out of his reach before he could even touch me.

"Please," he said, the word cracking to pieces, and I stopped so quickly it almost tipped us both over. "Joanna, I love you." My eyes rested on his throat, unable to rise any higher. "Look at me, please… Joanna, there's not a fraction difference in how I feel for you. Nothing changes that."

His hands were hovering at the edges of my vision, begging for permission to touch. I lifted my gaze with an actual struggle, finding it difficult to look at him in this moment. His eyes were red, lined with exhaustion and tears and strain, his skin gray and tired. Through all the pain there was a familiar focus, the way he watched every flicker of movement on my face, eyes scanning and memorizing, studying with reverence.

Whatever Corina had done, whatever she'd written, it hadn't corrupted the coven bond but had tried to worm its way inside.

"Have you seen her?" I asked.

"Not since you and I left the classroom," Isaac said. His eyes grew wide. "I don't know what to do, I would never jeopardize our *home*, but I…"

I reached up, stroking away a tear with the pad of my thumb, and his words trailed off. Oh, how I wanted to reduce Corina to ash for this trouble, not just her words.

"Let's go," I said, turning away when I realized there was no promise I could make. I would not love Corina for him, not ever, not after this. And I wasn't certain I could even promise not to hurt her, my hands itched to do exactly that. I only wanted to find her words and erase them from the world.

Aiden was stopped in front of a small door between two pubs, and Callum was undoing the lock with a spell.

"We'll knock at their door, but I'd rather not waste time waiting to see if they let us into the building," Callum told me, swinging the door in as I reached them. "If they aren't home, we'll search it anyway."

I swallowed. Was that too extreme? I couldn't judge in the moment, Corina's violation was too strong.

"Third floor, left door," Aiden said to me, and I ran up the stairs, skirts in hand, chalk in pocket.

Corina wouldn't be the only Scrivens inside, and while I knew she would likely put up a fight, I wasn't sure what the family wouldn't think of us barging in. Perhaps I should have gone to Myles first. This was his jurisdiction now. Or perhaps, if I'd been thinking straight, I'd have written my way to Corina's words, and saved the trip.

My fist was knocking on the door before I caught my breath from the journey up the stairs. I could hear the family murmuring inside, soft steps pausing on their way to the door.

"Who ess et?" a creaking voice called from inside.

"Joanna Wick."

I heard a scuffling sound against the wood of the door and then it swung inwards. A petite older woman smiled at me and nodded, stepping back to make room for me in the small apartment space.

It was one main room with a small wood-burning stove at the

heart, and a narrow table pressed to the left wall between two doors. On the right wall, four pallets were lined up together, where three younger women were sitting with bowls of steaming stew in their laps. I remembered them now, the mother and her three daughters, one of whom—Lora—was a Scrivens, all living with Corina.

"Joanna," Callum murmured and I turned. My covenmates had followed me inside and Callum was pointing to a smear of chalk on the door, words written and then erased over and over.

"They have no lock," I said, and my eyes started to fill up again, the anger of the night mixing together with my indignation for the women. I'd known the accommodations for the Scrivens and their families had been thin to find, but I hadn't imagined they'd been without locks on doors or beds to sleep in.

"I'll call Hildy," Aiden said. "We'll get that fixed."

The mother murmured and patted Callum's hand, waving her hands in the air as if to say it wasn't trouble to write the door shut. And truth be told, the words were probably better security than the door itself, which was rickety and thin and had a drafty gap at the bottom. But my coven could, and would, fix that problem too. Callum looked as if he were already mapping out the space and thinking up ways to make it more useful to the women.

My eyes drifted back to the two doors on the other side of the room. "Where is Corina?" I asked in Vermenian.

"In her room," one of the sisters said from the floor.

"She has a room to herself?" The words came out in the wrong language, my ire rising with the pitch of my voice, but the sisters smirked as if they knew exactly what I'd said.

"What a generous, lovely young woman," Callum muttered in Isaac's direction.

I couldn't look at them, I couldn't tear my eyes away from the door. That brat had shoved four women out of a bedroom that could have been shared. She'd stuck her nose up at me in my own work-place. And she'd tried to steal Isaac. I didn't doubt for a moment that if she'd been able to, she'd have unwritten our coven bond. I was relying on that bond in this moment, drawing Callum's strength and Aiden's patience—and I felt his tremulous fear in the line too, something I'd make up to him later when we were alone and Corina was no longer an issue.

"Have Bryce come too," I directed, thinking of my promise to the dragon. Maybe they would eat Corina.

I marched over to the door and stopped, nose to wood. It was locked. The magic didn't curtain over the doorway as it would have if it were one of Callum's wards, but was woven into every grain. It would open for Corina and only her. I moved down to the next door, leading to a modest little bathroom a small basin shower in the corner. There was a narrow strip of connecting wall with Corina's room before the sink counter, and I pulled my chalk free of my pocket, tracing a sloppy rectangle on the wall.

DOOR I wrote in block letters, and then the line was a seam. I knocked it open with my hip, finding satisfaction in Corina's resulting screech as I came barreling into her bedroom. She leapt up off her bed, a wide and accommodating piece of furniture that the mother in the next room could have easily shared with at least one of her daughters.

Corina was spitting at me in Vermenian, storming over to where I stood, but I spied the open notebook laying on her bed. There was a small pencil rolling off on page onto her mattress, the kind the library had sitting on tables for any forgetful student.

"You little witch," I growled. Her words died off on her tongue as she realized what I was staring at and with a quick glance at each other, we both ran to the bed.

Behind me, I could hear Callum and Isaac shout, but I was busy throwing my elbow in Corina's side as I lunged for the bed. The corners of the notebook pressed against my breasts as I landed, and on my back Corina began to claw and scream, her knees digging into my legs.

"Enough!" Callum shouted.

"Joanna! Corina, please!"

All at once, Corina was snatched off of me and, more gently, Isaac pulled me off the bed, my arms cradling the notebook to my chest. I stumbled back to the floor and turned, finding Callum holding a terrifying version of the girl in his arms as she kicked and writhed. He narrowly missed snatching his fingers out of reach of her teeth.

"Callum, let her go!" Isaac's hands steadied me with care as he yelled to our covenmate.

"Find the page, Joanna," Callum said, grunting as one of Corina's heels connected with his knee.

She was cursing in Vermenian, words I'd heard my uncle use when he was in pain, as I tried to calm my racing heart enough to see the words clearly in front of me.

"All of you, this is absurd, we should be talking, not treating each other like alley cats!" Isaac said at my side.

Crowded in the makeshift door I'd drawn in the bathroom were the sisters, looking gleeful and entertained.

I skimmed through the notebook so roughly a few of the fragile pages formed little tears near the spine. Maybe I needed to repeat the phrase I'd used to in the classroom so I could read the diary, if that was what it was. But then my eye caught on the name.

Isaac Metclaffe.

His name was on the center of a page, the whole cluster of words seeming to take up handfuls of pages before and after the one I'd found. His name popped up twice more and I tore every last mention free from the binding. Corina growled, one long exasperated sound, and gave up wrestling Callum.

"Isaac," she whined, voice so pathetic it made my hair stand on end. "Do you love me?"

Isaac was staring at the pages in my hand, his forehead knotted as his eyes lifted to mine, mouth parted but no words coming out.

"Let's find out," I said to Corina, my bones rattling with anger.

Her door out to the main room worked from this side and I went straight to the stove, where the wood had gone red and black with coals. I sank to my knees, the heat drying tears out of my eyes as I turned the handle and opened the door to the belly, fingers fisting slightly around Corina's writing. I threw it inside, watching, the threads of smoke rising first, and then the pages wrinkling. Black, burning lace grew over the curling corners and the crumpling center. Flames flickered up and within moments, the words were eaten in fire.

I shut the stove and looked over my shoulder. Isaac was standing in the center of the room with Callum watching his back, and Corina slumped in the doorway to her bedroom, lips frowning. She looked bored, not devastated, as if I'd just ruined a game for her.

Isaac groaned, bending forward and bracing his hands on his knees. He was staring at the stove, the gray cast to his skin turning green.

"Do you love me?" Corina repeated, words sickly sweet and mocking.

Isaac heaved, and then raced to the small bathroom, the sisters darting out of his way. I winced at the sound of him gagging.

"Watch her," I whispered to Callum, forcing myself up from the floor, my body aching like it was made out of stiff, heavy logs. "I'm so sorry," I said to the sisters in stilted Vermenian.

One of them shrugged as they stepped out of my way and muttered something about Corina. Maybe that they didn't mind watching the fight. Or were glad to see her plans ruined.

Isaac was bent over the toilet, back rolling with dry gags. I found a washcloth on a high shelf and rinsed it under cold water, taking it and pressing it to the back of his neck like my mother used to do for me when I was sick as a child. He moaned, body sagging at the touch, and he leaned his head back as I ran my fingers into his hair.

"Are you alright?" I asked as he took long, slow breaths.

He pushed away from the toilet, leaning into my skirts, and I lowered myself to the floor, wrapping my arms around him, covering him, and running my palms over his back.

"I feel disgusting," he hissed against me. "We should burn the whole book."

I nodded, resting my cheek on the top of his head. In truth, I wanted to know what else was written inside so that I could enjoy the unraveling of each of her spells. So I knew what else she might have manipulated for herself. Surely the bedroom of her own was on one of these pages.

Callum appeared in the door behind us. "The others are here."

I kissed Isaac's back and then untangled him from around me, his eyes falling shut as I propped him up against the wall.

"I feel as if someone's just carved aimlessly through my head and heart," Isaac murmured.

"I'll get you a glass of water," Callum said, his tone not entirely unsympathetic.

Isaac squeezed my hand as I rose up from the floor, his eyes flying open again. "Joanna, the things I said—"

I cut him off, "This isn't your fault, Isaac."

"That doesn't mean you aren't angry," he said, watching me.

I took a breath, slow and deep until I was about to burst, and then released it. "Let me finish this night and then sort out what I'm angry at. I don't think it's you."

Callum returned, water glass in hand, and he and I switched places. "Aiden says he'll get you something stronger if you need it," Callum said.

"Right now I'm not sure I could hold it down," Isaac admitted as I left the room and found the tiny apartment occupied to the brink.

Hildy and Bryce had brought Gwen and Tatsuo along, and it put thirteen of us in a space that barely housed the five original residents. I squeezed past Bryce where they had Corina cornered against a wall.

"What's the book smell like?" I asked, sticking the pages under the dragon's nose. Bryce grimaced and, without looking, swatted Corina away from the pages.

"Lies and roses," Bryce said. My eyebrows raised and they added, "Who made you cry, witchling?"

The endearment startled me for a moment, it was what the Hollow had called me while taunting me, but from Bryce, it seemed like a simple thing. I opened my mouth to dismiss the question, I didn't want to offer Corina the satisfaction, but my eyes flicked to hers, and then Bryce was rounding on the girl, a growl rising up from their throat that made my ears ring.

"Not in here, Bryce," Gwen warned.

The growl was muffled away, but Bryce kept Corina in their sight.

"She's been manipulating things," I said, showing the other coven the notebook. "I want to know what before I take this to Myles." In case, once he had the news, he shut me out again. "But first, Tats, can you tell me if there's anything inside that keeps this family out of a bedroom they ought to be allowed to use."

Hildy was looking at the pallets on the floor with narrowed eyes. "I don't believe that was the arrangement we recommended when they moved in."

Corina muttered at the huddle of us, and then jumped back as Bryce snapped their teeth in her direction.

"She says she's used to better accommodations than Canderfey cares to offer," Tatsuo translated for us. He was skimming through the pages and stopped near the front of the notebook. "Ah, here it is. 'No one but I will get any sleep in the bedroom we are meant to share.'"

"Thank you," I said, holding my hand out for the book. I tore the page free and went to toss it into the fireplace, weaving past Aiden.

"Is he alright?" Aiden asked, following me.

"I think he will be," I said, opening the stove and tossing the paper in, watching it burn. "Something made him sick. The magic or sudden shift of emotions. I don't know."

"Here's this," Gwen said, joining me at the stove, the small library pencil in her hand.

I rolled the pencil between my fingers for a moment and then flipped to the back of Corina's notebook, finding a blank page.

Corina Trier cannot write.

Neither Gwen nor Aiden made an expression if they saw the words. "Just for now," I said. It felt vengeful and cruel to take her power away. And I was not sorry. If I hadn't done it myself, I would have asked Bryce to. I wasn't even sure if I would tell Myles, or if I'd tuck the note away somewhere safe and let it stay.

"I've talked to the others and we've agreed, she'll stay at our house. I don't know that she'll find the luxury more of a comfort than being monitored, but this family certainly deserves their space without her," Gwen said, looking around the room. "And we can handle her better."

Bryce was grinning and I wasn't sure if I was sorrier for my friends at putting themselves out in such a way, or pleased with the thought of Corina being hounded by Bryce at all hours.

"I don't think there's a better solution," Gwen said, nodding to me. "You can trust us."

"I know I can," I said. I jumped forward, wrapping her up in a tight hug before she could shake me off. "Thank you."

"Oh, enough," Gwen murmured in my ear, hand patting at my back. "Get your coven home. We'll finish up here."

8

JOANNA

The house was dark and Isaac—who had come to bed like a ghost of himself, letting us bundle around him—was now missing from the room again. I sat up and Aiden rolled until his back was to me, letting out a sleepy huff. Callum's arm over my waist squeezed tighter for a moment until I pried myself free.

"Whu…where's Isaac?" he mumbled, nose wrinkling and eyes staying shut.

"I'll go find him. You sleep," I whispered back, bending and kissing his forehead before crawling out of the bed.

My heart sank when I saw the light on in his studio. Not again. Not after everything. What if I hadn't erased the power of the words over Isaac's heart after all of that? This time though, smoke drifted down the hall from the room. I ran to where the door hung open and Isaac looked up from his spot, cross-legged over a spread canvas sheet, a tin bucket in front of him holding flames that licked up a collection of drawings. The largest was the one I'd seen him working on the night before.

"I'm sorry, I didn't want to wake you," he said. "I needed them gone."

His hair was loose and still damp from the shower he'd taken after arriving home—scrubbing himself until his skin was pink, without a single drop of paint or smear of charcoal. There was a bottle of wine on the floor by his foot.

I sagged against the doorframe, catching my breath, my racing heart slowing with relief. "Can I join you?"

Isaac moved the wine bottle out of the way and held his hand out to me. "Please."

I joined him on the floor, his legs spreading to make room for me between them, arms circling my waist. The fire was climbing up the long wave of Corina's golden locks and my anger swirled in the pit of my stomach.

"I'm so sorry, my love," Isaac whispered in my ear.

I covered his arms with mine, turning my head and pressing my cheek to his mouth. "It wasn't your fault. You weren't really in love. You never betrayed us."

Isaac was silent, arms holding tighter, as the fire dragged the last remnants of Corina's influence down into the tin tub. Or so I hoped.

"I was," he whispered, body tense around mine. "Maybe not of my own choosing. And only for… for a day. But that's the worst part. I *was* in love, and after you burnt those pages that feeling ended, but it didn't erase what had been there. Now I think of her as someone I- someone…"

Someone he *loved*. Past tense, but all the same.

"How do you feel now?" I asked, turning in his hold so I could see his face.

"Still a bit sick," he said, with a smile that wasn't a smile at all but some kind of soft expression of sorrow. "Terrified… Angry. I haven't felt so angry in a long time and it's an emotion I try to avoid."

I squeezed his hand in mine. His father was not someone he spoke of, but I knew he'd been an angry man, vicious even.

"I… I wrote her unable to write," I said to him. It was wrong to ask Isaac to be my conscience after everything he'd been through today, but he had more right than any of us to decide Corina's fate.

His shoulders sagged. "Well, now a bit terrible and a lot relieved. I *hate* her Joanna, believe that."

"Easily. I hate her too." The fire crackled into ashes, and Isaac and I watched each other.

"I don't love her," Isaac said, gray gaze catching mine. "If it weren't for her words I *never* would have."

Some tight strain in my shoulders loosened and I turned, burrowing into Isaac's chest, my arms knotting behind his neck, and he drew me closer, balancing me on his lap, his hands tangling in my hair.

"Joanna, love, I'm sorry," he said.

I found the collar of his shirt and tugged it out of my way, wrapping my lips around his skin to taste him, dragging my teeth over the muscle of his neck.

"Stop saying that." I pressed the words into his skin. "I can't forgive you for something you didn't do."

"Then tell me you still love me," he pleaded, mouth pressing to the top of my ear. I froze and then leaned back, as Isaac combed strands of hair off my face. "You haven't said it since I told you all that I was—"

"I love you! Of course, I love you," I said, one hand rushing up his neck to his cheek, his face leaning into the touch like a cat, the shadow of a day's worth of beard scratching at my palm. "Nothing would have changed that. I… don't know what I would have done if it weren't a spell. But I'm not falling out of love with you, Isaac."

His fingertips were stroking a pattern behind my ear, tucking in a lock of hair over and over as he absorbed my words. The lines around his mouth and eyes were softening, the gray in his gaze warming. My heart felt crushed, or too full, I didn't know which, only that it was straining, wanting to be closer to him.

"Sit for me tomorrow?" Isaac asked, as his hand slid down my throat. I tilted my head to give him more to touch and he continued in the same path over to the strap of my nightgown, pushing it off my shoulder, his thumb digging into muscle.

I smiled at the thought, the sensation of his eyes on me for the day, and nodded. "The others too?"

Isaac's own mouth curled, a real smile this time. "Yes. But right now, I only want you. Is that alright?"

I answered by pulling him down to meet my lips, the pair of us making desperate sounds with the first kiss, hands clutching needfully to one another. Isaac's hands stroked over my back, squeezing at my hips and then wrapping around the sides of my thighs, lifting me off his lap just enough to spread my legs apart, my knees bracketing his hips. Then he was reaching up, holding my face to his, tongue licking into my mouth, twisting against my own until I was whimpering into our kiss, panting against his lips, my own hands holding his hair in fists.

When I started to squirm on his lap—heat and molten desire pooled between my legs, desperate for friction and to be filled and stretched and claimed again by him—he pulled away, lips wet, red, and swollen. My mouth burned from the scrape of his stubble and I craved more, chasing after him until he was grinning, holding me still.

"Lay back, lay down for me," he said, eyes bright.

"Not now, please, I want you," I said, grinding my hips onto his lap and feeling his cock twitching in response, needing me as badly as I needed him.

"You'll have me," Isaac answered, all the fragility of his voice this evening now softened back to his usual rasp and purr. "Lay back, my love. I want to look at you."

I huffed and started to fall back to the canvas when he stopped me again.

"Take the nightdress off."

"No sketching," I warned, narrowing my eyes. "You can't hang my nudes around the campus." He had more than enough here in the studio anyway.

Isaac grinned, leaning forward and sucking at my bottom lip briefly. "No sketching," he promised.

I slid off his lap, pulling my nightgown up over my head by the hem and tossing it aside, off the canvas sheeting. Isaac nudged the tin away, only ashes and smoldering scraps now, and then stood up, his gaze tracking me as I lay down, propping my arms underneath my head and crossing my ankles with a smirk. Under my back, the spot where the fire had sat, was warm—almost too much so—making an interesting contrast on my skin when the air above me was so cool, sliding over skin that was craving touch.

"Where are you going now?" I asked, watching as Isaac turned to his shelves, grabbing up a palette, and flicking dabs of paint out of tubes. "No paintings either."

"I want you to be my canvas," Isaac said, smiling at me from over his shoulder.

My eyes widened as he continued collecting color on the palette and then grabbed a brush from his collection. "How long have you been thinking of this?"

"It's not the first time I've thought of it, I'll be honest. But it struck me again seeing you sitting on that canvas. Do you mind?"

"I suppose it's too much to ask you to be tidy?" I asked, trying to hide my smile.

Isaac turned, twirling the paintbrush around his fingers while eyeing me as if I were somewhere between a blank canvas in need of his concentration and a feast to be devoured. "I promise I'll be very thorough when I clean us both up after," he said. He stopped at my feet, balancing on one foot, and tapped at my ankles with the other. "Open up."

I couldn't have explained what I had left to feel shy about, Isaac had seen every bit of me plenty of times before. Maybe it was that this was a new kind of study in his gaze, eyeing my skin with an intent to embellish. I uncrossed my ankles but Isaac only lifted an eyebrow at the small space I afforded him. I sighed and slid my heels wide apart, and he sank down to his knees in front of me, palette set to the floor near my hip, air rushing against the exposed skin of my pussy and making me shiver.

"You're beautiful," he said, his stare following a familiar path up from my ankle, over my knees, between my thighs with rapt attention, on and on up to my face, which was now flushed, my lips pressed tight as I tried to keep from taking heavy breaths.

His paintbrush flicked over my stomach, dry and tickling, and my body flinched and followed the touch. It traced patterns on my skin as Isaac watched my face until the gentle flick and tease had turned erotic, and I was whining behind clenched teeth, body squirming on the floor.

I sighed as the brush traveled to the palette, watching it dip into the black paint.

"For protection," Isaac said, a shadow passing over his eyes, and then he was leaning forward, one hand balanced above my shoulder. The paintbrush paused above my throat and then retreated. "Wait, this first, before I can't."

Isaac ducked down, mouth latching onto my pulse point making me moan in surprise, back arching up to brush my breasts against his chest as he sucked and nibbled and licked over the skin of my throat. I was gasping when he stopped, and the feel of the brush on my skin, as wet as his tongue but shockingly cool, was a stunning contrast. I froze, holding still as he painted swirling patterns over the spot where he'd marked me. Beyond the warm throb of my pulse in my neck, and desire in my cunt, there was a soft curtain of magic that fell over me with the marks, the feeling of being sheltered.

He studied my face as he finished. "Alright?"

I nodded, feeling the paint as cold lines against my skin, and watched as Isaac nodded, swiping the brush through the air, dense black vanishing off the tip and leaving it clean again. He dipped it into a cobalt blue next.

"Fidelity and harmony," he explained and then he bent again, leaving soft, wet kisses like a collar from one shoulder to the next, and then following them with a swirling, spiraling pattern of paint. His hair caught in the marks on my neck, and I was hyper-aware of every flicker of contact, the muscles in my back and thighs straining to keep from rubbing myself against him.

There was an expression Isaac had when he was sketching us because he wanted to try and translate an emotion he had when he looked at us, and a different expression for when he was trying to capture a line or composition, or a stroke of light passing through a window. His face now was some mix of the two, turning soft as he traced the curve of my breast with the pointed handle of the paint-brush, focus sharpening as he mixed colors on the palette and came up with pink.

"Love."

His voice was hoarse and he lowered himself onto me, his stomach against the aching lips of my sex, free hand cupping one breast and drawing it to his lips. His tongue laved over a taut nipple, drawing it into his mouth to suckle, to nip, and kissing a trail down to my belly button. He swirled the spot, making me quiver, and then dragged up to the neglected breast, mouth harsher, some veneer of patience breaking as he made me shout. My hands flew up to hold him to the spot, hips twisting up to rub myself against him, and he escaped my grasp with a laugh, drawing back. When he painted, he spent a long time on fine details, the wet paintbrush like a tongue against my skin until I was whining at the back of my throat.

I looked down my body, seeing a pattern like abstracted florals, my heart pounding and squeezing, my eyes watering. I was flooded with the emotion, thoughts swollen with love.

Isaac's eyes were shining and he flicked away the pink paint and dipped the brush into goldenrod yellow.

"Happiness," I rasped, breath ragged.

"For us," he agreed, and then he lifted my right leg up from the floor bringing my ankle to his mouth as he stroked color onto the sensitive skin behind my knee and up my thigh.

I was soaked, my cunt already fluttering, begging for release and to be filled. But Isaac had set some plan for himself and even though I could see his arousal, bobbing in the loose fit of his pants, he was focused, kissing skin and painting my legs until they were shaking.

He dropped the paintbrush to the floor.

"Finally," I gasped, my head dropping as I reached out for him.

"Not yet," he said, and then his fingers dipped into paint so red it glowed. "Passion."

"Isaac, I have passion, you can feel it," I said, laughing, reaching for his clean hand and drawing it to my pussy.

He grinned, fingers stroking through my wetness, dipping inside of me and then drawing out to swirl around my clit, my body chasing as he pulled away. The red-painted fingers landed on my hip, a curling flourish making my skin flush and the desire in my belly double, until I was moaning and writhing, helpless with want. He mirrored the shape on the other side and I reached back, fisting my palms in canvas.

"Isaac please." I felt near to coming, my body hot, little licking flashes of pleasure stroking at me every time the air brushed over the marks on my skin. When he stroked the insides of my thigh, leaving drumming fingerprints behind, I felt it start, every bit his intention to draw me over the edge before we'd ever really begun. He repeated the smear and dots on the other side and I came, sobbing and begging, rocking on the canvas, as my hips searched for a rhythm to follow.

Isaac wiped his fingers off on my belly and then pushed his sleep pants down off his hips, pressing against me, the paint wet and slippery between us as he lined himself up at my entrance.

"Don't you dare tease me ano—Ah! Isaac, yes!" My body was bowing toward his as he thrust inside of me, the way slick and swollen with my release.

"No teasing, love," Isaac said, hands holding my face as his lips stroked over mine with the words. "Oh Joanna, I need you too."

The pace was harsh and fast and clumsy. The floor was too hard beneath us, the canvas sliding with every thrust so that Isaac stayed deep, thrusts shallow, pelvis grinding against my clit. He hooked an arm beneath my knee, drawing it up to my chest, and braced his foot near my hip, driving into me, mouth hard on mine, voice grunting against my lips.

It felt wonderful and rushed after all the teasing, uncommonly rough for Isaac, but it left my body singing, rising to meet his, my feet slipping in smears of paint, skin sticking and sliding.

"I love you," he gasped out, tearing his lips from mine and pressing them to my ear, cock stroking inside me with that perfect twist he used to undo all my senses, dragging it high and making me see stars.

"I love you. Isaac, yes! I love you, please don't stop."

He drew back, hands wrapping around my hips, lifting me to meet his thrusts until I was shouting, unable to take him deeper, unable to see clearly, my body trembling as every crash together left me quaking and soaking around his length.

He groaned, a long deep sound, and then we landed hard against the floor, his body heavy on top of mine as he finished with shuddering nudges, warmth spilling in my belly, dribbling out from between us. I wrapped my arms and legs around his back, and Isaac laid open mouth kisses against my temple, my jaw, my shoulder. Our chests were glued together with paint, breaths returning unevenly, and I traced my fingers down his spine until he settled.

"I love you," I repeated to him, and he nuzzled closer as his cock softened and slipped free. "Nothing will take you from me."

There was a long sigh, and then Isaac was leaning back on wobbling arms, one hand stroking over my cheek as he retreated, a soft smile on his lips as he studied his handiwork on my skin, the colors somehow all smeared together now.

"Nothing could," he said. "Come on, let's show the others what a mess I've made and see if they'll shower with us."

He lifted me up from the floor, cradling me in his arms with a grin as he stumbled out to the hall, and upstairs to the rest of our coven.

9

AIDEN

"I can't believe you let her in your house," Hildy marveled, watching Corina Trier sitting at the table in our dining room, eyes fixed on the teacup in front of her.

"We left the decision up to Isaac," I said, my eyes drifting over to where my coven stood together by the kitchen door, Isaac between Joanna and Callum, their arms behind his back. "I'm not sure if he wanted to make a point of being unaffected or is just too agreeable for his own good. But you took her into your own house. It can't be easy."

"Actually… it has been rather easy," Hildy mused and caught my eyebrows raising. "Don't get me wrong. She's not pleasant. But when she saw the house, the guest room, and the bathroom she has to herself? Well, she brightened up. If Bryce wasn't having such a delightful time playing the monster, I'd say she was having too good a time for it to be a decent punishment."

"Joanna took her ability to write away," I said.

"Yes, and Tatsuo has heard a great deal of moaning on the subject," Hildy said, lips twitching.

"Are you always so sympathetic?" I asked, grinning.

"My coven likes trouble," Hildy replied with a shrug.

"Don't get me started," I muttered.

Hildy patted my arm. "You learn to take your amusements where you can."

She left me, joining Bryce at the window behind Corina. The rest of the Scrivens sat around the table, enjoying tea and lunch, with Myles at the head of the table. Well, most of them seemed to be enjoying themselves, Corina looked like she was attempting to imitate a queen at her own beheading. Every time Joanna passed her, the younger girl flinched. I couldn't say I minded.

My coven ducked back into the kitchen after serving out the sandwiches and I followed, nodding at Myles as I passed him.

"How is everything?" I asked, and then turned to Isaac who was filling the kettle for another pot of tea. "How are you?"

"Come here," he said, raising an arm out to me. "I'm fine, honestly. In a way, it's a good reminder to see her, helps correct the memory of those feelings."

He took my hand when I reached him, pulling it to cover his chest as I stood close at his back. Joanna and Callum smiled at him from across the counter. It'd been a week since Corina's spell, and while the weekend after he'd seemed jumpy and alternately distant or desperately close, he was himself again now. Or very close to it. I rested my cheek atop his head and watched Joanna and Callum attempt to make an attractive platter of cookies, one which was currently turning into a lopsided pile.

"I think they need an artist's eye," I said and caught Joanna's flickering glare and faint twitch of her lips.

"They'll manage fine," Isaac said, glancing at the pair. "My cookies won't stay on the plate long. Oh, hello."

The little Scrivens girl, Bekka, was wandering into the kitchen as if it were her own, walking up to the counter—which was as high as her nose—and studying the progress on the tray of cookies. I'd escorted her family to their apartment the day they'd arrived and Bekka had been dressed in dusty rags, the toes of her shoes flapping open as she fidgeted behind her mother's skirts. Now the girl was bright cheeked, blonde hair twisted up in braids on her head, and dressed in a pale purple dress. The style was frilly and playful, but undeniably Hildy's handiwork. Her shoes were a bright polished black, clicking with each step closer to the counter.

"Hello, Bekka," Joanna said and then asked something in Vermenian.

Bekka shook her head, rose up on her toes, and pointing to the platter, said something that ended with the word "Koeki."

One slid off the uneven pyramid in her direction and she looked up at Joanna. "Oh, alright," Joanna said, turning and lifting the girl up onto the counter, before passing her the cookie. "Don't tell your mottar," she warned, tapping the girl on her nose.

Bekka nodded solemnly, seeming to understand, and my heart swelled in my chest, my fingers squeezing tight around Isaac's. He laughed, back shaking against my chest as he set the tea to brewing.

Would Joanna be an indulgent mother? Playful, and dry as she was with Bekka? I wondered how we would ever manage any discipline between the four of us. Isaac would be too gentle and skittish, Callum would observe them like a work of magic, Joanna would tease and dote in tandem. I couldn't imagine not being wrapped around the child's finger. We would simply have to do our best with terribly spoiled children.

Joanna's finger knocked another cookie down to the counter and Bekka snatched it up, stuffing it behind her lips with a quick hand. Joanna grinned and glanced at me, and then immediately blushed and turned away.

"You're crushing my hand," Isaac murmured, turning his head to drop a kiss on my jaw.

I loosened my grip, watching Joanna open our junk cupboard, rifling through and pulling out a handful of loose papers Callum had left on the counter—because the mess couldn't simply remain confined to his offices and bedroom. She returned with the paper and a few stray colored pencils that Isaac must have left lying around. Bekka watched her as Callum passed the little girl a broken fraction of cookie and ate the other half himself.

Joanna smoothed the paper out on the counter and then rested the pencils on top. She nodded at Bekka.

"Draw."

"Tokahal?" Bekka asked, touching a pencil.

Joanna nodded, picking up the red and drawing a quick, simplified flower. Bekka chewed at her thumbnail for a moment, and then snatched up the green pencil and set to scribbling.

Joanna smiled and carried the tray of cookies out of the kitchen and into the dining room, Callum following with the tea.

"Don't get carried away," Isaac said to me, raising an eyebrow.

"I wasn't."

He only smiled and pulled me over to join Bekka in her drawing of a strange, jolly-looking creature on the page.

ISAAC MET me outside the Burgess building later that week, the pair of us crossing campus to surprise Joanna for lunch, when we heard the screams.

His hand clutched at my sleeve, as our feet stopped dead on the path.

"Go get Callum," I ordered, my body straining toward the shouting. I looked back to him, taking his arm in one brief squeeze. "I'll get to Joanna."

I turned back to the lawn, students were sprinting away from the source of the shouting, others stopping in their path and staring in the direction they'd come.

"Should we—?"

"I'll make it to the library before... the library is safe," I said. It had been ever since Joanna had written the words there this past fall. "Go find Callum, if he's not already on his way we'll need him."

Isaac took off in the opposite direction as I ran toward the library, the way clogged with gawking students.

"I've never- it wasn't- what *was* that?" a young man with a lopsided sweater shouted, rising up to his toes to see over the crowd. "Oh, where did it go?"

"Excuse me. Excuse me, please," I called out, shouldering my way through.

The students were packed tighter together the closer I moved to whatever held their attention until I felt as if I were swimming upstream. They shifted, a wave of startled cries and shrieks echoing out from the front of the line. I broke through and stopped. My way to the library was blocked, partly by the students across the way, clinging to one another and too scared to come closer, but too fascinated to run away. And partly by what sat before me.

Squatted before me.

What *was* it?

Low to the ground with short legs bent outwards like elbows, its body was as long as a carriage and as wide as myself. Shaggy hair hung in clumps over the creature, the color of moss on stone. It had a smushed face, nostrils flaring as it sniffed the air and stared at me with bulbous eyes in an unnatural shade of orange, the richest shade of a flame. There were two bright fangs hanging on either side of its wide, gaping grin, head twice as large as my own with soft ears that curled down. It took padding steps toward me with paws that looked strong enough to crush, and a strange flopping motion to its steps.

Behind me, the students shouted at the movement, and it carried around the circle, making the creature twist and stare and scurry in a new direction, its long feathery wide tail flourishing through the air.

And then I recognized it. Not as something there was a name for, but as a creature I had seen before. Smaller and two-dimensional, sketched by Bekka's hand at the kitchen counter with me and Isaac.

Shit.

"Aiden!"

I didn't dare tear my eyes off the animal as Callum shouted for me, only reached my hand up behind me, palm flat. He ignored it, the willful ass, and darted in front of me.

"Don't hurt it," I said, grabbing his sides and keeping him from charging. There was that sword of his in one hand, a knife in the other, but the knife vanished at my instruction.

"What is it?" Callum barked. Isaac caught up to my back, breath catching in his throat, and I knew he saw it too.

I stepped close, ignoring Callum as he tried to shake me off, tried to maintain his defensive position, ready to attack, protect. "Bekka's drawing," I whispered in his ear. "She drew it, put up trees behind it like our woods, a little sketch of herself. She *wrote* this in pictures."

Apparently, the childish misuse of scale applied to the creature's creation, because she'd held her hands a little over two feet apart to explain its size to us, although on the page it was four times the size of her own stick figure.

Callum's eyes flashed to mine, wide, compiling the information—with the crowd around us, this would be impossible to hide. Not like Corina's manipulation, this work of magic was far too visible.

"It isn't dangerous," Isaac said, stepping up to Callum's other side.

"You don't know that." Callum's back was tense, voice thick, body ready to spring into action at any second.

"She called it her friend," Isaac said.

In front of us, the beast was circling, tail alternately coiling in the air—in what *might* have been a playful manner—and drooping down, curling around its back ankle. It was starting to look nervous, every shift in one direction or another drawing new screams from the students.

"You can't know," Callum warned, but Isaac was sinking to his knees, and Callum scrambled to grab his collar.

"Just be ready," I said to Callum. "He's right. If Joanna had written that thing, called it her friend, would you be afraid of it?"

Callum held his breath as Isaac sat down on the ground, waiting until the creature turned to face him, then caught its gaze. He patted his knees, hands trembling, and the crowd went quiet. The curled ears perked up into tufted points and a black tongue lolled out from between the fangs, its dull teeth smiling, tail swishing like a fan through the air.

It ran, or did its best impression of running, in our direction, legs flopping out from its sides, body wobbling and tail...wagging.

Callum's shoulders relaxed. He knew the look of a predator, and while this creature was strange and monstrous, it was not on the hunt. Or it was very good at disguising its intentions.

"That's a very wrong dog," someone said from the crowd behind us and Callum snorted.

"Oh, quick, before Joanna sees it," I said to Callum, horror freezing on my face. "We'd better find somewhere to hide the beast or she'll try and adopt it."

Isaac hesitated on reaching out at the end, but it didn't matter. The creature rolled straight to its back, head landing in Issac's lap with a heavy thunk and bits of leafy debris falling loose from its fur. It panted happily and Isaac sighed, fingers digging into the dreadlocked strands. The beast squirmed, a paler green belly exposed, and somewhere in the crowd, a girl cooed. The students were loosening their formation, braver ones moving forward—the others, who had only come to witness the danger, losing interest and leaving.

"It's soft," Isaac said, smile growing as he settled down and the creature...the not-dog, squirmed its way over his legs, melting under his scratching fingers like a noodle.

Callum's sword was hanging in his grip, face baffled and torn with confusion.

I nudged his side. "Go on, pet it."

The sword vanished and Callum landed in the grass next to Isaac, a wet black tongue lapping at his palm before he reached the chin and scratched, making a leg twitch wildly in the air.

"Aiden, Iss-"

I looked up and found Joanna wrestling her way past the remaining milling students, and then stopping short at the sight of us.

"What on earth is that?" she asked, eyes wide. I was relieved to see she looked a little disgusted at the sight of it licking around Callum's wrist.

"A friend of a friend," I said, nodding her over.

The beast rolled up, with a helping hand from Isaac, at the sight of her. Joanna, obnoxiously brave creature that she was, let it ramble its way to her, sniffing at her boots and waddling around her in circles as she came closer.

"Bekka drew it, on Sunday," Isaac explained when Joanna was close enough that we could speak softly to one another.

Joanna's eyes widened and she wobbled as the beast tipped over, rubbing against her like a cat. It did look more like a cat. Not a great deal, but more than a dog.

"Oh dear," Joanna whispered, pressing her lips together as she stared at the beast.

"We need to learn what it eats, if it eats," Callum said.

"It's *not* coming to live with us. I've accepted the cats, but not this," I said.

Callum looked up at me, crooked smile growing. "So when Anders asks what kind of threat it might be we can be prepared. Also, I'm curious."

"Can't we just...destroy the drawing?" I asked.

"Aiden, look at it! It's a living creature now!" Joanna said, tone hot with anger.

It was a living creature polishing her boots with its black tongue.

I covered my mouth with my hand to keep the arguments inside. My body felt jittery from the initial panic, and relief and all I could think of was the consequences. Yes, we were lucky the beast was gentle...amusingly so. But Anders would see the potential danger of such an ability. Bekka would face the restrictions to her magic and her trust from the community.

"Can we get it back in the woods for the time being?" I asked.

"Too late," Isaac said, nodding behind me, the beast nudging his chest with one enormous paw. The thing had claws the same alarming orange as its eyes, but they were dull and rubbery, and when Isaac rubbed the soft belly, the claws wiggled like happy toes.

I turned and found President Anders storming toward us, thin hair flipping in the wind, acting almost like a sail on his head. His glamour was fixed on neatly, a glossy version of himself. Behind him, Elizabeth Bonde raced along at his heels.

"Spin this for them," Callum said to me. "Make it sound like something positive."

I ran my tongue over the tops of my teeth, trying to think faster than Anders and his VP could run. Students were joining Callum and Isaac in the grass, the beast looking wildly happy, licking hands and faces. Joanna stepped to my side, her hand wrapping around the sleeve of my jacket.

"I've written to Myles," she said, staring up at me with those brassy bright eyes. "And you're right. We'll do whatever we need to do to keep the Scrivens safe."

"It's not the Scrivens Anders is concerned for," I warned her.

She nodded, chin lifting. "I know." But her stare was trusting and confident, probably more than I deserved. I kissed her forehead and she released me, as I left to meet Anders and Bonde halfway, my mind racing.

"What in the gods above is that thing, King?" Anders growled, loud enough to catch the attention of the students in the grass. One young girl leaned protectively over the beast and then giggled as it cleaned her face.

"A drawing, by a little girl," I said. "Entirely harmless and a fascinating experiment."

My voice had taken on my father's deep, sharp demand.

"It's alive?" Elizabeth asked, finding a pair of glasses in her pocket and perching them on her nose as I nodded.

"As far as we can tell," I said. I waited until Anders opened his mouth to argue and then spoke over him, just as Marcus had taught me to do when dealing with an adversary, to rile them into being spluttering and senseless. "No one had any notion that the power translated to images. Canderfey will be credited with the discovery," I added, finding a smile stretching on my lips.

Anders crossed his arms over his chest and narrowed his eyes at me. "There were screams."

I looked around us at the campus with exaggerated slowness. Most of the students had moved, the rest were playing with the creature or watching with grins.

"Does anyone look terrorized?" I asked. I raised my hand as Anders started to speak again and enjoyed the red flood of color up his neck, breaking the magic he was forcing over his image. "Consider it a... mascot, of sorts."

Elizabeth Bonde snorted and rolled her eyes at me, but she looked more amused than judgmental.

"You're saying we should keep it," Anders scoffed, rolling his eyes up to the sky. "Honestly, King, are you trying to pretend this was intentional?"

"We assumed these results were unlikely," I said. Half-truth. We hadn't considered the possibility.

"I want it destroyed," Anders said.

"Of course, if that's your decision. I don't know how the students will take it, but..."

"Stuart, I think that's rather harsh," Bonde said. "It *is* fascinating!"

"Oh, please," Anders growled, but his eyes skimmed over my shoulder and there was laughter coming from behind me.

"It's the clearest physical manifestation of the Scrivens power yet, and with the added ability to study it as an organic creature. Does it eat? Does it exist indefinitely?" I watched his eyes narrow and continued, "Certainly a paper worth publishing."

"Contain it," Anders said, mouth twisting in a grimace. "I don't care how. And bring the Scrivens to my office."

He turned away before I could ask which of the Scrivens he meant. Myles would have to take the brunt of his ire. We wouldn't put Bekka in a room with the man just to be berated in a language she didn't understand. Bonde and I nodded at one another, a moment of understanding passing between us. She was an odd match for Anders as a Vice President, but there was a balance between them and I was discovering I much preferred her to him.

I walked back to my coven who rose out of the pile on the grass and met me away from the ears of the students.

"I've bought it...*us* time," I said and Joanna pressed into my side, her arms squeezing around my waist. "Can you confine it to the campus?" I asked Callum, waiting till he nodded to add, "And someone should go find Bekka. She ought to meet her beast."

10

JOANNA

THE DOOR OF THE ROW HOUSE SNAPPED SHUT, ANNOUNCING MY UNCLE'S return. Adele, who'd been keeping me company across the small table, set her teacup down on the saucer with a smile. She reached past the tea things, patted my hand, and pushed up from her chair, taking her cane and tiptoeing into her makeshift room as my uncle appeared in the small dining room.

"Leina!" He stopped in front of me, his eyes tracking his retreating mother.

"Hello, Uncle Myles. I was hoping we could talk," I said.

He exhaled heavily, hands bracing his hips, and scanned the small room as if searching for an escape route.

"Irene is upstairs. Napping, I think." I held my breath, wondering if he would really refuse to talk with me, or finally let me in on his worries.

Then he nodded and came over in slow steps, taking his mother's seat and pouring himself a cup of tea, drinking it down in one great gulp. "Irene is not… liking the move," Myles said. "She never learned Enmarian. She misses her friends from the village."

I looked down to my teacup, running my thumb around the lip. I'd seen very little of Irene since the first week after the Scrivens' arrival and done less to reach out to her and make her comfortable. We had a limited means of communication together and hardly anything in common from what I could tell, but she was family and she had given up everything from her home for Myles. Maybe I'd been too focused on the Scrivens and not enough on the others, the families.

"You know that I want the best for all of you," I said, grimacing when the words felt too trite to suffice. Wanting was not enough and I was floundering on how to help.

"Leina," he murmured, his expression softening as his hand patted mine in an echo of his mother's.

"And I thought that meant... guiding you all, with our magic. Learning the most about ourselves together." I chewed the inside of my lip, glancing at him out of the corner of my eye. "But I think instead, I should have you tell me what would be most helpful at the moment. For you. The Scrivens. Your families."

Myles poured another cup of tea, then refilled mine, and sat in silence for a long spell.

"Your covenmates convinced Anders that Bekka's monster was not a problem, which is more than I could have done," he said eventually, thumb tapping on the handle of his cup and making it rattle on the saucer.

"Lars isn't a problem." Bekka had named the creature, and the students on campus had taken the moniker up with a resounding cheer. Callum still wasn't certain what Lars would eat in nature, if he ate at all, because he was now so well fed on soft buns, sticky rolls, and snacks from the campus canteen.

"Have you edited your restrictions on Corina so she can't draw either?" Myles asked.

I blinked, heat rising in my cheeks. "As soon as we realized what it might mean."

"Then you know, leina, that it could have been a problem," Myles said, staring down his wide nose at me. "In hands other than Bekka's, with intentions other than playful."

"Did you know it was possible?" I asked. When his expression shuttered I added, "I'm not asking for research, I just—"

"I know, I know," he said, patting my hand again and then waving the awkwardness in the air between us away. "It's *possible*. It's not... common. Bekka will be a very strong Scrivens. Her parents worry for her."

"Then we aren't all... the same." I'd never considered that, but it made sense. Just as Callum was exceptionally powerful and clever, and Aiden's music was more moving than technically perfect, as he always told me. As my writing and Corina's tasted different to Bryce.

Myles laughed, "No, leina! I'm rather weak, and I use blunt words, wide sweeps. Corina is detailed. Nora is precise. You are clever," he said, pointing a finger at me. "You write *smart*. Clean. It's good."

I tucked my chin, trying to hide my smile and failing as Myles chuckled. I was flattered, but in the back of my mind, I also wondered, did that make me *powerful* or just tidy? I tossed the thought aside. I didn't need immense power, it probably only landed you in more trouble.

"What's Daniel?" I asked, wondering about the quiet, skittish man. The troubles his writing had already given him.

I half-expected Myles to become guarded again, protecting his people, but instead, he wobbled his hand between us. "So-so," he said, grinning at my surprise. "You wanted a big secret, didn't you, leina? No, Daniel is a good Scrivens too. He doesn't write now. Not much."

I sipped my tea and thought, Myles joining me in quiet, some of the uneasy distance from the past weeks softening after our conversation.

"I know... I know in Vermenia Scrivens were treated poorly because you were the only ones with magic," I said, catching and holding Myles' gaze. "But here, magic is everywhere."

"Here, it is that we are Vermenians," Myles pointed out.

"Yes. It is. And since that's not something you can change, I think it's simply better if we make them accept both parts. The Scrivens magic works under different rules than the magic they teach here, but that doesn't mean you shouldn't be allowed to use it."

"You think they will trust us?" Myles asked, eyebrows raising.

"I think that with time and *exposure* to each other, you will all become a part of this community." Maybe I *was* being foolish or optimistic. I knew it would take time and there would be hiccups like this week with Lars, but with the exception of Corina, all the Vermenians I'd met were pleasant people. I had to believe we could make a place for them here in Canderfey. And since belief wasn't enough, I needed to make a plan.

"Will you come with me to speak to Nora?" I asked. "I have a favor I'd like to ask her."

"I would, leina, but she will always welcome you, and she'll listen better if I'm not there to argue with her," Myles said, pushing his chair back. He added, grinning, "She likes you as much as she likes anyone."

I frowned and he laughed. I wasn't sure "as much as anyone" was a great deal in Nora's book.

"You want me to what?" Nora asked. She was tending a window basket of herbs while the other Scrivens—Daniel, Ella, and Kristin—hovered near the kitchen.

The row house was new, built after the Hollow destroyed the originals, but still a near-identical match for the one my family lived in. It boasted even less furniture from the residents, all of us choosing to stand rather than sit on the sleeping cots at opposite ends of the room. A curtain hung across the room to separate Daniel's space from Nora's. I wondered if we couldn't scavenge from what the graduating students would be giving away at the end of the year.

"I want you to teach Vermenian to people in Canderfey," I said, tucking my hands behind my back so I could wring them without Nora seeing. "Callum thinks we can work a budget to pay you to teach, and Myles said you taught in a grammar school."

Nora didn't do more than blink for a full minute. "Vermenian school children know more of the language than any Enmairian does. Who would come to these classes?"

"I... I would," I said, conjuring a weak smile. "And the classes would be free, so I think... some people would give it a chance. And we've already talked to one of the professors about free Enmairian lessons for any Vermenians who want them."

Nora's lips pursed as she stared at me.

I sucked in a breath and squared my shoulders. "The best way of helping you all assimilate here is to ensure communication. I know it can't only work one way. And I don't think I'm the only one who understands that. You might be surprised by how many people here would be willing to learn. Just give it a chance? If I'm your only pupil then we'll forget the idea."

Nora turned away, watching me from the corner of her eyes as she pulled the window nearly shut until only the breeze came in, carrying the scent of rosemary and mint along. When she faced me again, her lips pressed firmly together, I braced myself for her refusal.

"Alright, Miss Wick. I suppose you're determined enough to make it work," she said.

A brief, surprised laugh escaped me. "I usually am," I said, deciding to take that as a compliment.

Nora smirked and Daniel, who I'd assumed didn't speak Enmairian, snorted from the other end of the room. Kristin spoke and I was learning enough to know it was a question about me.

"Are you staying for tea?" Nora asked me, adopting Kristin's own benign smile.

I was three or four cups of tea deep from my visit to Adele and absolutely buzzing with caffeine. Now that Nora agreed to teach the classes, I wanted to run to find Callum, and pester him until he final-ized the last details we needed to start the classes.

"Not today, but thank you. I'll get back to my coven now. Thank you, Nora, for considering this. I think it really could help," I said.

Nora's smile softened into something honest and she followed me to the front door. "I appreciate all the effort you're putting into making us a place here. I hope for all our sakes it works out."

I called goodbye to the others and made my way across campus to the coven house. I'd made it as far as the common grounds in front of the library when I saw Callum out in the grass with Lars the monster. He looked a bit like a boy with his dog, if that dog was something that had crawled out of a swamp after eating everything that lived inside.

I stuck two fingers between my lips and whistled sharp and high, watching and laughing as Lars jumped, knocking Callum on his back, before scrambling over him and running toward me. I braced myself but he only bumped into my side, a little drool narrowly missing my ankles as he bounced in circles around me. We walked together back to Callum who was flicking grass out of his hair.

"What are you doing out here?" I asked, sinking down next to him, Lars falling over between us, belly exposed for scratching.

"I saw him on my way home," Callum said, fingers digging into pale green fur. "Thought I'd take some notes."

If Lars hadn't seemed so perfectly happy to wander wherever he pleased and visit whoever he liked, I suspected Aiden would have been forced to put up a strong argument against the creature moving into the house. I supposed there was always the matter of winter to deal with at the end of the year.

"Notes on his favorite spots for being scratched?" I asked watching him grin down at the beast.

Callum glanced at me over the rim of his glasses, his shoe nudging my hip. "If I was, I'd call it something scholarly like 'signs of autonomous nerve response,'" he said, keeping his face straight until I burst out in laughter.

"How is he then?" I asked.

"He doesn't have a pulse that I can find," Callum said, fingers combing through fur as Lars sighed and grinned at me. "Doesn't produce waste that I can tell, only eats what he's offered. He's more detailed than Bekka's drawing, certainly, but it seems like his core characteristics are her intentions. Friendly, affectionate, playful, sociable."

"But not his size," I said, thinking of the drawing that now hung safely in our kitchen.

"No, the scale comes from the drawing," Callum agreed.

I looked around us to be sure there was no one near enough to listen, and then turned to Callum. "Myles says that Bekka is more powerful than most Scrivens."

Callum's eyes widened and his gaze went distant. He was starting to reevaluate whatever ideas he'd had on our powers, just as I had done. "So we know Bryce can differentiate your signatures. And I suppose this means not everyone could make a monster from a drawing. Let's get home. I want you to draw me a teacup."

He stood up, Lars rolling to his feet and loping off in a new direction as if he knew we were done with our visit. Maybe he did, maybe that was just another piece of Bekka's magic. Callum pulled me up from the ground and took off toward home, my hand clutched in his and my feet stumbling as I caught up with his racing plans and pace.

"Do you think it's intention-based?" I asked. He'd always said that was the majority of magic, but we'd never had something like Lars to study before now.

"Of course it is," Callum replied with a shrug, and then a sheepish smile as I bumped my hip against his. "I think Lars is, in disposition at least, exactly what Bekka pictured in her mind. I don't think she *meant* to make him. And I don't know if every detail was planned or subconscious but…"

"But we'll start with a teacup," I said, squeezing his hand.

It was warm, and Callum was pulling me along fast enough that I was starting to sweat by the time we made it back to the house.

"Dinner in ten," Aiden called from the front room as we started to race up the stairs. "Don't you dare miss it for sex!"

"Unless you're inviting us," Isaac added from the kitchen.

"Don't let Isaac see my drawing," I whispered. "Even if it works, I'm not sure I could draw a teacup you can actually drink out of."

11

ISAAC

"Joanna, don't twist my words, please!"

I twitched, my fingers tugging on Callum's hair as I started to sit up from the couch, but he reached his hand up and pushed at my chest.

"Leave them to it," Callum muttered, hand covering mine in his hair, patting my knuckles to bid them to continue. We were off dish duty for the night, curled up together on the sofa with Callum's head in my lap. For an hour or so I thought it might end up a lovely evening.

"Not tonight," I said, but I didn't try moving again, even as Joanna's feet thumped down the hall toward the stairs.

"You say you don't want to argue but the second we stop the whole thing starts over again," she shouted back into the kitchen.

"It's been peaceful since the whole mess with… you know," I said.

"You being in love with someone else?" Callum supplied, a teasing lightness in his tone even as he squeezed his fingers around my knee. I hummed and retaliated by tugging at his hair until he huffed a laugh. He looked up at me and added in a whisper, "I knew their stalemate wouldn't last long. Not until they've had it out with what's really bothering them."

I raised my eyebrows. "Do you *know* what's bothering them?"

Callum shrugged, shoulders bumping my thigh. "With Aiden, I can make a guess. Joanna… the more something bothers her, the less likely she is to mention it. I think she's ignoring it herself."

"I *don't* want to fight but—" Aiden started, following Joanna down the hall to the stairs.

She spun on the landing and snapped down at him, "But you want me to tell you you're right when you're not!"

I sighed, feeling a headache coming on. "Can't you…I dunno, distract them? For the night, at least."

Maybe Joanna and Aiden had put the bickering aside recently for my sake, but if that was the case, I wish they hadn't called an end to the truce so quickly. I may not be feeling that same fragile nervousness that plagued me after Joanna burnt Corina's words, but I was sick to death of the tension between them.

"Course I can," Callum said, then he sat up and called to Joanna. "Jo, I'm going to show Isaac our new project."

The sniping words stopped as Aiden and Joanna both looked at us, Joanna's eyes growing huge with horror.

"Callum Pike, don't you dare," she whispered.

"You've been working on a new writing experiment?" I asked. Aiden and I had watched some of the experiments first hand if we weren't talked into participation, but there'd been nothing new since the Scrivens arrived.

Callum turned to me and winked. "Want to see Joanna's idea of a teacup?"

"Callum!" She turned and started racing up the stairs, Callum hot on her heels until Aiden and I caught up to them, wrestling over a childlike drawing of what was meant to resemble a teacup and instead looked a bit like a mirror that'd started to melt.

Aiden leaned against the doorframe, rubbing his temples.

"We can make an early night of it," I offered him.

"I think I'd better before this headache really sets in," he said. His eyes slid across the room to where Callum had Joanna laughing and blushing. "We can leave these two to their fun."

I wondered if Callum was right to leave Aiden stewing in this doubt he was nursing lately. But then Joanna yawned and stumbled away from the desk, tucking herself against Aiden's side as if she'd forgotten the fight from minutes before.

"Did someone say bed?" she asked.

Aiden's frown vanished as he kissed the top of her head. We trudged up to the attic together, barely making it out of our clothes and under the sheets before a drugging sleep claimed us.

DAMN DRUMMING IN MY HEAD—AN endless, incessant beat. I tried to roll away from the sound but my head weighed a hundred pounds and that drumming...that drumming was me. Pulse.

Shit.

One of my arms was numb, trapped beneath me, but I slid the other across the... I was in bed, the sheets beneath me were clean and cold. They...*she* wasn't nearby. I pulled in a slow, thin breath, smelled my own sour taste on the air. And no sweetness.

She probably hadn't even slept in the bed.

My fingers clenched in the sheets and I forced myself over, one slow inch at a time, eyes squeezed shut against the thin line of sunshine sneaking past the curtain. I peeled my eyes open one at a time, frowning at the ceiling, wondering if I was sleeping in the wrong direction or... the beams had moved. The roof was in the wrong shape, flat and caving in at the center, cracks in the plaster. No, that *was* my ceiling. I blinked and realized the light was dim, the curtain was closed. Maybe she had been here after all. My feet twitched, loose, boots off. Pants unbelted around my waist.

My stomach churned and I leapt from the bed, ignoring the way the room tipped, the floor dropped out beneath me, just forcing myself forward until I was falling into the dresser, vomiting up cheap swill into the washbasin.

Flickers of the night before came up with the sour, bitter, wasted alcohol. Drinking at the pub until the sympathetic ears ran dry and their pockets were no longer open to me. Stumbling back to home in the evening just in time to catch that couple, that pair of pretty men, clicking the gate of my house shut behind them.

"She's held dinner for you, Metclaffe," the big one, Aiden, said to me, his eyes dressing me down with scorn as his husband turned away from me entirely.

Anger and shame stirred together in my belly and another bout of sick struck me hard, splashing off ceramic and onto my cheeks.

The wood creaked behind me and then a cool damp cloth stretched over the back of my neck, another wiping at my cheeks as I pushed myself up. She was dressed for work already, tidy and sweet, with dark circles blooming under her eyes.

"There's toast downstairs for you. And tea," she said, eyes on my jaw as she finished cleaning my face.

"When's the last time you looked me in the eyes?" I asked, and my voice was harsher than I meant it, scraped raw from the sting of bile.

Joanna flinched and her jaw ticked, but she raised her chin high. The stretch revealed a bruise beneath her collar, fresh, and that too came back, her throat in my fist.

I would never. I would never. I would never.

"Don't stay out tonight," she said softly, her lips pressed hard together, and I watched with every little flinch of her eyes, how hard it was for her to look at me.

She thought she was worth more than me. Better for men like Pike and King. Men who didn't have to work a day in their life to have fine houses and money to spare.

She's worth everything. That's not who Aiden and Callum are.

"I'll have dinner and we'll... just have the night together," she said, gaze finally falling, words sweetening.

"If you don't get to work we won't have food for those meals you feed the *gentlemen*," I countered.

"It's not like—"

"You take their charity. And what else, Joanna?" I stepped toward her and she skidded back, hurrying to the door.

"Don't say things like that," she said, and then she dashed out of the room.

She was gone when I was dressed. The toast and tea were cold.

☾

MY HEAD THROBBED, swollen and aching. My throat was dry from road dust, digging out old wasted farmland for some new track to come through the village.

"Pint, Metclaffe?" Houser asked, slapping me on the back and making my eyeballs pound in their sockets.

I watched his back as he headed toward the village, the sun still over the horizon in front of us. Joanna wouldn't have food ready yet, she barely bothered to get home from the library before dark anyway. One cup would soften the steel hammer drumming through my skull. Would smooth the tear in my throat. And there were coins in my pocket now that we'd been paid for the week.

"Just one, then you lot send me out on my ass," I said.

Houser laughed ahead of me, a stupid braying sound that left me wincing. One pint and then home before those louses from down the road stopped to pay their respects again.

12

———

CALLUM

"General Pike, they're waiting for you in the command tent."

I woke from the dream, still tasting the woman's kiss in my mouth, feeling her hair running through my fingers, the men's hands on my skin. The sweetness faded quickly, replaced with dry, cold air and the stale smell of my tent. My eyes felt bruised, glued shut from sleep and I winced as I rubbed them open, crust against my fingers. I shivered as the frigid breeze flooded in from the open flap, carrying with it a scent that brought bile up my throat.

The sharp and bitter tang of blood layered with the too rich stench of shit and piss, meat burning over fires and stale ale soaking into the mud. A second breeze brought the backlash of magic hitting magic, my wards layering together at the edge of the field until they formed thin lines of electric storms.

I gagged and the corporal waiting for me turned away, clearing his throat over the sound.

"Breakfast, sir?"

"No," I said and the low tenor of my voice struck me as strange. I pushed my legs off the cot and they landed with a squish against the sinking rug on the ground. "Tell them I'm coming."

"Yes, sir." He vanished and I wondered how many soldiers along the way he'd tell about the Toy Soldier being too delicate for the battlefield.

I stared down at my feet, remembering to breathe through my mouth, that I should have put my boots on before getting out of the bed. Outside, men shouted as they passed, arguing over a woman in a tavern, and one of them was shoved roughly against a support pole, making my whole tent shake.

"Take it elsewhere," I bellowed and then winced, as pain stabbed through my skull and straight into my eye sockets.

Fuck. I really was going to be sick. And my breath reeked of alcohol, tongue dry and gummy as if it were wrapped in cotton.

I wiped my feet on the end of the sheet and shoved them into cold boots, pushing myself to stand. My lips firmed into a hard line as I waited to see what came next, balance or vomit. At least I was still dressed after the horror show of drinking from the night before. It was coming back slowly, replacing the fantasy of my dream with the bitter aftertaste of a bender. I brushed my uniform tidy enough, fixing my tie in the small camp mirror clipped to a pole, and then grimaced at myself.

The circles under my eyes were bruise-blue, cheeks hollow, and lips chapped to splitting. I scrubbed my hand over the shorn hair on my head, cut so close I could see my scalp, and frowned. I didn't recognize myself, could have sworn I was…younger the last time I looked in this mirror. Which was absurd, I didn't remember any other face. Maybe that was just how people felt as they got older.

I blinked and the faces I did remember weren't mine at all. Sweet brown eyes and a wry smile. Full lips and black stubble on dark skin. Black curls on a neck smudged with paint.

"Callum, where the hell are you?"

I spun, my brother James standing crooked in the opening of the tent, the flap draped over his shoulder as he leaned heavily onto a crutch. My chest froze at the sight of his left leg, the pant tied off at the knee, and my thoughts scrambling. He'd lost his leg? It was right and wrong all at once in my head. Just as quickly as the confusion and guilt sank heavily in my gut, churning in my stomach. That was my fault. I knew instinctively that it was me who'd put him in the line of fire and known the risk. Known it was *more* than a risk.

"Father's waiting on you, idiot," James growled, his body turning away so his amputated leg was out of sight. "The whole damn army is."

"I'm ready," I said, voice rasping.

James huffed and turned away. "You look like *shit*. But I suppose no one will care since it's *you*."

I followed James out, flinching at daylight even though clouds stretched over the sky in long, thick strips like bandages.

"If you're going to be sick, just keep it out of the path," James muttered. "Troops don't need to be trucking around your bad decisions from the night."

"And where are your decisions from last night?" I asked, the words falling out unbidden. "Did you send them up to the frontlines as usual or did you take a liking to one and get him tossed out of the ranks?"

James stopped still, his crutch sinking deep in soft mud as I reached his side. "You keep your fucking mouth shut or I'll tell Father about—"

"Or what?" I asked, the soft morning feeling from the dream distant now. Real life returning with every bitter, nasty word. "You know as well as I do there isn't a single discretion that would make Father see me as anything less than his prize pony. Not while this war goes on. And I don't know if you've noticed, but it's been twenty years, James. This war is never-ending."

"You fucked his new little bride," James hissed, face pushing into my space, eyes swollen and bloodshot.

My heart stopped. No. No, it wasn't possible.

They would never forgive me.

And then I realized, finally, painfully. There was no *they*. They were a dream.

I raised my eyebrows at James. "Well he's certainly not bothering to."

I carried on to the command tent without him. I knew the way.

"Fine fucking weather for this plan of yours," my father growled at my side.

We were at the top of the hill, icy spittle raining down on us from black night. We stared down at this month's battlefield, or what was left of it. We'd have to be moving on soon, but I was determined to gain ground in Vermenia before we did. Enmaire had seen enough blood for the year and if I was going send men to tear the earth into muddy pits, I'd rather it be far out of the way of my backyard.

"This is exactly the kind of weather we want," I retorted.

One ward pushing the ice and sleet onto the Vermenian troops, blinded by the cloud cover over the moon. Another keeping our soldiers out of the weather, dry from the mud. A third for brightening their vision. More still, to build rage against our enemies in their minds. To banish fear. The magic would work on them as long as they stayed in formation.

It only ever lasted for the first few minutes of battle before that same rage and fearlessness sent them scattering into the opponent. And it was a waste of magic to cover our men when the enemy was sheltered under the same wards. But it started us with an advantage and we won more than we lost.

Most days.

"If we lose as many men as your last plan we'll have to draw back," my father growled in my ear.

"If you distract me, you'll lose twice as many," I answered, voice hard, shrugging off the hand that pressed down on my shoulder. "I have a battle to win for you. Call home for more soldiers."

"They won't *give* me more with the way you spend them," he said.

"Tell them they'll have twenty miles of Vermenia to cover the loss," I called over my shoulder.

His footsteps squelched in the mud, pausing at the offer. "If we don't follow through…"

"Tell them and leave me to my *fucking* work!" I snapped.

My father left, steps slow and breaths heavy. He'd retire to the manor before long, and then the army would be mine. Unless they tried to appoint another weary old bastard to rein me in.

My fists clenched, fingernails digging into the skin of my palms, and I stretched my neck until it cracked and shook the tension out of my shoulders. This was all I wanted, these moments of magic and power, letting it take over my pounding head and aching body, erasing everything but the electric thrill of control.

I raised my hands, spreading my fingers out until they covered the width of the field below me. Metal clanged behind me, troops readying to rush the line on my order. I put them out of my thoughts. I had no speeches for these men, only a handful of minutes under safety before they took their chances against the Vermenians, with guns and swords and mallets in hand, whatever they still had and could carry.

Fire ignited in my bones, sparking at the bottom of my spine...

...the words tracing in black letters down my spine, her words...

...and rushing quickly up and over my shoulders down to the very tips of my fingers. Amber light gathered over my wrists and palms, threads twining in the air, spreading out like a spider's web, following my gaze down the hill.

It was as painful a feeling—forcing the power through me, shoving it out onto the battlefield—as it was a relief, like releasing an immense pressure through needle-thin points. When the power hovered in front of me I traced my fingers through it, like painting... like painting...

"Quit fidgeting," he said, eyes crinkling at the corners.

...smearing the color into sigils glowing in the air. Protection. Strength. Energy. Rage. I spun them together until the map of the ward was as intricate as lace like...

...lace on his collar, velvet on his jacket, like no one I'd ever seen before.

"Now," I barked over my shoulder.

The earth shook beneath as men charged past, rushing to take their place under the curtain of magic, shoulders knocking together as they tried to keep in the center, stay safest longest. Others, with blank gazes and grimacing mouths, took their places at the front of the ward. They knew what that position meant, they'd be out of safety soonest, least likely to return to their cot by morning, by tomorrow's noon, by evening, whenever the fighting ended.

Vermenia answered the screaming charge, fire stakes in hand. Those flames would wick out as soon as they touched my ice.

My body jarred as guns fired, the blasts clanging against my wards, echoing in my bones. Rust orange frontlines fell first, screams shattering through the air along the centerline.

Every blade striking off the ward brought copper to my tongue. Any minute now, they would break the lines, soldiers would charge out of position onto their opponent, blood boiling with the anger my magic drew out of them.

I ignored the ice sliding through strands of my hair, ringing down into my collar, beneath the cuffs of my coat, down into my boots.

Any minute now they would start falling, one by one, until I couldn't tell who was who for all the red on their coats.

13

AIDEN

There was a knock on the front door, echoing down the dark, empty hall. I stood at the counter of the kitchen, staring at the shadow of their outlines waiting outside, and took a deep breath. My stomach was still queasy from waking up with the hangover I didn't remember giving myself—although the bottles of evidence were in the sink when I woke up.

I tugged at the hem of my dinner jacket and started down the hall. They knocked again.

"Coming! Just a moment," I answered, my voice ringing off the walls and back into my tender eardrums. I should have found new art to hang after Isaac had left with his collection, the place just looked bare now.

I opened the door just in time to see Callum soothing an anxious Joanna, his fingers stroking through the dark curls she'd cut short again, her teeth digging into the corner of her lip.

"Hello you two," I said, trying to produce a smile as they straightened and blushed, eyes darting down to their toes. So perfectly in sync with one another.

I hated it. I craved seeing them and then hated the reminder. They were together. I was alone. Why had I agreed to this dinner in the first place?

"Is… is Isaac here?" Joanna asked, and I didn't miss the shiver of pain that swept over her face as she said his name.

"Not yet but he knows he's expected," I said, stepping aside. Callum had said it needed to be the whole coven, digging himself out of his books long enough to track me down in the conservatory to ask for the dinner.

They came in with soft steps, eyes studying the entry hall as if they didn't recognize the space, as if it hadn't been their home only a year ago.

"He's not bringing her with him, is he?" Callum asked, arm wrapping around Joanna's shoulder protectively.

"I never took down your wards," I told him, "Corina can't step a foot onto the property."

"Let's not talk about her," Joanna breathed, shrugging out of her coat and draping it over the banister just like she'd done in the beginning, when she was ours. All of ours. "I just wanted to see you both. It's been too long since we've spent time together and we are a- a…"

"Coven," I suggested as Joanna finished with, "A family."

I blinked at the word, my shattered heart slivering my chest with delicate wounds. I turned away from the door and lead them back into the kitchen. A family. That felt even less appropriate a word for us now as 'coven' did. We were a fractured thing—*why wasn't I putting us back together?*—and while Isaac had made the leaving easier for Joanna and Callum, he certainly hadn't started the dissolution of our coven.

I thought we'd make it out of Corina's spell…

…the words burning up in the fire…Joanna bringing Isaac back to bed and tucking him between us…

…Corina's hold over Isaac's heart, becoming his *muse*.

The wine I'd picked out for dinner was waiting on the counter and I poured us all steep glasses. I would need another bottle at least to get me through this night. I slid the glasses over to them, forcing my smile back onto my face.

"I don't know if I'll live up to Isaac's cooking, but I did my…"

Joanna was staring at the wine, chewing at the inside of her lip again in her nervous way. Callum looked back and forth between her and the wine, his eyes lighting up, mouth twitching with the words just waiting to burst out.

My stomach turned to stone and the wine was sand in my mouth. Joanna glanced up at me, eyes widening, filling with tears, a wobbly, hopeful smile spreading over her lips.

They said they had news to share. Wanted to see me and Isaac together before they said anything.

"You're pregnant," I said, my mouth turning paper dry, stomach churning as if last night's wine was rearing its head again. A baby. Joanna and Callum were having a baby. Living in a little row house together like packed sardines, too busy reading to cook themselves anything but plain pasta and tomato sandwiches.

"I wanted to say it," Joanna said, voice whispery, breaking. Somehow the sympathy on her face was just as painful as the joy.

I woke up with a heave, bile and bad wine and sorrow in my throat. Joanna was sobbing on the mattress at my side, Isaac scrambling across the sheets away from her. Callum lay with eyes open wide at the ceiling, his fingers fisting so tight in the sheets I thought he was likely to tear through them.

"Did I… did I hurt her?" Isaac whispered, face bloodless white.

"You *left* her, you left *us*," I snarled.

"You…all…left," Joanna gasped through wracking cries.

Callum twitched at that, rolling to his side and gathering Joanna up tight in his arms until she was clinging to him. With every broken moan from her lips, Callum returned to himself, his face softening from the frozen shock, until he was sitting up, Joanna bundled to his chest.

"Nightmare," I said, blinking. We were in our bedroom, together, and my mouth was dry as dust and horribly stale, but this was *our* home. Not mine alone.

Isaac looked like he was about to fall off the end of the bed, expression stricken and fixed to Joanna. I grabbed his wrist, his whole body flinching in response.

"Ise, it was a nightmare. Just a nightmare, come here. Come here."

Isaac remained stiff and frozen, watching Joanna sniffle into Callum's shoulder.

"That wasn't just a nightmare," Callum said, voice hollow.

"No," I agreed. It was my worst fear, played out over the course of a day. Living alone in the tower house, our coven in pieces, a child in a family I didn't really belong to, would only know in a cursory way.

Isaac exhaled and fell forward onto the mattress, tugging on my hand until I knew it was safe to go to him. I could guess what he dreamt of—turning into his father, hurting Joanna. I wrapped him up in my arms, a mirror of Callum and Joanna, and that was not enough to soothe the terrifying sense that my dream was waiting just around the corner. That I might blink and find myself awake in the wrong version of my life all over again.

Callum caught my glance, jerking his head, and we scooted closer. Under his breath, Isaac chanted, "I'm sorry. I'm sorry." Until all at once Joanna twisted out of Callum's hold and into mine, her arms circling Isaac's neck. Callum followed, the pair of us framing Joanna and Isaac. The bond thrummed and I shivered. Together our heartbeats slowed and steadied to a perfect, even pace with one another.

"I know who I would be without you," Callum whispered, a shadow passing over his face.

"You are a good man," I said, seeing the doubt flickering back in answer. "That's not who you would be, it's who you refuse to be."

Callum swallowed, head ducking down to rest his forehead against the back of Joanna's neck. Joanna was whispering in Isaac's ear, sweetness and trust, until he was soft, kissing the skin of her shoulder, vowing gentleness.

"We're all going to be alright now," I promised, hearing the catches in their breath as they settled back into calm, all of us surrounded by one another.

The words I'd said to Callum rang in my own head. I refused to let my coven fall apart, to let anything come between us. It didn't matter if Joanna and Callum operated on a level of understanding I hadn't reached with her yet. It wouldn't matter if a beauty caught Isaac's eye in the future. I was going to do whatever it took to make sure we were safe, we were together, and that our love for each other stood against any obstacle.

Starting with whatever had thrown us into those nightmares.

⁂

"THERE IS ABSOLUTELY nothing pointing to this being Scrivens!" Joanna shouted. Isaac's fingers threaded through hers were all that kept her from storming into President Anders' face, nose to nose, and beautifully furious.

We were in the Mayor's office in City Hall, summoned barely an hour after waking up from the nightmares. An entire day was lost to the spelled sleep and my coven wasn't the sole victim. All throughout Canderfey, every single person lay trapped in a nightmare replica of their life.

"It's unidentified magic, Miss Wick, and you'd do well to let your coven speak for you on this matter," Anders said, glamour shimmering with the effort of maintaining his illusion of serenity. His magic was fraying at the edges, and I wondered what kind of strain he'd survived in his sleep.

Joanna caught a ragged breath, falling back into Isaac's chest, where his arms closed loosely around her.

"She's one of two Scrivens you allowed in on this discussion," Callum said, barely restraining the snarl. "She has every right to defend herself and her peers. There's plenty of forms of magic capable of casting dream states over a population. I've used them myself."

"And did you use them yesterday?" Mayor Sewell asked, his voice cutting through the shouting with quiet efficiency.

My head was spinning. The Mayor looked as if he hadn't seen a wink of sleep, eyes red and skin that same haggard pale as the rest of us. He was still calm, though, still guarded and stoic. Whatever he'd lived through in his sleep, it hadn't visibly shaken him, only drained away some of that clean, dry look of his.

"Of course not," Callum said, steel covering the tremoring voice he'd woken with. His hands were knotted behind his back, knuckles white, and I knew his dream was following his thoughts even now. I remembered the early years with him, the stretch of lost time where he sat in silence, mentally replaying scenes from a battlefield. Startling from sleep, screaming.

Sewell's dark eyes passed over Callum, and then Joanna, before landing on Myles Kershaw. The man looked about twenty years older than the last time I'd seen him, all of his joy washed out of him from that drugged sleep.

"Is it possible that this was Scrivens magic?" Mayor Sewell asked him. Callum, Joanna, Anders, and I all rushed to answer, but Sewell held a hushing hand up, his eyes fixed onto Myles' face.

"I believe it is possible," Myles answered, his strong, wide features as still as stone.

Anders made a triumphant sound but was silenced with a glare from Sewell.

"And do you believe it is likely?" Sewell asked Myles.

I held my breath and found Joanna staring at me, a little furrow between her brow and a question in her eyes that I had no answer for. Was there any hope? I had no idea. I couldn't read Sewell. I couldn't even read Myles for that matter.

"No, sir," Myles said, taking a slow breath. "My people came to me frightened, believing *we* had been the focus of the attack."

"That is easily faked," Anders rushed to say.

"Will you look into the matter?" Sewell asked Myles.

"Of course."

"Look *into it?*" Anders shouted.

"I would like it if you or your department would investigate as well," Sewell carried on, now to Callum before turning to Anders.

"But of course the faculty is your domain, just as we agreed the Scrivens would be mine."

The glamour wavered, thinning and revealing the sweat and boiled red anger on Anders' face. He looked every bit as bad as the rest of us, and under the flush, he was gray with exhaustion. "Then I want them off the campus."

"Not without an investigation," I said, finally finding my tongue. All the heads in the office turned to me, but I soaked up their focus instead of shying away, and stepped forward. "This is why Myles was appointed, to represent the refugees and—"

"As if he were going to be *honest*—" Anders scoffed.

"*And*, a professor from the wards and warfare department of the university," I added, rushing over Anders before he could put another asinine objection together. "Of your choice, President Anders, of course. It's simply important that we not make this a *witch hunt*. Not in this town."

At the sudden flare of pride rushing down the bond from Joanna, I had to freeze and stop myself from puffing my chest out.

"I'll ask the police chief to make inquiries in town," Sewell offered, nodding at me. "For now I'm inclined to see this as a possible student experiment gone astray. I don't want action taken against the Scrivens."

My coven bond rang like a cymbal, all of us struck hard with surprise and confusion, and it cleared away some of the fog left in my head after the attack of magic. I was less and less certain that Sewell was aligned with Anders. He seemed to be more aware of what moves we were all making than we were of his maneuvers, but this was a conclusion to the discussion that worked in my coven's interests and the interests of the Vermenians.

The meeting wrapped up in the wake of shock, Anders requesting further word with Sewell. I watched as the Mayor steeled himself with a long breath before agreeing, and then I followed my coven out of the office into the bustling City Hall corridor.

Joanna wrapped her arm around Myles in a quick, tight hug. "We'll make sure nothing happens to any of you," she said.

"I know, leina, but take care of yourselves right now," Myles said, brow furrowing. "Don't anger that boss of yours."

"There's nothing Anders could say or do that would ever manage to get Woolard to part with Joanna," I said. And nothing was going to get Gwen out of that library before she was ready to leave.

Joanna squeezed Myles once more. "Let me write you a door back home. We'll make sure it's cleaned away."

"Here?" Myles asked, eyebrows raising, watching city officials passing us. "I'm not sure that's a good idea."

"Come with me," Isaac suggested, stopping in front of a door to a men's restroom. "I'll help. Joanna's right, you should get back to the others sooner rather than later. Let them know what was decided."

It was enough to sway Myles and he kissed Joanna's cheek good-bye, before following Isaac into the restroom. Joanna rounded on us as soon as the door was shut, skin still pale, but eyes sharp with new plans.

"Who will Anders leave in charge of the investigation on campus?" she asked Callum.

He scratched his fingers through his hair, body nearly tipping over before Joanna propped him up, her palm sliding up his spine and covering his tattoo.

"If he's solely determined to persecute the Scrivens, he could put Greensmith on the case. He'd certainly bungle the investigation into a problem for us," he said.

"Talk to your department," I said. Callum blinked at me, mouth frowning and gaze unfocused. "See if someone less biased can't make an argument to Anders before he makes a decision. Someone who will do the work *right*."

"No one in the department is going to get to the bottom of what-ever that spell was on their own," Callum said. *Except me*, was left out of the sentiment, for now.

"As long as the hunt doesn't lead directly to Myles and his people, I'll consider it a success," I said.

Joanna chewed the inside of her lip, glancing back and forth between me and Callum. "Maybe we should all go back to the house and… and rest…together?" she suggested.

Callum shook his head, squeezing her to his side, as Isaac reemerged from the restroom alone. "No, Aiden is right. I'll go talk to my department now while Anders is still speaking with Sewell. Frost has a halfway decent brain when he bothers. I'll meet you all at home." He kissed Joanna's hair and then stumbled out of her hold and crossed the hall to me.

I was watching Isaac over his shoulder, still too skittish around Joanna after the nightmares, and I didn't realize Callum was studying me until his hands were raising up to hold my face. He leaned in, placing a fragile kiss on my lips.

"I'm glad you found me," he whispered, with a swift, second press of his mouth against mine that I returned.

"Don't waste any of your time arguing if you think they won't listen," I said as he drew away. "Just come home, be with us."

He nodded and left, jogging down the stairs. Joanna pulled me closer by my shirtsleeve, her arm wrapped tightly around Isaac's.

"I'd write us home too if I could," Joanna said. "But we might end up with some city official wandering in after us."

"I don't mind the walk." I thought of my dream, feeling sick at the memory of the house empty, the color washed away with Isaac's departure, the rooms quiet without Joanna's playful bickering, too clean without Callum's stacks of books toppling over.

"I just want to be alone with my coven," Joanna murmured, resting her head against my shoulder.

My feet stumbled as we reached the stairs and my heart soared, the nightmare's barbs softening at her words.

14

JOANNA

None of us were eager to go back to sleep that night. I had a book in my lap, but the words might as well have been in one of Callum's favorite ancient languages for all I understood of them. Aiden picked up his guitar for a moment, barely checking it was tuned, before putting it away again. Isaac sat at my back, fingers sliding around my curls in a rhythm that left me almost dozing. If that weren't such a terrifying prospect. Upstairs, I could hear Callum pacing.

"Come on," I said, pushing up from my seat on the couch. Isaac was too fast to release me, usually he'd hold on longer, so I reached back and tugged him up after me.

"Where are we going?" Isaac asked.

"Up to Callum to help him research," I said, heading for the stairs. I nodded at Aiden in his chair by the window. "You too, come on!"

"He *likes* his work, leave him to it," Aiden growled from his seat.

I spun in the doorway and resisted the urge to set my hands on my hips—he'd teased me for that enough over the past couple of months.

"I just lived a life where none of you wanted me," I said and Isaac crowded my back, his hands on my hips as if to make up for that injury. "I don't know what you dreamt of, but I think we can all guess where Callum was. We should be together tonight. And I may not know exactly what I'm looking for as I help him, but I can still *try*."

Aiden sat as still as a statue through my tirade, and it took every bit of strength I had to stare back at him when the words ran dry. Foolish. I was only proving to him that I was still new in this house. That I didn't know them as well. That I threw temper tantrums and picked fights and—

Aiden sighed and groaned as he pushed out of his chair. "You're right, darling."

Isaac's hands squeezed my waist and I resisted the urge to ask Aiden to repeat himself. Instead, I turned and rushed up the stairs with clumsy feet, letting my steps cover the sounds of Isaac and Aiden whispering as my cheeks flushed.

Callum was standing still in his library office when I arrived, his stare traveling out the far window and I winced at the state of the room, books strewn about, stacked open face on top of one another, or laying about on the floor. If he weren't so clearly in a bad state of mind, I would have given him one of Gwen's patented lectures on the proper care of books. There was a pot of tea sitting on top of one of the open books in an armchair and I went to that first. The pot was empty and there was a drained cup in a stained saucer on another stack not far away.

"You have an odd taste in bookmarks, Callum," I said, glancing at him and seeing him jump as if he hadn't noticed me come into the room before then.

He blinked at me, watching as I cleared the tea things out of the way, passing them to Isaac as he and Aiden came into the room. Callum's hand shook as he combed it through his hair. Pinned to the window frame behind him was my terrible scribble of a teacup— thankfully no lopsided dishware had turned up in the house in response.

"No more caffeine," I said to Isaac under my breath. I raised the book I'd rescued from the teapot up to Callum, and showing him the spine I asked, "Anything useful in this one?"

"I- I can't remember," he said.

"I'll skim," Aiden offered, taking the book from me and settling into the armchair.

"What are you all doing up here?" Callum asked.

"Helping," I said.

I'd spent enough time in Callum's office that I was familiar with his shelving system, and I started sorting through the discarded books, returning them to their homes. Behind me, Callum stumbled over to Aiden's seat and collapsed on the floor. I looked over my shoulder to find him leaning against Aiden's legs, his head drooping to rest against Aiden's knee.

"I honestly can't remember anything useful from these past few hours," Callum muttered, lips mumbling over a pant leg.

Aiden shut the book and tucked it against his side, his fingers sliding into Callum's hair and scratching at his scalp until Callum's shoulders were sagging. "I'm not sure now is the time for research," Aiden said, a weak, wry smile on his lips as he looked at me.

"I don't think I should sleep," Callum whispered, one hand clutching around Aiden's ankle. "But it's been a long time since I've felt this tired and I can't focus for shit."

I opened my mouth to say we would take over the work when Aiden leaned forward.

"What do you need?" he asked, tugging slightly on Callum's hair until the younger man's head tilted back to look at him.

There was a stretch of quiet as they stared at one another, something passing in the silence that I couldn't name, but made my body perk into attention. Callum shifted on the floor and Aiden spread his knees apart to give him room. "You," Callum said, chin lifting up, voice soft.

All the words in my head died on my tongue as I watched Callum's hand slide up Aiden's thigh, covering his crotch and squeezing there. Aiden grunted softly and bent forward, dragging Callum up by his collar and kissing him with licking strokes of his tongue, the sound loud in my ears as I held my breath and watched.

I'd played the voyeur with them plenty of times before, but this felt different, more private. They hadn't said a word to me and I wondered if I shouldn't leave the room. Aiden was groaning into Callum's mouth, body just beginning to churn in his seat, folded uncomfortably, when Callum pulled away with a gasp and a high groan. Aiden's hands braced on the arms of the chair as he lifted his hips, Callum's fingers scrambling to undo the button on the waistband in front of him, face nuzzling into the crotch of Aiden's trousers.

Isaac reappeared in the doorway, surprise softening into a knowing smile, and my eyes darted between him, and Aiden and Callum fumbling together to free Aiden's stiffening cock. On the second pass, Aiden caught me staring and turned his head to Isaac.

"Kiss her," he ordered, my body warming at the command in his voice.

Isaac's smile froze and Aiden tilted his head. "You would never hurt her, Isaac. Go to her."

Hurt me? Isaac? The notion was almost laughable if not for the sudden fall of Isaac's smile. I reached my hand out to him and his shoulders sagged as he crossed the room to me. There were still books cradled in my other arm and he took them with one hand, setting them on a shelf above my head, his free hand sliding behind my waist to hold me to his chest.

"Are you afraid of me?" I asked.

Isaac's smile was bitter. "No, my love. Do you want to watch them?" he asked in my ear, hands distracting me with light, teasing scratches of his nails up my ribs and down over my ass.

Aiden seemed satisfied with us, his body dropping back against the chair, Callum's head ducking to press a line of kisses up the length of his dark cock, thumb swirling the seeping liquid over the thick, blunt head. Aiden groaned as Callum reached the tip of him, mouth enclosing him with a wet suck. Aiden's eyes opened, locking with mine.

"Answer him," Aiden ordered.

"Yes," I whispered to Isaac, feeling useless and dumb in my own body as I watched Callum teasing and torturing Aiden with a practice that must have been built over years. A flush rose in Aiden's cheeks as his hands stroked through Callum's hair and down his neck, caressing more than guiding, eyes watching Callum's mouth with heavy-lidded focus. When he looked up at Isaac and me again, the heat in his gaze left me melting.

"Lift your skirts," he said to me. "I want to watch as Isaac touches you, turns you pink and needy until you're begging us to fuck you."

There was a challenge in his stare and it made me twitch in excitement. Weeks upon weeks of us arguing, stubbornly resisting one another, and I finally felt like the game could be used for something we might both enjoy. I raised my brows in tart refusal, watching his stare darken, and then twisted my hands behind my back, smiling as I pulled the zipper of my dress down.

Isaac's breath sighed against the skin of my neck, his thumbs hooking into my collar and pulling the dress forward, down my shoulders. I pushed my underwear off over my hips with the dress, letting it all fall to the floor at my feet. Skirts down, not up. Isaac's warmth surrounded my back, goosebumps trailing after his hands as he stroked them up my waist and over my breasts, fingers slowing to toy at my nipples.

Aiden's chest was rising and falling in time with the bobs of Callum's head and he grinned at me with gritted teeth. "Always the clever girl."

"He only teases when he knows you'll take the bait," Isaac said, lips against the lobe of my ear. He nuzzled against the back of my neck and then caught the lobe between his teeth, making me turn soft in his arms, my head tilting in the hopes he might treat more skin in the same fashion.

"I'm an easy target," I breathed.

Aiden frowned briefly and then his eyes slammed shut as Callum crowded closer between his legs, both hands working, tongue lapping, claiming more.

"You have more power over him than you realize," Isaac whispered in my hair. "Just watch."

His hands slid back down to my hips, nudging open my legs with a gentle touch. He didn't tease me, not that I needed much encouragement after watching Callum and Aiden, but instead left me shouting out in surprise as two fingers plunged deep into my soaked core, his other hand pinching hard at my clit. My knees shook and Aiden's eyes flashed open, landing between my legs where Isaac was working at a fast speed, trying to take me apart before I even enjoyed the build-up.

"No," Aiden barked, voice rasping and throat bobbing as he tried to fight off pleasure in favor of controlling the moment. "Slow. Make her soak your fingers first."

Isaac hid his laugh in my hair and then his fingers drew slowly out of me, carrying the trail of wetness on them up to my breasts, leaving me shivering as he kissed my neck and shoulders. He softened the touch on my clit, drawing patterns on my pussy and pulling every sound free from my lips. My toes were curling into the carpet and I was jealous of the distance between us, and Aiden and Callum across the room, left exposed and greedy for their attention.

Callum was groaning as Aiden resisted the urge to thrust his hips up into his mouth, both of their hands roving, clutching, twining together.

"I want to touch you," I called to Aiden, letting my voice crack with the plea in the hopes that it would weaken him.

He swallowed, his hips jerking in the seat as Callum rose up around his length, his body squirming where he knelt, trying to find some of his own relief.

"Darling girl," Aiden gasped, a long rattling groan following the words. "You can wait your turn."

I turned my head away, finding Isaac waiting there, his mouth soothing mine with more care and tenderness than the bite I craved in the moment. I whimpered, wrapping my hand over his on my breast and squeezing, forcing his grip until he was hissing into the kiss. His body pressed tighter against my back, fingers diving back into my cunt, making me cry out and arch in his hold, nearly throwing myself forward.

"She's soaked," Isaac growled against my cheek.

But Aiden was occupied, hips bucking as Callum's fist pumped and squeeze around his base, tongue licking swirls around the head and then sucking hard.

"Fuuuck," Aiden moaned, the word falling out with a tremble, his head pressed against the back of the chair as Callum let him thrust into his mouth in a rough way I couldn't manage. Isaac's fingers were a steady pump inside of me, thumb barely brushing over my clit, just enough to make me twist and whine as I watched our lovers.

Aiden's eyes popped open with a shout, his whole body shaking as Callum finished him with eager whines, his hands sliding up under Aiden's shirt to scratch at his stomach as he swallowed inch after inch of throbbing length. Aiden's body went limp with slow quakes until he was hissing and pushing Callum back. Callum surged up, bending over Aiden in the chair, and I could see a brief glimpse of the tight stretch at the front of his pants where he was hard and ready for his own attention. They kissed, a sloppy but thorough care of each other's mouths, before Aiden pulled Callum in a clumsy landing to his side.

"Watch Isaac finish her off, then you can clean her up and have whoever you want," Aiden said to Callum.

"Oh, and what do I get for my efforts?" Isaac asked. His hand at my breast rose higher, fingers spreading across my collarbone to hold me steady as my legs shook, my orgasm edging closer with every pump of his fingers inside, every flirt of his thumb near my clit.

My breaths stuttered in my chest, whines held tight behind my lips, breaths uneven, my hips circling into Isaac's touch.

"Make her come and I'll tell you," Aiden answered with a grin, his arm wrapped around Callum's chest as if to hold him back.

"Please," I whispered, head tilting back to rest on Isaac's shoulder. "Please."

He pressed his mouth to my cheek as his thumb swirled hard over my swollen clit, his fingers crooking and stroking inside me until I was sobbing with relief and stars burst in my eyes, hips chasing his hand as I shook with release.

I didn't see Aiden give Callum permission, my vision was still dancing as Isaac held me up, his thumb pushing me through the after-shocks, one stroke after another. All I heard was the thump of knees landing on the floor in front of me and then a hand gripped my thigh, lifting and pushing it aside as a hot tongue was sliding over my sensitive flesh.

Callum licked and sucked and cleaned me with an urgency belying how badly he needed his own turn, hungry growls reverberated off my wet skin as he huddled closer, his tongue dipping inside of me to draw out more of my flavor. I shouted, bucking softly against his chin, and Isaac held me up, arms wrapped around my chest. My trembling fingers tugged on Callum's copper curls but instead of drawing away, he lifted my other leg over his shoulder, lips wrapping around my clit and tongue lashing until I was twisting on his mouth. He sucked hard until he threw me into an unexpected and harsh climax. Ecstasy burned through my veins, my muscles taut and strained, and my voice choked in my throat.

I was a weak mess as Isaac and Callum lowered me to the floor, but when I saw Callum's hands undoing the front of his pants I squirmed up to one elbow, determined to help him.

"Can you take me?" Callum whispered to me, and without meaning to my eyes slid to Aiden, asking for a permission I never would have questioned before that moment. But he was the conductor of this experience as if we were all his instruments to arrange into some new masterpiece. He smirked as I found myself waiting for his agreement.

"I told him whoever he wants," Aiden rumbled.

"If she's tired—" Callum began, ready to object on my behalf.

I sat up, taking his face in my hands and drawing it to my own, pulling his lips between mine and drinking the flavor of myself from his mouth. "I want you," I promised him.

He pushed me to the floor with a pained sound, his body landing over mine with a beautiful weight. Our hands fumbled between us, pushing his pants far enough away to release his cock, hot and steel hard as it landed against my belly, a droplet of precum wetting my skin. I was trying to undo the buttons of his shirt, craving more skin, when Callum was tapping at my entrance, pushing in without warning, both of us moaning.

Isaac had readied me, but two orgasms in and I was swollen and oversensitive. I wrapped my arms and legs around him as he pressed me to the floor, his hips kicking and pumping, the carpet scratching at my back as he fucked me.

"Gods, Joanna," Callum panted, heart beating hard enough for me to feel it against my breast.

"I have you."

He groaned at my words, head dropping to my shoulder, cock driving in steady, quick plunges. He was like a drumbeat inside of me, the rhythm matching the pound of my blood in my ears. I wasn't sure if I was numb or drowning in sensation, but the sound of Callum's broken shouts in my ear were satisfying a new kind of craving. I wanted his pleasure more than my own in that moment.

Above my head, I could see Isaac and Aiden embracing. Aiden was whispering in Isaac's ear, marking up his throat with biting kisses while Isaac nodded, chest heaving. I reached one arm back to the chair, wanting them closer, to have all of us together, and Aiden smiled. He nodded to Isaac who stood, pulling his shirt off over his head, pants already unbuckled. He pushed them down and kicked the legs off, coming to straddle the backs of Callum's knees. My breath caught in my chest as Isaac winked at me, sucking his fingers into his mouth and wetting them.

Callum shouted, thrusting deep with Isaac's first touch against his ass, and it left me arching with a muffled scream. Callum's arms circled my back, thrusts slowing as if he was working himself onto Isaac's fingers as he drew out of me, his brow furrowed, breaths short and rapid.

"Aiden," I called, until he was kneeling over my head.

"I'm here, darling," he soothed, smiling at me upside down, his head ducking to lick and kiss at my lips. Callum was curling on top of me, teeth digging into my shoulder as he grunted with every roll of his hips.

Aiden's fingers tangled in my hair, lifting my head slightly to take his kiss, his tongue flicking over the backs of my teeth.

"You have to make her come," Isaac said at Callum's back.

I wanted to protest, I was more than well cared for, but Aiden kept my lips busy, muffling my words. Callum sat up, pulling my hips onto his lap, his cock still nestled deep in my cunt, but the angle left the head of him dragging along my front walls and Aiden pulled away to let me shout delirious praises at the ceiling, numbness turning into sudden, explosive pleasure, the wet slap of flesh echoing with our heavy breaths.

My legs shook, my hands scrambling at Aiden's thighs behind my head, and Callum set his hand over my mound, the heel of his palm grinding dully into my aching clit. I was a wild, animal thing, my skin aching and tender. I made a strangled sound as Aiden started to pinch and pull at my nipples, his breath huffing with laughter. I couldn't think or speak and I had no leverage to control Callum's striking cock inside of me. The room seemed to tip, floor dropping out beneath me, and I came with a scream, the explosion cascading into a soft, glittering feeling stroking through me, head to toe.

No, it wasn't the floor dropping away after all. Aiden was simply drawing my shoulders onto his lap, hands soothing through my hair. Callum bucked and groaned, head thrown back and throat flexing as he filled me up with four hot pumps and then came trembling down to lay at my chest. My breath was still shuddering, cunt still fluttering, and Callum whimpered into the skin of my throat.

Isaac was fitting himself against Callum's exposed ass, hands holding his cheeks apart, cock glistening with lubricant although who knew where he'd found it. Callum hadn't softened as Isaac eased himself inside Callum's ass, and I laughed in dazed wonder to feel Callum twitching in pleasure.

"You alright, darling?" Aiden asked me.

I bit my lip, watching Isaac's eyes flutter shut, his lips parted. Aiden's fingers tapped my chin softly, a reminder, and I looked up to him, smiling and nodding.

"I want to watch," I said. Callum was heavy against me, but Aiden pressed to my back kept me from being crushed to the floor, or the carpet from scratching me raw—I could feel a tender burn there that would leave me daydreaming tomorrow.

Callum made a sound like a sob by my ear and I pressed my cheek to his face. "We have you, my love," I murmured in his ear, his arms clutching tight around my waist, hips making abbreviated little nudges as Isaac rocked against him. Callum was staying hard inside me as if the stimulation was prolonging his arousal, and when I squeezed around him, his mouth opened on a wobbling moan, and then his lips wrapped around my shoulder, tongue lapping sweat from my skin and teeth clenching just on the wonderful side of aching.

"You're so good to us, Callum," Isaac rasped, hands running a path up and down Callum's back, leaning forward to pepper kisses down his spine.

"We love you," I said, as Callum gasped and groaned and squirmed between us.

"You're ours, Pike," Aiden growled.

"Fuck, fuck, Isaac, please," Callum begged, his body bucking back and forth in earnest now.

I hoped no one demanded I come again. Callum's movements were soft enough not to leave me aching, but I knew I was pushed past a limit already. I stroked my hands up his side, teasing at ticklish places, pulling one of his wrists up to my mouth to kiss and suck. Isaac's rhythm echoed inside me until Callum was tense and rigid on top of me, and Isaac was gasping high and anxious.

"Beautiful."

I said it without meaning to, watching them, feeling them, knowing the exact moment it would happen when they both froze and shuddered, their voices chorusing in relief, Callum's cock twitching inside of me, and his hot release dripping out from between us. I held my breath as Isaac collapsed. Now the weight really was too much, almost oppressive.

Aiden pushed Callum back slightly, the younger man hissing, and pulled me free from beneath them, scooping me up against his chest, his hand cupping between my legs to stop the rush of fluids. My eyes went wide as he slid three fingers inside me, my mouth falling open and my chest stilling on a caught breath.

"I'll take you upstairs, clean us both up," Aiden said, gaze locked on mine. His fingers stroked softly inside me, a calloused thumb scratching over my too sensitive clit, every brush an electric spark of nerves that fluttered through me. "But first, you should know. I dreamt of losing you too."

My breath released on a shaky huff, as Aiden drew me hard against his chest, thumb working faster as his mouth took mine with a desperate hunger. The touch was painful and stunning, and I knew, *knew,* he would have me falling to pieces for him if he just *didn't stop.* Or I would be trapped in this exact pressure of perfect sensation until I lost my mind. I wrapped my arms over his shoulders, held him so tight I thought we both might stop breathing, and when he sucked my tongue into his mouth I burst, my body hot as flames, a mingling of mine and Callum's juices coating his hand.

"Good girl," he growled in my ear, my body shivering in response as if I had more to give, would start the whole evening over again just from those words. His eyes were warm on my face and I felt stunned and taken apart as if Aiden knew some wonderful secret about me that I'd been entirely unaware of until now. I don't know that I fully understood, even in that moment.

"Take me up to bed," I whispered.

He smiled, kissing my nose, and nodded, lifting us both off the floor with a grunt, Isaac and Callum rolling to their backs on the carpet, their chests rising and falling with their breaths.

"Come on, lads," Aiden said, grinning at me. "Catch up."

⚫

SOONER OR LATER sleep had to come for us, and the interlude in Callum's office had settled some of the emotional bruisings from the day before. Isaac fell asleep with his cheek pillowed on my breast, and then Aiden not long after him with his arm slung over my belly. I must have dozed too because I don't remember Callum leaving the bed, but when I woke with the need to pee, he was gone. I left the bathroom and stared at the mattress, my spot between Aiden and Isaac still open and waiting for me, and then at the cracked door to the bedroom.

I tiptoed down the stairs to his office, but it was every bit the mess we'd left it and I resisted the urge to reorganize his books in the dead of night. My steps creaked back out of the room and I chewed my lip, wondering where to find Callum.

"Joanna."

I jumped at the whisper and followed it to the stairs, seeing Callum's tired face looking up at me from the second story landing.

"Go back to bed, Jo. I'm alright," he said, wearing a frail smile.

"Where were you hiding?" I asked.

"My bedroom," he replied, a wry quirk turning up the corners of his mouth in earnest.

It was too late an hour to understand something so strange. Callum had never, in all the time I'd been a part of their lives, slept in his own bed. He seemed to use the room as a closet. Or a bit of extra storage for his books.

I hurried down the steps, ignoring Callum's shaking head.

"No, love, go back to the others," he coaxed as I reached him, leaning into his chest and smiling as his arms circled around me in reflex.

"You shouldn't sleep alone," I said, pushing him into the hall in the direction of his little back corner room.

"Joanna, I'm not sleeping," Callum said, words sighing out. My feet paused and then continued forward, dragging him along with me. "Joanna, I'm going to have night terrors."

The words were sharper, his hands landing on my shoulders and holding me still. He was a shadow in the dark of the hallway and our faces bumped together as he bent down, his nose nudging mine before he pressed a soft kiss to my mouth. "I don't want to hurt you or the others. And sometimes… I shout. I don't want to wake anyone up. It'll be alright. Aiden and Isaac will understand. Go back upstairs."

I chewed my lip, as fresh bitterness at Callum's father rose up, at the war Callum had been forced to be a part of, the scars it left in his mind. They had come back to haunt him with the enchanted nightmare, and it wasn't like the passing distraction and worry I was so used to with him. Aiden and Isaac would understand because it had been Aiden and Isaac who'd known Callum first, still years after the war. But I wasn't willing to sacrifice my covenmate's rest and peace if there was an alternative.

"What if I wrote something for you?" I asked, and I kissed the corner of his mouth. "You can help me pick the words. Something like… Callum sleeps peacefully without bad dreams or…"

"Joanna," Callum sighed, arms wrapping around my back and hugging me to his chest.

"Callum couldn't ever possibly hurt Joanna," I added, as a suggestion.

He jerked against me and then his breath puffed in laughter against my lips, his back softening under my hands. He scooped me up, my toes dangling to the floor.

"Alright you lovely, mad creature," he said, grunting as he carried me down the hall. "We'll try tonight, but if you feel me start to kick or moan, out of the bed you go and I don't care how tired you are."

I smiled, kissing his cheek. We found a spare bit of paper on the bedside table, and a pen in one of his jacket pockets. The room, which was smaller than any other in the house—and consisted of a bed, side table, and closet—smelled stale and unused, and I cracked open a window as I thought of what to write. Callum piled books off the bed, into his arms, and then set them down in a wobbling stack on the floor by the closet.

"What about this…" I started and then hesitated. I always found it harder to speak the words out loud before writing them down, but Callum liked to remind me that it was better than risking a slip of a word that might have the wrong results. "There are no nightmares in Canderfey tonight."

I could see Callum's expression by the moonlight falling through the window, saw the way the tense lines in his forehead smoothed away, mouth softening with a smile.

"Why take care of one covenmate when you can help a whole town, eh Jo?" he said.

I blushed and turned my face down to the page, taking his teasing as an agreement that the words would suffice. I scribbled them out, squinted and checked for errors, and then rested the pen on the page. I would burn it in the morning just to be safe, but I was satisfied it would keep Callum's night terrors away.

He shook the sheet loose, dust glittering silver by the moonlight, and then waited for me to slip beneath, following me after. The bed was narrow, barely wide enough to fit us even when I curled into Callum's shoulder. He was stiff on the bed and I wondered if I ought to write him to sleep, just to be sure he got the rest he badly needed. Instead, I rolled closer to the wall, pulling him with me until his cheek was against my collarbone. I scratched my fingers through his hair and heard his almost silent groan.

"Witch," he whispered with affection.

"Sleep, Callum," I answered, making patterns on his scalp with my nails, knowing the way it made him soft and easy in my arms. "I have you."

15

AIDEN

I was flipping through dresses on Hildy's rack, trying to decide which might suit Joanna's taste well enough to allow me to get away with the minor extravagance. Her new shop girl, the youngest of the Vermenian Grivet sisters who'd been living with Corina in the little attic, watched me from behind the counter with a coy smile, as if she knew I was entirely on the wrong track.

"I don't think I have your size, dear," Hildy said, appearing from the back room.

I grinned at her. "You most certainly do not," I answered, eyeing the fragile laces and thin silks that draped like water to the floors. "The Faculty Ball is next week after the students leave and I overheard Joanna saying she'd wear a dress she already has…"

Hildy raised an eyebrow. "It's not as if the dresses she has are shabby."

"Of course not," I said, rushing to cover myself, and putting a table between us just to be safe. Hildy had made all of Joanna's dresses. "I only thought… just something new to surprise her."

"Mmhm," Hildy hummed, smirking. "Because Joanna loves surprises."

I frowned at that. "She doesn't *mind* them." She didn't always see the need for the finery I tended to tuck into her closet, but she never refused a gift and I hadn't seen that old misfitting wool skirt of hers in months.

Hildy finally laughed, shooing me away from her display of hats and gloves. "If it's the Faculty Ball, you'll want the other side of the shop. I'm not sending Joanna out in less than she deserves."

She pointed over to the opposite wall where her individual pieces, works of art really, hung facing out for full appreciation. My eye caught on a glittering gold gown, gilded with beadwork that mimicked the rays of the sun over a dense bronze fabric. I reached for the hanger when Hildy made an odd sound behind me, something between a 'hmm' and a huff.

I let my hand drop. "Oh just say it."

"Joanna doesn't want to be sent out into a crowd glittering like a crown for you," Hildy said, walking up to my side.

"You said I should come to this side of the room. All of these dresses are *statements*," I said, staring down at my old friend.

Hildy only smiled up at me, serene and knowing. "Yes, but some are louder than others. Come on, King, I know you love your clothes."

I stared down the length of the wall, wondering how I'd landed myself into a pop quiz with Hildy on fashion, of all things. I walked over to a long, simple, black gown, draped to exaggerate a woman's curves.

"That one's too quiet," Hildy said and when I turned to glare at her she was grinning and shrugging. "Oh, I'm sorry, but *everyone* wears black at the Faculty Ball. Do better."

"Why don't you pick the dress out for me? I know you have one in mind for her."

The sweetness was syrupy on her tongue. "Because I know you can do this."

I breathed out through my nose, glaring at her. Our families had always thought we'd be a perfect match for covenmates—raised together, our tastes equally artistic. But Hildy was a pest, if not a genius, and I loved her like a sister. Besides, our covens weren't too shabby as they turned out.

I stepped back from the wall, scanning the line up again, resisting the urge to snatch up the blood-red gown I would have loved to see Joanna in, and easily passing over the austere steel gray. It took three passes, and Hildy's smirk only grew, distracting me from my goal and building my frustration until finally, my eyes stopped on a pale gown with an airy, full skirt. What color was that, really? Not quite pink, not properly purple, almost nearly a shade of brown. The waist was embroidered with buds so faint they almost blended into the fabric and were lost, and they carried down into the skirt, falling under layers of sheer fabric, making it look as if a breeze had caught petals up in the wind.

"There you are," Hildy said with a nod. "Let me make the tailoring changes and then I'll send it to your door. If Joanna balks, you can blame me. If she likes it, feel free to take a modicum of credit."

I laughed, skimming my fingers over the skirt, watching it follow the touch like mist. Hildy carried the hanger back to the counter, talking to the girl there—Abigail, her name tag read—in a playful mix of Vermenian and Enmarian.

"Does she have shoes?" Hildy asked me and laughed as my face went blank. "I'll manage it and the rest too. Just put your money on the counter, you old fool."

"You're six months older," I said quickly, an old refrain she'd used against me as children. It was a mistake to use it now if her narrowed eyes were anything to judge by. "Don't put the receipt in the box."

That made her laugh. "Of course not. I look forward to seeing you all there."

Callum claimed he wasn't going. Social events were never his strong suit and his moods had been uneven since the nightmare event the week before. He'd taken to sleeping on his own or with Joanna in his old room. The master suite upstairs seemed hollow without the pair of them.

I was betting on Joanna coming with Isaac and me to the Ball, as an enticement to get Callum out of the house. With the three of us dressed to impress, Callum would find himself in one of his old suits, tagging along. I didn't mind if he tucked a book in his pocket as long as he wasn't sulking at home, alone, trapped in his own thoughts.

I thanked Hildy and left the shop, stopping at my favorite grocery to see the new wine shipment and pick up Isaac's list. I was nearly home when I found myself crossing the street, heading in the wrong direction down a block that lined the perimeter of the main area of campus. I'd walked all the streets of Canderfey in the past twenty years on my own, with my coven, and earlier lovers before them. But I was halfway down the block before I realized I was wandering aimlessly when I didn't *want* to be. The groceries were heavy on my arm and I had every intention of going home and finishing my grading.

I tried to cross the street and stopped in the middle of the road, my feet carrying me backward, my thoughts skirting away from my goal of 'home' and drifting toward 'walk,' but this time I felt the magic catch, a wall in front of me. I growled briefly and then whistled a piercing, wavering note, sweeping my hand over the air in front of me. The ward glittered in answer, a complicated web beyond my skills that stretched in either direction, too far to see its end.

I turned back to town, rushing to Hildy's shop. She had a telephone in her office for taking new orders. She rolled her eyes as I entered but something in my face stopped her teasing.

"What is it?" she asked, head tipping.

"The campus is blocked off. At least from this direction. I can't get back in," I said.

Her eyebrows raised. "Today's the day students start leaving campus. Come, put your things down back here. I'll call the Library."

Joanna was at one of the Vermenian lessons in Callum's classroom, and he was probably with her as he always was these days. Isaac might be home to answer a call, but what could he do?

I followed Hildy into her workspace with bolts of fabric hanging on the wall, some velvet garment in the midst of being cut out on an enormous table, and half-finished dresses hanging in a row together. Hildy spun into her chair at her desk, dialing the rotary with quick fingers, and I could hear the ringing over the line.

"Yes, hello dear, find me Gwen please," Hildy said and then shook her head lightly. "Woolard, love. Your boss." There was a pause and I snatched a pen up from her desk, pulling my notebook out of my back pocket and flipping through the pages.

"Gwen, yes, I'm calling- Ah. Oh, I see. No, it's closed in this part of town." Hildy hummed and frowned, glancing at me, worry sneaking into her usual serenity. "Alright. Yes. I'll talk to you soon, love." She hung up the phone and turned to me. "Campus is… aware. It started right as the flood of parents started arriving. Callum is at the front gates, more of the faculty are tracing the path through the woods but it seems to be…"

"A complete cage," I said.

Hildy picked up a pen, tapping it against the wood of her desk, and I looked down to read the most recent message.

Joanna and Myles are up against Anders. From Isaac.

My stomach dropped and my head started to pound. *I'm stuck outside of this damn ward. Can you help them?* I scribbled, staring at the blank page. Anders was dead set against the Scrivens and entirely unimpressed by Joanna.

The words came in slowly. *Professor Frost is here. He insists this is a ward and nothing related to writing.* I sighed, they had an ally at least. Hopefully, Anders would listen.

I'm sorry you aren't here to see Joanna, Isaac added. *I know you love when she's efficient and ferocious.* I smiled in spite of the moment and looked up to find Hildy watching me.

"All is well?" she asked.

"No, but it could be worse. I'm going out to the road. See if I can't chip away at the ward."

"It's a ward then?" Hildy asked, her voice lowering, and eyes flicking to the front room.

My throat tightened at the question and I forced myself to nod, clearing away my surprise before I answered. "Frost is speaking to Anders now. It's nothing like Scrivens magic."

Hildy sighed, relaxing into her chair. "That's good," she said, rushing to add as my eyes narrowed, "It's good that Scrivens magic is so clearly different."

I crossed to her desk, finding a small space clear of sketches and pincushions, and perching myself there. "Hildy, tell me you don't think—"

"I don't," she said, eyes widening. Then she swallowed. "Except... Corina already *has* tried something, hasn't she?"

"Corina can't write now."

"Trust me. I know that," Hildy said drily, collapsing into her seat and shutting her eyes, mouth grimacing. "I didn't think that it was them. Not really," she whispered. "Anyway, it doesn't make sense for it to be Scrivens. Plenty live in town here. Why put a wall up between themselves? It's just... showy and disruptive."

I frowned. "More inconvenient than malicious," I agreed and Hildy nodded, her eyes still shut. It was as if someone was *trying* to be annoying. But were they trying to implicate the Scrivens or was it only...?

"Probably just a student prank," Hildy said.

I grunted, letting Hildy think I agreed, and made my way back out to the streets, my thoughts racing while I worked against the ward.

MY BONES FELT like lead by the time I made it home. Callum had broken the ward at the gates of campus and, with the help of other locals, I did the same in town, untying the messy knots of magic for over two miles into the woods. The lights of the house were on when I entered, the sound of water running in the kitchen.

"Aiden?" Isaac appeared in the doorway, and then rushed down the hall, grabbing the bags of groceries out of my arms and kissing my jaw in greeting. "I was worried about you."

"I was helping with the last of the ward in the woods south of here," I said. The kitchen was warm with the oven going, something boiling on the stove, wine breathing on the counter, but the house was quiet. "Is Callum still out?"

"Joanna dragged him back," Isaac said with a faint smile. "She took him up to the bath. You should join them."

My whole body groaned at the thought of taking the stairs, but the bath would do twice the good after working all that magic. Isaac poured me a glass of wine before unpacking the bags. My mouth felt bruised from all the whistling and singing and humming I'd done, and I wish I'd thought to carry some kind of instrument around with me, the way Callum carried knives in his magical pockets.

"I think I'm getting too old for this house," I said, wondering how I was supposed to make it up to the master bedroom tonight when I felt this tired. Maybe I shouldn't even bother, chances were Joanna and Callum would end up in his room again. Isaac and I might as well stay in mine.

"Joanna said she thought we ought to have a designated door for shortcuts," Isaac mentioned as he added salt to the sauce he was stirring. "That way we can skip the stairs when we need to."

"Did she?" *See that, you great growling bear? She's thinking of you too*, I thought. "I'll go up and join them if you don't mind working alone down here."

Isaac raised his eyebrows. He always did the majority of dinner without us. "I'm not touching a dish tonight after dinner."

"Deal."

I dragged myself up the stairs and down the hall, stopping at the door to the bathroom, as I heard the soft splash of water from inside, contentment emanating from Joanna and Callum's part of the bond. I cracked the door open, peering inside, my heart twisting at the sight. Joanna's eyes were closed, head resting back against the ledge of the tub, fingers combing through the wet, dark copper strands of Callum's hair. He was reclined against her chest, her free hand tangled with his, resting over his heart.

They were beautiful, water steaming faintly around them, lights off and the pair of them resting together, perfectly at peace. I shut the door as silently as I could and retreated back to the stairs. The shower would do me enough good on my own.

16

JOANNA

The house creaked overhead and I slid one eye open, and then the other.

"Aiden's home," Callum said with a sigh.

I touched at the coven bond gingerly and frowned at what I found. Disappointment again. I sighed and Callum shifted, turning between my legs and sitting up to look into my face.

"What's wrong?"

"It's nothing," I said and Callum raised an eyebrow. "It's just... today was *another* problem. And I know it had nothing to do with the Scrivens, but Aiden will probably have to deal with Anders again. Maybe Sewell. It's not... going how I hoped."

Callum floated away in the water for a moment, pushing my leg aside so that he could pull me to his chest, trading our positions. I curled into his warmth, my hands clinging to his shoulders.

"Aiden would gladly argue with hundreds of administrators for you," Callum said, splashing some of the warm water against my back as if we were really in the tub for washing rather than comfort.

I searched his face, reaching up to smudge away some of the bubbles stuck in his beard. "Every time I catch a glimpse of the bond

645

from him it's always… frustration or disappointment. I think- I just wonder if he—"

"Joanna," Callum growled my name with a gentle warning. "Aiden's been waiting decades for you."

"I know," I said, biting on the words. Callum stilled beneath me and I regretted my temper. But so often recently, I wondered if Aiden was satisfied with me as the fourth coven member.

He was quiet, but his hands stroked over my skin, cupping water and running it over my shoulders and down my skin to keep me warm.

"I liked Isaac when I met him," Callum said, lifting my chin and kissing me softly before continuing. "I had the craving to spend time with him at the start of the bond. But it wasn't the same as how I felt about Aiden. Aiden made me understand myself as someone other than the Toy Soldier. After a while, I wondered if there was really love between Isaac and I. There was friendship certainly. It took us a long time to learn who we were together and it was…not always painless. What we have in common are experiences we would both rather forget."

Their fathers. Callum's eyes darkened as he watched my face go lax with understanding.

"I don't know when it happened exactly. I picked a fight and Isaac got angry, and I saw how much it cost him. It made us really talk to one another, see each other." He went quiet, focus distant, and I set my chin on his shoulder.

"You're saying Aiden and I haven't learned each other yet," I said.

He shrugged. "Maybe. Or you're in the process. It doesn't happen immediately. This is a stressful time for you both right now, but I can promise you one thing. Aiden couldn't be less disappointed to have you in the coven, and I mean that as *you* yourself. Not just our fourth."

"Maybe I should pick a fight with him then," I said, shying away from Callum's sweetness.

He laughed, a startled, happy sound bursting free. "Maybe you should," he said, grinning with a wicked laugh I didn't understand.

Before I could ask him, he ducked down and locked our lips in a heady kiss.

CALLUM and I slept with the others that night, and I could see the flash of surprise on Aiden's face as we surrounded him. He laughed when I curled up around as much of his back as I could reach, pressing my cold nose to his spine, and his hand covered mine on his stomach. It wasn't the prescribed argument, but it made Aiden's side of the bond thrum in pleasure so it must have helped.

I woke, cradled like a beloved teddy bear to Aiden's chest, and smiled against his chest. His hand slid up to the back of my neck, massaging away some of the soreness after sleeping awkwardly. The shower was running in the bathroom, Callum and Isaac laughing under the spray of water.

"Our turn next," Aiden said, sleep scratching through the words.

He tugged me up his chest, our noses bumping together as we kissed with closed lips. Downstairs the phone rang, a dull echo carrying up the stairs. One of the cats squawked in surprise or warning, and Aiden's chest rumbled beneath mine, an irritated growl.

"Ignore it," Aiden said as I started to move.

"Stay here." I kissed his cheek, rolling off his chest and making him grunt. "I'll get it."

"Whoever it is will have hung up by the time you get downstairs," Aiden said, pushing up to one elbow, nearly distracting me with his bare chest, looking soft and warm and ready to envelop me.

"No one ever calls. It could be important." I hurried down the stairs, cats dashing in front of me and the phone continued ringing. It sat in the hall by the stairs, and the little black and white cat flopped onto his back, kicking his legs at the hem of my nightgown for stopping my journey before attending to their food bowls.

"Hel—"

"Joanna, the staff houses are on fire," Gwen rushed out on the phone. "I can see the smoke from the library."

The silence that followed was hollow, like the echo of white sound that came after a deafening noise. My throat felt empty, tongue useless, and my heart was still as stone for a moment. And then it beat again, faster than before.

"We're on our way."

I hung up, not even certain that the phone made it back into its holder, and started to take the stairs up two at a time, my toes stubbing in the rush. Aiden was in the doorway as I made it to the last flight, my breaths panting, and his face hardened in expectation.

"Fire at Myles', or near, or... I don't know," I said, stomach full of rocks tumbling over one another as I pushed past Aiden, then standing in the heart of the room, looking blindly around. Why hadn't I gone straight for my coat and shoes?

Aiden understood something in my panic, grabbing up the closest dress and helping me change as Isaac and Callum came in from their shower, steam clouding behind them.

"Get dressed," Aiden said to them as I scrambled into my sleeves. "Joanna will write us a shortcut to..."

"Isaac's office." I couldn't write us to Myles if my family's home was one on fire. But the Burgess building was near the street, and safe for us to come and go in.

I was heading back to the stairs before Aiden caught me around the waist, his pants up to his waist and unbuttoned. He wrestled up my zipper with one hand and waited until I met his eyes.

"Wait for us," he said in the same stern tone he'd taken with us in Callum's office, but without any of the affectionate heat. Callum passed him a shirt, helping him into the sleeves as Aiden released me.

"I could write out the flames," I said. There was a brief siren in the distance, and Isaac took my chin and turned my face to see him.

"The department is on their way. Let's go downstairs and get our shoes on, love," he coaxed. He was still buttoning his shirt but I followed him, glancing over my shoulder to see Aiden and Callum throwing sweaters on over their heads.

I nearly turned straight around on the second story, realizing I had nothing to write with, when Aiden stopped me, a stick of chalk held in front of my nose. I snatched it, giving him a wobbly attempt at a smile, and ran down the rest of the stairs.

I stepped into Isaac's office on the other side of campus, one boot still untied, and the sirens were blaring, making the glass panes on the window vibrate. Callum muttered a quick charm at my feet as I started to run, the laces tying for me as I skidded out into the hall and down the stairs. Even from inside the smoke was harsh on the air, drying my throat and making tears well in my eyes. I caught a brief glimpse of black clouds billowing outside the main window in front of the staircase, and then my heels nearly slipped.

"Careful!" Aiden barked behind me, but he didn't ask me to wait again, his steps thundering close after mine.

The street was dark with smoke, figures wrapped in blankets walking backward away from the scene, faces lifted in horror as fire-fighters and faculty fought the last flames licking up a line of houses on the right side of the street. My heart stuttered in my chest and suddenly I was breathing too fast and heavy, body bending forward as I braced my hands on my knees. Callum and Aiden rushed on without me, and Isaac gathered me in his arms as my knees gave out.

The fire was on the wrong side of the street, or the right side by my thinking, safely away from Adele, Myles, Irene, and the other Scrivens. I was weak with relief and sick with guilt for that very same reason.

"It's alright, love," Isaac whispered in my ear, and I didn't know if he was telling my family was safe or that it was alright to be so grateful that it was someone else's home on fire.

"Leina!"

My head lifted from Isaac's chest and there was Myles in the crowd I had skimmed over, his great baggy coat covering Adele and Irene. Isaac steadied me down the last steps of the Burgess building and over to the lawn where the residents of the staff houses stood huddled together, a clear barrier up between the Scrivens and staff residents.

Myles scooped me up in a bear hug when we reached him, and then dragged Isaac in for good measure.

"What happened?" I gasped, catching Nora's eye over Myles' shoulder.

"Everyone got out safely," Myles said in my ear. More relief, this time without the guilt attached.

"The fire didn't catch. It went up, all at once before dawn," Nora said. "I saw it from my bed."

Myles was still squeezing me tight as her words caught in my thoughts. That wasn't right. That wasn't how fires started.

"Not our words," Daniel said in Vermenian, his vividly pale eyes meeting mine for what seemed like the first time in our entire acquaintance.

"Of course not," I answered in the wrong language, but Daniel seemed to understand, staring around the crowd near us, pointing out to me the way their eyes skirted away as we looked.

The locals thought this was Scrivens magic?

"Callum's magic isn't working against the flame," Isaac announced, pulling back from the hug and taking me with him.

Callum was standing against a blaze, firemen hosing flames with water that evaporated before ever breaking the force of the fire.

I squeezed Myles' hand. "Can we write it out?"

"That's not a natural fire, leina," Myles warned.

Isaac's eyes skimmed my face, his brow folding. "But your words fought the Hollow," Isaac said.

I swung back to Myles, heard the shouts from the street, glass shattering. "Come with me." I pulled the chalk out of my pocket, broke it into three pieces, and held the two fragments out to Myles, catching Nora's eye. "Please help."

"Tell us the words," Nora said, tying the belt on her robe and stepping forward, plucking the chalk from my fingertips.

Myles grabbed the other piece just as quickly and we ran off the grass and onto the street, stopping at the line of firefighters. Smoke was stinging my eyes, and I held my arm over my mouth to try and keep the worst out of my lungs. Callum's hair was streaked black and I nearly tripped over Aiden's abandoned sweater, a wet stain on the spine of his shirt from the painful cloud of heat.

Nora and Myles sank to the road on either side of me, the three of us on our knees. Their eyes watched my face, waiting for my words, and for a moment I could think of nothing. Nothing but the roar of the fire in my ears, the creak of wood groaning under the pressure.

"Simple, clean, leina!" Myles shouted.

"The fire is out!"

The resistance made the first lines of my writing slow and clumsy, but then Nora and Myles' hands were working in tandem with mine, the struggle crumbling under our combined work. Fire spat and crackled, and Callum's magic shimmered in front of me as a shield. Another window splintered, glittering glass over the brick road. But the roar dulled to a fizzle, and then to brief spits and pops and finally to nothing, the world all around us brackish with smoke.

Callum's palms raised in front of him, and I winced and blinked away irritated tears while watching him. He coughed once, his hands vanishing in the dense smoke, and then he ground out one long word that left my head dizzy. Air kicked at the hem of my skirts and tossed my curls forward into my face as a great breeze gathered at my back and rushed forward, taking the last of gathered smoke up into the air and out toward the woods. Callum's right wrist twisted, fingers stretched apart and pointed down to the ground, and the smoldering coals of the houses, skeletal black things now, dimmed and settled, the oxygen sapped away.

"That wasn't a natural fire," one of the men, the firefighters announced to Callum. His voice was too loud and the words carried back to the crowd on the lawn, starting whispers.

"No," Callum agreed. "It fought interference until the Scrivens put it out. Do you mind if I go and—"

"We'll take over the inspection," the man said, stepping in front of us. "Go wait on the lawn with the others."

Callum bristled at the order and Aiden's arm wrapped over his back, lips going up to his ear. Callum relaxed after a few words, and Isaac and I followed them both over to the opposite side of the street.

"I'm going to listen in," Callum said, a hand reaching up and tracing over my collarbone. "Joanna, I want you to take Myles and the others to the library. Or back to our house. Alright?"

The warmth of Callum's protective warding trickled over my skin at the same moment icy worry ran through my veins. "Why? What's happening?" I asked.

Callum frowned, hand reaching up to his ear, already focusing on the men inspecting the scene. "It's a precaution," he said.

I looked to Isaac who seemed as worried and confused as I was, and then to Aiden, whose frown was so deep, it dug lines into the skin around his mouth. I was crossing back to Myles when one of the men near the charred ruins started shouting, calling to the others.

"Over here! I found words."

The sudden burst of frustration was stark, like a lightning bolt running through my mind, and it came directly from Aiden. Just as fast, he shut me out.

"There's more here too, sir!" another man called from farther down the row.

My eyes drifted to Myles, one big hand covering his mouth, weariness turning his expression lax and blank. Time seemed to slow as I walked to my uncle, wanting to run and somehow forgetting how to rush.

"Gentleman! May I be of some assistance?"

My throat swelled shut, heartbeat thumping loudly in my ears as President Anders strode calmly down the sidewalk, crossing in front of me without a glance on his way to the firemen. He was wafting perfume, hair slicked back and still damp like he'd taken the time to shower while his campus was on fire. Behind him Vice President Bonde rushed to catch up, her hair like a dark bird's nest on top of her head, arms bundled with blankets that she carried to the residents waiting in the grass.

Urgency flashed inside of me, a reminder from Callum, and I rushed behind Anders' back over to my uncle.

"Quickly, come with me," I whispered. "I'm taking you to the coven house."

"Leina, it would be better for you if we stayed," Myles said, blue eyes watery and reddened from the smoke.

"You're leaving now before someone says you can't," I said, staring back at him until he was shuffling his feet. I glanced at Nora long enough for her to nod in agreement. "We'll take a shortcut."

I escorted the Scrivens and my family around the corner, catching Bonde's eye as I passed, and wondering if I imagined the faint nod of her head. We cut past a line of trees to cover our sudden disappearance, and back to the Burgess Building. I wouldn't even bother asking Myles to follow me all the way up to the office, not when a perfectly good supply closet would do.

"I'm going back to my coven once you're in. Help yourself to anything in the kitchen or around the house," I said, all but *pulling* Myles up the stairs and into the building. "Oh! And would you mind feeding the cats?"

"Of course not, Joanna," Myles said, voice softened with the concern grooved into his face.

"It's going to be alright." I found the words were easy to say even while my mind was racing.

How? How would it possibly turn out alright when there were words scrawled on the burnt buildings? I could be willfully optimistic, but this was too great a strain, even for me. Someone had written…

I understood suddenly Callum's concern, Aiden's frustration.

Someone had written words with the intent to implicate the Scrivens.

I scrawled over the door to a classroom and then swung it open, the wood polish, hint of paint, and herbal whiff of home settling a bit of panic in my nerves.

"Go on," I said, twitching my lips in the semblance of a smile and nodding my head inside, counting the heads in front of me to make sure we hadn't left anyone behind. My family, Nora, Daniel, Kristin, and Ella—all the others were in town. "I'll come back with news as soon as I can. Make yourselves comfortable."

Seven grim faces stared back at me, each of them in their nightclothes, bundled against the morning cold. I grabbed a shaky breath, strengthening my smile with a Herculean effort, and nodded.

"It will be alright," I said again.

"Be careful, leina," Myles whispered and then he ducked inside, followed by Irene as they helped Adele.

Nora studied me anew, head to toe, and walked in after my family without another word or twitch of her expression, the rest of the Scrivens trickling in after her. I shut the door without looking back, resting my back against the wood. A sob struggled up my throat and I swallowed it down, squeezing my eyes shut tight, one tear squeezing out and escaping. I wiped my cheek against my shoulder and then turned around, licking my fingers and scrubbing away the chalk marks on the door until it was nothing more than a smudge.

I raced back to the street, the sharp smell of char and ash still clogging the air, even after Callum had cleared away the smoke. More people had gathered on the sidewalk and lawn in front of the street, mostly faculty and locals now that most of the students had left for the summer. They handed out food and coats to the residents waiting in the grass, huddled together and whispering. I could guess what those whispers said and it made my heart burn.

On the street, Callum and Aiden stood opposite Anders, hands flying and voices raised. Isaac met me on the way, my feet stalling at the line of rope stretching across the road. Callum and Aiden were just inside, fighting for me.

"And I'm telling you, that isn't Scrivens magic," Callum said, uncharacteristically loud against Anders' determination to see the worst conclusion in the fire.

"We have investigators on the scene for a reason, Professor Pike," Anders answered with a poor impersonation of patience.

"You also have the premiere expert in offensive magic," Aiden said, one palm splayed against Callum's back as if to rein the younger man in. "Why not take advantage?"

"Why not step back behind the line like you were asked, King?" Anders snarled, facade breaking.

"Scrivens magic isn't simply marked by words," Callum barreled on. "There *are* rules."

"Except you keep learning surprises, don't you?" Anders asked, eyes narrowing, lips curving a cruel imitation of a smile. "That was your selling point for me, correct? The discovery of Scrivens magic! Should I bill this fire to that academic paper that's supposed to do us so much good?"

"Stuart, perhaps this would be best discussed in an office away from listening ears." Elizabeth Bonde was standing behind Isaac and me, her eyes sliding in the direction of the listening locals on the grass.

"I agree, it is a distasteful scene," Anders said, but he turned back to Callum, his mouth opened to argue.

"What do the words say?" I asked, ducking beneath the rope, ignoring Anders' squawk of indignation. None of the real officials on the scene said anything to me. Perhaps they'd given up after Anders, Callum, and Aiden helped themselves to the investigation.

"This house burns," Callum said, pointing across the road to the base of a house, one area clear of smoke black stains. The words were easy to make out, enormous block letters of chalk ground into the cement.

"President Anders, if a Scrivens wrote that, the house would still be burning," I said, turning to the man and raising my chin, hoping my voice carried back to our audience on the sidelines.

"Is that a threat Miss Wick?" Anders asked, mouth still twisted into its unkind grimace.

"Of course not," I said, eyebrows raising. "But the only way to undo Scrivens magic is to destroy the words that set the spell into motion. If you can read those words, then no Scrivens wrote them."

"I really only have your word for that," Anders hissed, shoulders leaning in my direction as my coven crowded around me. "It's time for action to be taken to protect the campus."

"This is not *decidedly* proof of Scrivens involvement," Bonde said as Aiden barked out, "You need to examine the facts, Anders!"

"Why don't we wait to see what Sewell thinks of the facts, as they are written on that house, hmm?" Anders said, chest puffing out, and victory sparkling in that glassy gaze of his. He turned away from us, marching back to the crew of firemen making notes and examining the damage, and his Vice President rushed after him, belting her coat tighter around her waist.

"Where did you take them?" Callum whispered to me, turning his back to the scene, lines tight around his eyes.

"Home."

He nodded. "Let's get back to them. We need to prepare."

He and Isaac slid back under the rope, but I couldn't tear my eyes away from the ruins of the little staff houses, with their shattered windows and strange, shadow-black soot streaking up the sides to roofs chewed open by flames. Aiden stepped in front of my view and I leaned back, his thumb reaching up to stroke away a tear I hadn't noticed falling.

"There's still time for things to turn right, darling," Aiden said, words hushed.

I didn't know if I believed him, but I snatched his hand from my cheek and held it tight in my own as we left.

17

AIDEN

"WE ARE CAUSING YOU A GREAT DEAL OF TROUBLE," MYLES SAID, SEATED across from me on the front window bench. He had a mug of tea in his hand which Callum spiked with a little whiskey, but he nursed the cup like he was waiting for someone to take it away from him.

"No." I shook my head and found with some embarrassment that I genuinely meant it this time. "No, someone *is* causing us all serious trouble. But it isn't you or your people, Myles."

Callum came in from the hall, arms crossed over his chest, eyeing the room full of Vermenians, and leaning against the wall near my shoulder. "I told Sewell to meet us here."

My eyebrows jumped high and I opened my mouth to ask if he thought that was wise but shut it again just as quickly. I'd learned by now not to question Callum's judgment when it came to strategy. I scanned the room and wondered if I was seeing the same argument he was planning on. A room full of terrified friends and family huddled together in a safe space, a home.

"I called Marcus too," Callum said, softer, and he grimaced in apology as my head jerked up. "He said early on that there was a fund we could use in a moment like this. Donations for the refugees that might be offered to the campus in…"

"In recompense of a crime they didn't commit?" I hissed. "Is that the message we want to send?"

"I know," Callum said, frown deepening. "I know. And maybe… maybe we should let them use it to…relocate."

Escape. Before Canderfey came with torches and pitchforks? Had the environment heated so much? It was possible if Anders' version of the fire was successfully spread. No matter what, the Scrivens were in danger.

"We need to know who set that fire," I said.

"And gave us those nightmares," Callum added. "The ward around the campus."

"All of it's connected?"

"It was difficult to get a read on the burn site today. I'll go back later to be sure, but I'm almost positive the source magic had the same signature."

I reached back and Callum's hand squeezed mine. "Where's Joanna?" I asked. I'd expected her to be at his side and for once it wasn't jealousy following the thought.

"Upstairs in my office with Nora," he answered. "I think she's trying to think of words that might…help find whoever is responsible."

There was a strange twist in my gut at the thought of Joanna trying to use Scrivens magic to fix the situation—how it might look to a man like Anders—and I hated to find the response in myself. I wasn't sure if by thinking *like* Anders I was giving credence to his logic.

Callum straightened, eyes staring out the window. "He's here. Adele, take the others into the dining room. Myles, wait here with Aiden. No more self-sacrificing. You helped put that fire out today when the firemen couldn't, and we'll remind him of that."

I stood up and went to shut the door on the dining room as Callum whistled up the stairs for Joanna. Isaac reappeared from the kitchen just as the Mayor made it to our front steps and knocked. I nudged my coven back into the front room to wait before answering the door.

"Mayor Sewell."

"Professor King." He waited on the step, taking off his hat and folding his hands politely in front of him.

I wanted to gauge the likely outcome of this meeting solely by Sewell's expression, except his face offered nothing to judge his mood by. I stepped aside, gesturing him in, and caught the way he paused at the sight of my coven gathered in the room beyond, waiting for him. I took his coat and smiled as I watched Joanna square her shoulders at the exact same moment as Callum, a perfect pair of matching warriors.

"Mr. Kershaw," Sewell greeted Myles last, with a slight but polite bow, one Myles echoed while bracing himself on a cane.

"Before any of you start your arguments," Sewell said, pivoting in place to look at each of us. "I'm not inclined to believe it was Scrivens magic that started the fire. And the fire department has already attested to the fact it was certainly the efforts of your writing which put the fire out. They're still trying to ascertain if your words can be safely removed without the flames starting up again."

"Oh, I hadn't thought of that," Joanna murmured with a frown, glancing at Myles.

"We appreciate you taking the matter seriously," I said.

Sewell raised his eyebrows at me. "That's my job, Professor King. But I understand that you are currently up against a particular individual who is less inclined to look at the situation…objectively."

"Anders is blatantly prejudiced," Callum said, his hand resting on Myles' shoulder.

"Yes. I pushed him on moving forward with this project when perhaps I should have considered what his retaliation would cost the refugees," Sewell confessed, head nodding.

Isaac's gaze snagged against mine, our faces both going stiff, and I wondered if we shared the same thought. How far *would* Anders retaliation go? Enough to risk the safety of his campus?

"I've talked Anders off the warpath," Sewell announced and we all released a sigh of relief. "He's putting up a stink about the displaced staff. It will be a few weeks before they can have the houses in repair, even with good witches on the task, and this is the second time this year staff houses have been destroyed."

Joanna blushed and ducked her chin. The first bout of destruction had been due to the Hollow on the hunt for Joanna after she'd accidentally let it out of its cage.

"We have a fund we can use to help contribute to the construction," Callum said.

Sewell hummed and nodded. "Money always helps smooth a difficult situation. Very well. I'll find somewhere for the staff to stay without much trouble if you work on helping the construction." He turned away from the room, making to leave us in a relieved stupor, when he stopped and spun back. "I hope you'll understand, this isn't a warning meant in aggression but… this *has* been the third strike."

"The only Scrivens magic was Lars and that was—"

"Amusing, yes," Sewell said with a closed-mouth smile. "The timing of the rest has been unfortunate. And I do believe that the responsibility for the rest lies elsewhere. But we can't convince every mind in Canderfey, and the damage has already been done. Mr. Kershaw, please caution your people."

"My people have always lived in caution, Mayor Sewell," Myles said.

My respect for Myles never failed to rise with every hour I spent with him. Joanna, at his side, clenched her jaw and I was proud of her too for sitting on the words I was certain she was clamping away.

Sewell had brought us peace and disrupted it just as quickly, and it was on that unfortunate last note that he left us. I followed him to the hall, retrieving his coat and passing it back with a heavy heart.

"We meant to offer you tea," I said, the thought striking me too late.

"I've never been much for wasting time with a nicety," Sewell muttered with a shrug, a rare release of the calm, impenetrable mask slipping away to reveal someone a bit more practical and country than I would have expected.

I shut the door behind him and returned to my coven in time to catch Joanna pulling Myles into a seat, her voice hushed.

"We'll just have all the Scrivens meet here, together, to practice our writing," she said, eyes wide and Myles' hand clutched in hers.

"After what Sewell just said?" I asked, feet stopping like lead weights on the floor, voice raising.

Joanna looked up at me, her expression open with surprise as a flush rose up her neck. "It was the three of us working together that put the fire *out*, Aiden."

"I know that. And it will be the three of you who are blamed first for starting the fire by the more ignorant people who are determined to believe the worst, Joanna," I said. My own face was hot too, worry and annoyance mixing together into a combustible temper boiling in my veins. "Now is the time for caution, not conspiracy."

"It's not conspiracy to study your own magic," Joanna answered, words as high and clear as the warning ringing in my ears. "That's what Canderfey is for."

Something awful swelled up in my chest, an answer to her chastisement that I would have regretted before I'd finished speaking—that Canderfey hadn't been built for *them*, for Scrivens—and Isaac jumped between us, his hands lifted to parry the arguments. But my throat choked as I swallowed. I'd known what might have come out and Joanna looked struck, as if she somehow knew too.

"This is not the time," Isaac said, gentler and wiser than I was inclined to be in the moment.

It seemed, for a half-second, like the fight might wash away. And then Callum stepped forward.

"Joanna is right," he said, an arm wrapping around her shoulders. "The Scrivens are under attack and we don't even know who's responsible yet. Their only option is defense, and the best thing they can do is work together. Not shrink into hiding and wait for the next blow."

Joanna softened into Callum's side, her cheek brushing once against his shoulder, eyes flashing at me in a taunt. The knot in my throat went down like a rock and my eyes narrowed.

"If you draw attention to the Scrivens, you'll be putting your family, their friends, yourself, and our coven at risk. The world doesn't revolve around your high expectations, Joanna Wick," I growled.

"My expectations?" Her voice cracked as she jumped out of the shelter of Callum's arms, and past a grimacing Isaac to stand chest to chest with me. Her hands were clenched into fists at her side, eyes so wide I could see the whites all around. Her words shook and battered at me. "And what of your expectations, Aiden? That things *must* go poorly? That certainly someone will cause problems? Most especially your foolish, naive, brat of a *fourth* who makes scenes and talks out of her place and is so determined to believe that something *good* can be done for the people who need it?"

"What good has been done for the people who lost their homes today?" I shouted, hearing the thought the moment after speaking it, damning my mouth for not catching it before it was out in the world.

Silence followed and Joanna's face went slack, color fading too quickly. "Who do you blame for the fire?" she asked, voice wilting, body seemingly shrinking before my eyes.

"I- no one- that wasn't—" My brain stuttered over the argument, wondering where I'd lost my way and landed in such shit.

Callum interrupted me with a frustrated growl, and Joanna dashed out of reach and up the stairs. I turned, but Callum caught my shoulder and jerked me back to face him.

"What are you doing?"

I gaped at him for a moment and then the fire rose up in my chest again. The conversation, the argument, had gone horribly awry, but I meant what I'd said in the beginning before everything went twisted.

"Trying to protect my coven, to protect the Scrivens," I said, looking past Callum. "Myles, I'm sorry."

"I may agree with you," Myles said, although he was looking at Isaac for some kind of direction, whether to step in on Joanna's behalf, perhaps.

"Well, for the record, I *don't*," Callum snapped.

"You told me this was politics, not warfare," I barked back.

"That was before the nightmares, before that fire. The Scrivens are being framed. That's an attack, Aiden!"

"I know! And the last thing we need to do is make them look guiltier as if they're plotting their next act. We're part of this community too, Callum, and we don't need to be giving the wrong impression either."

Callum scoffed, and I resisted the urge to punch him, just a little, for how exaggerated the sound was. "You need to make up your mind about whose reputation you're concerned for. The Scrivens or ours. I personally don't give a shit what the locals think of me."

I growled, some new curse gathering in my lungs, ready to explode, and at the back of my mind I wondered if it wasn't for the best that Callum ignored me, chasing up the stairs after Joanna.

Myles cleared his throat in the quiet that followed, and my head was too heavy to lift and meet his eyes. "I'll take my people back to their homes."

"Myles, I…"

Myles lumbered to me on uneven steps and I forced myself to meet his gaze, wincing and expecting to see anger. But there was none. He patted my shoulder once. "We have the same concerns," he said with a half-smile. "For the same people."

Somehow the forgiveness made me feel worse. I'd spoken thoughts I hadn't wanted to give validity to, and I didn't know how to take the effect of those words away. They couldn't simply be erased or burned or washed off like the Scrivens magic.

Isaac released a rattling breath, hand reaching up to dig his fingers into his dark hair, eyes skidding over me to speak to Myles. "I'll help you, I need to pack up some food for everyone."

"That's not—"

"It's what I'd like to do," Isaac said, smile brittle, and then they left me with myself.

I found I did not like my own company at that moment.

18

AIDEN

I STOOD AT THE BOTTOM OF THE TOP FLIGHT OF STAIRS IN THE HOUSE, the ones leading up to the master bedroom, and tried to decide if I was angry or annoyed or aching with worry. Joanna had written…*something*, and now nothing went in or out of the room but the cats. And presumably her, if she were inclined to come out of isolation. Which she was apparently not.

It was immature and petty, and it made my heart feel like it had been placed inside a slowly tightening vice.

Isaac had called to her for dinner earlier in the evening, and his voice had lobbied back at him as if bouncing off a wall. He'd ground his jaw as he turned around, eyes avoiding mine. The meal had been quiet and I felt as if Joanna had placed a spell over my tongue as well. Words stewed inside of me, arguments and defenses and accusations, but none made it to my lips before being batted away. I didn't want to make a mistake and say the wrong thing again, and I had no idea what the *right* thing was.

"Leave her be."

Callum was at the other end of the hall by the stairs.

"I'm surprised you aren't with her," I said.

Callum only cocked his head. "Are you? Or are you fishing to know if she's locked me out too? She has and that's fine. She can have a night to herself if she needs one."

But she and I had started an argument and not finished it. No, it wasn't that. It was that we had argued and I needed to know if the damage done was irreparable. I hadn't liked her sleeping out of reach the past few days, and I liked it even less knowing she was alone and angry or hurt.

"We need to talk," I said, turning my back to Callum. There was no way in and I was only standing there as if waiting for her to appear at the top of the steps, forgiveness at hand.

"She needs a break, Aiden," Callum said, words hard against my spine. "Don't hound her for her attention when you haven't even decided if you want to continue arguing or apologize."

"Her attention?" I echoed, nearly a shout, spinning on my heel to face him. There was a cunning sharpness on his face, a shadow casting harsh angles. "As if I have been hoarding her attention recently? I've received a fraction of it compared to you."

There was a twitch of his lips and he lifted a brow. "Is that what these moods of yours have been about?" he asked.

"Moods?"

"Yes, moods." He was taunting, cocky, and obnoxiously calm, so unlike the Callum of a year ago whose only pretensions tended toward the academic. Certainly never the emotional. "Prowling around the house like some great injured beast. Picking at Joanna at the slightest hint of her ideas differing from yours."

My feet were carrying me closer to him, my shoulders stretching to fill the hall. "That's nothing like—"

"You can't orchestrate her, Aiden. She's her own person and I think you hate to hear it, but she's *right*," Callum snarled.

"I don't want to control her, you idiot!" I bellowed. On the second story, Isaac's studio door slammed shut, ignoring us.

"Tell me then," Callum hissed, eyes narrowing, "what is it you want?"

"I don't want the pair of you leaving me! Breaking the coven!"

He didn't look surprised. Instead, all the menace washed out of his expression, a soft smile spreading in its place. "Oh, you and your fool head," he murmured, and then his hands were cupping the back of my neck, pulling my face roughly to his, lips taking mine in a demanding kiss.

I snarled against his mouth, my hands fisting in the back of his shirt, tearing it loose from his waistband, slamming our chests together hard enough to make our breaths knock loose. He still smelled like smoke from the morning and I groaned at the bite of his teeth on my bottom lip. My feet were slow in following him as he pushed me around a doorway and into my own bedroom.

"We aren't leaving you, Aiden," Callum said, smile against the corner of my mouth, his legs kicking between mine, leaving me stumbling backward to my bed. The room was dim, sunset coming in through the window, and turning the faint light a violent red.

"You have a connection," I said, shutting my eyes as he pressed my spine along one of the bed frame posters.

Callum laughed, breath puffing over my cheek, and tilted his head to bite at my jaw. My hips kicked forward into his and I groaned out a frustrated tightness in my chest.

"A connection, hm? And what do *we* have?"

"I'm not saying—"

"Stop for a moment, Aiden. I'm not sure you know what you're saying today," Callum said.

I opened my eyes to glare at him and found him smiling. There was tension around his eyes, some hint of the concern I knew he *had* to be feeling with Joanna locked away from us.

"We love you," Callum said, hands running slowly over my shoulders and down to my collar, fingernails clicking over the buttons, magic popping them loose. He drew back enough for his blue eyes to clash against mine. "It wasn't the nightmare talking when I said I knew who I'd be without you, without Isaac. I am not the man I want to be for Joanna without the two of you. And she's helped me become the man I wanted to be for you both."

Happy. Callum was so much happier, brighter, at peace with himself since Joanna had joined us.

Callum's fingers dug into the muscles of my chest and my head thunked against the wood post behind me as they traveled lower. I was stiffening in my pants, Callum's own cock nuzzling against my thigh, twitching with interest.

"I love the way she softens for Isaac," he said. "And I love the pair of you pecking at one another like hens, but I wish you could see *why* you do it."

My brow furrowed, lips parting to snap, make him tell me, but I was interrupted by another kiss. Callum's hands pushed my shirt off my shoulders, catching at my elbows as my fingers snagged in the front of his own, undoing the buttons in the wrong order and nearly choking him when I forgot to tackle the one at his collar.

I was equal parts relief and need. He wasn't leaving. Which meant Joanna wasn't leaving either. But the confidence was wavering inside of me, and the only thing that seemed to distract that feeling was more touch. Callum's hands were at the buckle of my pants, and I pulled him down to the bed with me as I fell backward, hissing and moaning as our hips ground together with the landing. I tried to roll us on the bed but Callum drew back, kneeling over me and tugging his wrists out of his shirt sleeves, knees on either side of my thighs.

"No, you've bossed me around in this bed plenty," Callum said, settling on my lap with one palm grinding over my half-hard cock, the other tugging the waistband slowly down my hips until I was arching, helping him free me. He slid off the foot of the bed, tugging my pants down my legs.

"I recall you enjoying that bossing, as you put it," I said. It felt almost odd to be alone with him this way, stranger to have a playful tussle while Joanna was upset and Isaac was angry. But Callum looked as if we had the house to ourselves, or at least that this moment belonged to us alone.

"Well look where it's gotten you now," Callum answered, eyebrows dancing.

I grunted, sitting up and ready to object, when he kicked himself free of his own pants and jumped back on the bed, bouncing us both on the mattress and tackling me back into my sheets. His mouth latched onto my throat, palms pinning my shoulders down, and all my growls turned into a moan. One knee wedged between my thighs and I took the cue, bracing my heels on the bed and spreading myself open for him.

"I would never be happy living apart from you, Aiden," Callum whispered into my neck, his breath cooling against the wet marks he left on my skin, a shiver rolling down my spine. "You are not my friend, not only that. You're my home."

My breath hitched as his hand rubbed down my chest and then long, nimble fingers enclosed the head of my cock, swirling the slit against his palm, beads of precum slicking over my skin and his.

I turned my head, putting my lips against his ear. "It's not like you to be effusive and sweet."

"It's not like you to be insecure," he answered.

I wrestled beneath him. He was toying with me! Pricking annoyance up, then soothing it away with sincerity. His chest dropped to mine, hand stroking my cock until I went still beneath him and watched his face, the pace of his fist around me too good to interrupt. I bit at my lip and watched his eyes darken.

"You're trying to take charge of this too, aren't you?" Callum asked, his grin spreading. His own length was tapping at the cheeks of my ass. "I won't let you. I want you at *my* mercy for once. I want to take care of you. Show you what you mean to me."

"You do," I said, the words a rasp. He asked my opinion when I knew he'd already made decisions, and sometimes it made me roll my eyes, but it was more than he asked anyone else.

He leaned up, fingers squeezing around me, and licked his way into my mouth until our tongues were teasing and curling together, hums of appreciation echoing in the kiss.

"I know you like that control," Callum said, lashes tickling against my cheek, mouth mumbling against mine. "I know it's a way for you to care for us. But I'm having my turn."

He leaned back—a little drop of fluid from me now shining on his stomach—and pulled a bottle of oil from one of his pockets of space.

"Planned this, did you?" I asked. Inside my stomach flipped

happily. My palm landed over my heart, rubbing the spot, wondering if it minded all this abuse, the clenching worry and swelling relief.

"Tactician," Callum said, dropping a dense pool of oil into his palm and then coating his own cock until it shone, all of him lit up fire bright from the dying red and fuchsia glow coming through the window.

His fingers were slick as he finished, hands rubbing briefly together before one returned to my aching cock, the other beneath me, squeezing and massaging my sac before sliding below. I twisted away from the penetrating touch at first but Callum had me pinned, pumping at the base of my length, and that was a touch I had no interest in escaping. With the first slide of his index finger inside of me, a gentle plunge, I was entirely his to torment.

Sweat broke out on my forehead and chest, eyes fixed to his as he watched my uneven breaths, watched me lick my lips, wishing for another lover to kiss, to focus on. Callum knew me too well, knew exactly how far he could push, how tight to squeeze to hold me at the edge and keep me there, seeming content to fuck my ass with one slender finger. I was hot head to toe, and then I was whimpering, body squirming between his two hands, fingernails scratching at my fine sheets.

"You like the power too," I accused, when it was almost too much, too much of the same decadent pleasure at the same torturous pace.

"I do," Callum said, wearing a quiet smile. A second finger joined the first and I bounced until his palm slid up my length, squeezing my tip and making me arch with a shout, expecting to come. By some wicked magic trick of his, the ecstasy stopped there.

His thighs pressed to the back of mine, his fingers drawing free and carrying one of my ankles up to his shoulder, the tip of him nudging at my opening.

"I love you, King," Callum said.

For a moment everything was softness, the urgency of moments before easing as he relaxed his hand around my length, teased a touch down over my balls, turned his head to kiss my leg. And then he was pushing inside, my body pushing down the bed to meet him, the stretch both easy and stinging, the fill of him echoing through me. His hands held the back of my thighs, propped me up so he could press in deeper until my voice was crying out to the ceiling.

"Open the bond," Callum said, his own voice struggling to remain even.

I did it without thinking, Callum had me under his orders now, and there was a flicker of irritated amusement from Isaac, and a brief and tiny hint of Joanna, curious and pretending not to be. She vanished just as quickly but Callum only laughed.

"Let her hear you," he said.

"I'm not your soldier for commanding, Pike," I growled, clenching around him, reveling in his groan.

He retaliated too fast, hips surging in and out, no more teasing or stretching or prepping, just pure thrust and retreat, a smooth even pace that left me twisting and doing exactly as he bid, gasping and shouting. I was afraid to touch myself, afraid of coming before I was ordered, and my cock ached with a deep, hollow need, with every shift and bob, bumping against my own stomach, swollen and leaking onto myself.

Callum grunted, fingers digging in tight on my thighs, narrow hips slamming against my ass. He hitched my hips against his once more, softening his thrusts, and then I couldn't resist. I released the knotted sheets from my fist, stroking and pulling and squeezing myself at his rhythm, our eyes locking.

He shifted his angle to the perfect spot, gripping me in place, and fire flashed at my spine, pressure tight in my cock. My blood pumped and my voice shook as I chanted his name, the beat echoing in my center, in my head, in my bones. The burn burst out, warmth exploding, sticky release landing on my chest.

Callum bucked frantically, following close, and then stiffened, deep enough to make me grunt even as I was unwinding, my muscles loosening and going soft, the bed warm and a little damp from sweat beneath me. I wrapped my legs around Callum's hips, digging my heels into his ass and chuckling as he grimaced, his pleasure in conflict with the sting of my ass clutching too tight around him. He dropped my thighs and braced his hands on my chest, pulling free and panting, his body collapsing slowly on top of mine, ignoring the mess he landed in.

I opened my mouth to ask him if he felt better, and then realized that was simply a reflex of my using sex to help him relieve tension too often. This time it was *me* that needed my stress untangled between us. And he'd done it for the most part. I shut my mouth instead of telling him so.

Callum groaned and rolled away, his nose wrinkling as he looked down at his chest, now peppered with my cum. I huffed a laugh. My legs were shaking and I wasn't about to get up and go looking for a rag for him. He muttered a bit of magic and with a bubbling flicker over our skin we were clean enough for the moment. My legs were dangling over the edge of the bed, pillows pushed in odd directions from my clasping fingers. Callum collapsed at my side and I tugged him against my chest, my hand fisted in the hair at the back of his neck, dragging his mouth to mine for a slow, nibbling kiss, until release made me too drowsy and lazy.

He rested against me for a moment, a hand covering my heart, and then spoke. "Do you know why she belongs with us?"

I blinked. I'd been ready to doze. "What?"

"Do you know why Joanna is our fourth?" Callum asked.

"What's that supposed to mean?" I asked, frowning, and annoyed at the interruption of the peace. I thought we were done with the arguing and this felt like a new topic.

"The bond is there, the connection, like it was with us," Callum said, turning on his side and resting on his elbow, propping his head up on his palm. "I'm not arguing that she belongs with us. I'm asking if you've taken the time to think about why."

I groaned and scrubbed my hand over my face. "Callum…"

"I know you've been waiting for our coven to be complete, and I know that you love her, but I think you let that immediate connection get in the way of the process of falling in love *with* her," Callum said, hand fisting on the center of my chest, keeping me from sitting up and pulling away.

I grimaced as I met his gaze, his expression open and calm. "What are you trying to tell me, Callum?"

"She thinks she disappoints you. Frustrates you. That you want her here as our fourth," there it was, that word again, the one she'd spat at me, "and not for all the wonderful reasons a woman like Joanna can do us so much good."

I sat up and this time no gentle touch could stop me, but Callum only rolled to his back, inching back on the bed and into the pillows. "Disappoints me?"

He half-smiled and it wasn't a happy expression. "Yes. I thought it was ridiculous too, but that doesn't mean anything to her unless you're the one to get through to her."

"Because we argue?" I asked. I didn't mind the bickering, not really. No that was a lie. Every time it started up again I was less certain of where we'd be when it ended.

"You like to argue," Callum said. "Joanna does too. Your brains like that kind of work, hunting down points and counterpoints. It's not far from strategy, so I understand. You push each other. But she needs to know that you aren't pushing her because you're unhappy with her as she is. And I think you need to know that as well. She isn't going anywhere, Aiden. She wants you to be happy."

I stared at him. Callum was giving me romantic advice. Eight months ago was the first time he'd even *asked* for any and now… I might have laughed, but instead I was cataloging in my mind all the times I'd told Joanna how grateful I was to find her, to complete our coven. And how rarely I'd told her how she surpassed my expectations, how she made me laugh, and Callum smile, and Isaac easy.

"We should go upstairs now," I said. I needed to talk to her.

"Let her be," Callum said, sinking into the blankets.

"She's alone."

"Isaac's up there now."

When had that happened? But he was right, I could feel the shift in the house, they were together, their emotions softening and soothing one another.

"I wasn't joking when I said take the time to think," Callum said, yawning. He stretched an arm across the headboard and I sighed, crawling back so we could push the sheets down and slide underneath. "Our coven isn't breaking. I don't know if you've noticed, but we're all a bit obsessed with each other. We *certainly* aren't platonic."

Something near enough to a laugh escaped me and I pushed Callum back to the pillows, holding his face in my hands and kissing him before he delivered any more of this smart-ass nonsense.

THE PHONE RANG in the dead of night and I sat up with a start at the noise. Not again. Whatever it was, whoever was calling, there was no good news at this hour. Callum jerked up off his pillow just after me and I felt the others waking at the top of the house.

My body complained with cracking bones as I scrambled out of the bed, grabbing an abandoned robe off the back of the chair by the door and swinging it on as I headed for the stairs. Overhead, the door to Joanna's room creaked open.

"I'm getting it," I called, words cracking with sleep and gravel.

Steps padded, Isaac's slow, soft gait instead of Joanna's sleepy, uneven thumps, and I ran down to the first floor. The cats circled around the table, screeching in alarm.

"Hush. Scoot. Hello?"

"Aiden." My spine straightened like a schoolboy at the first note of my father's voice. "I need you and Callum to come to the city."

"Of course," I said, a reflex. I cleared the grit out of my voice and looked up, seeing Isaac, Callum, and Joanna lined up the stairs. "Why? What's happened?"

If my mother wasn't calling did that mean…

"The Vermenians are sending a surprise convoy to Rhodantis. Likely looking for their Scribes. Duncan Pike's on his way too and if Callum can manage it, I'd like him to head his father off. Keep him out of everyone's hair and the countries out of war. I need you to come make your arguments again on why the Vermenians are worth protecting."

Would Sewell hear of this? Worse, Anders? Not if I could manage to keep it a secret.

"We'll take the first train," I said, nodding up to Callum.

"Will Joanna and Isaac be with you? Your mother will worry about the house."

I nearly said yes when I remembered the climate of Canderfey. Joanna would want to—need to—stay with the Scrivens. And I wanted someone here with her.

"No, not this trip. I'll see you soon." We made our goodbyes and I hung up, delivering the news to my coven.

"Do you think they'll change their minds?" Joanna asked, hands wrapped around the banister, close enough to touch.

I shook my head. "I'll make sure they don't. Even the worst argument leaves us better defended if the Scrivens aren't in Vermenia."

She nodded and I searched her face for our earlier fight, but her expression was slack with exhaustion.

"I'll pack…prepare," Callum said, turning up the stairs. "Maybe if I play my cards right we'll be uninvited for the winter solstice."

Isaac followed after Callum, but Joanna waited for me halfway up the first flight. I joined her there. She looked especially small, pressed to the wall in her nightgown.

"I'm sorry. Some of the things I said today were… not sentiments I was aware I was even holding," I said. "I want to say more, but from now on I better take the time to think before I speak."

Joanna's head thunked softly against the wall as she looked up at me, one hand reaching out to tangle our fingers together. "I do believe our concerns are the same, even if our solutions aren't. Thank you for all that you've already done."

The breath slipped out of me in a shaky release and I ducked my head to hers, resting our cheeks together. "Joanna, I…" Callum's words were circling in my head. "I want to talk more when I get home. Clear things between us that I've left foggy for too long." When I leaned back I found her eyes wide and stricken, and I rushed to add, "I love you, darling."

She stared at me for a brief pause and I saw it there, the way she gauged the words, like she didn't know how to believe them. "I love you too," she said.

I considered taking the second or third train for the day instead, as long as there was a little time to talk. She kissed me, a soft tentative thing, and hummed as I wrapped her up and held her closer, returning the caress with a longer press.

"Don't stay longer than you have to," she whispered as I caught a breath.

But go, I heard in the words. I nodded and kissed her cheek once more before running upstairs to fix whatever disaster Callum had made of our packing.

19

JOANNA

The Hand Woods was calm, fragrant with early buds, and rich with wet earth and the summer fresh leaves. There was a woodpecker not far away, its persistent percussion covering the sounds of our feet crunching over the ground.

"What about here?" I asked, stopping and looking down to detangle my skirt from a briar.

Daniel stopped at my side, arms crossing over his chest, and Nora was just behind us. I wondered if she wrote herself impervious to all the reaching branches and snagging thorns, or if she was simply a more careful walker than I. We were in the woods south of town, far from the campus and away from any wandering faculty or spying university presidents.

"Here is safe," Daniel said, squinting at the small space between towering trees, only underbrush and delicate saplings in the way.

"Do we just…write it?" I asked them.

"We mark a symbol on the trees," Nora said, pointing to the slight outline of larger trees that surrounded the space. "And use that in the writing to define the structure."

I nodded. "Clever."

Daniel pulled a pocket knife out of his jacket and looked to us both, waiting for instruction. I went to the nearest trunk and imitated a set of slashing, crossing marks that would be distinct enough to avoid confusion and simple enough to carve or write quickly. He set to work.

"It would be better if we had someone to write us drafts," Nora said, walking up to one of the trees and resting her hand on the trunk. "Someone not Scrivens."

I chewed the inside of my cheek. I'd thought that might be the case and nearly asked Isaac that very morning. But I didn't want my coven forced to keep secrets from each other, and I especially didn't want Aiden responsible for keeping a secret that might land him in hotter water with the University or the Mayor than he already was. He and Callum had left campus the morning before, and Aiden said to keep their departure a secret as long as we could. Maybe Gwen would...

"I could do it."

The delicate lilting voice was too familiar, and my teeth gritted. Nora and Daniel jumped and spun to face Corina. She wasn't having an easier time trekking through the woods. Her soft shoes were soaked with mud and she held her skirts up to avoid catching them on branches and thorns, but they found the flimsy fabrics all the same. Her curls were tangled and there was a twig hanging in one. The sight made me smile.

"What are you doing out here?" I asked, eyes sweeping the woods. "Where is Bryce?"

Corina narrowed her eyes in response, and then huffed and yanked her dainty foot free of a tangling root. Bryce and their coven had kept the girl under careful watch for the weeks since she'd written Isaac in love with her and it shocked me to see her out on her own.

"Not home," Corina said, shrugging. "And I saw you going into the woods so I went for a walk."

"She's a good writer," Nora said softly. "Certainly practiced. We could change your spell so her magic doesn't take."

"I can talk it out for you," Corina tilted her head coyly, not realizing that the twig was even more noticeable that way.

I laughed and rolled my eyes, crunching through the brush to stand in front of Corina. She cocked her chin at me and met my gaze for a handful of seconds, before flinching and flipping her long blonde curls over her shoulder, catching strands in the branches of a sapling.

"I want to protect you," I said and Corina's head whipped back around to me, wincing as her hair caught, gaze fastening to mine. "Not because I have any fondness for you, but because it's important to me that Scrivens, you included, are safe here in Canderfey. But if you hurt anyone again, I will hand you over to the authorities. We have laws in this country about the use of magic and manipulating others, and I am not afraid to see you subjected to them."

Corina's lips pursed and she nodded once.

"We shouldn't work here," I said. "It's safer back at the house."

"No one followed me," Corina said.

"It's not people I'm worried about," I said. "These woods already have occupants."

The other Scrivens all looked dubious at that. The woods were thick, but not enough to hide a crowd of people that might be lingering. But the Hand Woods were full of old cages containing ancient beings, and while they might be safely trapped, that didn't mean they weren't paying attention to what went on in the woods. I'd felt one of those cages, an eerie, still grove of trees, on our walk to this spot, and rejected the thought of building our shelter there. Too risky.

"I'll explain on the way back to the library," I said to the others.

Nora and Corina balked at the notion of building a structure in a woods filled with sleeping monsters, but Daniel seemed pragmatic about the whole thing. Or he didn't understand what I was saying, it was difficult to tell.

"Why worry about the ones in the woods?" I asked Corina, raising an eyebrow as we walked out of the woods and onto a sidewalk leading to town. "You're living with one of their descendants."

Corina's eyes grew huge at the revelation, and I nearly teased her some more when Daniel nudged Nora on the sidewalk. Their steps ahead of us stopped as Daniel passed Nora his notebook. I pulled my own out of my pocket and found the message.

They've come to our home. Mother is frightened. - Anya Grivet

"My locks were better," Corina said, an unhelpful note for the moment.

"What's the fastest way there?" Nora asked me.

"There's no door to borrow nearby," I said. We're were in an unfamiliar part of the neighborhood and I didn't think anyone would appreciate us writing on their front door. "We'd better run."

Corina and I were fastest, but the message arrived too late. The street outside of the pub was flooded with locals, and I realized I was seeing the fire department for the second time in as many days. I was pushing through the crowd up to the barrier, when hands gripped my waist. Isaac tugged me to his chest, the pair of us barreling through the gawkers.

There was smoke churning out the tiny top window, the room of the Grivet's apartment, and the air was already stinging at my still sensitive lungs. The crowd around us was hushed, faces lifted, holding its collective breath.

"This one's not magical," Isaac told me. "But I overheard the fire department say their safety wards aren't working and they aren't sure how to get up the stairs without them."

Two of the sisters were pushed back on the sidewalk, tucked behind one of the department men, sobbing, but there was no sign of Anya or her mother. Down the row, a sooty-faced man shouted at a police officer.

"It wasn't us that set the fire! There was something on the stairs. I didn't see!" His eyes were huge, jumping over the crowd with a skittish urgency.

"They're inside?" I asked Isaac as Corina reached us.

"Yes," Isaac said, voice rough.

"Do you have paint?"

"Pai- what?"

"Paint, Isaac. Do you have paint or charcoal? Something to write on me."

"Joanna, no!" He turned my face to his, nose to nose, his eyes huge with shock. "No, you can't."

"I *can*. I have to." I reached into his pockets and, sure enough, found a thin tube of ochre paint, likely forgotten there weeks ago.

He tried to snatch it out of my hands, but my fingers were quick, untwisting the cap. It landed on the ground and was kicked away as someone bumped into my back. I held the tube in my left hand, shoving the sleeve of my dress up past my elbow to bare my forearm.

"You're crazy," Corina murmured lightly at my back.

"Joanna, you don't even know what you're walking into," Isaac said.

I didn't answer but began to smear paint over my skin, hoping I didn't run out of room.

"Something's wrong with magic," Isaac hissed in my ear and I looked up, finally, at that. "What if yours isn't working either?"

"I'll know soon enough," I said, the letters growing down my arm, sloppy.

"It's wet," Corina said. "Be careful."

"Absolutely not!" Isaac shouted, but she stepped between us to keep him from ruining my work.

I DO NOT BURN.

"That doesn't mean something else won't catch fire," Corina muttered. "Your skirts."

My skirts. She was right. But there wasn't time to think about skirts and hopefully, this would... Oh gods, Aiden would kill me when he found out.

I lifted my arm far over my head and when one of the firemen turned away to speak in his coworker's ear, I dashed past the barrier and into the stairwell, ignoring the shouts behind me. I made it up the first flight and turned the corner into dense, scorching black smog.

I did not burn, but that did not stop my lungs from screaming in the smoke. It didn't stop my skin from sweating in the heat. It didn't keep the stairs from moaning underneath me like a threat, or a charred fragment of roof to come clattering down the opening of the stairwell and nearly braining me.

Callum would probably kill me too when he heard. It was good they were away still. Already the words on my arm were looking smudged, the edges blurring too close together for comfort. I ran up the last flight of stairs and stopped on the landing. The door in front of me was blazing, cracking and crumbling, the flames catching on the connecting walls. An inferno waited between me, Anya, and her mother.

"Are you—" I couldn't catch my breath, there wasn't enough oxygen, and my vision swam in front of me. "Are you alright?!"

It might have been a creak of wood, but there was a sound from inside and I wanted to believe, so badly, that they would be alive when I found them. That there was someone inside to hear me, to answer me. There was only one way in and I didn't have the time to worry if my words would hold up. I barreled my side into the door, felt it shatter, sparks and coals and splinters kissing the skin of my legs, and scratching my cheeks as I stumbled through.

The room was hazy inside but I heard a rasp, an attempt at a cough from inside the bathroom, and ran for the sound. Anya and her mother were inside, soaking themselves in water, their cheeks sooty and streaked with tears. Anya screamed when she saw me, splashing at me, and then tugging me forward and soaking me, my head. I looked in the mirror and saw, my braid charred and tangling, burnt.

"They saw me write," Anya said in Vermenia. And then what I thought must have been, "They took my pencils."

She'd been defenseless against the fire. I dug in my pocket and pulled out the tube of paint, nearly squeezed empty, passing it into her damp fingers. She blinked at it and then gave up trying to put out all the little smoldering bits of me—the hem and hip of my skirt, the ends of my hair, my left shoulder— and turned to the wall, writing in quick even letters.

Anya's mother stroked wet hands over my cheeks and outside the bathroom the building went quiet, crackling flames dying away.

"The smoke," I said, and Anya nodded, paint growing thin on the wall but doing the necessary work all the same. I turned to the running sink cupping my hands into the water and carrying it up to my lips, choking and coughing on the first swallow. Outside there was a cheer and downstairs footsteps began to run up the stairs.

I hadn't taken enough time to think. To try and put the fire out from down on the ground. I'd only thought of the fact that there were people trapped up here without anyone coming for them. I winced and splashed my face with more water, taking another gulp.

"Good girl," Anya's mother said, patting my back.

I laughed, a panicked nervous sound, and wondered if she would defend me to my coven when they took me to task.

The fire department made their way upstairs finally, now that the fire was out, and a medic took Anya and her mother aside immediately, another reaching for me when Isaac barreled into the apartment. He pushed them out of the way, hands grasping my face, then my shoulders, twisting me around for him to examine me.

"Your hair!"

"I do like it short in summer," I rushed to say, but my voice cracked and I bent forward, wracking coughs seizing in my chest.

WHEN THE MEDICS finished checking us out, and the fire department finished questioning the Grivets, Isaac took us all back to the tower house. He let the Scrivens find their own way into the kitchen and took me upstairs, double-checking me head to toe and helping me cut away the most ragged ends of my hair.

Myles was coming in the front door as we made it back downstairs.

"Leina, silly girl," Myles hissed, coming forward and scooping me up. I grimaced in the hold. I had not burned in the fire but my skin felt painfully tender and raw now. "You have to use the words *smart*."

"There wasn't time," I said just as Isaac ground out, "I can't talk sense into her so you'd better try."

I dragged them both into the kitchen. Nora passed me a cup of tea, her steely gaze meeting mine. I nodded at her and she turned to Myles.

"Kershaw, it's time for the Scrivens to write."

20

AIDEN

"The safety of the Scrivens in Canderfey is the safety of Enmaire as a whole," I said. "With no record of the-the—"

The panic spiked hot in my chest, choking off the words. I was finishing the 'informal lunch' with my father and the rest of the ministers of defense, and somewhere in the bond, terror was reining. My fist whitened around the napkin in my lap, eyes drifting over the men watching me, waiting for me to gather my thoughts when my thoughts were spiraling in my head.

"The refugees were never recorded as Scrivens, you see," my father continued in my place and the room around me turned into white noise as my heart raced.

I reached for my water glass, hand shaking, and clutched it in my grip to hide the tremor as sweat beaded down my temples and I tried to trace my frenzied heart to its source. Callum was feeling the dread, the worry compounding as it hit him, and I couldn't untangle Isaac and Joanna from one another.

My father's elbow nudged my side as he made goodbyes to his peers and I stumbled through the same sentiments until he was leading me out of the restaurant.

"You did well till the end," he said. "Your Scrivens project should remain safe."

"Something's happened in Canderfey. I need to call," I said. "I have to get back."

He stopped us on the sidewalk, examining my face, and my eyes searched the street as if I might find my coven there in front of me, safe, when I knew perfectly well *someone was in danger*.

"I see. Here's a cab." He helped me into the back and I collapsed in the far corner, my hands clenching the bench for grounding as my father passed the driver directions back to his home.

Minute after minute of heart pounding, anxiety thrummed through me. The sweat trickled down my spine, and I realized this was another symptom from my coven rather than just my own fear. It was heat. Scorching heat, like the blaze from the other morning. Another fire? My notebook was upstairs in my old bedroom at my mother's house, but I knew with all the panic coursing through me this was not the moment Isaac or Joanna would take to write to us.

"If something happens and it gets back to the capitol," my father said under his breath.

"I'm more concerned with getting back to *Canderfey*," I growled.

We pulled up to the curb in front of my mother's house just as the worst of burning and terror collapsed inside of me. Callum's feet were slapping down the sidewalk and I jumped down from the carriage and into his arms.

"What is it? What's happened? That heat!"

"Upstairs. Grab the notebook. I'll call the house."

We rushed through the house, passing my mother as we split off at the staircase, and I picked up the phone. It was only a little comfort to feel the rush of relief from Isaac, Joanna's embarrassment and giddy adrenaline. That woman, I'd have her over my knee when I got home, and this time that was no empty threat.

"Aiden, what on earth is going on?" my mother asked, watching my fingers shake as I dialed the house.

"Checking on the coven," I said briefly, and then it was ringing... and ringing...and ringing. I listened for too long, as if any minute they would walk through the door and pick up the phone. Finally, my mother passed my back, reaching up and prying the phone from my ears.

Callum came down the steps, notebook in hand. "No message. But they're…they're alright now."

"What's happened, loves?" my mother repeated, hanging up the phone.

"We don't know. But there was…"

"Panic. And burning. Adrenaline," Callum said and my mother's eyes widened.

"I see. You're going home already then," she said, nodding as if it was already decided.

I twisted, my back to the wall, knees finally giving out as I sank to the floor. Callum came to my side and I leaned my head against his knee.

"I'm too old to pick him up off the floor," she said to Callum. "You'll have to do it, honey. I'll order your tickets home."

Callum let me rest until the tickets were ordered and then heaved me up to help with the packing. I tried to call the house again and it went on ringing for another handful of minutes before I caught my mother eyeing me from the kitchen. I hung up again and went to her, sighing as she bundled her arms around me as far as they would go, her fingers nearly touching.

"I don't like to see so much worry on that fine face of yours," she said.

"I know they're alright now. I'll feel better when I see them."

She pushed and shoved, a comical little grunt digging a smile out from me, until I was facing her, her chin lifted high to look up at me. "You showed up on my doorstep with that worry. Is it all this politics with the Scrivens?"

She'd heard Joanna's correction of the name once and adopted the words for the Vermenians easily ever since. My father had yet to call them anything other than Scribes.

"It's Joanna," I said, although what I'd meant to say was 'Yes, it's a complicated situation and I'm sick to death of it.' My mother raised her eyebrows, lips twitching, and I realized she heard exactly what she expected. Mother's magic. I cleared my throat and continued. "We're having…growing pains."

"Pfft. I always knew if you three found yourselves with a woman in the house, it would turn your heads upside down," my mother said, grinning.

I shook my head and she pinched my chin between her thumb and index finger.

"I'm afraid I'm going to lose her. That the coven will split," I said.

If I didn't know my mother's magic so well, I would have said it was the ability to drag the truth right out from behind your teeth.

She blinked at me, and then her lips pressed together and her eyes narrowed. "Aiden King, do you think I *lost* your father? He lives next door to me! I couldn't lose that man if I *tried*."

"I didn't- It's just that—"

"Your father is a good man and I do love him, but I never felt about him the way you feel about Joanna and Isaac and Callum. Covens are not all made the same way, baby," she said, face softening into a smile. "We wanted a child, the four of us. And we got the perfect child who was just right for us. And when this little house was just too crowded and the water heater wasn't keeping up, and the house next door went up for sale, Darren and Sarah moved. We're still a coven. A family. Are you telling me we haven't let you feel that?"

Marcus had always been my father. Sarah had tucked me in as a child as much as my mother.

"You…argued," I said, and the word sounded lame on my tongue.

"Yes, we did, and do. Darren's got a certain way of looking at things, and I have a certain way of looking at things and those don't always match. And we argue. You and Joanna argue?" I nodded and my mother nodded with me. "Do you ever think she's right?"

"Almost every time," I said and my mother beamed. "But she risks so much. She's constantly sticking her neck out for practically anyone she meets. It drives me mad."

She hummed and squinted at me. "Well, that kind of communication is for you two to sort out. But for the record, I'm not worried. I knew as soon as I met her that you two would better each other. Enrich your lives, sweeten Callum and Isaac's."

Callum's steps were thudding back down the stairs overhead. Despite the sudden shock of worry, and still not knowing what had happened, my load was lighter after the conversation with my mother. She smiled, seeing that ease, and patted my cheek, rising up on her toes as I bent to kiss her cheek.

"You better come visit soon," I said. "The others are sorry not to see you."

"I will. Get home and give them my love."

Callum left our bags in the hall, scooping my mother up in a tight hug until she was giggling and soothing her fingers over his hair, her toes dangling down to the floor.

"Catch your train, honey," she said to him, kissing his cheek.

WE LEFT the notebook sitting open-faced on the window ledge during the train ride, and the words appeared halfway home as the sun was setting.

Home safe. I frowned and glanced at Callum until more appeared. *Fire at the Grivet's apartment. No one badly hurt. Joanna's fine.*

"Joanna," Callum growled. "Fine, my ass."

I wrote back our arrival time and Isaac answered that he would meet us there. *Joanna too*, Callum scrawled, but there was no reply.

"She's done something terrible and heroic," Callum said in a low tone and I grunted my agreement, thinking of the heat that had stung my skin and drawn a sweat through the bond connection alone.

Joanna was not on the platform as our train pulled into the station and Isaac's expression as we descended the stairs was skittish.

"Where is she?" I asked, tugging him to my chest and wrapping my arm around his back. At least he didn't smell like smoke.

"With the Scrivens. At the house, I think."

"You think?" Callum asked, joining the embrace. "Catch us up."

Isaac pulled away, taking a deep breath, shoving his hands into pockets. "Some townies got riled up at the pub last night and someone let it slip that a Scrivens lived on the top floor of the building. When the pub closed they broke in. Started to harass Anya and her family, took Anya's pencil when she wrote to the other Scrivens. They claim they saw her writing their names but Anya swears she doesn't know their names. And her family didn't see the fire start so… the investigators are still looking into that since the men won't admit to it."

"And Joanna?" I asked, eyes narrowing.

Isaac winced. "Anya and her mother were still inside when she arrived, and the fire department's wards weren't working. She panicked, wrote herself unable to burn." His words rushed as my teeth gritted. "She got in, they wrote out the fire. Everyone is okay."

"That woman is insane," I said as Callum's fingers dug into his hair, tugging hard at the roots.

"There's more, not about Joanna exactly, but I want to get back to the house. It hasn't been a good day," Isaac said.

I caught a black cab idling in front of the station, the three of us packed together into the back seat.

"Why aren't you certain Joanna is at home?" I asked.

"She and the Scrivens were there when I left but…no, she's written it a secret now. I can't say."

My eyebrows rose and I nearly took my frustration with Joanna out on Isaac when we crossed into the perimeter of town, but Callum stiffened at my side.

"What is it?" he asked Isaac, voice harsh and hushed. "What's happened, there was a… I can't feel anything."

"I'll tell you at home," Isaac whispered, eyebrows raising.

I glanced at the cabbie, who seemed entirely uninterested in our conversation, but took Isaac's word. I hummed, a quiet feeler, wondering if I could sense whatever pricked at Callum and there was—

Nothing.

The hum was just a sound. There was no spark of magic on my tongue. I met Callum's eyes. He was tense and alert like a prey who knew it was being watched by the predator. The coven bond was gone now too, and my heart shook in my chest like a wild animal when I realized that I both did not know where Joanna was, but also could not sense if she was safe.

I understood what Isaac had been not quite telling us. The department's magic, that Enmarian magic, hadn't worked that morning. But Joanna's had. It was still working when ours wasn't. It was no secret that Scrivens magic operated under different properties. Enmarian magic was dampened by the presence of Rixon but Scrivens words still held power.

"Has anyone come to the house since the fire?" I asked, keeping my words soft, sliding my hand off my lap to brush against Isaac's, linking our fingers together.

"Not yet," he said.

Joanna and the Scrivens were together. They knew the magic was missing from Canderfey, but not theirs. How long before the rest of Canderfey, the town and campus would realize?

We pulled up to the house in near dark, the front window glowing faintly with a light left on somewhere farther back on the first floor. It didn't look like enough activity for Joanna to still be at home, but now I had no way of knowing. A collection of officials stood together on the front steps. The pit in my stomach hardened to heavy rock, sinking low in my gut.

Anders was there with Elizabeth Bonde at his side. Sewell with another of the councilmen. More concerning to me were the two police officers at the top of the step. Isaac paid the cab fare as Callum and I stepped out from either side of the car, bags over our shoulders.

"Gentlemen," I said before Callum could start the conversation on the wrong foot. "I hope you haven't been waiting long. Callum and I just returned from a visit to the capital."

"And your fourth?" Anders asked. He looked queasy and pale, hair thin and faded, skin papery and slack, and it took me a moment to realize that this was President Anders without a hint of glamour. He looked ill, worn down, and it almost drew my sympathy for him. But I didn't like the way he called Joanna the 'fourth' of our coven, as if that somehow put her in last place. And I realized why it'd become a term that left her prickly and insecure.

"I believe Joanna is with her family tonight?" I glanced over my shoulder at Isaac. The black cab was driving away and I tried to smile at Isaac, reassure him enough to keep some of the nerves out of his expression before it gave too much away. He nodded briefly, hands fisting back into his pockets again to keep them from fidgeting.

"And where is the Kershaw family, Professor King?" Mayor Sewell said.

If he was ever our ally, that treaty was expired now. There was no apology in his expression. I respected that he had never offered us more or less than what he thought was truly fair and best for everyone involved. And I understood too. Canderfey was essentially defenseless now, something had to be done.

"I'm afraid I don't know," I said. "Would you come inside?"

They were all too eager and I held my breath, hoping I was right and the Scrivens were long gone by now. The house was silent and I flipped the light on in the hall.

"We're looking to speak to Myles Kershaw on a serious matter, Professor King," one of the police officers announced. "Do you mind if we look around?"

"Not at all," I said, trying to sound even, casual.

"Stay here, Anders," Sewell said just as the other man started to follow the officers up the stairs. "Let them do their job."

Were Joanna's words on a door in our house somewhere, leading to the Scrivens? I waited, feigning calm as Callum and Isaac appeared, dropping our bags on the stairs. I wished I'd pried the secret from Isaac, or that she'd at least thought to include me and Callum in on the plan. I could protect her better that way.

"I hope Miss Wick and her family aren't out long," Vice President Bonde said to me, a placid smile on her lips. "There's been reports of activity in the woods."

"Don't be absurd, Elizabeth," Anders hissed.

The officers were down in a moment, glancing briefly into the kitchen, and the dining room before rejoining us.

"We appreciate your cooperation," one of the officers said. "We're also out tonight delivering an official notice. Scrivens magic is now prohibited in Canderfey. That includes your Miss Wick."

I swallowed, ignored Anders' triumphant expression, and looked to Sewell.

"The sooner they come in for questioning the sooner we might be able to put things back to rights," Sewell said.

"Of course. Thank you, gentlemen. We'll let Joanna and her uncle know the news as soon as we see them again."

"Do you have any idea where they might have gone?" the officer asked. "We might run into them while we're out."

"Knowing Joanna," Callum said, cocking his head and managing a faint smile, "probably the library."

I nearly laughed when the whole group blinked, sincerely surprised by the idea, and resisted the urge to touch Callum in thanks. It was a good guess. Now I just hoped he wasn't right. I locked the door behind them.

21

JOANNA

It was... not quite a house. Really it was a bit of a mess. Nora's caution to consider our words carefully while writing the structure into the woods was tossed quickly aside when we realized that Canderfey's magic was missing. Being terrorized by drunk locals was bad enough, being terrorized, or worse, by the authorities was exactly what the Vermenians had come here to avoid. Isaac left the house to meet our covenmates at the train station and I wrote with the Scrivens.

There is a door in the Hand Woods between two trees marked with...

On and on, the notebook passed from one Scrivens to the next as more details were added, rooms upon rooms, running water, a working stove, each addition bound with a secret kept between the group of us.

Someone—Daniel, I suspected—had the notebook now, writing roofs onto the last of the rooms at the top of the strange house. I stood in the kitchen, which was also currently a sitting room, and very nearly a shower if not for a hastily added corridor putting it back down the hall with the rest of the bathroom. The walls were littered with doors, leading to different stories of the house so that the elderly visitors didn't have to worry about stairs.

Corina was making tea, humming something sweet. I had let her write a tea set and it was the prettiest work of porcelain and prose I'd ever seen in my life. I was keenly aware that I admired her skill enough to be jealous, just a little. The sitting room in front of me wrapped out of the kitchen and around a flight of stairs, with mismatched chairs contrived for the individuals who wanted to sit in them.

Since the house went to the very edges of each of the trees we placed it inside, it ended up shaped as an uneven octagon. Without proper measurements nothing seemed to match or make sense, windows all set at different heights. The ceiling of Bekka's bedroom came to everyone else's shoulder height and her mother begged three times for the girl to rewrite the words, but the child was too delighted to be swayed.

"I should get to my coven before anyone realizes I'm with you," I said to Myles as he appeared from down the corridor that led under a staircase, and over to the bathroom at the other end of the house. I knew someone had written a laundry room in somewhere, but it could have been in the attic for all I knew at this point. I looked around the odd room, where counter space was multiplying at an alarming rate, and realized I wasn't entirely certain which door led back to the tower house now.

"You should get back to your men before they lose their minds with worry," Myles said. He laughed as he caught me chewing anxiously on the inside of my cheek, reaching up and patting at my cheek.

I scoffed and then cleared my throat. "Keep the notebook," I said to Myles and he nodded.

"Are you sure this is what you want to do?" he asked. "If there's trouble and they find you..."

"Do the others feel safe?"

He sighed as he looked around the house. Everyone was talking, Vermenian layered from the first floor to the top, and laughter was running down the stairs.

"Yes, leina," he said, smiling.

"It won't be a cage," I said. "You won't *have* to stay here. I'll fix things for us."

"That's not your job, leina," Myles said, settling large hands on my shoulders.

"It is if she says it is, Kershaw," Nora snapped from the kitchen. "Where's the notebook? We have an oven that doesn't heat."

"Go on," Myles and I said in unison, grinning at one another, and then he left for the kitchen and I turned back to the wall of doors. "Which of you is it then?" I whispered to myself.

It was squeezed between two others, short and narrow, just the same size as the pantry door. I swung it open, the kitchen dark, and stepped inside. I could hear Aiden down the hall and almost called for them when I realized my coven might not be alone. I tucked myself out of sight and then flipped the light on. Footsteps followed.

"Joanna? Is that you?" Callum called out and the others were rushing down the hall

"Who's home?" I whispered, wincing and hoping I hadn't given myself away.

"It's just us," Callum said, and then he was running into the kitchen, freezing for half a moment before seeing me and charging. I was tangled up in a hug before I got the chance to say hello. "Don't you dare leave without one of us again, not while the coven bond is missing."

Aiden was squeezing past Callum, circling to my back and joining the embrace until he stopped short. "What have you done to your hair?"

"Trimmed it," I said, twisting to look at him.

Callum put me back on my feet and then leaned back, blinking at the odd, chunky cut Isaac and I'd patched from what was left after the fire. "You burned your damn hair off, didn't you?" he asked.

"I like it short," I said and Isaac huffed a laugh in the background.

Callum and Aiden stared at one another over my head, and then Callum nodded once, and stepped back. I turned to Aiden and his eyes were narrowed.

"Are the Vermenians safe?" Aiden asked.

"Yes," I whispered, inching back until I bumped against Callum's chest.

"Myles is wanted for questioning at the police station," Aiden said, words turning deep and stony in the tone that gave me shivers and made the hairs on my skin stand at attention.

I raised my chin and gritted my teeth. "He won't go," I said. "I'll go myself—"

"You'll do no such thing," Aiden said, hands flying to my waist, holding me tight. My feet stumbled to him, toes stubbing against his shoes until he was arched over me, a thunderous expression digging lines into his forehead. "I've had just about enough of you throwing yourself into trouble with your hand slapped over your eyes."

I raised my eyebrows and pursed my lips to keep them from twitching. "*Just* about?"

His growl was feral, but his grin made my skin warm and expectant, waiting for touch. "If you want to play the brat, darling, I'll take you upstairs and put you over my knee."

"Maybe if you did instead of just teasing me with the idea, I wouldn't keep misbehaving," I snapped back. My eyes widened a fraction as the words escaped, but not nearly as wide as Aiden's. I stifled my own surprise and stared back at him.

He swallowed, throat bobbing visibly, and then I squeaked as he hauled me to his chest, one arm wrapping around my legs just below my ass. "Very well."

Isaac and Callum were grinning, near to laughter as Aiden carried me out of the kitchen, the hand on my hip sliding back to squeeze at my flesh and make me squirm.

"Have fun, love," Isaac said, "C'mon, Cal, let's make them some dinner."

"Give him hell," Callum said, winking at me as we retreated down the hall.

"Even if you didn't mean it, I still want a little time alone with you," Aiden said, low and quiet for my ears only.

There was a giggle in the back of my throat and I let it out, a high, giddy sound, arms twining around his shoulder as he grunted and carried me up the stairs.

"I did mean it though," I assured him and he paused on the landing, studying my face with warmth in his gaze. "Is it like… like in Callum's office? Where you were in charge of how… we found pleasure?"

The warmth spread down to his smile and he started up the stairs again. "If you want it to be. Are you going to be my clever girl, fighting my orders?"

I bit my lip as I smiled back in answer. "If you want me to be."

"I think it's time we got one thing clear Miss Wick," Aiden said as we reached the hall, striding down to his own bedroom. He turned, pushing my back against the door to open it, making me laugh. He walked us over to the foot of the bed, and then let me slide down to the floor, his hands lifting to hold my cheeks as he spoke. "I want you, every inch of you, exactly as you would like for me to have you."

I blushed, finding it impossible to meet his eyes, my chest growing tight as he stared at me.

"Whether that is screaming at me for compassion before our morning coffee, or sweetly curled against me at night," Aiden continued as I rolled my eyes, pushing gently at his chest, "or naked on my bed with your pert little ass up in the air begging for my palm to strike it, I don't care. As long as I know that you love me."

Now suddenly I couldn't look *away* from him, my voice lost as my thoughts bounced between the vivid image he'd placed in my mind and the immense love and affection he'd stirred up in my chest.

"I'm not sure I like you so quiet though," he said smiling, bending down. His hands squeezed around my ribs and I gasped, my lips parting just in time for him to claim my mouth with his. He sucked hard on my bottom lip and I fisted his shirt in my hands, whimpering at the slight nibble of pressure. He released me with a pop and his eyes traced over my face. "Better," he said. "Not quite as loud as I'm hoping for."

"If you think I'm going to scream for you with one little kiss," I said, that tartness rising back up at his teasing. His eyes were bright as I spoke, but his lips pressed together and I realized he was waiting for me to answer. Not the teasing, but the demand of emotion. I leaned into his chest, pressing kisses up his throat and then tilting back to meet his eyes.

"I love you, Aiden King. You challenge me and nurture me and I only...I only want to make you proud. I hope that I don't disappoint you. I know that I can be—"

"Stop, right there," he growled, eyes narrowing. "I will tolerate you rushing into enemy country to protect Callum, and even into a burning building to save others. But I won't hear you berate yourself on my behalf. Lift your skirts or drop them, I don't care, but up on the bed with you."

I held my breath for a moment, suddenly nervous. Not that he would hurt me. Aiden was more protective than anyone else I knew and harm was an impossibility, not to mention I had learned enough by now to relish the little flashes of pain in the midst of dizzying pleasure. Only, I didn't know what to expect or how to be *good* at it, and I didn't want to do the wrong thing.

Aiden's head lowered. "It's alright, love. We can—"

"I *want* to, I just- Oh!"

Aiden scooped me back off my feet, tossing me onto the mattress and following me down. His hands took my hips and rolled me onto my belly, my heart racing as he rucked my skirt up my legs and over my hips. I squirmed, trying to push myself up on my hands and knees, find my way to his lap, and then *crack!*

"Ah!" I stiffened, heat blooming over the right cheek of my ass and directly into my core. My arms fell out from underneath me in the wake of shock.

Aiden's palm covered the spot, circling the muscle gently, spreading the sweet ache deeper into my skin. My breath hitched and then I moaned, pressing my face into the bedding.

"Too much?" he asked.

I shook my head, lifting it up and turning so he could see the flush in my cheeks. "More."

"Undress first."

I rolled onto my back and found Aiden kneeling in front of me, one hand cupping himself through his pants, backlit by the hall light. He slid off the bed and rounded near the window, turning a lamp on, and brightening the room in shades of red.

When he stopped at the side of the bed, eyes skimming over me with laughter, I realized I hadn't moved.

"Now, darling."

I scrambled, hunting down my zipper. It'd twisted somewhere behind my back with all of Aiden's mistreatment of my skirt, and I got it halfway down before he barked a laugh, joining me on the bed.

"Come here, I can't have you tearing Hildy's lovely stitches." He sat at my back, helping me up to my knees, lowering the zipper, and then lifting the skirt up over my head. His hands dipped down into the back of my underwear, squeezing the soft flesh, and pushing the fabric down until cool air was rushing over my skin.

My breath was coming in deep heavy pants. When one of Aiden's hands slid between my cheeks, down, down to my wet pussy, I moaned and pushed back into the touch, wanting his fingers to dip inside me, fill me up.

Smack!

I cried out, body bowing forward and nails digging into the bedding, head dropping as my chest heaved like I'd been running for my life instead of simply waiting for that bright, shocking touch.

"You're right," Aiden said, voice ragged. "I should have stopped teasing you months ago. Gods, Joanna, you're soaked."

"More," I said again, dragging the word out and pushing my hips back into his hands, clamping the next moan into a tight sound at the back of my throat.

"You forget who's in charge," Aiden murmured.

I turned my face on the bed, seeing him out of the corner of my eye, and I smiled. "I can always ask the others."

Slap! It was softer, making me jump, and Aiden laughed. We both knew that was an empty threat. There was no way on earth Isaac would ever agree to spank me, and Callum was more likely to ask for himself than to offer. I sighed and smiled, and then Aiden surprised me with a loud cracking whip of his hand over the right cheek again, making me howl and twist.

He pulled my legs out from under me, tugging and yanking my underwear down, and I wrestled myself out of my blouse, tossing it over the side of the bed in front of me as I lay on my belly, the sheets scraping wonderfully against my skin.

"I thought I wanted you over my lap but I quite like this view," he said. I wiggled on the bed and he swatted me in that same burning spot. His hands cupped my knees, pushing them forward and apart until my breasts were pressed to the bed, my ass in the air and slick cunt exposed to his view.

My heartbeat was pounding in my veins. In this position I didn't feel like teasing, I felt owned. And when Aiden's fingertips reached beneath, stroking from my belly button, over my clit, and around my pussy, I *knew* that I was worshipped. One hand settled on my left cheek, squeezing and stroking, while the others played with the lips of my sex, pinching and pushing and dipping into my opening, dragging wetness back and swirling it over my clit.

"Breathe, darling," Aiden whispered.

I hadn't realized I'd stopped, but as soon as I exhaled he struck—two fast, hard snaps against one cheek and then the other. The shock was immediate as my body tensed and shook, cunt clutching on nothing like it was begging to be filled, even as I tried to jump away from the strikes. But Aiden had hold of me and he was quick to soothe the fiery ache.

Before I could recover his right hand, damp with my own arousal, landed once, loud and sharp on the other side. The slap stung, wetness cracking noisily against me.

This time my body melted, my moan long, ending with a whimper as his soft touch slid back down between my legs and two thick fingers pushed inside of me, pumping until I was rocking, and then pulling out again.

It went on. Electricity against my skin, shocking me and making me writhe, followed by a gentle care that left me shivering until he was fucking me with his fingers, taking me to within an inch of release. And then back to the beginning.

"Tell me, Joanna, do you disappoint me?"

The words were low and steady, drawing me out of a daze, my throat rough from shouting and pleading. His fingers inside me pulled away and I cried out, hips chasing them.

A soft, teasing swat. Just a reminder. "Tell me."

"Nooo."

"Good girl," he said, mirroring the swat on the other side. I flinched, the burn now a little too close to unpleasant. His hands dipped back between my legs, circling over my clit. "Do I love you, darling?"

What was he doing? I wanted to crawl away from the questions, but the touch on my clit was too wonderful and when it stopped I blurted out his answer. "Yes! Yes, you love me!"

"I do, so much. You've no idea," he said, voice thick. I twisted to see him and found his dark eyes on my face. "Tell me why I love you."

I gaped back at him, and then his hand picked up the pace, and my eyes fluttered shut.

"Quick, Joanna. Tell me why and I'll fuck you right through that orgasm you have."

"I-I don't know!"

His fingers pressed harder and I choked out a dry sob as the waves of pleasure pounded through me, my knees turning weak and body nearly tipping over if not for Aiden's steadying hand.

"That's not your fault," he whispered.

His hands drew away and I fell onto my side, peeking at him from over my shoulder as he unbuttoned his shirt with fingers glistening from my juices. He pushed his pants off next, shifting on the bed and kicking them down to the floor until he was entirely bare, huge and beautiful, and shining in the red light. He crawled over me and I rolled onto my back, mind cleaned out from his treatment, humming softly as my tender flesh hit the fabric of the coverlet.

He covered me, head to toe and then some, and I pulled him down to my sweat sticky chest, running my knees over his hips as he lined his cock up at my entrance and sank in slowly. His gaze locked with mine, watching my lips part on a silent 'o' as he filled me up, stretching me as I arched up to take more, touch more.

"I love you, Joanna," he said, sweeping curls off my forehead with a warm palm. I wondered if his hand still burned as much as my ass, and the thought made me smile as I started to answer him. But he hushed me with a deep, stroking kiss, the flick of his tongue matching the soft pace of shallow thrusts.

"I love you," he murmured against my lips, "For charging into battle for us. And even for taking up that shield against us when you knew someone else needed it more. I may not always agree with you, but I will *always* listen. Alright, darling?"

I blinked away the tears pricking in the corners of my eyes and nodded as he leaned back to look at me. "Alright. Yes. I love you."

"But. If you ever," he punctuated the word with a thrust. "Risk." And again. "Your safety." My nails dug into the planes of his back, and he continued as I panted. "So *carelessly*." He stroked deeper than before making my legs tremble. "We will have a serious argument on our hands, my darling. One that a handful of spanks won't cure."

"Aiden," I whined, weak legs trying to help me push and rut and ride along his length.

He grunted as I began to rock, and then pulled free of me, flipping me back to my belly and then pressing immediately back inside. I groaned into the bed, squirming as he caught my wrists before I could push up onto my knees, dragging them above my head and trapping them there. His hips dug into my sore flesh, coarse hair scratching over the ruby red handprints he'd left on my ass.

My clit scraped against the fabric beneath me as Aiden sucked a mark onto my shoulder, hips churning in heavy, slapping rhythm, the collision of his skin against mine like soft, fresh spanks. His cock struck perfectly inside of me, the angle of his head exactly aimed for making me shout, as stars burst behind my eyes. His mouth traveled, one hand taking charge of both my wrists while the other tangled into my messy hair, tugging it until my face was turned, our mouths catching clumsily at the corners.

"Oh gods, Aiden, please. I'm so close. I'm so close!"

"Promise," he said, rutting pace slowing, softening, until he was vibrating with tension over my back, holding still.

"Please!"

"Promise. You have to be careful. We can't lose you!"

"I promise," I shouted, rambling the words as fast as I could if it meant he would finish me, finish us both. "No more- more fires, or crossing borders, or- oh, Aiden, please!"

He swallowed my sobs with another deep, messy kiss, and then started to move again—long rolls of his hips, punctuated with snaps inside of me to make me squeal into his mouth. He left my hands hanging at the edge of the bed, and his now worked its way beneath us, pausing briefly at my breasts to squeeze and then down, straight to my clit, working it in fast, rough circles, fingers crushed to me between our weight and the mattress.

The bed was creaking, my voice breaking in the same rhythm, and Aiden pinched gently at my clit as his hips started to stutter. I came, body stretching into the touch, blood rushing in my ears, Aiden's palm stroking over my throat as he shouted in the tangles of my hair. He finished in a warm flash inside of me, his arms circling my chest and turning us onto our sides as he slowed with soft jerks against me.

We curled together, breaths slowing, Aiden shifting me in slow, gentle nudges until I was turned into his chest, my cheek pressed over his pounding heart.

"I love you, darling girl," he said into my hair.

"I love you, my King," I answered, lifting my chin for a soft kiss.

The bedroom door creaked open and Aiden lifted his head. "Hello. What is it?"

"Bringing some ointment for her," Callum answered, sliding onto the bed behind me and passing Aiden a glass jar of bruise cream. "This is pretty," he added, skimming cool fingers over the rosy marks on my ass and making me shiver. "Isaac wants to know if we want dinner in bed."

"Not *my* bed," Aiden growled and then seeing my brightened expression he huffed. "Fine. But someone else will change the linens."

2 2

———

AIDEN

I was sipping coffee at the kitchen with Isaac the next morning, wondering if I could find a way to enjoy the slow summer pace in spite of magic being missing and the current conflict between Canderfey and the Scrivens, when rapid knocking interrupted the fantasy.

No, it didn't seem likely that there would be any peace this summer.

Callum thundered down the steps, shirttails untucked. "Coming!" he shouted.

I braced myself for Mayor Sewell or the police officers again or, worst of all, Anders. And then deflated when the door swung open and Hildy stood in its frame, pale and fretful and underdressed—at least for herself—a package tucked under her arm.

"Hildy?" I called, as Callum stepped aside to let her enter. I met her halfway down the hall, resisting the urge to scoop her up in a bear hug and distract the frown stretching across her face.

"Hello, I'm sorry for coming so early but... have any of you seen Bryce?" Her hands were twisting the fabric of her skirt around and around her fingers, and then pulling them free and starting over again, brow furrowed.

"Not this morning but are they with Joanna at…" My throat choked a little as I tried to say the words. Joanna and the Scrivens had written their secret tight and I was unable to break the silence.

"Joanna mentioned running into Corina yesterday," Isaac said. "Corina couldn't find Bryce and struck out on her own."

My eyebrows shot up at that.

"Yes," Hildy whispered, eyes wide. "They went to bed with us the day before yesterday and left sometime in the night. Which isn't entirely uncommon for Bryce, really. But to not have come home last night…"

"They might be with Joanna," I said. "She didn't mention but we… were occupied with discussing the fire last night and she left early this morning."

Hildy nodded weakly, swallowing, an unfocused stare fixed to the wall behind me. "Alright, well. When you see her pass the question along for us, will you? It's all a bit much going on this week."

"Agreed," Callum said.

"Oh, and here, Joanna's gown for the ball tonight," Hildy said, passing me the package. "It took extra time what with magic missing now, but I- I didn't sleep much last night anyway and it should still be perfect."

"I wouldn't expect anything less from you," I said, trying to reassure her but not knowing how. Bryce Gast was an entity unto themself as far as I knew. If they weren't with Joanna then they were entirely a mystery to me. I only knew they were as devoted to their coven as I was to mine. "There's not much worry about harming Bryce, yes?"

Hildy huffed a laugh and rolled her shoulders. "True. I'll see you all soon."

"We'll ask around," Isaac promised her, leaning in to kiss her cheek as she turned to leave.

We opened the door to let Hildy out and found a less pleasant visitor on our step. Elizabeth Bonde, hand poised to knock, eyes wide with surprise, and a bag bursting with paperwork hanging at her side.

"What do you want?" Callum asked, eyes narrowing.

"Back so soon, Ms. Bonde?" I added, hoping it might smooth some of the rudeness. I wasn't entirely certain what to think of the woman. She wasn't afraid to disagree with anyone *including* Anders, so even if I couldn't count her as an ally at least she seemed to have some sense.

"Yes, with… bad news, I'm afraid," she said. "May I come in?"

She and Hildy swapped places, and my coven let Bonde in only so far as to close the door behind her. She glanced at each of us and smiled at me. "Is Miss Wick not at home?"

I opened my mouth to say no, when Joanna called from the kitchen, the click of the pantry door shutting behind her. "I'm just here! Hello, I was just…organizing." Her cheeks were pink with fresh air, and she had mud on the toes of her boots, but she jogged down the hall to my side, taking the cup of coffee from my hands and stealing a quick sip.

"Very well," Elizabeth said, eyeing Joanna's boots with an amused twist of her lips. "Anders left me a memo last night. You've all been issued a warning by… well, by the University."

"I'm on the school board," I said. "When was the meeting."

"There wasn't one," she said, in clipped, clean tones. "But that was the memo and Anders filled out the paperwork as if his signature were the only one necessary."

"Then we aren't really on warning, are we?" Isaac asked, looking between the Vice President and me, his forehead tangling.

"You are according to President Anders," she said.

"I'm surprised he didn't come himself to give us the news," I said, studying Elizabeth. She looked frazzled but that was her norm, wasn't it?

"He says he's sick." And she stared back at me with wide eyes and something that was almost a smile. "Here's the paperwork if you'd like to object with the school board."

"Of course we will," Callum spat, and Elizabeth's lips twitched as she passed me a crumpled mess of papers, the chicken scratch writing frantic and blotchy with ink. Anders' handwriting turned mad, it looked like.

"He's been… off his game recently, hasn't he?" I asked, voicing the question slowly as I read over the accusations. 'Negligence of duty' and 'endangerment of the student body' were included on the form.

"Mmm, I thought it was stress at first," Elizabeth said, nodding. "But now I wonder if he hasn't over-taxed himself."

I blinked. I wasn't certain if she was referring solely to Anders' workload, but before I got the chance to say anything she continued.

"I've got to get into his office and my own for that matter. Try to stay out of trouble before you get that warning cleared up," she suggested, clicking the heels of her shoes together before turning to the door. "See you at the Faculty Ball."

My coven gaped at her as she left and I barely noticed as Joanna pulled the package from Hildy out of my arms.

"What on earth is this?" she asked, flipping back the lid and allowing yards and yards of gauzy pastel fabric to spill loose.

JOANNA WASN'T happy to hear about Bryce missing, and she left straight away with Callum to go see Gwen at the library. Isaac took me through the pantry to visit the Scrivens.

Joanna had described the house to me the night before, but I was already certain there were changes and revisions in the planning. The space inside was impossibly large to manage fitting between a circle of trees, and sure enough, when I finally found the front door and stepped outside, I saw Joanna's boot prints traveling through the mud, examining the dimensions. Back inside, Isaac sat with Nora and Myles by a sunny bay window.

"We're on a warning," he told Myles, who frowned. "It can't really mean anything. Aiden and Callum both have tenure, really."

"Anders has lost his mind," I said, falling into a fluffy armchair that faced the others in their seats. And damn, I was fairly certain whoever had written this armchair knew exactly how to describe a cushion because it was perfection.

"A powerful madman is dangerous," Nora said.

"That's what I'm afraid of," I muttered. "I've been thinking of him as an idiot this whole time and I worry I may have…underestimated him."

"You don't think he's responsible for everything that's happened?" Isaac asked.

"Maybe not every little thing. Lars was Bekka. That fire yesterday morning was locals. But if Anders was responsible for the dreams, the ward, and now…" But how did magic erase magic? I didn't see any logic in that.

"He'd be responsible for the fear that stirred hate against Anya," Nora said in a tone that stirred at the forgotten childhood terror of a disappointed grade school teacher.

"It would take incredible power, yes?" Myles asked.

"President Anders is known for having a remarkable magical well to tap from," Isaac mused, fingers scratching at the stubble over his jaw. "We need to discuss this with Callum."

I nodded my agreement and, like magic, a crash came from the kitchen and then Callum and Joanna were rushing in.

"Did you find Gast?" I asked them.

"No! But Frost and Woollard helped us find the spell that put the town under the nightmare," Callum said, eyes gleaming bright and excited with triumph. "Same book as the ward put up around the school. Recently reappeared in the lost and found bin!"

My eyes popped open wide and Joanna bounced on the balls of her feet, her smile giddy. "Gwen was furious! But without magic, she can't get a read on who might have nicked it off the shelves."

"Did it have a spell for hiding magic away?" Isaac asked, sitting forward at the edge of his armchair.

Joanna bounded forward, landing in a heap on my lap and knocking an 'oof!' out from my lips. I wrapped my arms around her waist and she tied her fingers with mine.

"No," Callum said, frowning and going to lean against Isaac's chair. "But it looks like the ward was a means of setting a boundary on a further piece of magic. Just… not one I've found the source of yet."

"It's nearly time for us to get back to the house, we need to get ready for the Faculty Ball," I said.

Nora's eyes were narrowed and focused near me, and then Myles blurted out, "Leina! What happened to your hair?"

"Oh, it's just hair!" Joanna huffed, tossing the uneven mess about.

Nora snorted and pushed up from her chair, snagging Joanna's arm and pulling her up from my lap. "Come on, I'll clean that mop up for you. I'll send her back through your pantry and you lot can worry about the rest."

◦

JOANNA SLIPPED her fingers into her hair at the base of her neck, wincing as she touched the roots. Light from the chandeliers overhead glittered off the jeweled pins holding her hair into a smooth twist. Corina was the one who took charge of the styling when Nora's 'trim' became a little too enthusiastic, and the younger girl had written Joanna's hair to grow back down to her shoulders. It looked natural, but Joanna claimed it made her head hurt.

"Everyone's looking at me," Joanna whispered.

The Grand Hall was dusted off for the evening, filled with candles, banquet tables, and a bar in every corner, sure to help lubricate the pockets of attending donors for another season of funding. Every year before this one my coven would have split up, been in charge of schmoozing with interested parties to chat up our departments and raise a little money. This year I was keeping my covenmates close, and by the looks we were receiving, I wasn't sure that anyone minded.

"Because you're beautiful," Isaac said, taking her hand from her hair and curling it around his elbow.

"That's not true," she hissed back.

They were both right. Joanna was exquisite, delicate and feminine in the gown Hildy had guided me toward choosing, ethereal even. But that wasn't why people were staring. It was that everyone knew she was Scrivens, knew that we were the ones responsible for the Vermenians arriving in Canderfey. I suspected the suspicion was we were the ones to smuggle the Vermenians out again too. Little did they know, their supposed enemies were now dining together like a family,

712

tucked away in the Hand Woods just south of town in a strange, but cozy, house.

"Look, Woollard and her coven are there at a table," I said, pointing to the far corner of the room, through the crowd of dancers. The university had brought in a string quartet from the city for the music this evening, giving the university orchestra a rest to enjoy the night.

We rounded the floor of couples dancing and my heart sank a bit to see Hildy and her coven without Bryce Gast.

"Do you think Gast left?" I asked Callum under my breath. "Maybe they realized the magic was fading and got out?"

"Do you think they would?" Callum answered. "I wouldn't have. You wouldn't. No. I think they're still in Canderfey. I just wish we knew what they were up to."

"You don't trust them?"

"I suppose I do. Joanna does. But I wouldn't put it past Gast to keep a secret until they absolutely had to share, and if they know something, then *I* want to know it too," he said.

I grinned at that, wrapping my arm around his back and knocking against the sheath belted at his hip. I rolled my eyes. "Did you really need to bring the sword?"

"In this climate?" Callum scoffed as we reached the other coven. "Yes, absolutely. And I don't have a pocket to tuck it into, but at least I can get away with wearing it as a war hero."

"Any news?" Joanna asked, pulling out the chair next to Gwen.

"Not exactly," Gwen hedged, "but these were on our doorstep as we were leaving." She opened her purse to reveal a handful of golden feathers and when she dropped one into Joanna's palm I could see the weight of it as it landed.

"One of Bryce's treasures?" Callum asked, picking up the feather and brushed the edge against his fingers, each fiber clicking as he moved them.

"No!" Joanna gasped, eyes wide with wonder. Her voice was breathy and she took the feather back from him. "The magic is gone, Callum. Bryce's shape-shifting is *gone*."

Gwen nodded, "That's what I thought too." Joanna handed the feather back to Gwen with great care and I suddenly understood.

"You mean—" I lowered my voice, "You mean those are...bits of...Bryce?"

"Like stray hairs," Hildy said, eyes tracking the feathers as Gwen clipped the purse shut again.

"What I don't understand is why they didn't just come home, as is," Tatsuo said, his covenmates smiling fondly at him for the thought.

"Have you ever seen them, in their natural shape?" I asked.

"Bryce grew up imitating their parents who were imitating humans," Gwen said. "It was a very very long time before even they saw what they looked like as...well, they *are* themself, however that looks. I've always felt that way. But yes, I saw them once without the shapeshifting magic." She parted her lips as if to explain the sight, but no words arrived and she only shook her head, pulling the purse back into her lap and covering it with her palms flat, as if to protect the contents.

23

JOANNA

"Where's your head, love?" Isaac asked me, turning us slowly on the dance floor.

"In the woods," I whispered, watching the room spin around me over Isaac's shoulder. Keeping my eyes high above the heads that stared in our direction. "I keep feeling as if I'm…missing some important bit of information, and it's sitting right in front of me."

"About Bryce?" Isaac asked. "We know they're safe, don't we?"

"Not about Bryce," I said, and then I pursed my lips because that wasn't quite right either. "Maybe. I don't know."

"I miss the covenbond," Isaac whispered, smiling at me. "I could sort through your troubles for you."

I squeezed his hand, my eyes tracking past strangers to find Aiden and Callum returning to our table from the bar. My eyes narrowed as the university Vice President met them at their seats.

"Oh, what does she want now?" I sighed.

"You're not getting off the dance floor that easy," Isaac teased. "Whatever it is, Aiden and Callum can manage it for the next few minutes."

He tried to twist me away from the sight but I craned my neck, watching as Elizabeth Bonde pointed through the crowd to the front

715

doors. Then Isaac spun me out on the floor and I saw why. President Anders was storming into the Great Hall, headed directly for me. I gasped and stumbled back into Isaac's chest, and his arm circled my waist to steady me.

Anders looked as if he'd been wrung out. His skin was gray, hair in disarray, clothes rumpled and sweat-stained. One of the party guests stepped in his direction and Anders' shoulder plowed into the man, knocking him aside, gaze fixed to mine, sweat glimmering under the candlelight.

"You!" he shouted over the soaring strings behind me. The hall gasped as he stumbled, one leg giving out and nearly sending him sprawling to the ground. "This is your fault! You brought them here! All of this happened because of *you!*"

He was limping and as he crossed over a tile, I saw the streak of red that followed in his step. It was not mud or sweat that darkened that pant leg, but blood.

"Joanna, get back," Isaac whispered in my ear as the room hushed around us, musicians falling silent on the small stage.

"He's injured," I said, finally seeing the tear in the fabric near his knee, the wound black with welling blood.

Callum came skidding up to my side, sword drawn, looking strange and almost comical—freshly shaved and brandishing a weapon in his lovely black suit. Aiden arrived on Isaac's far side and I skirted out of their reach before they could try and tuck me safely behind them.

"President Anders, what's happened?" I asked.

"It's all gone wrong," the man wheezed as guests and dancers fell back into the corners of the room to avoid him as if this sudden appearance of madness might be contagious.

Others came closer, surrounding Anders—Mayor Sewell, Vice President Bonde, Gwen and Hildy and Tatsuo.

"Anders, I think someone better see you home," Sewell said, hands outstretched, voice placating.

"No, no. NO! Listen!" Anders shouted, words brittle. "My brothers *died* in that war. All to keep them out. And she- and- and *you* brought them here," he spat at Sewell. "It wasn't going to work. It was not going to work but now- now..."

The candles overhead fluttered and spat, sparks flying down onto the heads of guests who cried out in surprise.

"You've done something," Aiden growled, eyes narrowed on Anders.

"They could have turned right around again," Anders said, skin paling further, eyes so wide I saw the bloodshot whites all around. "Gone back. Gone anywhere else."

"You're ill, let's get you to a doctor and then we'll have a serious interview about what's been going on," Sewell said, finally stepping close enough to catch Anders by his shoulder.

But Anders twisted out of reach, a high panicked laugh escaping his throat as he stared out across the hall back to the doors.

"It's too late," he said, and then his injured legs gave out and he fell to the floor with a pained shout. "They're here."

There were shadows in the doorway.

The guests who heard Anders' warning gasped, skirting away from doors, clustering together between tables and near the bar. I heard the word carried on whispers around the room. *Scrivens.*

But that was not who was stepping into the Great Hall. Not *what* was stepping in.

For a moment, everything inside of me was quiet, calm, all of the thoughts of Anders and concerns for the Scrivens and worry for my coven just swept away in stunning, brilliant confusion. What on earth was I looking at? With thoughts washed clean from my mind, there was now room for a simmering, slithering anger, heat rising up my neck, an alarm sounding in my ears as I stared at the creature crawling through the doorway.

It was shades of stone black and bile green and blood red, taller than the workhorses back home, broader than a carriage. Massive bones stretched at leather flesh that shone like polished jewels. Looking at it made my fists clench and my eyes burn. The head was huge, flesh pulling back over thin, bloody gums and razor teeth, bone showing around an enormous jaw, large enough to take a chunk of a man's leg. Large enough to do worse.

The jaw lifted high into the air and the room filled with the smell of carnage as the beast took a deep inhale, a flap of skin on its throat expanding, fire gleaming through the thin flesh. It exhaled and the air around us trembled. Out of the corner of my eye, I saw Callum's grip tighten around the hilt of his sword until his knuckles were white.

Behind the creature came others, each so strange, so horrifying, that I had no notion of how to look at them. One made my stomach churn and my skin clammy. Another left my heart in shattered bits in my chest, hopelessness soaking my eyes. The tears blurred the image of their arrival, and suddenly I could think again. Turning fast on my heel, I put my back to the door. Callum covered me and I reached back, clutching at his jacket.

"Don't look at them," I whispered. "Don't look at them, it- it changes you."

His free hand found mine and he squeezed once in understanding. Isaac's eyes met mine and a tangle of angry lines softened on his face, his mouth parted on panting breaths.

"You did this," Aiden said, rage thick on his tongue, and I couldn't tell if he was looking at the beasts or at Anders.

"It's your fault!!" Anders answered, close to sobbing. "I wanted- I wanted people to see what might happen if they were allowed to stay."

"But that magic was yours! Not the Scrivens!" Aiden bellowed.

Isaac tugged at the lapel of his jacket forcing his stare off the beasts, and some of the anger bled off his face. "Don't look at them," Isaac warned.

"What are they?" Aiden asked.

I turned back slowly, keeping my eye on the glossy tile floor where I could watch the reflection of the creatures as they tread closer, claws clicking against marble, heat fogging around one's steps, ice around another's.

"Like the Hollow," I said. "They're what was trapped in the woods."

"You opened the cages," Callum said to Anders, eyebrows raising.

"No, no." Anders' head whipped back and forth. "I made a new one out of them, all around—"

"Canderfey," Aiden finished for him. "And it didn't occur to you that pocketing away magic throughout Canderfey would risk what was in those cages *coming out*?!"

"I didn't know," Anders wept, frail and thin on the floor. "I didn't know. I didn't—"

YES, HE DID.

The voice was such a shock, grinding bones and clashing metal, echoing like drums off the walls and floor and ceiling, that for a moment it drew my eyes back to the great ugly creature leading the parade of others. My throat tightened with fury and I tried to force my eyes away.

HE JUST DIDN'T CARE.

And then the creature bowed on legs that bent in the wrong direction, springing up and pouncing, his jaw scraping against the floor and teeth crashing around Anders' waist. Callum leapt forward as the room screamed, and I tried to catch him and stop him. The tip of his sword pressed to the bony jaw of the creature, and then there was a synchronized chorus of *crunch*! A soft whimper fell loose from Anders' throat as his face went slack, hanging from the corner of the beasts' enormous mouth. Blood dribbled in bright rivulets over wet gums and down to glossy puddles on the tile.

Callum's back was heaving with hard breaths, arm steady, sword poised against unrelenting bone.

The beast dropped Anders back to the floor and I winced, and turned my face away, feeling bile stinging the back of my throat, my lungs full of the stench of violence.

YOU SMELL LIKE ME, YOUNG ONE, the beast said to Callum. *THAT'S MY BLOOD THAT HOLDS YOUR SWORD SO WELL. I AM WARFARE. WE ARE THE ANCIENTS.*

Someone was retching by the door, standing too close to the gray-toned lizard-like thing that slinked along the floor—the one that made me feel ill when I looked too long in its direction. There were eight in the room behind Warfare and I glanced at them as little as I could, cataloging the sensations that followed.

Illness was the reptilian one. Sorrow came from the towering shroud that swayed and shivered with weeping. Jealousy from the eerily beautiful cat-like, prowling beast that gleamed in jewel-toned iridescence. Terror from moonglow, spindle thin, insect-like thing skittering up the wall and into the chandelier at the far end of the room. Suspicion from the dark, feathery swath that clung to the wall out of the corner of my eye. Shame, a sickly yellow groveling slither on the floor that tracked Warfare's steps and then squirmed away just as quickly. Bright, startling, toe-curling *Ecstasy* from the glittering silver and electric blue and sunset pink winged bird-like creature that swooped around the room, dizzying us all.

The last one was there, standing right in the doorway, and while I knew that I *was* seeing it, I could not process it in my head. It was made of a type of seeing I wasn't versed in. I called it Confusion and wondered if I wasn't right.

"Where is the Hollow?" I asked, my eyes searching for a safe spot to land and settling on Warfare's flank.

SISTER STARVATION IS WHERE YOU LEFT HER LITTLE WORD-SMITH, Warfare growled, snout lowering, pushing Callum's sword down with it. I tugged Callum back to my chest and kept my eyes traveling along the floor, watching the progress of the Ancients. Watching Anders' blood pool out toward my boots. *YOU ARE NOT ONE OF OUR BLOODKIN, BUT I'M SURE YOU'D TASTE THE SAME.*

The other Ancients were creeping closer to the rest of the guests, weeping breaking out near Sorrow, swooning beneath Ecstasy, and at any moment I was certain that whatever game they were playing with us would end, and more blood would be spilled.

"You won't harm a soul in this room," Callum snarled up at the beast.

MY MAGIC MAY BE MUTED, BUT I HAVE CLAWS AND TEETH ENOUGH TO PROVE YOU WRONG, BLOODKIN.

"I have claws too," I said and Callum jumped forward, swinging his sword to distract Warfare as I knelt into the spreading pool of blood, gagging as I dipped my fingers into the cooling fluid.

Isaac, Aiden, Gwen, Hildy, and Tatsuo surrounded me, Hildy screaming herself ragged as the long-legged, spindly, white Terror fell from the chandelier, but she kicked her leg out hard, tripping the beast to the floor and smashing her heel against its many-eyed face

I wrote quickly, not caring if it was smart, not caring if it was clean —my hands were soaked in red, red blood, it was not *clean*—or clever, or right.

The Ancients cannot come inside. My skirt soaked up the blood in gauzy sheaths as I smeared it over the floor, around the curve of feet that kept me caged safely, while the room burst into screams, Callum roaring in front of Isaac. The letters were crude in method and design, but the claws of Ancients scratched deep gouges in the marble as my magic dragged them backward out of the Great Hall.

"Joanna!" Aiden screamed, and then I was lifted from the floor as Ecstasy swirled overhead, tearing one of the chandeliers from the ceiling. It came crashing down on Anders' body, narrowly missing my words on the floor, my coven standing just outside the shattered fragments on the floor.

The doors slammed shut behind the Ancients and I caught my breath in Aiden's arms, staring through the dark glass at the creature I could not understand when I looked at it. I thought, for half a second, that it was wonderment squeezing at my heart when I caught its gaze, and then in the next moment, it was confusion again.

"The Scrivens," I said. "We have to get to the woods before the Ancients do. I need a pen…or chalk."

"Sewell, Bonde," Callum barked, and the pair—both were staring at the trapped body of President Anders beneath the metal skeleton of the chandelier—jumped and stared at him. "Keep those words clear and visible or the magic will be useless. Do you understand?" He pointed at the bloody finger-painted smears of my writing.

Sewell nodded, once, looking down at the words and then again, his throat clearing to call out to the room. "Everyone, we are safe here, inside. Please, remain calm!"

"We need something to write with!" Aiden yelled.

The room was silent in answer and I stood, feeling the stares on my face but not seeing beyond the red stain dripping down from my fingers to my palm. Callum stepped in front of me and covered my hand with a white handkerchief, wiping the worst of the mess away.

"I'm more tired than usual," I said, blinking at Callum's collar.

"The magic worked faster than usual," Callum answered softly.

Writing in blood. It must have made the difference.

Callum was ready for what came next, turning me away from my words as I bent over, heaving my wine back up and onto the floor, closing my eyes against the purple stain. I gagged again and then he was there, wiping my lips with the cuff of his sleeve.

"Done?" he asked, voice soft like he knew my ears were ringing. I nodded.

"I have a pencil," someone called from the stage, voice small and timid. Callum hustled me away from the wreckage as Elizabeth Bonde started calling orders to the faculty, and Sewell herded a group on the other end of the room. Gwen and the others followed my coven, Aiden taking a pencil from the violinist and passing it to me.

I held it in my hand for a moment, and my fingers, wrapped around the wood, were carved with thin red lines where the blood had soaked in. I sucked in a breath, shaking the stupor off, and looked up. There was a door off to the left of the stage.

"There," I said, pointing. We ran in a crowd, and my left fist clenched as I stared at the blank wooden door.

If I wrote the way, someone else might follow, giving up the secret of the house, the safe space for the Scrivens. Was what happened here tonight enough to prove their innocence? Even with Suspicion lurking nearby? That was what had been creeping in the apartment building with the Grivets during the fire, I was sure of it.

"Joanna," Callum whispered.

I blinked and raised my hand. I couldn't waste time.

Door to the secret house in Hand Woods surrounded by trees marked with, and I scratched out the symbol on the wood grain.

Inside the house was dark and quiet.

"Hello?" I called.

"Leina?" Myles whispered back, appearing from around the bend in the staircase. "Leina, there's something in the woods."

I ran to the nearest window, prepared to face the Ancients again. Prepared to cut into my own skin to write against them if it would work. How would we trap them? We'd written the Hollow's—Starvation's—cage shut with their true name, but I didn't have a connection to these Ancients. I didn't have time to be falling into trances to dig their secrets out.

There *was* something prowling in the dark woods with big, clawed feet reminiscent of a hawk, but the body was soft and feline and enormous, great wings stretching up off its back glittering dull gold in the moonlight.

"Bryce," I breathed out, thunking my forehead softly against the glass. The beaky face turned to the house, lamp yellow eyes blinking, wings flapping in greeting. Just as quickly it swiveled out to the woods, body lowering onto its haunches, claws digging into the undergrowth. "The Ancients have come. Bryce is guarding the house."

I squeezed past Hildy, Gwen, and Tatsuo as they rushed to the window.

"We have to stand with Bryce," I said to Callum. He nodded, hand fisted around the hilt of his sword. "Myles, I need paper."

"You need us, leina," my uncle said. He turned to the stairs, calling up in Vermenian. "Scrivens! Bring your tools!" There was more, words I hadn't learned yet, monsters included.

"Write me a damn sword while you're at it," Aiden muttered.

Nora came down the stairs with Daniel at her side, and Myles passed me one of the notebooks out of their hands.

"Can you write our magic back?" Isaac asked.

I tried the words. *Isaac Metclaffe has his magic. The dampener cage does not work on Isaac Metclaffe.* But neither brought results.

"When it was the Hollow who had escaped, you weren't able to put it back in with just a phrase," Callum said. "It took the name."

"We can write them into knots," Nora said. "With enough of us working, one phrase at a time, we can keep them in line."

"I'm coming," Corina called, rushing down the stairs.

"No," Myles answered and I almost spoke up on her behalf when he added, "You stay and keep Bekka and the families safe."

Her nose wrinkled, but she plopped down into a cushioned chair in front of the window, a new diary and pen in hand. When she caught my eye on the diary she tossed her hair and huffed. "I'm behaving."

I would have to believe her, at least for tonight. I followed Callum out the narrow door that led to the woods, where Bryce was already surrounded by their coven, fingers digging into feathers and faces pressed to fur.

"I never meant my no-pets rule to apply to you, you know," Gwen murmured up at Bryce, a hand stroking over the metal sharp beak of Bryce's face.

'You're so amusing when you're concerned,' Bryce answered in trills. They eyed me, head cocking in a perfectly avian manner. *'Witchling.'*

"Dragon," I said, smiling to see my friend again, whatever shape they were in. "Or should I call you Ancient?"

'Child of Ancients,' Bryce answered. *'But not one of* those.' The Ancients were crunching through the woods on their way to us. *'They are aching. It's uncomfortable to be what we are without our magic.'*

"But are they weak?" Callum asked.

'No,' Bryce answered. *'You should start writing.'*

All around the house, feet planted in leaves and briars, our pencils began to move.

YOUNG KIN, Warfare greeted Bryce as they neared. Shame was twined around the larger Ancient's leg, riding along, tucked quietly in hiding.

'Hello, Old Beast,' Bryce answered, a long tufted tail twitching, legs tensing.

YOU PROTECT YOUR BREEDERS? AND THESE WORDSMITHS TOO? THEY ARE NOT OUR KIND.

The Ancients spread through the woods, Ecstasy roosting up above the house, Terror tucking behind trees. Anya nodded to the shadow sifting through the darkness, Suspicion, speaking quickly in her own tongue.

"She says that was what was on the landing the morning of the fire," Nora told me.

As I had guessed. Suspicion, stirring up the locals against the Scrivens and her family in the attic.

'They are the only ones who can let you out of this cage,' Bryce reasoned to the Ancients.

AND THE ONLY ONES WHO CAN RESURRECT THE ONES WE HAVE BEEN FREED FROM, Jealousy spat, teeth shining like daggers and spit sizzling on the forest floor.

'They are under protection,' Bryce said, a yowling growl rising up deep from the back of their chest.

YOURS, YOUNG KIN? Warfare laughed at the notion, branches overhead shaking in the rumble. WE HAVE STRENGTH ENOUGH FOR ALL OF THEM. AND YOU.

'Their own,' Bryce said when I nodded.

My pages were flooded with guarding words, keeping the Ancients from touching us, careful to name them individually, to keep Bryce safe from my tangling sentences. When Terror came scrambling out from the tree line, it charged toward Isaac who held a sword in front of him like a shield more than a weapon. Isaac's hand shook and my heart trembled in my chest as I watched, but the bony white legs skidded in the earth and the bulbous body tipped, and then the Ancient was scrambling back again.

Our words held.

AND WILL WE LIVE LIKE THIS? Warfare asked. OUR COMPANY WILL WEAR ON YOU, I THINK.

I didn't doubt him. Nora was weeping softly, her eyes caught by towering Sorrow, and Daniel was crumpled to the earth, head in hands as Shame circled the ground in front of him, glistening like sour tears.

"Everyone go inside," I said. Illness was out of sight, but that didn't mean it wouldn't find a target and that was an encounter I didn't want to risk. I'd tried to write away the effect of the Ancients but nothing was sticking. It seemed to be what they were intrinsically, and perhaps that was something that couldn't be written away. I would try every word again just to be certain.

"We could fight," Callum said, voice grinding with tension, and when I looked at him I found him staring at the grinning maw of Warfare.

The Ancient was right. Magic or no magic. Unable to scratch and bite and tear at us, they would still do harm. I stepped in front of Callum and it was enough. His arm circled my back and he twisted us quickly, keeping me from presenting an unarmed front to the beasts. I put my hands around his face and held his stare until the rage had passed.

"Not tonight," I murmured, watching as his eyes widened with understanding. "Enjoy your freedom, Ancients. While it lasts. Every-one, let's go inside."

Callum nodded and he passed me, pushing Aiden back, pulling at Isaac's sleeves. Others followed, Myles gathering Daniel up from the forest floor and dragging him back to the house. Bryce and I remained longest, facing the Ancients in the woods, my eyes lowered to their feet, my friend warm at my side.

I DO NOT LIKE THE FLAVOR OF STALEMATE, WORDSMITH, Warfare said, heat steaming off his hide, clouding the air with metallic mist. *IT WILL NOT LAST LONG.*

I lifted my chin, meeting the Ancient's gaze, feeling the wrath rise up in my chest as I stared into smoke pit eyes.

"No," I agreed. "Not long."

Bryce nudged my shoulder with a sharp wingtip, and together we turned and left the Ancients in the woods.

EPILOGUE

ISAAC

JOANNA RETURNED FROM TOWN BY WAY OF MY BEDROOM CLOSET AND I reached up to wipe the chalk words away. *Door to Inky's Parlor.*

"Did you see anyone?" I asked, wrapping my arm around her waist and tugging her tight to my side, pressing my face into her hair.

I hated when she left the house without us, but Callum and Aiden would be coming back from the Scrivens and someone had to stay and watch the house, keep an eye on all the doors that led from our home to around campus. Make sure nothing unwanted came in.

"Only the Ancient I can't recognize," she said, brow furrowing. The one she called Confusion. "But town was empty. Which I suppose is for the best."

The Cage kept the Ancients inside but it didn't trap the residents of Canderfey, and most had left as soon as Joanna found a way to write a safe doorway into the train station. The Scrivens, our coven, and Bryce's remained, as well as Elizabeth Bonde—now the acting President of a desolate university—and a few other faculty. Sewell was in and out with council members, as they searched for solutions.

The Ancients remained, lurking through the woods around the Scrivens' house, over the paths of campus, lounging in sunspots as if they were contented cats rather than beasts waiting for an opportunity to maim and destroy.

"Will you tell me what you're planning to do with that?" I asked Joanna, nodding to the sack she'd retrieved from the townie tattoo parlor.

Downstairs a door shut, and Callum and Aiden's voices floated up. Joanna smiled at me and turned me in the direction of the hall, pushing me forward.

"Let's go see the others and I'll explain," she said.

Aiden and Callum were in Callum's second-story bedroom and we joined them there. We hardly ever went down to the first floor now, not when it seemed like an Ancient was waiting on the street outside the house, watching us every hour. I had a sneaking suspicion Ecstasy had taken to roosting on our roof at night if the regular frenzy of lovemaking was anything to judge by. That, or the recent circumstances made us desperate for one another.

"How is Bryce?" Joanna asked them.

Aiden opened his arms to her from where he sat on the bed and I smiled, watching her go and curl into his lap, dropping the sack on the floor at his feet.

"Keeping spirits up with the Scrivens," Callum said, toying with the hem of her skirt. "I think their coven is…managing. What's that?"

He bent and flipped the bag open, revealing a familiar looking collection of tools, including a rotary motor tattoo needle.

My eyes widened. "Are you thinking of *writing* on people?"

Joanna chewed at her lip. "Maybe. Carefully. It would be better than worrying about a protection charm wearing or sweating off at the wrong moment," she said. "And that wasn't what I was thinking of starting with."

"What then, darling?" Aiden asked, palm squeezing at her hip.

She looked up at me and smiled. "Our coven bond. I can still feel Callum because of the sigil on his back. I want it to be on each of us. I think we'll have our bond back."

Aiden's breath caught in his chest and my heart swelled in my chest. Callum grinned and shifted, leaving me room on the bed to join them.

"You knew about this?" I asked him.

"I wondered," he said. "I can't feel her, but when she has the sigil too…"

"When can we do it?" I asked her, my hands cupping around her knees to draw her legs onto my lap.

"Now," she said and Aiden's eyes fell shut, his face pressing against her cheek. "As soon as I set everything up. I don't know if you think there's anything else I should write first—"

"No, love," I said, smile stretching and heart pounding. To feel them again, heartbeats entwined with mine. I couldn't think of anything that felt more important at the moment. "This first. Please."

ANCIENTS

THE LIBRARIAN'S COVEN, BOOK 4

1

———

ISAAC

JOANNA's FINGERTIPS SETTLED AGAINST MY RIBS, BOTH OF US HOLDING our breath in the still air of the woods. She was invisible in front of me—our skin marked with fresh paint in her handwriting—and I reassured myself of her nearness, brushing one hand against her stomach. I couldn't wait to wash the words away and be able to see her again. Hand Woods was as quiet as a mausoleum around us. Our coven bond—sealed with the knot tattoo on my left rib—thrummed with Callum's tension and Aiden's worry from where they hid not far away.

A carrion bird screamed overhead and my stomach turned, nausea adding to the uneasy twist of anxiety that lurked in me.

Illness was approaching.

Joanna's breath caught and she brushed against me, swaying with the same wave of queasiness. I stroked my hand up to her neck and felt the fever in her skin. The coven connection wavered, Callum working to block himself out so we weren't all multiplying the crawling sickness that bubbled up with every step closer Illness slithered through the woods.

It's getting stronger, I thought. The Ancient wasn't even in sight yet and its effects were already leaving my knees weak, bones tired, and head dizzy. The change was so gradual over the weeks since the boundary had gone up that we'd barely noticed what was happening. It wasn't until the pattern of sickness became so plain in the Scrivens house that understanding finally broke through the haze of fever and headache.

"There," Joanna breathed, barely a sound against my ear.

Illness reached the clearing, its strange, elongated body scaled in green that shimmered wetly and nearly disguised the creature as part of the woods. It undulated as it walked, rising onto its hind legs and arching its head back, those orb-like eyes splitting open with a needle-thin black pupil that grew wider as it sniffed us on the air. I forced my eyes away as bile rose in my throat and sweat dewed on my head. Joanna was stiff at my side.

Meals, Illness called, the word pounding in my head and making the woods flash bright and dark through my dizzy vision.

"Now!" Callum barked from the other side of the clearing.

Now, before we grew worse, if it wasn't too late already for the others.

My fist clung to the back of Joanna's dress, feeling her own sweat against my fingers as we charged out of our hiding place.

Illness released a rattling noise, a combination of a purr and the screech of nails running down a chalkboard. I swallowed down the need to gag, keeping my eyes on the forest floor, watching the rot-brown claws that dug into the earth, the flurry of grass and leaf and twig that signaled my covenmates' approach from the other side.

Joanna screamed as we charged closer—an aching, woozy sound that sent my heart leaping into my throat and my feet stumbling beneath me. Illness echoed her cry, body swaying on its hind legs, and I lost my grip on Joanna, unable to keep myself from bending over and dry heaving to the forest floor.

There was a shocking crunching sound and my head flashed up— Hand Woods tipping in my vision—only to see black sludge oozing from Illness' side, blood landing on the earth with a sizzling spit. New, strange growth spiraled up from where Illness' blood landed, warped and dark vines, and the bud of a wine red flower, sure to poison anyone who dared step too close.

Joanna had done it, more black blood dripping from the end of her invisible sword into the grass. I scrambled to her back, hands fumbling desperately at her waist as Illness screeched again. My vision blacked at the sound, and Illness scurried away, dodging wildly through the trees, deeper into the woods.

"Keep pushing!" Callum called, voice close.

Joanna was panting and I heard a brief moan from her lips, her clammy fingers brushing over my hands at her waist.

"Are you alright?" I asked. *I* wasn't, and I hadn't made it nearly as close to the Ancient as she had.

"I will be," she rasped. "Come on, before it turns in the wrong direction."

We raced through the trees. I caught a brief glimpse against the forest floor of Callum charging forward as he made sure to herd Illness to our secret destination. Aiden passed behind me, a brief grunt of sound as our bodies bumped together.

"Not much further," he growled.

There was no sign of the trap as we neared the spot, although I recognized the wild rose growing up an oak, pink buds wilting as Illness screamed again. More blood spilled, a heavy slash across its side, black splattering over the roots of the rose bush. Illness spun, lurching after Callum's blade to answer the attack, but the trap was sprung.

Light glittered down from the tree branches, like sheets of glass shattering in reverse, forming themselves around Illness. The ground crunched beneath the cage, shards growing into the earth and transforming into a geode at the base of the cage, milky blue and sweet pink crystals blooming up as Illness thrashed behind a hard shell of Scrivens magic. Along the base of the cage, sigils shone. We'd found Illness' true name in an old text in the library, built out of the same symbolic alphabet as the Hollow's. Starvation. *Gvisaidravig.*

And now Illness. *Axition.* Spiraling woozy symbols and shapes that appeared to be inexplicably facing the wrong way.

I tore my gaze off the cage, taking a deep breath and opening my eyes up wide at the sky, the blur of my vision clearing.

Joanna gasped, shoulders relaxing back against my chest, as all the compounding symptoms vanished at once. No pounding headache, no feverish blood, no stomach that coiled and turned like a snake in our guts. Illness was caught in a prism that shimmered in sweet shades of violet and pink and blue. My lips twitched as a playful glint of light shimmered off the peak of the cage. Bekka's design was more beautiful than the Ancient deserved, but it would keep us safe and that was all that mattered.

"We need to go," Callum said, blade tapping with a hollow *clink* against the surface of the cage. Blood sizzled on the surface and evaporated in an awful stench. Behind the cage the rose bush rustled, branches already wrapping thorny teeth around the crystal. Illness pressed one bulbous eye to the hard opalescent interior, fury stirring in the slitted black pupil.

"We should burn the roses," I said, watching as blooms burst larger and darker than before, blood red and muddy brown swirling together on petals, struck through by inky veins.

A familiar, grinding roar echoed in the distance, and I heard Callum's huff. "If we can come back. Right now we need to get to safety before any of the others arrive. We only had the one name for one cage."

Joanna's fingers stroked down over my sleeve, tangling with my own and tugging gently. "He's right. This is only a first test. If it doesn't hold at least we know it works to cut off their influence completely."

A loud crack rolled through the woods from the southern edge of the boundary and Callum bumped against my shoulder.

"Time to move," he said.

For the first time in over a month—since the night the Ancients crashed into the Great Hall of Canderfey University—my body felt whole and healthy again. Joanna squeezed my hand and the strength in her grip made my heart pound with relief, the beat picking up as I followed her urging tug to run.

After the month of occupancy with the Ancients, it was clear they didn't seem particularly interested in each other's company. Now, thankfully, there were none close enough to Illness to catch up with us before we were within sight of the Scrivens house. It was a topsy-turvy little building in the corner of the woods, its strangely angled frame tucked into the outline of surrounding trees. A lamp sat in one of the low windows, the glow illuminating a small face pressed to the glass. I grinned as I saw Bekka waiting for us, answering her wave before I realized she couldn't see me.

My heart pounded in my chest, body thrilling with the run, with the sudden memory of strength and *health* that was returned with Illness now trapped. Joanna hummed, a sweet and almost whimpering note, and my cock twitched at the familiarity of the sound. All at once there was a woman in my arms, our feet jumbling and skidding dangerously in the tangle of weeds and roots on the forest floor. Lips caught mine in a needy hunger, teeth scratching and tongue laving in their wake.

A tree trunk scraped my knuckles as I pressed Joanna against it, my eyes slammed shut against the confusion of having her surrounding me and not *seeing* her. One perfect, long leg twined itself around my hips and I nestled hard against her, hand searching for the nape of her neck to fit her mouth more firmly against mine.

"Don't get yourself caught, you fools!" Aiden bellowed from the Scrivens house.

"Ecstasy," Joanna moaned, tearing away from the kiss even as she rocked herself against my stiff length.

"Damnit," I mumbled, biting down on the curve of her neck.

It was an effective and tempting trap, something so exquisite and affectionate, desire complimenting perfectly with the adrenaline of the chase.

"We have to..." Joanna began before tugging at my hair and sliding our lips together again, tongues stroking.

"We have to get inside," I finished for her, words rasping. I had to get inside of *her*, I thought, but I forced myself away. There would be time for that later, tonight, together with the others in our bed.

I still suspected Ecstasy had made themself a roost on our roof for how much I needed my coven in the past month. Or maybe it was only fear that drove us together, for comfort and reassurance.

Joanna's breath kissed my cheek, and for a brief moment she pressed herself against my chest as I backed away, the draw of the nearby Ancient too strong. I risked my own control and wrapped my arms around her waist, dragging her with me toward the house. Her boot kicked against the blade she'd dropped to the ground in our mutual frenzy and I waited for her to retrieve it before we rushed inside together.

An invisible Aiden held the door to the house open, voice laced with irritation and amusement. "Get inside, you two."

The door shut behind us, the space inside warm and dim enough that it was too dark to see after the bright day outside. Desire waned now that we were in safety, but not enough to make it easy to let go when Joanna pulled away. Ecstasy might have lit the match, but my love for any of my covenmates was enough to keep a blaze burning long after an Ancient's influence was safely locked out.

Aiden's hand stroked down my back as I caught my breath. Joanna paced to the kitchen, her boots clapping on the wood floor, and my eyes adjusted to the low light of the house.

"Did it work?" Bekka asked us in Vermenian, her native tongue, perking up in the bench seat of the window where she'd waited, eyes searching for us.

Footsteps stumbled into the front room. First Gwen and Hildy, followed by more of the Vermenian Scrivens, appearing at the announcement of our arrival.

"Perfect," I answered Bekka, my tongue clumsy on the foreign language. "It was as pretty as your drawing."

Corina slid out from behind Joanna's Aunt Irene, joining the little girl in the window, sunlight haloing around her blonde curls. "And my pretty words?" she asked, lips twitching with a smirk and gaze hovering in my direction without landing on my skin.

Anger spiked in my blood, so hot and sudden, I glanced out the window expecting to see Warfare. My vision simmered and I left the room, tracing Joanna's steps. Corina meant as little with her teasing as she'd meant when she'd written me in love with her. What was an amusing game for a bored and shallow young woman had nearly broken my heart and left me at terrifying odds with my coven just months ago. I hated her and that hate, the rage it drew up in me—and the urges to lash out—were impulses I'd battled my entire life to suppress.

My breath caught in my chest as I stepped into the kitchen. Joanna stood in full and perfect color at the round stone sink, hair tangled with a twig caught in her dark curls and a sprinkle of black blood spattered on her cheek.

"There you are," I said, muscles easing at the sight of her.

Her lips curled up and her eyes flicked over her shoulder, skimming the air and missing me. "Come here and I'll fix you too," she said.

There was a tear in her skirt, one of her old ones Aiden was always trying to hide at the back of the closet. It was hard to believe I'd had Joanna in my life for less than a year. Love was a natural reflex to any of my covenmates, and for a decade I'd lived every day with the understanding that I was blessed to know Callum and Aiden, to build a life with them. But the minute I'd first seen Joanna, standing in front of my painting of the wheat fields of Hammish, it was as if the work hadn't been complete until she was there. It was the same to see her sitting at the dinner table with us, or in the living room curled up in a chair reading. We'd left room for her in our lives before ever meeting her, and having the space filled went beyond a sense of rightness.

"You don't know how much I missed the sight of you," I said as I reached her at the sink, sliding my arm against her hands so that she could find the place where she'd painted the words.

I watched her blush flood her cheeks with pink, enjoying the last seconds of being able to observe her with all the hunger I had and not making her feeling shy.

"It was only an hour or two," she said, taking the damp cloth smudged with ink and stroking it over my skin.

"You're one of my favorite views," I said, studying her delicate smile as she cleaned away her magic.

There were many more of her words now tracing my skin that couldn't be washed away. Words of protection carefully arranged to keep some of the Ancients' forces at bay without risking any unnatural repercussions. The tattoos had hurt, even tenderly applied by a lover's hand, but I was growing fond of the sight of them. Especially the ones that bound our coven together, a knot of Joanna's own design.

Her eyes lifted to mine, brightening as they caught my gaze. "Yes, I know what you mean," she said, her gaze soaking me up now that I was visible again. She leaned in and I caught her kiss against my lips, humming in pleasure, some of the craving that had struck me senseless outside returning at the taste of her on my tongue.

"Don't forget the rest of your coven, Jo," Callum teased, his hands stroking down my back.

"This first," I said, taking the cloth from her hands and cleaning away the fine drops of Illness's blood from her skin, relieved to see they didn't seem to leave any trace behind.

"I'm afraid I'm more of a mess than that," Callum said as I rinsed the cloth.

"I'm going to go check on Adele," Joanna said, hand hovering in the air until I hear Callum drop a kiss against her palm.

She 'oofed' on her way out of the kitchen and I turned to catch the strange sight of Joanna rising up to her toes, eyebrows lifting in surprise and lips compressing as the fabric of her shirt bunched under invisible hands. Then Aiden rumbled and I laughed as he released her.

"We'll let you know before we're ready to leave," Aiden said to a blinking Joanna. She nodded as Callum nudged against my hip, reminding me he was waiting.

I took his arm in my hands, frowning at the slippery, oily feeling of Illness' blood on his wrist, and worked quickly to scrub away Joanna's words. Was the sudden squeeze in my lungs worry, or an effect of the blood?

Callum looked gruesome, blood splashed across his white shirt and his hand in mine coated in a thin layer of black.

"Oh gods, Pike, what did you do?"

Callum huffed, a sweaty strand of copper hair falling against his glasses as they sat crooked on his nose. "I got a good swipe in at the right moment."

I couldn't resist washing my hands and I dragged Callum's grip under the spray of water with me. "Do you feel alright?"

"I didn't until the cage sealed," he said with a shrug.

Aiden's warmth appeared at my other side and with a brief nudge of his arm against my knuckles I washed away Joanna's magic on his skin, sighing at the sight of him fading in before me. Our foreheads bumped together and we both closed our eyes, a commiserating stress at our more reckless covenmates echoing through our connection.

"Fusspots," Callum mumbled under his breath.

"Speaking of, did you see what the Ancient's blood did to those roses?" I asked. "There was another spot, where we hid."

"I'll go back and check," Callum said with a nod. "It could be an issue, for the cage at least. If not the woods."

"Not alone, you won't," Aiden said, face torn with a frown.

Callum's hands braced the edge of the sink as he pushed his shoulders back into Aiden's chest. I smiled as Aiden's hand cupped around Callum's hip.

"You can come if you like," Callum said, head tilting just enough that Aiden could rest his forehead against Callum's temple. "I'll take Gast and Ito and a couple of the Scrivens with me. But not today. Everyone will stay inside for the rest of the day."

"Joanna and I have patrol," I reminded them both and raised my eyebrows as Aiden's grumble grew in volume. "You'll stay home and *rest*. We take shifts for a reason. You can't be out all night with us every time."

"I don't like having any of you out of my sight," Aiden whispered, and Callum took his hand, wrapping it across his chest.

"Keep me company at the house tonight," Callum coaxed him,

winking at me as Aiden's face turned away. "We'll make sure Warfare doesn't tear the neighborhood down."

The Ancients had torn down the staff housing after it was evacuated. Joanna's writing ensured they couldn't come inside any building in Canderfey—with the exception of Bryce. The Ancients found a way around those words, destroying two dozen homes, university properties, and storefronts before the Scrivens spent a long day and night scribbling words on floorboards in every standing structure that remained. No building had been destroyed since, but as Joanna's Uncle Myles took care to remind us, no words were a guarantee. Scrivens magic was a constant riddle, a balance of how to make language as tight as a lock, but still allow nature to breathe. There was always a chance the Ancients might out-think the Scrivens.

"It's getting late," I said, glancing out the window.

The sun was only starting to set, turning Hand Woods golden and bronze, but something about the cage sealing out magic seemed to play with time. A sunset could last for hours one day and minutes the next. Better to be cautious.

"Go check on Joanna," Aiden said, his chin resting on Callum's shoulder, the two fully wrapped up in one another. "Now that I don't feel as if I might be sick any moment, I find I'm quite starving. We'll have dinner before your patrol starts."

I nodded and left them, relieved to find Corina missing from the window and only Bekka sitting in the frame, curls shining with sunlight and fingertip tracing drawings on the glass.

"Have you run out of your special paper?" I asked her, mixing Enmarian and Vermenian together where I could. Language was often jumbled in the Scrivens house, what with our coven and Bryce's and the remaining Canderfey residents passing in and out so often.

Bekka chewed at the inside of her lip, suddenly reminding me of Joanna in a way that struck me hard in the heart, and then nodded.

"We'll make you more," I said, referring to the paper Joanna marked carefully with a little symbol she'd designed to prevent Bekka's playful drawings from becoming accidental reality.

Speaking of which, a snuffling huffing sound followed by

galumphing steps down the stairs heralded the arrival of Lars—the world's most unusual house pet—heading directly for his young owner, mossy green head dropping into Bekka's lap. She scratched her fingers into his knotty curls and Lars huffed once more against her lap.

"Next visit," I promised the girl, and then turned to take the strange, curling hall—that shouldn't have lead anywhere if the house followed any logic—to Adele's room. Myles and Irene were inside, curled together on a long couch against the wall.

Adele was sitting up in her narrow bed, some of her color returned to her cheeks, although she still looked weary and pale. Joanna sat at Adele's side, their hands linked on her lap, and beamed at me as I entered.

"It worked," she said, leaning into my touch as I reached her and stroked my hand down her back.

"Just in time too," Myles murmured and I met his gaze with a nod of understanding.

Illness had an effect on us all, but it had taken Adele nearly to death's door before we'd found a solution. I hoped she was able to recover fully before our first attempt at a cage failed.

"Sunset has started and we need to eat before we patrol," I said to Joanna.

"Go on, *leina*," Adele rasped, smiling at her granddaughter and adding in Vermenian, "This old woman needs another nap."

Joanna kissed her grandmother's cheeks, rising up from the bed, and then tangled her fingers with mine on our way out the door.

"How long will it last, do you think?" she whispered.

I resisted the urge to sigh, wrapping my arm around her shoulder and kissing her temple. "Long enough for us to find another solution. We're good at those, love."

Joanna smiled and gazed up at me as we reached the kitchen where Aiden and Callum waited for us. "I love you," she said, the emotion ringing through the bond. She turned to smile at Aiden and Callum, adding them to the declaration, all of us answering the words, and together we took a cupboard door home to our kitchen.

2

JOANNA

Even with all the lamps unlit, the stacks missing the soft whispers of students, and the eerie weight of the air after keeping the building locked up for so long, the Canderfey Library was still magical. If anything, having it all to myself and Isaac, walking over the tile and hearing every step echo, gave me a possessive kind of thrill. The Library was ours alone for the night. We'd have to pass through more buildings before morning came, my chalk words creating doorways to rooms whose walls didn't connect, but my coven knew I liked to spend any idle hours of patrol in the stacks.

There were other advantages too.

Isaac pressed me up against the end of a bookshelf, arms circled around my waist, our lips linked in a lazy dance of strokes and nibbles and long, aimless presses. I ran my palms over his shoulders, up his neck, tracing his sharp jaw with a fingertip, combing through his long hair and clutching as he teased his tongue against mine.

My boss, Gwen Woollard, would be safely at home with her own coven for the night, but there was still a playful charge racing in my veins at the thought of being caught necking like students in the stacks. And lovelier still was the simple joy of kissing Isaac, talented as he was at the act, and knowing that there was no race to a destination.

Only the pleasure of closeness and affection, our love echoing between us and down the coven bond to Callum and Aiden at home.

I leaned my head back against the wood to catch my breath and Isaac's lips traveled to my cheek and down my throat, voice humming as he stopped at the curve of my shoulder. His hips pinned mine to the shelf, just like he'd held me to the tree that afternoon as Ecstasy soared above us. Now any desire was our own, tempered by the long day and our own patience, willing to wait to return home to our covenmates.

"You know I'll make you check those books of yours out, right?" I asked, grinning and eyeing the stack of old art texts Isaac had collected before we'd become distracted with each other. They sat waiting at the corner of a small desk, ready to topple with a wrong nudge.

"Ever the librarian," Isaac said, pressing another kiss to my skin, one of his fingers creeping around to unbutton the collar of my shirt. He pushed fabric aside and leaned into me, making me gasp as he licked along my collar bone, body hard against mine.

Not *quite* a librarian yet, although without our usual work to do, Gwen had made a point of focusing on my training when we needed breaks from researching the Ancients. It was turning into a strange kind of summer, the threat of the creatures we were fighting against dimmed beneath long lazy days of reading and the eerie emptiness of Canderfey.

Isaac lifted his head, nose nudging at mine, stealing another kiss from my lips just before I broke out into a grin. "Will you write us to the studio? I have some supplies I want to rescue."

I nodded, sliding out from between Isaac and the shelf, scooping up his books and carrying them over to the main desk. I drew out Gwen's tome of check-outs and returns, flipping it open to a new page.

"You were serious?" Isaac's laugh was at the edge of his words.

"'Course I was. I know my coven. We're book hoarders, even you and Aiden." I looked up from my careful accounting of the texts as Isaac reached the desk and added, "Someday soon we're going to find an answer to this situation and then Canderfey will go back to normal and the students will come back and this library will need to be fully operational again."

Isaac stretched across the desk, hands reaching for my face and dragging me to meet him halfway for a long, deep caress of his mouth against mine. "I love you, Joanna Wick. You are the most practical woman I've ever met, and if anyone can defeat nine ancient beings set on revenge, it's you."

The heat of my blush seared up my cheeks and I pushed Isaac back across the desk, my eyes rolling at his grin. My gaze froze as movement flickered behind him on the other side of the enormous wood and glass entrance to the building. I gasped, brow furrowing and brain fumbling, as Isaac whipped around.

"Do you see it?" I asked.

"Yes and no," Isaac said, shoulders broadening so that I had to lean to keep my gaze fixed on the creature.

It was the strangest of the Ancients, the one I called Confusion who was somehow impossible to look at and *understand* what I was seeing.

"Let's move to the next building," Isaac said, voice low.

But his words were interrupted by a bright chiming sound, bone or nail or metal against glass, and he and I both froze, staring at the Ancient outside the doors.

I beg an audience with the Wordsmith.

The voice was gentler than Warfare's, and easier in my head than Illness'—although, like the appearance of the Ancient, it didn't fit together quite right. It wasn't a voice like a human's, but instead a collection of sounds that might conveniently be misheard as words. Wind in the trees, or a symphony of instruments.

I walked out from behind the desk and paused as Isaac's hand wrapped around my arm.

"You can't come in," I said.

And it would be safer for you to stay inside, the Ancient said. *That doesn't prevent us from communicating, so if you are assured, then I am satisfied.*

"Let's go," Isaac whispered. "We don't know enough to be certain this isn't a trap."

"Callum was sure the library was safe," I answered back, not taking my eyes off the murky spot beyond the glass. "Better to speak here in this way than anywhere else."

Isaac sighed, the small fold between his eyes appearing, but stepped closer and wrapped his arm around my waist.

"What is it you wish to say?" I asked. I didn't bother raising my voice. I wondered if the Ancients needed us to speak aloud at all, but I didn't want to offer any kind of accidental link to my thoughts.

I am often called Mystery, the Ancient said and I stiffened at the sudden explanation. It fit, and my guess hadn't been so far off. *I would offer you an easier illusion to look at, but this is all I am without my strength.*

"How you look isn't my greatest concern at the moment," I said, unable to resist the dry tone in my words.

I tell you my name as a gesture of goodwill, the Ancient continued, a little bite of irritation streaking through the words in my head. *You will find me buried in your book shrine somewhere no doubt, my true name tucked between pages.*

I stiffened and resisted the urge to glance at Isaac. His fingers squeezed at my hip in understanding. If we had Mystery's true name we could do the same to them as we had done to Illness. This was either a trap or a peace offering and, based on our experiences with the Ancients, the former certainly seemed more likely.

"What do you want us to do with your true name?" Isaac asked.

Nothing, I only offer it as a reassurance so you might hear what I have to say next. We are not the only Ancients in your world. We are only the ones who were caged. You may find allies in our siblings if you search for them.

"Allies for you, or for us?" I asked, eyes narrowed.

It would depend on who you found, Mystery answered and Isaac bristled at my side. *I will not lie. When your ancestors offered us the choice between disguise and entrapment, there were those who chose to blend in with great reluctance. Time may have given them regrets. It has given me many.*

"And where would we find these sympathetic siblings of yours?"

Isaac asked as I mulled over the creature standing on the other side of the glass. It was impossible to know if Mystery was telling us the truth —it was in the Ancient's nature to be a secret. I wondered if they even knew what side they were on.

Have you forgotten? I have been in a cage for hundreds of years. Ask the Child without Nature, they may know.

That was what the Ancients called Bryce and I could see the way it prickled at my friend. Bryce had a great deal of nature, but—as they had explained—was apparently somewhat of an accident. Their two parents had taken on the disguise of humans, not realizing their new forms might lead to other human biological norms. Namely, conception and child bearing. Bryce hadn't told me what Ancients their parents were, or ever mentioned them still being alive or around, but that didn't mean they didn't know. Bryce's information came and went based on their moods.

"What do you want from all of this?" I asked.

I will hide like my free brothers and sisters, Mystery said. *I want my freedom, Wordsmith.*

"You're going to have to do more than offer us hints," Isaac said.

Perhaps. We'll see if you stand a chance of winning.

The tangling pressure of staring at something which refused to be seen relaxed as Mystery retreated from the doors of the Library and into the dark night.

"Do you trust it?" Isaac whispered to me.

"Of course not," I said, leaning into his side, letting him pull me against his chest. "They as good as told us they'll choose whatever side looks like it has the advantage. I think they only came to us tonight because we managed to trap Illness."

Isaac sighed, a weary, frustrated sound, and I tore my eyes away from the door, tipping my head back to look at him. He was tired. No, more than that. There were new lines digging into his forehead, and a sprinkling of gray around his hairline I'd caught him frowning at the other morning in the bathroom mirror. I understood why. The past year had been packed to the brim with the worst kinds of conflict. The Hollow—Starvation—escaping its cage and terrorizing the campus, Callum captured and kept prisoner in Vermenia, all of the recent turmoil with the Scrivens, and now this. Being cooped up in Canderfey, without his magic, hunting and hiding from Ancients.

For all of that terror and trouble, it had still been the best year of my life. I had my coven and, good or bad, I was learning that adventure made my blood sing in my veins. I just wasn't certain if Isaac felt the same. I knew he felt the same about me, about our coven. But I suspected when it came to the adventure, it was taking a toll on his happiness.

I rose up to my toes and immediately his face relaxed, the right corner of his mouth twitching with a smile before he met me halfway in a kiss. It was gentle and steady, but I shivered as Isaac's hands mapped up and down my back, settling just above the swell of my hips. His shoulders softened under my touch and he sighed against my lips as I stroked the back of his neck, but this time the sound wasn't unhappy.

"Worrying can wait until the morning," I said, drawing slightly back before pressing in again for another sweet pull from his mouth, humming into the kiss as he dragged me closer, tongue flicking the seam of my lips.

"I think it *is* morning," Isaac said, glancing over the top of my head to the front doors. "Or very nearly. Let's finish our route through town and get home, hmm?"

"What about the studio?"

"Let it wait for daylight," he said. "I'd rather be home with the others."

I kissed his chin, thrilled to see a real smile bloom on his face, and nodded. "The Solstice is tomorrow," I said, leading the way to the door behind the front desk where I could write us a way into town.

Isaac grunted in agreement. "I don't think we'll be spending the night out of doors this year," he said.

That was true, and it would be Bryce and Gwen's night for patrols, but perhaps there would be a way for everyone to celebrate together. I hated to waste the holiday feeling as though we were hiding. I would have to think of a way for us to stay safely inside, but undeniably happy. I scribbled our way to the grocer's at the farthest end of town. It sat on a triangular corner and had wrap-around windows, giving the best view of the street. We emerged out of a stock closet and made our way into the front room, hands linked.

As a straggling community, we'd long since cleaned away the last stock of the grocery and parceled it out amongst ourselves. The Ancients had barreled down the phone lines running into Canderfey, trying to cut off our contact with the outside world. With the help of Corina's carefully detailed attention to words, I was able to write our way into contact with Aiden's parents. We received bi-weekly rations of supplies and food now by meeting someone at the edge of the boundary, three of us standing guard as two others exchanged the cart.

"One of them is in the street," Isaac murmured, standing back from the glass windows where it was darkest in the store.

"Can you tell which one?" I asked. I liked the quiet nights when the Ancients kept to the woods and we could walk down the street and take in the fresh air. I wasn't as attracted to the outdoors as Isaac was, but a month of keeping indoors, in the summer no less, was starting to make even me stir crazy.

Isaac's back heaved under my touch and he spun quickly away from the window. I thought I caught sight of Terror's bone white, spindling leg ducking down an alley, but Isaac only said, "Sorrow," his throat tight. "Let's get home to the others."

I glanced out the opposite window. The sky wasn't even pink yet, barely dusky purple, but nothing had been destroyed in the night and it was nearly morning. I nodded and took Isaac's hand in mine, our fingers linking as I led him back to the supply closet, wiping away the last Scriven's words and writing out our way home, back through the pantry door in the kitchen that'd become our most common pathway.

The cats met us at the door, now used to the routine, immediately crying out for their breakfast.

"You go on up," I said to Isaac, nudging him toward the hallway. "I'll follow once they're fed, and we'll convince Callum and Aiden to sleep in with us."

Isaac's mouth opened briefly, an objection on his lips, and then he looked around the kitchen and realized there was no need to protest. We were home again. We were safe. "See you upstairs," he said, brushing a kiss against my cheekbone and then heading for the stairs.

I filled the cats' bowls and freshened their water. I glanced at the kettle on the cold stove and considered making myself coffee. Despite my words to Isaac, I knew he'd be asleep by the time I made it upstairs and I wondered if I might find the answers to Mystery's clues in any of Callum's collected texts. Before I'd decided, a yawn crawled its way up from my chest, so long and deep my jaw cracked.

To bed it was then. I made it to the stairs before I heard the scratching on our doorstep. Awareness shot up my spine, tightening my muscles as I took careful, silent steps closer. It was more than scratching—the sound extending over the entire door—and I held my breath as I crept into the front room and over to the bay window that would give me a view of our doorstep.

A red and black gleaming hide took up most of the window. Warfare, curled up in front of the entrance of our home like a block-ade, or the world's most horrifying dog. He turned and turned, body shifting grotesquely in front of the door, and then settled with his enormous face pointed to the window, as if he'd known exactly where I would be standing. Perhaps he could smell me.

Fury burned through me, making my hands itch to pick up one of Callum's swords from the front closet and swing open the door and go to battle. One acid yellow eye, slitted like a snake's, blinked at me and I stepped back. I refused to look away, even though I knew it was my own fixed gaze that kept the fire building in my chest, Warfare's rage coursing through my veins. I forced my feet one after the other back to the hall and out of sight of the window. Then, with every bone in my body protesting, I went to the stairs and up to my coven.

Warfare could build himself a nest on our roof too, if he liked. He wouldn't trick me into a battle before I knew exactly how to go about defeating him. For good.

3

———————

JOANNA

It was pouring rain on Solstice Day, the sound thunderous against the glass roof of the Library. Callum didn't even seem to notice. He woke me earlier than I wished, fidgeting in bed in the way that meant he was trying to let the rest of us sleep while being unable to keep still himself. I took him downstairs for coffee and then out of the house before he could wake Isaac, using the bait of Mystery's conversation from the night before.

"What did it say, exactly? That you could find the name inside pages?" Callum asked.

I blinked and realized that I'd been dozing with my eyes open, staring at a page I was sure I'd read more than once, but couldn't remember a word of. "Umm... no, no it was 'tucked between pages,' I think," I said. I ran a hand over my face and realized it was Aiden's gesture. "Do you think it was being literal?"

Callum grunted. "I think that an Ancient called Mystery is likely to leave us some kind of riddle. Although I'm having a difficult time believing it would really offer up its true name."

"It was... different than the others," I mused. "It felt more like talking to... another person, I suppose. The conversation was more human."

"Like Bryce?" Callum asked, looking up from his book. I smiled at the sight of him, glasses crooked on his nose and hair mussed from his habit of running his fingers through the strands as he worked puzzles out in his head.

"More human than Bryce," I said. "As if it were trying to imitate us."

Callum frowned at me. "I'm not sure I find that reassuring."

"I agree, but it makes sense if it was trying to convince us that it wanted to blend in, like… the others."

"That is my next question," Callum muttered, going back to his book before adding, "but I'll save it for Gast."

Footsteps clicking on tile echoed up from the front of the Library and I rose from my seat, trying to hear through the storm crashing overhead.

"Joanna, wait," Callum said, pushing his chair back.

"Hush," I answered him, already rounding the table. "It's probably nothing. I can manage it."

I didn't mention that between the two of us, I had magic and he did *not*. I knew he'd been training in combat again since the boundary had buried his power, but my magic was faster and tidier than his swordplay. He'd never been a slouch physically, but I was growing fond of the new, denser layer of muscle he'd been building with his training. I'd have to tease him into keeping it up after we restored Canderfey.

Despite his objection, Callum stayed seated as I crossed over to the balcony that looked down to the circulation desk. My shoulders relaxed and I smiled. Gwen and her coven were walking through the staff lounge doorway, my pleasure at seeing them only slightly dimmed by the fact that Corina was with them. Of course she was; they needed a Scrivens to travel anywhere.

"Hello there," I called down and Hildy looked up first, her smile tight but genuine. She was like Isaac, managing this catastrophe because she had to, because her coven was involved, but wishing to be anywhere else. Speaking of her coven…

Bryce tilted their head back, gold feathers catching the faint light of the day and glinting like hundreds of delicate daggers. Their yellow eyes blinked at me, hawk head tilting in greeting.

'*Witchling*,' they called.

Another reason for Hildy's weariness, no doubt, was having her covenmate trapped in a form so unfamiliar to them both. Raised by two Ancients who'd chosen to blend in with humans, Bryce's human shape was built from the Ancients' natural shapeshifting magic. Bryce told me it had taken them a long time to discover their fixed, hereditary form. Shapeshifting was like breathing to the Ancients. Losing that skill, the magic, was a cage of its own.

"What are you doing here?" Gwen and I asked each other at the same time.

"Come up and I'll explain," I told her.

"Tatsuo's concerned about the dampening boundary," Gwen answered.

I heard Callum drop his book, a soft curse falling from his lips, as his chair scraped against the floor and he came to join me at the railing. "What's wrong with the boundary?" Callum asked.

"I think it might be growing weak," Tatsuo answered and as a group the coven and Corina headed to the stairs.

"I'll write to the others," I said to Callum, returning to the table.

If the boundary was breaking down, then all we'd accomplished this summer was stalling, giving Warfare something to do while he waited for freedom. The waiting game we'd been playing had to end.

IT WAS NOT QUITE the Summer Solstice celebration I had in mind, but after a little wheedling on Aiden and Hildy's part Gwen waived her restriction against food in the library—under very strict regulations—and we'd gathered everyone together for a dinner party. Mayor Sewell arrived back to the University with the latest food supply and he sat with Uncle Myles and the rest of my family, huffing into a cup of ale at something Elizabeth Bonde said, a hint of a smile on his lips. Isaac sat at the end of the table, Bryce curled on the tile floor at his side, their enormous, lethal beak resting on the edge of the table and grabbing up the bones Isaac slipped to them.

Down the long row of tables we'd pushed together I spotted another professor from Callum's department, Ethan Frost, sitting with Pablo Banaker, one of Aiden's friends in the music department. And amongst them all were the Scrivens, finally looking at home in the community, a strange and clumsy combination of languages exchanged around the table. The circumstance of our summer had taken the tentative truce between University and Scrivens and transformed it into friendships and mutual respect.

My heart felt especially tender and vulnerable at the scene of us all together. Aiden reappeared from the staff lounge door—now leading into our kitchen again—with a large dish of roasted vegetables in his hands. He met my eyes as he set the dish down at the center of the table and then came to find me at the far end where I sat alone on a bench, a seat saved for him at my side.

"I can't tell if you look happy or scared," he said, one arm wrapping around my shoulders and pulling me into his side, lips pressing to my temple.

"I'm not sure either," I said, a smile shaking on my lips. I closed my eyes and pressed my face to his throat, breathing him in and feeling some of the tension drain from my shoulders. "I'm happy right now," I murmured.

Aiden kissed the top of my head again. "But?"

"But I'm worried about the boundary. This hasn't been an easy month, but now that Illness is trapped everyone is well again and it's been..." It felt wrong to say it'd been almost peaceful. Not when Isaac was so stressed and Bryce was uncomfortable and everyone was scared. "Is it too soon to start hoping we'll have our lives back again?"

"Never too soon. I make a regular practice of it. Callum and Tatsuo will think of something to hold the boundary until we know what to do about the other Ancients," Aiden said, soft enough so our discussion was only for our own ears. "When they aren't butting heads, the two of them can be very clever."

I grinned against Aiden's neck and then kissed the skin over his pulse for good measure. I wanted to crawl up into his lap and wrap myself tight around him. Not simply because of attraction or sexual interest, but because when I was tangled up with Aiden I knew there wasn't a thing in the world so terrible that he would let it interrupt our care of one another. Hildy's burst of laughter reminded me that we were at a table full of our friends. So I kept to my seat.

"No research for you tonight," Aiden said and before I could object his voice hardened into the tone he'd started taking recently, the one I was apparently hardwired to find thrilling. "You're tired." Except when he said I was tired in that voice, I felt the exact opposite. His hand reached up, thumb sweeping over my cheek and drawing my gaze up to his. "Our coven needs rest," he purred.

My eyes flicked back down the table, checking on Callum first. He did have dark circles under his eyes and his hair was even more mussed after talking with Tatsuo about the boundary. If we weren't especially persuasive in dragging him home after dinner, he'd be sneaking off to the woods alone to investigate. Isaac was yawning as I looked to him next, equally tired, although I knew it would take no convincing to lead him home.

"But if the boundary is fragile…" I mumbled, but I was already feeling warm and relaxed as I turned to Aiden again. He had won the argument before it really began.

He leaned down, enfolding our lips together in a perfect, chaste kiss that made me want to grab him by the collar and drag him home for much less chaste activities. "It will wait until morning," he said, eyes warming my cheeks with their intent stare.

I thought Callum would put up more of a fight as we gathered together, arms full of our dishes while we waited for the others to make it through the staff lounge doors one home at a time. Instead he only frowned and tried to balance everything in one arm as he pulled his glasses off and tucked them away into his pocket, little indents marking the bridge of his nose. Balancing an armload was a trick he excelled at…*with* his magic. Without it, Isaac and I had to crowd his sides to keep the whole pile from toppling to the floor.

"Ito's going to keep an eye on the boundary tonight from the outside," Callum said, Isaac's stretching yawn catching him into one of his own before he continued. "He's competent enough to hold it."

I snorted. That was faint praise, but praise at all showed progress in the boyish animosity between the two men. Aiden raised a damp cloth to wash away the chalk words Corina had scribbled on the door before us and then helped me rearrange my burden of dishes so I could write us home. The house was quiet and peaceful as we returned, our kitchen a mess from the flurry of cooking for the dinner party.

"You can be sweet and tell me not to worry about the dishes, but only if you promise they aren't still in the sink tomorrow night," Isaac grumbled as Aiden hurried to unburden us.

"I promise," Aiden said, smirking.

"I've just thought of a book that might have—" Callum said, taking a step to the door.

"No," Aiden growled, raising his eyebrow at me.

I smiled and caught Callum by the sleeve, forcing him to pause and wait for me. I slid my hand up his spine, smile growing as his body straightened with attention, and then leaned into him, cheek pressed to his sleeve. "Come upstairs with me and start the bath? It's the solstice, after all."

"Is that a tradition?" Callum asked, brow furrowing but following my nudges down the hall to the stairs.

I shrugged. "Not that I know of. We could make it one." His eyes lit up at the suggestion and his hands linked with mine, books and research forgotten for the moment.

THE NEXT DAY I watched Callum's back as he crossed over the boundary, checking for the fraying Tatsuo had warned us of. We'd marked the line with gold painted stakes in the ground earlier this month. My lips pressed between my teeth as he paused, shoulders shifting with a deep breath. His entire body seemed to flex and then he spun around, facing us on the other side, eyes bright and excited.

His hand flicked at his side and he pulled out a long dagger from the air.

"Lost that over a month ago when the boundary came down," he said, grinning at us.

Aiden sighed and grumbled something under his breath, glancing back at the dark wood around us, waiting to be interrupted by an Ancient.

"Don't play too long," Aiden said, perfectly dry with the faintest tense edge.

Because we could be found at any minute, and we didn't have another cage ready for an Ancient if we were.

"You could cross over too," I said to Aiden and then glanced on my other side to Isaac. "It's been weeks since you've had your magic."

Isaac shifted from foot to foot, standing with his back against my shoulder, fingertips resting against my left hip. "It's only color magic and I still have my art," he said. "I'm fine as long as our bond is still working."

"I'll be all right," Aiden echoed. "I'm more interested in heading back to safety than I am in whistling charms on the other side of that line."

"I'll be as quick as I can," Callum said, tucking the dagger into his back pocket in a way I found both amusing and concerning. What were the odds of him remembering he'd put it there later? Not high enough. I'd have to take it from him before he accidentally sat down and stabbed himself in the ass.

He raised his palms and for the first time the boundary became visible, a prismatic tangle of threads in a repetitive collection of colors. Black, sour yellow, white, rot green, dull blue, and more.

Isaac stepped forward as Callum shifted down the boundary, hunting for where Tatsuo said the threads looked frayed.

"Those colors," Isaac murmured at the wall. "They're..." He traced a finger over a thread of electric yellow, wincing at the touch but following the line over to where it crossed with another of the same shade. "These have to do with the Ancients."

"It's not just one boundary," Callum said and we followed his route, curving around trees and untangling ourselves from weedy undergrowth. "It's all nine of the cages for the Ancients, stretched and combined into one beast of complicated spell-working. How Anders managed to make something so grotesquely effective with such incompetent magic…" He frowned as his words trailed off, and I knew he was remembering that horrible snap and squish of Anders being crushed in Warfare's jaws.

"So it might not be all nine cages growing weak," Isaac said.

Callum stumbled over a tree root and then stopped, spine straight and eyes wide and blinking. "Damn. I hadn't even thought of that."

"Light up as much of that as you can and we'll all look," I offered.

"You three look and I'll keep my eyes on the woods," Aiden corrected. "I don't trust any moment of peace we have without one of *them* appearing to breathe down our necks."

"He's right," Callum said. "I'm not even sure I'm looking in the right direction."

"I was right that we should have brought others for help too," Aiden said, his back to us.

I stroked my hand down his spine, smiling even as he grumbled, and I watched some of the tension bleed out of him at my touch. "If it takes too long we'll get back to the Scrivens house and wait until a larger group can help," I said.

Callum's nose wrinkled at my declaration, but he nodded in agreement. His version of 'too long' was sure to be different than Aiden's, but between Isaac and I, we'd reach some compromise.

"You focus on lighting up as much of this as you can. Isaac and I will hunt for loose threads," I told Callum.

He arched an eyebrow at me. "Our darling authoritarian." His lips twitched as I rolled my eyes and then he stretched his arms and raised his hands back in the air.

I was learning more about sigils from Callum, finding ways to use them in our Scrivens magic as a link to the others'—more familiar—Enmarian Magic. The first time he'd shown me the twirling symbol he traced in the air, I thought it was meant to reveal something hidden, and it did in a way. Callum explained afterwards that it worked not to reveal something hidden, but to reveal the inner workings of a spell—like pulling open the back of a watch to look at its gears. He added two more symbols after the first, one for broadening the scope of a spell and another I hadn't seen before but which made the threads of color shift apart, less tangled and easier to see as layers.

Callum's forehead was furrowed with concentration and he nodded at me and Isaac. The web of the cages was now visible almost out of sight in either direction.

"Let's head in opposite directions?" I asked Isaac.

"No!" Aiden barked. "Don't spread out. You don't need to be more vulnerable than we already are standing out here."

"Don't walk farther than I can see either of you clearly," Callum compromised.

Isaac and I took off in opposite directions with slow steps. The cages stretched far over our heads, higher than the tops of the enormous, ancient trees in Hand Woods. Bright shimmering strands of magic hung throughout the air like decorative spider silk. It was dizzying to look at and I didn't know if that had something to do with magical resonance, or just the confusion of fine line and color layered together.

I focused hard on the work, trying to follow every thread to its next join, combing through the cage one layer at a time before shuffling a few feet farther and starting over again. By the time I was twenty or so feet away from Callum, the woods had softened around me and the whole mess of magic started to grow blurry and unfocused, like a word you'd stared at too long until it lost its meaning.

"Joanna," Aiden called in a warning tone.

Callum's magic was still making the threads shimmer at least another ten feet further away, so I hummed and waved at Aiden, trying to hold my place in the web of magic.

"Something's…wrong," Aiden said, and I was so consumed with my work that it took too long for the words to sink in.

I tore my gaze away from the cages and found myself farther away from my coven than I expected. Callum's focus was on holding his magic, but Aiden was shifting in place, his body tense and alert as he searched the woods. I glanced back at the threads, no tear or flick-ering color jumping out at me, and then started back to Aiden.

"I think- yes! It's here," Isaac called to us. "But it isn't all the threads. Just one is torn!"

"What color?" Callum asked. "I'll let the others go."

"I—I'm not sure. It's… shifting."

"Joanna," Aiden repeated.

I dug into my pocket, pulling my notebook and pencil free as Callum released one cage at a time. I jogged to Aiden's side, eyes hunting through the woods around him. There was no hulking Warfare or swooping Ecstasy, only the complicated clutter of trees. My heartbeat began to race in my chest, Aiden's urgency and my own confusion making worry rise.

"Why can't I tell what color that is?" Isaac asked.

I stepped back and looked to where he stood in front of the remaining cage, threads shimmering in a strange light that was not quite one color but neither was it many colors. My eyes widened with understanding.

"Mystery!" I hissed, running to Isaac.

But I was too late. Out of the clutter of trees in the wood came the Ancient, racing me to where Isaac stood in front of a frayed link of magic.

"Isaac, Callum, watch out!"

Seeing Mystery standing still was one thing, watching it move was even harder to look at, as if the entire woods was rearranging itself around the creature to confuse and disorient me. Worse, the Ancient was faster and much closer to Isaac than I was. Callum was running to the weak spot from the other side of the boundary as Isaac spun around, arms and legs spread.

I could see it on his face, the startled shock and the way his eyes flickered. Any other Ancient we would have *seen* earlier, *felt* earlier. Mystery blended in and stood out all at once as it rushed at Isaac. I wanted to scream at him to run—we didn't know enough about this Ancient to have any sense of how to fight it—and for a moment it looked as though he would. Then his expression hardened, eyes narrowed, and he bent his knees, bracing for impact.

Mystery's soft laughter shivered through me. Isaac charged forward and I saw it at the last second, the way the Ancient shivered past him, just out of reach, clear for the time it took me to blink. Slender and almost childlike—if children looked like little beastly things. Mystery made it to the tear in the cage, almost running into Callum's arms outside of the boundary.

"Catch it!" I cried, regretting the words as they fell off my tongue. Catch an Ancient, but then what? We hadn't had to deal with one in control of their magic since The Hollow, and those times had nearly killed us.

I'd never seen an Ancient shift before. It wasn't a bodily transformation the way I imagined. It happened even as Mystery passed through the cage. There was a scream in my head scratching through me, leaving my knees weak and legs crumpling to the forest floor. One beautiful delicate white arm stretched through the boundary and I could *feel* and *hear* the pain it cost Mystery to force itself through the narrow gap. Callum reached for the arm but all at once it was an arm *and* a frothy blue wing, sky bright and delicate.

First a body, not entirely inhuman, forced itself out of the cage, and then a bird. Or parts of a body that quickly turned into a bird. Either way, I was on the ground, hand clutched to my head and Aiden close behind me. Callum's arms swung uselessly around a form he couldn't catch and Mystery took off into the air. A pale blue bird, fantastical and sweet, floating away with soft curls of its wings, like a butterfly with deadly silver talons catching the sunlight the higher it rose.

Callum turned, palms raised, magic glowing at his fingertips. Above him Mystery circled, careful not to come too close to the boundary.

"Callum, get back inside!" Aiden shouted. "We don't know what it can do."

Isaac reached through for him, fisting the back of Callum's shirt in his hands and dragging him backwards, the pair of them stumbling down to the ground.

"Damn!" Callum hissed.

"It's my fault," Isaac said, a dirty hand reaching up to push dark strands away from his face.

Aiden helped me up from the ground and together we ran to our covenmates.

"Are you alright?" I asked Isaac, sinking to his side, running my palms over his shoulders to check for any damage. It hadn't looked like Mystery even touched him, but the contact soothed me if nothing else.

"I'm fine," Isaac said, catching my hand, but I could see the frustration and the nerves on his face and I pulled his hand up to my lips, kissing his knuckles.

"We should hurry back to the Scrivens house now," Callum said, that same frustration clipping his words. "I don't know what that felt like for the other Ancients, but we're better off without them knowing exactly what happened. If they haven't realized the cages are capable of fraying, we're better off keeping it a secret."

4

ISAAC

"Do you have any idea where Mystery might have gone?" Joanna asked Bryce.

My coven was squeezed together on one of Hildy's voluptuous velvet couches, not for the sake of space, but for closeness. Aiden's arm stretched across my shoulders, his fingertips resting against Callum's sleeve on the other side of Joanna. She sat all but curled up in my lap, her touch playing with the fabric of my sleeve. Bryce lounged on the carpet in front of us, Gwen's eyes narrowed in on where their dark talons curled into the dense weave.

'*That old thing is going to have less of a chance of finding its siblings than I would,*' Bryce answered, with an annoyed toss of their feathered head. '*More likely, it's gone to hide. Or to cause trouble.*'

"You don't think Mystery will run errands for Warfare?" Callum asked.

'*Ancients aren't a pack race,*' Bryce said and then shifted, tail thumping on the floor as Hildy cleared her throat. '*Usually,*' they amended and if it weren't so impossible with that hawk's beak, I would have sworn they smirked.

"Bryce suspects any truce between the Ancients at the moment is tentative at best. They are, essentially, working together in the hopes of making their currently narrow food source much larger," Tatsuo explained.

My stomach made a queasy swoop at the announcement. *Food source.* How pleasant.

"If that's true, that must mean we have a better chance of finding other Ancients who won't be sympathetic with Warfare," Joanna said.

'It means you have a better chance of finding other Ancients who won't care either way,' Bryce corrected. *'Most will refuse to help. Some may resent being found at all.'*

Aiden shifted uncomfortably at my side. "What if their freedom was put at risk by Warfare and the others?"

Bryce froze on the carpet and Joanna leaned forward to glare and hiss, "Aiden."

He raised his palms, "I'm not saying that's something we put forward. Only that if Warfare were to escape and the others with him, and if they attempted to take revenge for those centuries locked up, it's going to draw the whole conflict back up again."

"And if we were able to defeat the Ancients once, we could certainly do so again," Callum said, quiet and heavy. His breath huffed. "It's not a very good olive branch as things go, but I suppose it's an argument that might sway a decision. I'd be *more* reassured if we knew *how* humans did it in the first place."

"But are we decided?" Tatsuo asked. "We'll send someone to find other Ancients?"

'Me,' Bryce announced. Their coven stiffened, but no one looked surprised. *'They're used to hiding, but I'll be able to find them. I know of one or two.'*

"You won't go alone," Gwen said, firm enough to skip any argument. "Hildy will go with you."

"I will?" Hildy asked, eyebrows raising.

'Keep me company,' Bryce said and I suspected that there had been some prior discussion of the idea between their coven. What I didn't expect was for Bryce to turn their feathered head in my direction, and to blink that glowing gaze at me and add, *'You too.'*

I stiffened. "Me? Shouldn't it be... I don't know, Aiden? Someone with influence?"

"I have influence," Hildy said with a roll of her eyes. "And if you come we'll have your covenbond connection running back to Canderfey so we'll know if anything is wrong."

Joanna's hand reached to lift mine from her knee, wrapping her fingers around mine and drawing my gaze to hers, our faces close together. She was chewing the inside of her lip, eyebrows drawn together, and I couldn't read her expression clearly enough to know what she was thinking. I touched the covenbond with my thoughts and the immediate response was Callum's agreement with the others, then Aiden's reluctance to have any of us out of reach, and Joanna's perfect compromise between the two. I smiled in spite of the tension between the four of us.

"What do you think?" I asked her and then glanced at Callum and Aiden to include them.

"It's a good idea," she said, brow furrowing deeper, "even if I'd rather it wasn't. Do you want to go?"

I took a breath and opened my mouth to say 'no,' thinking it was the obvious answer, but the word never came out. Canderfey was an oppressive place with the magical boundary in place and the Ancients breathing down our necks. I missed being outside. I missed painting and having time to think about something other than the magical tangle I was trapped in. I didn't want to leave my coven, but...

"I would like to leave Canderfey," I said slowly and Joanna's expression relaxed into a gentle smile. She'd likely known as much before I did. I turned to Bryce, studying the tension in their form and the eager glint in their eye. "If you really think I can be of some help, then yes, I'll come."

Bryce blinked at me and I realized it had never been a matter of whether or not I *would* come, just how long it would take me to agree. *'Time to go pack,'* Bryce said. *'We'll leave in the morning.'*

"Just like that?" Aiden asked, chest puffing with irritation and worry.

"If Mystery has gone to help Warfare, they won't wait for us to catch up," Callum said, frowning. He nodded at the other coven and rose up from the couch, the cozy press of us together falling loose. "We'll see you in the morning."

WEATHER HAD BEEN strange inside of the boundary—as if the magic of the cage was not quite sure what to do with natural phenomenons. I wondered if that was one of the many questions about their construction that kept Callum up at night even when, as a coven, we did our best to wear him out. Even now, it was raining but only half the rain was making it inside, the rest washing down the boundary to create deep puddles all around Canderfey.

Aiden's fingers clamped a little tighter around my shoulder as we reached the edge, not quite as committed to letting me leave as Joanna and Callum. I turned to him, stepping into his chest and tilting my chin up for a kiss. He frowned at the offer, knowing it was only an attempt to soothe his nerves, but lowered his forehead. His nose brushed against mine twice before he caught my lips, hungrier and more demanding than I expected, a kiss meant to persuade me to change my mind. I let him make his argument as long as he wanted, soaking in his smell and taste. Callum's humor in the bond stirred a grumble in Aiden as his tongue stroked softly against mine, warmth coiling in my stomach. I ran my hands up and down his sides, felt his shoulders drop and his heartbeat slow as I rested my palm on his chest.

The kiss slowed to a stop and Aiden sighed against my mouth before either of us spoke.

"I'll be safe," I said. It was what worried me most, I would be safer outside of Canderfey than they were inside. And I understood why it had to be me who left. Callum and Joanna, our fearless warriors, couldn't be spared. And while they were throwing themselves headlong into danger, Aiden would never rest with them out of sight.

"You'll be missed too, so don't let Gast dawdle," Aiden whispered.

Bryce made a soft growling sound from where they stood close to the barrier, although it might have been a chuckle for all I knew.

"Don't close the bond," I whispered back. Of my three covenmates, Aiden was the least likely to cut his feelings off if he didn't want me to worry and I knew he would be my guaranteed line back to feeling the environment in Canderfey. He nodded and we both leaned in to kiss each other's cheeks.

I turned and found Callum and Joanna waiting for me, Callum's hands hidden behind his back and Joanna bouncing on her toes.

"We made you something," Joanna said as soon as they had my attention.

Callum's head tipped in her direction. "Joanna wrote it."

"Yes, but Callum gave the instructions," she rushed out and then nudged him lightly in the side with her elbow. He and I shared an amused and enamored glance—Joanna had done more than complete our coven when she'd joined, she brought out new facets in our relationships with each other.

Callum brought his hands out from behind his back, and I stared blankly at what rested in his palms for several moments until Joanna's nervous fidgeting brought me out of my daze. It was a dagger. I blinked up at them and then back down at the weapon. It was beautiful, certainly, the hilt light and simple silver, twisted up with gold and carved with sigils. The kind I might expect to see falling out of Callum's closet collection of weapons. What I didn't understand was why they were gifting it to me.

"I told you he would rather have a paintbrush," Callum said, smiling at me.

"It's very impressive," I said, realizing that Joanna's excitement at presenting the gift was starting to wilt under my confusion. "I'm not certain I... know what to do with it."

"The sigils will keep you safe around any reluctant Ancient," Joanna said as I stepped closer and lifted the dagger from Callum's hands with all the confidence of a skittish child. "And it doesn't *have* to be a dagger."

She took it from my nervous grasp, squinted slightly, and I

watched the delicate blade and hilt transforming into a pen as she slid it into my coat pocket.

"Now just make sure you keep thinking of it as a pen until you'd like it to be something else," Callum cautioned.

My eyes widened, gaze falling down into the dark hollow of my pocket, seeing the ornate silver pen gleam. "You made that? With words?" I asked them, all caution washed beneath awe.

"We've been experimenting," Callum said, shrugging. "It should help dull any influence."

"Then you should keep it," I rushed out.

Callum's hands caught mine before I could grab the pen to return it to them, his fingers squeezing and drawing me to his chest. "We'll make more. Keep it," he said, and then he was leaning in for a brief, tender kiss. His head turned, lips pressed to my ear. "And don't be afraid to use it if you need to," he said.

I frowned at the thought, knowing he didn't mean for me to use the pen to write with. No matter how it was disguised, and what protection it might offer, Callum had designed it as a weapon first and foremost. He moved away before I could answer and Joanna was in his place, arms wrapping around my neck and body leaning in. She hugged me tight and I ignored my troubled, turning thoughts, lifting my hand up to her neck and turning her face to mine, drawing her into a long kiss until she was heavy and relaxed in my arms.

"Take care of them for me," I said, leaving another brief kiss at the tip of her nose.

She hummed her agreement and an ache in my chest eased at the flicker of stubborn refusal I saw sweep across her eyes as her fists dug into the shoulders of my shirt. She would release me in a moment, kiss me goodbye once more, but the brief glimpse of her mind changing, of her thinking of asking me to stay, was enough reassurance.

"We'll come back with help, put them back in their cages, and then we shall have ourselves a very peaceful few weeks before summer is over," I said.

Joanna nodded, lips twitching and hands unclenching. "I love you," she said, and then she kissed me once more and stepped away.

'Better hurry,' Bryce announced from the border. They stepped over and for a brief second there were two of them. The glorious, golden, griffin-like beast, and the diminutive and wonderfully familiar monster I was so used to. And then the Ancient form was gone and there was Bryce Gast, slender and pale and undefinable, hair ever so slightly more golden than I remembered.

Hildy was on their heels and I followed after, as Gwen and Tatsuo crossed for brief, tight embraces around Bryce in their human form. My coven stood side by side in the woods, the light strange and dappled as rain continued to trickle through gaps, coaxing Joanna's hair into dark ringlets.

"Get home," I said to them. I didn't want to think of them caught by Warfare or Terror just for a sentimental last glimpse of one another.

"Same to you," Callum said with a tight smile.

I crossed out of the boundary as Gwen and Tatsuo passed me with a nod. My magic hovered under my skin, like the pins and needles of a waking limb, and I resisted the urge to reach for my sketchbook in my bag. In my pocket, Joanna and Callum's silver pen burned bright like a star, so heavily burdened with Scrivens and Enmarian magic I thought it might turn out more like a beacon for trouble than a shield against it.

5

———

ISAAC

I STARTLED IN MY SEAT, TEARING MY SHOULDER OUT OF THE GRASP THAT woke me. The roar of the train on the tracks bled into the memory of the dream, the growling whisper in my ear and the stench of beer in my face dissolving into reality. Hildy stood at my side, eyes wide and hands raised in reassurance.

"I'm sorry," she said. "You wouldn't wake."

"Funny dream." It hadn't been funny at all, but painfully familiar. I cleared my throat and shook my head, clearing the memories out of their cobwebs and rolling the tension out of my shoulders. "Are we there?"

"Nearly," she said with a half-smile. Her eyes were picking me apart, like I was one of her designs, refusing to meet correctly at the seams. I nodded at her, forcing my face into its usual benign expression.

"Alright. I'm ready. Didn't mean to nap, really," I said with a laughing huff.

We'd hiked over to the next town and caught a train south, although when I'd asked Bryce what direction we were going in they'd only answered, "The right one."

"We haven't really gone far," Hildy said, frowning and glancing out the window.

I'd thought we were getting sleeper rooms because we were headed all the way to the coast, but judging by the direction of the sun outside my window, it had probably only been a few hours. Hildy looked somewhat disheveled, her hair down from its previous knot and her dress a little less crisp in its edges. I smiled to myself as I realized why Bryce had insisted on separate compartments. I'd want the same if any of my covenmates had just been restored to their own lovely forms.

The countryside began to slow in its streak past my window and I reached up to grab my bag down from the rack overhead. "I'll meet you in the hall as we stop."

She nodded and ducked out of my compartment. I dug into my bag, pulling out my coven notebook. The pages were more than halfway full now with love notes and urgent messages and teasing. On the freshest page there were already new words waiting for me.

Miss you already, from Joanna, followed quickly by her scribble of, *Don't let Bryce bully you. They like a bit of push back.*

Callum had written only, *oh if you could see Aiden's moping.*

And Aiden had answered with, *I love you and I've forgotten how long I leave a roast in the oven.*

I laughed, the sound a little watery, and my fingers brushed the pen in my pocket before the magic sparked against my fingers and I remembered that it was a weapon more than a writing utensil. I dug a pencil out of my bag and answered the messages, hesitating over what to say for myself.

I settled on, *May Bryce know many helpful Ancients in a very close range. I want to be home again as soon as I can.*

It was true, although even more than being home, now I wanted to be home and have everything be *right* again. If I could help that happen it would be worth staying away. Glancing at Aiden's note I added to mine. *One hour, let it rest for twenty minutes, don't cut it just to check if it's done.*

The train slowed to a stop in a small country station that looked as if it might have been Hammish or one of the other little villages from near home. It sent a little sliver of ice through my heart as I left the compartment, the nightmare Hildy had roused me out of still too close in my thoughts. My friends were waiting at the end of the hall for me, ready to disembark.

"Who are you taking us to see?" I asked Bryce who was standing perfectly still, nose to the door and unnerving the car guard.

"An old friend. If they're still here," Bryce said with a shrug.

I looked to Hildy but her lips only pressed together in a poor attempt to hide her smile and she shrugged one shoulder in an imitation of her covenmate.

"If? You didn't think to check before we left?"

Bryce turned their head to stare at me. They'd kept their hawk eyes and their hair was a brighter gold shade than before and almost feathery, as if after spending so many weeks in their other form they'd grown accustomed to certain features and decided to keep them. Or maybe they just enjoyed the way those smooth yellow irises made the rest of us twitch.

"I told you. They're solitary. Not the sort to stay in touch."

"But you think they'll be here, or else we wouldn't have come," Hildy said, balancing between pride in Bryce and reassurance for me.

"He was…rooted when I met him. I doubt he decided to leave," Bryce said, flashing their teeth as we stopped, the train releasing a great exhale of mechanical groans and steam.

The guard opened the door and we stepped down to the platform, my nerves easing as I realized that no, wherever we were was not like Hammish. It was busier and the people passing us looked more like the kind who came to Canderfey than the farming folk of where I'd grown up. I followed Bryce and Hildy out of the station and up to the bustling town full of red brick buildings and smiling foot traffic.

"I hope you don't mind a walk," Bryce said.

"I don't mind a walk if we stop and eat first," Hildy said, eyeing the restaurants with a unique kind of greed. "It's been ages since we've eaten without worrying about rations."

She was right, I was starving and we were finally somewhere *safe*, out walking amongst other people.

The whole thing struck me as wrong, a sharp *clang!* of discomfort in my bones. Rushes of frustration, of anger, rose up inside me. My coven was as good as trapped inside Canderfey spending every waking moment—and in Callum's case some of the sleeping ones too, I suspected—trying to ensure the safety of everyone outside of the boundary. Mystery's cage had already unravelled. What would it mean for the world if Warfare's did too?

Yet here, less than a day's ride away from the trouble, no one seemed to notice. To care.

I understood, of course. It was one thing to hear the strange news and another to feel the weight of it on your back, Terror's claws digging into your bones. Maybe these people spared five minutes of their day thinking of it, maybe an hour. It wouldn't be real unless we failed and the Ancients were loose, and I knew my coven didn't intend to fail.

Bryce stopped ahead of me on the road, staring at my frown as Hildy peered into shop windows, her smile bright. "We'll eat on the way," Bryce said.

Hildy spun, lips parted to object, but Bryce's gaze cut to her, stern and sharp. I'd always considered Bryce Gast an intimidating person. They resonated with magic, skin shining with it, and there was an unpredictable energy running through them, warning anyone who stepped too close. But I'd never seen them wield that energy with their coven before.

Hildy's pout vanished and her excitement settled into focus. She nodded and then pointed across the street. "There's a little sandwich shop there that should suit us for the walk."

THE SUN WAS ALMOST TUCKED beneath the horizon and we'd walked for so long and so far out of town I wondered why we bothered with the train stop at all. We were journeying deeper and deeper into the country until there wasn't a building in sight all around us. Hildy kept sucking in long, deep breaths and then holding them in her chest, sighs constrained as if we couldn't tell how weary she already was of walking.

The earth was sandier and rockier this far south, although we were still miles and miles from the coast, the fields around us weedy and sparse. The ground was beginning to slope down and every step felt a little like falling, but at least the direction made our momentum continue. My back ached and my shirt was sticky with sweat against my spine, even the setting sun made my skin flush with summer heat.

I'd asked earlier how far we had to walk, long after I thought we'd have arrived, and Bryce had said they didn't remember how long a walk from one hundred years ago took.

One hundred years. Wherever we were headed, would it even still be standing?

Bryce stopped at an outcropping of rock, and I shifted the bag on my back, sharing a brief glance at Hildy, who swept damp hair away from her face and swatted away one of the many flies that had taken to following us on our travels.

"Not far now," Bryce announced, patting the rock with slender fingers.

Hildy's reserve of calm broke as Bryce dove into the high grasses and started marching northwest through the field.

"Oh Bryce, honestly, you left this part out on purpose," Hildy snapped, hands on her hips.

I ducked my head, hiding my smile and started after Bryce, who called back, "There used to be a path. Now there's not."

"Well, if there used to be a house and now there's not, we're going to be rethinking who's in charge of planning," Hildy growled and then I heard her boots stomping down through the grass as she followed after us.

"Watch out for snakes," Bryce said, just loud enough to be heard.

"You better sleep with one eye open, beast," Hildy muttered, and Bryce snorted.

I missed my coven. I wished Joanna was here with me to enjoy the spectacle of Hildy and Bryce's bickering. I wished Aiden was at my side complaining every bit as much about his dress shoes and Callum was tramping around, catching up on all the magic he'd missed for the past few weeks, trying to keep us all comfortable.

The sky was bleeding red along its edge and soon we'd be walking in the dark. There was a shadowy line of trees ahead of us, growing taller and denser until it looked like a jagged, black wall in front of us.

"The house is just past those trees," Bryce said. They stopped as they reached the overgrown brush row of trees and weeds and bushes that'd been left to their own devices instead of mowed and tended like the nearby fields. Bryce tilted their face up to the tops of the trees, eyelids shutting and dimming their eerie glow. "Feels like he's still here. Come on."

Hildy held in her irritation as she wrestled herself through a thick border of bushes, Bryce returning to her side to help her through. Their hands stayed linked as they continued forward.

I turned to face the clearing we'd walked into. There was, in fact, a house. A cozy-looking stone building, with a small horse stable and an old-fashioned well on the side of the house. There was a chimney piping out smoke and a glow in the windows of the first story.

"I just hope they have a guest room or two because we are not walking back to town tonight," Hildy said softly, but her smile had sweetened and her shoulder was leaning into Bryce's side.

I wasn't sure if it was relief that the hours of walking hadn't been for nothing, or anxiety at the thought of how this Ancient might receive us, but something about the stillness in the clearing left me uneasy. It was like being back inside the boundary at Canderfey, the sense that we were standing in a place cloaked in magic.

The door opened and a figure stood, backlit by the warm light of the house. He was as tall as the doorway and half as narrow. He slouched in the light, legs and arms a handful of angles. My hand twitched for the pen in my pocket and I felt the weight of its transformation tugging on my pocket before I wrapped my fingers around the hilt of the dagger I'd transformed it back into.

"Shift it back," Bryce whispered to me.

I did, shocked at the impulse to reach for a weapon, and then Bryce nodded and started forward to the house.

"You ghastly thing," the man in the doorway drawled, head bobbing in time with his words. "You're back."

"You said I would be," Bryce answered.

He was easier to see by the light, drowsy eyes and wispy hair and cheekbones that jutted out from his long face. Grandfatherly, almost, if not for the way his lips pursed in question at the sight of us, dark eyes narrowing with a light in them like stoking coals. He didn't move out of the doorway to let us in either.

"This is Hildy Samanta, my covenmate," Bryce said.

"Not the old coven," the man said, head tilting, and wariness prickled up my spine.

Bryce's gaze narrowed back but Hildy only smiled her professionally gracious smile—flushed cheeks and flyaway hairs and all. "No, I'm one of the new lot," she answered easily. "And this is our friend, Isaac Metclaffe."

"Isaac, meet Anger," Bryce said.

Anger. Bryce had brought us to Anger? I could almost feel Terror and it's spiny legs scuttling in my heart, my body bracing away from the news.

The old man smiled as my spine straightened and my muscles stiffened.

"Well you all look like you could use a soft chair and a cold glass. Come in," he said.

Bryce followed Anger into the little house, lamps lighting up a small sitting room that looked better suited to Adele than an Ancient. I stared at Hildy and she squeezed my arm.

"I trust them," she whispered, nodding once. She stepped inside and for a moment I was left there in the dark, wondering if I could find my way back to Canderfey, to my coven and the Ancients who were at least confined to their monstrous forms and limited influence.

"Well, lad? In or out. Don't let the bugs in," Anger called, cheerful and snapping.

AT FIRST GLANCE Anger didn't fit his... his purpose? It wasn't his name, really. That was some secret and strange old language of symbols.

I waited for him to yell, to throw us out into the woods and chase us away, fire in his eyes and strength in flying fists. It was the kind of anger I'd grown up oppressed under, constantly on the watch for, skirting away from with careful words and hunched shoulders. Instead, Anger led us to soft armchairs, the perfect number sitting together in the front room as if they'd been waiting for us. He brought us icy glasses of water, his head bowed to keep from brushing against the low ceiling of his own home. He even pushed a little footstool over to Hildy's seat with a gentle smile.

"So the cages finally rusted, hmm?" he asked us, lowering himself into his own chair, a lumpy looking thing that was so low to the floor it left his knees almost as high as his shoulders. It looked as if it could have been as old as he was.

"You heard?" Bryce asked.

"Felt it," Anger said with a nod. "I don't bother with towns if I don't have to and no one's found me out here who wasn't meant to yet."

Hildy was toeing off her boots, body easing into her own velvet seat, and I could see the weariness of the road rolling off her in Anger's cozy little sitting room. I sat, tense and ready to spring, in my own chair, although it was so comfortable that every second passing made it harder not to sag into the cushions.

"We'd like to put them back into those cages," Hildy said. "Without sacrificing all of Canderfey in the process."

"We found Illness' true name and fashioned a new cage for the moment," I said and resisted the urge to flinch as Anger turned his attention to me, black gaze still shining with hidden heat. "If we knew the others' we might be able to restrain them too."

Anger smiled at me and it was docile and almost dotty. "Oh, if I had any names to offer, my own would be under a pen just as quickly.

I don't know how your kind learned them in the first place, but it wasn't by asking siblings."

"We want to find more of the Family," Bryce said, and the hairs on the back of my neck rose at the name.

Bryce was tight-lipped about the Ancients, unwilling to share more about their race. I'd heard the Ancients refer to each other as siblings and knew Warfare considered Bryce lesser in some fashion. But to think of the Ancients as a Family, with who knew how many members, was a chilling realization.

"Haven't you kept in touch with your… sires?" Anger asked.

Bryce blinked and then shrugged. "They're too far. We need ones on the continent. Or near enough to travel quickly."

Anger's lips pursed again, long knobby fingers reaching and curving around a narrow jaw. "You're asking us to fight our own kind."

"Only the willing," Bryce answered quickly.

Anger made a choking, huffing sound which was probably meant as a laugh. He sighed and stared at each of us in turn for a long stretch of quiet, and then turned back to Bryce. "You came here because I have a soft spot for you," he said, bushy gray eyebrows lifting on his face. "Yes?"

Bryce didn't smile or preen the way anyone else might have. "Yes."

"And you know every door will slam in your face if you go without a Sibling."

Bryce's eyes blinked slowly and for a moment, anger was a taste in the air, hot and metallic. "Yes," Bryce said, slower.

"So ask me your question, Ghastly," Anger said.

Ghastly, I realized, was a name for Bryce, not a teasing barb. Gast.

"Will you fight the Ancients for me, my coven, and my…friends?" Bryce asked, hands poised on their knees, spine straight, and a heavy weight in the words falling from their tongue.

"Of course I will," Anger answered, voice lowering. "I have a bone to pick with Brother Warfare." And then he laughed, and no matter how cheerful and genial it sounded, it left dread churning in my gut.

6

———

CALLUM

I SNUCK BACK BENEATH THE SHEETS, TRYING NOT TO WAKE JOANNA AND Aiden. I held my breath, hoping to land so slowly on the mattress she wouldn't even feel me. Her smooth back was facing me, chest pressed to Aiden's side, one breast smushed against his dark skin and making my fingers itch to touch them both.

"You've been out of bed," she whispered.

The sun hadn't risen and the room was still dark. Joanna didn't move an inch aside from the soft blink of her eye, lashes brushing her cheek. At least if she was already awake I could press close without worrying about rousing her.

"Just to the bathroom," I said.

"Liar."

I grinned and ran my hand down her arm that crossed over Aiden's chest, lowering my head to the curve where her neck met her shoulder. Her hair had grown a little since she'd shorn it off after nearly setting herself on fire. I grinned as it crowded my face, curls teasing against my nose and lips as I peppered kisses over her skin.

"Did you find anything useful?" she asked, turning her head into her pillow to offer me more terrain.

"No," I breathed. "Another dead end. I woke up thinking I was a genius though."

"Mm, you usually do," she said and my heart swelled at the sound of the smile in her voice.

"I know we're essentially under attack every hour of every day," Aiden said, words thick and gravelly with sleep, brow furrowing and eyes refusing to open. "But does that mean you both must wake up so damned early?"

Joanna tried to muffle her laugh against the skin of Aiden's shoulder and I caught his lips twitching at the sound.

"I did find word from Isaac though," I said, snatching both their attention in one easy sentence. "He's fine. Bryce led them on what sounds like a joke of a journey, but they're at the home of an Ancient."

Joanna's shoulder pushed against my chest, rolling to face me. Aiden rubbed sleep out of his eyes, grimacing and following close at Joanna's back.

"Which one?" she asked, eyes wide.

I brushed back a lock of hair from her cheek that was waiting to fall in her eyes. "Anger."

She frowned and Aiden's eyes finally opened, wide and worried.

"That's why he felt so tense last night," Aiden said.

"Is he alright?"

I nodded. "Anger agreed to help them. Isaac said he's not what you would expect. I can tell he's still cautious, but I'd ask him to be if he wasn't, so that's alright."

"I wish we could have gone together," Joanna murmured. She pressed her forehead to my chest and Aiden and I wrapped ourselves tighter around her until we were embracing each other too.

"I considered it," I admitted, "but I think Warfare would've taken our absence as an opportunity." I certainly would have, and if Warfare's claim from so many weeks ago was to be believed, I was his descendant. I wished that meant I was capable of coming up with a solution to defeat him, but so far I'd failed at producing anything truly useful. I would just keep brewing ideas until something worked or we had new information.

One of those ideas now needed addressing. "In the meantime, I was thinking it might be smart to call in more assistance."

Joanna's head shook against my chest. "I don't want to risk anyone else's safety. It's bad enough that the Scrivens are here. I've been thinking of sending my family out to see my father. And Bekka and her parents. Anyone who feels ready to leave."

Aiden's hand wrapped around Joanna's shoulder, fingers brushing briefly against my own chest as our eyes met above her head. "My fathers will help anyone who needs somewhere to stay. It might be for the best to have them leave. At least until Isaac gets back and we know what to do."

"I've been trying to come up with ways to find more true names," I said and then winced. Fool mouth. I hadn't wanted to tell them the plan brewing at the back of my thoughts.

Joanna's head tilted back, face twisted in confusion. "You didn't say anything."

"He didn't think we'd like what he had to say," Aiden said, words gritty, at the edge of a growl.

My eyebrows raised, shoulders drawing up to my ears. "It's just… we do know *one* way of finding their names."

Aiden rolled to his back with a groan and Joanna sat straight up in bed, nearly kneeing me in the groin as she shifted. I was momentarily distracted by the sight of her breasts, soft lines pressed in from the bedsheet, and perfectly at eye level.

"Uncross your eyes. You said that was out of the question. You barely let me do it the first time and only gave in because the link to the Hollow was already formed," Joanna said, voice raising and turning blade sharp. I thought I caught Aiden smirking, pleased to be the one of out of Joanna's firing range for once. Not that Joanna and Aiden hadn't recently found ways of making their bickering a game between the two of them.

"Would it even work? There aren't any links formed now," Aiden pointed out.

My eyes shifted sideways and Joanna bristled in front of me. "You're researching ways to *create* links aren't you, Callum Pike?"

I pushed up from the mattress and wished I'd been more careful about waking them up when I'd returned. I hadn't planned on sharing these secret plans quite so soon.

"Only as a last resort."

"Do you know how risky that is?" Joanna hissed.

I arched an eyebrow at her. "I remember very clearly how terrified I was for you when you used that link."

"And I remember exactly how close I was to letting Starvation destroy me," Joanna snapped back.

My heart stopped in my chest and my mouth hung lamely open. Twin spots of red appeared at the top of Joanna's cheeks and her eyes shied away. Aiden's chest rose with a deep breath and then he sat up and kissed Joanna's spine, leaving his lips pressed to her skin until she relaxed with a shuddering sigh.

He slid out of bed. "I'll go make the coffee and feed the beasts."

I waited for Aiden to leave the room and for Joanna to speak again, but she remained still, chin tucked and cheeks blushing.

"You told us what happened, that the Hollow presented itself as us, tried to convince you that we were…" That she wasn't enough for us, that we were abandoning her. It was unthinkable. "You never said you almost believed it."

"I *did* believe it," Joanna whispered. I shuffled closer to her, bent until I could see the slight shimmer hanging at the edge of her eyes. "Part of me did. I chose to listen to the other part."

"Joanna." My heart ached and the bruising spread through my chest, into my lungs and up to my tongue. I reached a hand up, some of the pain softening as her cheek turned into the touch, her eyes shutting before the waiting tears could slip free. "You know that we would never…"

"I do, really," she said, nodding. She blinked rapidly and raised her eyes to mine. "I do. There's… maybe a little part of my brain that still lets those doubts eat up room. I promise it gets smaller every day." She lifted her own hand to mine, drawing our fingers together. I wrapped my other arm around her and drew her to my chest, her legs wrapping around my waist until we were as close as we could be in the awkward position.

"It isn't easy to separate yourself from them once the link is there," Joanna said. "I found the name by luck more than anything else and—"

"It was only an idea," I said, soothing my hand down her back.

Joanna leaned back, gathering a soft smile on her face before saying, "I did make it look easy."

I laughed and turned us, planting my feet on the floor. "Come shower with me." I stood, Joanna wrapped around my front, her arms tightening around my neck as I grunted and stood. I squeezed two handfuls of her ass in my hands, grinning as her breath caught and her eyes narrowed. Aiden had long since won the argument of us all sleeping bare and my skin stuck pleasantly to hers where we touched.

I carried Joanna into the cool tile bathroom in my arms and only let her feet touch the floor as we stepped inside our large, open shower stall. Joanna huddled behind my back, using me as a shield as I turned the water on, the first spray too chilly.

"You know... you can tell us when you feel uncertain," I said, turning to face her, feeling the water warm against the skin of my back. Joanna's smile began to retreat and I wrapped my hands around her face, leaning down until our noses almost touched, let my eyes stray down to admire her naked skin. "We're more than happy to reassure you of our love."

Joanna laughed at that, tipping her chin up to be kissed. I accepted the invitation greedily, my hands stroking back to her neck, over her shoulders and down her spine to pull her against me, let her feel my cock stirring at her closeness. Her lips parted and I followed quickly, enjoying the tease of our tongues together, the flavor of her in my mouth again. It had only been hours, I realized, my smile spreading and distracting me from the kiss. She leaned away to catch her breath, gaze tender.

"I know you and Aide and Isaac would argue reason with me if you could," Joanna said. "I promise I fight any worries away on my own. I'm really the only one who can."

She let me turn her until the spray of water was making her hair dark and heavy, water running rivulets in tempting paths over her skin.

"All the same, I feel a responsibility in showing you now," I said. And while I was tempted to drop to my knees and offer my affection in a decidedly more explicit manner, I settled for reaching for the little bottle of Isaac's posh shampoo we all liked to steal.

Joanna moaned as I dug lathered fingers into her damp hair, scratching my nails into the roots at the back of her head, working my way up. She purred and desire won out for a moment, my head dipping and the tip of my tongue licking up the water that ran down her neck until it tasted soapy and bitter. I drew back, rinsing one hand in water before running careful fingers around Joanna's face, keeping any shampoo from dripping into her closed eyes.

All the tension in Joanna's expression softened as I washed her hair until she looked like she was almost sleeping, except it'd been a long time since I'd seen her sleep without hints of worry on her face. I nudged her gently backwards, trying not to prod her with my cock, which was fully committed to presenting its case that there was more than one way to make our girl relax. She arched her neck, water rinsing the shampoo down the drain, and then opened her eyes, sly smile curling up her lips.

"Wash next," I said, my voice hoarse and hands ignoring the order to reach for the soap in favor of mapping the curve of her waist.

"Washing will have to wait," Joanna said, reaching between us to wrap her fingers around the base of my cock, my hips bucking against her in reflex at the gentle tug that ran through me.

She rose up on her toes, the head of my cock notching between her thighs and her eyes turning drowsy and warm. I steadied her against me, my hands cupping beneath her ass, ready to scoop her up and brace her against the wall at the first command.

"We ought to get a bit dirtier first, don't you think?" she asked, eyes wrinkling in the corners with laughter.

I narrowed my eyes, pushing forward so she walked backwards on tiptoe until her shoulders hit the tile wall, shivering at the contrast in temperature.

"You're trying to distract me from my goal," I said.

"What was that again?"

"Appreciating you," I said, hands smoothing around to her hips and pressing them away from mine to help me avoid the temptation she presented. I arched forward, shower running down my back, and trailed open mouthed kisses down Joanna's throat, paying special attention to the spot over her pulse that always left her trembling.

"I don't see why we can't appreciate each other," Joanna said, and I reveled in the breathy tone her voice was taking.

"I'm sure you'll appreciate me by the time I'm done," I said, laughing and sinking down to my knees, hands running up to tease at her breasts. I nipped and kissed across her hips, waiting for her to start her sweet pleading. She knew those whimpers had her coven wrapped around her finger.

I paused in my goal, Joanna's belly button eye level, and pressed my lips to the skin of her stomach before gazing up at her.

"Whatever doubts sneak in, there are no spells, no words, and no beasts that can shake the faith I have in you," I said, watching as Joanna's lip trembled and her hands covered mine on her hips. "We are unbreakable now that we have you, Joanna."

"Hush," she said, voice breaking. Our grins spread and I kissed her skin once more before lifting her thigh over my shoulder, drawing out her laugh as she gripped me tight for balance.

⊛

"Can you mimic the magic without knowing its exact structure?" Elizabeth Bonde asked me.

She was just outside the boundary, crouched in the grass in front of the spot where Mystery's cage had come loose. I hadn't had much respect for the woman while she was serving under Anders, but since his death and the Ancients' siege—if it could be called as much—she'd proven herself not only a keen commander of the remaining staff, but a fair hand at any kind of magic. I suspected she was what kept the wheels of the University turning while Anders had played the face of the leadership. She might be interim President now, but she'd be promoted before the end of her first year.

I flicked at a loose thread in front of me, but there was no response from the magic and no flicker of power inside of me. "Not from this side," I told Elizabeth. "What I need is a way to discover if this is happening anywhere else on the boundary."

Behind me, Daniel's pacing quickened, his boots stomping noisily over the same circular terrain of the woods. Myles told me it was a good day for Daniel, and he'd been chatty when I met him at the Scrivens house, but the longer we lingered at the border, the more restless he became. I looked up and Elizabeth's eyes were fixed to the man, her brow furrowing with worry.

"Should we switch places?" she asked me.

"Are you getting any sense of usefulness?"

She frowned and reached out to touch the cage, shaking her head. "No, as soon as I touch a strand it wipes any magical sensory I might use. And without touching all I feel is… well, that it's an irritatingly powerful and cryptic kind of magic."

I grunted my agreement and then stilled as Daniel began to mutter in Vermenian, still pacing. I turned in place, studying the other man for a moment. His shoulders were up near his ears, gray and dull brown hair rumpled with agitation, his eyes flicking through the woods, never landing anywhere for more than a second.

"Perhaps we should get back," Elizabeth said softly. "At least we know none of the other Ancients can escape out the same spot."

I raised my hand to stop her from stepping through, my eyes fixed on Daniel. He hadn't looked in our direction yet, his feet pausing every other breath and his back hunching as he stared through the trees.

"Stay outside the boundary," I said to Elizabeth, keeping my voice lowered. "I think we aren't alone. Daniel? Is everything alright?" I repeated the question in broken Vermenian and Daniel twitched, his pacing breaking away from his previous circle, moving deeper into the woods. I followed him with soft steps, trying to catch any sense in the flurry of words, but they slurred together, tumbling out in an uneven pace.

"I should get one of the others," Elizabeth whispered.

"No, I don't know which of them we're dealing with yet. We don't know that you wouldn't be caught too."

My heart drummed in my chest and I picked up my sword from the forest floor. Joanna had written protections into the blade and hilt with my help, but it wasn't the same as the magic I was used to and now craved having back again. As much as I now trained with the weapons I'd only studied before, my skills were in strategy not combat.

"Daniel, *es hamman*," I said. It's fine. It's fine. Safe. "*Besvigich.*"

Daniel's steps slowed, but his back heaved with heavy breaths. I knew these symptoms, had experienced them after witnessing the battlefields I'd built for my father and seen them in the men who returned home from the war I'd orchestrated. Daniel wasn't here in the woods with us and I wasn't entirely sure how to draw him back.

"Daniel," I said, keeping my voice gentle, hoping he would turn and see me, let me draw him back into our surroundings, dangerous as they were in this moment.

There was a prickling at my back and to the right, but with the sword in my hand and Joanna's magic keeping my head clear I understood the feeling for what it was. Not suspicion with Elizabeth or Daniel. Suspicion, the Ancient, black feathers no doubt hanging from a tree branch overhead of us, flooding our minds with its influence. Ahead of Daniel there was a spike of Terror too, trying to dig its way into my heart. The pair were a potent combination for a man like Daniel. For a man like me too, for that matter.

"Daniel es Callum," I said. "We're in Canderfey. We're safe." Which was not really true and he must have known that. I kept my breaths even, holding onto calm and not wanting to worry my coven through the bond.

Daniel's feet stopped, back straightening, and for a moment I thought I'd reached him. Then he turned, face red and tangled with so much fear it had pushed him to rage. He was a soldier, if only by force, and he knew how to transform Terror into a personal defense, to fight against what he feared.

"Callum," Elizabeth called, warning laced with worry.

"Stay where you are," I called, raising my free hand again.

It was a mistake, my body twisting slightly away from Daniel, sunlight falling through branches to bounce off the blade of my sword. I was armed and all Daniel saw in that moment was the threat of me. I tried to pull it back, hide it behind me, but it was too late.

Daniel snarled, heels lifting and arms tense and wide at his side ready to charge. If I defended myself, Daniel would be harmed or worse. If I dropped the sword, Suspicion and Terror would have two victims.

"Daniel, es Callum. It's alright. You're safe, Daniel," I said, trying to hunch, to make myself small and unthreatening.

It was too late. Daniel charged and I braced myself, slamming the coven bond shut before I was thrown to the ground.

7

JOANNA

"I FEEL AS IF WE'RE READING THE ENTIRE LIBRARY," I SAID, FLIPPING A book shut. "And I can't believe I'm saying that as a complaint."

Gwen snorted, sitting across from me in the rounded window of the Scrivens house, another text laying open in her own lap. "It would be more enjoyable if it hadn't proven so fruitless thus far."

"I suppose it's an interesting experiment for my studies. How many different directions can I take the concept of Jealousy in the hopes of finding information on an ancient mystical embodiment of the feeling." I glanced at the stack of books waiting for me on the side table and sighed, the prospect of reading for once a burden instead of a pleasure.

"The University has a limited collection of romance novels, but I'm sure plenty of them touch on the subject at some point," Gwen mused with a humored glance.

Most days it felt as if we lifted every book off a shelf and scoured it for clues. I'd taken to skim reading, a despicable habit, in the hopes of finding my way to something useful sooner.

"You're doing very well in your studies by the way," Gwen said, eyes on her page as she flicked it to the next.

Well, that did make me feel a little better.

793

"And now you'll have the advantage of knowing the entire catalog," she added in a tease. "None of the other clerks can boast that."

I laughed and reached for the next book, taking the break to reach down the covenbond in search of the others. Aiden was well, at home or traveling through some of the pathways I'd made in order to keep an eye on town. Isaac was distant but calm. Callum was... I frowned. Callum was closed, which wasn't unheard of but left me chewing my lip, eyes unable to focus on the page in front of me. I would keep reaching out to him. Sometimes one of us shut the bond when frustrated or irritated, to keep from affecting the others, but I didn't like that he was missing when I knew he was out in the woods.

There was a thump, muffle, thump, muffle sound coming down around the hall, the sound of Myles' footsteps and I looked up from the book, a little grateful for the interruption.

"Well?" I asked as he appeared from around the corner.

He smiled and nodded, coming to lean against the wall near me. "Irene and Adele will leave," he said. "Ella and Kristin too, if that's alright."

"Of course," I said. It might have been a risk to let some of the Scrivens leave, but I hated to ask anyone to stay who didn't want to. Speaking of which... "Gwen, do you know if Corina will want to go?"

"I was hoping so, but she said no," Gwen said, restraining her smile as Myles snorted in amusement.

"I'll tell Daniel when he gets..." Myles' voice trailed off and I looked up, watching him frown as he stared out the window. "Daniel. Daniel's..."

I followed his stare out the window and my blood froze in my veins at the sight of Daniel racing through the woods, face red and dewy with sweat, his eyes turning wildly around him. He stumbled over a fallen branch, and caught himself by planting the blade of a sword into the earth.

I stood, worry pounding through me like thunder. That was *Callum's* sword! I bumped into Myles as I pushed past him on my way to the door. Panic laced my muscles like lightning.

"Leina! Wait! He won't be himself."

I didn't care who Daniel was. I only wanted to know *where* Callum was.

"Leina!"

The door of the Scrivens house swung open and I left it hanging loose behind me as I ran out to meet Daniel, hearing Myles follow behind me as fast as he could manage with his limp.

"Where is he? What happened?!"

Daniel snarled at me, body hunching, and I resisted the urge to snarl back. "You hand that sword over to me right now!" I cried.

"Leina, hush," Myles said, hands cupping my shoulders and drawing me back before I'd launched myself at Daniel. "He's not himself."

"That sword should block any of the Ancients' influence," I hissed, struggling against my uncle.

"It's his own mind that's influencing him," Myles said gently. "Let me help him and we'll get the answers. I promise."

I dug through the bond, rattling at Callum. My arms wrapped around my waist and held myself together as Myles left me standing, placing himself between Daniel and I, his hands raised and open to reassure the frantic man. As Myles spoke to Daniel in dulcet, slow words, I reached out for Aiden in the bond. His concern echoed back immediately. He'd meet me on my hunt for Callum.

Daniel was sagging on the other side of Myles and my uncle took the sword from him at the first chance, holding it behind his back to me. I ran forward, wrapping my hand around the hilt and froze briefly at the sound of Daniel clearing his throat.

"By the tear in the border," Daniel rasped.

I nodded to him, too frightened and desperate to see Callum to say more. I spun, the woods wavering around me, until I was sure of which direction I needed, and then took off running, sword heavy in my hand.

"Leina, wait for us!"

"I'm not wasting any more time!" I answered, rushing in the direction of the border. It was less than a mile to the spot, but if I needed to I would have run to the opposite end of Canderfey, through doorways and shortcuts. Halfway there Callum roused in the bond, anxiety spiking high, and I pushed myself harder. An animal cry echoed ahead of me and then Aiden came crashing through the undergrowth on my left, eyes so wide the white showed all around his irises.

"Where?"

"Border!"

A high-pitched scream streaked through the woods, followed quickly by another until it turned into a series of brief and breathless shrieks.

"Terror has someone," Aiden whispered, a shiver in his voice.

"Get to Callum," I said. "Let me deal with the Ancients." At least I would be immune to their influence while I held the sword.

"Joanna," Aiden bit out, glaring at me, but the rest of the words died on his throat as the view ahead of us cleared.

"Do it," I snapped.

Elizabeth was writhing on the ground, crawling on her belly, trapped beneath spindling and spidery Terror. Her face was sheet white despite her shrieks, pale and shining with tears. Callum—my heart stuttered in relief as I found him. Callum was upright, braced against a tree with his back to us, the enormous black feather form of Suspicion sweeping its wings against the border, blocking Callum from dashing across to safety.

There was blood running down his neck to his shoulder from a head wound and his movements were jerky, a little like Daniel's as he ran to the Scrivens house.

"Be careful with Callum. Focus on him and not the Ancients," I said to Aiden.

"And Elizabeth?"

Getting to Elizabeth would put Aiden too close to Terror. And selfish as it was, I wanted Callum safe first. I wouldn't leave the woods without Elizabeth, but I wouldn't be able to focus until my coven-mates were out of danger.

"I'll get to her," I said.

The choice between listening to my instructions, or arguing for my safety, warred on Aiden's face. Callum bellowed, drawing both our gazes as he rushed to Suspicion before being knocked back by black talons. I ground my jaw and snatched Aiden's hand in mine, wincing as I ran past Elizabeth, still pinned and screaming. Aiden's feet dragged behind mine and I pulled hard, forcing him to follow me to Callum who was on his back, scrambling away from Suspicion, his breathing labored and uneven.

I left Aiden at Callum's side and ran between them and the Ancient.

"The way isn't open for you here," I snarled, thrusting the sword between us, the tip clipping against a black feather and making Suspicion screech. "Go back to your roost and stay away from my coven!"

I lunged forward and Suspicion's black wings—wide and airy, like a dark moth made of raven's feathers—wooshed, raising the Ancient out of reach with another layered scream. I stumbled, keeping the sword raised over my head, but Suspicion didn't dive back down again, instead flying higher and deeper into the woods.

"Joanna," Callum gasped.

I spared him a glance. His eyes were glassy and it looked like the wound on his head was still bleeding, but he was whole and safe enough for the moment. Elizabeth's scream interrupted my relief and I spun to face her. Terror had scuttled himself around to face me, furry white head and milky-pink faceted eyes watching me, flickering in an uneven tempo of blinking, so that part of his stare was always focused on me.

Interesting that one so brave has a mate so susceptible to my gifts, Wordsmith, Terror hissed in my head.

"She's not my mate, but that doesn't mean I won't attack you on her behalf," I answered.

Not this one. This one is unclaimed. No, you belong to that frightened one. His heart is as weak as a child's.

Isaac. The Ancient meant *Isaac.* A startled laugh burst from my mouth at the very thought of Isaac's heart being weak. Isaac's heart was the strongest of all of us, its rhythm was the one our whole coven beat to.

"You are a very poor judge of character," I said, and then frowned. I hated every word wasted speaking to the Ancients. It was only their version of baiting and buying time. "Let her go."

I didn't wait for Terror to comply, instead running forward with a roar and a wild swing of the sword in my hand. Terror reared back on his hind set of legs, front claws kicking and stretching for me. I ignored them, and the fear clutching at my heart, making it beat so fast I thought it might take off into the air like Suspicion. I dug the blade deep into the underbelly of Terror. Foul and sour, pale white pus spurted from the wound and Terror chattered like a hoard of crickets all singing in chorus. Aiden took the opportunity, scrambling over and dragging Elizabeth away even as she fought him, still caught in the Ancient's hysterics.

I pushed harder, a shout of pain and rage clenched behind my teeth, until my hand was slick with Terror's blood and the Ancient was toppling backwards. I pulled the sword loose, meaning to strike again, but Terror was faster, chattering and skittering away up into a tall tree, pale blood trailing after.

"By gods, you're terrifying," Callum said in appreciative awe.

My hands were shaking, my grip weak around the hilt of the sword, fingers slipping in blood. Elizabeth's screams had turned to whimpers, eyes squeezed shut where Aiden held her upright. Callum pushed himself up from the earth and approached me with slow steps, eyes watching my face.

"I'm all right," I said, but all the strength had left my voice.

"We need to get back to the Scrivens house before any of the other Ancients come to the scene," Aiden said.

I nodded and Callum reached me, arm wrapping around my waist. His own grip felt weak too, fingers digging into my side as if to reassure us both. "Not that we have any doubts of your ability to protect us," Callum murmured.

"Here," Aiden said, producing a handkerchief. He looked uncertain of which of us to hand it to. Callum's head needed it more than my soaked hands, and I didn't think a single handkerchief would leave me feeling clean after what I'd done. I nodded my head in Callum's direction and Aiden pressed the fabric to his head.

"Are you all right?" Callum whispered as we began to walk. We leaned into each other for support and Aiden was practically carrying Elizabeth Bonde as her steps slid in the grass.

"I will be. After a very hot shower."

"Not what you meant about needing to be a bit dirtier, is it?" Callum asked.

My laugh was strangled in surprise but I grinned at him, grateful for the humor to help distract from the horror. A shadow swept over the forest floor and I twitched. Suspicion had their eye on us.

"Keep moving," Callum said to us all, firm and quick as Aiden's feet stalled.

We made it back to the Scrivens house, Ancient eyes on our backs but without another altercation. I dropped the sword as soon as Callum shut the door behind us and rushed to the kitchen, barely making it in time before heaving bitter vomit into the sink.

"Joanna?" Myles called.

"'M fine," I rasped, reaching blindly for knobs to crank steaming water into the basin, washing away the sticky blood on my skin and shoving my arms under the water, wincing at the burn. I flinched as a hand settled on my spine and then forced myself to relax.

"Water or spirits?" Aiden asked softly.

"Spirits," I said. Something to rinse the taste out of my mouth. I was soaking the sleeves of my shirt in the water, but since they'd been splattered with Terror's blood too it was probably for the best.

"A little for each of you would be good, I think," Aiden said and then stepped away.

I opened my eyes again, pushing myself upright by the elbows. The kitchen was bustling at my back. Gwen had Callum seated on the edge of the table, pressing a cloth to his head wound and leaving him hissing. Irene and Nora were fussing over Elizabeth Bonde, Aiden passing them a small tea cup of potent smelling alcohol.

He returned to my side, his fingertips brushing over my shoulders. "It tore your shirt but it didn't break your skin," he said. I lifted my chin and he brought another cup up to my lips, helping me drink so I could leave my hands under the streaming water.

"Where is Daniel?" Callum asked. "It wasn't his fault."

"He's resting," Myles said. "This is a… setback for him. I'll let him know you're all safe. Leina?"

"I'm fine," I said. In truth, I felt like I might be sick again, although I couldn't say for sure why. I had no regrets about stabbing Terror. "Do you think I might have killed them?" I asked Callum.

He grimaced and Gwen pressed harder on his wound, making him squirm. "I wish it were that easy."

I nodded and Aiden offered me another sip of the drink. I shook my head. It smelled a little like gasoline under my nose and wasn't doing my stomach any favors. "I just want to get home," I murmured to him.

He nodded. "As soon as you're ready… and Gwen finishes with her patient."

"Ah! It wasn't *that* bad a wound," Callum growled.

"Don't be squeamish," Gwen snapped back.

I huffed a weak laugh and turned the water off, letting myself fall into the comfort of Aiden's chest. Rest and tea, that was what I needed.

"Write to Isaac," I said to Aiden. "He's bound to be worried."

Aiden nodded and moved away with a last kiss to the top of my head. I braced myself against the counter and waited for my stomach to make up its mind.

8

AIDEN

J OANNA APPEARED OUT OF THE BEDROOM, WRAPPED IN A TOWEL, A cloud of steam licking the air after her. Her skin was pink and tender, like she'd rubbed it near to raw in the hot water. I opened my mouth to ask if she was all right, but I'd said the words a dozen times already and she was at her breaking point, as likely to pick a fight with me as she was to burst into tears. If she wasn't all right, I wasn't helping by asking one hundred times.

"How's your arm?" Callum asked, the pair of us wrapped up in each other on the bed. We'd ducked in and out of the shower earlier and I'd been tempted to linger and wait with Joanna, but her expression had been guarded and preoccupied. Now she smiled at us, gaze softening.

She rolled her right shoulder, a faint wince on her face. "Sore."

"If I'd known you planned on such a physical approach with the Ancients, I would've had you training with me," Callum said and I jerked to glare at him.

"Don't give her ideas," I said, barely joking.

"Not sure it's my favorite method," she said. She glanced down at her towel and then at the pair of us, naked atop the sheets, and abandoned the cover into the laundry pile before climbing in after us on

Callum's other side. "How's your head?" she asked, stretching up and pressing a kiss to Callum's forehead.

Watching Joanna stretch, her soft curves going taut and tense with the motion, always sent dozens of wicked ideas through my head. Callum laughed under his breath, one hand reaching between us to cover my twitching cock, rubbing aimlessly against it as it jumped and begged against his palm.

"My head is well enough," he said.

"Well enough?" Joanna arched an eyebrow, cheek propped up in one palm, her breasts catching my gaze and making my hands itch to cup and hold and tease their fullness. "Well enough for what?"

"For whatever Aiden's cooking up in that insatiable head of his," Callum said.

"Ah. I'm the insatiable one, am I? And what were you two up to this morning while your coffee was growing cold?"

Callum hummed in thought, his hand abandoning its attentions on me in favor of dragging Joanna's thigh over his as he shimmied down the mattress to kiss her breasts. I guided one to his mouth, watching Joanna's eyes grow heavy lidded as he licked a circle around her nipple.

"It's never as good without your direction, Aide," Callum said, a smirk in the words and spreading across Joanna's lips. That was entirely flattery without truth, but I didn't mind hearing it.

"Oh is that so? Do you like my direction too, Joanna?" I purred.

Callum had his fingers between her legs and Joanna's lips were parted, breaths turning heavy as she tried to keep from squirming into the touch.

"You know I do," she said, ending with a gasp. Her hand reached out, clutching to Callum's ribs as she rolled to her back. He'd be inside her in a moment if I left them to it and I toyed with the idea of watching the pair of them together, a favorite duet that I could orchestrate, setting their pace and directing their motions.

The idea wasn't enough. I craved the same closeness after the danger in the woods, the fright of seeing Callum injured and the shock of Joanna's rage as she fought the Ancients back. They had surprised me today, for good or bad, and I wanted to surprise them in exchange. For the sake of our combined pleasure, if nothing else.

I pushed myself up, sliding off the bed to the sound of Joanna's stuttering breaths, and walked over to the cabinet where we kept the oil.

"Are your fingers wet with her, Callum?" I asked.

Joanna's eyes fluttered open, tracking my movements, smile curling as she saw what I was carrying back. I'd never been more convinced of how perfectly designed we all were for each other as the moment I'd realized Joanna was as avidly enthusiastic for watching us enjoy each other, as she was for any attention lavished upon herself.

"Yes, she's soaking them," Callum said, nuzzling his face against her breasts. Joanna blushed prettily at the praise and spread her legs wider, eyes fixed to mine, waiting for her instructions.

"Touch your hole," I said to Callum. "Use her slick to get yourself ready for me." It wouldn't be enough but it would start him and I would make sure I was plenty ready by the time he needed me. "Scoot down on the bed and put your mouth where your fingers were. Joanna, no finishing until I say."

Joanna nodded, bottom lip tucked between her teeth as Callum groaned and moved into position, face hovering over Joanna's damp pussy, as his hand reached down between his legs, past his cock and sac to his asshole.

"Spread your legs." I meant the words for him, but I grinned when they both obeyed, the inner muscles of Joanna's thighs taut and stretched as her heels dug into the mattress. I poured oil into the palm of my hand, reaching down to stroke myself, and then dribbled a little more between Callum's cheeks to help him stretch himself. He wouldn't get very deep from that angle, but the initial stretch would do the trick.

Callum was licking around the edges of Joanna's sex, careful not to carry her too high too fast, and the frustration of the gentle exploration turned her cheeks beautifully rosy. Her hands reached for his hair and then—remembering his injury—grabbed at his shoulders, nails digging shamelessly into his muscled back.

"That's good," I said, brushing Callum's fingers away and replacing them with my own. One pumped easily. Two and there was resistance, but also Callum's eager sounds as he rocked back against the touch. "I want you to put two fingers into Joanna. Focus on her clit with your mouth until she's ready to come and then draw back."

"You're trying to kill me," Joanna hissed, hips rolling into Callum's kiss as he slid two fingers from his other hand into her weeping cunt.

I grinned, twisting my fingers in Callum's ass, spreading and stretching him as I pumped my cock until it ached. Callum took my orders easily, lips latching around Joanna's clit, her back arching and voice crying out. She'd leave marks on his shoulders before we were over. And I'd leave my own brands around his hips, remind him that he was ours and safe. Remind *myself*.

I drew my fingers out and immediately pressed the head of my cock to his opening, gritting my teeth and running precum around his rim before pushing in past the initial tightness.

"Fuuuck," Callum sighed, cheek resting against Joanna's thigh, his brow furrowed and lips open on a pant. Joanna whimpered and wiggled and Callum stilled her with a hand around her hip. "Gods, Aiden, don't just *stop*."

I laughed, rubbing a little more oil around my length before dropping the jar to the floor and slowly churning my hips. Callum clenched gently around me, making my breath short and my eyes want to cross. His ass rocked with faint jerking motions, trying to draw me deeper. I reached my hand around his hip, ready to wrap my fingers around his cock, but he shook his head.

"Wait, no, I want to fuck her next. Is that all right?"

I was torn between laughter and flattered affection. Perhaps a bit of eager arousal too. "Fine with me. I'll be careful," I agreed, settling my hands on his hips before drawing back. Callum hissed and turned his face back to Joanna's cunt, sucking greedily at her clit and burying a moan into her as I sank back in.

"Uhn! Yes, *please*," Joanna begged, eyes seeking mine as her sweaty palms slid on Callum's skin, one heel slipping against the bed as she tried to buck.

"Not yet," I told her. I continued an agonizingly slow rhythm inside of Callum, enough to make us both tense and frustrated, as he continued to torture her at the edge of orgasm before pulling away with a gasp. I rewarded his restraint with a series of fast hard snaps, the smack of skin chorusing with Joanna's whimpers. Stars burst in my vision at the explosion of syrupy heat and spiky pleasure as my balls hit Callum's.

Joanna pressed to us her desire and need through the bond and I groaned, potent need flaring in my groin and licking up my spine. My hands were too tight on Callum's skin, but there was no pain in the covenbond, only frantic desire.

"Push her to the edge again," I rasped.

Joanna whined, trying to scoot away, but Callum hooked one of her thighs over his shoulder and buried his face into her skin, lapping noisily until Joanna was twisting on the mattress, eyes slammed shut and body arching.

"She's too close," Callum said, drawing away after a moment, and Joanna growled in frustration.

"Let me come, damn you both!"

Callum grinned and I laughed. "Fine. Don't stop, Callum, even when she begs."

It was a matter of a handful of breaths and then Joanna was bowing on the mattress, shouting praise to the roof. I closed my eyes, soaking it in, the obscene wet noises, my cock so deep in Callum I thought I could feel our hearts beating in tandem. Joanna began to plead for a break but Callum pushed her further, fingers pumping and lips sucking until soon she was clinging to him again, face torn with agonized delight.

I chased my own finish, plunging and retreating deep and quick, grinding myself closer until Callum was forced against to Joanna. He clenched around me and I bellowed, head thrown back and thighs trembling, as a spike of electric pleasure raced from the base of my spine up to my head, leaving me dizzy and breathless. I pumped my hips even as relief left me drowsy and sated, my release dribbling out and down between Callum's cheeks.

Callum's back was tense as I pulled away, resting on my heels and catching my breath. He didn't hesitate, one hand wrapping around Joanna's ankle as he rose up. She was limp, hair rumpled from tossing her head on the pillows, and she looked at Callum with a gaze begging for reprieve.

"Are you too tired?" He asked, throat tight and voice rasping.

She blinked and then grinned and shook her head, reaching for him. He kissed her lips once and then flipped her onto her belly, drawing out a squeak of surprise before spreading her legs and thrusting inside.

My jaw dropped a little and even though there was no chance I'd be ready to join them before Callum was done with her, it didn't stop the stunned appreciation. Joanna's fingers clawed at the sheets, but a moan of relief and satisfaction fell from her lips as Callum fucked her with abandon. I watched the muscles of his back churn and flex, ass clenching with every snap of his hips. They were a little different from Isaac and I, a little wilder and with more fight in them. Where I wanted to pack my coven up and carry them away to safety, Callum and Joanna wanted to battle for that safety. Even the way they worked together during sex was as hungry and animal as it was loving, the pair of them clawing for comfort between their bodies.

"Aide," Joanna breathed, and I crawled to her side, tracing my fingers over the red prints I'd left on Callum's hips and the dig of nails she'd marked on his shoulders.

Callum's eyes were half-lidded, sweat dewing on his brow and mouth still slick with Joanna's arousal. I reached my fingers into the hair at the back of his neck and drew him to me for a kiss so I could taste her on him, interrupting his rough rhythm.

"Finish her," Callum said, eyes dark on mine, his words an echo of my own order.

I laid down at Joanna's side, her gaze vacant as she moaned again, Callum shaking the bed beneath us with his urgency. I kissed her, licking into her mouth and letting her taste all of us combined. My hand burrowed beneath her hips, pinned to the mattress by their combined weight, seeking her clit clumsily.

"Oh stars, yes," she hissed as I rolled the tender little bead beneath my touch. She writhed between my hand and Callum's body, her cries stuttering in time with the sound of Callum's cock working in and out of her.

"Fuck, fuck, yes!" Callum groaned, his stomach landing against her back, the last handful of thrusts uneven and gentle until the pair of them were collapsed. My hand wiggled, fingertips still teasing Joanna, and Callum hissed through his smile as she squeezed around him. She was floating in that place where every other touch might send her over the edge and I was tempted to continue the game a little longer, but she looked beautifully ruined and a few minutes away from falling asleep.

Callum slid sideways onto the mattress, his chest heaving, hand soothing down her back. His cock rested against the back of her thigh, shining wet. I pulled my hand away from Joanna's pussy, reaching for Callum's hand on her skin.

"I'll go get a washcloth," Callum said, smiling at me, all the wild energy burned out of him again.

"And snacks," Joanna mumbled.

"And snacks," he agreed.

I scooped a limp Joanna up and settled her against my side, her head resting against my chest, one arm draped over my waist.

"I think I'm getting tired, Aiden," she whispered.

She didn't mean sleep. The declaration brought me some relief. I was proud of my ferocious covenmates, I loved them for their bravery even when it left me worried and anxious. That didn't mean I wasn't looking forward to a time where there was no call to battle they felt the urge to answer.

"Then we will have to find some time to rest, my darling," I said. She cuddled closer and I wrapped my arms around her. She was asleep before Callum returned with the tray.

I frowned, halfway between dreaming and wakefulness. The sounds of someone retching echoed from the bathroom and Callum's elbow nudged my side again.

"It's Joanna," he whispered. I peeled my eyes open, wondering if the gray light in the room meant it was dusk or dawn. Callum was sitting up in the bed, hair rumpled, one eye still squeezed shut and the other staring at the bathroom door. "Think she's sick."

There was another bout of coughing from the other side of the door and I huffed. "What makes you say so?" I asked, glaring at Callum as he flopped back down into his pillows.

He hadn't really woken up; when he did he'd be fussing over her. I rolled out of bed, legs clumsy beneath me, and grabbed my robe off a chair, wrapping it around myself as I walked to the bathroom door.

Joanna was rinsing her face in cold water as I walked in, the toilet flushing beyond her. She glanced at me out of the corner of her eye and then spit a mouthful of water down the drain.

"I'm fine," she said, voice sore and strained. She winced, bracing herself against the edge of the sink. "Maybe. I might be sick again."

"I'll make you mint tea," I said. I frowned and hesitated in the doorway. "Do you think Illness is out of the cage we made? Or that this might be a reaction to Terror's blood?"

Joanna's smile was weak. "I think it's just old fashioned stomach flu, to be honest. Tea sounds nice."

"Wha's happened?" Callum slurred, falling out of the bed and stumbling over to us, naked and eyes still squinted shut with sleep.

I held my sigh in and Joanna paled and scuttled back to the toilet, landing on her knees. "Joanna's ill. Watch her while I go get water and tea. Find her robe."

Callum grunted acknowledgement and ran to Joanna's side, smoothing her hair out of her face as her back heaved with a gagging cough. I hurried downstairs to the kitchen, trying not to feel too relieved that this meant Joanna would be off patrol duty for the night.

9

——

ISAAC

Kilburn was a port city like Rhodantis, but unlike Enmaire's sparkling seaside capitol, Kilburn was industrial and dark. There was no artist's influence in the arrangement of the streets and buildings, and while I'd smelled the brine of the sea as we approached through the narrow alleys and streets of the city, I had yet to see a glimpse of any water. A greater contrast too was the fact that Kilburn appeared to be almost wholly working class. Bryce had coaxed Hildy out of her silks and into a simple black dress and heavy coat, her long black braids tucked beneath the collar, determined for us to not stand out.

There were taverns at every street corner and not one of them appeared to lack a generous number of patrons. Locals shouted to one another out of apartment windows, their eyes tracking us, strangers, as we wove through the city.

"Keep your hands in your pockets and your eyes off any faces," Anger murmured in my ear.

I drew in on myself, not due to any fear of local thieves. Anger, upon noticing my reserve around him, had taken to keeping me company as we travelled. It didn't help that Bryce and Hildy were fit as a unit to start with. While Bryce might have trusted the older Ancient, I couldn't reconcile myself to the idea of Anger as an ally. I didn't want to bring him home to my coven and risk their safety if he couldn't be relied on to stay on our side. Why couldn't Bryce have taken us to Protection or Gentleness.

Does Gentleness really sound like the man you want in a battle? Callum's voice asked at the back of my mind.

My stomach churned in my gut, worry transforming to nausea. The smell of fish was growing so strong in the air I was tempted to cover my nose. I'd never minded the smell before but something about the heaviness of it as we walked closer to the dock made it nearly unbearable.

We continued down a crooked alley, tall black brick buildings crowding us into single file, and finally I caught a glimpse of the water, far on the horizon past the clutter of ships waiting in the bay.

"We won't be welcome visitors," Anger said as we reached the mouth of the alley, the fresh whip of wind beating away some of the heavier stink of fish from the air.

"Should we send word first?" Bryce asked.

"No," Anger scoffed. "She'll take off like a shot if we do. Better to be a surprise. Just let me lead and be ready to fight our way out."

"Fight?" Hildy asked, eyes growing wide and glancing to mine.

Sometimes being a human traveling with an Ancient seemed to involve a little less exchange of information than I would have wished.

"Who exactly are we dropping in on?" I asked.

Anger lifted two bushy eyebrows and sauntered down the salt slick cobblestones. "Secrecy," he called over his shoulder.

"That doesn't sound *so* bad," Hildy murmured to me as Bryce followed Anger ahead of us.

"Depends on how committed they are to their purpose," I said. I reached my hand into my pocket and wrapped my fingers around the pen my coven had gifted me.

Anger led us through the bustle of activity at the docks—heavy nets burdened with the morning catch and men unloading cargo from trading ships—down to a red brick warehouse with dusty, thick-paned windows. Wide garage doors were pulled open as bulky, tattooed men carried in boxes and a foreman counted inventory. We traveled past the open entry to a small side door, so narrow and thin it looked as if it'd been out of use for decades.

Anger rapped twice with his knuckles on a fragile-looking board and then turned the handle and let himself inside, the three of us following him into the murky dark.

"I can't see," Hildy whispered as softly as she could. Her hand gripped around my elbow and she bumped into my side as someone shuffled closer.

"With me," Bryce hissed to her and then I was alone in an abyss of shadow.

My fingers tightened around the pen in my hand, grip so fierce I thought I felt Joanna's words imprinting against my skin. With that scratch of magic in my palm the darkness cleared. The room was bigger than the hallway I expected, although not a great deal. I flinched as the dark cleared and I found myself startlingly close to a man at my side, a towering figure and twice as broad as me. He was surly looking, skin tattooed from his knuckles up to his chin, with greasy knots of hair hanging down to his ears. His eyes were fixed over my head and I realized he was as much in the dark as Hildy. As I had been before calling on the pen for support.

Of course. Joanna had told me it would protect me from Ancients' influence. Secrecy was cloaking the room in their power.

"Who's there?" the man in front of me grunted out, eyes squinting as if to dig me out of the heavy black surrounding us.

Hildy and Bryce were ahead of me, shuffling into the dense dark, and I hurried after them, glancing over my shoulder to see the guard —if that was what he was—gazing blindly in our direction.

"Sister, I hope you don't mind the visit," Anger called ahead.

The room was deep, another two guards stationed against the walls before I caught up with my party. A wide desk stretched across the back of the room, a figure seated behind in the dark, dim light glowing at the surface in an attempt to throw their face into shadow.

Secrecy was a plain looking woman. So plain, in fact, it was difficult to look at her for more than a second, my eyes constantly drawn elsewhere—a strange stain on the wall behind her head, a stack of papers at the edge of the desk near me, a folded map beneath her hand. What I was able to put together was a nondescript face with shoulder length hair somewhere between blonde and brown. Where Mystery drew the eye to a puzzle, Secrecy deflected my attention.

"Brother, I think you know I *do* mind," Secrecy answered, voice more pleasing than her chosen face. She spoke in a whisper that tugged at my ears, the urge to listen an itch in my thoughts. "I would have preferred a warning."

"Well, I preferred actually finding you here," Anger answered, cheerful and baiting, with just the faintest edge to the words.

"What do you want and why have you brought company?" Secrecy asked. I kept my eyes lowered as she scanned the group of us, although when she looked away I caught a glimpse of heavy lidded eyes burdened with dense black lashes.

"I've come to call in my favor," Anger said.

Secrecy leaned across the table and hissed, "*Conditional* favor, Brother. *What* do you want?"

The answer to her question was clawing at my tongue, begging to be spoken aloud, and Hildy was squirming at my side as if she were fighting the same compulsion. Our private thoughts weren't safe around this Ancient.

"The Siblings in the woods are near to escaping their confinement, Sister," Anger said, the cheer leeching out of his voice. "We should act. They risk our place in this world."

"Do you really think so?" she asked, brows lifting and hands gripping the edge of her desk. "You think the humans will come for you in your little cottage on a plot of land no one has ever written onto a map. Do you believe they will find me too, Brother? Am I such a weakling as to be chased out by little witches?"

My gaze had fixed to the map on the desk during the Ancients' conversation, the lines and muddled shapes organizing themselves in my thoughts into a familiar outline.

"It's none of my concern," Secrecy hissed, and it was a tone meant to shut the door on the argument.

"If you aren't concerned, why are you studying a map of Canderfey?" I asked.

Secrecy's body tensed like a cat that had just spotted a predator and Anger stiffened at my side. Secrecy's eyes met mine and there was a digging, scratching sensation in my head, but it was dulled and distant and I knew Joanna's magic was protecting me from Secrecy's hunt through my thoughts. The Ancient growled, face shifting into something more feline than before, and her gaze slid to Anger.

"You brought a spy into my territory?" Secrecy snarled.

Anger sighed. "He's not a *spy* you paranoid beast, he's just a fool who *doesn't know when to keep his mouth shut*," he said, the latter part spoken from the corner of his mouth and directed to me.

I swallowed, and fought the plea for help on my tongue. Prickly energy was making the air crackle around me, concentrated between Anger and Secrecy.

"If you want to keep your little operation running without inconvenient attention, it's to your best advantage to help us keep Warfare in line. He's done none of the Family any favors."

"Threats and snooping," Secrecy snapped, standing from her seat.

She wasn't much larger than Bryce but her body shone darkly in front of us, obscuring the room more deeply. Hildy gasped, eyes searching the dark as Bryce held her tightly by the waist, ready to run.

"Think with the *useful* side of your brain for once," Anger snapped, fists thumping on the desk, his namesake temper finally revealing itself.

"You've overstayed your welcome, Brother. You have seconds to leave. Your friends have less."

Bryce was already drawing Hildy back with careful steps, their eyes hunting through the dark for a safe route out. I glanced over my shoulder and found the guards stationed along the walls having moved out of position, bodies filling the narrow room to block our way out.

"You really have grown *simple* in your old age," Anger huffed, his laughter growling with irritation.

Secrecy's hiss turned to a yowl, body springing up over the desk, lamp knocked to the floor with a clatter and a swoop of light. Anger's hand fisted around my elbow, dragging me away.

"Go on, witch," Anger shouted at me. "Use that magic of yours. Mine won't do us any good in close quarters."

Secrecy was sliding in and out of the corners of shadows as we retreated on stumbling heels.

"I'm a *painter*!" I cried.

"Color magic is as good as any other!" Anger answered.

Was it? I knew how to conjure a shade without inks or oils or canvas or brushes. I'd used my magic under Callum's instruction in the past, but never without him and there was no time to focus in the panic!

Secrecy appeared too close and our bodies stumbled into the blockade of a brawny guard. The lamp was rolling back and forth on the floor behind the approaching Ancient and a strange color twisted on the wall. By instinct, and feeling deeply foolish, I held tight to the pen in my pocket with one hand. I swiped my free hand over the spot of color in my vision, a dark yellow-gray that read as hiding. It caught in my mind, a thread snagging, and I wrapped it around Anger and I, throwing it back to Bryce and Hildy too. It landed against my skin like a cloak and Anger laughed as Secrecy's stare turned loose, skidding away from us. She growled, so low it was almost silent.

"My gift," she hissed. "You use *my* gift against me?"

"Another!" Anger said, dragging me alongside him by the strap of my back. "With more punch this time!"

There was a drowsy blue dragon twining around one of the guard's arms and I lifted the color, brushing it over his eyes and dodging out of the way as he stumbled and crumpled against the wall in a dead sleep. Secrecy screeched and raced to the door as if to trap us inside.

"You chose your allies poorly, Brother," Secrecy called by the door.

"One more, put a little fire into it," Anger whispered in my ear before answering his sister. "Think on who you really want to be dealing with in the future, Sister. You've flourished in their world. How would you fare in Warfare's?"

I found the last color on Bryce's collar, a deep and vibrant red-orange, and hesitated with my hand outstretched.

"Go on," Anger urged.

Uncontrollable rage. I picked it off a little hint of pattern and flicked it right into Secrecy's eye. The Ancient screamed, body rattling against the frame of the door, muscles tensed to resist the call. All at once she was in motion, tearing through the room, hunting for us as we skidded out of her way, her body crashing into every surface, arms and legs spread and power scraping shadows through the air.

We escaped out of the doorway, Secrecy's shroud evaporating and leaving me blind to sunlight. Anger dragged us all down the dock away from his sister's warehouse, the door banging shut behind us and silence sudden on the air.

"Well that was fun," he said, laughing. "Better reception than I expected and we've given her something to think on."

Hopelessness swooped in my chest as the glare of daylight began to soften in my eyes. "We left empty handed."

"I haven't even the faintest clue what happened in there," Hildy snapped, swooping a hand over her hair.

"Your friend learned a lovely new trick," Anger said, hand clapping on my shoulder and rattling me with a strength unsuited to a gangly old man. He looked at me and winked. "A temper isn't so bad in small doses, now is it?"

I ground my teeth and looked back over my shoulder, expecting Secrecy to chase us down with that tornado of rage I'd thrown her into. But the cobblestones were only occupied by the usual business of fisherman and import.

BY THE NEXT morning I was beginning to think of Anger like a slow-developing infection. He snored in his sleep and it left me stewing in irritation deep into the night. He picked his teeth with anything thin enough to fit. He'd stolen three half-finished cups of ale in the tavern below where we rented rooms, and I was fairly sure he could be held responsible for the two bar fights that broke out during dinner. A hot, itching, binding emotion I'd worked all my life to avoid was growing a nest inside of me and it had only been three days. How many more of our searches for Ancients would turn up as fruitless as Secrecy and how long would I have to suffer Anger's company?

"Come on, lad," Anger said, clapping that hammer of a hand down onto my shoulder again after I'd finished dressing. "Bit of breakfast will do you good."

I was queasy again this morning although it was probably more to do with dealing with Anger and bottling my reactions. I followed him down to the tavern. There were still a few bodies propped up in booths, stale beer left in mugs in front of them, their snores symphonic in nature. Bryce and Hildy had taken a table near an open window, a pot of coffee on the table the most welcome sight I'd seen yet today. Hildy poured me a cup and I kissed her cheek in thanks and greeting. Behind me the tavern door opened, a colorfully dressed man in a brilliant blue cloak and comical mustache entering and heading toward the bar.

"Where are we off to next?" Hildy asked Anger as he sat next to me. "Are there any other... of your siblings here in Kilburn?"

Anger rubbed at his jaw, finger turning his coffee cup idly on its saucer, a painful ceramic scratching sound building from the treatment. Bryce smirked at my frown and I scowled into my coffee.

"None that I know of," Anger said slowly. "May be some in cities along the way to the capitol. Of course we are looking for a certain kind, ones who'd be handy in a fight. Truth be told, Secrecy has us all pegged down on one of her little maps. Yesterday could have gone better."

I swallowed a sigh. That was partly my fault, pointing out the map of Canderfey. Anger hadn't helped by goading her though either.

"Anyone care for a card trick?" The bright blue cloak slid up to our table, a dark haired man grinning beneath his twirling mustache, golden waistcoat stuffed near to bursting with a generous belly.

"Not this morning," I said, trying to soften the sharp edge in my voice.

"I love a good card trick, show us then!" Anger said, and I could feel more than hear his laughter at my expense.

The magician dragged a chair to the end of our table, plopping himself down backwards on the seat and procuring a deck of cards with a rustle and a flourish. The cards spread across the end of the table, and then back into a neat pile, squat fingers with dirty nails manipulating them in quick, swirling motions.

"This is a game of balance, you see," the magician said, voice proud and droning. "Not a simple matter of 'is this your card, good sir?' No. We are looking for the pairs who make things even."

Hildy's lips were quirked in amusement, but both Bryce and Anger had their eyes narrowed at the man, paying closer attention than I thought the showman really deserved.

"You may be thinking 'why, this fellow has a funny deck, that's all,' but here milady, I'll hand it to you and you may inspect it yourself and choose the card that suits you." He handed the deck to Hildy who turned the faces up to her private inspection. "Please reassure yourself that this is a simple, trustworthy deck. One you could find in any corner shop. And then pick your card."

Hildy drew a card free and held it to her chest, the entertainment of the game brightening her eyes. She handed the deck back to the magician with several compliments on his part, and some of the irritation that tightened my shoulders began to ease with humor.

The magician turned to me, penciled black eyebrows raising high on his forehead. "Now this young man here shall pick a card for himself *without* looking and we shall see how balanced your table is, hmm?"

"You don't have much work to do in this game, do you?" I asked and the showman's smile cracked with a real laugh for a moment.

"Go on, Isaac." Hildy said, grinning.

I grabbed a card from the middle left and glanced at it in my hand. It was a snarling black mask of a face, crown atop his head thorny and dark, eyes sinister. The Black King. I supposed that would make his balance the White Queen, by the magician's logic.

"Now, if you would please satisfy our table's curiosity by turning your cards face up for everyone to see," the magician said, a flourish of his hand over the empty space. Hildy and I turned our cards over side by side and my breath caught in pleased surprise. The Black King and White Queen laid out on the table.

"Ahh, you see. Perfect counterpoints," the magician said, voice warming and turning silky.

Anger huffed at my side. "Mystery, you slick bastard. I knew you'd show up sooner or later."

My back straightened and Bryce hunched, a low growl in the back of their throat. The magician only rested an elbow on the table, chin propped in his hand, and winked at me.

"Hello again. I was hoping it'd be your pretty covenmate who went hunting, but I suppose you'll do." There was a wobbling distortion of the magician's face and then it returned to place.

"You escaped the cage," I said. "What are you doing here?"

"Same as you, isn't it obvious?" Mystery asked, brows raising.

"Are you here on Warfare's behalf?" Bryce bit out.

"I am not," Mystery said, simple and clean. "But you'll do his work for him if you go after siblings like Secrecy and ruffle their feathers in that way. You *need* the counterpoints."

I glanced down at the two cards still lying face up and frowned.

"That lot won't be able to help against foes like Terror and Jealousy," Anger said, waving a hand in the air.

"That *lot* is the best chance against our caged siblings. And the easiest to find. Aside from Peace, of course."

Peace. Peace to Warfare. The Ancients had opposites and Mystery thought they'd be able to help us defeat Warfare and the others! I sat up sharp, the first glimpse of hope burning in my chest.

"I haven't kept in touch with them," Anger said, raising his nose in the air. Bryce narrowed their eyes on the old man, who refused to meet any of our eyes.

"You need me," Mystery said, catching my eye. "Ancients are cloaked in mystery and it happens to be my area of expertise. For instance, I know of one particularly helpful sibling who arrives in port this very afternoon. We can catch her before her next adventure if we're quick."

"Who?" I asked.

Mystery beamed at me, finger reaching to twirl that silly mustache. "Little Bravery, of course. Terror's counterpoint."

THANKFULLY THE DOCK we were waiting on was a safe distance from Secrecy's warehouse. Just as Mystery predicted, a large ship was lowering a walkway down to the dock as we arrived. Mystery had called Bravery a 'her' so I scanned the ship's deck for any female faces but all I saw were burly men like Secrecy's guards, tattooed and sunburnt and looking like they hadn't finished sleeping off the previous night's gin. Or maybe that was just the sea legs.

"Get your clumsy paws off me!" a voice squeaked. A small boy was being carried like a parcel beneath an enormous man's arm, heavy boots stomping down the walkway.

"You've picked your last pocket on this ship, you little runt."

"I'll slit you from chin to belly! I'll eat your eyeballs like gumdrops! You just wait till night, I'm gonna—"

The boy's language was darker than my father's on a bender and I wasn't sure who I was more concerned for, the frail-looking but ferocious child or the enormous man who was taking elbows and feet to some tender places.

"I present to you, Bravery," Mystery said, he and Anger both grinning.

The boy was dropped to the dock like a sack of potatoes, landing on his feet like a cat, and then out from under his hat appeared a long blonde pigtail. My eyes widened and my lips twitched. She, not *he*, stared at us with narrowed eyes, poised on her tiptoes and ready to bolt.

"Settle, Sister, we're here as friendlies," Anger said, grinning at the child.

"Whatchuwant?" she asked, words stretching together.

"We have a battle for you," Bryce said, crouching down to the balls of their feet. Bravery's chin lifted, dark blue eyes studying us each in turn, grubby hands on skinny hips.

"Brother Warfare and the others have nearly escaped their confines, Sister. Will you fight them or join them?"

Bravery strode toward us with long, loping steps, her feet kicking out ahead of her. She barely reached my hip and I had the urge to lift her up into my arms so she didn't have to crane her neck as she examined us, but she didn't look cowed to be smaller and I suppose if she wanted to she could do her fair share of damage to us.

"I'll fight with you," she said. "But only cause you asked first."

In spite of the poor promise of loyalty, I smiled. We had three Ancients, none of whom I was completely confident in, but three all the same. It was better than we'd started with at least.

10

JOANNA

"Are you sure you wouldn't rather go with them?" I asked Myles, at his side in the doorway as Irene and Adele finished gathering up the last of the possessions they would take with them to Bridgeston while staying with my family.

"I would and I wouldn't," Myles said, patting my shoulder. "I would hate to sit on my hands knowing you had a fight on yours. And I'm confident that we'll win and they'll come home soon. Unless Irene likes it too well." He winked to assure me he was joking.

Irene hadn't been happy in Canderfey when they'd first moved, but the Scrivens house—living together with the other Vermenians—seemed to turn her mood around. I'd seen her laughing and chatting a bit more every day, even with the present danger surrounding us in the woods.

"Camma, leina," Adele said and I crossed the room to her. "I found this. Should be for you, I think."

Pinched between gnarled fingers was a picture of a young girl with hair a little lighter than mine. My nose was more prominent than hers, more like my father's, but otherwise she looked a great deal like me as a child.

"My mother," I said, stroking my thumb over the image.

Adele hummed and nodded and then wrapped me up into a tight hug. "Keep it safe," she said.

"I will." I squeezed her back and then smiled as she pulled away. "Tell my father not to worry."

Adele laughed. "This is a father's work, I think. But yes."

After Aiden received final word about where the Vermenians would go, if they chose, our numbers were cut in half. Myles was staying, and Nora, which I'd expected. Corina was a surprise but even more so was Daniel. He was still skittish after the incident at the boundary, but he seemed determined to prove himself trustworthy, for his own sake if not ours. The last to decide to stay was Lora. I'd saved her and her mother from the apartment fire Suspicion had stirred up in the spring. I wasn't sure if she felt she was repaying the favor or seeking her own revenge against the Ancient, but I was glad to have her. She was a practical writer, good with Daniel, and suspicious of Corina—all qualities I admired.

"It's time," Aiden said, leaning into the room, soft creases of sympathy at the corner of his eyes.

I wrapped Adele's arm around my elbow, escorting her out of her room and to a spare cupboard door of the Scrivens house that would take us to the grocer's at the edge of town. The hall was crowded with hugging figures and my heart ached for a moment. It had been hard to say goodbye to Isaac at the boundary, but I knew nothing would stop him, Bryce, and Hildy from returning to us as soon as they were able. I was less certain if I would see some of these familiar faces again. What if they found new homes outside of Canderfey where they were more welcomed than they had been here? What if we failed to defeat the Ancients?

I pushed the melancholy thoughts away as a small hand slipped into mine. Bekka stared up at me with wide blue eyes. As Adele left my side to hug Nora, I knelt down, squeezing Bekka's hand in mine.

"I'll miss you," I said in Vermenian.

"I'll miss you," Bekka said, staring at her feet. Then her head lifted and she spoke in a rush. "Feed Lars treats from me and tell Isaac I will keep practicing while we are away."

I grinned and nodded, a shocking rush of tears rising up to my eyes as Bekka threw her arms around my neck and held me tight in her grasp. Tears were springing up often lately, not to mention the persistent bug in my stomach, and I thought it might be time to spend a day's research in the comfort of my own bed instead of running pathways through Canderfey at all hours. Exhaustion was hitting me hard and my moods were running wild in the wake.

Nora led the way through the door, Callum armed with his sword at his side. Sure enough, as if they heard our whispers through walls or sniffed us out through all of Canderfey, Warfare was visible through the wide glass windows. He was charging up the street, paws raising smoke from the brick road, Ecstasy swooping around his head, and Jealousy and Sorrow trailing behind him.

"Joanna!" Callum called, running for the front door.

"Get them across," I shouted to Aiden, his jaw clenching as he nodded. "We'll hold them off."

I pushed through the families, giving Adele a quick, shaking smile in goodbye before bolting out the door. I made it across the sidewalk, stomach flipping inside of me as I dug chalk out of my pocket, silver clinking in its depths. Callum was nearly to Warfare as I bent in half, arm stretched down to the brick. I pressed the chalk hard against the ground, drawing a heavy line across the road, careful to not let it break in any spot.

"Joanna?" Callum shouted and I heard the first clash of his sword against a leather hide, his answering 'oof.'

"Almost!" I answered, refusing to let myself be distracted by the terrifying sight of Callum battling a beast ten times his size.

I ran back to the middle of the line I'd drawn, a shivery pleasure stirring on my skin as Ecstasy flew closer.

No Ancient may cross this line by foot or feather, I wrote. It had been Corina's words and I found them a little flowery, but overhead Ecstasy screamed and I reared back to see their flight spiraling out of control, sharp claws scratching at my invisible boundary, golden wings twisting to catch the air again.

"It's working!" I screamed to Callum. I turned and waved my arms at the grocery windows, a flood of friends running out the door and to the cage boundary where six figures stood on the other side. "Don't dawdle in goodbyes," I warned them and then stood, my legs wobbly beneath me, Ecstasy still close even if she was unable to reach me.

You have such pretty pleasure, Wordsmith, she cooed to me. *And such handsome covenmates.*

I growled under my breath and she swooped away, back in the direction of Warfare, where Callum was trying to safely retreat. I had no weapon but the silver charms in my pocket and if I ran to Callum now, away from the protection of my line, I'd likely only distract him. My nails bit into my palms as I watched, heart hammering in my chest. Warfare was crouching, armored head butting against Callum with every swing of his sword, his feet skidding over the brick. Any moment and he might slip, leaving him to Warfare's mercy.

I could write another line, or test a new phrase, *anything*, but I hated leaving Callum on his own and out of reach. Aiden would murder us both if I crossed the line.

I clenched my jaw and stepped forward, but a hand caught me by the shoulder drawing me back.

"Not so fast," a gritty voice said in my ear.

I spun and nearly laughed with relief. Geoff and Sabine York stood behind me, both armed with long and deadly blades.

"Let us handle the beasts," Sabine said, eyes warm on my face, calling up a blush that I blamed on Ecstasy's influence, or giddy relief.

"Wait!" I said, before they crossed my chalk line. I dug in my pockets and drew out two silver bracelets. Geoff scowled and Sabine beamed at me.

"No one ever gets me jewelry," she said.

I ignored her tease and pushed one over her free hand and then switched to Geoff. "They'll protect you from the influences, for the most part. They can't be killed easily, if at all, but you can injure them. Worry less about that and more about driving them back until we can all get safely inside."

"I told you she's bossy," Geoff said to Sabine.

"Thank you for coming," I said, and then they were running to

Callum, Geoff scooping him up from a near slip as Sabine lunged for Jealousy's toothy smile, a matching grin on her face.

When Callum had suggested calling in reinforcements, I never imagined he meant this coven. Of all the help we had in our corner, they were the only people I was willing to drag into the mess with us. We *needed* fighters and I suspected that Sabine York craved a good fight.

Samuel and Darin were ushering the remaining residents of Canderfey back into the grocer's and I joined them at the doors, repeating my warning to them as I passed them each a silver bracelet. Corina was lingering in the doorway, batting her eyelashes at Darin. I pinched her elbow and dragged her inside with me, my eyes on Callum as he ran in our direction.

"Don't think for a second I won't bind you up so tight you can't even *think* of words, crisis or not," I hissed in her ear.

Corina rolled her eyes and shrugged me off. "Can't I even *look* at men?" She huffed and stomped her way back to the door, scrubbing off the old words I'd written to my own house and replacing them with the way back to the Scrivens house.

Callum came in after me, bells ringing behind him. One of his hands was held out in front of him, bleeding faintly, and Aiden grunted and rushed to us both. "It's only scraped from the pavement."

Sabine and her coven were across my line, Warfare hanging back but refusing to run. Ecstasy was flying high and far away from town, deep into the woods. Sorrow and Jealousy waited behind their leader.

"I can't believe Sabine came," I said. I pinched the inside of my arm as my throat tightened and *another* bout of tears tried to spring to my eyes. This was getting ridiculous.

"I plan on milking their guilt over that kidnapping any time we find ourselves in life or death situations," Callum said with a shrug.

"Any time?" Aiden groaned. "Can't this be the last?"

Darin was flipping Warfare a rude gesture with his free hand, his coven turning and walking calmly back to the grocery.

YOU ARE CLEVER, WORDSMITH. BUT THE CAGES ARE FALLING AND YOU WILL NEVER FIND OUR NAMES IN YOUR

PAGES. IT IS ONLY A MATTER OF TIME BEFORE WE ARE FREE. WILL YOU GIVE CHARMS TO ALL OF MANKIND?

I opened the door to the grocery for Sabine and the others and spoke softly to Warfare. "I am clever, and you are only good at one thing. I think I can come up with more than a few charms to stop you."

Warfare roared as the bells on the door chimed and it swung shut behind me.

"YOU REALLY DO FIND the strangest trouble to get into," Geoff said, passing me a cup of the mint tea I'd asked for.

"One of those was your fault," I muttered, lifting the cup up to my nose and taking a deep breath. The smell settled my rattled nerves and I ignored Geoff's side-eye stare, snuggling deeper into my favorite of the armchairs at the Scrivens house. Samuel, Myles, and Aiden were up to something in the kitchen and my stomach hadn't decided if it approved or not. Corina had Sabine and Darin cornered somewhere and I decided that if Sabine decided to collect the selfish girl for her coven, it would be no problem of mine.

"Do you believe what the beast said? That there's no finding their true names?" Geoff asked, his tongue unfamiliar around the last two words. Callum had caught their coven up to date, but it'd been plain on all four of the warriors' faces that they were here less for the magical puzzle and more for the chance to tackle a new kind of foe.

I sighed. "Yes. We're still looking because, well, it gives us something to do. I don't think we expect results at this point. I'm hoping that when Isaac and the others come back, they bring an Ancient back who either *does* know the names, or knows how they were found in the first place. A spell... or vision."

"You look tired," Geoff said, his keen stare studying me and ignoring my speech.

"I am, thank you," I snapped, bright heat flooding my cheeks. His eyebrows rose and I swallowed. "I... I am. It's been a long two months."

He nodded and sipped from his own mug of mead—Darin had insisted on bringing casks with them, and Myles was thoroughly grateful. "You could have sent word sooner."

I smiled, hoping it would suffice as an apology for my sudden burst of anger. "You feel that guilty for handing Callum over to Pearce?"

"Don't be a brat, you know we're friends," Geoff said, but in such a rush it was as if he didn't really want me to hear the words. I grinned at him and he growled and got up from his chair, moving quickly into the kitchen.

Callum came to take his place, bringing a heaping plate for us to share with him. I took a tentative breath and my stomach growled in hunger, thank the stars. He scooted the chair closer to mine, balancing the plate on his knees between us.

"You took your time dealing with Warfare," I said, watching him as he lifted a chicken leg to his lips, fat dripping to his fingers.

He stared back at me for a long moment and then rolled his eyes, lips quirking. "You're as bad as Aiden. I *promise* I wasn't trying to build a link to use later and find his true name. Cross my heart."

"We don't know what information Isaac and the others will bring back with them. Or which Ancients."

"I know, Joanna."

"There could be a dozen other ways to solve this we haven't even thought of yet."

"I *know*, Joanna," he said, laughing and pushing the plate into my lap. "Eat. You look pale."

I took a few tentative bites, not trusting my fickle stomach, and Callum picked up an olive. "I think I need to take it easy for a few days," I said.

Callum's eyebrows raised, olive poised at his lips. "Of course. Are you all right?"

I smiled at his sudden frown and his squaring shoulders. "I'm tired and I think I'm fighting a bug."

"I was thinking about those roses near where we left Illness," Callum said, head tilting. "I'll go and look at them tomorrow. They might be leaving some of his influence out in Canderfey."

I nodded. "I honestly think I'm just worn down, but Isaac was worried about that before he left and it should probably be looked at."

"I'll take our brute squad," Callum said, nodding towards Sabine and her coven who were catching up with Myles, Daniel, and Nora.

Aiden joined us, sitting in the windowsill, and then Gwen and Tatsuo followed, bringing chairs with them. I grabbed a chicken leg before Callum could steal it from me—we fought over the dark meat like a pair of stray cats unless Isaac doled it out fairly.

Somewhere in the evening, after seats had rotated and company had changed again and again, and after I was pleasantly full with no signs of regretting it, I nodded off to sleep in my chair. Strong arms lifted me, but my eyelids were too heavy and the smell of Aiden's cologne was lovely and familiar, so I only tucked my head against his shoulder, listening to the murmur of his and Callum's voices.

"Should we call in a doctor?" Aiden said, the words a rumble against my cheek.

"Let's give it a few days and make sure she doesn't push herself," Callum answered.

Even falling into sleep, I knew we were home the moment we crossed the threshold, the smell of spices and paint and wood polish feeling exactly *right* all the way down to my bones. I only needed Isaac to return. My head rolled, a stray thought passing, wanting to ask if he had written, and then I was deep in sleep's embrace.

11

ISAAC

I OPENED MY EYES THE NEXT DAY IN THE DARK CARGO SHIP compartment we'd rented to ferry us around the coast to Rhodantis. Across from me, in the lower bunk, an unfamiliar woman sat with one of Bravery's thin legs dangling in her face. She was dressed in mourning black and, despite the shadowy darkness of the room, wearing a veil over her eyes.

"Who are you? Where's... where's the man who was using that bunk?" I asked. Because you couldn't call someone by the name *Mystery* to everyday people, could you?

The woman's head tilted, a swath of shining black hair rushing over her back, like the sound of silk. "It's me, darling," she said, her voice at the edge of tears, or near a hiss. "Just a new face, love."

My mouth hung open as my brain stuttered over the information. I knew the Ancients could shape-shift at will, but I'd gotten used to their faces, and in the case of Bryce and Anger, it seemed they had too. It hadn't occurred to me those faces might change at any moment, but I supposed it suited Mystery.

Anger came in before I could come up with a sensible answer. He took one look at Mystery and huffed.

"Bit overdramatic," he said.

"Don't be unkind," the woman, Mystery, said in her new, miserably dangerous way.

Anger crossed the small space and knocked on the bunk above Mystery. "Wake up, you old beast."

"Bugger off," a small voice mumbled.

"We're docked and if you stay on this boat, I won't feed that belly of yours."

Bravery sat up like a shot. Her mop of blond hair missed crashing into the beam above her by a mere fraction of an inch. "Wha's for breakfast?"

"Come up and get some fresh air," Anger said to me.

I stood up just as Bravery's legs swung over the edge of the bunk, accidentally—or maybe not—kicking Mystery in her newly veiled face. I reached out for the little girl's waist and small dirty hands swatted me away.

"What're you doin'?" she growled, leaning her face near mine.

"Helping you down," I said. The floor was quite a jump down from her spot on the bunk and the boat was still rocking.

Her eyes narrowed, staring down her small pert nose at me. "I'm over ten thousand years old," she said, but then her hands braced my shoulders and I lifted her off the bunk, setting her gently to her feet. Ten thousand years old or not, Bravery was seventy pounds soaking wet and I couldn't shake the impulse to take her hand to guide her upstairs.

She settled the debate by biting my hand with a sharp set of teeth, making me yelp and release her. She landed on light feet, rushing up the stairs and out to the deck without me.

"She's always been a menace," Anger said fondly.

I grunted and grabbed my pack, pulling my notebook out of the front flap and turning the pages as I walked up to the deck. When sunlight hit the pages as I found the place where I'd written my coven the night before, I frowned.

Seven oxen dribbling underwater gravy left Contean by yesterday's moonlight... On and on it went, swirling nonsense. I scanned the deck, as if searching for the culprit, but the words were in my own handwriting. Beneath them, in Callum's, was something equally ridiculous about a murder of crows.

Mystery rose up from the belly of the ship, black veil sparkling with beads, her mourning garb doing nothing to distract the eyes of all the crew and passengers from staring at her.

"Is this your doing?" I asked her, thrusting my notebook in her direction.

She glanced at the jumbling words. "Ahh, it may be a bit of my magic, love. I promise it's entirely unintentional, *of course*. Nasty little side effect."

I narrowed my eyes at the Ancient. "If I find out otherwise, I'll be hunting down your true name or your counterpoint or a plain, old-fashioned iron cage. I don't care."

"Simplicity," Mystery said, black hair swooping through the air as she turned. I rolled my eyes as one of the crewmen behind her swooned and braced himself against the ship railing. "But he's such a bore."

"Can my coven see what I've written them at least?" I asked. Mystery shrugged and my jaw ground. "Why were you put in that cage in the first place?"

She stilled and I felt the gaze on my skin through her black veil. "We were asked to be less than we were. I thought if we stood our ground together, a better compromise might be reached. Warfare led me to believe we had stronger numbers. I regret my alliance with him now."

And with that she left me standing alone, stewing in my own thoughts, her skirt swishing like whispers as she crossed the deck to where the others stood, waiting for the walkway to be lowered.

My breath caught as I saw it, Rhodantis, displayed in the stunning view it was always meant to be seen—from the water. A perfect growing mountain, glittering with all the jewels of architecture and color the city had designed itself to perfection with. Despite only having come on visits to Aiden's family, returning to Rhodantis felt like finding myself at home again. The colorful arts district rose up on my right, government at the left which put the King family some-where dead center ahead of us and up the hill.

I joined Hildy where she stood at the railing, trying to coax Bravery down from perching herself at the edge, legs swinging over the water.

"You're going to fall in," Hildy said.

"So what? It's a warm day and I can swim," Bravery said, shrugging Hildy off.

"Leave her," I told Hildy. "They're basically immortal aren't they?"

"I wish we'd had a better idea of who we were bringing with us when we asked our families to put us up," Hildy said, glancing down the line of our party. Anger looked rough around the edges, Bravery was a filthy little creature of a girl, and Mystery was… well, who knew what they would be in an hour let alone by tomorrow.

"Did you speak to Bryce at all about the true names?" I asked in a whisper.

Hildy nodded and shrugged. "Yes, but they don't think anything is likely to shake loose on that end. We'll see."

"I know of a counterpoint here in the city," Bravery said, balancing herself with a leg on either side of the railing, the boat rattling as the walkway was lowered to the dock.

I raised my eyebrows, "And you'll take us there?"

"I said I'd help," Bravery said, nose wrinkled in some expression of distaste, either at my questioning her, or at her own agreement to come with us.

"I don't doubt there'll be another hiding somewhere," Anger said.

"Let me be the one to wander," Mystery said, waving a pale hand across the view of the city, black rings glittering.

"Not on your own," Bryce said. "Hildy and I will hunt with you. Isaac, go with Bravery and Anger."

I didn't know whether to blame the sudden flare of anger on the Ancient bearing the same name, or my own exhaustion. "Wouldn't it be better for us to all search together?"

"It's a waste of time and energy, darling," Mystery purred.

Hildy's smile was sympathetic. "The sooner we find the counterpoints in the city, the sooner we can rest with our families, have dinner…bathe," she added with a speculative glance at Bravery.

Her hand squeezed my arm and Anger's eyes fixed to my face as I resisted the urge to pull myself out of her grasp. I wanted to shout. I was less concerned about resting and bathing than I was about returning to Canderfey and seeing my coven in peace. But that same worry lined Hildy and Bryce's eyes. I wasn't alone in my exhaustion. I was just less composed than Hildy.

"Come on, kid," Bravery said, fraying boot nudging my thigh, before she swung down from her perch and headed to the walkway. "Let's go fetch Health from his hospital."

THE RHODANTIS CHILDREN'S HOSPITAL was on the north end of the city, high up the hill and away from the heavy bustle of traffic and business, tucked near a beautiful residential neighborhood. It had an unobstructed view of the ocean over the entire, long, western side of the building, and a large tiered garden with little plots of flowers and herbs and vegetables, tended by the patients well enough to be out of doors.

Bravery strode in through the front doors, filthy enough to be a walking infection, and I wondered if it wouldn't have been better to take Anger and Bravery back to Claudia's first before coming here. As much as Bravery looked like she hadn't seen hot water in a year—which she probably hadn't—Anger and I weren't much better as her companions. We were lucky security wasn't escorting us right back down to the docks.

The reception of the hospital was bright and cheerful, a clutter of toys in a cozy sitting area to my right, the ocean view displayed in floor to ceiling windows on the left. Bravery stomped right up to the front desk, her chin barely clearing the top, and the young woman on the other side stared back, eyes sparkling with good humor.

"I'm here to see Doctor Honeyman," Bravery said.

"I'm afraid Dr. Honeyman isn't taking any new patients," the receptionist answered, trying not to smile. A nurse came down from the wide, dark wood staircase leading up, files piled in her arms.

"Tell him Snapper is here to see him." Bravery glanced over her shoulder at Anger and I, then added, "And a couple other friends."

The nurse snorted, less amused with the three of us than dubious. She and the receptionist shared a glance, shrugging at one another.

"I'm on my way back up, I'll mention it to him," the nurse said, eyeing us again.

"If you'll wait until he comes down," the receptionist said, gesturing to the sitting area.

Bravery eyed the stairs as if judging how fast she might make it up them before being caught. I risked having her take my hand off my arm, catching her by the shoulder and pulling her after me and over to the chairs.

"Snapper?" I asked.

She shrugged. "I have to go by something in front of your lot," she said.

"When's the last time you ran into Health?" Anger asked her.

She shrugged. "One or two of men's generations ago. He always turns up around these places though."

Footsteps clapped in a rush on the stairs and Bravery bounced up out of the chair I'd pushed her into with enviable energy. A young man—handsome, with rich brown skin, thick black hair, and a full dark beard—was tearing down the stairs, eyes scanning the front room until landing on Bravery.

"Snapper!"

"Honeyman!" Bravery's voice sounded bright and girlish for the first time and she took off in a run, leaping into the young doctor's arms.

Except that he wasn't really young, of course. And who knows how much of an actual doctor he was, I realized, the health of his patients not withstanding.

Honeyman, Health, lifted Bravery up onto his hip, white smile brilliant. "You look well," he said, which was generous. "Who've you brought with..." his words trailed off as he took in Anger. The old man disguise was placid, hands tucked into his pockets, eyes wide and innocent, but I was relieved to see Health's eyes narrow in recognition, his easy demeanor with Bravery vanishing. Anger and I walked over to the pair of them and Health stiffened, arms holding tight to Bravery.

"Brother," he said softly enough that no one else but us would hear the greeting.

"Brother," Anger echoed. "May I introduce a new acquaintance of ours? Isaac Metclaffe, of Canderfey."

Health's eyes widened as he took me in, his lips parting. "Ah. Yes. I see. Why don't… the three of you come up to my office? As a matter of fact, Snapper, I have a few patients who I'd like you to meet."

"Happy to help," Bravery said with a firm nod, her voice sweetened in the presence of a friend.

We followed Health upstairs, the receptionist watching us with curious attention, to an office on the east side of the building overlooking a garden. Health set Bravery down and she marched down the hall on her own.

"She'll find the ones who need her," Health said with an easy smile, then his gaze slid to Anger and the smile dimmed. "Come in. Sit down. I've wondered if someone would remember me."

"You're Illness' counterpoint," I said, taking a seat in a leather armchair near the tall windows.

"Yes. But I won't kill them."

I startled in my seat, looking between the two men. Health was staring back at me, his expression earnest and skin glowing in the warm sunlight. Anger's gaze was in his lap, head hanging with sudden exhaustion and a red hot fury in his narrowed eyes that I was afraid to address in case it might turn in my direction.

"I… I didn't know that was possible," I said. Even Mystery hadn't said as much.

Health's eyebrows rose, head tipping to the side. "I assumed that- Well, yes. That's… that's what happened to Peace, of course. And… others. Ones whose counterpoints were convinced by Warfare's early arguments."

Anger looked up and the air simmered around him, as if reality was at the edge of splintering by the sheer force of his rage. "Happiness is dead too, lad. I told you I had a bone to pick with Warfare."

I couldn't tear my eyes from Anger's, even as understanding sank in my chest like lead weights. Warfare had convinced Anger to destroy his counterpoint?

"Happiness still exists in the world," I said.

"We aren't the producers of these things, of course," Health said quickly. "Just avatars. We amplify, but we don't supply."

"It seems hard to find, to hold onto, for all your chasing though, doesn't it?" Anger asked, stare still locked with mine.

I had happiness with my coven—every day, even apart, even in the worst situations, but I understood what Anger meant. It was a fleeting feeling and it took reminders or suffered distractions from moment to moment. Had it been purer once, hundreds of years ago when Anger's counterpoint was still alive?

I meant to say that we only wanted the Ancients in Canderfey bound up again, but what came out instead was, "Why did you do it?"

Anger swallowed, face flinching. "Warfare's strategy was far beyond any of our guesses at the time, a millennia ago when they told us we could shift to fit your kind and withhold our influence, or we could find ourselves a new world to roam."

"You didn't want to shift?" I guessed.

Anger scoffed. "I did. This was my home. Humans were easy feeding for me, so prone to their own tempers. Happiness… she thought if she just proved what she was capable of in her own strength, your kind would change their minds. She could make them *happy*." Anger's thin fingers scraped over his chin, eyes turning distant. "Brother Warfare was in both our ears. She overstepped. There *is* too much of a good thing. And with a little nudge from Warfare and at the risk of being exiled I… lost my temper," he said, words falling slowly from his tongue.

"Many counterpoints were tricked to similar ends," Health said softly. "But to destroy the other end of yourself is…"

"You don't know what it is, Brother," Anger snapped, hot stare flicking to Health, whose lips pressed into a firm line. "It is like carving yourself into pieces, all your nerves begging for relief, for mercy."

"I won't do it," Health whispered.

"We aren't asking for that," I said, waiting for Anger to look at me, and then nodding to Health, watching his shoulders soften in relief. "We only want to keep everyone safe. If that means returning the cages to the way they were or… or something else if you don't agree to that."

"I never objected to the cage," Health said, shaking his head. "It was a relief. Illness was unruly. It never took Warfare's whispers to sway her. She is an infection of her own making."

"Will you come with us to Canderfey?" I asked and then I remembered where I was and what Health must be doing for the children here. "If it… I mean, if there is time and you won't be missed."

He smiled, sagging back into his chair. "My patients will be fine without me for a few weeks. I try not to influence more than necessary. I do human's work here, maybe a little better than most, but that's all."

"If there was ever one of the Family whose gifts the humans would encourage, it was yours, Brother," Anger said, voice settling to a soft rumble.

Health huffed and nodded. "There's a kind of danger in that too."

Bravery came bounding into the room a moment later, eyeing us all with her nose wrinkled. "You lot don't have anything better to do than just sit about on your bums in here?"

Health laughed and turned to me, releasing a long breath before speaking. "I will help you in whatever way I can, I just need a few days here before I leave."

If it had been Mystery, or Bravery, or even Anger who'd asked for time I might have asked for reassurance, but there was something irresistibly reliable in Health. I nodded and told him to meet us at the edge of Canderfey in four days' time. It was a deadline to our adventure, and even if we hadn't found all the counterpoints I was happy to put a date on returning home.

Upon our arrival on her doorstep, Claudia King—Aiden's mother—challenged Bravery into a bath in a deft game of wit and the girl came out looking halfway tamed. Hildy conjured up a new set of clothes to tempt the little Ancient—leather leggings, a loose tunic, and a vest with plenty of hidden pockets—and between the two women Bravery seemed gentled and cheerful.

By dinner, we had a new member to the party. The Samantas and the Kings had just gathered in Claudia's courtyard for the meal, a long table laid with heaping plates, when the bell rang in Claudia's house. Trust, Suspicion's counterpoint, arrived still in the suit he'd been wearing when Mystery found him at Hildy's family's bank. He was tall and he looked exactly as I might have imagined a banker, average and easy going, every bit the human with gray streaks in his brown hair and a rounded belly. He apologized three times for interrupting the meal before he was convinced to take a seat next to Hildy's mother, his own boss.

Anger kept Mystery company with Bryce at the far end of the table, and I felt a moment's peace at the other end sitting with Marcus and Lissa and having my head to myself and my emotions settled for the first time in days. I wanted to sketch the scene, but I wasn't sure if there was time enough in the world to catch the strange dynamic between everyone present, certainly not enough time for me. Hildy's mother alone was struggling to grasp that her employee of the month was a magical being of unknown age and origin.

"Oh, I've worked at your family banks since your grandfather first opened the original branch," Trust said, smiling with rosy cheeks and dimples, his sherry glass held out for a refill.

"Do you know where you're headed next?" Marcus asked me.

I shook my head. "Mystery says their instinct will take us in the right direction." Marcus raised his eyebrows and I nodded. "I know. I agree. I worry we're being... distracted from what's happening at Canderfey."

"Well, we heard from Aiden last night," Marcus said and smiled as I perked up. "Sabine York and her coven have arrived to help and some of Vermenians are on their way here, or to Bridgeston in the case of Joanna's family."

There was an ache in my smile. I wanted to be there with my coven, be with Joanna as she said goodbye to her grandmother for the moment. I looked down the table at Bravery as she snuck a sip of Claudia's wine and Trust in his cheerful and placid smile.

"I feel like they're doing all the work without me and I'm here collecting..."

Marcus followed my gaze, forehead quirking in amusement. "Yes. They are odd. But that doesn't mean they won't be helpful."

I hummed with an agreement I *wished* for rather than felt.

12

JOANNA

I GAGGED, STOMACH SORE FROM ALL THE VOMITING I'D DONE IN THE past week, arms clinging to the cool porcelain of the toilet. Even the smell of my own sick made me want to puke again. That didn't seem fair. I pushed myself away, flushing the toilet and dragging myself up to the sink, scooping handfuls of water into my mouth to wash away the bitter taste of bile and then splashing more over my clammy face.

Days of rest only confirmed how tired I was and I'd yet to make it through a day without something setting my stomach off. I was starting to wonder if Callum wasn't right about there being something left of Illness's influence in Canderfey. The Ancient's blood had landed on my skin, had it infected me somehow? If that were true though, Callum should have been right at my side and twice as sick as I was. He'd been gory with the stuff.

Thankfully neither of my covenmates were home to hover around me and my only company down the stairs to the kitchen was Molly, our orange tabby. I set the kettle to brewing and dug mint tea out of the cupboard.

My contraceptive tea I took every morning was sitting on the counter, cold from when Aiden must have brewed it for me before leaving. The whistle of the kettle began to hiss, muted beneath the

841

warning tone ringing in the back of my mind. I lifted the cup to my lips in my shaking hands as my eyes slid away from the kettle. The calendar was on the wall, just out of the corner of my eye and my blank stare strayed to it, tracking the weeks gone by.

The cages spread out over Canderfey nearly two months ago and my last period had been…not long after. I was late. Understanding sank in slowly, and embarrassment not long after. There was no Enmarian magic in Canderfey which meant that there was no charm working on my contraceptive tea which meant I was…

Late. Late or—

"Oh stars," I whispered as the kettle screamed and my stomach dove to the floor. I stared at the cup in my hand, thoughts spinning. It was a stressful two months with who knew what influence from Illness playing on my body. Even simple exhaustion might make me late. The herbs in the tea were meant to promote health, but the charm was the guarantee against pregnancy.

I tossed the tea down the drain, wondering if I was wrong, what if the charm worked differently? Except the evidence of my body seemed to argue the proof. I made myself a new cup of mint tea with trembling hands.

What if I was pregnant? There would need to be a doctor and what doctor in their right mind would come *here*? *Now*? I needed to tell…

Oh gods, Aiden. I was both terrified and thrilled at the thought of telling Aiden. I took the brewing tea over to the table and sat myself down in a chair before my legs gave out beneath me, the kitchen growing fuzzy as all my thoughts turned inward. He would absolutely melt with happiness. Or would he be so worried about me now it would drive us both insane?

And *Isaac*. He wasn't home. I couldn't tell Aiden when we had no word from Isaac. His last message had arrived as gibberish, although Claudia wrote the night before to let us know he was well. Mystery had returned and was garbling our words to one another.

My hand was hovering over my stomach and I set it flat on the table, taking a deep breath. If I *was* pregnant, it was a couple years earlier than I'd thought it'd be and at the worst time, perhaps it would be better if I wasn't. There was so much to consider. The Ancients. I was still training…

A small smile was creeping onto my face, turning up the corners of my lips. I remembered—months ago when we were searching for a solution to the Hollow— connecting with Isaac in Gwen's living room during a trance and finding the pieces of his true name. I'd seen the vision of the child that would be ours and the color of absolute familial devotion, had reveled in his love, felt it echo in me.

The doorknob of the pantry cupboard rattled and I sat up, pin-straight, a strange impulse to suck in my stomach coming over me. *Calm down, Joanna,* I thought, trying to relax my expression. It was something between a grimace and a smile as Callum came through the door, and I knew in that moment I had to wait for Isaac's return before I spoke to my coven. It would offer me a little more time to be sure too.

"Ah, awake finally," Callum said, smiling at me. There was sweat on his forehead and he smelled like a bonfire but there was no sign of a struggle on him. "You slept through all our bustling around this morning. Feeling better?"

"I'm- I- Yes, I think so," I said. My voice was too high and I cleared my throat. "Having tea just in case. Where were you?"

"I burnt down the roses and all the others spots of corrosion I found in the woods," Callum said. "Didn't feel anything unusual around them, but I'm working blind without my magic, anyway."

"Sorry," I said, head still reeling. What would Callum think of a baby? Between him and Aiden, would I ever be allowed outside again? Even if we did defeat the Ancients and Canderfey was set to rights again, they were bound to be so protective of me I'd be lucky if I was allowed to walk down a flight of stairs on my own.

"What are you sorry for?" Callum laughed.

That same strange smile was starting to stretch over my face and I forced it away, biting the inside of my cheek to restrain the urge. "Um. Nothing. I just woke up and haven't had any coffee yet. Babbling."

A baby. Aiden would have to stop laying his instruments every-where. And oh gods, all of Callum's weapons.

Callum crossed to me, slipping one hand into my hair and then tilting my head back. He bent, cheek pressed to mine briefly before kissing me, slow and gentle until my head was back in the present again. The caress ended with a nip at my bottom lip.

"I do have some bad news," he said, pulling away just a fraction.

My eyes widened and I nodded to the chair next to mine. He took a seat and I slid my hand into his.

"I think Illness' cage Bekka made is starting to fracture. I don't know if it's that she left and maybe Scrivens magic relies on a certain amount of proximity, but it means we need to act."

"Do you think you can separate the cages again and we can fit the original around Illness?" I asked.

"I don't think we could cast anything stable inside the boundary. *If* we decide to put Illness in a cage, we're going to have to take down the one involved in the boundary and somehow catch Illness outside the line."

"It sounds risky."

"Yes," Callum said, lines digging into his forehead with his frown. "I don't know how to guarantee we don't lose track of Illness. Or keep the other Ancients from distracting us or catching us between one step and the next. I don't even know if the cage is our best option."

I squeezed his hand. "Then we'll speak with the others and decide as a group. Sewell is still out with the Vermenians who left. How is Elizabeth?"

"Fully recovered from the attack in the woods," Callum said. "Embarrassed but ready for action again. She's getting a lot of questions about whether the delay for next school year will be lifted or not."

"Pfft. She should suggest anyone with questions come to Canderfey to see the circumstances for themselves. Is there any word from Isaac?"

Callum frowned and shook his head. "There were words, nothing useful. Have you checked the messages from the Kings?"

"Not yet."

"Stay here, I'll go look," he said, rising in a jump and kissing the top of my head before running out to the hall to find the notepad by the temporarily useless telephone. "Claudia says they left this morning but they don't know where to yet. Isaac told her to tell us to expect a… Dr. Honeyman by Wednesday. And him too."

"A doctor?" A doctor *and* Isaac? Which meant on or near Wednesday I would tell my coven what I'd only just realized this morning.

"An Ancient who is a doctor," Callum said, notebook in hand as he reentered the kitchen. "Doesn't say which Ancient but that's… promising, I think?"

"Useful if nothing else," I said. I took a sip of my tea to distract my mouth from the words it wanted to shout.

A baby. We might be having a baby.

Which meant it was really time to find a solution to the Ancients. We couldn't raise a child in Canderfey as it stood. And I wasn't about to give up my library to the likes of Warfare.

<hr>

"Look at his face," Darin whispered to Geoff as Samuel's teeth gritted, my tattoo needle thrumming against his upper-arm.

We were all gathered together in the Library, the largest and safest space for everyone to share, with plenty of room for opposing personalities to keep their distance. Like Aiden, who glanced at the speaking warrior out of the corner of his eyes, gritted his teeth, and got up from the table to disappear behind a bookshelf.

"It'll be your turn next," Samuel said to his covenmate, and I pulled away to give him a moment to breathe and shift in place, before getting back to work again. Silver charms were useful in an emergency, but my tattoos were better protection against influence. It was half measures but it got us this far.

"She'll be as gentle as she cares to," Geoff said to Darin, faint smirk on his lips.

I wasn't remotely interested in being gentle, especially not to

Darin, but I expected Geoff—and Darin for that matter—knew as much.

"It's not that I mind getting this done," Samuel assured me. "If I'd known there were Ancients out in the world, as you say there are, I'd have wanted as much earlier."

"I think the ones you need to be concerned about are the ones we're trapped with, I'm afraid," I said, finishing off the last line of the sigil with a soft flourish. "All done. Keep it clean."

"I assumed the point of us coming here was to help you all *fight* against these creatures. Not just for us to sit inside and wait for your research team to think of a solution," Sabine said to Callum.

They were a table over with Myles, Nora, Tatsuo, and Elizabeth, strategizing what to do about Illness' soon-to-be disintegrated cage.

"Fighting is all well and good if we have a plan designed to succeed," Callum said, voice tense in an attempt to hold onto his patience. "What we have at the moment is a rough idea at best."

Tatsuo leaned forward between the two, blocking their glaring views of one another. "We do, however, have an end goal in mind. Illness caged, outside of the current boundary. Surely if we start there and work our way back, we might find a solution."

Aiden appeared out from one end of the shelves near me, catching my eye briefly with a smile before we both held our breath, waiting to see if Callum would respond with irritation or praise.

"It's certainly preferable to running into the woods, blades drawn," Callum muttered. "I know how to cast the cage, so do you and Gwen. Aiden can manage the music."

"I know color magic," Elizabeth said, drawing over the sheet where we'd made notes on Illness' true name. Her lips pursed at the color splotch Isaac had left there. I'd seen it earlier and nearly thrown up, although it took very little provocation now to make me sick.

"Joanna will manage the words of course," Callum said.

"Let Corina do it."

All the heads in the room turned to me at my sudden outburst. My heart was running wildly in my chest at the thought of repeating the exercise of the spell. Even if we already had the name and I didn't have to dive into Illness, the magic was taxing and I'd been struck uncon-scious the last time. And now... my hand was on my stomach, fingers twitching, and I dropped it to my side.

"What?!" Corina squawked, and I wasn't sure if it was in excite-ment or horror.

"Corina?" Callum asked, derision lacing his voice.

"I'm still tired and we only get to do this once if it's going to work," I said. I looked to Corina, her lips parted to object. "You're a better Scrivens than me anyway, aren't you?"

Aiden murmured my name under his breath, but I ignored him. Corina's eyes narrowed, but her chin tilted up with pride.

"I am," she said, as if waiting for someone to correct her.

"Then prove it. Besides, you owe my coven."

"Oh, it was just a little diary—"

"Write the name for the spell, Corina," I snapped and her lips slammed shut, eyes widening.

"Fine," she answered, equally surly.

"Switch places," I said to Darin, glaring. He got up without a word and took Samuel's seat as his covenmate moved out of the way.

"Geoff always says you're a terror," Darin said. "Didn't believe him."

"Well, he's right," I said, enjoying my current temper and that it seemed to be doing a little work to keep Darin in line. "Now don't fidget."

He grunted as I started the tattoo, eyes searching the room for some sign or mercy or assurance. Geoff only grinned at me and Aiden went to join the planning at the other table, dragging Corina over with him.

"You can be rough with him," Sabine said, crossing over to us and folding her arms in front of her chest. She smiled at Darin and added, "He likes it."

For the first time since I'd met the man, I caught Darin blushing.

Hours later, after the plan was formed and I'd nearly fallen asleep at the table, Callum and Aiden surrounded me at either side and escorted me home. I cradled books in my arms, one on magic in infancy that I tucked into my pile in the hopes the others would assume I was only indulging in my usual generalized curiosity.

"I can't tell if you're trying to punish Corina, or redeem her," Aiden murmured as we returned home.

"I'm not sure either," I said.

I bit my lip. A week ago I wouldn't have hesitated to be the one writing Illness' name and sealing that cage, but now the very idea, the risk, terrified me. *A child, we're going to have a child.* It had always been in the plan, of course, not just to satisfy Aiden's burning desire for a full house and family. I wanted all of it too, although maybe not a house *quite* as full as he dreamed.

This wasn't a someday child though. Or it might not be. I looked up at my coven in the gray evening light falling through the kitchen windows. Callum's copper hair in a tangle from all his thinking and planning and bickering. Aiden shrugging off his vest and rolling up his shirtsleeves to make do for us for dinner—we were all missing Isaac extra on that front. They would be good fathers. Isaac would be a good father.

Tears began to fill my eyes and I turned away before either of them could see.

I loved them. I knew in that moment, regardless of everything at odds against us, I didn't want it to be stress or a flu or a late period. I wanted this child more than anything else. I hoped Isaac made it home soon before the news came spilling from my mouth. And I hope he brought us a solution to the Ancients with him.

13

ISAAC

"DO YOU FEEL AS THOUGH WE'RE LETTING THEM DOWN?" HILDY SAID softly, sitting at my side at the front of the horse and cart wagon we'd rented to travel the country side.

Hildy's mother had been ready to purchase a train car to ourselves, when Mystery announced that trains only went in two directions and we would need to be ready to head down any road at all in our search. Since there were no cars that would fit two human adults and five mystical beings—regardless of their chosen age and weight of the day—a wagon it was.

"In Canderfey? Yes. And then I hope I'm wrong," I said, shrugging. "We said we'd find Ancients and we certainly have. If Mystery isn't lying to us, then at least we know we're finding the *right* ones."

Hildy hummed in agreement and quiet bickering broke out in the wagon behind us. "I think I was just enjoying being out of that boundary so much, having Bryce's familiar face back," she said. "What will you do if it doesn't work? If we can't cage the Ancients?"

"I don't think that boundary will hold indefinitely, Hildy," I said. She frowned, hopelessness and weariness mixing on her face as her shoulders sagged. "Not that I'd want to abandon Canderfey even if it would."

849

"I think the country would be a lot more interested in helping find a solution if the boundary *did* come down," Hildy said.

The wagon cover flipped back and Bryce clambered onto the bench between us, a snarl on their lips. "Millenia-old children."

Mystery woke for the day in a middle aged man's form, looking a bit like Marcus, if Marcus were constantly smelling shit somewhere nearby him. He spent every quiet moment seeking philosophical debates. Trust was either too good natured to mind the drone, or was encouraging Mystery for the fun of it. Anger and Bravery were less patient.

"Oh, shut your gob, you old dust bag," Bravery yelled in the background.

"At least Bravery has the excuse of appearing as a child," I said.

Bryce glared at me out of the corner of their eyes. "She chooses that form for a reason."

I bit my lips closed and focused on the road ahead of us. We were nearing a crossroads, arrows pointing to towns in the north. A large boulder rested at the southern corner, and propped up against it was a crumpled figure, a pair of weather beaten crutches propped up against the rock next to him, matted light hair covering his face. With a glance at Bryce, who shrugged, I slowed the horses to a stop.

"Are you all right, sir?" I asked.

The man looked up and I flinched back, jumping down from my seat. He had a wound over one eye, blood caked on the skin around his temple, and his cheeks were gaunt.

"Let me help you." It would be a risk with the company we had in the wagon with us, but I didn't want to leave someone wounded on the side of the road if we could offer them a ride to safety, or at least a doctor.

Long, thin fingers lifted, raised to stop me. "You'd better not," the man said, lips dry and cracking, voice rasping to match.

I glanced at Bryce, who I knew had some gifts at healing, but they were staring at the stranger, eyes narrowed and head cocked. Behind them, the wagon cover flipped back and Anger's face appeared, grimace already twisting on his mouth.

He stared at the forlorn man in front of me for a long moment before heaving a sigh. "Agony. I wondered if we'd run into you."

An Ancient. *Of course* he was an Ancient. Just as Mystery had promised us, if we travelled with them, we'd find ourselves running into more of their kind.

Agony's head lifted, eyes growing wide. "Brother?"

"Get him in the wagon," Anger told me. "Keep yourself contained, Agony."

I braced myself as I stepped closer to the Ancient but there was no pain or misery, and he looked more terrified of me than I was of him. I wrapped my arm around his back, shoulder blades pronounced and digging into me as I lifted him. He whimpered as he stood on one leg and I helped him to his crutches.

Hildy caught my eye as I led him to the back of the wagon, where Trust and Bravery held the curtain open. I understood the look in her eyes, flinching and skeptical. Was *this* an ally, a broken man barely able to stand?

"You're... what are you all doing here?" Agony asked, breathless and weak, groaning as he was pulled into the back with his siblings. "Is this about...*Warfare?*" he whispered. "I was on my way to Canderfey to see if I could help."

The pinch between my brows eased at his words. Yes, this was an ally, the definition of one if maybe not the one I'd dreamt of bringing home with me. At least he *wanted* to be involved.

"We'll be going there soon, Brother," Trust said, patting his shoulder. "We have a few more of the Family to find first."

"But... Peace," he said, looking at the other Ancients with woeful eyes.

"Yes, we know," Bravery answered with a solemn nod. "We'll do what we can without her."

It would be a rough ride for Agony if he was injured, but I wasn't sure what was to be done for him. I made to leave them, but Agony stopped me, a soft touch against my arm.

"Head north, into Greensville. Ask for Lord Nettleham."

Mystery's smile was smug as he watched me leave. Maybe I would be home before our four days were up. I tried not to worry about who I'd be bringing with me.

GREENSVILLE WAS QUAINT AND PRETTY. Its farms were lush, strawberries glowing in tidy lines like rubies glittering under the sun, and we passed two orchards perfumed with the promise of peaches. The scenery was idyllic and happy people waved to us from the streets as we passed them, the friendliness almost strange after Kilburn and the distracted bustle of Rhodantis. When we stopped to ask for directions to Lord Nettleham's estate, we sent a woman into effusive praises, information sprinkled sparsely through.

"Oh, it is the prettiest place you might imagine, just up northeast of here. The pond has the freshest fishing of the district and the creeks are quite the cleanest. You just take the left fork. And Lord Nettleham *is* a charming man," she said, nodding so hard I worried for her neck, cheeks straining with her smile.

"Maybe this is Sorrow's counterpoint," Hildy whispered to me as I led us northeast, hoping I'd chosen the correct forked road to ride left on. "It certainly seems happy enough here."

"Perhaps the cheer will balance out our new addition," I answered.

"Yes... at least he seems able to keep his gifts to himself, so far," Hildy whispered. "Oh! There it is, I think. Seems grand enough for a Lord."

Nettleham's home was not simply a house, but a sprawling structure in bright limestone. The sun was setting somewhere behind us, casting the house in pinks and golds, candles lit in every enormous window. The road curved around a pond in front of the house, white pebbled drive leading up to an enormous staircase.

"Do you think Nettleham is the Ancient? Or someone working for him?" Hildy asked.

I shook my head. "I don't know. It's not subtle if it is him."

The front doors were opening as we reached our destination and I knew by the breadth of the shoulders and the jaunty run down the stairs that we were being greeted, not by the butler, but the master of the home.

"Hello there, welcome visitors!" a strong voice called to us.

Anger leaned out from the wagon to mutter in my ear. "That's him. Poncy bastard. Pride."

"Are you lost good friends, in need of rest? Please, come in. Let me show you my home!" Pride looked about Hildy or Aiden's age, handsome with easy features and dark curls haloing around his head. His eyes twinkled and his smile shone and even without Anger's warning, I knew there was something distinctly... irksome about the man.

Anger groaned. "He'll have us up till sunrise if we let him go on in this way. I'll handle this."

The wagon shook and then stones skidded, Anger leaping out of the back.

"Brother?" Pride asked, a frown marring his handsome features. He fell back a step as Anger stomped in his direction.

"Oh! No!" Hildy cried, standing up from her seat.

But it was too late. Anger's fist flew through the air, landing on Pride's square jaw and sending Lord Nettleham sprawling across his beautiful, white, pebbled drive. Anger shook out his hand, sucking briefly on his knuckles, and turned to us with a careless shrug. "That should keep him in line for an hour or so. Long enough to get him packed into the wagon at least."

The wagon rattled and soon all the Ancients were standing together on the drive, Hildy and I following after.

"That was maybe not the way to handle the conversation, Brother," Trust said softly.

"It saved us listening to the sound of Pride's voice rattle on for another three weeks straight," Bravery muttered.

Pride sat up, hair ruffled and cheeks flushed, hands rushing to brush himself off. Hildy ran to his side and offered her hands, but the Ancient only snapped at her. "I'm fine. I'm fine! I can manage myself."

Bruised Pride then. Anger smirked at me and I wondered if he could read the joke running through my head.

He caught sight of Agony in the group, whose shoulders hunched and head ducked. Pride's lips pursed. "A Family reunion then is it? Agony, I told you to go and find Sister Generosity. You overstayed your welcome here in Greensville."

"Generosity is nearby?" Trust asked, and he turned to me, smiling as if no one had been punched and Agony wasn't wilting in his arms. "She'll join us, of course. She can't say no. And she's Jealousy's counterpoint."

"Did Agony ask you to go to Canderfey with him, Brother?" Anger asked Pride who spluttered.

"Well, yes. And I would have, of course, but you know how he is," Pride said, hand swiping in Agony's direction. "Any mission of his was sure to go awry and I can hardly be spared here."

"Oh? What is it you do exactly, here in your lovely house?" Bravery asked, toes kicking pebbles at Pride's feet as she stomped through the crowd to stand at Hildy's side, arms crossed over her chest and eyes flashing at the other Ancient.

"Sister," Pride said, forcing a smile and a brief bow. "You're looking well. I keep things running smoothly, successfully, here in Greensville. This is a very nice village, you know. Very prosperous, very industrious."

Bravery sniffed and tossed her blonde braids over her narrow shoulders. "Never heard of it." I buried my laugh and Pride's smile soured.

"Yes, well. Why don't you all come inside? I can offer you refreshments. Wonderful accommodations." Pride tugged at the hem of his jacket with one hand and gestured up to the house with the other.

I glanced at Anger, who met my eyes and jerked his head in refusal and I thought I understood the meaning. We'd be wasting time and the only benefit would be to Pride's ego. While I knew Hildy might enjoy the rooms offered, and Agony might benefit from a good rest, I was inclined to agree with Anger. I would rather keep moving, keep searching for the others we needed. If Generosity was nearby, then that was where we would go.

"I take it by your refusal to join Agony, you won't be interested in joining us," I said to Pride, who raised his eyebrows. "We'll be returning to Canderfey to stop your siblings. My coven is there waiting for us and I'd rather not delay unnecessarily." I turned to the wagon, gratified to hear the others behind following me, and Pride called out.

"Wait! No, no. Of course I'm happy to assist in such an endeavor. I'd consider it my responsibility, if nothing else," he said and I faced him again.

"It's been over a month," I said, raising my eyebrows, letting that anger I strived so hard to keep at bay turn my hands to fists at my sides and drive my words. "Your responsibility hasn't urged you to Canderfey yet."

His face flushed red again, but his shoulders squared. "Yes, I understand. It was only," his eyes flicked to Agony and he cleared his throat, "It seemed a little hopeless before. I am bolstered to see so many of the Family together this way." Anger scoffed and rolled his eyes and Pride pressed on. "Please, come into the house and we'll prepare for the journey."

"Get your things, P," Anger said. "We leave tonight."

Pride searched our faces, looking for one weak link in our resolve, and maybe it was his influence, but I *was* proud that not one of us seemed swayed.

"Yes, well," he said, smile mixing with a grimace. "I'll get my car."

He left us in the drive, Trust following him with a reassuring smile.

"I think you should ride with him," I said to Hildy, nodding Bryce over to join us. "The pair of you go ahead to Generosity, with Trust. I'll follow with the rest."

"You're taking on more than your fair share," Bryce said, looking at the other Ancients.

"Bryce is right," Hildy said, hand squeezing my arm. "That's quite a handful."

"It'll keep Anger from punching Pride again," I said, shrugging. "Agony knows where we're headed. Who knows. Maybe we'll find another on our way to meet you." Hildy nodded and I turned to the others. Anger, Bravery, Agony, and Mystery. I took a deep breath at the sight of them and then spoke. "Alright you lot, back in the wagon. We'll meet the others at Generosity's."

Anger grinned at me and Bravery whooped, running past me and launching herself into the front seat of the wagon.

"We'll have ourselves a little adventure," Anger said to me, winking.

"I certainly hope not," I answered, dread pitting in my stomach as he shrugged and heaved himself into the back.

WE MADE it as far as the other end of the village before Agony's apparent bad luck caught up with him. With us all.

I was turning the wagon onto the main road again when the back right wheel hit a pit, the entire wagon rattling dangerously for a few turns before the corner end collapsed. The horses whinnied and reared, and my arm wrapped reflexively around Bravery, tucking her into my side before she scoffed and wrestled herself free.

"Don't be an idiot," she grumbled at me and then threw herself out of the wagon and onto the road, walking back to the busted wheel.

"Oh no," Agony moaned from inside. "This is my fault, isn't it?"

"Don't fret, Brother," Bravery said. "I saw a spare wheel fastened under the belly. We'll fix it up as quick as can be."

It was dark already and while I'd resigned myself to a night of trying to stay awake, I'd hoped it would be while making progress on the road. I jumped down and joined Bravery at the back of the wagon, Anger sliding out of the crooked belly. Bravery was crawling beneath, quick fingers working to free the spare wheel.

"Keep your eye out for any locals," Anger said to me. "Bravery and I will have this done without any trouble." He crouched on the ground and, despite his disguise as a frail old man, heaved the corner of the cart up onto his shoulder, leveling it with the rest of the wagon before it could stress the frame. "Told you I would come in handy."

I snorted, shoulders relaxing, and turned myself to the road, relieved for the moment. There was a tavern on the opposite corner, noisy with activity inside, but the windows were obscured and otherwise the village seemed quiet. For a moment, I rested in the reassuring thought we'd be on our way out of town again without anyone the wiser.

Then the tavern door opened, six broad bodies stumbling out into the night, voices loud and slurring. My spine prickled in reflex, the sounds and smells—beer and spirits wafting across the road on a breeze—painfully familiar.

"Almost done," Bravery said, just a hair too loud, and one of the men leaving the tavern backtracked on his heels.

"Any trouble friends?" he asked.

I shook my head and waved my hand. "Just fixed, thank you. No trouble."

Maybe it was something in my voice, too tense for their ears. Or maybe they were bored and would've wandered over regardless. They came, still laughing at whatever joke passed between them moments before. Anger shifted behind me, the wagon settled and Bravery hidden behind us, finishing her work fastening the wheel in place.

"Strangers again," one of the men said to the other.

"We passed through earlier today," I said, ignoring the frantic rhythm of my heartbeat, the way my blood turned hot and cold in my veins. "On our way out now."

"What's going on?" Mystery asked, jumping out of the back of the cart. He held the cover open behind him, revealing a sprawling Agony peering out from the shadows.

"You!" hissed one of the locals. "It's that vagrant again!"

"We told you not to come back here," another snarled, rushing toward the wagon, his shoulder crashing into mine as I stepped into his path to block his way.

"We're taking him out of town with us," I said, raising my hands up to try and stop the others. "We only stopped to fix our wheel."

"That man is bad luck," said the largest of the group, spitting onto the ground by the wagon as Agony flinched in the back. "We nearly lost a third of our crops this year because of him."

"Well he's leaving tonight," I said, but the man in front of me—my height but with a good fifty pounds on me—was pushing me back, chest to chest. "There's no need for worry or any argument!"

"Oh, there's no worry," said the largest. "We tossed him out on his sorry ass once, we can do it again."

"You lads better walk on home and leave us be," Anger said, hands in pockets, body relaxed. "There's no fair fight for you here."

"We aren't going to fight you, Grandfather Time," the one at my chest said, laughing and the scent of his breath washing sour ale across my face. "We just want him."

"You'll have to go through me first," Bravery said and I whirled around, scooping her up off the ground before she could charge into one of the men and get herself hurt. She stared at me, indignant and angry. "I have millennia on you."

"Well, I have a good hundred pounds on you," I said, even if she was right.

"Grab the curse from the back," one of the locals said.

"Now wait a moment, if you please," Mystery began, before promptly being shoved to the ground out of the way of the men.

I passed Bravery into Anger's arms and caught the approaching man by the sleeve of his shirt, turning him in my direction, fire running through my thoughts and muscles. Hard hands hit my shoulders, beer breath in my nostrils, and dark eyes ringed with red clashing against mine.

"You fuckin' idiot," the man said.

He looked like my father, or he smelled and acted like him, and I did what I had never done as a young man. My arm swung, fast and sudden, before I had time to breathe or think or regret. The punch landed high on the other man's cheekbone and I shouted at the lightning strike of pain that rocketed up my hand to my arm all the way to my shoulder. The man stumbled back, feet slipping on the ground one step after another, until he landed on his ass with a grunt.

Chaos broke out, Mystery up on his feet, and Bravery tearing around the legs of the locals. Anger cackled as a younger man barreled into his ribs and didn't budge him an inch. Another man came for me but Bravery had him falling face first, caught by the ankles before he ever reached me.

"Get the wagon moving," she said, childlike giggle ringing in the air, before running for another man. "Quick, before any others come out."

I caught my breath, head clearing from the haze of my past, and I ran to the front of the wagon, jumping in and nudging the horses into action. They jostled in complaint as the Ancients jumped into the back of the cart, one after the other, Mystery with a grunt of great effort, but we were well into speed and the shouts from the men we'd left behind grew fainter with every second.

My hand screamed with pain and I stared down at it in my lap as if I didn't recognize my own fingers, hadn't drawn them hundreds of times in introductory classes and idle boredom. Anger climbed out from the back, still chuckling, and took a seat next to me.

"That was a bit of fun then," he said.

"I've never hit anyone. Not in my entire life," I said.

Anger startled and turned to stare at me with eyes wide. "You're serious?" I nodded. "I don't see why you're so skittish around me."

"I don't *want* to be an angry man," I spat out, voice raising.

Anger only blinked at me. "It doesn't sound as though you are." It blew all the furious wind of my mood out across the strawberry fields and into the night and we sat together in quiet, wagon rocking and road vanishing beneath us, for a long time. "Everyone is angry sometimes. Fighting it doesn't change *feeling* it. You're not an angry man. You're just human."

My fingers flexed in my lap, but my tongue lay numb in my mouth and Anger let the conversation pass as we rode on.

14

CALLUM

"ARE YOU READY?" I WHISPERED TO THE OTHERS. THE SUN WAS BARELY cresting the horizon down the road and we were waiting outside the boundary for Sabine, her coven, Joanna, and the Scrivens to arrive, herding Illness with them.

Aiden, Elizabeth, and Tatsuo nodded, but Corina sniffed and tossed her blonde hair.

"It is only writing," she said. "I'm not as weak as your Scrivens."

Aiden swallowed and I knew he was resisting the urge to snarl at the young woman. I kept my own tongue still. Corina might be creative, but I was nervous about Joanna choosing her to be the one to write Illness' true name, *Axition*. She was clever, detailed, and delicate when it came to spinning the world around her little finger in her diary. I knew that was no guarantee she had enough personal strength to withstand the physical battle Joanna forced herself through with the Hollow.

"We'll see," I said instead, hoping skepticism would scratch at her ego enough to push her to prove herself. Otherwise we were making an incredibly risky choice, one that would likely cost us our lives and anyone else's Illness sought out in freedom.

A branch cracked deep in the Hand Woods and Corina's breath

861

caught, the sound carrying from where she sat behind me, slate at her knees and chalk in hand. I stared into the darkness, the shapes of the trees blurring together in the inky blue light before dawn. Another crack cut through the air, echoing forward to where we waited, and a roar followed, leaves rustling in the branches overhead.

Aiden moved behind me. "Should we—"

I raised a hand in his direction to stop him. "They're coming. We need to be in formation when they get here."

I ignored the way my muscles burned with the urge to run over the boundary to hunt down Joanna and the others. They would be fine, *Joanna* would be fine. She was the most capable person I knew. A large part of me wished it was her writing instead of Corina. I trusted her—all my covenmates—more than anyone else in the world, but she had said no and it was a decision I wouldn't argue with. She knew her limits. That she was worried for them now terrified me. I swallowed down the lump in my throat, fingers flicking off stray wisps of magic hanging on my fingers, waiting for their work to begin.

The sound of voices, whispering and calling to one another, filtered through the increasing crunch and snap of foot traffic. I didn't know if I was imagining the approaching shadows, or if it was our friends running closer.

"Are you sure you can take the cage down and put it up again in time?" Aiden whispered.

I was not sure. I wasn't sure about any of the plan. I'd been floundering since the moment I crossed the boundary two months ago and my magic fizzled to nothing in my bones. This *was* my best plan for the moment and I would put all of my energy and magic into its execution.

"Get it to the border!" Joanna's voice rang like a bell in the shadows. "We'll hold them back!"

"Joanna!" Aiden shouted, and I fisted my hands so hard I thought my knuckles might snap.

"Go!" Another person cried. Samuel, I thought.

Figures were forming out of the shadows, three running ahead of the others, the writhing form of Illness dragged between them. Nora,

Daniel, and Lora. Joanna's leashes—words scratched into the leather with a sewing needle—wrapped around their fists as they hauled the Ancient with them to the boundary. Behind them loomed a hulking figure, steam rising from the familiar black and red hide.

"They're being followed by Warfare," I called to the others.

Joanna's shout of effort rang out and my entire body jumped in the direction of the boundary.

"Wait!" Tatsuo warned.

Joanna wasn't alone. Sabine's own war cry was calling through the air, answered by her covenmates. My body warred with itself, the instinct to run and help Joanna, tear her out of harm's way, battling with the knowledge that I needed to be *where* I was. Joanna knew what she was doing.

But she's tired. She's been sick.

"Callum, we're coming!" she called and I saw her, behind Illness and the Scrivens, hair a wild, dark tangle, her cheeks flushed.

They were weaving through the trees, Joanna nearly tripping over a fallen branch. I needed to be ready, we didn't have a second to spare to get them across the line with Warfare at their backs. I raised my hands, the warm buzz of magic singing in my blood, fingertips writing the sigils in the air until the cages were lit up in front of me, slowly untangling from the single layer into many. I'd removed Mystery's days ago when we heard from Isaac that the Ancient was traveling with them, and it offered practice for the moment, working the kinks of dismantling out ahead of time.

My eyes were distracted from my work as Suspicion swooped down from the branches, aiming for Joanna, my tongue stone in my mouth as I tried to warn her. I didn't need to. She was ready, spinning on her heel and thrusting my sword at a frothy wing, the winged Ancient barely retreating in time. The monster screeched and a fistful of black feathers floated down to the forest floor.

Focus, I hissed to myself, trying to stamp down the pride bubbling up as I watched Joanna fight off our enemy. I wrapped my fingers around a thread of Illness' cage, humming softly, calling *Axition* in my thoughts, tugging at the line. The cage resisted and I poured in power, trying to ignore the sight of the Scrivens coming closer with Illness in tow, of Joanna turning back to Warfare and Sabine's coven.

I'd work magic in the wrong direction if I wasn't careful and end up freeing the wrong Ancient, or get someone hurt if I didn't have the cage down at the right moment. I tugged harder and behind me Aiden raised his violin, a whimpering note assisting my work. With a rough yank and a lick of power that I felt from the base of my spine straight up through my eyes, the thread snapped, the broken tension rippling around the boundary. Illness' cage collapsed.

Behind the Scrivens, Joanna was speeding to the line, skin shining with summer heat and effort. Warfare charged after her, the warrior coven caught up with other Ancients.

"Hold Illness!" I shouted to the others, my gaze fixed to Joanna's face, her lips pursed tight but panic flooding her eyes.

"Pike, there's no time!" Tatsuo snapped.

"Then stall," Aiden answered for me, and his music rose high and terrible, threatening to take the strength right out of me until I blocked it out, my entire vision swallowed up as I waited for Joanna to reach us.

"Don't you dare," Joanna rasped, too far away from safety, too close to Warfare, his teeth dripping with venom, snapping closer to her skirt with every bounding leap. Twenty feet away from her. Fifteen. Ten.

Any magic I sent to aide her would fizzle to nothing before reaching her. Panic ran like lightning under my skin, urging me to action, and I responded to the call without thinking. My fingers grasped around a blood black thread of an Ancient's cage.

"What are you doing?" Aiden hissed.

I didn't really know, only that I felt Warfare in that line of magic in my fist and I wanted him to feel me too. I threw power into the thread, amplifying it one sigil after another. Joanna reached the Scrivens, her hands joining Nora's in dragging Illness out of the boundary. I shoved forward at Warfare's cage, the framework pressing in to crash against his snarl, hot breath and stinging spittle licking my knuckles.

Warfare leaned into the web of the cage, color fizzling around the contact, and my vision flashed blackened soot and bleeding red. He would break the cage and then we'd have two Ancients loose and I'd have ruined everything. There was agony and fire vibrating lines through me, my scream gritted behind my teeth, Warfare's bile yellow eyes swarming and taking up the whole of my vision.

Soft hands wrapped around my shoulders, interrupting the radiating pain and Joanna's soft scent of pages and vanilla cleared my head.

"Enough," she said, fast and hard, pulling on my shoulders. "Illness. Illness' cage, Callum!"

I released my hold on Warfare, felt him splintering out of my head, leaving shards behind, and turned to where the Scrivens held Illness taut on leashes at the center of our ring. Aiden was holding notes longer than they should've been able to hang in the air, and Elizabeth had sweat dewing on her temples as sick yellow swirled the circle, binding in the Ancient.

I stepped forward, knowing I'd wasted too much magic holding back Warfare. There was a new pacing scratch in the back of my head, wrathful and patient, those slivers I'd made room for in the conflict. I'd formed the link between us without meaning to, the one I'd promised my coven I wouldn't try to find.

"Callum," Aiden said through a clenched jaw.

I stepped into position at Corina's back and raised my hands, the chant falling from my lips in a barely steady rhythm, hands tracing magic in the air until we were working in unison.

Corina's back was flexing and I thought at first she was writing. Then I heard the soft whimper, her head shaking side to side. Joanna shifted in the corner of my eyes, sinking to her knees, leaning in to speak.

"One line at a time, Corina," she said gently. "Just focus on the shapes. The pain will pass, I promise.

New lines of magic were weaving in the air, trying to fulfill our commands, but we needed Corina to lock those threads together and seal the Ancient inside.

"I can't," she whispered, head shaking. "I can't. I can't move."

The magic poured out of me, a faucet running on an increasingly shallow well, taking all my energy and ability to think clearly with it. Aiden's color was turning gray and Elizabeth swayed, the color she spread starting to flicker. Tatsuo and Gwen tried to shore us up, but sooner or later they'd weaken too. Without the lock of the name, all we'd be left with was a massive drain on ourselves.

Joanna's eyes traced the group and I nearly told her to stop when she crawled forward to Corina's side. We needed her, and anyway my tongue felt useless in my mouth.

"Together," she said, pulling chalk out of her own pocket, her free hand grabbing onto Corina's.

She started from the other end, and I stumbled closer, wanting to see, wanting to drag Joanna away to safety, to consider the whole mission failed. Joanna's shoulders tensed and she gasped with the first line. Corina broke into sobs, but her fingers twitched on the slate and her hand squeezed so hard at Joanna's both their knuckles turned bone white.

I held the chant, tried not to think of the way Elizabeth's eyes fluttered and rolled, the way the leather leashes looked ready to snap with strain and break Joanna's magic, that Aiden's music was wobbling nervously.

Corina moaned and Joanna was eerily silent, body faintly shifting, and I wondered if she was breathing at all. Their chalk scratched and then there was a soft tap, the two lines meeting, and the threads of yellow tangled together. Three of Aiden's strings broke and Elizabeth landed on her knees in a faint. The cage was shut.

Illness screamed as the threads squeezed around their skin, body shifting from reptilian to human-esque to almost liquid, as if it could escape the magic through a crack. The more Illness moved, the tighter the weave grew until the magic worked into the Ancient, dragging them down to the slate slab where their name was written.

Corina scuttled away and then collapsed, still crying, her arms wrapped around herself. Joanna lurched to her feet and stumbled out of the circle. My body was too sluggish to catch her and the sound of her throwing up left me wincing. Aiden and I turned our backs on the vanishing Illness and walked with uneven steps to our covenmate. She was bent over just before the boundary, one arm around her waist and the other wiping at her mouth. Just left of us, bloodied and catching their breaths, Sabine and her coven crossed the line.

"I was going to give you shit for letting us deal with the Ancients, but it looks as if we got off easy," Darin said.

Black spots filled my vision and my knees rattled as they hit the ground, my body falling before I'd even realized.

"Is anyone injured?" Sabine asked me.

I shook my head, thought I felt a long, black tail lashing through my mind, and slammed my eyes shut. "Magical depletion," I said.

She nodded. There were two of her, and then one, and then two again.

"You're turning green," she warned me.

I joined Joanna in heaving into the grass. The work was done. One more Ancient out of the way. *Just survive*, I thought. *Survive seven more.*

15

JOANNA

I woke up in bed, Aiden and Callum pressed close on either side of me. My memory of returning home was hazy. Lora found us a door to write through somewhere outside of the boundary, so we didn't have to tempt Warfare to a second fight for the day. I'd written us a second door straight up to bed, all of us too weary to walk our own way up to the top story.

Callum's eyes were already open, staring unfocused above my head, and Aiden's breath puffed damply against my shoulder, his arm around my waist almost uncomfortably tight.

"You didn't have to do that," I said to Callum.

He blinked, returning to the present, and he looked almost surprised to see me.

"You nearly hurt yourself pushing at Warfare that way," I added. Even now he looked as if he might be sick at any moment, somehow the wrong color, or maybe that was the storm clouds hanging out the window, turning the light strangely soft and green.

"He almost had you," Callum said.

I opened my mouth to object and Callum's eyebrow twitched. He was right. I'd run through the woods, heart pounding and knowing that one step more, one more second, and Warfare would snap me up, cut right through me and break me in half the way he had with President Anders. I stared back at Callum in the following quiet. The baby, my suspicions that there *was* a baby, was on the tip of my tongue as we stared at one another.

Not yet, I reminded myself. *Isaac will be home any day. We should all be together.*

"You aren't arguing," Callum said, frowning.

"No," I said, the word coming out breathy, salt stinging at my eyes.

Horror struck Callum's face at the sight of my tears and it drew a choked laugh up from my throat.

"Hey," Callum whispered, one hand reaching up, thumb stroking away wetness, his head scooting closer on the pillow until his nose nudged at mine. "Today was a win. We have Illness locked up for good."

I nodded, squeezing my eyes shut, the stranglehold on my throat of worry and fear still gripping me. "I miss Isaac," I forced out, the only truth I was prepared to share. "I want us all together again."

"Just a few more days," Callum said, nodding. "I know. I'm sick of the separation too."

"I agree," Aiden rumbled, lips kissing my skin. "You saved the day again. As usual."

I assumed he was speaking to Callum, until Callum grinned at me and said, "She did, didn't she? Wonder how highly Corina thinks of herself now."

I blushed and shook my head. "I shouldn't have goaded her into it like that. I know how impossible, how painful it is to write one of those names. It should have been me from the start."

"Actually," Aiden said slowly, head lifting until his chin was crooked around my shoulder, cheek pressed warmly to my ear. "If we had more Scrivens, pairs might be a better idea. Faster, offer each other support, or at least a back up Scrivens. It worked today."

"No, think of Bekka, or Kristin and Ella. They wouldn't fare better than Corina and I. Besides, we don't have anymore names," I pointed out. Callum stiffened in front of me, his eyes sliding away, and my heart skipped with worry. "Callum?"

"Something… may have happened when I manipulated Warfare's cage."

I blinked and froze, body going cold, and then jerked up in bed, squirming my way out from between them.

"A link," I said, turning to face him, eyes wide, waiting for him to correct me. The fear trickled in, ice dripping in my veins. "Callum, you didn't."

Aiden sat up and Callum grimaced, hand running over his face and rumpling his hair. I was going to be sick again.

"We agreed, Callum! We said that wouldn't happen," I said, voice high and tearing in my tight throat.

"It was an accident," Callum said, words muffled behind his hand.

"Was it?" I asked, small and quiet.

He sat up, eyes wide, hand reaching for mine. "I swear, Joanna. I… I'm embarrassed to admit it, but I didn't have the faintest clue what I was doing in the moment. Not that I regret stopping Warfare from taking a bite out of you. I don't even know if it would work for the others, or if it was because somewhere in my ancestry there's a little link to him. I just… got lucky?"

"This doesn't sound lucky," Aiden said with a heavy sigh.

"I'll figure out how to undo it," Callum said, but his eyes flinched.

I tucked my hands underneath my thighs, my skirt rumpled from sleep and the turmoil earlier in the day. "You mean *if* you don't end up having to use it."

"It's the only lead we have so far," he whispered.

Aiden's lips were pressed together, head shaking slowly. "That doesn't make it a good one."

Callum was looking to me for an answer, but I didn't know what words I had to offer. I shrugged my shoulders and his expression sank. I debated staying, arguing, but instead the worries just raced a track through my mind. What if we lost Callum to Warfare? Did Callum's being a descendant mean he had an advantage to defeat the Ancient, or was more likely to succumb to him?

"I'm going to the library. Write if you need me."

There were unlikely to be answers, but maybe there would be

distractions. As it was, I needed walls between Callum and I to keep me from throwing myself at him and refusing to let him risk himself, or telling him all he stood to lose if something went wrong.

I ignored their sighs as I left the bed and went down into Callum's office, gathering up a few books I'd left in corners before heading to the library through Isaac's closet door.

I wasn't alone in the building. A familiar set of footsteps clicked against the wood flooring in the wings overhead.

"It's only me," I called.

"Come to read, or for a bit of work?" Gwen answered from within the stacks.

I was too tired and terrified to read for pleasure. "Work, please."

Gwen hummed overhead. "Come and join me, then." She was up in the rare historicals, an area I'd grown familiar with during our hunt for Ancient names.

"Are the books misbehaving again?" I asked.

"No, your notes keep them in line. Elizabeth and I cleared out Anders' home the other day and I found a hefty collection of formerly missing texts," she said, turning her head to me and wiggling her eyebrows.

She was standing on a stool, one arm cradling three heavy old books and her other hand balancing at the top of the shelf. She laughed at my expression and I realized I must have been wearing a greedy look as I eyed the cart at the end of the aisle.

"I was going to put them back myself, but they're rather interesting pieces. Most could go one of a few different directions in the catalog. Why don't I let you work on them for a bit of training?"

"I would love that," I said, feeling a simple, giddy thrill rising up in me. New books. New *old* books that I hadn't met yet, with strange and interesting contents. "How long have they been missing?"

"Oh, some of them probably left the catalog as long ago as when Anders was a student." She sighed and added, "The University has a tendency of hiring book thieves."

I grinned. My coven included. Best of all, if they'd been out of the library so long, that meant even Callum and Aiden hadn't seen them before. Callum would be green with envy when I told him. I wondered what that might mean for the Ancient, Jealousy, out in the woods and then brushed the thought aside. I didn't want to think of Ancients or even Callum for a few hours.

Gwen stepped down from her stool and brought me the three books in her arm. "Start with these since you've already seen where I was heading with them. Let me know if you have any trouble with the others. A few belong in Staff only."

I took the books from her. The first, a text on the history of the University, was easy to place, and the other two were within reach, both about other local landmarks. Neither would leave my coven-mates too jealous. Back at the cart were the real gems, and I was tempted to find a nice corner to curl up in and read through the collection, the call of reading offering a respite from all the stress still lurking in my thoughts. I resisted the urge. Gwen said this was training and I didn't want to have the reputation of being the slowest librarian at Canderfey University.

It was as if President Anders had never once followed the rules of borrowing and returning, amassing himself a collection of texts to see him through his studies, and even his career at the University. The subjects were varied, editions old and rare, from biography to reference to theoretical. I marked a few to come back to, for my own sake or for one of the coven.

Gwen was right, too. There were a few puzzles. One was an autobiography of a witch whose coven reached a total of twenty-three people and supposedly claimed an island for themselves off the coast of Enmaire, except I was fairly certain the account was fictitious. Another almost certainly belonged in the staff library, considering it was a cookbook of poisonous pastries. My favorite was the last, a children's pop-up book with spectacularly detailed artwork, all about the things in the world for which there was no explanation. Except Canderfey Library didn't have a children's section.

I took the three puzzles up to the Staff section to an open table and sat down, determined to put in a decent effort at shelving them myself before asking for Gwen. After studying a map of Enmaire's coast and determining there was no such island, I chose romantic fiction for the first. The second would go in the dangerous herbs catalog. The third I let myself enjoy.

I was reading the tale of a small pool of water in a little northern town not far from where Callum grew up. It was supposed to have temporary healing properties, and existed without a source—no hot spring, no secret well, just what might have been mistaken as a puddle of infinitely fresh water. Each of the stories included a visitor to the area, a stranger who came and went before the new oddity was discovered by a local most in need. The scene of the pool included a strange and filmy paper that shimmered as I twitched the pages, mimicking the surface of the water. The stranger was on her way off the page, a young woman dressed in a red cloak, when I noticed the pattern on the fabric. Sigils that almost squirmed as I looked at them, as if they were trying to escape observation.

I'm sure you'll find me tucked between pages.

"Mystery," I whispered, eyes growing wide. "Gwen! Gwen! I think I've found something."

I turned the page to a new story and looked for the stranger. This time it was an old man whose walking stick bore the same symbols ingrained in the wood. In the next tale it was a wolf whose fur gleamed with the shapes. Gwen arrived as I was closing the book, feeling the fever of excitement and triumph burn in my cheeks.

"What is it?" she asked, eyes worried and voice breathless.

"I've found a name," I said, laughing. I turned the book over and handed it to her. "We need to know everything we can about who made this book. The author or the illustrator or the publisher. Any of them. Just in case it's a lead to others."

Gwen took the book into her arms, frowning at the cover and opening the inside. "This wasn't even in our collection to begin with. I think it belonged to Anders. I took it so you could show Isaac for the art."

"Well I'm glad you did. It's about the Ancient, Mystery. And I'm hoping there are more."

Gwen's wonder washed away and her eyes glinted behind her glasses as she nodded. "I'll go search my references."

"I'm going to get Callum and Aiden and tell them," I said, my grin so wide it hurt my cheeks.

I rose up and started toward the stairs, Gwen's hand stopping me by my elbow. She smiled before speaking. "It's not as exciting news, I know, but I wanted to tell you, you did well."

She was right, it wasn't as significant as finding one of the true names we'd been searching for, but the praise still made me blush.

"Oh, good!"

"We'll talk more about your program later. Go gather the others. I'll see what I can find."

I nodded and ran downstairs, writing home and finding Callum and Aiden cooking together in the kitchen. Callum looked up from the vegetables he was cutting, apology on the tip of his tongue, and I rushed ahead.

"Can whatever you're making wait? I've found something at the Library. A true name."

Callum's knife clattered to the counter as he rushed to me, Aiden quick behind him, before doubling back to the stove to turn everything off.

"Whose? Where?"

"Mystery's. I know he's missing but if the author knew *more*—"

"Show us," Callum said, his hand reaching for mine. I squeezed and rose up on my toes, kissing his lips briefly before dragging him and Aiden back into the Library with me.

THE BOOK WAS a little bit of a dead end. Mystery's name was there but it was the only work by the author and illustrator, and any record of the publisher had been lost in history.

"Don't look so disappointed," Aiden said, still smiling and lifting my chin to stare back at him.

"I just want a solution," I said.

"I know. We all do."

"Mystery probably isn't even a threat. Isaac's *working* with him."

"I know," Aiden repeated.

"I don't want Callum to use that link," I whispered, swallowing hard.

Aiden's expression hardened, looking down to the tables below the wings where Callum had lost his focus to one of Anders' returned texts. "I don't either. *He* doesn't want to. But I trust in his abilities, just as I trust in yours, and just as I know that I will always be at both your sides, helping in whatever way you say I'm needed most."

Tension melted in me as I stared up at Aiden and his eyebrow ticked up at my softened expression. "I love you," I said.

Aiden's cheeks flooded with warmth. "I love you," he said.

It was a simple exchange, one our coven passed between each other every day, but in moments like this one I felt the weight of the words enveloping me. I knew better than anyone how powerful a word could be, and I felt the protection of Aiden's now when I needed it most.

The staff room door banged open, and my sense of safety wobbled before I squared my shoulders and faced whatever new disaster was on its way. Tatsuo ran in, Corina and the warrior coven close on his heels.

"It's Shame's cage," he said, the announcement filling up every dusty corner of the library. "It's starting to unravel."

16

ISAAC

THERE WAS A BLACK CAT PERCHED ON THE BACK OF ONE OF THE HORSES
when I woke the next morning, small body riding the muscles of the
beast like a ship afloat. Bravery had the reins in her small hands,
Anger dozing at her side, and the cat turned to stare at me as I peered
out from the car. Their pale silver eyes blinked at me, gray tufts of
hair sprouting from its ears and a dense black mane around its head.

It's going to get crowded in that wagon, Mystery said, cat eyes
blinking.

There was only Agony and I in the cart together, the Ancient still
sleeping. I sat up and drew the curtains back, letting sunlight and
summer stream in.

"Morning," Bravery said, smiling at me and looking deceptively
angelic by daylight. "How's your hand?" I lifted my fist, swollen and
bruised from the punch I'd thrown, and Bravery eyed it briefly,
nodding. "It was a good hit. We're almost to Generosity, just up
ahead."

I grimaced as I combed my fingers through my hair, tangled and
dusty from the road, and searched the scenery for our destination.
We'd reached a woody region in the night, not quite as dense as
Canderfey, but through all our circular travels in Enmaire I thought

877

we were at least getting closer to home. Up ahead was a wide cross-roads and on the far corner a large and somewhat shabby looking home sat on a plot of land. Leaning slightly to the left, the building was wide and cluttered with windows and rooms that stuck out at odd angles. It reminded me a little of the Scrivens house in the woods, as if someone had tacked on new spaces to accommodate need. In the overgrown front yard sat a shiny black and green car, Pride's no doubt. Our friends were waiting for us.

There was a large wraparound porch filled with people who looked only a little better off than Agony did, their clothes threadbare, a few on crutches or with arms in slings. Standing on the steps of the porch, waiting for us, was Bryce. Their bright hair glowed in the sunlight, skin impenetrably pale, eyes watching us in our slow arrival.

Anger sat up with a snort as Bravery turned us onto the gravel drive. He cleared his throat and squinted at Bryce. "Been waiting for us long?"

Bryce shook their head. "Your sister is… giving us a bit of trouble."

Anger grunted as if he'd expected as much and jumped down from the seat, passing Bryce on their way to the wagon. They looked at Mystery the cat, then at Bravery, and finally at me.

"How did it go?" they asked.

"We got into a bar fight," Bravery supplied.

I grimaced and nodded. "Fine, aside from that. What do you mean by trouble?"

"She says she'll come," Bryce said, eyeing the house. "She also says she'll do some woman's laundry, and dress another man's wound, and cook breakfast for whoever's last woke up."

"Generous to a fault," I said and Bryce snarled and nodded.

"Brother! No!" A woman screamed from inside.

Hildy appeared, rushing down the steps, color high in her cheeks. Her eyes found me and she smiled but it was a panicked sort of look. "Oh, hello, Isaac. Bryce, in the car. I think we're finally leaving."

"I could use a spot of breakfast," I said.

"Here," Bryce said, pulling an apple from their pocket and passing it to me, and then feeding two more to the horses.

"Brother, this is not the way," Pride said, his broad back walking the wrong way out of the house and nearly falling down the steps. In front of him came Anger, woman thrown over his shoulder.

"It is the only way," Anger said simply, small boots kicking against his hip, holes in the soles and laces untied.

"Put me *down!*" she cried.

"Will you come, Sister?" Anger asked.

"You know I will, but first I must—"

I caught a brief glimpse of reddish brown hair streaked with gray, strands falling loose from a bun that looked several days old and half-hearted, as Anger strode to the back of the wagon.

"Be ready, lad," he said to me.

"Your needy will still be here when we are done and you get back, Sister," Trust said, following the brothers arguing over Generosity. "It really is best if we leave first. Come." He took Pride by the arm and led him back to the bright car just as the woman, the Ancient, was dumped into the back of the wagon.

"Drive, Sister," Anger barked to Bravery.

I shuffled to the end of the wagon and caught the new Ancient by the waist just before she dove out. She struggled against me, overly strong hands trying to pry my arms away from her waist. Thinking of what Bryce said, I rushed to plead with her.

"I really do need you to come with us," I said, my voice muffled against a warm woolen shawl. She paused in wrestling me off and I continued. "My coven is waiting for me in Canderfey and I haven't been in touch with them. I'm worried. If you'll come now I can see them sooner, know that they're safe."

The woman sighed and relaxed in my arms and I drew away slowly. Generosity's disguise was middle aged, with large, dark eyes that were circled in tired blue. Those eyes and her mouth were lined, clothes patched together, and she was still wearing a mending thimble on one finger despite being thrown over Anger's shoulder.

"Oh, alright, darling," she said, voice surprisingly sweet and deep.

Motherly, I realized, sitting back on my heels. She relaxed against the frame of the cart and Anger jumped back onto the bench at the front as we pulled away from the house. She looked out the curtain at all the people standing on the porch and I thought she looked a little relieved.

"It'll be like a vacation for you, Sister," Anger said, echoing my thoughts.

"They *do* need me," she said.

"Everyone thinks they need you," Bravery said.

"Oh, Brother!" Generosity cried out, finally seeing the heap in the corner that was Agony, his eyes peeling open. She crawled over to him, digging into her pockets. "Here, let me help you."

Anger snorted on the bench and Mystery prowled down the flank of the horse and then leapt into the cart, coming to curl up at my side.

"How many more?" I asked, too tired to sort them out in my head.

Generosity would be... counterpoint to Jealousy. Agony, to Ecstasy. Pride, to Shame.

"One more," Anger said, voice turning dark. "Delight."

IT WAS ANOTHER SWEET VILLAGE, a little less grand than Pride's, but very familiar.

"We're in Carlton," I said, spotting a greenhouse I'd drawn on more than one occasion when I was younger. "I grew up near here."

"She always finds places like this," Generosity said, leaning up against the back of the bench and watching the town go by. She'd brightened along the road after tending to Agony, and was currently letting Mystery doze on her lap as a cat. "Where cheer is easy to come by from a reliable stock of sources."

I frowned and shifted back into the belly of the cart. "I don't remember it being that easy," I said. "Not until I arrived in Canderfey." Generosity reached her hand out and squeezed mine briefly.

"Last stop, lad," Anger said. "We'll have you home as soon as we decide who's in charge of wrangling Delight."

"Not a chance," Bravery said, scowling. "Can't stand her."

"Delight?" I asked, brow furrowing. "You can't stand *Delight*?"

"You'll see," Bravery said, turning in her seat. "She's exhausting! Ah, here's the car."

We stopped on a corner in the center of the village and I groaned as I crawled out of the back of the cart. It'd been almost a full day of riding in the wagon, with rests for the horses and a few short breaks. My back cracked ominously as I stretched, Bravery snorting at my groaning. Hildy appeared from around the corner, Bryce at her side.

She passed me a wrapped sandwich as my stomach growled in warning. Mystery leapt down from the back of the cart, twining around Hildy's leg until Bryce hissed at them.

She's in the tea shop across the street, Mystery said. Hildy's eyebrows raised at the voice in her thoughts and she skirted away from the cat she'd been about to pet. *But none of us will volunteer to go collect her. She's unbearable.*

I frowned and suspected I'd be left to go convince Delight to join us when Hildy cleared her throat. "I'll get her," she said. "I'm overdue for a turn and I'm used to talking women into things. Clothes usually, but this shouldn't be so different."

"We'll be close behind," Bryce said.

Hildy nodded, shoulders squaring and chin lifting as she crossed the street, looking like she was ready to go into battle. I followed with Bryce, breaking into the sandwich. Over my shoulder I caught the other Ancients, wary expressions on their faces as they hung back near the car and wagon.

"Do you think she's… dangerous?" I asked.

"Maybe," Bryce said. "If she wanted to be. More likely, she's annoying."

Hildy reached the door as two women about her age were leaving, giggles pouring out onto the sidewalk as they left. It was a group of ladies inside, visible through the wide windows, and their voices layered together, bodies bowing with the force of their humor. One laugh was louder and brighter, and I guessed it was coming from the woman with bright white curls and a round figure, her shoulders bobbing in time with the tinkling sound.

"Would you still like to knit together?" One of the exiting women asked the other, who sighed.

"Not today. I've got a splitting headache now."

"I know. She can be so…"

"Yes. Yes, she can."

The door shut behind Hildy, just as another pair of women stood from the table and made their way out. Their wide smiles grew tense with every step further from the table and I began to understand the effect Delight was having, why the Ancients were in no hurry to see her.

"You can take the car home with the others," Bryce said, watching Hildy smile at the group at the table, artfully able to invite herself into their circle.

My eyes widened and I turned to them. I'd thought for certain I'd be left in the wagon with the majority of the Ancients again.

"I can?"

Bryce smirked without glancing at me. "Yes. Take Bravery and Anger with you. They'll convince Pride to cross the boundary. Trust and I will manage the others."

I would get to see my coven soon. We were only a handful of hours away, I could be with them again before morning. The relief rushed through me, as heady as Callum's northern mead, worry and frustration unwinding from around my bones.

"I'll write ahead once I'm far enough from Mystery. Let them know we're coming," I said.

Bryce nodded, eyes fixed through the window to their covenmate. One of the women at the table noticed us staring and I slid out of frame as her smile slipped. I looked too rough from the road and travel, a dark beard starting to grow in on my jaw. Bryce was disconcerting enough on their own.

"Thank you," I added.

Bryce stiffened, eyes skidding over to me and then away again. "Don't mention it."

"I really do—"

"I was serious," Bryce snapped and my tongue went still in my throat.

The front door opened, more laughter pouring out, and a smile spread across my lips as I tried to bury my own laugh. I was hours from home, hours from my coven. That delight was entirely my own.

☾

We'll meet *you at the station.* Joanna's handwriting sprawled across the page, the covenbond thrumming with so much mutual excitement I thought I might jump out of the car, as if the energy of expectancy would let me reach them sooner on foot.

If nothing else it would offer minor relief from the bickering of my fellow passengers.

"If you would just drive at a reasonable speed," Bravery said, scooting across the front bench seat, toes stretching toward the gas pedal.

"I *am* at a reasonable speed," Pride protested.

I wrapped one arm over Bravery's shoulders and dragged her over to my side. "I'd rather not have us wrapped around a tree a mile before I reach home," I said, raising an eyebrow.

Bravery smirked up at me. "I might be a very good driver for all you know."

"I might believe you if you were twice as tall, but as it is I don't think you can reach a pedal and stare out the window at the same time," I said. Anger laughed, stretched out in the backseat dozing and watching the stars go by out the windows.

"I suppose there will be decent accommodations provided?" Pride asked.

I was watching the road go by, closer and closer to reaching the train station, and I hummed in thought. "There are rooms available with my coven, or with Bryce Gast's. Or you can stay at the Scrivens house." I looked down to Bravery and then to Anger. "I think the two of you might like it there." And I was certain Pride would not. Separate housing would be best for all parties involved.

"But all of those places are inside of the boundary," Pride said, frowning.

"Yes."

"Where we will be in our… less adaptable forms."

Bravery rolled her head to stare at Pride. "Afraid of looking foolish?"

Pride sneered down at her. "When was the last time you were stuck in your own skin, Sister?"

She shrugged. "Don't remember. But it won't be for long, and it's not as if we shift about properly while playing human. Aside from Mystery a bit."

I looked back to Anger, his arms crossed behind his head, light eyes reflecting the night sky. "I hadn't thought of that. Bryce says it can be uncomfortable. Will you be alright?" I asked.

"It would be better if we were staying *out—*"

"We'll be fine, lad," Anger said, cutting Pride off, whose sigh seemed to go on for an impossible stretch.

"We'll have to be, this looks to be the place."

The train station was a long building, the drive wide to accommodate the high traffic around school holidays. We pulled up, engine purring, and my heart pounded as if it were expecting some disaster or confusion, as if I didn't already know what to expect. Shock and joy struck me like lightning as the front doors opened, and Joanna appeared, face stretched in a wide smile and her curls bouncing. The tires of the car were still turning, but I was running out of the car, Pride sputtering in annoyance and the brakes screeching.

I made it halfway up the cobblestone walk before my arms were full.

Pages and ink and vanilla. Her warm face tucking itself against my neck, breath kissing my skin as we breathed each other in. Joanna's arms were around my shoulders, one of my hands sliding into her hair, the other arm wrapped tight around her waist. She spoke and the words were muffled into my throat. I was laughing with relief, eyes falling shut as I pressed my own face into her hair, the softness familiar.

My heartbeat felt *right* again, entwined with hers, with Aiden and Callum's. Their footsteps sounded on the walk. I'd barely lifted my head and Aiden was there, face dipping down, cheeks full with a smile as he kissed me, his hands joining Joanna's in stroking my back. Callum sighed, one hand squeezing my hip, his cheek resting on my shoulder. We were tangled together, finally, and I let myself forget about the boundary and all the Ancients and any time spent away.

"Hello there," Aiden said.

I grinned and turned my head, Callum lifting his so our noses bumped together, lips catching. He hummed, the sound vibrating into the kiss. I studied his face as he pulled away, expression too tense and worried, his eyes skimming over my shoulder to the Ancients who must have made it out of the car by now. It was going to be alright, I decided. Whatever he was worried over. We would fix everything.

Joanna was still pressed tight to my chest, face hidden, and I slid my hand down to the back of her neck, squeezing gently. "Let me look at you. I missed the view."

Her laugh was brief and her head tilted back, tears shining on her grinning cheeks. "I missed you looking, but I'm afraid we don't have time. We need your help." Her eyes drifted over my shoulder to the approaching Ancients and then widened as they landed on Bravery, flicking back to me.

"She's older than she looks," I said. "What is it? What's happened?"

The soft bubble of the reunion popped as Callum straightened and looked west to the woods. "Shame's cage is unravelling. We're not far from it here and I'm certain I can repair it from outside. Sabine and her coven are inside trying to hold the Ancients, but we're outnumbered and could use a little interference."

I leaned back into the arch of my coven around me, each of them finding somewhere to rest a hand, and I looked to Pride. He squared his shoulders, lifting his chin and unbuttoning the sky blue linen waistcoat he wore.

"Show me the place," he said. "I will keep Shame contained."

"Pride," I whispered in Joanna's ear.

Her lips twitched and she looked at me from the corner of her eyes. "Oh, I could tell."

"This way," Callum said, running into the night toward the black mass of the woods.

Pride, Anger, and Bravery joined him and I made to follow until Joanna tugged softly on my hand. She reached up, fingers scratching at the growth of beard on my cheeks.

"Aren't we in a hurry?" I asked.

"We should be," Aiden rumbled, guiding us after the others.

Joanna sighed, smile fading. "I know. I'm just glad you're home."

"Come on, before Shame breaks through and Callum does something ridiculous like force another link," Aiden said.

My feet stumbled beneath me at the news and Joanna's eyes rolled. "Don't get me started," she muttered.

The sounds of fighting crept through the night and the glow of the cages glittered ahead of us. Callum's back faced us, standing in line with the three Ancients I'd traveled with. My feet were picking up the pace and I found myself less reluctant to face the conflict. I wanted to see Anger in action, wanted to see if Mystery was correct about the counterpoints. If the time I'd spent away from my coven had been worth more than simply a reprieve from Canderfey.

Bravery looked back over her shoulder as we reached them. On the other side of the cage, steel flashed blue under moonlight, a sword striking against a steaming black shadow. Bravery winked at me and leapt through the boundary all at once. She was smaller than I expected, even in this form, a creature between a cat and a deer. Golden antlers sprouted from her head and she wore soft fur in shades of peach and orange and tawny brown. I was equally tempted to scoop her up and protect her from any harm as I was when she was disguised as a little girl, but she bolted fearlessly into the fray, yipping with excitement.

"I'll see her safe," Anger assured me.

BROTHER YOU HAVE ARRIVED AT THE WRONG FIGHT. YOU SHOULD BE STANDING WITH YOUR SIBLINGS. Warfare snarled into the air, a grunt coming from one of Sabine's coven, and then he stomped his way forward, out of the shadows and into a glimmer of silver moonlight.

Anger's head shook, his shoulders rolling as he walked nose to nose with the glowing cages. "I always wished you talked less, Brother."

He went through head first, landing on all fours, black as night and the largest Ancient I'd seen barring Warfare. He turned back to us once, his coal gaze flashing now with heat and flame, growled, and then bound into the woods.

"Here's the tear," Callum whispered.

"And there is Shame," Pride said, pointing to the slithering yellow figure that circled nervously closer to the border. Pride grimaced at the cage and then jumped through, feathers sprouting through his hair and over the back of his neck as he grew. A long inky blue tail of feathers followed him like a train as he darted on awkward bird's legs over to Shame, who made a strange moaning noise.

Let me through, Brother, Shame begged, so weak it left me flinching. *Let me be free again. I will vanish, I promise.*

I cannot. Pride dove towards Shame and they both cried out, the air wavering and sparking like lightning between them.

I looked to Joanna but she was already staring, watching Callum hiss through his teeth as he found the threads of Shame's cage and tried to force them together again. I stepped up to his side, picking up the mottled yellow from Shame's dewy hide with a flick of my fingers. I added it to the haze of Callum's power and then Aiden whistled, a weak and plaintive note.

"It's taking," Joanna breathed, "And Warfare is retreating. He didn't bring enough of the others with him."

Geoff stumbled through the boundary, hand cupped around a dark stain on his upper arm, and Joanna ran to him. The threads in Callum's hands twined together, coaxed under a last press of power from the three of us.

"Just a gash," Geoff said, catching his breath, huffing as Joanna yanked his hand away, revealing a deep, bleeding tear in the flesh of his arm.

Sabine and her coven bounced through the boundary, sweat gleaming on their brows and breaths panting. I caught the flicker of worry that creased between her brows before she forced her face smooth.

"I told you not to get so close to his tail," she said. Geoff grunted in answer and Sabine dug a bandage out of her back pocket, bullying her covenmate as she tended his wound.

I checked back on the woods, relieved to see Shame and the others following Warfare, my new allies lumbering—or in Bravery's case, prancing—back to us. Darin watched the trio with a wary expression, settling as they crossed back into their human forms.

"That little girl nearly took a bite out of me," he said, glaring at Bravery.

She shrugged. "You're so big I mistook you for one of the Family," she said.

I snorted and shook my head. She was in one piece, so were Pride and Anger. Joanna slid into my arms, face tucked to my throat and Aiden and Callum were quick to follow, wrapping themselves around us.

"Now I see why you were so eager to get home. Handsome bunch aren't they?" Anger asked me with a wink.

"I'm a lucky man," I said.

Joanna's hip nudged against mine. "We all are," she said, biting the inside of her lip. I wondered if this was a new confidence in my covenmate, or if she was feeling a bit of Pride's influence. Either way, I couldn't resist stealing another quick kiss from her.

"I hope none of us are staying with them tonight," Bravery said in a noisy whisper.

Joanna choked on a laugh and pulled away, untangling the group of us. "Ah, we should get back. Gwen and Tatsuo, Hildy and Bryce's covenmates, are waiting at the Scrivens house. They have room for at least one of you, and there's lots of room at the Scrivens house. I've written adjustments to allow you safe passage through the buildings, but your… siblings don't have the same luxury."

She led us back to the station, inside to a small office door, writing our way into the Scrivens house, Sabine dragging her coven in first so she could tend to Geoff. Anger stopped me at the doorway with a hand on my shoulder.

"You may not see much of me once we're inside," he said, frowning. "I don't want to cause any trouble, so I'll try and keep to myself."

Less than a week ago and I would've been glad to hear it, but I'd grown to like Anger's company recently. While he was suited to his nature, he was also in control of it and his assistance had never faltered, even though he wasn't one of the counterpoints.

"Joanna has ways around your influence," I said to him. "We'll take it one step at a time."

Anger's eyes widened at my answer, lips parting, but Bravery beat him to speaking, "We're growing on him. Told you."

I laughed and followed my coven through Joanna's door. My magic vanished in a blink, but my bond was in place and that was all I really cared about. There were friends to greet on the other side, Gwen and Myles and Daniel and Tatsuo, but I turned to watch the Ancients travel through.

Pride and Bravery stepped through together, Pride's oversized, avian form far too large for the narrow space and his jewel green gaze clearly suspicious of the homey interior. Corina cooed at Bravery, and was rewarded for trying to pet the Ancient by nearly having her fingers nipped off, which I found unnecessarily pleasing.

Last came Anger, head bowed to avoid knocking against the door frame, and then he landed on dark black paws, long fur hiding his face, voice grumbling in tones that echoed in my bones. His head lifted briefly, a beastly bear-like face, and then ducked away quickly.

"You're a little large for the rooms but the Scrivens can adjust if need be," I said, hoping to put Anger at ease.

He growled and the sound cut off abruptly, as if he'd forgotten the way it made the air simmer. *MIND YOUR OWN WORRIES*, he said, words careful not to snarl. *I'LL MANAGE FINE.*

"As long as none of you eat Lars, we should get along very nicely," Nora said, Bekka's pet curled around her boots. Bravery sniffed at the creature, was immediately and thoroughly licked, and then yipped and ran far from his reach.

GO HOME, LAD, Anger said. *WE'LL BE FINE.*

Whatever unease I felt at the thought of abandoning the Ancients evaporated as Joanna's fingers threaded with mine. They were right, I was ready to be at home with my coven.

17

———

JOANNA

T HE ENVIRONMENT IN OUR BEDROOM WAS ALMOST COMPETITIVE—
Callum, Aiden, and I all trying to touch our fair share of Isaac, eager
to reunite with him as a whole coven again.

My fingers were pulling at the buttons of his shirt, Aiden's
shoulder pushing me out of the way as he sucked along Isaac's neck,
Callum holding his face to Isaac's, tongues stroking together. Isaac
pulled away, head falling back and breath panting. I finished with the
last of the buttons, exposing his chest and caressing his skin in greedy
exploration, my fingertips studying the structure of him.

"If you lot think I have the stamina for you each to have a turn..."
Isaac trailed off with a needy hiss as my nails scratched gently over his
flat nipples.

"It wasn't what I had in mind, but now that you mention it," Aiden
said, grinning at me.

"Joanna will have to be first," Callum said, ever the strategist.

"No," I said, blinking and scooting back. "I think it's my turn to
watch. Isaac always seems to like it."

Isaac's flush burned a deeper color, eyes glassy as he lifted his head
to stare at me.

"I can be patient," I added, smile curling up my lips.

891

Aiden's fingers dug into Isaac's hair, catching his eyes, which dilated at the gentle tug on his strands. "We're going to make such a mess of you, my love."

Isaac moaned and I slid off the bed, watching as Aiden took Issac's mouth in a thorough kiss, tongue licking in with a slick sound that made me shiver. Callum pulled Isaac's shirt away, throwing it to the edge of the bed and then working quickly at the waist of his trousers. I unbuttoned my own blouse, fingers skimming my skin, tracing the rounds of my breasts and the sensitive skin of my stomach. Isaac's eyes opened, lips parted and breaths heavy, a long groan falling as Callum's hand slid down between skin and fabric to fist around his cock. Isaac's eyes tracked my hands as I undressed, my palms cupping and massaging my breasts, legs kicking out of my skirt. I dipped my fingers inside my panties as Aiden and Callum wrestled Isaac down to the mattress while stripping him, their mouths feasting on his skin until he was writhing on the sheets, cock seeping and bobbing stiffly against his stomach.

"On his knees," Aiden whispered, head lifting from Isaac's stomach, his index finger tracing a line up the underside of Isaac's length. "I'll hold him while you take him."

Callum nodded, teeth snapping at Isaac's throat and then pulling away.

"You're trying to kill me," Isaac rasped as they pulled him up.

Aiden's dark hands framed Isaac's face, his lips pressing over one eye, his cheek and chin, and then his lips in a gentle caress. "We're savoring you."

I tried to stifle my own whine, fingers slipping through arousal to circle over my clit, but the faint sound drew three pairs of eyes.

"How long until your patience runs out, Jo?" Callum teased, tugging his own shirt off over his head, scrambling on the bed to free himself of his pants.

"I don't know. I'm beginning to understand why Isaac doesn't mind watching with his sketchbook. It *is* a pretty picture," I said.

"It'd be prettier with you in it," Isaac said, hand reaching out for me. "Come closer."

I shook my head, trying not to thrill with thinking of how things would go if I was within reach of their hunger. "I will. First I want to watch. Aiden, make him focus."

Aiden had just finished stripping out of his own clothes and the sight of them all bare and pressed together pushed me to slide two fingers inside of myself, equally high on the dizzy rush of watching and wishing to be nestled between them. Aiden grasped Isaac by the hips, pulling him tight against his chest, kiss rough and hungry until Isaac was fighting back, crowding Aiden. The hands on Isaac's hips slid down to his thighs and then tugged him up, Callum helping so that Isaac was balanced between them in a crouch, his thighs spread around Aiden's hips, their cocks and chests pressed together.

I stumbled a little closer to the bed, afraid to miss a single sound or sight of them. The way Isaac stiffened as Callum began to toy at his ass, the clasp of strong hands on muscle, the head of Aiden's cock appearing, seeping lightly onto Isaac's stomach. The chorus of groans as Isaac arched and Callum began to fit himself inside, Aiden distracting Isaac with kisses on his throat and answering nudges of his hips. They were beautiful, so in harmony with one another. A visual feast for me to enjoy.

Isaac's head turned, his eyes fixed to where I touched myself. I shimmied out of my underwear, one foot propped onto the bed to offer him a better view. His gaze dragged up my body, tongue flicking out over his lips as he watched my free hand pinch at a nipple, plucking it to a point.

"You're beautiful," he whispered. Then Callum shifted position and Isaac's eyes slammed shut, shout echoing up to the ceiling, hands clutching to Aiden as Callum dragged his head back for a messy kiss.

"Come here, darling," Aiden purred, and I abandoned teasing myself, skirting the ticklish warmth of the precipice waiting inside of me.

I crawled to his side, one hand skimming his back, the other scratching softly on Isaac's thigh. I kissed Aiden's cheek, looking down over his shoulder to see where he and Isaac were stiff and red with arousal, pressed between their chests. The mattress bounced, breaths mingling, all three of my lovers' voices breaking with pleasured grunts and hisses.

"He'll come soon," Aiden whispered into my ear. "And Callum after him. Do you still want to wait?"

I nodded, pressing my lips to his jaw. "You're not the only one who has a bit of imagination in bed."

Aiden laughed. "Never doubted it."

Isaac's throat and chest glistened faintly with sweat, half-formed begging words beginning to fall from his lips. Callum's brow shone too, furrowed with focus, lips parted and strangled pleasured sounds trying to break free. Isaac dragged their joined hands up to the center of his chest, fingers squeezed tight together as Aiden held him up for Callum's taking.

"Gods, I love you. Love you all," Callum managed and then his spine was curling forward, hips jerking. I looked down between Aiden and Isaac, seeing Isaac's cock twitch, licks of cum paint his and Aiden's chest. A long and stuttered cry fell from his lips and I gazed up again to watch his face tear in relief and ecstasy.

They settled slowly, Callum's thrusts continuing in uneven, soft nudges until he pulled free and Isaac whimpered. Callum's slender fingers stroked up Isaac's shoulders and then he backed away, helping Aiden lower Isaac to the bed, sticky release shining on Isaac's chest. Aiden scooted forward on his knees, tugging Isaac up to his lap. Aiden's erection was nudging at Isaac's entrance, slipping in Callum's cum.

Isaac laughed, weary and baffled and I circled around Aiden's back to stretch out on Isaac's other side, brushing sweaty locks of hair off his face. He snatched at my hand, pulling it to his lips and sucking my fingers into his mouth, tasting my arousal. Then Aiden was pushing in and Isaac was arching, eyes shut and mouth open, my fingers abandoned on his tongue.

I bent my head, kissing his lips and cheeks, Callum joining me, as Aiden began to roll his hips. I leaned back, my hand sliding through the mess on Isaac's chest, his cock twitching weakly, as I wrapped my hand around its soft state.

"Fuck," he muttered, releasing a whimper.

He groaned and then pulled me back to his mouth as Aiden fucked him. I knew every time Aiden thrust completely in, because Isaac would whimper again and bite my lower lip. Every time Aiden was nearly out, Isaac would pant and squirm on the bed. Every time Aiden hit a perfect spot inside, Isaac's cock would twitch again, a little closer to half hard each second.

"Kiss him," I told Callum, sliding down the bed.

Callum followed orders neatly and I reached down to where Aiden was inside Isaac, stroking briefly against the base of Aiden's cock and making him purr with a lazy smile. Then I reached for Isaac's sac, rolling and squeezing in a slow pattern, watching Isaac's stomach clench, his fingers fist in the sheets, his cock stiffen.

"Wicked girl," Aiden said, voice strained.

"Determined," I corrected. In truth I was desperate. Even after I'd stopped touching myself, my body throbbed and craved more. The insides of my thighs were already slick with desire. I sat up on my knees and stretched to kiss Aiden, sucking on his tongue as it thrust into my mouth, holding his face to mine with tight fingers on his chin.

Isaac was almost entirely senseless, coaxed back into a needy frenzy so soon after finishing. Every limb and muscle was tensed and Aiden's breaths were hitching, his teeth gritted and eyes watching where Isaac was clamped tightly around him. He wanted to hold out but Isaac was squeezing too hard, nearly forcing him out. Aiden's will broke in four deep thrusts, dizzy pleasure washing over his face, hands petting every inch of Isaac he could reach as his thighs trembled and he nearly collapsed forward, catching himself by his palms at the last second.

Callum and Aiden drew away and Isaac stared at me through slitted eyes, a tired grunt in his throat as he lowered his heels to the bed and I threw my leg over his waist. I stroked his length, shifting to poise myself above it, and Isaac hissed, his hands flying up to my thighs and gripping tight enough to bruise.

"I'm going to pay you back for this," he said, warm and sweetly dangerous. "Turn you so limp and exhausted you can't even speak your own name."

"Tonight?" I asked, grinning.

He laughed and rolled his eyes. "No. When I can think straight. Another night."

I bent forward and kissed him, soft and tender and sweet, the opposite of the kind of touch I so desperately wanted, and then leaned back. "Fair enough."

And then I sank slowly down, Isaac's cock a perfect stretch, just on the right side of strain, my body pulling him with the same greed I felt racing in my veins, cunt fluttering and threatening to finish me early.

"Joanna," he whispered, eyes softening. "Love. I missed you."

"I missed you too," I said, voice strained in my throat. I rose up slowly, thinking at every second I might come, and then lowered myself even more slowly, catching Isaac grinning.

"Ride me, love," he urged, hips flexing.

"I don't want it to be over," I said, trying not to whine. Callum laughed at the head of the bed and then came to my side, hand stroking up my spine.

"Isaac's not going to be done with you for a bit," Callum said, pecking at my lips. "You wanted to wait, after all."

My lips pressed into a pout and Isaac's hands found mine, linking our fingers together.

"Ride me or I'll fuck you from below and you'll get whatever I feel like offering," Isaac said, smirking.

Desire took over the decision, my hips lifting and falling and a bright, sudden, flying orgasm washing through me. I pulled my hands free of Isaac's and planted them on his chest. I wanted more immediately, thighs burning as I chased the feeling, as if I could hold onto the pleasure if I was desperate enough. Isaac helped, heels planted in the bed as he bucked up into me. Callum was at my back, pushing my hair aside to kiss my throat, his hands sliding around my torso to my breasts. Aiden lay, sacked out at the head of the bed, watching us all with his lazy grin.

"That's it," Isaac panted. His throat flexed as he looked down between us. He shifted, hitting high inside me and making my arms collapse. Callum's hand lay trapped between us, rooting down for my clit as Isaac's arms held me tight to his chest.

I moaned, uncertain if I was still in control of the pace or if I was simply being taken. I didn't care. It all felt too good. Callum's touch, Isaac's cock, Aiden's kisses appearing on my shoulder as he shifted to join us. It burrowed through me, lighting up every nerve, blacking out my vision, until I was shouting into Isaac's chest, cunt clasping tight around him, his hips stuttering in response. It was the orgasm I'd wanted, deep and rich, curling my toes and turning me limp and useless, Isaac still rutting gently into me, warmth flooding my veins and sparkling under my skin.

He finished with a hot rush inside me and I tucked my smile into his skin, thinking of the secret I had. The one that would need to be shared soon. But not now. Hands slid me up and over to curl into Isaac's chest, Callum laying down at my back and Aiden on Isaac's opposite side.

"I have a million questions for you," Callum said, words mumbling against my hair.

Isaac grunted in answer, his fingertips skating over the arms I'd slung across his stomach.

"Tomorrow," I said, reaching back and pulling Callum's arm over my ribs to join Aiden and Isaac's hands.

"It's good to be home," Isaac whispered.

I tilted my head back to see his face, relaxed and sated, free of worry lines and the tension around his lips he'd carried before his travels. The bond, our heartbeats, even our breaths were all in sync again. I parted my lips to say something, that home was better now he was here again, and fell asleep on my next sigh.

* * *

CALLUM ROLLED, and his elbow nudged against my stomach, a woozy swoop running through me. I sat up with a start, hand over my mouth.

"Going to be sick."

"Mmhuh?" Isaac was just starting to wake, eyes peeling open and lips frowning. His hands reached for me as I started to scoot to the end of the bed.

Callum was faster, used to the warning by now, and he sat up like a shot. His arm scooped me up from the mattress and I grimaced, trying to keep from gagging, as he rushed me toward the bathroom.

"Again?" Aiden rasped from the bed. "I thought you were well again."

I couldn't answer, Callum skidding to the toilet just in time as I retched, last night's dinner landing with a splash. Callum hurried to the sink to wet a washcloth with cool water and I sighed between the next spell of sickness.

"This means it isn't Illness," Callum said. "Unless there's something we don't know, the effect of their blood or…"

There was definitely something they didn't know. This just wasn't the scene I'd pictured while I'd imagined telling them.

Aiden and Isaac came padding into the bathroom. Isaac sat down at my back, pulling my hair away from my face and soothing his hand up and down my spine.

"How long has this been going on?" Isaac asked.

"Since you left. She said she was tired. But it's been days now of this," Aiden said, tone grave and worried.

"I'll be okay," I whispered, throat scratchy.

"You said that the first day," Callum said, reaching over and pressing the cool cloth to the back of my neck, the gentle shivers soothing the uncomfortable twist in my gut. "I wonder if we shouldn't take her out of Canderfey. Send her to your parents in Rhodantis, maybe."

"Yes," Aiden answered, just as I huffed and said, "Don't be ridiculous."

"Joanna, if you aren't well—" Isaac started.

"I'm *fine*."

"You're sick," Aiden growled.

"You should see a doctor. At least get away from all this stress."

"It isn't stress!"

"You don't know that."

"I'm pregnant." And then I threw up again with a groan, cursing the timing of the morning. My covenmates were silent, their gentle touches paused as my words sank in.

"You're...what?" Aiden whispered, sinking down to the floor at my side.

I caught my breath, cheeks hot and tongue bitter, and looked up to his face. His eyes were huge, surrounded by white, and his mouth hung open.

"Pregnant... probably," I said, reaching back and pulling the cloth off the back of my neck, wiping my lips with it and waiting for a reaction. I turned to find Callum similarly stunned, although much paler. Behind me Isaac appeared thunderstruck and terrified.

So I explained. "I didn't realize at first. I was still drinking the contraceptive tea everyday. But the boundary probably—"

"Cut the magic off," Callum said, voice barely audible.

"Yes."

"That was almost two months ago," Isaac whispered.

"And I didn't notice my cycle skipping. It was maybe more of a relief that it hadn't turned up with everything we were dealing with so I just... And then I was sick and everything pieced itself together, but Isaac wasn't at home. I thought it should wait till we were all together again."

My heart was wild in my chest and my fingers clung hard to the porcelain of the toilet as I waited for one of them to respond in any way but shock. What if that was all they felt? I might be sick again. Despite everything going wrong for us in the moment, I'd latched onto the idea of a child with such *joy*. What if I was alone in that feeling?

"Joanna," Aiden whispered, hands reaching out and cupping my face, eyes watering and lip trembling as his mouth stretched into a beaming smile. "You... are you... really?"

My own smile emerged wobbling, Aiden's tears calling up my own as I nodded, blinking rapidly to try and keep from crying. "All but certain. I haven't seen a doctor yet, of course."

"We should go to Rhodantis," Aiden said, firm, making to rise as if he were about to pack right away.

I laughed, catching him by his arm. Gods, we were all just sitting here, *naked*, and I'd given them the greatest shock I could dream of. This wasn't at all how I'd imagined telling them. Maybe over a calm breakfast was expecting too much given how our summer had gone so far. "We can't leave now!"

"You shouldn't be *here*," Aiden said, understanding leveling on his face. "Gods, Joanna. Think of everything that might have happened."

"There's a doctor coming," Isaac said, so quiet it barely broke through Aiden and I. I looked to him, heart beating unevenly with nerves. He looked so serious, eyes touching every bit of me while he thought. "Health, the Ancient. He's a... pediatrician, but I'm sure, given who he is and... and how old he is."

"See?" I asked Aiden, smiling. "The immortal being of Health. Could we really do better?"

Aiden snorted but relaxed. "Fine. Let's clean you up. We'll have breakfast in bed. What would you like?"

"I honestly don't know that I'll keep anything down right now," I said and he frowned. "Mint tea?"

He nodded and hurried to stand, making for the door, before promptly turning around. His hands wrapped around my shoulders and he bent, kissing the top of my head with a long, firm press.

"I love you. You- well, you probably know how happy you've made me, but all the same I plan on showing you."

I blushed, eyes rolling. "I hardly managed it alone."

Aiden left us, laughing and grinning, shoulders straight and proud as he dressed and ran downstairs to make tea and probably more food than I could eat in a week. I turned around, facing Callum and Isaac, chewing on the inside of my lip as I waited for them to speak. Aiden was easy. Aiden had wanted children even *before* I'd joined the coven. I knew Isaac and Callum wanted children, but I think all three of us were more patient for the eventual occurrence.

"Are you all right?" Callum asked me, taking the washcloth and rewetting it before crouching down. He pressed it below my jaw and I leaned into the touch, nodding.

"Yes. Are- are you?" I glanced at Isaac too, whose gaze fell to his lap.

"Oh, *Joanna*," Callum said, drawing me back to him. "*Yes.* Yes, I'm happy." He leaned in and kissed my forehead and cheek. "Trying very hard not to think about all the risks you've taken in the past couple months, but yes."

I nodded. "I know. I've gone over everything more times than I can count," I said, watching anxious pain streak across Callum's expression. "I don't regret any of it. And I don't want to be kept here in the house now that you all know."

Callum looked at Isaac and out the bathroom door, his hand reaching up to his own hair and tugging at the strands. "You'll have to convince Aiden." I scowled at him and he shrugged. "I'm not saying I wouldn't feel the same in your place. I just... I just don't know how reasonable any of us are going to be given the situation. Gods. A *child*." A smile and a giddy laugh broke free and I joined him. "Come on, let's get you off the floor. Are you- will you be sick again, do you think?"

"I can't tell," I said, waving my hand away. "But I wouldn't mind being back in bed."

Isaac was faster, arms around my thighs and back, lifting me from the floor with a soft grunt of effort.

"I'd understand," I whispered in his ear. "If you... if you aren't sure."

Isaac jerked, hands tightening on my skin and his head reared back so he could look me in the eye, startled and solemn. "Don't think that. I'm terrified," his lips twitched and his gaze softened, "but I... I've dreamt of this too, love."

I sighed, curling into his hold even as he set me down on the bed. He slid in next to me, tucking me against his side, Callum bringing me my robe.

"Health should arrive today or tomorrow," Isaac said. "I'll bring him here as soon as he is."

"I hope I'm not wrong," I said, taking the robe from Callum and slipping it on as he hunted down some pants.

"Well, if you were wrong, I put in a valiant effort last night, so..." Isaac said, shrugging and smirking with a twitch of pride on his lips.

Bright, surprised laughter burst out of me and I reached over, pinching at the flesh on his side and making him squeeze me against him. He was smiling, teasing, and even though there was fear and nervousness and worry and insecurity buzzing quietly on his line of the bond, it meant a lot to me that he was willing to be happy, excited even, with the rest of us. I knew he was afraid of being a man like his father. The idea of having a child was probably stirring up those old wounds, but if he was already willing to overcome that fear I had no doubt that Aiden, Callum, and I could do our best to help him.

"If I am...pregnant," I said, tripping over the word now that the frantic energy from earlier had settled, "it will be a very lucky baby."

Callum lay backwards on the bed, resting his cheek on my calf, and wrapping a hand over my knee. "Very well read. Extremely spoiled."

"Well loved," Isaac corrected, one foot nudging at Callum's arm. His head turned and he kissed my forehead.

Downstairs a knock sounded on the front door and suddenly all of our peace and contented affection froze, the three of us stiffening on the bed.

"Damn," Callum said, rolling away. He grabbed a stray shirt, Aiden's maybe, from the floor and headed for the stairs. "I'll take care of it."

Isaac and I remained cuddled up together for a handful of tense seconds before scurrying out to find out what bad news waited for us on the front steps.

18

——————

AIDEN

A FATHER. I WAS GOING TO BE A FATHER. FINALLY.

I was existing in two separate worlds. One was the Canderfey outside of our door where enemies lurked in the woods, strange allies were arriving, and a battle I barely understood was looming over all our heads. And the other was this house, my coven together, happy and dreaming of—no, *expecting* a child.

I grabbed the wrong part of the kettle, scorching metal, and yelped, shaking out my hand and rushing for the sink.

Focus, King.

Except that I couldn't stop grinning and thinking of running back upstairs, two steps at a time, to kiss and cradle Joanna, to pull Isaac and Callum in close until we were one ridiculous cluster of limbs and laughter. Joanna's joy was tentative and shy, she was feeling our covenmates out. I knew what to expect. Callum would be pleased and every so often that happiness would stun him into confusion and planning, worry and shock. Isaac would be more of the latter and every so often that worry and shock and confusion would give way to joy. It was all tangled up in him and I would do my absolute best to sort the threads out, remind him of who he *was* and who he was not.

Namely, his father. Just as Callum was not his, thank Gods, and I was not mine, much as I respected him.

I dried my hands, poured Joanna her tea and the rest of us cups of coffee, and dreamt of the baby. Which of us it would look like, and whose habits it would take up. Something would have to be done with the back garden so there would be a place for them to play. I could cut down on my course load and stay home to care for them, so Joanna wouldn't have to interrupt her work at the library if she didn't want to and—

A knock sounded on the door and for a moment I forgot the other world I lived in, the one where people didn't walk outside if they didn't have to. I started toward the door, tying my robe around me, and it wasn't until I heard Callum thundering down the stairs that I remembered.

"Who do you think it is?" I asked.

Callum shook his head, wearing one of my shirts and his sleep pants, his eyes focused on the door as if he were expecting it to open on its own.

"If it's one of the Ancients we have to trust the Scrivens magic to keep them out," Callum said. "Hopefully it's friendly."

He pulled his sword out of the umbrella stand and I resisted my urge to wince, following close on his heels to the front door. I had no magic and no weapon, but I'd fight with my bare hands if necessary. Feet thumped on the steps overhead and I turned to find Joanna, still pale from her morning sickness but narrow-eyed with lips pressed together, hand in hand with Isaac on their way down.

"Stay upstairs," I hissed.

"No," Joanna answered.

Of course not, I thought with a weary sigh. But she stood behind my shoulder as Callum opened the door.

On our front steps, pink-winged Ecstasy waited, metallic silver eyes blinking, head cocking in an avian manner.

I have come to call a truce, Ecstasy whistled in our heads, shivers and heat running under my skin. *On behalf of myself.*

"I find that unlikely," Callum said, making to slam the door in her face.

She chittered but didn't move forward. *You bring my siblings to the woods, you offer them your homes. Warfare said such civility between the Family and humans was impossible.*

"Our courtesy to your Family doesn't extend to you if you intend to break the same oath they made centuries ago," I said.

I know. I will make myself a disguise if I am freed. I will take the oath and live in restriction. Better human skin and law than another cage. Ecstasy's head bowed and her wings spread for a moment, colors dizzying me and weakening my knees. *I like human appetites. Covens create attractive passion. If the Child of Nothing has one I may find one of my own.*

"Without manipulation or influence," Joanna said sharply, peering out from my side.

I understand the law, Wordsmith, Ecstasy said, the edge in her tone like nails running down my back.

"Will you fight Warfare and *those* siblings?" Callum asked.

I will fight them to cages, but not to death.

"We aren't asking for death," Isaac said. "Your brother, Agony, is coming here."

Ecstasy retreated down one of our steps, her shock like a white hot spike in my groin, before quickly burying her influence. *It has been a long time. I think I will be glad to see him. You can trust me. I will fight for you when you are ready. Until then I will keep out of Warfare's way.*

Callum looked down the length of the street. "Wise, I'm sure. I will trust you when you deliver on your promise. Not until then. But if we succeed you may give your oath and we'll take down your cage."

Ecstasy shivered at the promise and we all shivered with her. Her wings beat and she jumped from our front steps, taking to the air. *I shall fashion myself a very pleasing disguise.*

Callum slammed the door shut before she could continue, his back pressing to the surface and hand reaching up to cover his eyes.

"Do you believe her?" Isaac asked, the blush of her presence receding on his cheeks.

"I don't know. I don't even know if I *want* to," Callum said. "Warfare having one less reliable ally is good news but it doesn't offer us a solution."

"The others will have arrived by now," Joanna said. "Maybe if we speak to them, one will know something. We have Mystery's name."

"But Mystery is working with us," I said, frowning. "They'll probably take the oath too."

"We could use their name as leverage against them," Callum said, eyeing Joanna whose expression sank. She didn't like the idea but she'd thought of it and we were all desperate enough to use it.

"Mystery also thought that bringing the counterpoints would be a better tool than just Ancients to fight," Isaac said, gentle tone urging caution. "Let's hear them all out first before we decide where to apply threats."

Joanna's shoulders rose and Isaac turned her to face him, hands framing her face and lifting it up for a brief kiss. "I will do whatever I have to for this to all be over," he said, locking gazes with her. "I want Canderfey back to rights, and you safe, and our only worries to be students and… and nurseries."

A smile lit up Joanna's face and they both relaxed as she nodded.

"Come on, darling," I said to her. "Let's have a bath before we see the others."

Joanna took my hand and followed me to the stairs.

"I'll bring the tea up," Callum offered. "And some food."

I nodded, glancing over my shoulder at him and he smiled in thanks. Callum and Isaac needed time to discuss the part the Ancients would play and Joanna needed to be taken care of. Even if I knew it was a hopeless argument and that Canderfey and the rest of us needed Joanna to be a part of this battle, I was still going to put a serious effort into talking her out of it if I could.

Joanna brushed her teeth while I started the bath water, keeping it from getting too hot and adding in some soaps and oils I knew she liked.

"I know what you're going to say," she said, moving to sit at the edge of the tub as we waited for it to fill.

I grinned at her and nodded. "I know how you're going to answer, but let's go through the motions and see if we can surprise one another, hmm?"

Her lips pressed together, trying to tamp down her smile as she nodded. "Alright."

I pulled her up, my hands reaching for the belt of her robe and pulling it loose, holding her gaze. "I don't want you to fight against the Ancients."

She hummed, head tilting and reaching for the tie on my own robe. "I won't pick up a sword or put myself any closer than I have to be, but I *will* be there. I've done the math. If we can trust Ecstasy, that still leaves six Ancients. And we have six Scrivens, including me. I have to write." I frowned and she shrugged off her robe, letting it pool on the floor and then pushed mine off my shoulders, rising up to her toes and slinging her arms around my neck. "I can't stay here at home while the rest of you are out in danger. And I won't be any safer if something goes wrong and I wasn't there to help."

My eyes fell shut, a weary breath rattling out of my chest as I hunched and rested my forehead against hers. "Fine. But if you feel *any* discomfort—"

"Aiden, there will be discomfort," she said, frowning in apology.

"I don't want to risk…everything," I leaned back and wrapped my arms around Joanna's waist, lifting her into the water and following after. We slid down together, sides pressed to one another.

Joanna's smile was patient and I knew what she was thinking. There was no promise I could pull from her lips that would stop her, no safe room I could lock her inside.

"I won't gamble, Aiden," she said, earnest and sweet. "Not if I don't have to. But it isn't just me at risk. Callum is going to try and pull Warfare's name and I don't trust anyone else to make sure that name is carved in stone. I was always going to play this part, just as Callum was probably always going to be the one to deal with Warfare, much as I hate to admit it. I'll be careful."

Then she took my hand under the water and rested it over her stomach. My throat squeezed and our smiles shook as we stared at one another.

"I know you wanted more time," I said.

"We'll have more time," Joanna said, grinning. "With the baby. I want this. I want our life together and I'm not interested in my life going any other direction."

I pulled her to me, my lips sliding over hers, hungry and needy, my heart so painfully full it pushed new tears out. I shut the outside world out again and let myself have this moment alone with her.

"You're going to be a wonderful mother," I whispered, kissing marks over her cheeks, pulling her into my lap.

"Well if I'm not at least they'll have three very wonderful fathers to make up for it," Joanna laughed.

"How are the others?" I asked.

"Maybe not as excited as you and I," she said with a shrug, bending forward and kissing the end of my nose. "But happy. Callum won't really let it sink until he knows it's safe for us all. And Isaac will let himself enjoy moments as they come. He'll fall in love when he holds the baby."

"You've sorted it all out then, have you?" I asked, relaxing deeper into the water and taking her with me until our shoulders were submerged.

She nodded, her forehead on my cheek, our fingers layered together under the water. "Bryce will watch the baby when we are busy."

I stiffened in surprise, eyes going wide. "Gast?"

"They'll be godparent, of course."

"What if I want to retire and stay home with our child?" I asked.

"Oh, and will we never go out to dinner? No more concerts?" She pinched at my ribs and I laughed.

"Fine. Let the dragon be the nanny. If Gast wants to, I'm sure I couldn't stop them."

The bathroom door opened and Callum and Isaac came in, a tray of food and our drinks in their hands. They lined it up along the tub ledge and undressed to join us.

Don't be too happy yet, a small, scared voice whispered in my head. *It isn't over. It isn't safe. Anything could happen.*

I may not have been a warrior like Joanna and Callum, but I would fight with every last note of music and breath in my lungs. It was time to move forward and enjoy the best years of my life with my family.

19

———

ISAAC

WE GATHERED TOGETHER AT THE LIBRARY, A STRANGE CROWD OF humans and Ancients, and it took even me some time to sort out who was whom. Mystery was back to their unknowable shape, Tatsuo and Bryce had met Health at the boundary just hours before and brought him too—a sprightly and almost human figure, faintly green and with his legs hidden beneath a long borrowed robe, the knees bowing out unusually. None of them but Anger had the same strength of shape as one like Warfare and I worried all over again about their ability to help us.

Generosity was winged and wide and airy, more like a butterfly than a bird and certainly not as threatening as her feline counterpoint, Jealousy. Delight was smaller than the others, bouncing constantly on long legs and leaping to the tops of shelves, tall bright yellow ears twitching. Agony was keeping to a seat far from the others, an enormous snake strangling the legs and back of the chair. Trust was twice as tall as any human, a pillar being in an almost transparent silver blue.

I sensed Illness's cage as I reached here, Health said to me, taking a seat at the table where we were all settling.

"There were concerns about safety and their influence," Aiden

911

explained and Health nodded, his hair almost like Lars' green dreadlocks.

I am glad it was managed and I still offer my support. His eyes skirted to Joanna for the fourth time since he'd entered the library and I wondered if he knew already about the…

My heartbeat picked up a bit at the thought. Gods, I was going to be a father. *What if, what if, what if* chanted through my head. If I was cruel or short-tempered. If I failed my coven. If I was too scared to love the child. What if Joanna wasn't well and it wasn't a pregnancy at all?

"First of all," Joanna called, voice slightly raised to draw the attention of the crowd. "Mystery. We have your true name."

The Ancients hushed and stilled around the table and the air shimmered as Mystery circled us. *Found it, did you?* Joanna nodded and Mystery continued, *I gifted it to the artist for solving me during our friendship. Wrote the stories myself. What will you do with it, Wordsmith?*

"Nothing, I think," Joanna said. Her eyes tracked Mystery's movements. "We'll see."

The Ancients' laughter was in my head, but the tension at the table was dissolving.

And what will you do with the rest of us? Bravery asked, leaping up to the table and stretching in front of Joanna, rolling to her back and presenting a downy belly. I was fairly certain Joanna would lose her hand if she tried to pet the Ancient, but she was too smart to be caught, her hands folding in her lap.

"How are you willing to help?" Joanna asked.

Bravery purred and flipped back onto her paws, claws clicking on the tabletop. *I can hunt down Brother Terror, drag him back to you by his shaking bones. He can't act against you while I'm near.*

"Wait," Callum said, sitting forward. "What do you mean by that? Can't act against us?"

Our influence is empty when we are with our counterpoints, Health explained.

"It doesn't give us true names but it might be easier to create links, find those names, while they're in the presence of their counter-points," Tatsuo said.

"Links?" I asked, looking to Joanna. "You mentioned that when I arrived. What happened? I thought we weren't attempting that again."

Callum blushed and Joanna's lips firmed, her eyes down in her lap, and my stomach squirmed at the sight.

"It was an accident," Aiden said, "but Callum got tangled with Warfare. Either we waste more time hunting down names we can't find, or we try to recreate what Joanna did with the Hollow."

"I don't know if it happened because I'm some kind of descendant of his like he claims," Callum said. "I think it might be possible to force the connection. For all we know that's what was done hundreds of years ago."

The Ancients shifted around us and I wondered if it wasn't *exactly* how it had happened the first time around.

Most Enmairian magic comes from a bit of our blood trickling in one way or another, Trust said, pale pillar swaying over our heads. *You are reflections of us.*

Elizabeth startled at the declaration and stared up at the Ancient before turning back to Callum. "We had to take down Illness's cage last time. Are you considering risking that for the others? And one at a time?"

Callum shook his head. "One at a time gives too much warning, too much time for retaliation or attack. I think…We should act all at once. Call Sewell back with faculty who can help. If you will hold your counter-points we can break the cages and meet you inside to form the new ones."

"What about Warfare?" Hildy asked. "Peace is dead."

I'LL HANDLE WARFARE, Anger growled, pacing around the table. *BESIDES, HE'LL WANT TO FEAST WHEN HE'S FREE. HE WON'T GO FAR IF HE THINKS THERE'S AN EASY MEAL CLOSER.*

I frowned, watching Anger. He was the biggest of the Ancients in the Library, but he wasn't a monster the size of Warfare. And he wouldn't dull Warfare's influence like a counterpoint would. If Anger couldn't contain him we would all be at risk.

I'LL HANDLE HIM, LAD, Anger said, hovering at my back.

It burned in him, the pale center of a fire—rage and resentment and centuries of regret. I didn't know if it was enough to fuel Anger in fighting against Warfare, but he was right, there was no one else who stood a chance like he did.

"Let's plan our circles now," Callum said, taking Joanna's notebook and pencil, sketching out the names and organizing who we would need to return to Canderfey.

ANGER AND BRAVERY hunted me down in the upper wings. I was sitting on the floor between two bookshelves, a favorite book of color reference in my lap, my eyes unfocused on the page.

WHAT'S TROUBLING YOU? THINK I CAN'T TAKE THE BEAST? Anger asked, stopping at the end of the aisle, unable to squeeze his enormous frame between the shelves.

"I'm worried about that, yes," I said, waiting for him to react. He only grumbled, fiery eyes peering through shaggy strands of hair.

HAVEN'T SEEN MY TEETH YET, he mumbled.

That isn't it, Bravery said. *He's scared, I can sniff it from head to boots.* The Ancient slinked up the aisle, flopping down on the floor by my thigh, heavy paws landing on the book in my lap, chin tilting against her fur to stare up at me. The tease was there again, did I dare risk my hands against claws and teeth to pet her?

I did not, and she flashed those bone-bright fangs at me in what I was sure was humor.

"Joanna is pregnant," I said.

YOU'RE WORRIED SHE'LL GET HURT, Anger said.

"Of course I am."

No, said Bravery, *it's not that either. Tell us.* Her tail beat against the wood of the floor, her body heavy and warm against my legs.

"My father was an angry man. A drunk, and the drink made him worse, but it wasn't what caused the anger," I said. I'd said the words before. To my coven. To friends. Sometimes, like with Callum, Aiden, and Joanna, it was a burden eased. Other times the confession only felt as though I'd peeled back a bandage and exposed a festering wound.

"I'm worried I will be that kind of man. That kind of father."

Bravery purred and blinked at me, saying nothing. My hands were fisted against the legs of my pants, jaw clenched until my teeth hurt.

ANGER ISN'T CRUEL, IT ISN'T VIOLENT, Anger said. *THOSE BELONG TO CHOICES AND ACTIONS. ANGER IS ONLY SOME-THING YOU FEEL. HOW YOU RESPOND TO THAT FEELING IS SEPARATE. SO YOU FEEL ANGER SOMETIMES. DO YOU MAKE CRUEL CHOICES? DO YOU SEEK VIOLENT ACTIONS?*

I looked down at the colors on the page, vision blurring.

One day you will lose your temper and yell at your child, Bravery said. I jerked, staring back at her. *They will do something foolish, or rude, or cruel, and your patience will fail you. Your Wordsmith will do it too.* She grinned again, *Although my money is on it being Warfare's descendant first. The feeling will pass and it will come back. But I'll tell you a secret—our race can read a future as easily as a past. There's never a moment you will harm a hair on your family's head.*

I choked, a sob strangled in my throat, and swallowed it down. It could have been a lie for all I knew, but I didn't care. I *believed* the words as Bravery spoke them. I wouldn't hurt my family, my children. Burying the sudden crumbling in my chest and blinking away any tears in my eyes, I lifted my head and nodded at Bravery and then Anger.

COME DOWN. YOUR COVEN IS WAITING FOR YOU, Anger said.

I gathered up the book to study in preparation for our battle and followed my friends back to the stairs. Bravery leapt down by the twos and threes, but Anger in his enormous lumbering form looked as though he might begin to tumble and slide at any moment.

"I see now why you prefer to shapeshift," I joked.

Anger snarled and nearly skidded to the landing. *WATCH IT, LAD.*

"Is it just as hard on your knees as an old man?" I ran down the next flight as Anger roared, and caught a brief glimpse of that threatening maw of sharp teeth snapping in my direction.

Downstairs at the circulation desk my coven stood with Health, Joanna's cheeks pink with happiness. It was true then, we were going to have a baby! I ran to join them and Aiden's arm wrapped around me pulling me to his side, our bond thrumming with nervous joy.

Yes, you're pregnant. Health said, beaming back at Joanna. *Healthy and strong too, the pair of you.*

Joanna laughed, the sound full of relief and delight and I left Aiden's arms to go to her. She was shaking slightly as I held her, breaths uneven, but I could feel her smile against my throat. How worried had she been, keeping the secret and wondering all the while if it was even true? She'd waited for me to make it home and the thought left me slow and lazy and satisfied. I kissed the top of her head as Anger finally made it to the tile floor.

For once, I didn't feel raw after talking about my father. I didn't feel the weight of him like a chokehold around my throat. It would come back, stale old fear and the bruising ache of history, but it wouldn't stop me from moving on, continuing the happiness and the stunning breadth of love I'd found with my coven.

MY EYES DRAGGED open to the sound of scythes cutting through the wheat stalks under burning midsummer sun. Or was it a dry brush tracing the future of a painting on an empty canvas? The night was dark and heavy in our bedroom, Aiden's face blurry in front of mine. Again, the sound stirred overhead, but this time I understood it. Wings scraping over our roof, a warning.

I sat up, Aiden's fingers clutching at my skin and then sliding away to underneath his pillow. Joanna stirred beside me, clamped in Callum's possessive hold. For a moment the affectionate, shadowy, picture of them called a need for charcoal on a page, and then talons scratched above me, threatening the tile on our roof. Callum sat up, sudden and startled, and Joanna's irritated pout was as sweet as she had been in sleep.

"What is it?" she whispered.

Callum looked at me, copper curls almost blue in the dark, falling into his eyes and against the pillow marks on his cheek.

"Get dressed," he said.

He and Joanna rolled off the bed and I followed, glancing back to find Aiden groaning and sitting up, at least half-aware of what was going on as he thumped over to where he'd left his clothes. I found the pants I'd arrived home in almost under the bed, the day too busy for tidying, and jumped into them. In the back pocket was the silver pen Callum and Joanna had gifted me and I pulled it out, wrapping my fingers around it and embracing the sense of safety.

On the street in front of our home a sudden and bellowing roar echoed in the night. Warfare.

"Write to the Scrivens house," Callum said as Joanna pulled a dress on over her head. "We aren't ready to tear down the cages, we need to scare him off."

She nodded, heading for the stairs and Aiden stopped her, his fore-head lined with stress.

"I won't go outside," she said, staring up at him. Aiden's shoulders softened and Joanna jumped up to kiss his cheek before running down.

"She's going to have to write a name when we're ready," Callum said, voice low and gentle. Aiden glared at him and Callum ignored the warning stare, heading to follow Joanna. "We need six Scrivens. She'll be with us. We're stronger with her. She's safer with us."

"Let's just deal with tonight, shall we?" Aiden said.

Joanna was running into the hall from the kitchen as we made it downstairs, cheeks flushed and breaths short. Behind her appeared Bravery, leaping down the hall toward me and the front door. Sabine followed in her wake, and there was a giddiness in the warrior's expression that left me wondering if Bravery didn't have a descendant of her own.

"Anger is coming through the woods. He doesn't fit through doors," Joanna said, a little sheepish, as the rest of Sabine's coven appeared.

Agony slithered alongside their footsteps and Health followed a moment later. Callum rummaged in his closet, pulling out a sword and then passing a long axe to Aiden, who looked so stunned I almost wanted to laugh. Warfare roared again—a taunt—and a sound followed that I couldn't comprehend, a horrible crunching and tearing, the windows of the house rattling. Bravery stood on her hind legs pawing at the front door to be let out like one of our cats.

"Chase them off," Callum said to us. "Don't risk more than you have to."

He opened the door and Joanna muffled her scream behind her hand, ghost-white Terror hanging from the door frame. Bravery yowled and leapt for her brother, his bone thin legs kicking in the air and the two of them tumbled down to the street. Warfare had pulled the bricks up from street, rubble piling into a barricade just down the road.

Bryce and Pride were barreling down the road to Warfare's back. Suspicion swooped like a black cloud over our heads, almost invisible as it blocked out the stars and moon, and Jealousy raced towards Bryce, Sorrow swaying at the end of the street.

SEE, SIBLINGS? BETRAYAL FROM THE FAMILY! THEY ABAN-DONED US TO OUR CAGES AND NOW THEY'VE COME TO SEE US TRAPPED AGAIN!

"He's going to try and convince the Ancients to kill their counter-points," I said to Callum.

Bravery and Terror were circling one another on the ruined road, claws clicking against stone and dirt.

Callum nodded. "Then we'll make sure that doesn't happen."

"Be careful," Joanna breathed behind us. She stood, one hand clutching the railing of the stairs—I suspected to keep herself from charging after us—the other pressing her pencil and paper to her chest.

I concentrated on the silver pen in my hand, remembering what they'd told me, and it transformed into a long blade. Not quite Callum's sword, but I was more likely to trip myself with a sword I didn't know how to use. Still, the point was deadly sharp and it felt light enough in my hand to move and fight with. Agony slid ahead of us on the ground, heading for Warfare, and Callum, Aiden, and I followed with Sabine and her coven.

Pride took to the air, skirting around Warfare as he rose on his haunches, enormous jaw snapping at jewel bright feathers. Suspicion screamed overhead and Pride beat his wings, heading for his sibling.

YOU HAVE THE WEAKER SET, DESCENDANT, Warfare snarled at us.

It was a thought I'd fought since meeting the Ancients on the road. How could Delight fight Warfare? What would Bravery lead us to but possible danger? Now though…

"They managed to not land themselves in cages, at least," I said, thin blade raised in my fist, eyes fixing on Warfare's throat rather than his eyes.

Warfare's laugh was a growl, but in the bond Callum and Aiden sang with respect and I squared my shoulders in answer.

THEN WHY DOES LITTLE BRAVERY LOOK SO CAUGHT? Warfare snapped.

A pained yip rang out behind me and I spun to see Bravery pinned beneath Terror, its long white legs scratching and piercing at her pale fur, sparks of tension rippling like lightning around them. On the opposite end of the road, past the worst of the rubble, a horrifying howl and roar blended out of Anger's throat.

"Go help her," Callum whispered to me. "We'll deal with this."

I ran down the street, Bryce taking my place, feathers rustling with intention. Bravery twisted on her back, butting her antlers at Terror, claws scratching against the scaly shell of his underside. He jabbed her with another talon and my horror was entirely my own, fingers tight around the hilt of the long blade in my hand.

"Get away from her," I called, marching closer even as my veins turned to ice in my limbs, heart hammering unsteady and frantic, as if it might stop at any moment.

sheis minetoend. she woulddothesame to me, Terror rattled, their words running together.

You've let Brother Warfare corrupt your mind, Bravery answered and she sounded strained. *I came to try and undo his work. That's all!*

Shimmering silver blood hit the ground next to me in a sudden splatter, an Ancient's scream sounding overhead in the night. Pride or Suspicion, I didn't know, but I didn't want Bravery's mixing in. I lunged forward, catching the tip of my blade along one of Terror's legs, the sound of contact like a piercing whistle in my ear. Terror reared back twisting in my direction and Bravery sprung up with a sudden curl of her body, antlers pushing him backwards to hit the ground. I stuck the needle fine end of the blade into Terror's side as Bravery bit sharp teeth into another leg. She whimpered and I pulled the silver free, eyes going wide.

"You felt that?" I asked.

Terror took the opportunity of my retreat, scrambling backwards and Bravery ignored me to address her brother.

Get away from here. Keep your head out of Warfare's ass for a day and think of where you want to put your loyalty.

playinghumanmakes yousoft, sister, Terror rattled in answer, but then he was scuttling down the road, away from the fight behind us and diving into the shadows of the woods at the end of the road. Sorrow followed after him, bowing and weeping.

Bravery turned to me, blood darkening the fur on her side. She spit on the ground, her brother's blood, and spoke, *I keep telling you I am stronger than I look.*

"I'm learning I am braver than I feel," I said.

Then let's go and face Warfare before he gets his teeth into our family. She leapt past me and I spun to face the scene.

Warfare was surrounded—my covenmates and Sabine's with their weapons striking his tough hide along his ribs, Bryce snapping and clawing down the back of his thighs, Agony twisting around his ankles, his fangs digging into muscle. Anger paced in front of the larger Ancient and then rose up and roared in chorus with Warfare before lunging, long claws swinging in massive paws, dodging the snap of Warfare's jaw. I meant to join them when a tangle of feathers came spiraling down to the ground next to me, Pride bleeding silver, collapsing to the ground.

"Health!"

Coming, the Ancient answered from where he'd guarded Joanna at the door of our house.

I knelt at Pride's side, ignored the clashing of metal and the snarling of beasts beyond me. My fingers landed on gilded feathers, a delicate touch at first, the feel of them sharp and glossy.

I will heal, Pride said, voice tremulous in my head. Health reached us, one furry bowed thigh peeking out from the robe he wore.

I can do little in this cage, Health said.

"Can you carry him?" I asked. "Take him out of the boundary so he can heal faster?"

The ground beneath us trembled as Warfare's feet stomped, legs kicking out, nearly braining Callum until Aiden pulled him away in time. I stood, blade ready, and watched as Warfare kicked and snapped a path clear for himself, and then began to lope away from the road. He was nearly out of sight before I realized that, for once, he had no parting shot of words, no promise of retaliation. Good. Let *him* worry for once.

PUT HIM ON MY BACK, Anger said, limping over to where I stood with Pride, whose wings twitched uncomfortably. *I'LL CARRY HIM OUT.*

I would rather bleed to death, Pride said, but it was dry and almost humorous. Anger only snorted, fire eyes rolling behind dark hair.

I left Pride grumbling as Health heaved him onto Anger and I walked to Callum. He leaned into me, sweaty and rumpled and I reached up, frowning, to where his lip was bloodied and swelling. His forehead tapped briefly against mine before he jerked back, looking over my shoulder.

"Stay inside!" he called and I turned to see Joanna poised at the very edge of the doorway of our house, her lips pressed white, eyes wide and worried. "We don't know where Suspicion ran off to."

North woods, Pride said, hanging strangely over Anger's back, who began to lumber down the road. *I chased him away before crashing.*

"Thank you," I said, nodding at Pride and Anger.

Bravery brushed up against my leg before dashing over to the house and up the steps, nudging Joanna back inside. Aiden was halfway there already, the other Ancients and allies following in for the shortcut back to the Scrivens house. He turned and reached out his hand and Callum leaned into me, wincing, as we walked across the street to home.

It has to be soon, Bryce said, pausing on their way back to their own house.

Callum nodded. "Tomorrow. Or the day after. We'll end it."

We reached Aiden on the sidewalk. He stood gazing up at a bewildered Joanna, heartbreak drawing lines around his mouth and eyes.

"You're going to find Warfare's name, and she'll write it," Aiden said softly. Callum stared back at him for a long moment of quiet before nodding. "If anything happens to either of you…"

"I know," Callum whispered. "That's why it has to be done, to be finished."

"If a single whiff of trouble ever comes back to Canderfey, we'll be moving," Aiden said, grumbling low and groaning as he dragged himself up the stairs. Joanna pounced on him the second he was within reach.

"Oh I *hated* that," she said, gratefully scooped up in Aiden's hold, his borrowed axe dropped by the closet.

"I thought it went relatively well, actually," Callum whispered to me.

I swallowed my laugh and shut the door on the broken night.

20

CALLUM

Soft steps padded into my office, interrupting my frenzied rummaging through piles of books, their pace and weight so familiar to my ears.

"Joanna? Where is Heverley's *Archaicism and Cryptography?*"

"I returned it to the library," she said. "It was a week overdue."

"Overdue?" I landed in the chair behind my desk and faced her. "Joanna... I hardly think due dates are worth worrying over at the moment."

She cocked her head and flipped open the cover of a book at the top of a pile. Another library book I'd borrowed. Also *overdue* if her frown was anything to judge by.

"I'm trying to tweak the sigil for bindings," I said as Joanna closed the book and walked toward me. "I was thinking if I used a variation, something similar to the Ancients' alphabet—"

My words stilled on my tongue as Joanna's hand covered my lips. She bent at the waist, cheek pressed to the top of my head and her breath stirred my hair. I waited for her to speak and when she was silent I found myself sagging into the chair, the energy of my search fizzling away.

"I love you," she said.

923

The words beat like a drum in my heart every time and my mouth curled up behind her fingers. I kissed them and she pulled away slightly.

"You're brilliant, and I know that there is nothing in this world that would stop you from fighting for our coven, for Canderfey and everyone in it," she whispered.

My throat squeezed at her speech. "Of course not."

"But right now, all I want is for you to come downstairs and join us for dinner," she said.

I looked up as one of Joanna's hands slid through my hair to the back of my neck. "It's dinner already?" I asked. That meant it'd been over sixteen hours since I'd left my office.

She nodded, smile a little stiff. "If you come and sit with us, I will convince Aide and Isaac not to tie you to the bed tonight and keep you from researching."

"I think that choice of words was intentional," I said, narrowing my eyes at her, pleased as her smile widened into something genuine. I caught her hand as she made to leave the room, and she let me pull her back into my lap. "I love you too. I'll come down for dinner, and I'll even try to sleep tonight. Restraints optional."

"Don't be a tease," she hissed, leaning in to bump our noses together.

I squeezed my arm around her waist, watched her smile wobble and fall, her eyes drop. Joanna was one of the strongest people I'd been lucky enough to know in life, and any brief show of reservation or fear for the coming fight was a sign of trust. One I cherished. She'd buried them before, run away and tried to cope on her own in the beginning and later throw herself into arguments with Aiden so he couldn't see she was scared. If she was learning to be open with us, then I could learn to give my focus to the people who needed me.

"Everything is going to be fine. We've done this before, you know," I said.

She raised her eyebrows. "I remember. It wasn't easy."

I shook my head. "No, it wasn't. I know we're all tired. I know I'm terrified something will happen to you, or the baby, Aiden, Isaac. Any of our friends."

"But we don't have a choice," Joanna said, finishing my thought.

I nodded, the heaviness of understanding weighing every cell in my body.

"Dinner," she murmured, brushing her thumb over the bruise on my lip from where Warfare had landed a scant blow.

I lifted us both out of the chair, steadying Joanna on her feet, and we walked hand in hand down to the dining room where Isaac and Aiden were laying out a meal. Aiden's expression lightened at the sight of us, his hands circling Joanna's waist briefly, drinking her in before he came to kiss my cheek.

"Man cannot survive on knowledge alone," he said in my ear.

"Not when his coven won't bring him up a tray," I teased.

Aiden rolled his eyes, but his hand squeezed mine as he passed on the way to his chair. Dinner was quiet and peaceful, my head traveling up to my office more than once. Joanna drew me back, her toes nudging against mine, and Aiden kept my wine glass full, perhaps in the hopes of leaving me drowsy enough to sleep tonight. It was impossible not to talk of the day to come, impossible not to let it bleed into the tender mood and leave us clutching our knives in our hands, but then Isaac would coax us into a new topic.

Tomorrow had to be ugly, but for tonight at least we could have the harmony of the four of us together.

"The others are in place," Joanna said, her voice tight and quiet.

My coven and I stood together outside the edge of the boundary, the morning quiet on the peaceful side of the cage. All around the south edge of Canderfey stood clusters of witches and Scrivens, even a handful of Ancients, waiting for the sound of today's battle to begin. I looked to my right through the trees, spotting Tatsuo, Hildy, and Samuel listening in a tense quiet, bodies ready to act. To the left, obscured in the dense woods, Mayor Sewell stood with Myles, Pablo, and Agony—now healed and without his crutches, looking a little wild and poisonous with his matted hair tangled high on his head.

"What if Anger can't wrangle Warfare?" Isaac whispered.

"I'll hunt him down myself. The cages won't come down until it's safe," I said.

Aiden scoffed quietly and shrugged when I glanced at him. "Safe is an overstatement and you know it." He held Joanna's hand tight in his grip. Any moment he might change his mind about letting her act as our Scrivens lock to the cage.

I held my breath, bracing for the screams so we could begin our work. The sun beat down on our heads, sweat trickling down my spine, the air hazy with heat.

Even prepared, I hunched at the sounds, like every violent dream made into painful music on the air. Joanna flinched, turning her cheek away, but her shoulders squared and she lifted her notebook up.

"Now," I said, her pencil already scratching.

What if one of the cages stays locked? I worried, my palms raising, fingers casting the sigils I'd taught the others, my attention narrowing in on the blood black threads of Warfare's prison. *What if we fail?*

"Focus," Isaac whispered at my back. "You've thought of everything."

I hadn't. Some moments I wondered if I'd thought of even half of what needed done, but it was too late to back down.

"It's working," Joanna murmured, her eyes bouncing between me and her page and the others down the line of the boundary, our Scrivens all connected in writing to one another, communicating progress.

Deep in the woods ahead of us Warfare snarled in what sounded like a laugh and Isaac's breath went short. The cages were unravelling. If Anger and the counterpoints inside didn't have hold of our enemies...

You've never faced them with their full magic. You're in over your head. It sounded like my father's voice.

"We're ready," Aiden said, drawing me back to them.

"Seconds," I warned, teeth gritting. We were seconds from the cages' collapse. Seconds before we had to run. Run toward danger. The instinct to hold my coven back, to keep them from this idiot's mission—me, I was the idiot—struck me hard.

And then the air was clear of color and magic flooded back into Canderfey like a wave, beating at my back. I gathered up every scrap I could cling to, taking a deep breath. My coven ran ahead of me and my feet stumbled into action to catch up with them, running headfirst toward Warfare if only so I might buy them seconds if this all went wrong.

The woods were alive with our energy, noisy with storming feet and panting breaths. Each of us was armed with magic, ready for the moment we would reach the Ancients. Not far. Not far. Close enough to the Scrivens house if we had to get inside. Inside would still be safe, wouldn't it?

It startled me at first to see them grappling—the tall, frail, old man and the giant with flaming red hair and a thick beard—as we reached where Anger held Warfare.

Gods. It was clearer than ever that I'd tripped myself into a link with Warfare. He looked like my *father*, but huge and terrifying again, as Duncan had when I was a child. Some small, young part of me begged to turn and run straight to my closet library in my bedroom and hide there until his temper had passed. Joanna was catching up on my heels and the impulse, the imperative design of me since meeting her, demanded I protect her. Now our child, too.

Anger had his thin hands wrapped around Warfare's throat, the great giant laughing, eyes wide and red, but he couldn't pull free despite how weak Anger looked beside him.

These are only disguises, I reminded myself. They were not so poorly matched. Anger had succeeded in holding him here for us.

"Remember the illusion," Joanna said. I thought at first she meant their shapeshifting, as if she'd read my mind. Her hand wrapped around mine, squeezing tight and releasing me quickly and I realized she meant while I searched for Warfare's name in the link.

"Stay safe," I answered.

My coven spread out around Warfare and Anger, Joanna waiting at my back, and with a lift of my hands Aiden's bow was in the air, striking against the strings of his violin in a steady, urgent cacophony. All around us in the woods, music tore through the air, a shuddering weeping cry for Sorrow, a spiky crawl for Jealousy, shrieks for Terror. Isaac stood across from me, casting blood-black pools of color like a wound spilling in the air between his hands, different glows of magic blooming at every circle. The more the dark shade spread, the more the woods reeked of a battlefield and dark memories clawed at the back of my mind.

It was impossible at first to disentangle my head from the web of all the music, all the color, and then Warfare roared and light flashed with pain through my head, spilling darkness at the edges of my vision. I forced my eyes open, tried to ignore the clashing sounds building around us, and found Anger staring at me. I nodded and he began to hum—a rocky, rattling sound. Warfare bellowed over the drone, as if he could drown it out.

"Search for the place in your mind where you feel him dragging," Joanna coaxed at my back.

The headache between my temples that felt as if someone was trying to dig their way out. It drummed with Aiden's bow, pulsed with the violent color Isaac conjured, until the woods began to fade around me. My bones vibrated in my body and a scream fought its way up my throat, my gaze fixed to Warfare's red face. He was trying to dig his way out of me before I could borrow the link and burrow through him in search of the name. I slammed my eyes shut and forced my mind into the music, the color, and Anger's rattling drone.

Joanna had said I would find myself in nothing when the trance took. She was wrong.

I opened my eyes to the view that haunted me at night, blood and earth and shit in the air. Something worse. Rot—a horrible, sweet contrast to the violence. The ground was rocky with bodies already sinking into the mud, as if half an attempt to bury them had been made. Their uniforms were blind now, no colors of allegiances remaining in death, only black dirt and gory stains and bloodless pale skin.

At my feet lay a young man, one lifeless blue eye staring at the toe of my boot, the other submerged in wet earth. I knew his name, had sent him to battle the morning he died. This morning.

Remember the illusion, Joanna said in my thoughts.

The eye staring at my boot was brown, not blue, or was it green? And that morning had been decades ago. I swallowed down the trembling, queasy horror of my past and remembered I was here to find my enemy.

"I suppose you think this is a clever trap for me?" I called out, staring around at the sea of bodies on a gray day, all their faces familiar, but not distinct. It could have been any battle. "Trap me in my own nightmare?"

YOU FEAR WAR.

I turned and there he was, Warfare in his strange imitation of my father, boots mucked with blood, skin red with energy.

"No. I regret it," I said.

WAR IS INEVITABLE. IT IS ALWAYS WAITING.

"Maybe," I said, kneeling down, letting Warfare march to me, his boots pressing bodies deeper into the ground. I turned to the boy in front of me and rolled him onto his back, reaching out with my sleeve to wipe the mud off his face, hoping to find a clue. "My participation isn't, however. I study war, not to make it easier to battle now, but easier to avoid," I said.

THEN YOU ARE UNPREPARED FOR THE SLAUGHTER I WILL DELIVER UNTO YOUR FAMILY, YOUR FRIENDS, YOUR NATION OF WEAK-FORMED WITCHLINGS.

"My family, friends, and nation may have something to say about that," I said mildly. When I'd offered as much dignity as I could to the young man at my feet, I pushed myself up and moved onto the next, glancing briefly at their uniforms, the unfamiliar patches over their breasts.

Warfare snarled at my back. I looked at the patches on the uniform of the man in the ground in front of me and frowned. The symbols on the patches were broken versions of the Ancient's alphabet, none of the letters complete, and none of the shapes the same from one body to the next. Was it a puzzle to solve, or only proof that this was Warfare's mind? Even the nonsense of the illusion was built in his language. I tried to fit the pieces together, searching for a word, his name. I needed to be quick, faster than Warfare could break out of Anger's hold.

Boots thumped through the mud, snapping bones beneath their weight, stopping at my back.

PICK UP A SWORD AND FIGHT ME.

I stilled. He was as warm as a fire, scorching at the nape of the neck, reminding me of evenings as a boy, standing in front of the fireplace in my father's study, trying to find the right bits of my day to impress him with. I didn't want to let Warfare distract me, I wanted to hunt for his name.

It was too late. A sword dragged at my arm, my fingers wrapped around its hilt between breaths. He would have his battle whether I liked it or not. I took a breath, relaxed my shoulders, and spun to face him, blade swinging through the air. My heels sucked through the mud, body burning, and Warfare laughed, blocking my blow with a clash so strong it made my brain rattle in my head.

Illusion, I told myself, but the illusion was in *his* favor, not mine.

He barreled forward and I ducked and turned to his side, swinging again toward his ribs, blocked again with contact so fierce it rang through me.

MAYBE YOUR FATHER WOULD HAVE BEEN A BETTER OPPO-NENT, EH?

I laughed at the goad. He would not have, that much I knew for certain. Still, I wished I was someone like Sabine or Darin, constantly training, constantly pushing my strength.

This isn't about strength. This is strategy, I thought. Warfare was distracting me. I was hoping to distract him. How long could we last in this game before the outside world needed us?

I grunted as Warfare pushed forward, our swords locked, and tried to hold my ground even as the earth slid beneath my shoes. I stumbled backwards. I was outmatched. And if there was no chance at winning in sword fight, what could I win in?

Warfare swung his hammer of a blade and I dodged it frantically, my feet slipping. I landed in the mud, falling on top of a smaller, fragile body. I glanced down and my lungs turned to stone. Joanna's dark curls were soaked in mud, her brown eyes cloudy, lips blue, blood stained around her temple. My heart was cracking, the fissures spreading through me like ice. A strangled shout of horror clawed its way out from my throat as I pulled her slack body out of the mud.

SHE'LL LOOK WORSE WHEN I'M DONE WITH HER, Warfare growled. I was paralyzed, more screams trapped in my tight chest, releasing in a slow, pained whine.

Illusion, she whispered to me, but the reality of seeing her this way, feeling her cold under my touch, was too much. Blood crusted and dried over her chest, her blouse torn open. I brushed my fingers over the spot, knowing at any moment Warfare's blade would run through me. The blood flaked away revealing the deep gouges in her skin.

Illusion.

I'LL CARVE THEM UP INTO FINE MEALS AND PASS THEM AMONGST THE FAMILY, REMIND THEM WHAT HUMANKIND TASTES LIKE.

I tore my eyes off the symbol on Joanna's chest—a half word—and found Aiden in the ground next to me, his skin an eerie, dusty shade of brown. His eyes pecked out into pocked, gruesome sockets, another symbol carved on his cheek. A blade and a cross, marking my coven as Warfare's.

He was busy laughing as I pushed myself up, the frozen broken form of Isaac pinned beneath his boots. His palm stretched out to me, as if he'd been alive a moment ago, his gray eyes milky. A sob rose up, and the threat of bile with it. There was a symbol in his hand, an open grave.

A blade, a cross, an open grave.

"That was a mistake," I said, voice shattered and thick. I would never let my coven go when this was over. Never out of my sight.

The soldiers surrounding us were faceless, just impressions. But my coven had cost Warfare something, the perfect truth of them taking more magic than illusion. He'd put his name into their skin, hoping I'd be too grief stricken to see the truth. The truth was, I would never let my coven fall before me.

I WAS WRONG. YOU ARE TOO WEAK TO BE MY DESCENDANT, Warfare taunted.

"I will bury you," I vowed. "*Dormundun.*"

The ground trembled and Warfare hissed, eyes narrowing and face elongating out of my father's and into a snarling snout, his back hunching.

"*DORMUNDUN!*" I shouted. "Let me out so I can cage you!"

The sky cracked open over my head and I chanted his name on my tongue, watching Warfare transform back into the fanged beast of the woods. The illusion was crumbling.

21

———

JOANNA

THE AIR WAS TOO THICK TO BREATHE. THE MAGICAL CLASH OF THE SIX circles created flashes of lightning in the air, like a summer heat storm. My fingers dug into Callum's shoulders as he arched, body struggling against mine. His mouth was open in a silent scream and I pressed my face to his hair.

"Find it," I whispered, inaudible over the roar of music and clamor of Ancients around us. "Find it and come back."

Callum shook, trying to tear out of my grip, and I looked up, searching for Aiden's gaze and finding my worry compounded there on his face. Panic left me desperate for choices. Could I force a link with Warfare like the others, follow my way in to help Callum? Aiden and Isaac were sweating, Anger was bleeding, and I knew at any moment I might be sick.

I don't want this. The thought struck me hard. My gaze searched through the woods, seeing the struggle on all my friends' faces, knowing we might fail. *I don't want to fight anymore.* A month ago I'd found it all a little exciting. A horrible, terrible, tiny amount of fun. Not now. We couldn't go on like this. The odds wouldn't stay in our favor forever. I didn't want my coven at risk, I wanted us together, happy, safe. I wanted my child *safe*.

Callum's lips moved and I scrambled around to his side. Had he only been wetting them? The tension was shifting on his face, body still twisting in discomfort. I leaned in close as he swallowed and heard the whisper.

"*Dormundun.*"

"He has it!" I shouted, dropping my chalk to the slate and wrapping my hands around Callum's feverish neck. "Come back, Callum."

"*Dormundun,*" he said again, the word strangled. His eyes shifted beneath his eyelids and then they were open, staring in shock and horror at me.

"Write it," I said, but before I could move away he was groaning, surging up onto his knees, arms clamped around my waist and mouth slanting over mine, a desperation in the kiss that I tried and failed to match. I pushed at his chest and he only held on tighter, lips scouring mine, sucking and nipping, a moan rumbling in his chest. He sagged and I picked the chalk up, pressing it into his shaking fingers, a laugh on my tongue. "Write it, Callum. So I can."

He took a deep breath, eyes searching my face, and then he was bent forward around me, scribbling three symbols onto the slate for me to copy. He jumped up, body swaying as he stood, and his fingertips brushed faintly over my hair before raising to cast the circle.

Warfare's form exploded out of the shape of the giant man into some strange cross between it and the monster he'd been before, the movement tossing Anger aside. He had a thrashing tail now, tipped with spikes like a blade, and it swung menacingly through the air. The air wavered around him in some shift of power.

Callum's shouts were shocking behind me, his voice fuller, soaked with pain and relief, and I fought every urge to reach for him. I picked up the discarded chalk, ignored the way the entire woods seemed to spin around me, too polluted with magic to see straight, and forced my hand to trace the lines Callum had made.

Licks of heat ran through my veins with the first mark, like blades kissing under my skin. Isaac screamed ahead of me and my stare whipped up, to find him holding the color, crashed against the ground but still holding the magic.

"Don't stop," Callum rasped.

The next symbol crashed into me, body vibrating like an avalanche, eyes barely able to track the crisscrossing lines, and fingers trembling so hard I thought it would ruin the mark. The last came, stealing my breath from my lungs, all the light from the world, my heart beat slowing and body growing heavy. I would die by the last mark, I was sure of it, felt it threatening each of us.

A high pitched sound, more like glass breaking than a voice, cleared my thoughts and left me panting, Warfare's name complete on the slate. Callum collapsed behind me and Anger came rushing forward, rust orange light burning on his fingertips, sealing the name to the stone. I heard Callum's gasp as the woods shook, and I remembered the dragging, tangling feeling of being pulled under by the Hollow. I turned and pulled Callum to me, his face in my hands and my eyes holding to his.

"Let him go," I said. "Don't fight him, don't give him purchase, just let him pass."

Callum's eyes were wide with terror, voice and breath still in his chest, his gaze clinging to mine.

"Just let him go," I pleaded, unsure if I was speaking to Callum or Warfare. Whoever I could reach.

Aiden and Isaac reached us, surrounded Callum, our hands covering his skin, our bond enveloping him as if it could anchor him to us. Maybe it did. Callum gasped, eyes fluttering and rolling and I thought for sure he'd be snatched into Warfare's trap a second time like I was. And then his eyes popped open wide and he surged up in our hold, trying to wrap us all up against him.

Weak breaking sounds collapsed out of me, laughs and sobs mingling together, and I let myself be folded into them, hiding away from the woods.

"He's gone," Callum whispered. "He's gone."

For a moment, it was only us, the world blocked out by my covenmates, the music and fighting dulled beneath the sound of their breaths mingling, hearts pounding. Then the forest floor crunched behind me.

"Warfare is caged. But the others aren't," Anger said.

We separated, Aiden pulling me up by the waist, and I saw what he meant. Every other circle was trapped in a tense, frozen state. Colors pounding, music trembling, Scrivens waiting in the heavy fog of magic for their moment to write. Mayor Sewell, Tatsuo, Sabine, Gwen, and Professor Frost were all trapped, either in the links created or still trying to force them. Gwen looked too pale and I wanted to race and take her place.

"We can try and shore them up, but all of them? There's too many." Aiden whispered to Callum. "What do we do if they can't get the names?"

Callum frowned, scanning the woods. Ancients were locked together, counterpoints fighting one another in stalemates impossible to solve. They were meant to balance not compete.

"We have to get them out of the links if it's going to fail," Isaac said. "We don't know what it will do to them to stay like that."

"The music will fail soon," Aiden said, eyeing his friends who had come to help us as their instruments struggled to hold magical notes.

Callum's shoulders sank under the weight. His plan was crumbling and we hadn't found more names, more options. I stared at the circle lead by Mayor Sewell, my uncle Myles' lips pressed together as he watched the Ancients Agony and Ecstasy hold up a containment spell that was ready to shatter at any moment. His eyes met mine through the trees, and I understood the steady, even expression on his face. We had to do something. Not we, my coven. We, the Scrivens.

"Joanna," Callum murmured, and I tore my stare away from Myles to him, his brow furrowed and gaze aching. "What do we do?"

My eyes strayed back to Myles, where Terror and Bravery clung to one another, fighting and embracing at the same moment. Teeth and claws, arms and legs tangled.

"Did you know her true name?" I asked Anger. "Happiness?"

His expression hardened and he shook his head. "No. Only my own."

"Was it painful, to be with her?"

I regretted the question as I watched his face fall, head shaking.

"No, wordsmith," he whispered. "It was right to be with her. It was wrong for us to be corrupted against one another. Balance is ease, that's what we are to one another. You won't convince them to kill each other."

"If it's our only choice..." Callum said, not understanding the direction of my thoughts.

"What if it wasn't a cage? Would you offer your name for her?" I asked Anger, whose eyes narrowed. "Not to be trapped here in the woods alone. Not a cage. More like a... a leash."

"You want to bind the counterpoints," Isaac said. "Do you think it will really keep them in line?"

"We know it was Warfare who convinced them to refuse taking the oath," I said. "That we've been promising them the same cage all summer. What if there was an alternative one? They take the oath and they accept the bind. I can... I can already think of the words."

"Both would have to agree," Anger said, and I nodded. "You'd be willing to let them out in the world?"

I bit the inside of my lip and looked to my coven. "I just want this to *end*. I want peace. I trust the Ancients who came to our aid. If they agree...if they trust their counterpoints, then I'm willing."

Callum's brow furrowed and he watched the struggles continue with no change. How much longer could the circles last?

"It's better than this," he said softly.

Anger glanced down at the tile where Warfare's name was embedded in stone, a combination of our magics. He sighed and looked to me. "Peace? Alright. Ask them."

"Me?" I said, stiffening. I glanced at Isaac who was watching the woods, ready to intervene. He knew them better than I did. "Shouldn't it be... someone else?"

"I don't think it should, Wordsmith," Anger said, lips curling. "Offer them your choice."

I swallowed hard, the words that had been forming in my thoughts a moment ago fading under the notion of speaking. Aiden came up to my side, his fingertips glowing faintly, raising to my throat.

"So they can hear you," he said.

I gave him a panicked, pleading stare, and he shrugged. "No- I—" my voice died, suddenly twice it's usual volume, and Aiden raised his eyebrows. Snarls and snaps and horrid music full of threat hung in the air, and my coven waited for me to speak.

I stepped out of the crowd of my coven and Anger, my mouth working in silence, waiting for someone else to take my place. There was a nudge in the covenbond, Aiden or Callum, and the words burst out.

"Stop casting!" I shouted, voice cracking with nerves. "No more cages! Warfare is defeated!"

Music faltered in the circles but wavered on and I looked to my coven for support.

"Tell them," Isaac said, coming to my side and squeezing my hand.

I bit my lip. *Think of the words*, I told myself. *The right ones.*

"You don't have to be in a cage! You can live in the world, you can be free again!" I grimaced, expecting the fighting to continue, but in their tangled embraces the Ancients went still and the magic conjured throughout the woods softened with them.

"Hold them," Callum called to the circles. "While we talk. Just hold them."

But Terror and Suspicion and Jealousy, and all the others, weren't fighting now and it sparked hope in my chest. Pride and Shame were closest to me. Tatsuo was kneeling on the ground, eyes dizzy and skin pale as he emerged from the trance. I walked closer to their circle, my coven at my back, Anger pacing close and careful.

"I couldn't force my way in," Tatsuo panted.

I nodded. "I know. I think there's another option." I stepped between Hildy and Samuel until I was almost within reach of the Ancients. "Would you give your sister another chance?" I asked Pride, Shame now a thin almost feminine creature in his hold, her face hidden by dark hair and unnaturally long limbs that bent and twisted. "If you were… were responsible for her?"

"Gladly," Pride answered, shoulders squaring, head tossing his curling dark hair out of his eyes. Shame looked up and I had to catch my own gasp at her milky black eyes taking up half her face, no other features but her gaze.

"Would you accept a binding?" I asked them both. "Your names tying you to each other?"

Pride's face fell and Shame stiffened. *It's going to fail*, I thought. Then Pride looked to his sister, aching and tender, with eyes filling up. She leaned into him and Pride nodded.

"I don't think you know what you're asking," he said, "but yes, I would accept that." Shame curled in on herself and—just like a sibling might—Pride stroked her back and cooed to her in soothing words, "None of that now. Don't be sorry. Think of all we'll see together."

"I can write the words if you will help me with your names," I said.

"On their skin," Anger said to me. "I'll fix the magic. That way they know the names are safe."

"The others are relaxing," Callum whispered to me, hand squeezing my waist briefly. "It's going to work, clever girl."

I only had the chalk in my hand but with Anger's magic it would have to work. Gods, would it work? Pride held out his arm and with crooked fingers Shame rolled up his sleeve. I stepped to her side. Old familiar feelings of not being *enough*, not being important, licked up my side. They were hers, not mine, and I found the understanding held firmly like a grip in my mind. Even as a small country librarian, I was enough, and I was enough now. This would work.

Shame's fingers wrapped around mine, her touch clammy, and together we wrote.

I am bound by magic and body to... Shame's touch guided me and I tore my gaze from Pride's skin, his tan arm so human. I stared at her instead, the sharply pointed chin, eyes like black pools, and bones protruding at odd angles. Anger's magic burned over the soft chalk marks until they darkened, like a brand, or a tattoo.

She pulled her hand away and Pride said, "Now you, Sister."

The woods were silent as Shame turned her back on me. Pride's hand took his sister's place on mine, raising it up to write over winged shoulder blades and a knobby spine. He crowded close at her side as we wrote, replicating the words burned into his skin. She pushed against him and I looked away again as he began to write his own name on her back, accidentally finding myself staring at them in a kiss. Or as close as a kiss as you could have when one person was missing lips.

I gasped and stumbled back as Pride released me, the Ancients' faces pushing closer, an uncomfortable melding of skin. His arms squeezed around her and Anger guided me back, shimmering midnight blue and dove gray lingering in the air around them as they melded. It was almost gruesome, and nearly romantic. As much as shock begged me to look away, I fixed my stare, watching as Shame slid into Pride, his eyes growing larger but not as much as hers, his hair longer, the frame slimmer. He, *they*, inhaled as fingertips relaxed into one another, feet settling in the same shoes. They were different, a little smaller, more feminine, their stare skidding away shyly.

My hand covered my mouth. "I didn't know," I whispered. "I'm sorry, I didn't realize."

He'd warned me as much and I hadn't stopped to listen, too determined to solve the problem. It wasn't a leash at all. They were transformed.

"We did," they said, their voice gritty and layered at first, before settling into something gentle. "I knew. I made the choice."

I looked to my coven, faint-headed and fingers trembling, the circles surrounding us. I expected to see the fighting start up again at any moment, Ancients refusing what I'd just inflicted on Pride and Shame. There was no fighting, no shouting, just oddly matched pairs standing side by side in circles of magic, waiting for me.

"We accept," Sorrow and Delight said together, the dour vampiric figure and the cheerful old woman.

Callum squeezed my hand, Aiden smiled at me, but Isaac was staring in the other direction, to where Bravery and Terror leaned into one another, regret twisting his expression into pain.

"Do we write?" Corina asked, in the circle with Sorrow and Delight.

I didn't look away from Isaac, but I nodded, Anger walking over to fix her words.

"Wait," Isaac whispered as Myles approached Bravery and Terror, Agony on his heels. "Wait!"

Our coven followed him as Isaac rushed to the small girl. Terror's form was still monstrous and pale, towering three times as tall as his counterpoint, barely more human than he'd been before. He skittered backwards as Isaac landed on his knees in front of Bravery, but her hand was linked with the creature, holding him tight.

"You don't have to do this," Isaac said, tears clogging his throat.

Bravery smiled at him, a mix of melancholy and laughter softening her expression. "It's just another adventure," she said. "I've never felt scared before. It might be fun."

Isaac huffed, shaking his head at the ground, at her small feet in little black boots. "I don't recommend it, personally."

"Yes, but you're still so young," Bravery said, reaching out with her free hand and tilting his chin up. "I think it's time for a change. I'll be fine. You'll see."

Isaac's shoulders sagged and he twisted, begging me with a look, cheeks shining. I nodded to Myles, waved my uncle away, and joined them.

Bravery turned her chin up to Terror and grinned. "Don't worry. It won't hurt." She gave Isaac a brief hug, which he tightened, kissing the top of her head before rising up and moving away, and then she held out her free arm.

Terror crouched at my side, the pair of us wary of one another, and strong, bony fingers joined mine around the chalk, Agony's sharp silver magic waiting above us. The words came clean and swift, running down the length of Bravery's small forearm and across the tight muscle of Terror's ribs. Terror tried to pull away at the last second but Bravery 'tsk'd and held on tight till it was over.

"I hope I'm not a boy," she said at the last moment, and then she dragged Terror down tight against her, and he lifted her up in his arms.

There was a compromise, growing, aging, shifting, and at the end a pimply teenaged boy with short blond hair and broad shoulders stared back at me, nose wrinkled.

"Oh well," he said with a shrug.

I forced a smile, and walked back to my coven, chewing on the inside of my lip, searching for the words to say to Isaac. "I'm—"

He cut me off, arms around my shoulders and pulling me to his chest. "I love you."

No apology then, not today. The wood was five figures shorter than it had been minutes ago, ten Ancients gone and replaced with… we didn't really know what. Beings of unknown quality. The moment was strange, not the heaviness at the end of a battle, although there'd been losses somehow too. Not the joy of victory, either. A balance between the two.

"It's over," Aiden murmured, the same strange confusion lining the words.

Canderfey was restored.

"I really think we ought to get married," I said.

22

AIDEN

I FIDGETED WITH THE COLLAR OF MY JACKET IN THE MIRROR OF THE Library Staff Lounge for the fifteenth time.

"I think you're making it worse," Callum teased.

"If I didn't think I'd end up finding pins in all my suits for the rest of my life, I'd ask Hildy if this collar wasn't crooked," I said.

"You wanted her to focus on Joanna's dress," Isaac said, lips quirking. "There were bound to be some losses."

"If she didn't, Joanna would've volunteered to get married in a…" I didn't know what. Something she'd already worn, probably, maybe even from before Canderfey, just to torture me. "Honestly, that woman…"

That woman was going to be my wife. I stared blankly at myself in the mirror. These men my husbands. Finally. *Finally*.

"Happiness looks a bit strange on you, love," Isaac said, pressing to my side and stroking my cheek.

"I'm absorbing the moment." I turned my face, catching his lips with mine. A stray thought passed and I froze. "You don't think we'll walk out there and… and suddenly we'll be under attack by some previously unknown foe, do you?"

Isaac raised his eyebrows. "Why would you even put that out as a possibility?"

"Truth be told, I saw the Scrivens working together on something," Callum said. "I think today is well and truly secure in their hands."

I sighed. That was a relief. Nora and Myles and the others would see to this day going smoothly.

It had been two weeks since we trapped Warfare and bound the Ancients and I was beginning to believe that there were no more shoes left, they'd all been dropped. At least for a while. Faculty had returned to campus, which was under the necessary repairs after Warfare's occupation, and students would be here in another month, just a few weeks later into the season than a usual term. The Scrivens had returned, their reputations restored, and while some had taken their old housing back, most opted to remain in the house in the woods, now an official Canderfey landmark of curiosity. The two cages, Illness and Warfare, were thoroughly disguised and warded by Callum's magic.

Knuckles rapped on the door and Bryce popped their head in, examining us each in turn. I suspected that if we didn't pass muster, we wouldn't be allowed out.

"Your turn. Joanna's almost ready."

"You've seen her?" Callum asked, a little bite of jealousy in the question. Bryce only shrugged in response.

Isaac squeezed my hand, giving or taking support. Probably both. Callum led the way to the door, almost bouncing with every step.

We were different now, the three of us. Callum was more confident, more at peace with himself. He'd invited his brothers to the wedding and a few even waited outside with their wives. Duncan, thankfully, was not in attendance. Isaac was braver, more open. He'd started painting Callum's old bedroom into a beautiful panorama of Rhodantis for the nursery.

And I could admit what I'd always been afraid of—the same thing I'd been craving for decades—a family, capable of breaking apart, but strong enough to hold together. I had one now and I wasn't alone in making us whole, keeping us happy and in love. We carried that responsibility as a unit.

Joanna hadn't fixed us, just as we hadn't made her powerful and self-assured. We worked in a balance, pulling each other in new directions, supporting our weakest points. I didn't know if we were ready for the life ahead of us, but I knew we were prepared to find our way there, learning more every day.

I'd offered a dozen different locations for the wedding, but Joanna had been firm on one thing and one thing only, the Library. Gwen Woollard, unsurprisingly, had accommodated. The study tables were replaced with rows of chairs and the sun shone down on our guests in multicolored rays through the stained glass ceiling.

We rounded out from behind the circulation desk, seeing our audience for the first time.

"What a crowd," Callum sighed.

Our friends, Callum's brothers, my family and Joanna's. Sabine and her lot were here, which I couldn't quite wrap my head around except that Joanna and Geoff seemed to get along. All the Scrivens and the Ancients—bound and otherwise—watched from the back row.

What an odd collection of people. What a year we'd been through. The Hollow, Callum's capture, Anders fighting the Scrivens, Warfare and the Ancients. Joanna had asked us once about covenbonds, the old ceremonies of invitation and union and trial. If the strength of our bond was judged by the depths of our trials, then I was even more confident of our marriage's success.

Bryce led us to the front of the group where Gwen waited at a high altar, glasses perched on the end of her nose and book in hand.

The Librarian's Wedding, I thought, lips quirking. I wondered how efficient the ceremony would be. By the book, certainly. I grinned at Isaac, his own smile giddy and bemused, and wished I could share the joke, stupid as it was. Later tonight, if I remembered.

Pablo Banaker and friends of mine struck up a bright, easy melody from the shelves, a piece I'd thought was half-finished from earlier in the year until I imagined it playing at this moment. It was ready for us. We were only just beginning after all, our song wasn't about to end for a long time. We took our places at the end of the staircase to wait for Joanna. The four of us would walk up to the altar together.

Stares brushed against my skin but my eyes only traveled up, waiting for that flash of her to arrive. It came in a deep brown, the toe of her shoe the color of dark tea and leather bindings. I saw the tip of her shoe, her ankle, and then a rush of heavy fabric, all cream silk, whispering against itself like the pages of a book. Hildy was at her side, coaxing the skirt out of the clutch of Joanna's hands as she tried to navigate her way down the stairs in the gown. It was simple, by Joanna's orders, but decadent and beautiful, just as we saw her.

She bit red lips, fighting her smile and failing, dark curls framing her face and barely tucked away. My hands itched to touch her, to run up the stairs and lift her up into my arms. Instead I waited, we all waited. Isaac squeezed my hand at my side. Joanna fell in between Callum and I, her arms curling around ours, the clutch of her fingers the only sign of her nerves.

"I hope this is short," she whispered under the cover of the music.

"I hope it goes on forever," I said, watching her soften and smile.

Isaac took the lead, the three of us following him up the aisle to the altar where Gwen waited with books and cups and candles, a length of silk stretched across the front of the table to bind our wrists for our hand-fasting.

"Join hands and we'll begin," Gwen said, gentle and clear.

·

I WOULD REMEMBER pieces of the ceremony later—the sweat on Isaac's palm, the stick of Joanna's lipstick against my mouth, the way Callum's voice trembled as he recited the vows. In the moment it all blurred, buried under the pound of my pulse and the hazy perfect vision of my coven, our hands linked in touch and the tie of cloth between us.

"Congratulations," Marcus said at the reception after.

Gwen's hospitality of the library had not extended to the reception, and we'd moved to a local inn that had only reopened this week. Herbal garlands made by the Ancients strung across beams, replacing stale air with the scent of a garden, and drinks were passed liberally. I suspected the party was as much a celebration of Canderfey being restored as it was of us.

"Thank you," I said, shaking his hand until he pulled away laughing.

My cheeks hurt from smiling and I could barely keep track of who I'd greeted and thanked. There was still a wet mark from my mother's kiss on my cheek and I saw her across the room now, enveloping Isaac and Joanna in a tight hug. I smiled even harder and then searched the room for Callum. He was with Joanna's father and Myles in a far corner, out of sight of his family, drinking ale and looking peaceful and sleepy.

Pablo was playing something obnoxious on a fiddle, lively and bawdy and old, and I left Marcus to steal Joanna for a dance.

"Do you know a country jig?" she asked me, laughing as I dragged her to the center of the room. She pulled Isaac along in her wake.

"No, teach me," I said, bending down and pulling her into a kiss. She leaned in until the crowd catcalled around us and sent her ducking away, blushing.

"Help me show this city boy how to dance," she said to Isaac, who was jerking his head to Callum, calling him out to the floor.

We lined up together, arms around each other's shoulders. Joanna and Isaac dragged us into some ridiculous display of kicking and jumping where I was continuously offbeat, laughing through it all. Bryce and Tatsuo joined us in the line, caught up as Joanna spun past them.

"I think I'm better off on the stage," I said, as the music finally slowed.

Joanna's hands wrapped around my forearms, dragging me back. "No, not yet. Dance with me first."

One for just us, I decided. I'd catch Isaac and Callum on my own later. I wrapped an arm around her waist and caught her hand in mine, pulling her to my chest as we started to sway.

"I'll pick a fight with you next week," she said, resting her cheek on my chest. "Just for fun. To keep things normal. But for now I think we should all be very, very happy."

I laughed. She was a little giddy and tired, and tonight I would carry her home, keep the three of us tangled together and awake until dawn.

"What if I'm too sweet to fight with?" I asked, grinning. "What if I constantly please you and agree with you and make us the happiest home anyone's ever heard of?"

She tilted her head back, her smile sly. "I'll think of something."

I grinned and ducked down, kissing her until our feet stopped moving and even the sound of our friends' laughter couldn't interrupt us. It was a good promise.

EPILOGUE

JOANNA

One Year Later

I stopped on the walkway, students rushing past me, and gave myself a moment to drink in the familiar sight. The shimmering windows winking glimpses of the tall shelves, the lamps glowing at the circulation desk, a new crop of students as strange and charming as last year's and the year before.

"Soaking it in?" Isaac asked, one hand brushing across my shoulders, his other arm holding our daughter to his side. Julia was barely six months old, propping herself up with small hands on her father's shoulder, her curls darker than mine, matching his. She had his gray eyes too, and my freckles.

I nodded, reaching out and pulling one of those black curls out from the corner of her mouth, letting her catch my finger in her fist.

"I think I feel sort of spoiled from the maternity leave and summer," I said, smiling at my grinning daughter, feeling Isaac drink us both in with his stare. "I almost hate to go back to work."

"I'd like to think she'll miss us today, but I think Aiden has a very busy schedule planned for her," Callum said, crowding us and catching her soft cheek on his lips as she lolled backward. She screeched and babbled as he blew a raspberry against her smile, wielding my hand in hers against his nose.

"There you are," Aiden said, one hand hidden behind his back and a large bag over his shoulder stuffed with snacks and toys and who knew what else. "I thought you might have dragged her into that dusty place and set her to shelving already."

He came to join us, gaze equally drawn in by our daughter, but his hidden hand appeared, bouquet of asters and goldenrods in his grip.

"Was this your errand this morning?" I asked, laughing. He'd woken us all up, sneaking out of bed earlier than usual and hadn't made it back home before we had to leave for work.

He nodded and bent to kiss my lips, passing me the flowers. "For your desk," he said. "It's your first day."

I blushed and ignored their smiles, even Julia's. She took after her fathers.

"Give me my sweet girl," Aiden cooed, reaching for Julia. Isaac and Callum got in last kisses on her cheeks before she was scooped out of their reach. "Tell your ungrateful mother to have a lovely day."

"Oh, hush." I swatted Aiden and then wrapped them both up in a hug, taking a long breath of Julia, sweet and heavenly, before pulling away and blinking the threat of tears back. "Have fun and—"

"Keep her out of the sun, yes, I know," Aiden snapped, kissing me quick and firm. "See you at dinner."

I parted with my coven and marched toward the library, eyeing the books waiting for me through the window with excitement. My books—the University's, but mine. As the Assistant Head Librarian, they were something like mine.

I grinned as I opened the door, the scent of leather and dust and parchment and oil heavy on the air.

I wondered what I would find in their pages today.

THE END

ALSO BY KATHRYN MOON

<u>COMPLETE READS</u>

The Librarian's Coven Series

Written - Book 1

Warriors - Book 2

Scrivens - Book 3

Ancients - Book 4

Standalones

Good Deeds

Command The Moon

Say Your Prayers - co-write with Crystal Ash

The Sweetverse

Baby + the Late Night Howlers

Lola & the Millionaires - Part One

Lola & the Millionaires - Part Two

Bad Alpha

(Faith and the Dead End Devils, coming fall 2022)

Sol & Lune

Book 1

Book 2

Inheritance of Hunger Trilogy

The Queen's Line

The Princess's Chosen

The Kingdom's Crown

<u>SERIES IN PROGRESS</u>

Sweet Pea Mysteries

The Baker's Guide To Risky Rituals

The Knitter's Guide to Banishing Boyfriends

Tempting Monsters

A Lady of Rooksgrave Manor

The Basilisk of Star Manor

The Company of Fiends

Sanctuary with Kings (coming 2023)

Monster Smash Agency

Games with the Orc

Howl for the Gargoyle (coming Winter 20230)

ABOUT THE AUTHOR

Kathryn Moon is a country mouse who started dictating stories to her mother at an early age. The fascination with building new worlds and discovering the lives of the characters who grew in her head never faltered, and she graduated college with a fiction writing degree. She loves writing women who are strong in their vulnerability, romances that are as affectionate as they are challenging, and worlds that a reader sinks into and never wants to leave. When her hands aren't busy typing they're probably knitting sweaters or crimping pie crust in Ohio. She definitely believes in magic.

Sign up for Kathryn's newsletter or join her Facebook group Kathryn's Moongazers for sneak peeks of upcoming works!

www.ingramcontent.com/pod-product-compliance
Lightning Source LLC
Chambersburg PA
CBHW021238200726

48288CB00014B/1